POWDER

Kevin Sampson lives and works on Merseyside. His chequered career has embraced the production line at Cadbury's, film production at Channel Four, and the music business front-line of Produce Records, as manager of Liverpool band The Farm. His first novel, *Awaydays*, is currently being adapted for the screen.

ALSO BY KEVIN SAMPSON

Fiction
Awaydays
Leisure

Non-Fiction
Extra Time

Kevin Sampson

POWDER

An everyday story
of rock 'n'roll folk

V

VINTAGE

Published by Vintage 2000

6 8 10 9 7

First published in Great Britain in 1999 by
Jonathan Cape

Vintage
Random House, 20 Vauxhall Bridge Road,
London SW1V 2SA

Random House Australia (Pty) Limited
20 Alfred Street, Milsons Point, Sydney
New South Wales 2061, Australia

Random House New Zealand Limited
18 Poland Road, Glenfield,
Auckland 10, New Zealand

Random House (Pty) Limited
Endulini, 5A Jubilee Road, Parktown 2193,
South Africa

The Random House Group Limited Reg. No. 954009
www.randomhouse.co.uk

A CIP catalogue record for this book
is available from the British Library

ISBN 0 09 928996 2

Papers used by Random House are natural, recyclable
products made from wood grown in sustainable forests.
The manufacturing processes conform to the environ-
mental regulations of the country of origin

Printed and bound in Great Britain by
Bookmarque Ltd, Croydon, Surrey

For Jeff Barret

'You know from then on that this – all of it
– it's all fucking bullshit.'
　　　　　　　　Richard Ashcroft, September 1997

'No one got any more humble, more considerate
　or any nicer through getting famous.'
　　　　　　　　John Boy Walton, *The Waltons*

　'They're right, you know.'
　　　　　　　　Kevin Sampson, September 1998

Part One
Getting There

Keva had bought his *NME* twenty-five minutes ago, but only now could he bring himself to look at it. This was not something that'd just go away if he binned the mag. He could leave the café, walk back to the flat, walk away from it all, lock himself in, but this awful thing would still be there when he came out again. He was going to have to take his medicine and read the fucking thing.

He'd been all too well aware that Sensira were starting to do it, but this, the scale of it, the sheer *bigness*, was a total, total shock. From the moment he saw it, it made him ache to the pit of his soul. He'd bent down, half-genuflecting in the usual place on the usual bottom shelf in his newsagent, and there it was. There they were. Nothing could have prepared him for that stunning impact as he twigged who was on the cover. What he was looking at, there, then, in luscious, grinning colour, smiling from the front of the *New Musical Express*, from the *cover*, was Sensira.

Sensira! On the *cover* of the *NM*-fucking-*E*! Jesus! Was every fucking journalist and punter in this country a complete mug? Fuck! How could people fall for it? They're shit! They are *such* shit! *Sensira*, for fuck's sake!

They'd been cleaning his boots a few months ago. Now, Sensira, the eternal support group, were on the cover, in the middle, in the news. Keva, quite properly, felt his whole spirit sink again as he turned the page and forced himself to take it all in. It was too true. Sensira were news. They were Big. Thank Christ there was no one in there to see him like this. His face, he could feel it, was twitching with envy. He stared at the article vacantly, reading without taking in a word. This was it, then. This was how the end felt. There was no point, no point at all in his carrying on.

He looked at the picture of Helmet. The little twat even had his hair the same as his now. He was shameless. Keva tried to drink

3

his coffee but it tasted of nothing. This creeping realisation, this whole thing was horrible. He had to read on. He had to.

'What's so damn hilarious, handsome?'

Lorraine. One of the girls at Keith's. Gorgeous. Tall and fine-boned, with a bent nose that looked great on her. You couldn't call any of the Keith's girls waitresses or manageresses or whatever. They all seemed to do everything. Lorraine, at various times, had waited-on, cashed-up, grill-chefed, sung 'Kiss Me Honey Honey' for the students and chased out junior hoods trying to make a name for themselves in a soft establishment. She's one of the girls at Keith's.

He'd been potty about Lorraine, once. Plenty enough people had told Keva she liked him, especially since the band started gigging. He knew she liked him. But he knew, too, that if he were ever to ask her out, she'd put him down. No doubt about it and no matter, anyway. He was long past her. He lost interest once he knew he could have her. Suddenly, once the unattainable Lorraine, the object of much delusory masturbation, was within his grasp, there seemed no point to it. She'd end up leaving him.

Besides, the other thing about her, which people seemed to find cute but only made Keva wince, was her range of irritating Hollywood starlet accents, sometimes as many as three in one short enquiry. She could make 'Top up ya coffee, handsome?' start out as Melanie Griffiths and end up as Jean Harlow. Marilyn was never far away, of course, either. She used words like 'handsome'. He couldn't spend too much time with someone who did that.

Keva pushed the *NME* across the table to her, looking away in disgust as he did it. She clocked the accompanying shot of Helmet and snorted.

'Don't getcha knickers in a twist over him, honey. He's bogus.'

Coming from Lorraine it could've sounded pat, just another of her sayings. But she was dead on. That's exactly what he was. Helmet Horrocks was bogus. Seeing him there, now, the subject of an almost hysterical *NME* editorial, was actually painful to Keva. He picked up the paper again.

HELMETMANIA! ran the headline. Then:

'Sensira for Arena', and:

'It's all gone bonkers!' – Helmet.

The gist of this news-spread, inside the front page, was that the demand for a show by Helmet's band, Sensira, had been so enormous that they'd had to move it from the Forum to Wembley Arena. Wembleyfuckingarena! Sensira!

'With capacity limited to 8,000 by Brent Council for the show, tickets sold out within four hours of going on sale.'

What? *Limited* to 8,000. Jeezuz! Fuck! He felt dizzy. Just a couple of good club gigs would do the Grams for now . . . bring a few bob in, get a demo together, keep things moving, but . . . FUCK! Wembley Arena! For that stunted little get and his phoney strung-out waster hymns. Twat! He flicked a look at the black-and-white of Helmet, saucer-eyed, scared, intense – a sickly child grown big. Keva couldn't help himself. He gobbed on the photo then read the piece again, the bit where Helmet was justifying the switch from the intimate, punter-friendly Forum to the enormous fleeceadromes of the arena circuit.

It's like, the kids've made it clear that they want the big vibe, the tribal gatherings. They want thousands of kindred souls, all together, having the time of their lives. It's all gone a bit bonkers when Sensira go from playing to four men and a dog in Eccles to this – but it's just the way things are going right now. It ain't too big. How can a party be too big?

In how many ways could Keva despise him for this fake, cynical rhetoric? Seven. The seven deadly idiocies of Helmet fucking Horrocks.

1) The affected, and improper use of *like*. Either the *kids* have made it clear or they haven't. It is not like anything.

2) *Kids*? Fuck off.

3) *Vibe*. See *kids*.

4) *Tribal Gathering* with small initials. Pseudo-clever tapping of popular culture, letting the journo know that he's not a pleb, he can come up with the straplines, too, while simultaneously letting the reader see that he's 'out there'. With them. A well-deliberated, fake-spontaneous soundbite. Gobshite.

5) *Bonkers*. Slipped up there, tithead. Who the fuck says 'bonkers' except you.

6) *Four men and a dog*. Direct lift from Keva, whose fine band, the Grams, are loved by the grassroot fanzines and are just now starting, with three or four other similarly poetic, melancholic guitar outfits, to be touted by the music press as the New Underground. In the Grams' biggest interview so far, a splash in *Chasing Chaos* fanzine, Keva pointed to a gig in Carlisle as being epochal, in spite of being attended by 'four men and a dog'. Maybe Helmet was taking a swipe at him. As if he'd have time to, the twat. And that wasn't all he'd nicked. His whole look had gone from scruffy folkie in cord jackets to the cool, smart-casual look favoured by the Grams. Regardless, he still looked a Ted in low-cut trainies with no socks. He just couldn't carry it off.

7) *Ain't*. Nuff said.

That was just the news page. At the end of the report, readers were directed to an exclusive Helmet interview in the centre spread of the mag. Keva speed-scanned it for mentions of the Grams and the New Underground, but it wasn't so bad. Helmet was looking forward to Sensira's imminent tour of the States, which he expected to be *bonkers* and stressed, again, his bewilderment at so much happening so fast. He reminded readers that it was only six months since their first, independent single ('Noodle-doodled'. Crap. Helmet guessing what it's like to be out of it.) had dented the Top 40, signalling the start of this unplanned stampede to Wembley Arena, Los Angeles and fuck knows where else. It was difficult to keep a critical distance (not half!), difficult to take it seriously. It was bonkers. He only touched upon the New Underground reluctantly, and only then at the journo's behest, hoping that bands like the Grams, The Purple and Macrobe 'get to where they wanna be'. Helmet pointedly excluded Sensira from any 'scene', but it was not a bad interview. Not like last time.

It wasn't even a year ago. The Blackpool gig. Wheezer had cobbled together a mini-tour – Derby, Sheffield, Leeds, York, Manchester, Blackpool, Liverpool, then on to an earner at Bangor University that no one wanted to do. The venues were tiny, mostly, but the gigs were going well, over a hundred at each show, touching two hundred at a couple of them. Sensira were going on first every night, with the Grams and The Purple alternating the headline slot, on the grounds that they'd both had Radio One sessions – the Grams on Peel, The Purple on Lamacq. Helmet was just made up to be there. He'd written to Keva about twenty-five times, said how much he loved the Grams, thought they were the only new group worth bothering about, the only band that made a difference to him. Next thing he'd formed his own band, made a demo – any chance of any gigs, anytime, anywhere? They'd even roadie for the Grams. Be honoured to. Keva didn't much like the tape but, so what? Helmet seemed to have passion. He was a dreamer and he loved the Grams – and praise was something which Keva could always tolerate. So Sensira did a couple of farting little one-off gigs with the Grams, kissed their arses and humped their gear. And then came The Tour.

There'd been a great rapport between the bands, an atmosphere of shared destiny, with the Grams the unspoken topdogs. It was starting to feel like this was going somewhere. Three years of playing in shitholes in front of twelve, twenty, fifty people then suddenly The Wheeze had come on board and started to get the ball rolling. Local press and radio. Bit of a following in Liverpool, then the Peel session and this little tour. Decent PA systems. Soundchecks. Crowds which, though still modest, formed enough of a throng to infiltrate the Bermuda Crescent, that semi-circle of dance floor in front of the stage where no fan dared to tread. There'd been nights not so long ago, nights like Carlisle, when the Grams had been on fire and you could sense that the handful there just wanted to get into it, hurl themselves to the front and dance with the devil. But they were too few to penetrate the Bermuda Crescent and they settled, instead, for earnest head-nodding in the shadows of the bar to let the group know that their efforts were not in vain.

This time, though, the crowds were bigger, drunker and more willing to get into the music, right from the off, swaying, bouncing, punching the air. Each of the bands gained an extra yard of swagger from the headrush of seeing, for the first time, eddying mobs flailing to their music. And then, in Leeds, Keva McCluskey became a Star.

It was the Grams' turn to headline. The crowd was swelled by a boisterous but happy mob of Leeds fans looking for a drink after a midweek game. From the moment Keva took to the little stage, they were into it, identifying with his understated street cool, digging the searing guitars and soaring melodies of the Grams, dancing together in their own little pack. Everything clicked. Keva didn't give a fuck how he came across. He did everything he'd always wanted to do. He stalked the stage like a panther, staring through and beyond the crowd, smouldering, crouching, twisting himself into knots and pumping his little arse, lithe as a mamba, decadent, sexual. A Star. So much so, so obviously was something big happening, that the crowd, at the end of each song, was momentarily silent, just for a beat, just in case there was something to miss. Then they roared their throats raw. Even the ooh-ooh-oohing of the Leeds United crew sounded great. Everyone knew it. They'd just seen the Next Big Thing.

Andy Carmichael, the promoter, thought so too. Next day he phoned his flatmate, Cindy Hogan, a freelance for *Melody Maker*, who'd been back in Glasgow on the night, and told her to imagine having missed the Stones' first gig. That was enough for Cindy, who convinced her editor to let her run the first national piece on the New Underground. She reckoned that, two years on from uni, still covering the flotsam passing through Leeds, York and Middlesbrough was apprenticeship enough. This thing of Andy's, the Grams, The Purple — this whole scene was something she could get in on from the start. The New Underground. The way ahead. This was Junction 1 on the road to the journo Premier League. The *Maker*, the *Face*, the *Observer* in three cute hops, with a cause to call her own. She could go on *The Late Review* and *The Treatment* and be a pundit. Bunny Sawyer, get your arse out the way. Here comes Cindy!

Cindy went for the Blackpool show. She fancied the idea of Friday night in Blackpool as a setting for this new, Northern uprising which she was about to unveil. Far enough away from Leeds to wangle a hotel from the *Maker*, too. And it just . . . it felt good. She didn't warn the bands that she was coming. She never did. So while the Grams and The Purple were out in search of good fish and chips, the ascetic Helmet was driving his band through a second soundcheck. A second hour of soundcheck for a thirty-minute set. Cindy, primed by Carmichael, had reckoned on giving Sensira and The Purple a big picture caption each, maybe a hundred-word résumé, with the Grams getting the splash. But what happened instead was that Cindy Hogan fell in love with Sensira from the moment she walked in on their rehearsal at the Jinx Club.

Not that Helmet was to blame for this, except in so far as his band could whip up a fair melange of up-to-date influences. There was nothing original or frightening about Sensira, but they had a likeable, fashionably doped-out sound. They'd studied their masters well, and if the result was a little stage-manufactured, nobody seemed to care.

It wasn't Helmet's fault, either, that Cindy, looking every inch the club chick with her straight black hair, her black plastic jeans and her skinny dancer's frame, loathed and detested dance music. Cindy was a sucker for bands. Bands. Gangs of moody boys with scrawny arses and big dreams. She was into Mansun and Spiritualized. 'Cattle And Cane' by the Gó Betweens still got her crying every time, and she still loved the Mary Chain more than any band alive. But what she liked best, the thing that dripped honey through her veins, was a big, classic, atmospheric ballad. Rock bands with acoustic guitars. Neil Young – 'Only Love Will Break Your Heart'. Primal Scream – 'Losing More Than I'll Ever Have'. Echo And the Bunnymen – 'All My Colours'. Aztec Camera – 'We Could Send Letters'. Nirvana – 'All Apologies'. The Grams? Carmichael had told her yes, and she went after them in delirious hope.

Except that Helmet didn't tell her that his band was not the Grams. Not until right at the end of the interview, after she'd sat in on the soundcheck and taken them all out for a drink, and nodded and smiled and jotted down all the stupid, word-perfect quotes Helmet had always wanted to say to the music press. Only when it was no longer avoidable did he make his coy disclaimer:

'That's three times you've asked me about the Grams now. I'm beginning to fear you think we *are* the Grams!'

By which time Cindy was smitten. And that *was* his fault.

Keva stared out on to Lark Lane, seeing nothing. His dark eyelashes prickled with a stinging, panicky sweat. His right hand instinctively swooped into his pocket, feeling out Rizlas, grass, lighter. With the other hand taking the weight of his forlorn head, he knocked up a miserly one-skinner and sparked it. Lorraine'd let it go at this time of day. Feeling a deep sense of his own tragedy, Keva sighed out a slipstream of sweet smoke and, with his smoking fingers, lifted a swathe of sleek brown hair from his eyes and tucked it behind his ears. Bastards. This was so wrong. Sensira were taking on the world.

From that initial *Melody Maker* piece, they'd got a record deal and cracked the outer limits of the hit parade, but Keva had not the faintest indication that they'd become so huge. It should've been him. Those fans, those eight thousand going to Wembley and all the ones who bought 'Noodledoodled' and all the ones who, if the footnote on the news page was confirmed, would see them headline at Reading, next – they'd always been there, ready, just waiting for something to happen. He'd known that from the start. There was a whole mass of fans out there, *devotees*, real music lovers just waiting for the polarising fashions to be over, waiting for something they could call their own. It should've been him. It should've been the Grams. Something was going to have to be done. He left two quid on the table and headed back to Ivanhoe Road to call Wheezer.

Wheezer was late. Wheezer was always late. It wasn't an act. He had more to do, longer lists of things he *had* to do than anyone else any of the Grams had ever met. He was even late the night they got into all of this together. Beano had come back to the dressing-room at the Lomax to break the news. There was a pretty good crowd, but the funny lad in the mad cardigans, the one who always came to their shows, who'd been there from the start – he hadn't turned up. He was always there, near the mixing desk, slightly embarrassed at his own presence and never quite sure enough of himself to let on to them. That night he was nowhere to be seen. The Grams were queerly disappointed by this, and felt a little weird, they'd all confessed later, when they went on stage. When James finally spotted him and nudged Keva to let him know, they'd both been ineffably chuffed.

He'd come over at the end, this time, while they were loading out. This chain-smoking, slightly stooped lad, took a deep breath then spoke for the first time. They'd never heard anyone talk like him. He was over-articulate and he betrayed a slight impediment when he was excited, but it was the nervous energy of his speech patterns that took them aback. He introduced himself as Michael Finlay and he came on like Bertie Wooster with twice the bluster and none of the style. He was mad, but he was terrific. He heaped on the praise in tipsy, gabbled ejaculations, and what he said was that he thought the Grams were the best band in the world and that he knew a bit about contracts and business and did they have a manager and would they let him have a crack at it? The combination of stunned surprise and the feeling that maybe he was a bit of a talisman meant that no one said no. Keva liked the bit about the best band in the world. He thought so too.

His knowledge of contracts was yet to be put to the test, but the lateness continued. He lived on the Wirral. He wouldn't drive. All good reasons why nobody expected Wheezer – with his inhaler followed by cigarette routine he'd been Wheezer Finlay from that night on – to hit an appointment within half an hour of the suggested time, and why on those occasions when he was, more or less, punctual he was greeted with a standing ovation. It seemed perverse now to recall the reticent, reclusive fan of old.

Keva tossed his locks and flicked at the *NME* again. He wasn't that arsed sitting there on his own. With his uncommon dirty straw hair and freckled brown eyes, his gaunt, beautiful face and those big, vulnerable lips he'd long been used to girls sneaking a second look at him. But it was even weirder now. He was becoming enough of a face in Liverpool for students in Ye Cracke to point him out and start talking loudly about the bands they were into. He loved it when that happened.

And he knew everyone in there anyway, he was in the place at least three times a week, so it wasn't so much of a chore to have to wait in the War Office for Wheezer to show. He delved inside for skins and came up against the letter. He should have just sent it. Too late now. Fate, destiny, luck, whatever – it had long since averted its beguiling glance from Keva's coy eyes to favour someone else with its starlight. Not him, now. Or ever.

He could hear the Lovely Girls being adorable in the bar. He hoped they'd spot him and come over for a natter. The Lovely Girls were the twin, nineteen-year-old daughters, Eloise and

Madeleine, of Joy. Joy held legendary status in there. She was far beyond being a barmaid to her regulars. Joy was a sage, a cynic, a bit of a hippie and the mainstay of Ye Cracke. Apart from the bags under her eyes, which bore out many a late night, she looked more thirty than forty. The supple figure was still there, fighting for recognition under layers of sobering cheesecloth. But standing next to her girls, now, gently rebuking them for this or that misdemeanour, she could pass as their hip older sister.

They lived, had lived all their lives, in Canning Street, just up from Ye Cracke. Fine houses, big Georgian townhouse affairs, but – and no escaping it – smack bang in the centre of Central Liverpool. A few paces up the road and you're in Liverpool 8. Toxteth. Rogues with accents. But the Lovely Girls could just as well have been brought up in Saffron Walden or Cheltenham. They had no Liverpool accent – just happy, well-spoken voices which, if they had a fault, were a little excitable. The girls talked rather quickly and they *loved* music. They went to see all the local bands at the Picket and the Lomax. Eloise blushed once when James Love, the Grams' cherubic but perennially randy guitarist, pointed out that both Lovely Girls' names had impeccable rock 'n' roll lineage, even though Joy had already told them many times about all the bands that she and their father had known before the girls were born. Their father died a long long time ago.

'Hey! He's gone into my hole!'

Maddy's favourite joke. The War Office was a little side room in the pub, favoured by would-be bohemians and the Grams. Maddy always called it 'my hole', and liked to ask chaps if they'd care to come into her hole. At one time, Maddy and Eloise used to gigglingly volunteer to be the Grams' groupies.

'We'll be your groupiz,' they'd blush, meaning it. The amateurish, DIY nature of the suggestion – you guys are a band, now, so we'll play your concubines – used to irritate Keva. Music was not a game to him. From the moment that Syd, years ago, *years* ago, had played him 'Way To Blue' he had known the sound of his own pain and wanted to make a similar, yet different sound. A music that'd make it better. 'Groupiz' didn't even figure.

No reasonable person'd try it on with the Lovely Girls. James, though, had shagged both of them, after a gig at the Picket, on their downstairs couch. Eloise waited her turn. They'd been screwing since they were thirteen, they told him pleasantly, Maddy losing her virginity two minutes before Eloise.

Wheezer burst in, out of breath, sucking on his Ventolin, gesticulating for a pint. His loony Jerryhelmet cut looked more Luke Skywalker than ever, parted down the middle by the breeze as he'd run up the hill from Central. Keva got up to fire them in, pushing the *NME* at Wheezer.

'Seen it,' gasped Wheezer, smiling his twisted smile. 'Bonkers!'

Keva came back with another Guinness for himself and a pint of Timmy Taylor for The Wheeze. The Grams were fond of the ale in there, deeming it a drinker's pint.

Keva glanced at Wheezer's latest shapeless C&A jumper. He could never fathom, had never asked, what causes a person to choose, to *choose* to purchase clothing from C&A. Was it some subconscious – or conscious – tribute to his mother? He smiled but made no comment. He waited for the manager to pronounce, knowing that, whatever he said, it'd make him feel better.

'You're not bothered by this potherb, are you?'

Tended not to swear, Wheezer, erred towards quaint Monty Pythonisms and silly grammar school putdowns. *Potherb* sounded about right for Helmet, though. It suited his silly, poncey, contrivedly 'sensitive' face.

'He's going to LA, Wheeze. It's scary! He's playing to eight fucken thousand on Saturday. Where the fuck are we? No place! In the fucken War Office, planning things . . . planning, as usual.'

'Forget him. He's made of sand. There's nothing to back this up. He's got no tunes.'

This was more like it. Keva could listen to a lot of this.

'Doesn't help us, though, does it?'

'Not directly.'

'Not indirectly. The whole fucken world is into Helmet Horrocks and his band of . . . merrily bonkers minstrels. Where does that leave us? No place, is where that leaves us!'

'Wouldn't be so sure about that. Sometimes it's better to be second man through the door.'

'You what?'

'Let Helmet charge ahead. Use him as battering ram. Let him

use all his efforts for caving the door in. Then he's barely got the strength left to crawl through. He's got nothing left in the tank. You just coast past him. Second man through the door.'

'You're spooking me, la. What you talking about?'

'It's obvious to a blind man. Sensira are jumping up and down with their hands in the air going "Miss! Miss! Me, miss!" But when Miss decides to let Helmet answer the question, he can't. He wants the attention, but he doesn't know what to say.'

'Don't see where that helps us . . .'

They both slurped at their pints. Wheezer made a big thing of pondering deeply, and right now he was just happy to prolong the silence. He could feel it coming. Keva was building up to having another go at him. He was a fucking good manager, everyone knew that. Things had started to move for the Grams since The Wheeze got involved. Even the little club promoters took time at their shows to tug the band to one side and say, 'You got a good manager, there. Glad I let him talk us into doing this show. Don't forget about us when you're famous, eh?' All the same, flak from the boys came with the territory. Who else could they blame when things weren't going so well?

'Found an office yet?'

It always started with something general, some oblique attack on Wheezer's lack of orthodox professionalism as compared with other, usually anonymous, managers.

'Nope. Got a CD I can send out?'

'You know fucken well that I haven't . . . How the fuck are people gonna take us seriously while our postal address is L fucken 60? The tenderloin or what, la? Jeezuz!'

Wheezer held his hands up for calm.

'It's pointless us fighting each other. We're on the same side. If we're going to argue, we should save the fights for stuff that matters.'

Keva stared avidly at the young manager, unsure whether to continue his assault. Wheezer changed tack.

'It's down to money, Keva. That's all it is. How many times have we been down this road? Money to get you in the studio. Money to get the CD cut and manufactured. Money to mail the blighter out. An office comes a poor way down the list, hey?'

Keva nodded.

'Same again?'

Wheezer got up, then stopped in the doorway.

'That's the only difference between Helmet and you. He got that perishing record out. His timing was immaculate, true, but it was the . . . it was having got a record out that counted so much. Something . . . to *have*. We can do that, too.'

'How?'

Wheezer came back in and sat down, leaning his head towards Keva, beckoning him closer. Keva lurched forward.

'We need money quick, right?'

'Too right.'

'Will you do . . . will you consider *anything* to get that money?'

Keva grinned for the first time that day.

'Tell me what you have in mind, you fucking oddball . . .'

The walk was doing Guy good. Every stride of his well-worn Bass loafers took him further away from the Christian Vermeer clinic – from rehab – and back towards real life. Guy deBurret was determined, this time. His nightmare stay in detox, then the endless rehabilitation had been enough to persuade him there was no point in his coming back to say Hi to the nurses. If there was to be a next time he might as well go the whole hog and snort, slur, piss and vomit himself all the way to the crematorium. He'd spent so much of the past month hallucinating, nightmaring, obsessing about his funeral that he knew for sure that he wanted to burn when the time came. But not just yet.

He wheeled out of Flood Street on to the King's Road and, marvelling at the actual tackiness of cultural mythology's Trendiest Road in the World, set himself on course for the Bluebird. Guy would have liked to believe that his mother had chosen the venue so he could lose himself in its vastness, but no. She was sacrificing him to one of her big, clumsy, bosomy gestures of love. They were meeting in the Bluebird because, far from hiding him away, she wanted to show Guy off to the world, show he was better, show he was back. She wanted to show everyone that not only was she not ashamed – she was wholly devoted to her wayward son. This was to be a baptism of fire, with no end of familiar faces dotted around the place whatever the time of day, each intimately acquainted with the sordid details of the demise of one of the Royal Borough's most gilded youths.

He didn't give a shit. He was quite looking forward to it. It'd mainly be the Sloaney dames, young and old and indeterminate, any one of whom would dig out one of their gold fillings for a date with Guy. Whatever the stigma of rehab, it didn't harm your sex appeal. Not only was Guy rich and beautiful. He was Bad.

He didn't know what he was going to say to Ma. She wouldn't make it easy. Ron Lazarus had written a few times and Billy, Speed and some of the A&R boys had been in to see him. The job at MonoGram Records was still there – of course it was. How could a multinational record company sack someone for taking drugs? They were only less likely to sack you for being gay. He'd be quite Someone to sack, too. Nineteen when he signed Medsin, whose very first album went platinum in the UK and gold in Germany, Japan, Australia and the US. Their third album, *Year Zero*, had just gone platinum in the States. Platinum. One million sales. One million in the first ten weeks, MTV banging the hell out of the first clip and every prospect of at least another three hits to come from the album. Two at least. *Year Zero* was going to go five times platinum over there. Fuck Britain. Of course MGR'd have him back. His ears were worth millions.

But he didn't want to go back. In no sense was Guy going back, anywhere. Six weeks was a long time to do nothing but think. He hadn't thought about anything much before. Everything he'd wanted had come to him before he'd really had a chance to plan how he was going to get it. Everything was fast and now and plenty. He was blessed, and he knew it. Even the job at MGR had been set up by a family friend, after Guy had refused to follow his brothers into the Bank. His father had never quite understood why his son would *not* desire a position at Farquhar deBurret and, taking that as the ultimate rejection, had retreated from his family – all of them – spending more and more time alone. Guy felt bad about his old man, but there was no way he was working in a *bank* for the rest of his life, even if he did own a chunk of it. So he'd fallen into a job which was not a job, where the criteria for success were an ability to party and an ability simply to survive, to persevere, to still be around. But Guy had gone against the grain. He had talent. He was shit hot, and that was his downfall.

Nineteen years old and shit hot with the world at his feet. What more could he want? Not much. Only ways of expressing his misery. By his twenty-first birthday he was doing methadone with Evie and the girls in St Pancras. The new Medsin album was off to a flying start, and Guy just felt dead. On St Valentine's day this year he'd been found outside the Cross Bar choking on his own vomit. Food for thought.

So he wasn't going back. He wasn't going to be shit hot. He wasn't going to compete. He had vague thoughts of heading off to Deya or Ronda, maybe write or do a little painting. But more than anything he wanted to find Evie. Evie was the constant during his lost months. For the first few weeks he'd asked for her every day, then, when they couldn't find her, he made his plans. It'd work. They'd be great together. Rake-thin Evie, his favourite trick, his closest friend . . . He was going to find her and take her off the street and take her away with him. Abroad. Anywhere. Anywhere that was not this, here, now.

He'd thought about little else and the more he thought about it, the more he convinced himself it could work, him and Evie. It was the one real thing in his life. His royalties from Medsin'd pay his way, even if his father saw through his threat to cut him off. Whatever he did from now on, it'd have nothing to do with pressure, sales targets, commerce – and the further he got from the sultry insinuation of rock 'n' roll, the better.

He'd wondered, often, what made him do such things, why he went further and further and closer to the edge. Why did he do that? Why would he destroy himself? Often, too, he thought it was because of the music business. Music. Business. Two words which should never live side by side. Coming to MGR as a wide-eyed romantic, he was, at first, shocked, then quickly disillusioned by the callous disregard of his colleagues for the talent of their bands. In playground terms, it wasn't *fair*. Only when bands reached lunar earning potential were they given human consideration and even then it was a trade-off. It was all a bid to keep them sweet. At all times, all bands and artists were product and their treatment reflected their marketability. Whether the label sent you to

Glastonbury by helicopter or transit van, they were sending you there to do business. He'd seen it all – too graphically. Any notions harboured by Guy of sitting up until dawn smoking and arguing with like minds about the blues were all too swiftly squashed. The music business wasn't fair. He hated it. He wouldn't be going back.

He stopped outside the Bluebird and checked himself in the wing mirror of a crassly-parked Merc. Girls had fancied Guy for ever, but he didn't much care for his own face. His nose was a little pointed, he thought, and in his own mind he lacked character – he looked rich and spoilt. He had good, thick yellow hair and clear blue eyes, but, whatever he wore, no matter how street his clobber, his face gave it away. He was a toff. He smoothed down the Hackett blazer and skipped up the steps. He muttered his mother's name to the blue-shirted greeter and followed him across the endless blank white room. He prayed she'd be there but he knew she'd be late.

'*Guy*! Darling! Oh, God, I can't believe it . . . *baby*!'

Ticky Turnbull, a flurry of heels and hair, bounced into his path and smothered him with kisses. He could not have been gladder to see anybody.

'Oh, baby, I've *missed* you! You *did* get my letters? Sorry I couldn't get along to actually see you in the actual flesh . . . you know I've been tutoring? God, tell me about it . . . you're coming to the bash, of course . . .'

Guy held his hands to his ears and grimaced comically. Ticky stopped herself in full, gushing flow and stooped slightly, giggling.

'Put a sock in it, George,' said Guy, thumping her playfully.

'Oops! Am I terribly loud and embarrassing?'

'You're a trollop. Can we sit down, please? I'm sure Maria'll be delighted that I'm in the company of such a *solid* influence . . .'

Ticky prodded him in the ribs, jutting out her underbite in the way girls do when they're fighting boys.

'Less of the solid, matey. I'm a sex goddess. Can't, anyway. Got bloody Bundles on a leash up there.' She rolled her eyes skywards. '*Birth*day treat. I ask you. Like nothing more than to come and rap with you and Maria but I wouldn't inflict Bundles on *any*body. Better dash. *Do* say you'll come tomorrow. Ciao, honey.'

She kissed fresh air and was away, a riot of blondeness. She stopped and half turned.

'Hope he's not going to pro*pose*! Shouldn't have minded so much before I saw you, Guido . . .'

She rolled her eyes again, and clasped her hands theatrically to her bosom. Guy bowed gallantly. She blew him a kiss and shrank her head down into her shoulders girlishly, backing away to her table. Guy chuckled to himself, continued to his own place with the tutting operative and perused the wine list without taking in a single detail. Ticky was twenty-one already. Cripes! It seemed only weeks since they were shinning up trees together during those endless days in the New Forest.

'Oh! Foolish child!'

Maria deBurret's stentorian baritone brought Guy, and half of the Bluebird's customers, back to the present. Guy stood up to greet her, unexpectedly overcome, tears starting to moisten his eyes. His mum smiled lovingly.

'Come here, you wee eedjit! What are we going to do with you?'

Maria lapsed into her native south Dublin brogue and clasped her youngest and most dearly beloved son to her breast. She held him there, still, for a full minute. Guy was certain her cheeks, too, would be moist when she released him.

Maria and Guy sat and talked for three brief hours, pausing only to order, to say ta-ta to Ticky and her squire, Henry 'Bundles' MacCormack, and to greet other friends and gossips who passed their table. The heat had gone out of the early spring sunshine as they negotiated the last few steps out on to King's Road. Maria turned to Guy again and, clasping his face in her two hands, she pulled him close.

'Don't run away, darling. You think that's what you want, but . . . don't go to waste. Your daddy . . .'

Guy shushed her with his index finger.

'. . . your father thinks you're a wrong'un.'

Guy smiled. 'Well, I am, aren't I?'

His mother ran her fingers through his hair, her eyes watering up again. 'You're gorgeous.'

They hugged deeply. Maria stroked his temples with her

thumbs. 'If only he'd see that, hmmm? See all the bloody *good* in you . . .'

This hurt Guy more than he'd imagined it could do. He tried to smile at his ma. 'He will do,' he said. He wanted him to.

In a roped-off corner of a grand marquee in the village of Balmerlawn, Hampshire, James Love sucked on his seventh Players since soundcheck. He still refused to tie his cummerbund.

'Fuck are we doing here, Keva? It's like a fucken freakshow . . .'

'Five grand, that's what. I don't like it any more than you, Jimbo, but, you know – what can you do? We need the dosh.'

James snorted. 'Fucken Wheezer! Does he think we're a cabaret band?'

He eyed the rest of the band, already dressed in evening attire. He picked up the purple satin ribbon between thumb and forefinger, examining it with disdain. 'I mean, what the fuck *is* this? A *cummerbund*! What the fuck's a fucking cummerbund?'

He tossed it on the floor and started to build up with the bumper-sized patchouli skins he'd picked up in Macynlleth.

'Wait till you see the tott, anyway,' grinned Beano, the wiry, always animated drummer. Alan Miles to his mum; tight, harsh white curls, no eyebrows, good smile. 'They're howling for a bit of rough, this lot!'

'State of you, Al,' moaned James, lighting his preposterous reefer and inhaling deeply. 'Hardly out of *Das Kapital*, that, was it?'

'Beg pardon?'

'You. Sid the Sexist.'

'Well, they are. Have you ever seen a crowd like it at soundcheck before? They just kept walking over and catching your eye and, fuckinell, I'm telling you, there is some tott out there! They're just running their eye over us lot to sort out the men from the boys for later. I'm telling you.'

Tony Snow, the laconic bassist, wandered back in, sniffing exaggeratedly. 'What the fuck is *that*?'

'The hippies've taken over the asylum,' grinned Beano.

'*Pot*!' spat Tony, managing to invest the word with sinister, deadly implications. 'Yeuch!'

'*I'll* tell *you* why they're all here for soundcheck, shall I?' said James, ignoring the jibes and getting himself going. 'Because they've been here all fucken day nibbling roast wood pigeon an' that and sipping fucken Pimms, they're bored of the string quartet playing *The Four Seasons*, they're pissed, they're privileged and we're a change of fucken scenery. We're a spectacle! We're a fucken sideshow for the idle rich. It's . . . it's a grotesque carnival of pomp and privilege.'

He rocked on his heels and took another deep toke, seeming pleased with his diatribe.

'Blimey!' laughed Tony.

'Mr Love in Lexicon Binge,' teased Keva.

'Any more of that wood pigeon an' that?' grinned Beano.

'Don't get funny with me. You know the score. We're fodder. We're the fucken turn!'

Everyone cracked up laughing, making James even madder. He kicked the side of a speaker cabinet in vexation, and walked away stiffly, trying not to let the pain show.

'Look, Hector, why don't you just take the short cut. Apologise to Wheezer and admit that he was right all along. And put your fucken cummerbund on! You know you'll have to.' Tony's voice was deliberately, infuriatingly soothing. 'Hector?'

James winked and pointed at Tony with his roach. 'You don't get me that easy, you know.'

James Love, real name Hector Lovett. Named after Hector Chumpitaz, an undistinguished Peruvian footballer who'd appealed to his father's sense of the absurd around the time of James's birth. To this very day, Mr Lovett called James 'Chump', but he'd been James Love since the day he and Keva formed the Grams. That was a day of destiny, and a day, for James, to be who he wanted to be. From the moment Keva asked him his name, he was James Love. James Love, the Guitarist. The more he indulged himself in this womanising, axe-god fantasy, demanding Remy Martin on the rider in small Northern clubs, the more the band loved to bring him back to reality. He hated, more than anything, to be called Hector, but he hated to let them see it.

'Everything all right, darlings?'

Reality today was a shockingly lucrative, highly embarrassing gig for a load of toffs in a tent in Hampshire. Even James knew it made sense to get their heads down and get it over and done with. No one would ever know – and it'd speed up their response to Sensira's currently unobstructed view of the stars. Even The Purple were supposed to be talking to record companies. Why not the Grams?

'Do we have absolutely everything we need?'

Everybody turned to see who the owner of the cut-glass *QE2* voice was. They were met by the radiant face of Victoria Turnbull, twenty-one today, heiress to the Turnbull supermarket millions, aglow in all the simple good fortune of being who she was. Ticky Turnbull. Witty, glamorous, rich, connected, super at games and, while not strictly a heart-stopping beauty, she was pretty and made the most of an impressive bosom, bound high in a voluptuous Wonderbra. The Grams were speechless.

'Yes? No?'

James tore his eyes from her cleavage.

'Couldn't find us a bottle of that bubbly everyone's gassed on? Any old bottle'll do. One of your old fella's'd be sound – Dom Turnbull an' that.'

'HEC – TORRR!'

Ticky giggled enchantingly. 'Anything you want, sweetie.' She went to walk away then stopped and thought aloud. 'But then do we *really* want to be guzzling naughty champagne *so* soon before we go on? First set's less than an hour.'

Keva laughed and clapped his hands. Her rejection of James's ridiculous request had been charming and final. James gazed after her, puppy-eyed.

'Bottle of Remy, then? I can handle me Remy an' that. Doesn't do nothing to me . . .'

Ticky tossed her golden tresses and glided out of the marquee, smiling back over her shoulder. 'I'll see if I can find you some Guarana!'

James paused for impact. 'You can see your knickers through that, you know!'

'Perfect!' she tinkled, and floated off into the distance.

'Not that you'll have on 'em for long,' muttered James, and settled down to restringing his guitar.

'Knocking up or what, Kee?'

He was starting to look forward to this. Keva pulled out his tin.

'So, Hector, what was that about Sid the Sexist?' smiled Beano.

'What was that about *first* set, is all I'm worried about?' groaned Tony. 'She *did* say that, didn't she? Or am I making the whole thing up?'

'I didn't catch it,' said Keva. 'Where's fucken Wheezer?'

Fucken Wheezer was standing to the side of the main steps of Balmer Hall, smoking, smiling, watching the guests arrive. It was great. He'd already seen several thespians and seventies rock stars arriving early for the booze and, in between the debs and semi-aristos he recognised from *Tatler*'s Bystander pages, he'd bathed in the warm afterglow of self-regard. And while he didn't for a moment think of this show, this non-show, really, as any sort of career high for the boys, it was, undoubtedly, a management triumph. He'd got this earner for the lads, double quick, all by himself. They should think themselves lucky to have him.

Normandie Keith, actually lucent, passed right by him. These women, these incandescent beauties, had a shimmering allure unique to the world's most privileged. They were born lovely, but their teeth, their eyes, their beauty were enhanced by a short lifetime's exposure to the best of everything – except work and care. They were carefree, and beautiful for it. Their smiles, their perfect light tans, radiated fortune.

Tara Palmer-Tomkinson was Wheezer's favourite, twinkling with mischief and intelligence, naughty eyebrows and a luxuriant sheen to her skin. He was determined to ask her for a light if she happened by. Such infinite beauty could only be accessed by the very few. The extremely rich, of course, had no trouble pulling the Sophie Andertons and Laura Baileys. They, along with actors, politicians and rock stars, could take their pick. Simon Le Bon for God's sake, a provincial tubby if ever there was one, managed to cop for Yasmin Pervanneh off the hair adverts. Maybe the manager could get a bit, too, if his band did well. A girl like Tara would talk to you if you were manager of U perishing 2, wouldn't she? No matter if you were unremarkable and spoke through your nose – neither supreme wealth nor the veneer of power was a turn-off. A bit of deflected glamour'd do The Wheeze no harm at all. He set himself killingly high standards. If he couldn't have Tara, then it'd be someone like her.

Wheezer squeezed his Silk Cut Ultra for a better flow of toxins and dragged hard on it. He'd had asthma, really bad, lungy, bronchial asthma, since he was four and he'd been smoking since he was eleven. Sometimes he thought that was because his dad had been a chest specialist. Dr Finlay. It hadn't helped overcome his shyness in the playground. By smoking, now, he kept them all alive through the bitter remembered rows.

His family – mum, dad, three younger sisters and one little brother – were wiped out in the car crash. Six years ago, in the summer before he was due to go to university. The accident sent him, quite definitely, into shock. Emotionally he was immature anyway, but this had taken him right back inside himself.

The family had been well-off, comparatively, although Dad sent far too much money to numerous relatives in Ireland and insisted on putting all five kids through private school. They lived in a big, dilapidated Edwardian semi in Parkwest, Lower Heswall, and drove an ancient Volvo. The house was lovingly neglected – lived-in, every inch of it, and worn out through decades of family life. Dad never did so much as plaster over the crumbling walls and the house never saw a lick of paint in all the years they lived there. The car, too, went without services and seatbelts. He blamed Dad for the tragedy for years, for rubbing out his family, then blamed him some more for having no pension, no insurance, no provision. The house was paid for, just, when they died. Wheezer was left with just over £17,000 after death duties and expenses. With insufficient funds to do the place up and make it saleable Wheezer went to ground there.

Or rather he went to sky. The playloft in the roof of the house was converted into Wheezer's leisure suite. He scrubbed the place down and painted it white, spending cannily on a second-hand Technics system, complete with sub-woofers; a huge Sony home-cine Nicam Stereo telecentre with the full Sky Digital package and a vast, splitting, mustard-yellow chesterfield that he'd spotted in the *Globe* and sprawled upon which he spent the majority of his life. He was always scanning the Wirral *Globe* for bargains, useful additions to his squad, but he was pretty well content. He signed on, smoked thirty a day, bought records, kept the garden tidy, read *NME*, *Tatler* and the *Financial Times*. He watched pornographic videos, which he acquired by post from adverts.

He could go for days without speaking, letting the phone ring if he didn't feel like getting up off the sofa, or just didn't want to talk. His communion, his link with the outside and his means of expression was his PC. He had the full works, P400 chip, modem, quad-sound, everything. That was the thing he plugged himself into, the heart that kept him beating. It was through this, in the last couple of years, that he'd started to make a little extra money playing the stock market, investing modest amounts and generally performing above the market averages, and it was through his PC that he trawled a world of music on the Internet.

But when he went outside, what Wheezer lived for was to smoke and drink at rock concerts. He'd go anywhere, to any pub, any shithole to see a group. Live bands were the whole point of nightfall to Wheezer and by day he stoked his obsession. Communing with the global family of music lovers on the Internet, Wheezer was on top of every musical scene, everywhere in the world. He spent most of his dole money devouring websites about obscure bands in North Carolina or Oregon, writing to fellow devotees. He could get in touch with a promoter in Sioux City as easily as one in Hull. The rest of his time on the Net was allocated to his other interests – pornography and easy money. For a couple of years, now, on any given day, he'd play some tunes, e-mail a few of the more progressive indie promoters about the Grams, deal a few shares, peruse some porn and masturbate. Wheezer Finlay was a music nut, a miser and a relentless masturbator. He was a natural for management.

Five thousand pounds for an unknown band was not the work of a greenhorn. A casual enquiry from a tipsy Sloane at a gig in Durham last Christmas had been ruthlessly hunted down by The Wheeze the morning after his drink with Keva in Ye Cracke. He'd kept the kid's number, just as he kept every number, just in case. And this was a case in point. They desperately needed to get some meaningful funds together so that the Grams could get their own single out. A thousand sales through The Chain With No Name would get them in the indie charts, and who could say where that might lead. The toff came up trumps. He could get the Grams gigs right through the summer, as many society bashes as they cared to shake a stick at, and the wedge was top dollar. Wheezer had asked him to find them just one – one that'd pay them five grand.

'I can *do* this!' grinned Wheezer. 'I'm good at it. I can be a Player!'

He chuckled to himself and stubbed out his ciggie as a nimble MGF pulled up on the coral-pink gravel drive. If these aristos wanted to give him five big ones for a couple of sets out in the anonymity of the countryside, no danger of any music journos blowing their cred, then that was fine by him. This would be the last time he'd have to coax, cajole and railroad the boys into doing things they hated. It was for the best. From now on they could get things motoring, starting first thing Monday. This was the start of something big. A sleek, racing-green Bentley Turbo drew up alongside the MG. Shit! *Two* sets! He hadn't actually got around to telling the boys about that one, yet. He loped off into the dusk.

'We're not going on,' stated Keva.

'OK,' said Wheezer.

'Whaddyamean, OK?'

'I mean, fine. It sounds like a decision. So if it's a decision, it's a decision. Let's go.'

'The fucken uniforms are bad enough! Why didn't you tell us about the two-set malarkey?'

'Because you never would've agreed to the blinking gig in the first place if I had.'

'And you thought you'd just politely mention it before we went on, when there was fuck all we could do about it?'

'I don't do things to *humiliate* you, you plank. I do what I think is *right*, and if I have to keep checking every decision back with you then it makes for a bloomin' long day. There has to come a point when you potherbs realise we can't always have the highest principles. We're here because it's to all our benefit. Can you not see that . . . ?'

They looked at each other. Wheezer made big eyes and took a hefty drag on his inhaler.

'. . . and yes, I had intended to mention the two sets bit a *little* bit earlier than this. Clean forgot.'

'Can't argue with that, eh?' smiled Beano. 'Come 'ead. Let's just get the bleedin' show on the road.'

'No way.'

'Keva's right,' blustered James. 'This *is* a matter of fucken principle now!'

'Principle?' said Tony. 'The principle was always getting five big ones in our mitts. If it takes three hours to earn it instead of one, what's the problem? The principle is that we leave here tonight knowing that next week we start recording our first single.'

'I agree with you,' said James.

Keva shook his head in amazement. 'You're fucken scary, you are, Hector. You're a one-off.'

Wheezer stood up and looked directly into Keva's face. 'So what d'you want to do?'

Keva examined his manager's astonishing hairstyle and his suede-and-corduroy zip-up cardi and smiled to himself. 'Get you some decent swag with what's left over.'

Everyone laughed a little too loudly.

'But, eh!' shouted Keva, silencing them again. 'Make sure we get looked after proper, Wheeze. We're not doing them no favours here! No way are we driving back tonight. We want rooms and everything. Two fucken sets!'

James tied his cummerbund around his too-tight black jeans, left on as a silent protest appreciated only by himself.

'This isn't bad, eh?' gasped a sweating Tony in between songs. Keva took a slug of Hildon.

'They're all right.'

'They're fantastic!'

Keva had to allow that these toffs really knew how to party. The Grams were enjoying the sort of bacchanalian freakout usually the preserve of mushied-up drongos invading Stonehenge for the Solstice. Everybody, from eight-year-old boys in twee tartan kilts to ruddy-nosed elder statesmen, was leaping around gaily to the sexy white noise of the Grams. That these folk were some of the worst dancers in the world didn't matter a jot. They went for it like insaniacs, grimacing comically, their faces a study in agonised concentration as they punched the air and twisted with religious vigour, blissfully out of time, a riot of teeth and hair. The band loved it.

The one couple who could really cut it, dancing like they'd grown up in Havana rather than Hampshire, was Guy and Ticky. James had a fine view of Victoria's unfettered breasts as she threw herself into the music and grooved hypnotically. Guy rolled his hips, sliding from side to side like a boxer, grinding out a lascivious beat. He and Ticky were lost in the music.

The Grams paused for breath, sweat cascading now down their bodies. Only James, the love-Buddah, looked at home with his starchy dress-shirt stuck to his well-covered torso.

'Whoo! Sex!' screamed Ticky's pals and female cousins who had all mobbed up in front of the stage, casually ignoring the band at first, dancing with each other and facing away from the stage. After a couple of songs they'd had to listen as well as dance, and by now they had formed a knot of fomenting hormones, swaying down the front, taking the piss out of themselves and the band, but loving every second. James and Tony had had a marvellous time, pumping and thrusting in the general direction of the Sloanettes.

'Yo! More! C'mon, Sex Gods, MORE!'

'Yes, play some more, you work-shy Northern bastards!' boomed the Conservative MP for Eastleigh. Everyone hooted, Keva included. Smiling on stage. A first.

'I'm genuinely very sorry to say that this next one is going to have to be the last . . .'

'Boo! Shame! . . .' 'Ripoff!!' 'Whassis, Turnbull! Bloody skin-flint!'

'The licence . . .'

'Licence? Sod the licence! I'm the chap who wrote the bloody thing! Give it here!'

The tent rocked to the amplified braying of horsy laughter.

'Besides,' said Keva, holding up his hands for quiet, enjoying himself up there, 'we know that the Minister for Social Security is down there somewhere and we wanted to get away before he takes our dabs and rats to the soshe . . .'

The tent shook again with delirious laughter and synchronised stomping of feet.

'Have a whip-round!' 'Buy them some pies!'

'Anyway!' shouted Keva. 'This is it. It's a slower one. It's about how little things sort of . . . light up the world if you just open your eyes and see them. It's called "Beautiful." I'd like to see spontaneous hugging among you lovely . . . rather wealthy people.'

Guy went to take Ticky by the hand but found himself being pushed away by the clumsy, now inebriated, corpus of Bundles MacCormack.

'My dance, I think, deBurret,' he slurred, pulling Ticky away with force.

'*Thank* you, Henry, I *can* walk,' spat Ticky, shrugging herself loose and striding ahead of the sodden squire. She glanced back at Guy who winked happily. MacCormack's reddening face glowered at Guy, mouthing the word 'smackhead' as he passed. If it hadn't been Ticky's twenty-first, Guy might have had to lay the fat boy out, then and there. Serve the pig right for looking like a seventeenth-century assize judge at the age of twenty-eight.

But no. Nothing would spoil the evening. Guy was having a great time. And this band really were something else. They had it, he was sure they had. They were spiritual. The songs were instant and catchy, but there was a depth to them, too, a dark side that he couldn't immediately fathom. Maybe it was good that he should sit this one out and watch them properly. Fuck Bundles MacCormack. He wouldn't know soul if it woke him up in the middle of the night, said 'This your missus?' and screwed her right in front of him. This band had soul, spirituality, the lot.

Guy sat and watched as the Grams bridged the generation gap with this gorgeously soothing protest song. The younger guests grabbed candles off the tables and held them aloft down the front, while others waltzed gently and the remainder swayed together, slowing as the words began to resonate, then simply stopped and listened. Guy was not alone in biting back a swell of tears, smiling at the folly of it, and the act of his laughing loosened a gentle, gently intensifying espression of emotions held at bay too long. He felt drenched. The simple beauty of the ballad was more powerfully affecting than anything he'd heard, anything new, in years. It was as good as 'Imagine'. If 'Beautiful' was the only thing that these boys ever wrote it would still be more than enough. The melancholic refrain, asking for a love that can't be had, was almost too sad to bear. It was poetic. It was Great. It would add something which was not already there. And Guy had already heard more, as well, more than enough to know absolutely that this was a Great Band.

Who did he think he'd been kidding? To think that he could walk away from music was a folly. Most of it he could cheerfully dump – the packaged, niche-marketed, antiseptic dreck which constituted so much of his popmart world. But there would always be moments like this. There would continue to be, for always, that one track which transcends everything. This was his life. He slumped back and sobbed out of relief and happiness.

'S'matter, Uncle Guy?'

Little Giles deBurret stood on his tiptoes, dabbing at his uncle's eyes with the corner of his tiny lace handkerchief. Guy swept up the four-year-old and sat him on his knees.

'Nothing's the matter, Farmer Giles,' smiled Guy. 'Everything is just tickety-boo.'

Which it was. Guy was determined that this band, these songs, would not be twisted and manipulated and compromised by the music business. Guy saw a glimpse of a possible future and it liked him well.

Long after the end of their set, having been physically coerced into an hour's-worth of punked-up Beatles and Rolling Stones covers, the Grams would play no more. To hoarse cheers and lewd wolf-whistles the band trooped off-stage, Beano and James stopping to sign every arm, leg, paper doily and breast pushed in front of them. Keva and Tony forged onwards through the crowd, keen only to lie down, speak little and, in time, eat a few crisps.

James spotted Ticky at the side of the stage, hands on hips, head inclined, eyeing him with amusement. He made his way over to her as casually as he was able with a semi rock-on in those restrictively snug jeans. Bundles MacCormack was unconscious at her feet, his dinner jacket stained red with vomit.

'Hi.'

'Hi, you.'

'The birthday girl. Do I get me bubbly now?'

She smiled and stooped down to shift Bundles off her foot. James took another eyeful of her breasts. With her back to him and still pushing at the supine MacCormack, she reached behind and slid her hand between James's legs. He glanced back at the dance floor. Nobody was watching.

'You filthy bastard. You couldn't take your eyes off them.'

'They were there, like.'

Still bending over MacCormack, she worked the buttons of James's flies.

'Want to have them?'

'What?'

Only now did she turn round. 'Come on. You'll have to give me a hand with this bloody pig, first. That'll be our cover. We'll drag the fat fuck out the back way. Accept no offers of help. Come on!'

James stood there, the tip of a lycra-shrouded erection peeping from his unbuttoned jeans. 'Sound an' that. Yeah. I'll have that . . .'

Tony reappeared, wet hair sticking up, white towel around his shoulders, spraying deodorant into the T-shirt he was unravelling.

'Coming to have a look?'

'Nah. You go. I'll wait for The Wheeze to come back. Might do a runner with the lolly.'

'Sure?'

'Yeah. Fucked.'

Tony shrugged his shoulders and made his way out of the old gypsy caravan they'd been using as a dressing-room. Keva sank back into the bunk, started to wrap a one-skinner and thought about the dizzying array of girls out there. There were some real little babes down the front, knowing Roedean types you knew'd do anything for a *rock star*. He smiled to himself. It was too easy. And after the spangling high of the show, he felt deflated. He was tired.

He smeared Clinique's M Lotion over his face and neck and left it to soak a while. Body Shop under-eye firming gel went on, as did their wheatgerm oil around the eyes and temples. He popped a couple of zinc tablets and washed them down with V8 just in case he changed his mind about the floozies. But it seemed unlikely. He almost never thought about sex these days, and initiated sexual encounters even less frequently. When sex visited him, it was in the form of brief encounters which were easier to accept than decline. Girls after shows were his most likely outlet, but even then they'd have to hunt him down and do all the work. He couldn't be arsed. It was more a case of keeping face in front of the band.

And now, recently, more and more he *couldn't* be bothered. Twice on the last mini-tour, in Dundee and Newcastle, he'd been summarily incapable. In Newcastle the girl had apologised and gathered her things and rushed out, upset, but to the Dundee girl it was a challenge. She was up and down him, flickering at his nipples, caressing his balls – and still nothing.

'Will I stay the night?' she'd said.

After that, Keva thought he'd only go after sex – and everything – when he really wanted it. He wasn't doing anything out of habit, or because he felt he had to, or because everyone else was doing it. Eating, sleeping, watching *South Park* – he'd do it if he wanted to.

Keva alone knew the real reason for this almost permanent state of ennui. It was to do with the encroaching horrors of age. He'd been thinking about it constantly. Nine months from now, on New Year's Eve, Keva McCluskey would be saying ta-ta to his twenties. To his youth. Of this nobody but his mother had an inkling, and he hadn't seen her in years. Just that thought, that little broken bit of a notion sent his spirit plummeting down, down, deadly down. He had to kick back against it, drive it out and away.

Keva only ever mentioned his birthday in the vague context of star signs and never at all when it was near. Any celebration of the day itself was always neatly outshone by New Year revelries. That there was no focus on his own Big Day, allied to his preternaturally boyish looks, meant that Lark Lane and the world took Keva McCluskey for twenty-three or so. James Love, at twenty-five, was the daddy of the group, while both Alan and Tony had only turned twenty in recent memory.

It had been gradual, this running down of his motor, but with the waning of his third decade it all seemed so final. It wasn't just his genes. Nothing was fun. He couldn't get worked up about anything but the band. Keva's sole obsession was the band, the band, the band – and even that was going down the pan. Few things gave him pleasure. He could not get fired up. Clothes, maybe. He could get a fixation on a shirt or a pair of trainies when he first clapped eyes on them in the shop, but even then it was a quick thrill. He'd obsess about it until he'd got the money together to buy the thing, then he'd wear it once and think it was just all right.

He was trying everything to boost his vim. He took zinc, liquidised carrots and spinach, meditated, tried to work out what he needed more of. But nothing worked. His overall feeling was a sullen listlessness. The songs he wrote had, for a long time now, a sense of sadness which was easy to miss in the maelstrom of the clubs, live. On stage and with the group he came to life. He was angry. But when he sat and played alone, on the Martin, his songs made him ache. The feeling that things were coming to an end would not go away, and this stuff with Helmet was making it so much worse.

It hurt him that he'd been used by Helmet, had unwittingly helped this inferior band along the way. But it hurt more that this was to the exclusion of his own talent. Sensira did not deserve all this acclaim. It was that simple. It was, simply, not fair. It was so, so wrong that the Grams had been trumped by such a negligible force. If the Grams didn't, very soon, start to receive the acclaim they deserved, Keva couldn't see them carrying on. As a band they'd be over, but for him, more than anything, what'd be the point? Wheezer was off now, collecting the dough that'd finally turn into the Grams' first single, but what if people hated it? He'd probably, quite seriously, do himself in. There'd be nothing else to live for. The Grams *had* to make their mark. And they had to do it quickly.

He thought of the lads – the young *lads* – out there, charming the girls, taking their pick. It was so easy. He tried to remember that surge of desire, when you talk to a girl and your dick's already shooting up your stomach in anticipation. Another life. He loved women. He loved being in love. But it all seemed to be slipping away from him. All of it. A gentle knock at the door stopped him from having to think too hard.

Wheezer followed Lord Turnbull into his study. Out through the leaded, mullioned windows, Wheezer could see clearly the spectacle of James Love, encouraged by a guffawing female accomplice, bolting an inert figure to the lawn with croquet hoops. As the girl staggered to and fro, laughing, James secured each limb tight to the croquet strip with two or three hoops until the snoring bulk was imprisoned like Gulliver.

'Well,' said Turnbull, trying key after key from the immense chain he produced from his immense desk, 'that was hot poop.'

Wheezer, a collector of grammatic curios, was thrown.

'I'm sorry . . .?'

Turnbull, red-eared, turned back from the wall-safe, determined to be understood. 'The show. First rate. Bloody marvellous, actually. Very, ah, with it.'

Wheezer smiled. 'Thanks. Glad it worked out.'

The heavy door clunked open, taking Lord Turnbull, chain of keys still in hand, with it. He disentangled himself from the safe door and delved inside. He brought out a brick of banknotes. Wheezer tried not to gape. Turnbull whizzed the crisp notes against his thumb and plonked them on his desk. He looked at them a while.

'Five, we said?'

'Yes, sir. That's the fee I arranged with Hugh. Five thousand pounds.'

Saying it almost made him faint with pleasure. He was a Player. Lord Turnbull nodded and inclined his head slightly to the right.

'Mmm. Value Added Tax?'

'Not registered, sir. Not yet.'

'Mmmm.'

Turnbull stared back into the safe. Wheezer took a peek at the block of currency on the desk. Fifties. A hundred of the beggars. He wondered if now was a good time to broach the question of a few beds for the night. He took a deep breath. Turnbull brought out another brick of banknotes, thumbed through it, went to split it then shrugged 'what the heck' and threw another five thousand pounds on to his desk. Wheezer gaped. Sucks to the beds. He could hardly put the bite on him now. He'd book them all into some country pub for the night with the extra dosh and tell the band he'd had to make a gory scene to get it.

'Little bit extra, there. You must all stay over, too, as our guests. Appreciate the extra work you chaps did for us this evening. Could've told us where to stick it. Came up trumps. Excellent show.'

Wheezer dragged his eyeline away from the money. 'Oh, no, honestly, that's not necessary. Encores are all part and parcel of the show.'

Turnbull swivelled sharply, facing Wheezer now.

'Not exactly Prince Rupert, are you? Don't think I can quite understand chaps who go around turning down five thousand pounds. Tell you something. It's true. Don't be a nice guy. Be straight – but don't be nice. See? Take the cash and get out among those fillies before I change m'mind.'

Wheezer took it and walked, quickly, back out through the maze of corridors until he found himself once more outside the hall. Only then did the nervous, exhausted giggle steam out from his lungs like a boiling kettle. He got the money out again, and stared at it. He kissed it, laughing, and, checking that no one was there to see him, started to lick the thick pack of notes, chuckling bronchially to himself. This was fantastic! Thousands and thousands of flipping pounds! The most they'd ever been paid before was four hundred pounds for the student show in Bangor. *Now* look at them – they were up and away!

He wondered, as he ambled back to the caravan, whether the group needed to know about their windfall just yet. He could make out that he'd had to negotiate hard for the night's lodgings, but the extra lolly would be spoiling them right now. As of yesterday, there was £37.19 in the group's account. Maybe he'd just keep this bonus back for emergencies.

Keva had listened in silence and with mounting excitement, alien conditions both, as Guy deBurret had outlined his plans to him. He pronounced his name 'Ghee'. He wasn't one to fall for a line, Keva, but this bloke had a charm and a directness which would make you eat out of his hand. He'd worked in the music business since he left school. He'd signed Medsin for fuck's sake, not his own personal cuppa but fuckinell, Medsin, you know? This Guy, Ghee, good dancer, cool-looking fella, was now completely disenchanted with the record industry. He'd even got Keva laughing at the very idea of music, genius, creation, inspiration, being an 'industry'. He had him cackling at his impersonation of pimply A&R men in Patrick Cox shoes (the impersonation here involved a pigeon-toed-geek-in-big-shoes walk, which was brilliant) coming up and saying: 'Hi. I'm in the industry myself.' He was a passionate talker. Keva liked him. In particular he liked what he had to say about the Grams.

'You're unique. I mean that. I love the spirituality of your band. It's pure. It's the Emotion Signal. I mean, you saw some of those old dowagers out there, they were fucking *crying*. That's God-given. It's not something that anyone can just set out to do. You can't make that up with bits and pieces of what's gone before and give it a topspin, although I do see your Gram Parsons borrowings, I like the way you weave those bits in, it's nice, not retro at all. I take it that's where the name comes from? Nothing to do with barbiturates, I trust? You ever think about bringing in a little bit of cello on the last chorus to "Beautiful"? Now that *would* have 'em sobbing in the aisles . . .'

He'd gone on like that, gushing, lurching from idea to mad idea, full of himself and the Grams.

'*God-given* . . .'

And then he'd launched into the real soul-bearing stuff about his drug-taking, his personality changes and the gradual decline in his life, leading to attempted suicides and, ultimately, detox and rehab.

'ReHab Records. That's what I'm going to call my label. That'll stick it right up my old man and those fucking thick-headed heathen brothers of mine. ReHab Records!'

He paused and laughed. 'And we're going to have fucking principles. We're going to be the artists' label, man. ReHab Records. The artists' label!'

Wheezer came through the caravan door as the two of them cackled and clinked cans to ReHab. A sixth sense of jealousy shot through him, a reflexive possessiveness that anybody should try to make business moves, should be talking business, with his artist without his say-so. He felt cross with bloody Keva, too, for his disloyalty. He should've stalled the guy to wait until his manager got back, whatever he was talking about. He hadn't been gone half an hour and here he was drinking to some shady bloody relationship they hadn't seen the need to bring him in on.

That was so typical of Keva. From the start he'd let Wheezer manage the bits he wasn't interested in himself. Hustling for gigs. Hiring vans and PAs. But he'd been the last of the four of them to sanction Wheezer as sole signatory on cheques for less than two hundred pounds, which was just practical common sense. Who wants to be running to the band for approval of a cheque to Telecom for 107 quid? Even now, anything more than two hundred rips'd have to have Keva's counter signature and, even then, only after patient, paranoid, minute justification. If the band needed to get T-shirts printed and it was going to cost £279 for a hundred, Keva'd find a way of implying that the moment he countenanced the cheque the money would be sailing straight into one of Wheezer's many accounts.

So it shouldn't have been such a surprise that here he was again, encroaching on to managers' turf when it was sexy enough to take his fancy. He felt puny. Keva could flick him to one side anytime he fancied. Wheezer could wear his fingers down to the knuckles for this lad and he'd still swap him for someone else if the mood took him, or if he thought it'd give him a better shot at the stars. That extra five thousand – should he decide to keep it – and the certainty that nobody would ever find out about it, restored a chunk of his self-esteem. He flopped on to a bunk without acknowledging them, giving nothing away.

'You'll be Wheezer,' said Guy, smiling.

'The very same,' said The Wheeze, smiling back, offering his hand, hating the guy – and hating himself for liking him.

'Have a can, Wheeze,' said Keva. 'You'll like this.'

Guy played footsie under the breakfast table with a wan-looking Ticky. She stared at her plate. Of the assembled breakfast guests, only Guy looked remotely well. He grinned perversely.

'So what is it, then, Georgie?'

'Don't call her that, Guy,' boomed Maria. The nickname 'George' had stuck with Ticky for those who remembered her tomboy days, shooting rats with her air rifle and shouting 'filth' at the local bobby. Guy ignored his mother.

'It can't be the lightly poached eggs which are the cause of such distraction. And you've drunk gallons more champagne than that and lived to tell the tale. So why is the glamorous Lady Victoria, newly of age, such a study in repose? Could she still be in shock, perchance, at events which unfolded in the wee small hours?'

Maria scowled at him. Ticky looked up, snapping out of her reverie and smiled conspiratorially at Guy. She leaned forward, covering her breasts with one hand out of deference to Maria. 'Do you think he'll be all right?' giggled the meat 'n' veg heiress.

At dawn, Bundles had eventually managed to alert a groundsman to his lowing. He was almost rigid with cold and would have been soaked to the bone had there been less fat and fur to penetrate. Pneumonia was still an outside possibility as the groundsman, stifling chuckles, freed Henry from his improvised manacles and ran to call an ambulance. MacCormack was more concerned by the sounds of pleasure he'd been forced to listen to, at length, emanating from the boathouse by the lake. He had, thus far, been denied sight of his putative fiancée's flesh, but when he fantasised about making love to her, a pastime which was indulged in rarely but with gusto on those occasions when he was neither eating nor sleeping, she made sounds like those he heard last night. He had insisted on walking to the ambulance and collapsed spectacularly two yards from his target.

'He'll be in paradise,' sniggered Guy. 'Nice comfy bed, plenty of grub, tons of lackeys to run around for him.'

'Poor old Bundles.'

'Make someone a super husband.'

Everyone joined in the laughter, which seemed auspicious enough for Guy to spit out his news.

'Erm, Ma . . .?'

'Mm?' Maria looked up from the *Sunday Times*.

'I'm thinking of going into business.'

*

Wheezer read the first copy as the slothful Xerox churned out the rest. 'WITH LOVE ALL THINGS ARE POSSIBLE' it said at the top of the page. It was a good-luck chain letter. If you photocopied it twenty times and sent it out within ninety-six hours you would be enveloped by an ethereal spirit of good fortune. So many nice things would happen that you'd have to pick your way quite carefully through them, otherwise you'd be sure to trip over. But there was a flipside. If you failed to send out the letter of love to twenty people within ninety-six hours you were fucked.

'Carlo Daddit, an office employee, received the letter and forgot it had to leave his hands within ninety-six hours. He lost his job. Later he found the letter and mailed twenty copies. Within a few days he got a better job. Dalan Fairchild received the letter and, not believing, he threw the letter away. Nine days later he died.'

'Poor old Dalan,' muttered Wheezer.

Who the heck had slipped the ruddy thing under his door? Some crazy chambermaid looking for a change of life? He and Keva had both sat up until three, excited, and the note hadn't been there when he went to bed. He picked up the last of the copies and ran to join Keva, waiting outside the hotel.

'Wish me luck,' smiled Guy.

They got up to leave the little café in Liverpool Street. He'd explained it all to them, but no matter how many times he said it, it sounded to Wheezer and Keva like he was going in there to borrow money off himself. They walked out into the street, more nervous about this than anything either of them could recall.

'Ta for the hotel, by the way, Guy. Top of the shop.'

Wheezer didn't want to get too far up Guy's arse, especially now it looked as though the deal – the *deal*! – was going through, but the hotel, the Gore, right behind the Albert Hall, *had* been cool and it was only right to thank him. He'd paid for Keva and him to stay over, while Long Richard, their loyal driver-roadie, had taken the group back to Liverpool in the van.

'Pleasure. It's recoupable, of course,' he smiled.

Recoupable. Wheezer'd read up about things like that in *How to Succeed in the Music Business*. So far, he'd failed cosmically. Guy stopped opposite Finsbury Circus and turned to face them.

'Well – this is where I get off. Fingers crossed, boys . . .'

He pointed out a whitewashed pavilion in the gardens, to all intents and purposes a grander-than-usual storage shed.

'Nice place. Wait in there for me. Might be five minutes . . . might be three hours!'

He waited for the lights, and strode off towards the Circus itself.

They made their way over to the pavilion, an incongruous haven of calm amid the hurlyburly of the ancient financial seat of the City of London. All around them, billions of pounds, yen, dollars and marks were being made and lost without a nail being hammered or a nut being tightened. And right there, on the sixth floor of one of the oldest and loveliest buildings on the north side of Finsbury Circus, the immediate prospects of the Grams pop group were being divined. It would have seemed impossible a couple of days ago and still seemed far-fetched now.

'Well. It's out of our hands, now. Secret handshakes and all that . . .'

Wheezer and Keva took stools at the bar. Even though the place was deserted Wheezer felt out of his depth. He gave the wad in his navy gabardine 'manager's' jacket the gentlest touch, just to be sure it was safe. He'd have to get it to the building society soon. There was bound to be a branch round this part of town.

Wheezer couldn't see a price list anywhere. He ordered two cups of tea from the little bar. The tea, when it came, was served, with a fine array of biscuits, in a big, steaming Royal Worcester pot.

'What d'you reckon?' asked The Wheeze.

Keva looked away, then smiled. 'I reckon we're on. I really do, mate. I reckon this is it.'

Now Keva had made the privacy of tortured dreams into words, Wheezer allowed it, too. For the first time since he'd started managing them eighteen months ago – even though he'd pumped them up many, many times – for the first time Wheezer Finlay allowed the notion that he was working with a real band. A band that magazines would want to interview and photograph. One that put records out. One that people adored. One that made money. They giggled silently, giddy inside, relishing the moment.

Wheezer fished out the chain letter again, and read out the pay-off line, amused.

'Remember. Send no money and do not sign this. It works.'

There'd been an impasse at Farquhar deBurret. Guy and his brothers – sly William, pig Ralph and oaf Hilary, waited and waited for Lord Philippe to arrive until even William ceased to be amused by Guy's mounting irritation. Louis Buss, the family attorney, was drafted in to make the quorum and, even then, the brothers insisted that Guy make a formal presentation to the board.

'Look. The proposal's simple. Give me some of my trust fund now, in advance, on competitive terms. Make money out of me! Just do it!'

William smirked nastily and drawled, looking down at the table, shoulders hunched, swaying slightly, 'No can do, old boy. Not that simple, sorry. Procedure blah-blah.'

Guy turned to Louis Buss, helpless. He winked. If Guy, the only one of Phil's sons who was worth anything, wanted some venture finance he was damn well going to ensure that he got it. He stood up.

'I'm assuming that if we're interested in hearing Guy's proposal then we're *very* interested in supporting his venture?'

The brothers snuffled and coughed and grunted affirmation. Louis nodded to Guy. So he got up, looked at them all for a moment then commenced speaking. Guy made a passionate presentation for his proposed new business, pointing out his strengths and expertise in the music market and the potential advantages of a small, agile company with a commercial ethos. He also gave an honest representation of the record industry's inclination to absorb cash, and his intention to trade ethically.

'Part of my motive for doing this – the *main* reason – is to show that one can do business without one of the parties needing to be victimised. If this band goes to a major record label I'm certain they won't survive past their first big tour of the States.'

William was fighting to keep his face straight. 'Business with ethics, eh? Mmmmm, sort of a Body Shop vibe. What you gonna call yourselves? The Really Moral Music Group?' he snorted.

Hilary was beside himself with mirth, forcing the words out, 'No! No! Or . . . or . . . The Really Moral Vibe Co-Op!'

Guy silenced them. 'Actually, we're called ReHab. Whether you cough up or not, the label goes ahead. What you boys have to ask yourselves now is this: do you want the business? Or do I go elsewhere?'

'How much?'

'Guess!'

'I never guess.'

'OK. Lord Filthy's Devil Child, copyright all the Sunday tabloids you read so keenly, needs to draw down the modest sum of £666,666 to start up this venture. As you're aware, my trust fund matures, give or take a couple of weeks, a year from now. On my twenty-fifth birthday I shall be deemed responsible enough to take a seat on the board . . .'

Ralph went yellow. Guy grinned sadistically.

'. . . and to lay my hands on all that lovely dough you've been putting to work for me. So all I'm proposing here is that you advance a fraction of that sum from the bank on the usual terms of interest, with my fund as the guarantee. The slight difference is that I intend to repay nothing for a year. Not a bean. But exactly one year and one day from receipt of the funding, I shall pay back both the principal and the interest in one lump sum. Everything. If I fail, then I fail big. I forfeit my rights in the family interests. That's your incentive.'

'Say 'gain, old boy? You're ready to drop the lot?'

'Everything.'

While William said nothing, Ralph jumped to his feet, spluttering, 'Seven hundred grand! A gift of seven hundred fucking grand? Because that's what it is. We won't see a penny of that back . . .'

'On the contrary. You actually can't lose. When I succeed, you get back your investment plus interest in the usual way. Should I fail, then my trust fund will more than adequately cover the debt. Plus, I'll be handing over my share of the bank to you boys! It's a bet you're sure to win!'

'What happens to the balance of your trust?'

Guy smiled mock-pleadingly. 'Leave me with something, guys?

You're quids in whatever happens. Doesn't that sound like the sort of deal you boys like? Or do you want me to stroll next door and make exactly the same case to BZT and walk out with better terms, my trust untouched and my position here still intact?'

Ralph went to speak but William cut him short with his bored, dismissive drawl. 'Give him the fucking money. I vote yes. Let's get this thing done and dusted. Who says "aye"?'

'Ooh, not me, never,' said Guy happily, knowing he'd won.

'Louis? What does Pa say?'

Louis Buss looked at William with sleepy contempt and cleared his phlegm. 'Oh, I'd say that he's in favour of the deal. And . . .' He turned to Guy, a skein of moisture damping the bruised grey eyeballs. '. . . I think he'd want to wish you well.'

'I somehow doubt it,' sneered Ralph.

Guy stood up, relieved, but nothing like as elated as he'd expected.

'See you in a year!' smiled William.

It was a muted celebration for Guy. He wasn't surprised at the rebuff from his dad, but he still had hoped, right up to the last minute, that he'd turn up at the bank to support him in this, his first business venture. He'd never given the old man a hard time, not until these few fuck-ups with the drugs and the press and all that. But it was over. *All* of the boys had had their moments, although they'd all ended up acquiescing to family destiny. He'd expected his father to be there today. Louis' words had been well meant, but it would have been better if he'd said nothing.

He felt hardened to this whole thing suddenly, and couldn't feel a part of the hilarity around him. His family were hateful. He watched Wheezer and Keva bent over his mobile, giving the rest of the band the good news. This'd be Guy's reality from now on. He felt, for the first time in his life, real power. He was going to influence fate. Collude with destiny. Not a destiny put in trust for him at birth, but one he could take risks with, fly in the face of, for better or for worse. He was going to protect this band, look after them and take them wherever they wanted to go.

He smiled at Wheezer's twisted, enthusiastic face as he spoke. An amiable dunce. It was something to Guy that he could make a difference. Poisoned by his own life, at least he could make a difference to someone else's. That'd be his purpose. He was going to give other people something to live for. And there was not a day to lose. In every sense, the clock was ticking.

The first thing he did was to bring Ticky in. He fancied he was rescuing her from a similarly pointless round-dance – her excitement and gratitude in accepting told him he wasn't wrong – and Ticky found the offices and the place for the boys to stay. There'd been some debate about moving them down from Liverpool, but with action needed now, on every front, Guy wanted to direct operations hands-on. He'd have called the label Immediate if the bloke from the Rolling Stones hadn't got there first. Everything needed doing immediately, not just because of Guy's bet, but because the time for the Grams had come. Their time was now.

So he had the band in Whitfield Street recording the album with Andy Lachlan, one of the Big Three guitar producers in the UK, and Paul Morrow, a young engineer starting to get noticed for his tricks with feedback and wah-wah. They'd already recorded two tracks, 'Intermission' and 'From Now On', at the Pink Palace in Lark Lane, a stone's throw from Keva and James's front door, and Guy was pleased with the garage-band, almost mono feel to the tracks. He was weighing up the pros and cons of doing the whole album in Liverpool, bringing in a heavyweight old-school producer like Clive Linklater, who was getting all the wrong gigs and would jump at it and make a fucking tremendous album, when Andy, his first choice, had a cancellation.

Andy, a muse and a family man, worked ten 'til three and nine 'til two, weekdays only, only within a twenty-five-mile radius of London. He never touched anything stronger than super-caffeinated coffee, of which he drank many, many cups, each and every day. These distinctly un-rock 'n' roll conditions had conspired to make some of the enduring albums of the late eighties and nineties, and some of the handful which could properly be called classics.

So now Guy had the Grams here, under his nose, where he could regulate trouble, notoriety and genius. The album was shaping up, and there was plenty enough left of the night for the boys to kick up a reputation. It was good to have them out there, spreading the word and sowing seeds. The tatty mews house Ticky had found them in Farm Place, Notting Hill Gate, was perfect for London living – handy for the studio via the Central Line and a taxi ride from all the hotspots. The band loved it. Even Keva was having a good time, talking shite in Camden, pronouncing himself the bastard child of Nico and Nick Drake to appreciative Dutch backpackers.

Guy was happy enough in the new office. They were using the two small rooms at the back of Purvert PR. It was ideal – for now. He couldn't gripe. Fifty quid a week for a prime Clerkenwell address and, more importantly, an inbuilt entrée to Jeff Purvis, undisputed king of press agents, for sure, and a London legend. Ticky was close friends with Hannah Brown, one of Jeff's up-and-coming press officers, and she'd swung it that they could use the spare rooms while they were finding their feet. They were keeping illustrious company. Heavenly Records, Out Promotion and Creation had all touted their wares from these selfsame rooms at one time or another. Guy was hoping that Purvis would insist upon first option on the Grams PR as part of the deal, but this was a man who turned down more cassettes from more starry-eyed bands than the promoters at the Dublin Castle. He was a lanky, dishevelled figure who displayed none of the physical trappings of a premier league music entrepreneur. He was different in that he had integrity too. He only worked with bands that he loved. Guy knew better than to try to push a project upon Jeff Purvis. He'd let the Grams and Jeff fall in love with each other over the full course of time. For now, he had a load of pettifogging details to pin down.

Wheezer called from the studio to say that backing vocals on 'Beautiful' were going a treat. They still had Keva's main vocal to do, but they'd all be fine for the four o'clock meeting. Andy was off to pick his kids up from school and, besides, Keva had been putting down some of his most beautifully battered vocals last thing at night, often after a few drinks and a smoke. Guy was still very unsure about Wheezer. He couldn't fully trust someone who'd gone out, of their own free will, and actioned a haircut like that.

Worse, though, Guy sensed a resentment in him, a brooding, simmering dislike which was hard to simply ignore. On the other hand, he worked well with the band, got them places on time and wasn't afraid to sort out a lot of the mindless stuff which just had to be done. In a situation like theirs, Wheezer could prove to be a useful foot soldier, but nothing more. Guy could not see the Americans taking him seriously. In the perverse Oedipal world of the US music business, labels liked to work with big, stroppy managers who'd bawl them out and bully them. They responded to cats who 'went ballistic' on them. Wheezer could get Keva to an interview on time, but could he get Geffen Records Vice-President of Alternative Promotion to take his call? Unlikely. He just didn't have that big personality. He was insular. Given the extent to which Guy's investment depended upon a breakthrough in the States, he was going to have to keep an eye on that situation. If it came to it, he reckoned he could persuade Wheezer of the wisdom of appointing a co-manager for the US. He'd have to. Wheezer'd never hack the States alone.

The band were all drinking San Miguel and ordering various tapas when Guy trooped over the road to Don Pepe's. He'd considered having this meeting at Purvert (pronounced Pah-vert), but for all that he wanted Jeff and the boys to gel he couldn't make a case for holding a meeting like this on the premises of that most loquacious of operators. Don Pepe, deserted before the six o'clock rush, was as good a spot as any for this.

Beano and Tony gave him big grins and handshakes, still delighted with their new posh ally and very much out to please.

'A'right, Guy, mate,' gushed Beano. 'Got any cures for piles, an' that?'

Everyone laughed. Al's problem with haemorroids was celebrated. He told everybody about them, and invited girls to stroke his 'clit' during intercourse.

'Don't sit down so much,' deadpanned Guy to the drummer, drawing cackles.

'Hey, where's Ticky, Guy?' asked James, puppy-eyed. He'd started saying it *Ghee*, like Ticky and Hannah, who'd been down the studio a couple of times and had already made it back to Farm Place for a smoke. Hannah was a laugh. The Grams loved her.

Wheezer couldn't stop staring at her. She reminded him of Tara. She'd never look at him, though. She was cool.

James had reason to be grateful to Hannah too. She was a sparing user herself, but she'd introduced him to plenty enough folk who could get him what he wanted. And what he wanted was cocaine. For too long he'd had to scrape by in Liverpool on a bit of ganja, a line here, a weekend gram there. But this was it, now. He was here. He was James Love, the Guitarist, and that was a god that needed fuel. That was a god that needed coke. Lots of coke.

The boys hectored Hector and Guy got the drinks in.

'Right, guys . . .'

'Shouldn't that be ghees? . . .'

Wheezer silenced them with a variety of jabs and contorted faces. Guy nodded his appreciation and continued.

'Come on, boys. This is going to be the most tedious session you'll ever spend in a bar, but I guarantee you won't have a more important one. In many ways, this is the sum total – the thing you've been striving for for three and a half years . . . The Record Deal.'

He paused for impact. Nobody said a word.

'But what I'm going to do now is to try to persuade you that the Record Deal is *not* what you've been striving for at all. Of itself, it is nothing. It is a starting point. But it's fundamental, in my experience – so very, very important that the band knows all about their own deal. I want you to understand the actual nature of our commercial relationship . . . *intimately*.'

Guy could see Wheezer was looking irritated already. If he was the sort of manager who tried to keep the details, the options, the deals away from the band, Guy doubted the relationship would stand too much strain. Whatever. So be it.

'You wha'?' laughed James, looking round for support. Nobody made eye contact. Guy took a sheaf of papers out of his zipper wallet.

'This pile of papers is your recording contract, although . . .'

'Just gizzem here and we'll sign 'em and get back to the studio. I can't be arsed with this.'

'Shut the fuck up, Hector! Give him some fucking respect!' hissed Keva.

'And stop pretending to be thick! Stop swearing!' added Wheezer.

'Fuck that! No offence, Guy, mate, but I play guitar in a rock 'n' roll band. I don't need this commercial relationship shit. Fuck the money! I trust you, man. I go for you! Let's make music!'

The band went to round on him, but Guy held up a hand for calm.

'No problem, James. But will you just do me a favour? Just stay and listen. I'll try to be quick, but I can't scoot over this stuff. I'd like to just get on with it myself, but it's so important, this. Artists *must* have a knowledge of what they're getting into, what they're agreeing to. Believe me. It's everything.'

James shrugged, indifferent, and took a swig of San Miguel. Guy started again.

'I'm bound to miss loads of incredibly vital stuff out, so stop me if anything at all doesn't make sense.'

Everyone nodded.

'I'm sure you know the basic ways in which major record companies contract artists to record for them. They pay an advance to cover budgeted wages and studio costs. They pay for the marketing of the record – adverts, posters, video clips, press agents and so on. They recoup these costs, and an agreed proportion of the promotional costs from sales. If there is a surplus, the record company pays the artist a share – a percentage, a royalty – typically around fourteen per cent. Their justification for paying such a small percentage of profits to the artist is usually that the start-up cost, the cost of breaking a new band, is so high that their own margin has to reflect the risk. They'll also point out that distributors, publishers, various rights societies all want their piece of the action, but in many cases the record company is affiliated to the distributor, and in many cases the publisher too, so they're looking at a fuck of a good return if they manage to successfully market one of their acts. If they recoup on the first album then they're going places. With me so far?'

Everybody nodded. Wheezer and Keva knew this stuff backwards, but it was good to hear Guy simplify it like this, and good to know that he wasn't flannelling them.

'Good. Because we're not going to do it like a major record

company. We're going to try and do this in a way that protects and rewards both of us, equally.'

Guy could feel his top lip glistening with sweat. He brushed the back of his wrist over it and tried to focus on getting this right. He'd thought about it, the fairness of it, many times over since first learning the intricacies of record deals at MGR. He'd always had it at the back of his mind that one day he'd be cutting his own deals and he wanted his deals to be famed. He wanted to make *artists'* deals, deals that'd make the best want to come to him. He wanted to be fair. So he'd honed and refined his blueprint until it was watertight – honest, unsentimental and, he was certain, fair. He'd taken the best bits of a major's deal for a name artist and tacked it on to the sort of profit-share favoured by some of the more successful independent labels. The majors tended to screw their talent to the floorboards with big cash advances and low royalty participation. The indies were, often, a bit too reverential, attaching a cultural significance to artistic freedom that their bands didn't merit. Why come to a label if the band thinks it knows how to sell itself? Guy wanted to offer contracts that were a realistic representation of the various talents each participant brought to the mix. Deals where nobody felt shafted way after the event, like they'd been played for a sucker all along. Proper, happy, workable situations – not tight for the joy of squeezing every last point out of the negotiation but certainly not silly liberal-soft. He was as daft about music as any world-weary bedroom guitarist, but he could not go for this incontrovertible right of the guitarist to fuck with the sleeve art. Artistic freedom? No. No such thing. He was here to help them, if they wanted his help. And as for the supposed fucking sanctity of the publishing . . .

'I know you just want to get back to the studio and get the records out and go on *Top of the Pops* and tour America and Japan and shag as many groupies as you can get your mitts on . . .'

'Hear, hear!'

James had been doing quite well. Wheezer growled at him.

'Ah, turn it in, sad kecks!' hissed James.

He got up, held out his hands and shrugged to Guy and walked out, playing air guitar.

'Arsehole,' said Keva.

'It's a fat thing,' said Tony.

Guy waited to catch their eye. They caught his and over-compensated, concentrating hard.

'. . . if we get it right, you'll do all those things. And when we're doing all those things, all the time, like as though it were a proper job to be taken in a limousine to MTV to record a news item, people are going to be coming up to you, saying: "Saw you on *The Chart Show* on Saturday. You guys must have a few quid, eh?" And you won't have. And if you're in one of the ninety-nine per cent of bands who just go at it, head down, live fast, lap it up, you're gonna start thinking: "They're right. Where's all the money going?" Well, fellas, I'm going to tell you all that right now. Because the most time-honoured, classic, stupid reason for bands splitting up just as they're coming into their creative prime is that, once the rush of celebrity, sex, drugs, fame, adulation . . . just *doing it* has started to wear off, most bands start to wonder why they're still living in a bedsit . . .'

The band laughed nervously. He felt like the new, popular, trendy young supply teacher.

'. . . they get back from the gruelling, sell-out tour of Japan and Australia and the Far East and they notice that the singer, who writes all the lyrics and half the music, has bought himself a Merc. And then the shit hits the fan. So let's try and pre-empt all that now, shall we?'

Keva was blushing madly, while Beano and Tony nodded dumbly. Wheezer looked at his feet, redundant.

'Here's the basic thing. I'm putting up £650,000 plus interest to try and get this thing going. It's not money I can afford to throw away. I need to earn it back. So every pound that I cut loose for the Grams' recording sessions, video clips, wages, clothes, tour shortfall – the whole caboodle – I want you to know two things about that cash. It's not a gift. I'm taking a chance on lending it to you, and I want to get it back.'

More animated, sympathetic nodding.

'So I want the rights. I want rights to everything. The recordings, of course, but I want in on publishing, merchandising, touring profits, everything that brings in a fee –'

Wheezer stood up, smiling, both hands raised in a mock stick-up. 'Whoah! Slow down, man, hold it . . .'

'– Lemme finish, will you? I don't expect to get this dusted right here and now but I do want you to understand my principles . . .'

The rebuke from Guy made Wheezer bridle. He found his own voice, this time, his sense of outrage giving him a new self-confidence. 'Oh, I think we understand them all right . . .'

Wheezer's tone and the sarcastic way he'd said 'we understand', as though he was one of the band, as though he spoke for them, made Guy want to punch him. He understood nothing. He was there on sufferance. He was a joke.

'I don't think you do. Don't try and paint me as the bad guy until you've heard what I have to say. I want us to support each other. No hidden agendas. OK?'

'Sounds to me like you're having your cake and eating it. You rip us off and we have to like you as well. Nice deal.'

Guy was very close to walking out. Keva saw it, and placed his hand on Wheezer's sleeve.

He jerked his arm away, angry. 'I'm trying to look after you, here. Just because it's the first deal you've been offered, you don't have to swallow it whole . . .'

'Just let the fella speak, will you . . .'

'Is there a problem here, Wheezer?'

'I think there is. You're giving us this big one about trust and honesty and fair play, and you're trying to get us to assign everything – *everything* – to you. There's no *way* that's fair – and right doesn't even come into it. It's immoral. And all this rot about having to earn the dough back . . .'

'You don't believe that?'

'I don't.'

'You have to believe what I say.'

The two men glared at each other, Wheezer looking away first. There was nothing to be gained from driving Guy into a corner.

'OK. Continue.'

Guy continued looking at him for a moment, then composed himself. He was enraged at Wheezer's belligerence, his asinine inability to recognise the honesty of the offer. But the more he thought about walking away from the thing, the more he realised he was hooked. He wanted this. He needed it.

'I want to earn back my investment as quickly as possible from as many sources as possible. Sure, not great for you. But once I've recouped, once I've *recouped* . . . I mean – I'm putting into this band much more than a major would risk. You're getting a massive deal, with much bigger rewards at the back end than any major would ever let you near. Just let me tell you. Right . . . I'm not going to stand here justifying myself, you know. It's up to you. This is what it is, for me . . . I pay for everything upfront. I get first call on the dough that comes back in. Once I'm straight we split everything fifty-fifty.'

Wheezer was scribbling frantically in a new red memo pad.

'I don't need to flimflam you with examples of how a comparative deal with a major might work, because there *is* no comparison. And this is the only deal I'm putting on the table.'

Guy was getting a kick out of how tough he could be. Some of Lord Filthy's blood had found a way inside of him. He could see that Wheezer knew he was for real.

'But the publishing, Guy,' wheedled Wheezer. 'We can talk about everything else, but surely you don't need to slap a compulsory purchase order on the publishing?'

Guy was surprised by Wheezer's tenacity. Perhaps he had a future, after all.

'I'd go along with you that the writers have an inalienable right to their publishing under the restrictions of the usual artist–record company contract. But there's nothing usual about what I'm proposing . . .'

'I'll say.'

'I'm sorry you feel that way.'

Keva jumped up, his tousled hair falling over his face. As he raised his arms for peace, dark patches of perspiration were visible under the arms of the pale lemon Smedley cotton-knit shirt.

'Hey! Hang on, fellas! We're falling out with each other in our first proper meeting. Is this what we're about? Taking sides? Self-interest?'

'The very obstacles I'm trying to avoid.'

Keva turned to Wheezer. 'Come on, Wheeze. This sounds OK. There's a lot of sense in what he's saying.'

Wheezer gave Keva a curious look. This wasn't the Keva he knew talking. They'd spent many a tortuous night keeping each other awake as Long Richard drove a hire-van back through the night from some godforsaken venue and one of their most-requested conversations was the one about the publishing. Specifically, how Keva would keep on to it when the Grams finally Made It. It was his certificate, his medal, his proof of worth. It was a thing which songwriters always kept on to, for ever. The publishing was his.

Wheezer didn't mind being told to shut up. He didn't especially dig the confrontation part of the manager's job. He was happy to sign anything Guy put in front of him – not because he was a fool or a coward, but because he knew intrinsically that it'd be OK. And if anything anywhere could be taken for granted it was that Guy deBurret was a winner. He was an arrogant prick, but he was a winner and he'd drag them all with him. Wheezer was only speaking up now because managers – good managers – were supposed to fight over everything for their boys. He'd read *Nasty Habits* and he knew not to give in over anything without a full-blooded scrap. Also, he found that he enjoyed arguing with Guy, especially in front of the band. But he was mindful not to blow the whole thing. He'd give it one last shot then zip up.

'What about if you take everything until you recoup your outlay then the publishing reverts to the band and we split the remainder down the middle?'

Keva breathed a big sigh of relief that The Wheeze hadn't fingered him by name in his plan. Reverts to the band sounded good, for now. He could cross that bridge another day.

'You're missing the whole point of what makes my proposition unique, Wheeze.'

Wheezer felt woozy at the warm familiarity of Guy's use of his nickname and instantly despised his own weakness.

'If I don't put up money now, there won't *be* any publishing. Or any touring, merchandise, PPL, PRS, anything. There'll be no income. I'm giving this band a value. I don't just want something

53

in return for that. I want in. I want to be in the gang. Do you know what I mean?'

Wheezer knew what he meant. Tony, Beano and, finally, Keva nodded.

'There's no way,' said Wheezer. 'It's immoral. You're holding us to ransom.'

'I don't see it that way.'

Wheezer couldn't believe he was hearing himself come out with this, putting the entire deal in jeopardy. He couldn't stop himself. 'You've lured the lads down here, got them hooked with the cottage, the studio, the girls and everything, and it's only now you've chosen to show your hand. I'm sorry, Guy. We should've had this conversation sooner. Maybe we're all guilty of innocent things here, maybe we all got a little bit carried away. But the bottom line is we can't go ahead with this. You're trying to convince yourself it's fair, but in your own heart you must know it's hokum. I can't recommend it at all. Come on, boys. Sorry.'

Guy saw the dismay in the faces of the boys. They desperately wanted to say yes, get on with it, get to the next stage. He could probably have gone right through Wheezer, there and then. But he decided to leave it. He knew he had them. And he was starting to see good things in Wheezer.

'I respect that you're trying to protect the boys, Wheezer. But they only need protecting from predators. Sleep on this and you'll see that we're pulling in the same direction. Give it some thought.'

He nodded at the band and made his way out, glancing at his watch for effect. The bar was starting to fill up with after-work tipplers from the *Guardian* and ITN. Guy pulled up in the doorway and turned around. 'And to underline that last point, if you still need convincing about what I stand for, you can go and finish off at the studio without fear. If we don't reach agreement you can keep the masters. They're your songs, after all. Give us a tinkle tomorrow.'

He could see them going into a huddle as he crossed back over Clerkenwell Road. Wheezer was dragging on his inhaler and sparking up a fag simultaneously. He couldn't tell, and didn't care, whether the band were haranguing Wheezer or congratulating him or neither.

Guy hesitated at the foot of the steps to the scholastic old redbrick at number 83. The concerted efforts of the last couple of hours had left Guy wired, and he knew he wouldn't settle to anything. The early-evening sunshine gave London a hazy calm. Even now, the streets were emptying. In half an hour the area would echo with the crooning of pigeons and the rambling soliloquies of piss artists. He set off, aimlessly, back down the side streets and up on to Farringdon Road.

He felt the warm abrasion of his cock rubbing against his groin as he walked. It was growing heavier as each stride rolled it this way and that in the confines of his pants. He felt keen and sharp and powerful, swaggering on through his city, nothing to fear. Nothing to fear, and aware of the pulse of his knob against his jeans. There was a weird titillation as he walked on, not certain where he was going, not sure why he was so heady, so full of thrill. And then he knew.

The road sign offered a few destinations – The City, Islington, The North (M1). But all Guy could see was the bit that said *King's Cross*.

He'd had a fascination with hookers since he was seventeen, up from Eton for the weekend when Maria thought he was staying in the country with friends. He'd found what he liked all by himself, just by wandering around, riding the night buses, getting lost and turning down this street then the next, panicking, quickening his step and avoiding eye contact with all manner of night-time low-life. And then he started to recognise the streets and places, linking them together in his mind. So the terrifying alien magic of Soho became more familiar and, in time, it was just Soho – one of the places in London he used to go to and wander around, looking at girls, looking for sex. He could well have afforded the high-class, high-price call-girls of Park Lane or their niceprice cousins in Shepherd Market and Brewer Street. But nothing excited him like the wretched teenagers working the streets behind King's Cross Station and St Pancras. It was a new world to Guy. These girls were the lost souls, the lowest of the low. Skag-hags and jellyheads, emaciated young girls from Perth, Dundee, York, down for a trip which never took them home. They held a tantalising revulsion for him, drawn by a whisper, disgusted with himself for the hard-on raging in his pants.

They were cheap and fast and ready. They did it – anything, whatever he wanted – standing up with the lorries and trains thundering around them. He'd started that first time with a blow job from Moira, a wizened twenty-year-old from Paisley. She'd told him that, after he'd tried to make conversation, stricken after he'd come so quickly. She spat his load into the street and he said: 'Erm. Are you from Glasgow, then?'

He kept his hands in his pockets, rocking on his feet, not wanting to hurt her feelings by just paying up and getting off. The crazed eyes burnt deathly cobalt as she looked him up and down. He could taste the craven hot stench of her breath.

'I'm fae Paisley. Fifteen quid.'

'Oh. I thought you said . . .'

'Aye. But bareback's fifteen.'

Moira got him to fuck her the next few times and seemed to get off on it. Each time they did it she let him have a bit more. She'd pull down her shoulder straps and place his hands on her striated breasts, guide his fingers under the biting elastic of her panties and jerk his hand around her clit. Twenty pounds. He couldn't get the stink off his fingers. This one time she said Guy could have her bareback for the same price. She was whispering it in his ear, scraping his neck, that hard, cracked-out voice croaking to him, asking him to. He went to the place with her and that was when he first saw Evie.

From then on, right through the remainder of school and after, it was just Evie. Slim, pretty, honey-brown Evie from Leeds. Not slim, really. Thin, wire-thin with such taut, such perfect skin. No mottles, just one litle scar. She was beautiful. Somalia was where her ma and da had come from. They lived in Liverpool a while but her da had disappeared and her ma met a bloke from Leeds. They talked a lot. Guy would've loved to put her in a blood-red strapless Alexander McQueen piece and take her along to the Met Bar. She'd look, quite sincerely, a million dollars with those never-ending limbs, like Iman before she met Bowie. He told her that. He wanted her all to himself, all the time, and he wanted the reputation too. She had a tiny nose and devastating, slit-white eyes and dramatic cheekbones. She had a beautiful, tight-cropped head. Guy loved to kiss her skull. She showed off her bottom in tight cut-down jeans, and always the little red T-shirt displaying the emphatic jut of her tits. She was noiseless when he had her, a conscientious worker, determined to give satisfaction, but mindless of herself. He tried, he tried to speak to her, but there was nothing in it for her. He asked her lots of times to stay with him and be his girl but she wouldn't ever discuss it. She'd just look down and clam up.

The last few months before rehab when they were all partying hard, what Evie had been asking him to do was to have her backside. The first time had been unbelievable. He'd never known anything like it. This time she was animated like he'd never seen her before. She was an animal. It hurt at first, even through the drugs, hurt a lot, tearing his foreskin as he pushed and drove to get up there, but what heaven when he was deep inside, Evie backing into him, muttering and swearing. He'd brought lubrication after that, but it was never so good. The last time he saw her she was mumbling to herself, almost chanting this kind of verse or prayer as he was ramming her – then she burst out crying. It was the only time she ever let Guy hold her.

Over the following days and weeks he searched for her but no one would tell him what had become of her. He missed her badly. He couldn't do without her. Moira kidded on that she knew where Evie had gone and Guy took the hook, staying with her in her hostel for a couple of days. By the third day he was doing rocks with her, kissing her scabby lips, sliding his tongue inside that rotten stinking mouth, higher than the sun with this burnt-out Moira who loved him and left him puking in the gutter with not a clue who he was.

Guy felt dizzy as he crossed over Pentonville Road. Fuck the Grams and their dippy manager. Rock 'n' roll? They didn't know a single thing. He was going back.

Wheezer felt unusually energetic. Could be he was still pissed. The celebrations had gone on and on, only ending with the last of the Superbok and the chirruping of blackbirds. That four a.m. mix of 'Beautiful' had been too much. Round about one o'clock Andy had started shaking at the control desk as the mix came together, muttering, 'This is it, this is it.' You could actually see the hairs on his wrists stand up. He was manic, pulling up distorted guitar sounds and celestial backing vocals, this idea leading on to that, impervious to the rest of them in the studio.

The band and Wheezer watched and listened. It was joyous. Everything in all of their lives to date reached a collision point, a point of meaning when Andy, in tears, worn out, had played back the song. The gradual build of the guitars, James's chiming hook fading into the middle-eight and coming back under the swelling strings, lulling you, tenderising you, ready for the chorus:

> *So let's forget the you, the me,*
> *We know if that could come to be,*
> *It all would look so beautiful again,*
> *All this would be so beautiful again.*

For pure, innocent idealism it was up there with 'Blowin' in the Wind'. They hugged and held each other, feeling their own significance. They didn't give a fuck, at this moment, whether anyone else liked it. This was the song they'd honed and trimmed and loved for two years. Keva had brought it in as an uncut gem and they'd worked on it, together. This, the song it had become, was the way they had dreamed it could be. It was beautiful.

'Guy! He's got to fucken hear it! Let's get him down here!' screamed Keva. Even as he spoke his mind flashed through the release, the acclaim, Helmet Horrocks. No way would that cunt ever write something as good as this. The world was going to know that, at last.

'Cripes, yeah!' gulped Wheezer, unconvincingly, his voice low down in his thorax. He scrambled around for Guy's number. His knee-jerk jealousy lasted no time. Guy was in the gang. He was a believer. He was in on all this.

'Is right, Wheeze. Get Ghee de Ghee de Ghee down here, pronto an' that!' said James.

'Ghee de Geezer,' laughed Beano.

'Hey now! Fellas!' laughed Andy. 'I know we've made a killer record here but, like, it's getting on for five o'clock. He'll be in the office in a coupla hours. And I want him sweet!'

They laughed and bowed down in front of him, kissing his feet.

'Off, you dogs!' He gave James a little kick in the gut. 'I'm away to mah bed. Gents, it's been a rare pleasure. The honour is mine.'

Andy made his way to the staircase then came back.

'I hope you know you're a fucking brilliant band.'

James found himself tittering with excitement.

'And him . . .' said Andy, pointing at the mercurial guitarist. 'Lock him up.'

He gave a cheesy thumbs-up and was gone. There was silence for a second.

'YEARRGH!'

They danced round in a circle, dragging Paul by his ponytail and showering him with kisses. Ben, the spotty young tape-op was carried around the studio shoulder-high, bashing his head into door frames and stainless-steel lights. He begged for mercy, slid down and brought out the last of the beer from the fridge. No one wanted to go to bed. Tony and Beano walked down to Soho in search of an all-night breakfast. Paul started to build up. James got up and beckoned Ben to follow, furtive. He put his arm around him and guided him into the reception area.

'Can you get petty cash?'

Ben looked pained. His stilted Jamaican accent was dropped as he became a white wannabe from Richmond again for a second.

'Some. Why?'

'Sort us some powder?'

The young tape-op grinned. His Yardney accent returned. 'No probs. You'll have to sign for DATs or something, yeah? Ten secs.'

James went back inside. Paul, Keva and Wheezer were listening to the tune again. James was bored of it. He wanted to do another one. He wanted to do another line, too. And then go out and do some more. Hannah had had a bit, but she'd fucked off about two. He'd have to wait for Ben to get back, but it was going to be a long wait, listening to them lot creaming it over the fucking mix. It was good. But didn't they expect that? And bleeding Ben'd want to sit with him until all the coke was gone. Fuck it.

*

Keva and Wheezer walked in silence through the damp daffodils of Hyde Park. When they woke up tomorrow – today – they would each have in their hands a cassette of a song which would become known all over the world. An early-morning jogger passed. Keva felt for a moment as though the jogger would stop, turn back and shake his hand. It felt like everybody they passed already recognised them, knew what they'd just done. The realisation that only they, for now, knew just how the song was going to affect so many people made them feel almighty. Keva wished he could just walk, on and on. The sun burnt off the last of the slovenly dawn clouds and shone out above. It was going to be a glorious day.

Wheezer didn't sleep. His mind was electrified with thoughts of the contract, schedules, press, touring, offices. Should he set up down here, or was a bit of distance a good thing? Wheezer intended to commission the boys on their hundred quid a week, off the top, just to get them into the habit of shedding twenty per cent of everything they got, but London was expensive. Maybe he and Guy would work better together if they weren't in each other's pockets. Liverpool might be best.

He was elated. He listened to the chorus of snoring from upstairs and felt a fond, protective, paternalism. The boys needed him more than he needed them. He felt big and strong and able. People were going to hear of him, soon, and they'd talk of him as a sensitive, strong, sympathetic manager who had the ear and the respect of everyone, from local crew to Directors of Programming. He no longer felt that Guy and Keva could just push him out. Even if they did, the whole thing would crumble without The Wheeze. It wouldn't be the same. He wished the clock'd go round a bit faster so he could speak to Guy. Hearing the song now, he no longer feared him. They, the Grams, had brought this treasure to Guy. They were the unique factor here. They were the talent. Guy'd know, when he heard it, that he was just a bank and he'd feel humbled and honoured to do his bit. Right now, it was Wheezer who was the boss.

Evie had not been there. Moira was gone too. Guy, burning hard, found himself paining to unload. He found a sly-eyed trick with bleached, thinning hair. He clutched her ears as she gobbled, looked down on her pink scalp and, his tense buttocks oscillating wildly as he started to come, jammed himself hard into her head. He'd come in seconds, pushing too far inside her, pulling her on to him, choking her. She jumped up, gagging, crazy, ridiculous in the cheap lime-green minidress, spunk dribbling.

'Yow mad fucken bastard!'

'What?'

'Yow fucken know!'

He felt nothing. He looked past her, willing himself elsewhere. Empty now, he just wanted out. He stuffed his knob back inside his trousers and started walking away, buttoning his jeans.

'Giz another fucken tenner, you, you cunt.'

'You're fantastic.'

He quickened his pace. The disgraced Yorkshire tart followed, keeping her distance, shrieking at Guy as he passed another trick.

'See 'im! He ain't fucken right! Stay away from that fucken loon, I'm telling you!'

He pushed away from the area, his heart palpitating madly, and weaved his way through to Russell Square. He sat a while, breathless, lungs bursting. That was it. Finished. That whole caper. Over. He was not going up there again. Evie was gone. Probably dead. Didn't matter.

His breathing became more regular as he sat and collected his thoughts. There was going to be no more of this shit. His own needs were now in last place. He was going to channel everything into the Grams and ReHab. And he was going to do it right, in every sense.

Guy was going to make records. Only the best records. Big international hit records which were big international hits because they were so bloody good. And he was going to achieve all that without shitting on anyone. He was going to do it with style, with sensitivity, with humility. Everyone'd love him – especially his bands. He was going to do this, it would happen. He doubted whether Ahmet Ertegun or Seymour Stein sat plotting for years, getting the details right before making their move. They would have known instinctively what they were going to do. That's what happened with Guy that night in the marquee. It just came in an instant, laid out before him, people, places, everything – the whole picture. He just had to get up and move towards it.

As they ducked into the Blackwall Tunnel Wheezer prayed it'd be cooler down there, but there was no respite from the stifling heat. Even with the MGF's air-conditioning, the two of them were slick with sweat. The heatwave had carried on into May and London was suffocating.

'By jimminy! This is Hot hot!' wheezed Wheezer. He was having a bad time of it, but the Triludan Forte, the Becotide and the Ventolin were keeping the allergies at bay.

'Shoulda gone by train,' murmured Guy.

Wheezer nodded. The relationship was only a grade better than strained, but the two of them were similarly driven. Impatient to get their hands on the white labels, Guy and Wheezer were driving down to Beckenham to pick up the batch from COPS. The test pressings had turned out well, and they'd ordered two hundred seven-inch white-label vinyl EPs, sexy little things to mail out to radio, press and those with influence. They wanted to keep the batch smallish in order to stress the collectability of this release, in tandem with the EP itself.

Guy and Wheezer had both had the same idea once they'd agreed to hold off on 'Beautiful' as the first single. Wheezer originally reckoned it should be released in August, when business is traditionally slack and you could, with luck, get a Top Five with thirty thousand sales. 'Beautiful' could even get to Number One at that time of year. So while they all wanted to sell as many records as possible, whatever the time of year, Top Five is Top Five, it's noted in Europe and beyond and, crucially, it could help your case with MTV.

MTV, in Europe and even more so in the States, was always looking for the 'Story'. It was like you had to score a bare minimum of points in all sorts of categories: Tour Profile (how many people come and see you play?); Record Company Commitment (are you a big priority act?); Track Record; Chart Position; Prospects In General (if MTV grants you the all-important rotation, will you reward its faith by becoming Bon Jovi in the foreseeable future and participate in overblown MTV Awards

Specials in places like Luxembourg? MTV likes to see its babies grow).

Wheezer, confident of the potential for 'Beautiful' to appeal to a broad cross-section, had argued that they could get maximum exposure for the single, let it shine out as the big crossover hit of the summer at a time when there was little in the way of quality opposition – a few Ibiza hits making their way back to Blighty, and that'd be it.

Guy had shared his faith and raised it. He thought 'Beautiful' was a Christmas Number One. He didn't think it, he knew it, he was sure of it. There couldn't be a song anywhere to touch it and at Christmas in particular, the sentiment of peace and love and the simple beauty of nature would find a receptive public. Moreover, by Christmas, ReHab would have all its overseas licensees in place, including the Big Four – Japan, America, Germany and Spain. If you could crack Spain – and Portugal to a lesser extent – the mass markets of South America and Hispanic USA opened up for you. Guy knew that those territories would expect a synchronised, unilateral release strategy. No imports, no leaks – everyone looking after their own market simultaneously. Sure, they could get Top Five in Britain in the summer, but that would piss the Yanks off badly. You had to give them plenty of time to schedule the release properly, prep it, build a *story*. A bit of track record with their first release'd do that story no harm at all.

So they'd left the scheduling of 'Beautiful' as an open point, agreeing that the immediate concern was to make a big impact with the debut. Without a properly co-ordinated, successful launch, there would be no Japan or America to upset. Their aim was to have the country talking about the Grams as soon as possible. And humming their tunes.

They all agreed that a Limited Edition EP was the right way to launch. They were confident of airplay support from all the local Liverpool stations – City, MFM, Merseyside and Fibre'd definitely play it on Crash FM – and they reckoned they were within touching distance of Radio One. Most of the night-time DJs were aware of the Grams and it wasn't unlikely that, if the track was right, they'd get played. They could build pockets of support in various regional strongholds, places they'd played, cities whose local radio station had an indie show, concentrate their attack on those places and work inwards from there.

With 'Beautiful' out of the running, there wasn't much debate about the lead track. 'Desert Rain' was a highlight of their live set, a balmy, slow-building epic infused with soul-sapping melodies and sheet-metal guitars. Until this year it'd been first song of the set. It never failed to make its mark, whether that be the silencing of chattering art students at the bar in a crowd of forty-five at Derby or sparking off euphoric pogoing amongst the Leeds fans. Over Christmas they'd managed to finish three new songs, giving them seventeen in total on the A-list. When they went out gigging again in February they rejigged the set-list to close powerfully with 'Chimera', 'Desert Rain' and 'Beautiful'. For all that 'Beautiful' was the stand-out track, the one which could fire up a Lisbon sky with fifty thousand sparking lighters, 'Desert Rain' was always the signal for dance floor mayhem. During that last tour, the crowd seemed to know the track from the Peel session, grinning to their mates and singing along with the infectious chorus, a joyful scrum piling into each other down the front.

It was a hit. The only argument they'd had was whether the song's potential was being thrown away by limiting the issue to ten thousand. Guy had waved down the protests.

'Look, there's no conflict here. We need a fuck of a good track to let people know we're here. We're going to be banging the drum, telling radio, press, the world about the Grams and ReHab. They're gonna yawn and say, c'mon then, impress us. So what do we do? Give them an intro track and tell them wait till you hear the next one and the one after that? No one's interested in what's coming down the pipeline. They want *now*.'

Wheezer coughed. 'I'm not so sure. I mean, look at what Ocean Colour Scene did. They weren't arsed whether "Riverboat Song" was massive. It was a reintroduction to a band that'd been away. MCA tied radio into the plan from the start, collaborated with them. Said to them, try it out, give it a few spins, see if it works for you. If not, no probs. We've got an album full of killer tracks here.'

'So they say . . .'

'What d'you mean? It's well documented . . .'

'After the event . . .'

'I don't think they'd risk pissing Radio One off by implicating them in the story if there was nothing in it . . .'

Guy cut in, impatient, dismissing him. 'Doesn't make a blind bit of difference to our situation. We're not MCA. We get one shot at this, and it has to be right. Right marketing, right promotion, right track.'

Wheezer shot him a look. Guy continued. 'I hear what you're saying about throwing away one of our best tracks. We won't be doing that. What we're doing with this release is cultivating a fan base, a core that's going to grow with us. You've given me the database of . . . how many, Wheeze?'

'Seven hundred.'

He hated himself for his eagerness, his awestruck satisfaction at having a role in all of this, at being able to fire back an answer just like that. What he was doing with great competence was playing the role of the sidekick.

'Seven hundred. See? Fucking solid indie base. We'll turn that into five, six thousand after this EP. We'll put response postcards inside, get the names on the database, make sure those people are looked after. Nothing so cruddy as a fan club. Just treat them as the elite, the first few to get into the Grams, a privileged set who'll get, say, a specially commissioned photo, signed by the band, sent out with first news of tours, new releases, whatever.'

Keva couldn't stop grinning. He had to bite hard on his lip. He wanted to be on the Grams mailing list. He couldn't suppress his silent, hiccuping giggles. This was great. He was about to Make It.

'Sounds like a fucken fan club to me,' smiled James.

Relief! Everyone guffawed.

'Okay. So it's a fucking fan club. But they don't pay for the privilege. We value them. We never rip them.'

'Ah, c'mead, Guy, why can't we fleece 'em like everyone else?'

Guy smiled and carried on.

'What we're gonna do is a ten-thousand-limit, red vinyl EP.'

'Vinyl?!', huffed James. 'Who the fuck listens to vinyl these days? Dance-heads and auld-arses!'

Guy held his hand for silence. 'Vinyl, James. Luscious, rare, classic red vinyl. ReHab 001. Collectable as fuck. The songs you did up in Liverpool will be the bonus tracks, with "Desert Rain" obviously the key. Ten thousand is the absolute limit. We won't press any more than that. Once they're gone, they're gone. You can assume a thousand immediately being snapped up by collectors. They know their stuff, these fellas, and if press starts to kick in the way we anticipate, all these funny little *Record Collector* readers are going to be helping themselves to two or three each. It's a desirable product with immediate scarcity value. If we decided to reissue it on CD in a year's time, when the band are huge, none of the ten thousand who buy the EP will complain. It just adds value to their red-vinyl hard-on. It's like having "Anarchy" on EMI. It's saying, "I was into these before anyone else." So we can't lose. Not only are we *not* throwing the track away as a loss-leader, we're giving its eventual, its *inevitable* re-release the best possible talk-up. And, more importantly, we're introducing the world to the Grams with a fucking fantastic track. Give the radio bods something they actually *want* to play. What d'you reckon?'

'I'm in,' said Keva.

The others nodded. Wheezer shrugged. Why didn't the band at least confer among themselves, with him, before blurting out their compliance? He'd have to talk to them about this. Things were getting better with Guy but the boys had to realise that he was, nonetheless, the record company. The Enemy. Wheezer furrowed his brow.

'If we sell the lot, where do we . . . *chart*?'

'Well, we'll stick the whole lot in Chart Return outlets, so every sale is a tick, but it all depends upon who else is out that week and what numbers the Top Ten are doing. Who knows? Thirty-five?'

Wheezer seemed happy with that, then frowned again. 'What if thirty-five gets us *Top of the Pops*?'

Guy grinned. 'We turn it down.'

'You what! Turn down *Top of the Pops*?'

'Sure. It's not the cock-almighty now, anyway. Anyone can get on. What we'll do, though, to avert any misconceptions, is tip off Chris Cowie way up front. Take ourselves out of the reckoning, but involve Cowie in the process, yeah? Let *Top of the Pops* know this is just an introduction to the band and we'll be hoping to join their illustrious constellation with the next record. That sort of thing.'

Wheezer was all admiration and resentment. Guy, at twenty-four, knew it all. Wheezer was twenty-five and he'd *never* get to know all this stuff. He should just be thankful that Guy was on their side. He'd have to train himself to use his expertise rather than just militating against the boy as a matter of course. He could learn from him, though it pained him no end to have to acknowledge it. Knowing *The Guinness Book of Hit Singles* off by heart was one thing, or being able to quote whole tracts of *How to Succeed in the Music Business*, but Guy had been there. He knew first-hand how it all worked. Wheezer knew he should stop feeling so threatened by Guy's experience and start enjoying the ride.

So that was decided. 'Desert Rain', late June. They brought Paul back in to ply a track of squalling feedback, just under the surface, which gave an already catchy song a layer of desolate euphony, so that while its chorus was instant and penetrative, the whole was raw, bruised, unsettling. It sounded epic, like 'Bitter-sweet Symphony' with danger – hungering, yearning, broken-hearted and bloody hummable. Only Keva knew what the fuck it was about.

Wheezer waited in the car while Guy went to locate their consignment, turning up the radio when Sebadoh came on. This was the great thing about Radio One. They were taking risks, playing weird stuff on the flimsiest of criteria – that it was good. Not long ago you'd have to wait for the nation to be safely tucked up before the depraved outpourings of The Fall or Scritti Politti or Baby Ford could be unleashed. Even a sublimely depressive track like 'The Drugs Don't Work' couldn't have been played a few years ago. Now, since the new controller, you'd hear the Spice Girls next to Placebo with the Ramones thrown in for a laugh, and The Verve were the Biggest Band in the World. Radio was on a high. You could easily see the Grams fitting in. They'd fit in. They would.

Guy vaulted into the driver's seat and reversed cutely into the last-but-one loading bay. He disappeared into a doorway set into a huge steel roller-gate and emerged, smiling, with a small, flat cardboard box in each hand. Wheezer gaped.

'Go on, then,' shouted Guy. 'Help yourself.'

Wheezer jumped to it, disappointed that there were only two boxes left for him to lug. He got back into the car with his booty and sat, still, watching the box as though it was going to turn into a pumpkin. He slipped his fingers under the edges and prised the lid open. It was wondrous to him. What he saw was a neat stack of white-sleeved, blank white-labelled, black plastic records, some with vinyl trimmings still attached to their outer edges. The labels were unmarked as they'd decided to personalise and number each EP by hand. All Wheezer had on his lap was a box full of plain black records, undistinguished in their white, unembellished sleeves. But he was overcome.

'Guy?'

'Wheeze?'

'I know I'm sort of . . . superfluous . . .'

Guy groped for the appropriate denial.

'. . . so I just wanted to say that this . . .' He held up a box, looking straight ahead at a reversing transit van. '. . . is a dream come true. My own white label . . .' He turned at last to the reddening Guy deBurret. '. . . it's everything, Guy. It's fantastic. My own white label. It's what it's all about.'

Guy looked at Wheezer's flushed face and gave him a friendly prod. 'This is just the start of it.'

Wheezer gave an embarrassed little half-grin. 'Am I, sort of . . .'

'Involved? Or weird-looking? Both. Very. Come on.' He sparked up the MGF and felt its surge. 'We have plans to bestlay. Or whatever you do to best-laid plans.'

Wheezer, knocked back in his seat by the acceleration, let the wind lift up his fringe and have a little peep underneath. He was transported, like a kid on his first fairground ride. Guy sneaked a look at him. He still wasn't ready to trust anybody, anywhere. But he was coming round to Wheezer. If Guy could get him to actually start working *with* him they might make a good team. And The Wheeze, Guy thought, might just have what it took to become a very good manager. He was no pushover and, for all his idiosyncracies, he was a character.

The American side of things still worried Guy. There was a type of American record company vice-president who'd enjoy twisting Wheezer into knots, take advantage of his inexperience. But Guy had to admit he was wrong about Wheezer not having the big personality. He had a different sort of big personality. He was an English eccentric. He possessed that brand of quirky charisma which would work with the very top level in America, the people who actually ran the companies. Clive Davis, Howie Klein, Geffen himself – people like this, unthreatened by a precarious sense of self, would love The Wheeze. Most important of all, he had a good creative sensibility. He could do it, if he wanted to. Guy determined to treat him more as a partner, if he'd let him. He turned the radio off and shouted, to be heard above the wind.

'You're a music man, Wheeze.'

'Am I?'

'Sure you are. You know you are. Same as me.'

Wheezer was wearing his beige Pringle V-neck with the lion in contrasting brown, one of his favourite fashion items. James called everything Wheezer wore *fashion* items. Fashion slacks. Fashion zip-ups. And the Pringle was most definitely a fashion pullover.

'What was the first record you bought?' asked Guy.

'Human League. "Don't You Want Me".'

'Mmmm. Nice one.'

'What about you?'

'"Pump Up the Volume". MARRS.'

'Oh, aye . . .'

'It was!'

'1986 . . . you were how old?'

'Twelve.'

'So what was wrong with . . . Bananarama? Or Princess.'

Guy laughed at the recollection. 'You had the Human League, why can't I have someone cool?'

'They were Number One when I was ten. They weren't cool, they were pop!'

'So were MARRS, you tit!'

'MARRS weren't Number One!'

'They fucking well were!'

By the return trip through the tunnel, marginally less stifling this time, Wheezer was on to all-time best-selling British hits.

'Oasis don't figure, man. They're about number ninety-three.

The perishing Beatles only have two or three tracks in the Top 100. Ken Dodd, yes. Rolf Harris, take a bow. Benny Hill, Cilla Black, The Barron Knights . . . even The King barely rates a mention next to these giants of pop. And we're gonna have to sell some records if we want to topple The Tweets!'

Guy took his hands off the steering wheel to clap. 'I'm impressed, Mr Finlay. Very impressed. Although I don't believe a damn word. The Tweets outselling Oasis, my foot!'

He was even beginning to sound like Wheezer. They found a space in Back Hill and jogged back to the office, eager to start marking up the white labels.

Hannah felt as though she was starting to get to know the band. She hadn't asked Purvis, yet, if she could work on the project but she knew that here was a band she could really take into new areas. They had a weird charisma, four separate karmas working for and against each other in a way that fascinated her. And if it fascinated *her* . . .

She looked at them, arguing over the simplest of questions. Tony and Beano counted as one, really, their droll world-view so complementary that they were each other. Alan – Beano – was crude but even that was not without a certain charm. The real pull, though, the nucleus of what made these boys a prospect to her, was the smouldering rivalry between the twinkling, voluptu-ous guitarist and the prickly singer. She reckoned Keva was a honey with his long lashes, staring eyes and that wild mop. And his remoteness – even though he was talkative he always seemed distant, as though he was thinking of something else – only made him more captivating. Hannah was a tough girl, independent in every sense and, by choice, for now, needless of the draining plausibility of men. It was working out just fine. She wasn't going to give that up. But Keva was interesting.

It was rare to see Tony so righteous.

'You don't know what you're saying . . . it was the lightweight thing. We were all so . . . thin. Even I was, back then. We had no gear. Travel light. Thin gypsy thieves. The Grams!'

'Bullshit! I came up with the fucken name so I should know . . . Maybe I just never told anyone *why*!'

'OK, boys, cool it – while you're, like, deciding who thought of the name, does anybody need another drink?'

Tony jumped up. 'Here y'are, Hannah, we'll get them. Sit down.'

'You sure, Snowy? I'm a working girl, you know. I expect you to look after me when the millions come rolling in, but I can stand a round of drinks. Even on Purv's wages.'

She made the last two statements sound like questions, in the current Aussie-Londoner idiom. Ticky butted in, in her inimitably rich, manly voice. 'Very gallant, Tony, but until Guy signs some cheques for me we're all officially skint. I'll get 'em in. You can owe me.'

Tony looked relieved. 'All right then. But when we get our first wages we're taking you out. OK?'

'Fine. Sound.'

She smiled at him, bringing him in on her joke. Although the boys loved her rampant Sloanieness, she'd become more mellow, less hyper in the short time she'd worked with Guy. She was lovely.

'I'll give you a hand.'

Tony squashed up next to Ticky, fighting to get served in the Duke of York's six o'clock mêlée. He liked her a lot, but he knew she was out of his league. He was uncool, he knew that. Even the basic classics, as Keva called them, indigo Ted Baker cotton denim shirt, Evisu jeans, nooskool leather Adidas Campus shoes, looked sloppy on Tony. He just didn't have the figure. He was five foot three and, no getting away from it, stocky. Not fat, but broad, powerful. Not a fashionable shape. No way would the Hon. Victoria Turnbull even notice him in a crowd, or if she did she'd only think him sweet or cuddlesome. He felt like twatting James every time he blathered on about humping her in the boathouse that time. How could she? With *him*?

The band looked forward to their daily trip down to the Duke, during Sprogtrek, Andy's daily dash to pick up the kids or put them to bed. Keva admired him for the way his life was centred, but he didn't envy him. There was no gravitational pull in Andy's life, no schisms, no conflict. It was ordered. But it gave them a few hours every day to leg down to Clerkenwell, catch up with Ticky and Hannah, meet Guy and The Wheeze, whatever. It was getting to be a bit of a scene. Maxine and Celeste from the studio had started coming down with them, hanging out, talking about what was happening in London and who they'd seen and so on. The Grams were at the centre of their own little universe.

Tony watched Maxine, tall and elegant, make her way back from the loo. She always struck Tony as hard beneath the surface, as though she'd had to fight for every little thing she'd got in life. She was shallow too, a user, a trendy, someone who wanted to be in with the right people. He preferred to steer clear of her. She hardly noticed him, anyway, she was so busy fooling with James and trying to impress Keva. If a woman looked like anything then Maxine looked like she'd wither and die if she didn't suck Keva's cock soon. She leaned her manicured hands on Keva's shoulders as she cracked a joke with the table. Tony couldn't hear it from the bar, but it must've been a good one. Beano was hawking with laughter.

They carried the drinks back. A long-haired character was occupying Tony's stool, half facing them in that I'm-not-staying sort of way. Tony stood back, wanting to seem indifferent, looking for another space to sit but wanting the sweat to know he was in the way too. Celeste, always pure-looking and pretty in a slightly hippyish way, spotted Tony's impatience.

'Ally, this is Tony from the band.'

Her voice was cockney-posh. No pretensions, no voguish Jamaican inflections, her voice just told you who she was – a rich-kid runaway who'd lived among Londoners a long time. She missed out 't's, as in Uneye-id Colours of Benni-unn, but that was about it. She could have been one of the Lovely Girls' long-lost cousins.

'You're in his seat. Shift, man! Make room for the talent!'

The most handsome, most instantly likeable face Tony had ever seen turned round, smiling warmly, hand proffered. 'Hello, mate. Ally Bland. I keep hearing terrifying things about you boys . . .'

A confident bastard, but clearly All Right. Tony shoved up next to him. He was not given to warming to sweats, but this club hippie was a laugh, constantly doing himself down with tales of his inability to hold drink and drugs, his sexual failures and his disastrous club package holidays to Ibiza and Tenerife. Hannah was having none of it. Ally ran the best one-nighters in London, she reckoned. He'd come down the Duke to meet with Purvis who was, as ever, late. Ben came in, pleased with himself, and nodded James over. They disappeared to the bogs.

'D'you reckon you could come round to the idea of me as, you know, a Special Friend?' said Ally loudly, grinning at Celeste.

'Not likely!' Celeste smiled. She put her arm around Beano. 'I'm saving myself for little Al, anyway. Look at him. Isn't he lovely?' She squeezed his skinny frame in a bear-hug, capsizing his stool, and tickled his squirming body until he squealed for mercy.

'Look at his little buns! Bless! Come to Mama!'

To everyone's slight surprise, they started to kiss lasciviously. Nobody expected it of Celeste, who seemed too sunny and freckled to have thought much about boys. The band expected it even less of Beano, only because the kissing which now engrossed that corner of the pub was so tender. Beano always made a big deal of his rough-and-ready approach, putting himself down in the process, but always making out his women to be creatures who were 'dying' for 'it'.

Beano, in many ways, was the odd one out. The rest of the band were from north Liverpool, or had been before Keva and James got themselves a floor in the sprawling Ivanhoe Road manse in arty Sefton Park. Beano, though, he was from the Dingle, mongrel territory where dynasties of socialists still called black men coons and still fought shy of affectations. A non-Dingle accent was an affectation. Beano, when drunk, as he often was, would jerk his curly head to one side and stab away at Tony with unfiltered notions of the Working Class, his pride in his tough upbringing, how the world had it in for low-born urchins like him. He was naive, even for a twenty-year-old. Tony knew well that Beano was a council-estate misfit, burdened with all the prejudice and none of the nous of the street. He'd had it rough, no doubt, but any one of them could take him in a fight. Even Wheezer had made him back down and apologise over something he'd said last Christmas. But he and Tony were a team, the straight guys to the tortured poet Keva liked to play, and the ludicrous technicolour excesses of James. He was a great lad, Beano, and a fuck of a drummer.

Wheezer came in with Jeff Purvis. Tall, a speedball of dirty, sandy hair and knock-knee faded Levi legs, rangy, stooped like he wasn't quite used to his height, a magnetic storm of nervous energy. Another hippie, thought Tony.

'Evening, all,' he smiled, jumpy in the face of such a large and unexpected audience. That was all he seemed to say to them, when they bumped into him in the office. 'Good morning, sinners' and 'Evening, all.' He raised a quizzical eyebrow at the passion-play in the corner and pulled up a stool.

'Get us a Stella Dry, Hannah, love. I'm fucked.'

Wheezer hated Purvis for the alacrity in Hannah's step, the eagerness in her face. But he liked him moments later. Purvis leaned over to Keva, nodding conspiratorially at The Wheeze. 'Just been with this lunatic here . . .'

Wheezer liked being called a lunatic. It made him sound rock 'n' roll. It made him sound mad. Mad Ozzy. Mad Keef. Mad Richard. Mad bloody Wheezer . . .

'Heard the track. Fucking absolutely first-rate. Magnificent. I can only share his optimism. Tremendous.'

Ally leaned over. 'This the Grams? Give us a white and I'll get Sweeney to whack it on tonight.'

Keva liked to hear people like Ally Bland speak the band's name. It made them real. It was good. People were starting to have an opinion about his band. Hannah plonked Jeff's drink down.

'"Desert Rain"?' she interrupted.

'I'll have some of *that*,' said Ally, nodding his head dramatically. 'Nice.'

'Not sure it'd work down Marigold. I know you've been, like, dropping a few guitar tunes, yeah, but this is . . . *heavy*.'

She'd turned it into a question again, an option, but Keva came alive. He always thought of 'Desert Rain' as a burner, a gradually conflagrating epic which left you exhausted by its intensity. But heavy? He liked that. She was tuning into the undertones of the song. He took a good look at her while she argued with Ally, leaning one hand on her slim hip. She was gorgeous.

'Listen,' said Ally, leaning over and grazing her nose with a kiss. Wheezer bristled with indignation. Keva burned with envy. '*Everything* works down Marigold. Whatever we play them, they love, yeah? It's a very open-minded crowd we've got down there. And if it's one of Jeff's, it's going to work for them, yeah?'

All eyes were on Jeff. He made harassed eye contact with Hannah. She winked and pulled tongues at him. He nodded. 'I'd love to say it's one of mine, I truly would. But Hannah's beaten me to this one. It's her band.'

She wanted to be blasé about it, but her grin was not suppressible.

Keva, only a little bit disappointed that the main man was not to be *their* man, raised a bottle of Beck's. 'To Hannah.'

They all clinked bottles except Tony and Beano, who, unconverted yet to the joys of small, expensive measures of bottled continental beer, were on pints of Fuller's.

Guy and Wheezer had started off tying the band into every meeting, every decision, major and minor, but they soon got bored. They wanted to be in the studio, hearing the finished mixes, or out with the girls. Even Ticky was out of the office more than she was in. This suited them fine. The campaign they'd been drawing up was draining them. Every point was argued through until they were both satisfied the right course of action had been reached. To attempt it with six or seven conflicting points of view would have been agony.

Besides, the pressure was now on to complete the album. Andy, for all that he had become besotted with the Grams, had a big commitment to one of Parlophone's new bands. They'd been about to record at the time that Guy had first enquired after Andy, when the singer's father had dropped dead in the street. The album was put on hold. Andy had said, like, take your time, we'll do the album when you feel ready. And now they were ready. He wasn't someone who'd be willing – or able – to bullshit them or stall them, especially in circumstances such as these, and he wasn't someone who liked to turn down work. He loved the way the Grams album was sounding but, ultimately, it was a job. Guy wanted a finished album before they started stirring things up – it'd be hard to find time for the studio once the circus had started – so everyone was making the most of what little time they had left.

They'd worked out, minutely but with plenty of slack, a plan for the year ahead. 'Desert Rain' was the almighty calling card to the world. It was to be so rare, such a symbol of quality, that copies would turn up like masterpieces, in the most remote places. With this in mind, mainly, an ability to supply the Head of Programming in Nogales, Arizona, the venue manager in Osaka, the countless Internet contacts throughout the world who would love to be deemed important enough to receive this rarity of rarities as a personal gift from Wheezer, he opened up his own account with COPS and ordered another batch of whites along with five hundred CD promos. Wheezer was a habitual compiler of cuttings, ticket stubs, gig posters and had an acute sense of history in the making. 'Desert Rain' was, by far, his most historical moment and memento.

The magnificence of the track was instant, but ReHab still had to make the most of it. It had to be the most talked-about release, and the Grams the most talked-about band, of the summer. In order to do international deals with the calibre of company and individual Guy envisaged, 'Desert Rain' had to do its job.

After that, it'd be all systems go. They'd need to make a video for 'Beautiful'. Do the right press. Tour the UK and do selected one-offs in Europe. Foreign licensees would then be put in place, which would mean trips to New York, Los Angeles, Tokyo, Frankfurt, Paris and reciprocal visits, no doubt, to see the group live. The Americans, in particular, would want the group over there for pre-release promotion, and each other territory would expect their pound of flesh, too. And then they'd release the best fucking album of the year.

Wheezer was very hip to all this and the more he worked with Guy, the more he began to see things his way. But one part of the plan continued to disturb him. He didn't want to say anything at first – the relationship with Guy was starting to work, but when they disagreed it was war. But this thing now seemed so obvious, such a fatal flaw, that Guy must simply have got over-excited, or somehow just plain overlooked it.

'Hear me out, Guy, look . . .'

'Wheezer, shut it, will you? I ain't got time for this. *You* ain't got time . . .'

'. . . the gap between "Desert Rain" and "Beautiful" is too

perishing long. "Desert" will be over by the start of July, and we're asking them to wait 'til *December* for the follow-up?'

'Correct.' He was hardly listening to him.

'That's nonsense, Guy. I'm looking at this as a punter. It's the only way I *can* look at it. OK, right, we know that "Desert" is the big attack on the mainstream consciousness. It'll work, too – I think I believe that more than anyone. It'll get under their skin. With any luck, the punters who *couldn't* get the EP, because it sold out in two days flat, will be even more desperate to get their mitts on the next one. And the ones who *did* get a copy are now total fans, converts one and all, ten thousand of them eagerly awaiting news. So what then? We've got the great unwashed licking their lips, slobbering for the main course and we tell them, what? Supper's not quite ready yet? Won't be for quite a while, actually . . .'

'Fuck off! Jeez, Wheezer, you shouldn't talk about stuff you don't understand, sometimes . . .'

'So *tell* me! *Make* me understand! I want to, believe me . . .'

'We're putting them on *tour* . . .'

'Preaching to the converted . . .'

'Using your trite gastronomic analogy, in a five-course dinner the tour is a perky little sorbet to cleanse the palate, remind the gourmet of the delicacies which have gone before and prepare his tastebuds for the fucking feast that lies ahead!'

'The dish'll have gone cold . . .'

Guy sighed, deflated and patronising both at the same time. 'Wheeze. Just leave it. Honestly. Trust me.'

'Can't. Gap's too long. It'll be like the Big Tease. It'll backfire. Come across as phoney. Punters'll lose interest.'

'Bollocks!'

'Don't think so. Worried.'

'Total fucking bollocks!'

Guy's wavy *Brideshead* locks fell in angry strands over his reddening forehead. Wheezer was a little surprised.

'Look, I'm . . .'

'Talking shit!'

'Guy, I'm raising a perfectly legitimate . . .'

Guy slapped the desk hard with both palms. 'Fuck off,

Wheezer! You do not know what the fuck you are on about! Just SHUT UP!'

There was silence. Guy slumped on to his desk, head in arms. 'You're a bloody fool . . .'

This last hurt Wheezer more than the combined effect of Guy's gradually intensifying ranting. He was used to Guy getting stressed out over work things, but his railings against him were becoming more personal. He got up, collected his notes and slid them into his briefcase. Guy looked up.

'And that fucking *brief*case!'

Wheezer left, flagging a cab outside. He almost always used the tube, but was too bothered to make the walk down to Chancery Lane. He let himself into Farm Place, determining to find his own office and his own place to live immediately. He dialled up call minder to see if there was any word from the group. From now on, he and old spoilt deBrat were on opposite sides. Maybe they always were. He'd get back home and set the five thousand pounds to work for the band – give them the office and the cute assistant they'd always wanted. And give Guy deBurret hell.

James had left a message, waffling on about some club they were all going to. Wheezer could hear him smoking and exhaling dramatically, talking through his own fog. Meet them in there. Bring some PDs. James had got the hang of per diems all right. He was starting to do Wheezer's head right in. Even a Sunday trip to the bagwash would elicit a would-be businesslike look and: 'D'we get PDs?' James Love wittered on, sniffling loudly after every important bit then shouted: 'BUT YOU WON'T FUCKEN COME, WILL YA!' and slammed the phone down. Wheezer rubbed his ear and looked at the receiver as though he were in a *Columbo* movie. There was one more message.

'Message received today at nine – twenty – nine – from telephone number . . .'

It was Guy.

'Fuck, Wheeze . . . I'm really sorry. I ran after you but you got into the only cab ever to go west down Clerkenwell Road after six thirty . . . you need to get a fucking mobile . . . sorry . . . I wish I could tell you what's up with me . . . er . . . this is all getting to me a bit . . . er . . . call me if you get this before ten. (Beat). Oh.

You're absolutely fucking right. Of course we should put "Beautiful" out earlier. Still programmed into my MGR mode, see. Thinking of a single lasting four or five or six fucking weeks. But, by royal command, "Desert" will last a mere *one* week. So, yeah. Mud in your eye. We should think about . . .'

The message ran out of time. Wheezer was grinning enormously. He reached for the phone, wanting to scam up a new plan immediately, but hesitated and put the receiver down. He should leave it till tomorrow. And he should still think hard about basing himself back in Liverpool. It'd be much more . . . *businesslike*. He shouldn't feel too sorry for Guy. The episode served as a reminder as to the frailty of all human relationships and he was determined, now, to keep his distance. He ran his finger along the video shelf and located *Buttman in Europe*.

Wheezer was anxious about the Ally Bland show, but he was a lone voice.

'You're all too seduced by this whole London thing. You're allowing yourselves to become trendy . . .'

'Makes a nice fucking change from being totally fucking unheard of.'

It'd been Hannah's idea. Ally was taking over a disused Paddington hotel for one of his Marigold word-of-mouth parties. They were always brilliant, Ally's dos, with everyone from young clubbers to TV executives clamouring for invites. Hannah thought it was the perfect opportunity to launch the label. They'd give Ally a bit of a budget to make it amazing, and the band could come on at about midnight when everyone would be up for them.

'He's a club promoter. A bloomin' good club promoter but he has no expertise at all when it comes to live bands. The sound'll be awful.'

'Just tell him what we want. Anyone can hire a PA!'

'It's not just the PA, is it? It's the room. It's a deserted flippin' *hotel*. The acoustics'll be crap.'

'Acoustics!' scoffed James. 'Acoustics are what you make them!'

'Famous last words, Hector!'

'You're starting to do my head in, you!'

Hannah intervened, telling Wheezer that the Marigold crowd

didn't expect Albert Hall acoustics. They were a party crowd. They'd support the band. It was a great opportunity. There'd be journalists, DJs, radio people in the crowd, all delivered right to the Grams' doorstep. He wanted to believe her. He wanted to believe it because it was *her*. He loved her with all his heart. But she'd never know that, and he fought her even harder.

'That's me whole point. This is our big hello to the potherbs who control our destiny. We don't want to sound tinny. It's too much of a risk. Guy'll support me on this.'

Guy didn't. Andy's advance and the Whitfield Street bill had made a sizeable dent in the cashflow and here was an ideal way of holding a high-profile launch for the band and the label without spending crazy money. He'd bring along the sales team, pluggers, the whole mob, take them to supper, make a fuss of them. It'd be perfect.

He also needed a gig to bring Mack Hansen along too. Mack was a partner in H3O, the booking agency who represented some of the best live acts in the country. It was a young, hungry outfit but they were notoriously picky about the bands they took on. Mack had taken a risk with Medsin – the other partners didn't get it at all – but they'd gone on to become one of the biggest live acts in the world. H3O cleaned up. Touring was key to the gameplan with the Grams and an agent like Mack could take a lot of the pain away. With all respect to Wheezer, the band had only scratched the surface when it came to live work. It'd all been put together through like-minded Net nerds in out-of-the-way places. The nearest the Grams had got to playing London had been Angels in Bedford and the Crypt in Hastings. Guy wanted Mack on board as soon as possible. The Grams were doing the Marigold party.

Guy's mobile vibrated in his pocket. He recognised Mack's number on the display, but he couldn't get reception down in the basement of the hotel where gear was being set up. Wheezer and Long Richard were trying to shift a big cabinet so that it was tilted inwards slightly. Damage limitation, he said. He was starting to make Guy nervous.

He bounded up the steps and called Orange ansaphone. He had one new message. Mack couldn't make the gig. Shit! He was going to come to soundcheck instead. No! Call him back with a time.

Jeezuz! Without the crowd there, there'd be no vibe, nothing for Keva to bounce off. The band were tight, but part of their magic was the way they could transport a crowd. He wanted Mack to see that. Maybe Guy should stall him. Maybe he could still get him to come down tonight.

'Mack. Hi there, matey. Guy. Deffo no can do tonight?'

'Can't, mate. Helen's cooking supper for some Yanks. Plain forgot. These are, like, real players. Might be buying into me for a UK presence, know what I'm saying?'

'The Taurus guys?'

'The very same.'

'So bring 'em along. Have your supper then show them how London rocks.'

Pause. Eternity.

'Hmm. Quite like it. Lemme get back to you.'

The line went dead without Mack saying bye. Three minutes later he was back on.

'What time?'

'Midnight.'

'We'll be there. Me plus two.'

'Excellent. See you . . .'

He'd been cut off again. But Mack was coming. And one of the coolest agencies in America was coming, too. Better and better.

Soundcheck was amazing. The Grams tore into their set with deranged energy, Keva's jugular throbbing as he snarled into the mike. Everyone in the room, set dressers, caterers, helpers, stopped what they were doing and turned to the stage. Then they started getting into it. Hannah and Celeste jumped on to the DJ's podium and gyrated hypnotically. The band responded by cranking it up another gear, James going down on his knees, eyes closed, head rolling as he peeled out his squealing acid guitar and Tony, legs apart, jumped up and down with his back to the crowd. By the end of the session there was a crowd of thirty grooving in front of the band. They clapped and whistled and stamped their feet at the end, continuing the cheering as the band made their way through them back to their dressing-room, grinning at each other. Guy was wishing he'd let Mack come down now.

'Shit that, wasn't it, Wheeze?' smiled James. Hannah and Celeste burst in.

'Fucking hell, boys! Manics eat your hearts out! Rock and fucking roll! Whoo!'

Wheezer shuffled to the door. 'I'll leave you boys to it, shall I?'

The sound had been OK. Not brilliant. But who could say how it'd be with three hundred punters packed in, muffling the room? Wheezer was prickled. He couldn't get the band on their own these days. Every conversation was interrupted by Guy or Hannah or Maxine or some other hanger-on throwing their tuppenceworth in, and the boys seemed too inclined to take their counsel. They were being got at by people who liked being listened to. He hated to see how easily the boys were impressed. They were taken in by every new phoney who shook their hand, bought them a drink, offered them a line. He felt as though they were slipping away from him already. Emotionally and physically, he could not get close to them. He'd have to sort out some security with Ally for that dressing-room. The girls were getting more of the band's ear than he was. James, in particular, had started to turn his back whenever Wheezer started a lecture, talking over him, changing the subject, just not listening. Sometimes he'd just sit there with a stupid grin on his face as though whatever Wheezer was telling him was the most inane thing he'd ever heard. High on his list of recruits, up there with a proper road crew, was a security guy. That'd keep the parasites away.

The setting up of the gear had convinced Wheezer that their raggle-taggle crew of mates and semi-skilled associates was not up to the job, either. Long Richard was a hell of a bloke, but what use was he? Wheezer could set up the gear better himself and as for his driving, well . . . when did serial pot-smoking ever help sharpen your senses? Long Richard was never without a spliff on the go, either in his mouth or in the advanced stages of construction. The Grams were the best new band in the world and everyone around them, from now on, would have to reflect that. They were going to have the best. Starting with the appointment of an experienced tour manager. The TM could bring in a sound engineer, a backline bod to work with Alan and Tony, and a lighting engineer to work wonders with the fluorescents. Even if they were only doing club gigs using house rigs and lights, it was good practice to start working with pros and grow with them. He'd get on to it on Monday. James appeared at his shoulder, making him jump.

'Got any PDs, Wheeze?'

'Cripes, James, no I have not!'

'Why not, like? We're working, aren't we?'

'It's not a paying gig. It's your own blooming launch party. You shouldn't be seeing it as a chore.'

'Doesn't make no odds to me. Mr Love's at work. He needs bread. He can't live in London on fuck all.' His cheeky eyes were goading Wheezer from his round face.

'You only got paid yesterday.'

'Eighty fucken quid after you had your cut.'

'So aren't I supposed to take a cut? Am I robbing you of your hard-earned riches? What am I meant to live on, myself?'

'I'm not saying that, like . . .'

'What're you saying?'

'I'm saying, you know, eighty quid, like. You give us eighty quid.'

'Which is what *I* get from four lots of commission. We're all on eighty quid.'

'Commission!'

Wheezer ignored the remark. 'I've still got seventy-five notes left. Where's yours gone?'

'Mr Love's a rock 'n' roll legend, Wheeze. He has expenses.'

Wheezer snorted.

'I'll lend you twenty rips. But it's coming out the next lot, so, you know, don't spend it all at once. Yes?'

'Giz fifty.'

'That'll leave you with exactly thirty pounds next week, James. What're you going to do then?'

'Not arsed. Mr Love lives for the moment.'

Wheezer was exhausted. He handed over fifty pounds.

James was off, up Edgware Road and ringing at Jimmy's flat in Luton Street within minutes. He'd stopped sending Ben now recording was finished. The parcel always seemed a bit light after Ben'd got his mitts into it.

'This is really good coke,' said Jimmy, his Waterford accent making the word into 'cowke' as he unfolded a wrap for James to inspect. James chuckled.

'I've never met a dealer who said this is really shit coke, like.'

Jimmy looked offended. 'Please don't use that expression, James. I am categorically *not* a dealer. I supply a range of goods and services to a select clientele. Please.'

'Sound an' that.'

'Seriously, man. This is off the flake. It's the best cocaine in London – hasn't even been cut yet. I'm doing this for seventy-five, but I'll let you have a fifty-pound deal, just this one time. Because I like you.'

'I like me too.'

'Well, here's to friendship, because I'll never get rich while I keep giving the stuff away to me clients.'

'If you didn't keep devastating your consignments!'

'That as well. Stick the dough on top of the cupboard, there. And James – don't even bother fucken turning up here with fifty quid again, yeah?'

Beano had never known anything like it. He and Celeste were at each other every moment they were together. He'd never believed in love before, but he felt giddy when he thought about Celeste. He was mad about the girl. The moment soundcheck was over, he'd swilled down his armpits and the two of them were off in her little Fiat. Tony felt deserted without him.

'Anyone fancy a drink?'

Keva shook his head. 'I'm gonna go back to FP with The Wheeze and get a bit of kip. You should, too, you know. This is a big one.'

'Will do in a bit. Really fancy a pint, though.' He was almost licking his lips.

'There's a place called The Cow not far from here,' offered Hannah.

'When do we leave?'

'I'd love to, Snowy, but I can't.' She rolled her eyes. 'Things to sort out here, yeah? Then Guy wants me to come in on his big meet 'n' greet supper at Kettner's later.'

'Oh, come on, you bore!' hissed Ticky. 'I'm in on that as well. It's not for ages! Tony's asked us to have a drink with him. One won't hurt!'

Hannah looked at her watch and groaned. 'No. You two go. I might follow you down there. I've just got to, like, get this guest list confirmed with Ally. Where is the great studly one, anyway? You two go on. I'll try and catch you up, yeah?'

Tony was delighted. It was almost a date. He and Ticky made for the exit. Maxine was heading down the steps towards them and, checking to see whether Keva was with them, smiled brilliantly and swished past.

'See her,' muttered Tony to Ticky. 'I 'ate her.'

Ticky laughed out loud. 'Oh, Tony. You do make me giggle. You're such a little grump.'

'I like being grumpy.'

Wheezer came running after them. 'Eleven o'clock back here, then!' He turned imploringly to Ticky. 'Don't let him get drunk, will you? Please? Lot riding on this tonight.'

'Wheezer, why don't you come along with us and you can keep an eye on us. It'd do you good to let your hair down for a change.'

'Don't encourage him,' said Tony.

'I'd *love* a drink, but no. Thanks all the same. Lots to do. Look after him.'

They drove off. Wheezer walked round in a circle, nerved-up, wondering what he should do next. Keva whistled to him from a side exit and beckoned him over.

'Sexine's on me case! Can't handle her right now. Let's do one!'

They flagged a cab on Praed Street and were back at Farm Place in no time at all. Keva flopped back on the big, once-white sofa and chilled out with the spicy home-grown Long Richard had given him. Wheezer thought he'd seize the moment.

'The lads don't seem to be taking it very seriously. They worked harder when there was nothing at stake.'

Keva snuggled further down into his cocoon and blew a pillar of smoke straight up at the ceiling, holding the joint like a dart player. He seemed to think about what Wheezer'd said for an eternity, before angling his face towards him.

'Nah. They're just enjoying it all. That's all. They love the band.'

'They love *being* in a band. They've done nothing yet, and they're acting like rock stars. Beano'll be wearing shades next!'

Keva shaped smoke rings dismissively. 'Have you mentioned any of this to them?'

'Chance'd be a fine thing. I can't get near them for trollops and drug dealers and yes-people.'

Keva smiled at Wheezer's quaint verbiage. 'You're wrong, la. There's no way those lads'll go off the rails. They're having a grin. This is what they're in a band for. The band'll always come first, but if there's a bit of a hoot to be had, why not seize the opportunity? Isn't that why people start bands?'

Wheezer fixed on him, intelligent eyes peering out from under the brutal fringe. 'And why are you in a band? How come you're not prancing round town like Alex Graham?'

Keva blew his hair out of his eyes with the piquant smoke. 'There's a bit more to it than that, for me. I write songs. I want to know how good I am.'

Wheezer nodded. 'You're good. You're the best.'

Keva looked down. Wheezer persisted. 'Still need a hardworking band, though. I mean James . . . James is so flipping good. But he doesn't want it, does he? He doesn't want . . . *respect*.'

'I think you're wrong. Hector's weird. It's all an act, all that larger-than-life stuff. In his own way, he probably wants it more than all of us.'

'The way he's carrying on, he's going to be the one who stops you getting it. If he doesn't respect himself, he can't be too surprised when no one else does.'

Keva laughed and docked his spliff. 'Oh, he respects himself, all right! I think it goes beyond mere respect. Jimbo *loves* himself!'

'Well, there's a difference. There's a flipping big difference. I just wish the big potherb would stop putting the cart before the horse. That's all.'

Keva wanted to laugh, but not as much as he wanted to spare his manager's feelings. He was so fond of the nutty Wirral throwback when he said things like that. He smiled over at him.

'Wheezer?' said Keva.

'Yes?'

'Respect!'

James was earning considerable respect from Maxine. Disappointed to discover from Hannah that Keva had vacated the premises moments before her arrival, she'd been about to tag along with her and the quiet one to The Cow when James arrived back. He was cute, James. Cuddly, in that he made you want to hug him, and funny, too. She loved men who could make her laugh. And he always had a line for the ladies.

'Do you know Pedro?' he twinkled, tiny dimples puckering his cheeks. He was quite a honey.

'Alas, I know him well.'

'And are you a friend of Pedro?'

'Not too close, just at the moment. Sorry.'

'No matter. Come with Mr Love.'

She went into the dressing-room with him, where he chopped out the beak with a plectrum and beckoned her to go first. He passed her a little steel tube, only a couple of inches long, and she ducked into the cocaine, vacuuming it up in two robust snorts. Whomp! It was good. She dabbed up the remaining grains and ran them round her gums. James hoovered his line in one, languorous draught and exhaled with satisfaction.

'Ah! Very nice. Mmmm. Consider me suitably fluffed.'

He eyeballed Maxine. 'Now then, Maxine. How would you like Mr Love to go down on you?'

Keva and Wheezer were the first back at the venue. A long queue was snaking out into Praed Street, plenty of dressed-up kids, a few older trendies and some outrageous fashion casualties. Keva, dressed-down in Clark's desert boots, Newbold jeans and a vintage, nettle-green Gabicci, shook his head in despair as they passed two tubbies in grotesque tie-dyed silk.

'You two better not come down the front,' he muttered.

It was embarrassing having to walk to the front of the line and flash their Access All Areas stickers. A murmur of interest went up as security checked them out and then they were down there, slalomming through the busy bar and across the dance floor, feeling as though everyone was watching them go past, charting their path to the sanctuary of the dressing-room. It was bare. No cans. No sandwiches. No crisps, water, juice, ice or ciggies and no towels. It was all Wheezer needed. He hated scuffling with the promoter over riders. He went out to find him. He felt better, though, felt like The Man as Ally turned away from briefing his security to greet him.

'Heeey! My man!'

Ally greeted him with a funny, back-to-front, clenched-fist handshake. A big security guy watched, impassive, as Wheezer stared at Ally's syncopating hand, eyeing it like it was going to bite him. When the hand finally stopped still, Wheezer gave it a gentle shake. Ally was all animation.

'Are the boys here? I'll get the goodies over to the dressing-room pronto, man. Didn't want it getting too warm in there, growing feet and all that. Sorry, Wheeze, what was it? You're looking stressed there, man.'

Wheezer was glad he didn't have to take Ally to task over the rider.

'Just wanted to ask a tiny favour. I know everyone's all into hugging and telling each other they love them – and jolly nice it is, too. But can the band have a few minutes before and after the show on their tod?'

Ally looked hurt and puzzled all at once. 'Sure . . .'

'I mean, specifically, can we have a fella on the dressing-room door. Just to keep everyone out. Just for a while immediately prior to and after the show?' Wheezer glanced up at the hulking bouncer, who stared out past his shoulder.

'A rock-star sort of thing. No problem, man. I mean, I doubt they're going to be kicking the doors down, it ain't that sort of vibe in here, but if you're nervous . . . hey, we aim to please! Whatever, man . . .'

'It's not so much your crowd I'm bothered about.'

'Aha. Catch your drift, man. Whatever. We'll get someone sorted. They'll be there before you get back. Probably won't let you in, mind!'

He rapped the order into his walkie-talkie and gave Wheezer the thumbs-up. He found himself trying to think up things which'd make Ally mad.

Sure enough, there was a hefty young girl on the door by the time he returned. Wheezer introduced himself and gave her her guidelines. Band only until further notice. She wasn't overtalkative, but he could see that she was going to do the job for him. He was right. Ten minutes later he could hear the unmistakable sound of Beano, slurring slightly, demanding that he and his girlfriend be let in. Wheezer grimaced at Keva and bounded over to the door. Beano was incensed. Even behind his mirror shades, that much was evident. He was very cross indeed.

'What's all this shit, Wheeze?!'

Wheezer pulled an apologetic face at Celeste. 'My orders, I'm afraid. Biggest gig of your life, this. No distractions until after the show. Sorry, Celeste. You'll have to unhand the boy for now.'

'Bollocks!' He pushed past Wheezer, dragging a protesting Celeste with him.

'Hey! Leave it, Al, it's cool! Wheezer's right. I'll see you later.' She tried to leave. The security girl came in. Beano stood between the two girls, comically puffing out his slight chest as the yellow-shirted bouncer confronted him.

'Need me to deal with this, sir?'

Wheezer shook his head. 'Thanks. There isn't going to be a problem.'

Beano jerked his shades off in defiance. 'Fucking right there is! There's gonna be a big problem if you're gonna carry on with this shit! This is the fucking Grams, not fucking Pearl Jam! We don't do shit like this!'

Again Wheezer gurned apologetically at Celeste. 'Sorry, Celeste. I think Al and I need a word.'

'Sure. See you later, honey.' She went to kiss him.

'Don't call me that!'

Celeste held her hands up in mock-surrender. 'Woh! Touchy! Whatever, you know?'

She looked hurt as she strode out. Keva winked at Wheezer.

'See whatcha done, you prick . . .'

'Don't swear at me, Al.'

Beano ran at Wheezer, eyes aflame, and hurled a punch at his head, catching him just above the ear. It stung, nothing worse. Beano was in tears.

'That girl, right . . . that girl just cooked me the best meal of me life . . .'

Keva hesitated, to be sure that Beano had really said it, then shrieked with laughter. Wheezer, spluttering, tried not to join him. Beano glared at Keva, betrayed.

"Kinell, Beano – Monty Python!' cried Keva. 'Couldn't you come out with anything better than that?'

'You wouldn't understand, you twat!' He glowered at them, seething. 'You've probably never had a meal like that!'

That was it. The two of them were helpless, trying not to enrage Beano further but bent double with strangulated mirth. It was agony. Beano stormed out. Wheezer went to get him back, but Keva held up one hand to halt him, the other holding out Beano's discarded shades. 'I'll go. See if we can talk some sense into lovelorn Johnny. You can ditch the specs.'

The meal with the team at Kettner's was a great success, largely because of Tony Snow. Guy had appointed MSF as Sales and Distribution, with 180 Promotions coming in as Strikeforce. Gil Acton's company, Acetate, were plugging TV and radio in London, with Air-Aid doing regional. There was no need for regional press right now – not for a limited edition EP.

Ticky and Tony were late. Guy introduced Tony to the workers, excused himself and walked Ticky back outside the restaurant. He was annoyed, but very calm.

'I'm quite correct to say that you asked me for this job, aren't I? Begged, one might say?'

'Ooh, Guy, am I being chided?'

'I fear you are, Georgie. I'm honoured to have the pair of you on board, but it's a fucking job. You don't fit it around your social engagements. Clear?'

'But little Tony was . . .'

Tony came out. 'Everything OK?'

'Super-duper,' smiled Ticky.

'Good. Just that there's a large group of thickset men desirous of grub. Ladies, too. But they're thin . . .' He turned to Guy. '. . . Sorry I made her late, Guy, mate. I just fancied a bit of company. Everyone pissed off without me and Ticky took pity. She's a good 'un. I'm made up to be working with her.'

'Very noble of you, Snowy. I feel the same way, too. Honoured to be working with her. So let's *work*.'

Ticky charmed a variety of portly Brummies, who charmed her back with proclamations of ardour for the four-song cassette Guy had sent out. Hannah took care of the pluggers, assuring them that a raft of top-notch music press interviews was upcoming.

'Helps us build a story, obviously, if we've at least got *NME* on board. More the merrier, but *NME*'s a must for Radio One,' drawled Gil. His sidekick, Terry, a chirpy, tattooed cockney sparrow agreed.

'*NME*'s a mast. A *mast*.' He addressed Hannah's chest. She made cow-eyes at Ticky who signalled that she was going to the loo. Hannah met her on the stairs.

'How you getting on?'

'Oh, they're sweeties. It's only a matter of time before shipping, though. I can feel it. The drink's starting to kick in. Shipping's going to come any moment!'

'Good luck!'

'Yah! Go build the story, kid . . .'

They brushed cheeks. When Ticky got back to her table, Tony was thrilling six sales guys with tales of Paul McCartney.

'Seriously. He was at the Lomax gig. He come up and said . . . you guys, you're the greatest rock 'n' roll band in the world. After the Beatles.' His imitation of McCartney's American-Scouse accent was spot on.

'No kidding!'

'As I live and breathe,' nodded Tony, all dumbstruck sincerity.

'Wow! We can use that! You don't know what a cherry you've just given Midland sales force. That'll add another ten thousand albums to the ship . . .'

Ticky smiled to herself and gave Hannah a cheery hand-floating-on-water sign. Hannah mouthed 'shipping?' and Ticky grinned confirmation. Tony had these guys in his pocket. It looked as though Guy was getting on well with his table. Things were going fine.

'Did I tell you about me scrap with Liam Gallagher? Not so much a scrap, really, you need two for a scrap . . .'

Ally came back in. 'I'm not being funny, man, but the guys'll have to go on. The crowd're right up for it. Sweeney's whipped 'em into a frenzy, man, it's a fucking passionfest out there. We can't stall 'em any more. Seriously. Your guests'll be in there, somewhere. Their names've been crossed off the door. They're in here . . .'

Guy hadn't managed to locate Mack. Mack would've made a point of finding him at a normal gig, but maybe security had been weird with him. He prayed they hadn't been stroppy. It wouldn't take much to make Mack Hansen storm out, especially with people from the Taurus Agency to impress. Guy called Wheezer over.

'Beano OK?'

'He's smashing. He's been drinking nothing but coffee and water for two hours. He's speeding his nuts off. He's raring to go.'

'Cool. We'll go for it, yeah?'

'Yep. Let's do it.'

Wheezer was about to round the group up in the usual way when Guy clapped his hands together and shouted, 'OK, FEL-LAS! LET'S GO AND PLAY SOME ROCK 'N' ROLL MUSIC! ALL . . . RRRRIGHT!'

He said 'all right' the American way. It was all quite unnecessary and a terrible irritant to The Wheeze. The group seemed quite geed up by it, too, which was worse. Tony, Alan and James were already filing out, left hand on the left shoulder of the one in front. Where'd *that* beastly affectation come from, by Toutatis? Keva followed a moment later. Wheezer had just had a final word with the security girl and was struggling to catch up in the dim corridor when he tripped on something. It was Keva, bent over, hands on his thighs, retching. Nothing was coming out except a stringy strand of bile. This had never happened before. Wheezer was unsure what best to do.

'OK, matey, take your time.'

Long Richard ambled over, roach perpetually stuck to his

bottom lip. He stooped to inspect Keva through dangling, filthy dreadlocks. 'Nerves,' he said, and loped away.

The absurdity of Richard's prognosis wasn't lost on Keva, who lifted his head enough to grin wanly at Wheezer. 'Just gizza minute, mate. Nearly there.'

James was on stage, waving imperiously to the tightly packed crowd, who cheered back at him. The atmosphere was scintillating, the anticipation palpable. There was half as many again in the adjoining room, unsighted, hushed, craning for a view of the band who were, all of a sudden, the most talked-about in London. Tony, shitting himself, tuned in self-consciously, his back to the mob. Alan sat rigid, taking deep breaths. Keva nodded to Wheezer, who flashed his spotlight at the sound desk. The PA started to crank out the Grams' intro music, an intense, swelling vocal piece from Berio. The lights went down. Keva, a catlike silhouette, slunk on to the stage, one arm held high in a clenched-fist salute. The crowd yelled and whistled their approval. They continued to push forward from the back, already swaying and ready to dance, wanting to let go, sucked into the spell of the grotto and the sense of occasion. It was a uniquely terrifying and awesome moment for the Grams, who proceeded to blow it spectacularly.

Everything was wrong. The on-stage sound was a mess, booming hollow from the stage speakers. Beano couldn't hear his click-track and played a skittering, frantic improvisation throughout. Tony could barely pick him up, the two of them duelling hopelessly, trying to make up for their lack of cohesion with more and more energy and aggression. The crowd seemed to be going for it and the cheering at the end of each song was sustained. But Keva knew it was a disaster. He raked the crowd for Wheezer, trying to gauge his reaction, and saw him hovering by the mixing desk, alert, frigid, racked with worry. James went off into his own psychedelic garageland, strafing the crowd with blistering, corruscating solos. They stuck at it, but each of them was guessing what the other was playing. It was a tragedy. They went off to frenzied applause, but it sounded disembodied. None of them wanted to go back on again. Guy was waiting in the dressing-room, ashen.

'Everyone seemed to like it . . .'

'They must like shite, then . . .'

No one said anything for a minute. James looked up. 'Where's fucken Wheezer?'

Wheezer was on stage, ignoring the cheers and shouts for more, tracing wires with his torch and reconnecting leads into amps. He found the main problem, a loose connection into Tony's stage speaker making the bass supernaturally loud but muffled, too. He bandaged it with gaffer tape. Ally's people should've made double sure of all this after soundcheck. He knew what they'd say. Everything was fine in soundcheck. Yeah, and everyone knows that people tramp all over the stage after soundcheck – anything can happen. They should've checked it over. Hucksters! He went back to the dressing-room.

'I think I've fixed it. It was nothing. Case of very little, far too late.'

Nobody said anything. Guy was dreading having to find Mack and try and make some sort of a silk purse out of this shambles. He couldn't be bothered even trying to lift morale at the moment. Just as he was thinking how right Wheezer had been to preach caution about this show, The Wheeze spoke up.

'You should go back on, you know. I've got a feeling Ally and Hannah are right. I don't think that lot realise just how bad you were out there. They think that's how a real band sounds . . . they think that's just the energy, man, the dirty sound of a fast young garage band . . .'

'Fuck off, Wheeze! It's bad enough as it is . . .'

'I'm just saying. Your on-stage sound should be OK now. If they think that that was the real thing, and I'll grant you that's quite a big if, there's nothing to lose if we go back up there now and show 'em what it's really all about. Do it for yourselves . . .'

'I agree with him,' said James, jumping down from the dressing-table.

A knock at the door. Ally, beaming. 'Blimey, guys! What can I say? Crowd are mad for it! Any chance of seconds? Or shall I just hit the lights?'

The Grams trooped back on stage and, if the sound was only marginally less cluttered on stage, they still felt better about their encore. Back in the dressing-room, long after they'd come off stage, they were surrounded by well-wishers. Wheezer had told Aymee, the security guard, to let them all in six at a time, wanting the group to feel better about themselves. The sales team were the most muted of the handshaking, backslapping congregatation, but even they seemed impressed with what they'd seen.

'Not at all what I was expecting,' said one, Gary Hendry, the north-eastern rep.

'No, me too,' said Paul Parlour, East Midlands. 'You'd never've envisaged that . . . *anger* from the tape . . .'

'Mm . . .' continued Gary. 'It was quite . . . punky.'

'Mm,' agreed Paul. 'Yis. Pounkaye. Virry pounkaye.'

Guy had thought the whole thing sucked like a lemon and, having now patrolled the entire catacomb and found no sign of Mack, he knew it for sure. Mack would not have stayed for more than two or three songs. He'd give Guy the usual treatment – call him first thing Monday, sometime between nine and ten for bad news calls about groups he'd seen over the weekend, and he'd tell him for nothing that the Grams were crap. He couldn't face the rest of this sham party. The whole thing was blowing up in his face. Over 150 grand and what the fuck to show for it? His brothers'd be chortling into their chins if they ever got to know about what'd happened. What was that fucking group playing at tonight? Where was all Keva's . . . *charisma*? Guy knew, he utterly, utterly knew that if *he*'d been up on that stage tonight he'd have had the crowd eating out of his hand . . . He stayed and did his duty, gave every guest a bit of his time, but his heart was back home in Dolphin Square, away from all this, respectfully remembering that amazing group he'd seen at Ticky's party only a few months before. Everybody was chittering at once, full of themselves, full of being in the Music Industry.

'*NME*'s a mast. A *mast*!'

Guy spotted Wheezer chatting to Terry and Jeff Purvis, who seemed animated, and reckoned this to be the moment to slip away. Maybe he was just tired. He slunk out into the night and flagged a cab and, remembering his mobile, switched it back on. The New Message clarion screeched out almost immediately. Just one new message. Mack.

In a controlled, icy, very vexed voice he was telling Guy that he was outside this no-mark club, that someone had already pinched their names off the guest list, that they had been insulted and abused by security (Very Mack. Especially with Americans present. They'd more probably been informed in apologetic, embarrassed tones that, according to the list, they already seemed to be inside the venue.) and that he would never, ever take a call from Guy again. He could have wept for joy.

Hannah was making repeated trips back into the changing-room to usher everybody out to join the party when she caught sight of Keva, myxomatosed, fixated by a woman on the other side of the room. She found herself overcome by a searing flush of jealousy. Smiling pertly, she sidled up to Keva.

'Seen something you like?'

'Wouldn't put it quite like that.' He dragged himself away from eyeing the girl and turned, troubled, to Hannah. 'Was she here, like? Tonight?'

'Course! Don't be silly . . . She's here, isn't she?'

'Shit! Now we *are* finished . . .'

'What you on about? Cindy's a darling.' She gave a hollow laugh and pulled Keva by the wrist. 'C'mon! D'you want me to introduce you?'

'No thanks. We've already met.'

On the Tuesday everybody was up early, fidgety, unable to settle. Even James was restless, edgy from the non-stop smoking, boozing and snorting of the last few weeks. He threw his nervy, spasmodic cough and dragged hard again on his nasal cavities. He could not force air up through his nostrils. His nose was locked, blocked tight with hard-packed gack mucus. He pushed his thumb over one nostril and blew hard down the remaining cavity, trying to force a passageway, any airhole at all. Nothing. A dismal whine from his nose as the sinuses tried to recover from the assault. James staggered back to his bed, head spinning. He'd have to lay off the yaoh for a few days. He wouldn't be able to get much up there, now, anyway.

The other three had their minds on today's music papers. They wouldn't hit the shops until tomorrow, but you could pick up

NME, at least, from certain news-stands after three or four o'clock. The reviews so far had been impossibly good. It was like the journos were penning their own little personal letters to the group, telling them how great they were, hoping they could get to meet them some day. The *Observer* and the *Sunday Times*, always jousting each other for the first glimmer of the next new thing, had both run massively uncritical pieces about the night. the *Sunday Times* carried a whole page about Ally Bland and Marigold in their Style section, tipping Ally as One to Watch. Ally, in turn, tipped the Grams and the author of the piece seconded that emotion in hyperbolic terms.

For Keva, reading the reviews in Holland Park on a bright, early June morning, it was almost an anti-climax. Yes, the girl from the *Observer* picked up on some of the important points about the band, noticed their clobber, liked his presence and the way he dominated a postage-stamp stage. But she was so gushingly favourable about a band who hadn't even been interviewed by *NME* or *Select* that it all sounded like a fashion-pack flavour-of-the-week thing. Almost like reviewing Keanu Reeves' band. It didn't ring true. It sounded like she'd heard the name being tossed around at a dinner party and wanted to get her own byline on them before anyone else. And she'd misheard the one lyric she quoted, heinously. What should have been: '*Shadows taunt me – roaring, howling*' from 'Chimera' was printed as: '*Shadows draw me Robbie Fowler*'.

His temples flushed hot as he read it. It made the Grams sound like The Farm or one of those football bands. He hated football. He hated all manly, sporting pursuits. He wished the embarrassing fashion among bands for pretending to be into 'the footie' would die a natural death. As he ambled through the orangery and out towards the Holland Park Avenue gate, he saw Wheezer stumbling towards him, carrier bag crammed to bursting with the Sundays. Keva smiled broadly.

'Have you read it?'

'Robbie Fowler? Serves you right for singing like Joe Cocker!'

They slapped hands, cackling.

'Whoops!' smiled Wheezer.

'What?'

'That was a bit London, wasn't it? The gimme five.'

'I fear we are becoming wok 'n' woal,' laughed Keva, trying to do Guy's voice.

Over chocolate croissants in Cullens Pâtisserie they decided an early return to Liverpool would be A Good Thing. They'd finish off the various bits and pieces then go and regroup, ready for the big push.

Keva was certain that Cindy Hogan was going to annihilate them in the *Maker*. He'd written her a sarcastic letter after her Sensira piece last year. He regretted it almost the moment he slipped it into the postbox, but the girl was a shithead. If she was looking for any chance to snipe back at him, this was it. He'd handed her the pistol and a spare round of ammo for good measure on Saturday night.

The *NME* and *Melody Maker* would hit the streets of London at about four o'clock. It wasn't even eleven. They sat around Farm Place, restless, listening to Beano and Celeste arguing upstairs. Tony jumped up.

'I'm gonna give Hannah a bell, see if she's heard anything.'

'What like?' asked Wheezer.

'Dunno. Just, maybe her contacts might've given some indication . . .'

'I think we would've heard something from her if they had . . .'

'Mm. S'pose so.'

James got to his feet, shaking his head. He sniffed hard, this time feeling a squash-ball-sized pat of sputum hit his throat. He spat into his hand to examine it. Sand brown, and almost solid. Pure, thick, membrane mucus. He took it to the bathroom and ran it away down the sink, shouting back in a comically bunged-up drone: 'State of youze all. Shitting yourselves about a fucken review. Rock stars don't worry about fucken reviews! It's just an opinion. We don't give a fuck, do we? We don't even read 'em! Do we care? Coz I don't! Mr Love doesn't read reviews . . .'

'Look, Hector . . .', said Keva, pained, searching for the right put-down, '. . . just . . . *fuck off*, will you!?'

James came back looking sincerely hurt. 'OK. I'll do one.'

'Yeah,' said Tony. 'Go and do some more . . . *drugs* with your trendy new pals . . .'

James blinked at him and lit up a Players, shaking the match theatrically. He blew a jet of bluish smoke at Tony. 'Don't damn it till you've tried it.'

'Fat chance!'

'Exactly,' said James, pleased with himself. He turned and headed for the door. Tony came after him.

'Ay, bollocks, what d'you mean?'

James smirked and winked at him. 'Looked in a mirror lately?'

'You do enough of that for all of us. Face down!'

'Do yourself a favour, Snowy. If you can't cut down on the ale, choose something more in keeping with a rock god. Vodka or JD or something. All that Real Man's Ale's making you . . . *jowly.*'

He waved and smiled his aggravating, know-all smile, the chipped tooth looking like a perfect target to aim at. Wheezer pulled Tony back. James winked at them both.

'See yah, losers. I'm off to enjoy me life. I've got one, see?' And he was gone.

Tony turned to Wheezer. 'Am I getting fat?'

Wheezer blustered and before he could answer, Keva piped up from the couch, 'You are, actually, Tone. Don't wanna be taking up with Hector's fuckin nonsense, but you could do with losing a coupla pounds, you know. Chubby isn't wok 'n' woal!'

Tony grabbed at his cheeks and strained to see himself in a mirror which had been erected for a taller man. 'Yeah, well – that'll all go when we're on tour. It'll melt, hour and a half of jumping about under arc lights every night for six weeks.'

'Six weeks!' interrupted Wheezer. 'You guys are gonna be on tour permanently if I have my way. Your only days off are gonna be for telly and interviews. That's if our singer can help me get Mr Love back in line. Keva thinks Hector's still utterly and totally devoted to the group, don't you, singer?'

Keva bit back the urge to fight with him. He pulled himself up off the sofa. 'Hector's Hector. Don't worry about nothing, la. He's cool. He can handle anything, Mr Love. This is just his . . . this is his purple patch. Let him ride it out.'

They all laughed, unconvinced. Tony jerked his head at the door. 'Come 'ead. Let's have a nice long walk into town. Time we get there, they might have some news, eh? Maybe I can lose a few pounds on the way . . .'

They shouted to Alan and Celeste. Beano came downstairs in a disgusting, furious lemon Versace summer blouse, set with rhinestones and tortoiseshell buttons. Celeste had cropped his hair with the attachment on Tony's Remington. She'd also shaded in grotesquely arched eyebrows, drawn them over his wispy white tufts with thick kohl so that his affable, approachable aspect had taken on shades of Cruella de Vil. The whole effect was set off by a pair of rubberised Scholl flip-flops and jeans which would have been too wide and too baggy on the big one of Russ 'n' Jono.

'What d'you think?' beamed Celeste.

They all gaped at him. Tony spoke up. 'You look daft.'

Beano turned on Celeste, whose warm brown eyes were startled by his ferocity. 'I told you! I fucken told you!'

The dispute lasted all the way along Bayswater Road to Pret à Manger in Marble Arch, where they filled up on overstuffed butties and espresso. Beano darted into Selfridges to wash off his eyebrows and purchase a pair of Paul Smith jeans. He didn't hesitate in taking the forty pounds Celeste offered towards the cost. She was very quiet while he was gone. Tony tried to talk her round.

'He's feeling the strain of all this, you know. We all are.'

'It's not that.'

'He's mad on you, you know.'

'Yeah.'

There was silence, for ages. Keva and Wheezer glanced at each other. Tony, awkwardly, uncharacteristically for him unless drunk, reached out and took Celeste's hand. 'Come on. No long faces.'

She laughed. 'You sound like my dad!'

'Good. So long as I don't look like him. I think we all need a dad, round here.' He caught Wheezer's stung expression. 'Shit! Wheeze! Sorry, mate, I wasn't thinking . . .'

'No worries. Forget it.'

But Wheezer wasn't hurting over the clumsy reminder that his parents were gone. He was cut that the group didn't see him as their own father-figure. He sparked up a fag and sucked fitfully at it. When Beano returned sporting new jeans and no make-up, the flip-flops didn't look so bad. The shirt would have to be for Celeste days, though. She hugged him as though he'd been away a week and stared into his eyes. 'Ah, me little Scouse minstrel. Me little bard. You're gonna go away from me, aren't you?'

Tony leaned over. 'Er, your dad, Celeste . . . He's not, you know . . . *jowly*, is he?'

They ambled on down Oxford Street in much better spirits.

After an interminable wait at Purvert, Hannah got a mate on *NME*'s newsdesk to fax over the review. It was fine. Nowhere near as fawning – or as inaccurate – as the Sundays, but there was an undercurrent of support for the band. The reviewer slagged off the terrible sound and the fashion for sticking bands on in dance clubs, but gave the Grams full marks for a passionate and energetic attempt to rise above it. Wheezer looked for the byline. Pat McIntosh. They'd have to mark him or her down as a friend.

Purvis stopped by, smiling, 'I told you, Wheeze, mate – if they decide they wanna like you, they'll find a reason to like you. If they decide to shine their lovelight on you, you can put out overblown MOR shite, have an ale gut, look like an off-duty milkman whatever designer crud you wear, never say one interesting thing, ever, and the journos'll suck the fart sediment out of your crack. But if they're set against you . . . there's nothing you can do about that. You can bribe 'em, suck their cocks, make the best fuckin' record in the whole wide world, ever . . . but they'll still bury you. You Gram boys seemed to have passed whatever random sampling it takes these days. I'd say you're in.'

Jeff winked at Keva and loped away, each knock-kneed stride devouring a yard and a half. There was nothing from the *Maker*. At five past six, after conferring with Purvis, Hannah gave Cindy a call on her mobile. She was pleased to hear from her, very breezy and upbeat. She spoke guardedly about the Grams' gig. She hadn't put anything in the paper for a couple of reasons. One was that she'd thought the band sucked to high heaven that night, even allowing for the sound. If she'd reviewed the show she'd have had to damn them. Secondly, she'd seen them not a year before and was knocked out by them. She knew what soaring highs they were capable of. Whether it was she who came along to their next show, or somebody else, she hoped they'd be back on form. She didn't see the hurry to get the band into the paper if she couldn't genuinely mention them in a positive light. She put on a borderline Glaswegian, Thumper voice: 'If yah caint say sumthink nice . . .'

She didn't mention Keva's letter. Hannah, working on a hunch, asked if she fancied popping into the Duke for a quick drink.

'Are the band gonna be there?'

'They can be, if you want . . .'

Pause.

'. . . Aye. Why not. It'd be fun tae catch up with yez again.'

Keva was underwhelmed. Hannah pushed him into Purvis's empty office, half closing the door behind them. Keva kept up his mewling protest. 'You didn't tell her *I* was here, did you? I mean, the lads can go. I don't have to come, do I?'

Hannah smiled and pinched his cheeks. 'Why so bashful, angel? You're gonna have to meet her sometime . . .'

'Yeah, just not now . . .'

She imitated Tony, inaccurately. 'Don't talk soft, lad. Look . . .' she said, returning to her own businesslike tone. 'You simply can't afford to have enemies in the press, yeah? People who are indifferent are bad enough, but . . .'

'Who said she's an enemy? . . .'

'Right. But she will be if you carry on mysteriously disappearing whenever she's around.'

'I don't want her around.'

Hannah lost patience. 'Look! She was fine. She wants to meet up with you all again. Take it at face value! She's a journo, yes, and because she's a fucking *good* journo, yeah, she knows full well that, like, you boys are doing it and, like, she wants to stake her little claim in that. That's how it works.'

'*She wants to stake her claim? That's how it, like, works?*'

He mimicked her, smiling right into her eyes. There was a slight tic in the left. Her face was flushed with held-back anger. She was Fenella Fielding with attitude. A sensation of affection, real affection and desire overcame him. He wanted to hold her and kiss her. She looked ready to hit him, or smash something. He took her hand. 'Thanks. Now I know,' he said, as gently as he was able.

There was desire in his voice. She looked down. 'Don't scoff. That's what journos want out of the job. They want to hang with the boys. They certainly ain't in it for the money.'

Her own voice was starting to shake. Keva was standing inches from her. They were next to Jeff's desk, the rest of the party just outside the door. She wanted to shut the door. She wanted Keva to just kiss her, really kiss her. He met her look again. 'I hope you don't mind me saying this . . .'

'What?' She heard the vexation in her voice.

'I wish you weren't working with us. Do you know what I mean?'

She gave him a sad half-smile. 'I hope you mean what I want you to mean. And I wish you meant it.'

She pushed carefully past him and went to shoo the others to the pub. Keva saw Purvis watching him from outside. Five minutes ago he merely found Hannah attractive. Now he loved her.

Hannah seized the first opportunity to get Ticky to herself. Tony and Keva were sitting with Cindy, laughing about something or other. Purvis was at the bar with Wheezer, talking passionately about Tim Hardin, and Guy was up on the Caledonian Road, looking at a potential office. Beano and Celeste had gone to Don Pepe for an argument and James was at large. Locking the cubicle door behind them, Hannah accepted a ciggie from her friend and inhaled hard.

'Fuck, Ticky, I don't know what to do! He would've had me on Purv's desk if there'd been no one there! I know he would.'

'And you would've let him?'

'God, yeah! I'm fucking crazy about him! I mean it . . .'

Ticky raised her eyebrows at Hannah.

'Ticky, I swear, I wouldn't have, like . . . I wouldn't have wanted this for anything. Yeah?' She took another hungry drag, snatching a nervy look at her pal. 'I mean it's like, you *know* I would not go looking for this, yeah?'

Ticky touched her wrist. 'I know, baby. I know.'

Hannah threw her head back and blew a thin column of smoke at the ceiling. 'Shit! What am I gonna do? I don't fall in love with pop stars! Like, I don't fall in *love*, yeah?'

Ticky was about to reproach her, then stopped and stooped down, taking her by the hand and looking into her eyes. 'Sweetie, you've got to forget all this. It's just not gonna happen. You can't let it. Put it out of your mind . . . it's too soon, and it's just . . . *wrong*.'

'Easy for you to say. You're, like, the most in-control person I know . . .'

Ticky snorted. 'Not quite so, darling, actually . . .'

Hannah looked up at her. Ticky made an embarrassed 'yikes' face and took the plunge. 'You must know?'

Hannah was all eyes.

'God! I try not to make it obvious. It's Guy . . .'

'Guy! You *haven't*!'

'No!' she laughed. 'Not for want of trying. Been in love with him since I can remember, I think. I just don't think he sees me that way. D'you know what I mean?'

Hannah nodded.

'And now he's the boss . . . it's *too* weird!' She eyed her friend carefully, feeling her out. 'I'm quite unhappy, actually . . .'

Hannah didn't take it up. Ticky jerked out of her contemplation, clapping her hands once. 'Anyway. You and Keva. Forget it. You're not ready. He *certainly* isn't. End in tears.'

Hannah sighed. 'I know you're right . . .' She took a last resolute drag on her cigarette, belatedly hearing and processing Ticky's pleas. She was only half listening, and responded only dreamily, out of politeness. 'What about Bundles?'

Ticky groaned. 'Don't ask. Don't know how I let it get this far. Going to break it off. Got to.'

Hannah got up, shocked. She'd heard that bit, all right. 'No! It's not true! Darling . . . why didn't you say? Fuck! There's me waffling on about my stupid crush and you . . . you must be miserable . . .'

'Yes. I'm bloody miserable. But I'll feel a whole lot better once it's done. Poor old Bundles. Never did love him. Now I don't even like him. If nothing else, working with Guy and the boys, meeting people like little Snowy . . . it's made me realise that men can be . . .' She eyed her friend beseechingly for approval. '. . . *nice*. D'you know what I mean?'

Hannah nodded. 'What a pair of sad old maids.' She stubbed out the butt. 'C'mon. We better go and pander to the boys. At least we'll be doing something right.'

They shook little fingers and went back out into the pub.

James, Purvis, Maxine and Ben sat in the Hanway Street basement, brains zinging with clear, brilliant thoughts, hearts pumping with their pleasure in themselves.

'I think that's right an' that, Jeff,' James asserted calmly. 'I know it sounds big-headed an' that, but I may as well say it cos it is what it is. I agree with you.'

Maxine nodded along, all sincerity, wondering when James was going to get his charlie out.

'I think we *are* gonna be the biggest band in the world. It's just one of them things, innit? It's meant.'

'It's great,' nodded Purvis, grinning and grating his teeth. 'It's just, you know – *fuck off*! I fuckin' love it!'

'*Mad*,' nodded Ben. 'Too much, man.' He locked his eyes into James. 'Have you, er . . . ?'

James jerked into action, as though he'd just been prodded out of a prolonged reverie. 'Oh, sound an' that, here y'are, la, fill your boots.' He passed him the wrap and Ben was up and off to the bogs. Purvis watched him go, then fixed James with a quizzical look.

'Don't get me wrong, like, Jimmo, I know Ben's sound . . . but is he a *friend*?'

'Course he is . . .'

'But is he a *friend*? Is he a FRIEND?'

James gave a little shrug. 'I dunno, do I? I mean, does it matter an' that? I've got loads.'

'You won't have at this rate,' tutted Purvis.

Maxine interjected. 'He *never* has any! He'll sit here 'til dawn with you if you've got toot. Lovely lad an' all that, but I'm just saying . . . keep an eye on him. *I'll* tell him, if you want . . .'

'Nah, leave it, eh? It's only powder an' that, innit? That's all it is. Ashes to ashes, powder to powder. Who gives a fuck?'

'No, mate – we're just looking out for you, that's all. That's all it is. Friends.' Purvis was staring fanatically right into James's face, mad as sand.

'Yeah?' James met his look, equally enraptured by the purity, the sincerity of the moment. 'Nice one. It means a lot to me. I mean it. It does.'

Ben returned from the toilet, dabbing gently at his nose with a tissue. He pulled a comical, taken-aback sort of face. 'Like, wow, Scooby! Bit, er . . . harsh after a while, that gear. Bit bleachy. You sure the cunt didn't cut it with speed, man?'

As he went to hand the sachet back to James, Maxine jumped up and snatched it, her voice suddenly hard and cold. 'If you're too fucking soft to say anything, some cunt better!' She opened up the neatly-folded little envelope. 'I knew it! Look at that! Greedy little cunt . . .' She slammed the remainder of the coke out on to the baize table top, eyeing Ben venomously. 'You've got no fucking respect, you, you little toe-rag! You spoil every fucking thing!'

She stormed out. Ben threw an apologetic shrug at the others and ran out after her. Purvis leaned over to James. 'Probably worked that together. Probably out there now, snorting all your drugs.'

James laughed his incisive laugh and went to the bar.

It was a bad start to what was going to be a tricky day. Wheezer turned on Radio One to hear the outro of The Purple's new single, 'Bolero'. It was good. He knew they'd signed to Mantra, a big, sussed indie who would've been the Grams' label of choice, but he wasn't expecting the fruit of that deal to see the light of day for ages. Mantra were a no-rush, no-hype label who'd think nothing of remixing a track six or seven times until the group got the sound and the feel they wanted. They were an artists' label. By their own standards, this was a rush-release. He turned the radio up.

'. . . from Huddersfield, out on the twenty-ninth of June. Very fine indeed, and we're going to be playing it every day this week. Travel, and there's a tailback south of Junction 21 on the southbound carriage of the M1 . . .'

Wheezer didn't hear the rest. He was taken over by a desperate low. The Purple, playlisted on Radio One! Crivens. He was overwhelmed, too, by a nagging, visceral dread which he couldn't source. Something from last night. Something from last night . . .

Keva emerged from the room he'd had to himself all night, James having briefly turned up in the Duke of York with Ally Bland, Ben and a gang of girls before taking off with Cindy, Purvis and Maxine. Purvis tried to get Wheezer to split half an E with him, but Wheezer managed to ward him off. Wheezer hadn't really hit the drink badly since they'd been in London and the more the Grams' sideshow started to grind into motion, the more he felt like getting out of it. But the session at Mono and the trip back to Liverpool and everything else weighed heavily on him. There was too much to lose, just now, and if he couldn't stay strong how could he preach to James? Keva scratched his head and yawned, farted weakly and waggled his finger rhythmically in his arsehole. He looked every inch the sensuous rock star.

'Whatdja reckon to Hannah, then, Wheeze? Reckon she's up to it?'

Wheezer knew this was coming. He had to hand it to the singer, he didn't stand on any ceremony. Hannah, after her session in the bogs with Ticky, had been noticeably cool with Keva. At first he'd thought it was something to do with Cindy being there. But, bit by bit, she'd been addressing herself more and more to Wheezer. She seemed to find him captivating. She listened intently and laughed at his stories and told even funnier ones herself. He felt that there was something there, but he didn't want to push it, just in case.

The Cindy side of things could not have gone better – she was sharp and funny, but she was upfront, too, admitting that she might have a conflict of interest, hinting at a romantic interest in one of Sensira and thereby admitting what Keva already knew about Helmet. That he was poison. Helmet was using his closeness to Cindy to poison the well. There was no doubt about it now – he was an enemy. A nasty, over-ambitious, insincere, phoney, prick, hobgoblin enemy. He had it in for Keva and he intended to protect his new messiah standing – and bury the truth about his past – by any means necessary.

Cindy Hogan would have to be watched. She was a smart girl. She was keeping her options open, Keva reckoned. She was career-minded and she didn't need to make an enemy of a band who could be gracing covers before long. Who could tell when they might be approaching Cindy to write the first of fifteen dozen authorised biographies? Equally, Sensira might at any moment suffer a massive fall from grace. So he could see why she might want to court them. But there was always that nagging suggestion that she might be a virus. Cindy allayed any such thoughts with her gently jibing stories about Helmet's inability to take drink and his tendency to throw up after a couple of tokes on a doob. She was wickedly funny with her impersonations of Helmet screaming for the tour bus to pull over. Keva walked right into it. When Cindy mentioned Sensira's new single, 'Beta-Blokka', he took up where she'd left off to launch into a tirade about Helmet's plastic-hip obsession with things he'd never tried.

'Why's he always going on about drugs? And football? And living on the edge? He's a little grammar-school divvie from Eccles, he's never been to a match . . .'

'Actually, he's from Rochdale,' smiled Cindy conspiratorially. She was definitely on their side. 'He's got a gran who lives in Salford. He used her address to impress you guys.'

Keva felt as though he could afford to be gracious – condescend a little, even. 'Well, he shouldn't have. He doesn't need to. He's not untalented and he should have the confidence to show that talent in its own context. He's *not* a mad, telly-throwing binge-boozing drug monster! He's Helmet. A little prick from Eccles. D'you know what I'm saying?'

'Rochdale.' Cindy grinned and pulled tongues at him. She was cool.

Hannah, on the other hand, seemed to have gone mad. At the end of the evening, as the pub broke up, emboldened by drink, excited by the imminent prospect of Helmet Horrocks's defrocking and infatuated past caring about professional decorum, Keva asked Hannah if she fancied going on somewhere. Maybe get something to eat. Her reply was tart and crushing.

'Let's keep this on the level, yeah? Like, you've all got a big gig first thing tomorrow and I've certainly got enough on my plate.'

It was one of those statements-as-questions again. She left him gaping after her. What could've changed so drastically during the course of one short evening? He'd spent a bit of time with Cindy, yeah, but that was at Hannah's behest. She should be pleased by how well he'd done. He went back over everything that'd been said and came up with . . . nothing. She was schizo.

'Wheeze?'

'I think she's doing a brilliant job. We should leave her to it and concentrate on our own stuff. To wit . . .'

'Not till eleven, is it?'

'Not till eleven, but by the time we round you all up . . . Could do with getting down there early, anyway. Suss the place out. See what the sound's like.'

Guy had persuaded Mack Hansen and some of the other young agents from H3O to come and see the Grams in rehearsal at Mono Studios' rehearsal rooms in Old Street. He was desperate for Mack to represent them, snowing him with calls, faxes, flowers, cigars, champagne. Calling a truce, and still insisting on seeing the band play before he'd consider working with them, Mack told Guy it was the roses that swung it for him. The H3O crew were due to come over in their lunch hour, but Mack was a man who tried almost too hard to be larger than life. He was liable to breeze in there at eleven thirty and try to catch them unawares.

Wheezer had also put together a list of tour managers. Lina Braben, Mack's assistant, had faxed over so many names that the Wheeze ended up shortlisting candidates on the basis of surname likeability and place of domicile. He was seeing four guys: Eddie Hamilton from Derry; Marty Lynch from Dublin; Tom Stone from Glasgow; and Malky McHugh, also from Glasgow. Glaswegians make tremendous crew, and many of the best TMs have come from there. Wheezer harboured a little suspicion that he'd end up favouring one of the Scots, but it was going to be up to the band too. He was also seeing a woman, Donna Dramas, a young New Yorker who'd moved to the UK to be with her boyfriend, the sound engineeer Pat Blake. She had a rep for toughness, but her bands loved her. She sounded good. By any comparison, today was a massive one for the Grams.

They were taking no chances. Ticky ordered a cab to pick them all up from Farm Place at ten. At ten past, with no sign of James and no word from him, Wheezer sent the other three off. As he was leaving, Keva turned to Wheezer and said, distractedly, picking his teeth: 'You're right. We're gonna have to get the jolly one out of London as soon as. He's gone mad.'

Wheezer nodded and got back on the phone. Ticky had heard nothing. Hannah had seen him leaving the club with Maxine and a few others. Maxine left him in the Troy Bar at three thirty. Three thirty! He was going to be good for nothing.

Wheezer got Guy on his mobile. 'You've heard about James?'

'Yep.'

'So . . .'

'So what?'

'Whadda we do? Cancel?'

'Cancel now and that's it. Mack'll blow us out for good.'

'But we can't go ahead without James . . .' There was a lengthy pause from Guy. 'Hello?' barked Wheezer, vexed, knowing they hadn't been cut off.

'Just thinking, Wheeze. I mean, what is, is, yeah? If he shows up, we've got a show. If he doesn't, we haven't. But if we go calling Mack up now, putting the mockers on it, then we definitely *definitely* don't have a show. Yeah?'

Wheezer's turn to pause. 'Yeah.'

'So I'll see you down there.'

The connection went dead. Wheezer replaced the receiver. Jings! What a day this was turning out to be. The Purple playlisted and now Hector going AWOL. What a selfish, fat . . . *fool* he was! He was supposed to be the one with genius, the instinctive hookmaker who could make magnificent pop sculptures out of Keva's complex ramblings. He had so much to gain, such a name to make for himself. But he was just a silly, chubby, sybarite, with no more foresight than a gambler with a sure thing scrawled on a ciggie packet. Whatever loose connection was holding the rest of them together, James didn't seem to want any part of it. He was on a one-man mission to oblivion. Wheezer went to call a cab, then told himself he could get there just as quick by tube. Quicker.

Sitting on the eastbound Central Line train, willing it from station to station, Wheezer suddenly got to the heart of his unease. Something Purvis had said. Just a little nod, as he was getting ready to go last night, just after Wheezer had declined the tablet. The two of them stood at the bar, Purvis necking down the last of his Stella Ice, watching the huddle of chattering excitement in the corner. He stared over just a little bit too long and chewed his lips. He went to say something then just sort of half-nodded, half-shook his head. 'Mustn't interfere,' he'd said. That was it. Nothing really. But to Wheezer it was nothing good, either.

He got off at Bank and sprinted fanatically up Moorgate and into Old Street to find James Love sitting on the floor of Room 7, Mono Studios, sucking a Players, tuning his guitar and blinking innocently from beneath a preposterous Rastafarian hat.

'What's to do an' that? Where is everybody?'

'Where've you been!'

'Where have *I* been? I'm *here*, matey. Eleven bells, you said. Bin here since five this morning, truth be told. Wanted to make sure an' that, didn't I? Didn't wanna let the side down . . .'

'Jings, Jimbo!' Wheezer was laughing, but no sound was coming out. 'Couldn't you've . . .'

'Nah! Come 'ead, Wheeze, you wouldn't thank me for getting you up at five bells, eh? I knew this was a twenty-four-hour gaff so I just mosey'd down, had a bit of a kip then went for a sauna an' a bite of brekkie with Sandy. Feeling pretty damned chipper, actually, Wheezy, old thing. Any PDs?'

Wheezer stared at him, fascinated by the bulk of his hat, hardly noticing James's cheesy imitation of his accent. 'Who's, er . . . Sandy?' he murmured, absent-mindedly, then before he could answer, 'Cripes, James!'

James grinned his annoying chipped-tooth grin. 'Sandy's in charge here. Sound fella. Wants to see you when you get a mo.'

Wheezer continued standing there, still fucked from his run. James nodded, his sparkling eyes teasing Wheezer, challenging him to find a good reason to stick around. Wheezer went to find Sandy.

They couldn't have scripted it better. The Grams gave a blistering thirty-minute set which left Mack Hansen speechless. Bob Old, the 'O' in the partnership, asked if they could hear some more, for their own pleasure, but Guy was keen to get things buttoned up.

By four o'clock the Grams were proudly represented by Mack Hansen and Todd King, a thrusting young gun who was going to be their personal agent at H30. Marty Lynch was installed as tour manager. Wheezer had been very impressed by Donna, too, partly because she'd taken the trouble to come down and explain, in her laryngitic voice, that all men were assholes and Englishmen were flat-assed pricks with extra fries and she was off back to New York. She thought the band were sensational.

'Best fuckin band I seen in a fuck of a long time,' she said, breaking Wheezer's hand and staring menacingly right into his eye sockets, chewing remorselessly. 'Better dan dah Voive. Good luck, hey? Hope it works out for ya.'

The Glaswegians wanted too much money for the stage the group were at. What Wheezer wanted was somebody who was shit hot, but who was prepared to grow with the band. Both Tom and Malky had been very upfront, but they weren't prepared to take less than their rate now, even if it meant getting a rise when the band started to make money.

Big Tom Stone put it eloquently: 'Ah'm no a flamboyant man. Risk bothers me. Ah wantae know what am getting each week, every week. And ah'll work damn hard for that, nae matter how well the boys're doing. How rich they get is no mah concern. Ah'll get them to every gig. Ah'll make sure they're treated with respect. Ah'll get them the best sound and the best lighting that the budget'll stand. And ah'll make sure they're the best fuckin' rock 'n' roll show in town. That's mah deal. And ah ken what ah'm worth for mah end o' that deal.'

Wheezer was tempted, but ultimately it wasn't just the money. He was intimidated by the age and canniness and experience of both Tom and Malky, nice guys though they undoubtedly were. He couldn't see himself having the respect of guys like that. With chaps like that, he'd always find himself having to prove himself to them – their gauge was track record, track record and track record – he sensed this very strongly. He'd have to shout at them before they'd rate him, and The Wheeze wasn't one for going ballistic.

As Eddie turned up drunk and could do no more to convince the party of his worth than to loll against the back wall slobbering and sticking his thumb up after each song, the job went to Marty. He would have got it, anyway, by virtue of his personality, enthusiasm, wit, flexibility and a CV which would have been impressive for a forty-five-year-old veteran. For a twenty-nine-year-old, it was staggering. The fact that they hadn't invited another serious candidate made their decision simple. Wheezer was delighted.

The whole gang went out to celebrate, Mack treating them all to delicious, old-fashioned grub at St John. He wanted them all to know that the meal wasn't cheap, his Romford accent becoming more and more syrupy, the more champagne he drank. 'That's the last time you boys are billing me,' he laughed. 'From now on, the funds flow strictly inwards. Here's to rivers of the stuff!'

They toasted, just a little bit embarrassed. Beano sipped at his toasting champagne but ordered a bottle of noxious dark beer as soon as it was gone. He wouldn't order food, saying that he didn't feel hungry. Mack, Bob and Guy exchanged knowing looks. Mack, an unsubtle man who had come to estimate his own opinion almost as highly as he imagined his young charges must, felt that he had to speak out, now.

'Boys!' he rasped, banging on the table and looking into Beano's face with a deeply sympathetic understanding. He held up a hand. He was like Des O'Connor about to tell you a liddle story. 'I'll put this bluntly. I'm a simple guy and I don't know any other way. We all like to have a good time. I know I do . . .' He waited in vain for appreciative chuckling. His eyes went wide. '. . . and I love a nice meal too. But I don't wanna facken eat if I've spent all night on the powder!' He beamed manically at them, tapping the side of his nose, triumphant. 'Eh! Eh? Am I right?'

Puzzled shrugging and muted nodding. Nobody knew what the fuck he was on about.

'Good! So don't snort your bloody careers away, hey? Lecture from dad over.' He looked each one of them separately in the eye. It was difficult to hold his stare. He looked mad. Wheezer found him holding on him for an eternity. He looked away, and caught Guy and Todd choking back the giggles.

Mack continued: 'Not before you've made me a few bob, anyway! Hey? HA-HA-HA-HA-HA! C'mon, drink up, guys! 'Nother bottle, please my man! No, make it three bottles. And be a love and plonk us a nice bottle of Armagnac on the table, will you? . . .'

Todd leaned over to whisper to Wheezer. 'He's a great guy . . .'

Todd, a Londoner, spoke like a Brooklyn nutcrusher. He glanced furtively at his tipsy boss. 'He shouldn't drink.'

Wheezer nodded his absolution. Todd smiled. 'Mind you, you wanna hear him on the phone to some of our fucken promoters when he gets back from a lunch like this . . .' He screwed up his face. '. . . not pretty!'

Wheezer winced sympathetically, hating Todd already. He was not going to relish having to deal with this nakedly ambitious, hungry go-getter. He'd eat Wheezer alive – if he let him.

It was only on the train back to Liverpool that Beano spat it out. Keva, hair newly cropped after a dash to James Worrall before boarding the train, came back from the bar with three half-bottles of Virgin Rail Mâcon Blanc and a pint glass full of ice.

'Sorry, chaps. No full bottles. Geg in, y'all.'

Beano watched them fill their glasses and turned his face to the window in such a way as to invite questions. Nobody noticed. The wine was drunk quickly. Wheezer, happier than he'd been for a long, long time, got up to fire the next round in. They were all getting on well. That sense of a shared destiny was returning, and it was good to be heading back home. He had never really thought of Parkwest as being *home*, so steeped in sadness was the place, but he found himself impatient to get back, lounge on his battered old chesterfield, play his tunes, live his own funny life. He could happily do that for ever. At that moment he felt immortal. Nothing could touch him. He looked at the lads and was overcome with fondness for them. He watched James, ridiculous in his Rasta hat, drain the last of the wine, and he smiled at his boys.

'Same again?'

Lots of raised thumbs and approvingly nodding heads. Except for Beano.

'What about you, Al? Get you a can or something?'

'No, ta.'

Wheezer clicked. He was going to have to be a manager again for a few minutes. He sat down next to Beano and tried to sound worldly. 'Missing her already, mate?'

Beano turned to him, his face a map of scorn, voice a squeaky pitch of outrage. 'What'd *you* know about it, you fucken hom?'

Wheezer stood up, holding his palms out. 'OK, mate, I was only asking. If you wanna be left alone . . .'

Beano jerked his head around at them all, eyes flashing. 'State of you all! The fucking Grams! The fucking Grams drinking wine on the train! Is that what this group is all about, now . . . ?' They exchanged looks of puzzlement. Beano railed on. '. . . bottled lager . . . snorting coke with hippies! Eating fucking lamb's guts . . . how much was your starter, Snowy . . . what was it? Goose's gizzard? No, no . . . that's it, you were pig's trotters!'

Tony was indignant, not expecting his little pal to rope him into the tirade. 'I was hungry!'

'Pig's trotters me arse!! Twelve fucken quid for pig's . . . *feet*!' He was breathing hard and fast, totally gone. '*Soup* is what you have for a starter! Soup!'

He turned to Keva, his staccato Dingle accent adding venom to his fury. 'What's happened to youse all? We haven't been away from Liverpool for five fucken minutes and youse've all turned into Duran Duran! Is that what we're all about, now? Paying twenty rips for a fucken *skinhead*?' Keva blushed, touching his scalp reflexively. 'Poncy food and expensive haircuts and fucken drug habits? I can't believe what youse're all turning into . . . Youse're fucken *pop stars*!'

There was a long uncomfortable silence as they recalled images of Beano in a dark Paddington basement wearing shades; Beano refusing to lay down another drum track because he was late meeting Celeste; Beano in those fantastic clothes . . . they were all thinking these things when Tony spoke.

'Fucked you off, has she?'

Their hearty, generous laughter was just the ticket. After a pause, Beano joined in, shoulders juddering in spasm as he added his merry cackle to theirs. Later on, he took a gingerly sip of Mâcon Blanc and declared it piss before swigging off the whole half-bottle. During the course of a drunken and soul-searching sentimental journey home, it transpired that Celeste had indeed decided that it would be for the best if they saw no more of each other. Tony Snow could not have been more pleased.

The Caledonian Road studio suited Guy and Ticky well. Its

previous occupants, a growing video production company, had left a bright, sparse, airy loft space which needed little alteration. They kept the office open-plan, with all the sound and vision hardware grouped around an old Ligne Roset couch in the cul-de-sac of the L-shaped room. Rent was a workable £1400 a month – not extortionate for so much room in an area which was so close to everywhere they needed to be, and which was now coming into its own as a business and residential district. In a year's time that lease might go for over £50,000 per year.

Every morning on his drive to the office from SW1, Guy would take the backstreet route around Good's Way, telling himself it was a shortcut, hoping to spy a lissom black girl in a cropped red T-shirt. But if Evie was still alive, she was definitely not working King's Cross any more. He was in and out of the area at all times of day and night, on foot and in his car. Few of the gaunt faces were familiar to him. Once, working late into the night calling up associates in the States and talking up the Grams, he spotted the peroxide Yorkshire whore as he drove home, 'Desert Rain' drenching his senses. He could still play the track, having heard it hundreds of times, and succumb to a similar wave of despairing saturation as had overcome him during that first playback at Whitfield Street. It provided a poignant soundtrack as he slowed, thinking of apologising to the girl, wondering if she knew of Evie, knowing he was not yet rid of his street itching. He'd tried dating, tried all that, but no – it wasn't the same. Collapsing into his armchair in Dolphin Square, simultaneously banging Channel 5 News on, he was taken over by a great, dulling want. He could see no point, now, to any of this. He wanted more. He wanted love.

Over the following days and weeks he lurched from this morose fatalism to heights of overcharged enthusiasm. Only the Grams music could lift him and his positivity would come only then in spurts. He was getting the work done, everything was starting to move forward under its own momentum, he was able to delegate with confidence – but things were not right with Guy. On the Saturday evening of Glastonbury, having just known a fleeting spasm of joy on hearing Peel give 'Desert Rain' its first national play live from the festival site, Guy telephoned his mother to ask if he could come down. She was delighted, then carefully worried.

'Is everything all right, darling?'

'Just need to talk.'

They talked. He lay with his head in his mother's lap while she stroked his hair and tried to reassure him that depression ran rife in the family's lineage.

'It's nothing, these days, the Blues. You can pop along to the quack and he'll give you a script for Prozac, or whatever. I can call Jonny while you're here, if you like. I use it myself. It does a job.'

'I'm not taking pills, Ma. I don't need drugs.' Maria nodded. 'I know what I need – and it's not bloody pills. I need the truth.'

Maria looked, properly, as though a ghost had walked right through her. She clutched her breast like an amateur operatic. 'How do you mean?'

'You know what I mean.'

She couldn't look at him. She couldn't be sure whether he knew something, or whether he was just shooting off into the trees to see what fell down.

'Would it help to talk to someone else about this? A professional?'

'No, Ma. I need to talk to you.'

She took his hand, eyes watering. He sighed out loud.

'I've worked it out, anyway. Haven't I? What's a shrink going to tell me that I don't already know?'

But he took the card, anyway.

The longer they stayed in Liverpool, the more it felt as though none of this had happened. There'd been the horrid business of having to dispense with Long Richard. Everyone except Beano volunteered for the task, though nobody wanted it. Beano argued in favour of keeping Richard on in some reduced capacity, but Tony, more than anybody, argued against such cowardice. If Long Richard couldn't do the job he was supposed to do then he should go. Eventually they took a break from rehearsal at Crash and Wheezer and the group sat around while Marty explained to Long Richard that he was taking on the job of tour manager, thanked him for leaving the group in such good shape and he hoped that his own people, the crew he was bringing in from now on, would be half as conscientious as Richard had been. He never once let go of Long Richard's hand as he said all this, ocasionally giving it a hearty shake to emphasise a point of praise. As it slowly dawned upon Richard that he was getting the boot he blinked at the band, then Wheezer, in bewilderment, waiting for them to interrupt Marty and, with amused embarrassment, explain to Marty that Richard was one of their own. He was as good as one of the band. He was Long Richard, for fuck's sake.

Nobody said a thing. Tony and Keva picked a spot on the floor and studied it throughout the whole dismissal. James smoked three Players in ten minutes. Wheezer could see that Richard was choked, incapable of retort. If he'd spoken out he would have burst into tears. He walked briskly, stupidly tall, out of the room. Beano followed him. The others looked at each other in silence for a while, half expecting Richard to come back in and smash an amp or shout something vile. He'd been very, very upset at this dismissal from a job he must have loved more than anyone had guessed. After a minute James started guffawing, and this set them all off.

Beano returned, shouting: 'It's *that* funny is it, a bloke losing his job and his dignity in front of a kangaroo court?'

Everyone shut up. Wheezer spoke out first. 'Ah, come on, Al, you know what it's like . . .' Beano offered little encouragement. '. . . haven't you ever been at a funeral and found yourself . . . *struggling*?'

'Don't think I have, no. It must be fucking hilarious . . .'

Tony jumped up off his chair. 'Look, you, you little tit . . . turn it in! You're just angry with everyone! We all know why, but it's not our fucking fault! If you can't cope with this now, there's no point you carrying on . . .'

He stopped in mid rant because Beano, who had started tuning the skin of his snare drum, screamed an indecipherable word at Tony, flung a beefy drumstick at the wall and ran out of the room. Tony followed and cornered him at the big, heavy, steel-plate door, grappling with the slide bolt. Beano couldn't get it open.

'Hey! Mate . . . come on! What's going on . . .?'

The two of them went for a walk up Moorfields and along Chapel Street to the church gardens by Ma Boyle's. Beano reiterated his fear that the group were turning into phoneys.

'Laughing like that at a fella who's just had the boot . . .'

'You got that wrong, Al. We weren't laughing at him . . .'

'I suppose you were laughing *with* him?'

Beano looked at him with calm disdain. The look was laden with *et tu* censure and self-righteousness. Tony didn't miss a flake of it.

'What about you, then, Al?'

Beano forced a laugh. '*Me!*'

Tony waited for him to straighten up. 'Seriously. Who's the real prima donna here?'

Beano laughed more volubly.

'I'm not saying this for fun, mate. But you're the fella who's breaking rank all the time. You're the one with the ego. Keva can be a knobhead, but he's a team player, isn't he? He puts the group first. You *know* that Long Richard had to go. We *talked* about it!'

Beano held up his hands. 'I'm sorry! You're right! I don't agree with the way the group's going, but you're right. All for one, an' all that. Nasty habits an' all!'

Tony grinned. 'Good.' He hugged his skinny albino pal. 'We can't do this without you, you know. We need you. Don't be a prick. This is just the start of the madness. You wouldn't want to miss it for the world!'

Hannah had set Keva up with a couple of telephone interviews, and Air-Aid had taken them to Shrewsbury and Lancaster to record acoustic sessions for late-night BBC local radio indie shows. Hannah was coming up on Thursday to brief the boys for the Big One. *NME* was due to spend Friday night in Liverpool with the Grams. The word from Stamford Street was that 'Desert Rain' was one of the most played items in the *NME* offices, proving as popular as the new offering from Blur and attracting no end of offers to interview the group. Pat McIntosh, the guy who'd reviewed Marigold, was coming up. It was good timing. The sleeve art was just finished, and Hannah was bringing up master cassettes of the album. She would usually have travelled with the journalist, oil him up with drinks and coke, but this was so crucial to the entire next stage of the Grams' development that she'd decided to spend some time with them beforehand. She was concerned that, as a group if not as individuals, they came over a little earnest, a little too principled and *clean*. She intended to try and mix some sex up with all the ideology.

If there was euphoria at Hannah's news about *NME* it was doused by the reality of Wednesday's press. Keva and James were perched at a window table at Keith's, James drinking red wine and speed-reading *NME*, Keva flicking insouciantly at the *Maker*, prolonging the ecstasy. Today was the day the Grams, belatedly, began their long and loving relationship with *NME*. *Enn Emm Ee*. The Bible. Today, the Bible was reviewing 'Desert Rain'. Keva didn't mind James having first read – he wanted to stave off his orgasm for as long as possible. Both Hannah and Guy had tried to speak to him, yesterday, wanting to share the good news with him, read out their hot-off-the-street reviews, but the boys had hidden behind their ansaphone, giggling. Let it all wait until tomorrow. Keva had been unable to sleep, imagining the accolades. He'd finally dropped off, mind throbbing, at a quarter past four. James had to wake him. Tomorrow was today.

Keva got to the reviews. His heart was thumping. His throat was dry. The cover was trumpeting the story of Sensira's Wembley show, but no matter how great they called it, nothing was going to take from this moment: the Grams' first Single of the Week. He scanned the reviews and straight away his eyes told him that theirs was not one of the two photographs illustrating the singles column, his brain catching up seconds later. He looked again. He actually did that, double-checked, certain that, in his eagerness to suck it all in he'd missed something the first time. What *Melody Maker* was recommending was 'Bolero' by The Purple and 'Beta-Blokka' by Sensira. Was that out already? What was Guy doing sticking out a record at the same time as them? He searched for their own review. Maybe Guy had pulled strings to get it taken out at the last minute, realising they'd picked the wrong week to release. The Purple and Sensira obviously had the same idea about going out during the midsummer slack period when business needed a boost. He was just starting to breathe easier when he saw it. Five lines in the bottom right-hand corner of the page:

In another week this laudable debut might have seemed special. But placed next to former foils The Purple and Sensira, the Grams show how far they've been left behind by the new kings' pop precocity. All the right bits and pieces only go to make a dissatisfying whole. Terrific shards of tantalising guitar and a grand epic feel to the arrangement ultimately only postpone the reality – there's no song here. Useful intro to a worthwhile group.

Useful. Worthwhile. Laudable.

It was, of course, written by Cindy.

No tune. *No tune!*

'Bitch!' hissed Keva, throwing the paper down.

James smiled infuriatingly. 'Gone a whiter shade of there, old thing! Whassup?'

'That cow from the *Maker*! Fuckenell . . . I asked for that one, didn't I?' He pointed at his chin. 'Fuck! I sat there, didn't I, going "put it there! Put it there!" Shit! Bet she's laughing her fucken head off! Fuck! How *stupid* can you get. She's going out with fucken Helmet, isn't she?'

'Oh no, she's not, don't worry about that . . .'

James, missing the London highlife, had taken his money on Friday and gone to the Sensira show with Purvis and the mob. Keva didn't mind James being there as much as he'd thought he might. He liked the idea of the Grams having a social presence, even when they weren't there, and he had to allow that James, affable and easily liked, was a good ambassador. He was real too. While Helmet was dabbing coke on his tongue and pretending to have a fit, James would be eyebrow-deep in the stuff, hogging and snorting and laughing and *living*, staying up until there was no more fun to be wrung from the remnants of the dawn.

It also gave off a message, Keva thought: that the Grams were on their way. Helmet's card was being marked. He hadn't asked James much about the show when he got back. If he had, he might've been better prepared for this. He felt stupid. He saw himself in flashback, sitting there with Cindy, slagging off her boyfriend's band. She'd been quite charitable, considering.

James grinned infuriatingly. 'It's the drummer she's seeing . . .' He picked up the *Maker* and squinted at the review. 'I think she's right.'

'You think everyone's right.'

'It could be worse. I mean, it would be a downer if this was, like, a *proper* single, hoping to stay in the charts and sell loads an' that. But it's not, is it?'

Keva snapped. 'It's a fucking great *song*! She's saying there's no song there! Fuck's she on about? The one thing you can say about us over everyone else is that we've got tunes, la! The shite we throw away is more tuneful than all that sampled cack Helmet's fucking with . . .'

'Maybe people like sampled cack. Maybe Cindy Hogan's a secret cack fanatic . . .'

'She's fucking us up, James. Cleverly, very cleverly and very deliberately. She even says, like, if this was any other week . . . the fucken record's not out for two weeks! She coulda left it 'til next week or whatever, but she obviously wanted to review us next to that lot . . . The New fucken Underground. My arse!'

'Well, wouldn't you if you were her?'

'Fuck off will you, Hector! Take *our* fucken side for once! You're *in* the fucken band! Don't be embarrassed by it . . . you're not in Soho now!'

'I agree with you.'

Keva went to launch into him again and caught his flatmate's teasing expression. They both pointed at each other – gotcha.

'Come on though, Hec – what's this shite about us lagging behind? That's crap.'

'Well, we are – I'm not being funny now.' He lit a ciggie, blinking, thinking how he was going to put this. 'I'm just saying, like, we've only just really started. We *are* that little bit behind them an' that. I'm not saying that we won't catch them up and overtake them . . .'

He snuffled and tugged on his fag. Keva studied him.

'Do you believe in this band?'

'Don't talk soft.'

'Do you really want it? More than anything else in the world?'

James met his look face on and blew smoke above him. 'More than anything, mate. I want it. Especially now.'

'Good. Because this is going to be a fucken war.'

'Bit Velvet Underground, isn't it?'

She looked again at the colour copy of the sleeve. It was strikingly similar to the banana theme of the Velvet Underground & Nico album, but where the Warhol sleeve displayed a fresh, exuberant sexuality, Keva's sleeve featured only a limp, wilting banana skin. The company winced at Hannah's directness and waited for Keva's reply. They'd all beaten about the bush since he'd picked up the artwork from Miles, wanting to point out the obvious plagiarism but too fearful of another debilitating row so close to the big interview. Keva looked up at her.

'At last. Someone with a record collection. You're the first one to get it, you know . . .'

'Well, actually . . .' said Wheezer.

Keva silenced him with a look. 'Of course it's a pastiche of Andy Warhol . . . but I don't think he's going to be suing us,' laughed Keva.

'Is there any, like, *story* behind the choice of image?' asked Hannah. She waited for Keva to reply, eyes locked into his. He stared back, misty freckled eyes saying nothing. Hannah looked away, eyeing the sleeve again. 'Anything we can use to tell *NME*, I mean? No matter if there isn't, just that there's often a good story behind these things.'

Keva wondered whether to tell her. A confession to the nation. Keva McCluskey, soon to turn thirty, can hear the footsteps of his awful, awful past stealing up on him. He doesn't have the energy to keep running. Run, run, run. Don't look back. Keep on running and it won't catch up. But he can't any more. He's slowing down. He *feels* down, always. He's tired. Catch him and kill him. He's had e-fucking-nough.

'It's just a great image, that's all. Sorry. I thought it'd look smart as a T-shirt.'

She smiled at him. It was as though she knew. He was back in love with her again, her petulant mouth and the little squiffy tic in her eye.

Walking down to Albert Dock for a drink in the sunshine, Tony dropped back to chat with Hannah. 'I'm glad you're here. It's nice to have you back.'

She was supernaturally pleased by this. 'Why thank you, little Snowy. It's good to see you too. I've missed you. I've missed all my boys.'

'Some more than others, I bet.'

'Now, now. My love is given equally to each and every one of you naughty Grams.'

Tony laughed and linked his arm in hers.

'Welcome to Liverpool, anyway. I was starting to think none of this had really happened.'

'Oh, you'll know about it soon enough, all right. These are the last few days of normality you're going to spend for, like, many, many years, you know. In a few weeks' time you won't be able to come to places like this – and I'll be spat on by envious groupies, yearning for your gold-plated nuts.'

He smiled, and hoped that some of them would like stocky fellows.

Sitting outside the Pumphouse, four pints into a session on a scorching June afternoon, it was easy to feel good about the world. It made it all the more mystifying to Hannah that the group were so boring when it came to the subject of themselves. It was as though they'd made a contract and signed it in their own blood, agreeing to be as pedantic and as ordinary and as matter-of-fact and as unquotable as possible. She was pretty sure, too, that she'd hit upon the reason for it – and it was the oldest and easiest stumbling block of all. They were worried about what the others'd think of them if they came out with anything too pretentious. Keva was a natural. Mystical, poetic, given to long, dreamy pauses as he reached for the truth, he was a press officer's dream. He'd go off into his little dreamworld, then, with a lazy shake of the head, he'd be back with some nonsensical, existential claptrap. It was a brilliant act – he should definitely do most of the talking. But all of the others were good value, too – Tony's little one-liners, in particular, were the sort of thing which would make a good foil for the metaphysical outpourings of the lead singer.

The problems came when they were all together. James had this irritating way of snorting a little cackle out, a hyena-pitched, one-note bark of disdain whenever Keva said anything romantic. Beano, too, was forever butting in about the dockers' strike, or the militant traditions of Liverpool and the Grams' revolutionary agenda. She'd only ever heard the others mention this sort of thing in passing. If it was such an issue then Keva ought to make more of it, bring it right to the fore. He'd make a good revolutionary, certainly a much more believable rebel than Helmet Horrocks.

James gazed out over the Mersey, exhaling loudly. 'It's beautiful, Liverpool, isn't it?'

'It is,' said Hannah, sharply. 'And you're a great, beautiful pop group, yeah?' She turned her attention to Keva. 'But you're going to give the most boring interview in the world if you lot carry on like this.'

'How'd you mean?' complained James.

'I mean . . .' she turned away, exasperated. 'I mean, you are what you are, right, and everyone should respect that and not try, ever, to make a group of people into something which they're not and which is uncomfortable for them . . . but, like . . . you're so *different* and yet . . . you want to come across so *ordinary*! It's, like – this is where people form their *opinions* of you, yeah? And you can control that. You can decide exactly how you want to be seen. Once you've started doing interviews, real interviews, that's it, yeah? You're public property. You've given them enough to make their minds up. But as of now, it's a blank sheet. You can be cynics, dissidents, agnostics, whatever – you can be who-the-fuck-you-want-to-be.'

She spoilt it by stabbing the table with her forefinger on each of the last few words.

'If you wanna be cynical about it, this thing we're doing tomorrow with *NME*, yeah . . . that's your chance to scam up a nationwide appraisal of everything which is weird and wonderful about the Grams. It's your chance to tell everybody why they should buy your single, why they should buy into *you* instead of the half-dozen new bands being touted this week. So you can't waste a word, yeah? There's no such thing as a throwaway line. You've got to think about what you're saying – about what you *want* to say. Everything has to be remarkable, yeah? You can't afford to say anything that, like, you don't wanna see in print. Yeah? You've got to have your soundbites ready, whether they fit into the context of the interview or not. Just jam the fuckers in there! You've got to make sure, as far as you can make sure, that you stand out. And at the moment, instead of telling the world that "Beautiful" was a psychedelic dream about an unattainable utopia, right, you're going to make out it's a paean to the minimum wage. You're boring, lads . . .'

They looked at each other, and their drinks. Keva, in particular, listened with a disembodied patience, humming almost inaudibly, flicking the side of his glass and watching the ferry boats with distracted interest. He brought his attention back round to Hannah.

'And what makes you such an expert, Miss Brown?' said Keva.

Hannah bridled. 'What are you *talking* about, Keva? We're not on different sides! I'm trying to help here.'

'Oh, I don't doubt that for a moment. I just wonder whether you *can* help. If you thought that your plan of getting us all to go for a drink with Cindy Hogan was going to bear big juicy bundles of fruit then maybe we're all talking about different things.' He looked right into her eyes before delivering the final cut. 'Yeah?'

'Come on, Keva, that's not fair . . .' started Tony.

Hannah interrupted. 'No, leave it, he's right. Right to raise the point, anyway. Cindy Hogan was there for the taking. The thing that fucked it up . . . was not my deft conjuring of the opportunity, which was – and should be – taken for granted. It's my job, after all. No, the fuck-up was your obsession with fucking Sensira! Forget that, like, Cindy's shagging one of the band and she thinks they're the Acid Test anyway – how d'you think *you* come across, Keva, when you bitch so much about someone else's success? Do you think that's a fucking endearing quality? Do you think, like, it displays lots and lots of belief in your own band? We may all know that Sensira are a crock, yeah? But the fact at the moment is that the country likes them. We love them. We don't want to hear some jealous shit who's done fuck all himself sounding off about how jammy and fake and clueless they are. It just makes you look . . . pathetic!'

It wasn't just the heat of the sun burning Keva's face up. He was flayed. He scowled at Hannah and stared off at the river. She looked away. Tony, James and Beano all slurped at their beer at once, staring intently at the river, desperate not to catch Keva's eye. He smiled. 'I suppose that's one way of looking at it.'

They guffawed, slapping the table for mercy.

Keva smiled resentfully at Hannah. 'OK, Spinmeister. We'll do it your way. You just tell us what to do.' Tony winked at Hannah. Keva caught the exchange. 'I mean it! In for a penny, in for a pound, what?'

Guy walked away from Dr Zwimmer's. He hadn't been at all sure that Dr Zwimmer would be able to help, but zapping his car open now – he was liberated. It had been reassuring to sit there and just talk and answer the occasional question. It showed Guy that he was not a bad person, that he had done few bad things in his life. It showed also that he had some dormant issues. Rejection was a recurring beast, but he knew that already. He knew that. In an hour they had barely got started, but for the first time in a long while he was walking to his car without that sense of foreboding. There was no knot in his abdomen which he had to trace to source before he could continue with his life. He felt better. He knew what was going to come out of these sessions. He just hoped that Zwimmer would help him rationalise his feelings, channel his thought-flow to places where he could do good. For now, though, he was renewed. He had a record label to run and he felt like being there, now, in Caledonian Road, like no other place he could imagine. He was high. He was ready to take the Grams into orbit.

The muffled, remote sound of a clankering diesel engine brought James round. Someone was hammering at the door. Fuck it. Let someone else go. It wouldn't be for him, anyway. The pummelling on the door persisted. A reedy voice was gasping through the letter box.

'James! Keva! The darned taxi's waiting here! Open up, you chumps!'

Shit! It was Wheezer. Everything came back to him at once. He groped for his jeans and worked his fingers into the tiny hip pocket. Aha! Gotcha, you boundah! James dug out the little wrap Paulie had slotted him last night and sat up in bed, positioning an old football annual on his knees while he lined up the last of the coke. There was a decent little stack there, enough for a bump now and another little livener in an hour or so.

'All right! Coming!' he bellowed down the stairs. He ran down, vaulting the stairs three at a time, and opened up for Wheezer.

'You blimmin' potherb! Where's Keva?'

It was the same story with Keva, again. Mind numb with worry, he'd only given way to sleep after dawn. He'd lain awake all night, tossing over Hannah's broadside against the group. Against him, really. He'd been unable to put Hannah out of his thoughts. One kiss, he knew it, and this warm fondness would fan up into something he couldn't answer to. He knew he'd have to go careful with Hannah. He wanted her so much. She'd give him the energy. Every time she was near he wanted to touch her and kiss her. He was hard now, grinding his pelvis into the mattress as he squeezed his pillow tight. She was right. They should stay away from each other. Neither of them had time to put into it what they'd want to put into it. They both had too much to do.

Ten minutes later, Wheezer, Keva and James were stepping inside the Co-Operative Bank's Castle Street premises. After Hannah's attack yesterday, they'd spent the afternoon planning the biggest party Liverpool had seen since Cream's birthday celebrations. The Ivanhoe Road pile was enough of a rambling gothic monstrosity to provide the perfect backdrop for unrestrained bacchanalia. If Hannah wanted rock 'n' roll then rock 'n' roll she should jolly well have, with the Grams at its swirling, illusionary epicentre. Today and tonight they were going to paint a tableau of Liverpool bohemia for Pat McIntosh such as he would talk about for many moons. He would want to talk and talk and talk about it, and then he'd remember things he'd forgotten and talk about his stay in Liverpool some more. He wouldn't want to leave. By the time he got back to London, the Grams would be the coolest fucking rock band in the galaxy.

But first, they were going to have to spend a few quid out of the

Turnbull twenty-first fee in making this party swing. Wheezer would've come clean about the supplementary payment from her pa, but he'd already, out of sheer blind panic and Wheezeresque superstition, put it into a Farquhar deBurret tracking fund which had the potential to double its value in a year. It could also, equally, spunk the lot – so he was saying nothing, for now.

They drew out a thousand pounds in twenties and fifties. Once Wheezer had their signatures on the cheque they were free to go and meet Hannah, Beano and Tony at the Adelphi. Pat McIntosh was due in at 12.48. Wheezer slapped their backs, wished them luck, arranged to meet them later and went off to confirm DJs, lights, PAs and risers with Marty, and to purchase lots and lots to drink.

Everyone was immediately at their ease with Pat. He was cool. In that first ten minutes, as they ambled up Mount Pleasant and cut across to the Pilgrim, he made it clear that he was a fan, that he got the whole deal with the Grams, knew what they were trying to do and wanted to see them do it. He even went to the bar to get the first round in. Hannah tugged Keva back as he tried to insist upon his native right to buy the drinks.

'This is going to be a cinch. He wants to be your mate. This is, like, more than just a job to this guy. He's honoured. It's, like – he's doing the first big interview with the fucking Beatles. He's in Liverpool, it's, like, 1963, yeah – and he's about to sit down for a bev with John fucking Lennon. So don't disappoint him. Don't matey up to him too much. I'm not saying you need to be an asshole, but don't be a pushover. He's looking for a Star. D'you read me, Keva? Yeah?'

Keva nodded. Hannah arranged the courtyard table so that Pat had to sit next to her and opposite Keva. The others would have to lean over and shout if they wanted to get in on the act. Pat picked his way up the steps with a laden tray and took some pleasure in having remembered everybody's tipple correctly. He delved into his duffel bag, bringing out a microrecorder.

'No objections to my recording this, anyone?' he asked, looking at Hannah. She smiled her permission and they were off.

*

Afternoon tailed into early evening and still they didn't want to leave. Wheezer had been there for the best part of an hour, gently suggesting they might like to attend their own party, but nobody wanted to move. They were groggy, lazy and happy, but more than anything they were exhausted from laughing. After an hour of intensive questioning about such concepts as fate, eternity, cosmology and soul, Pat took a deep slurp on his pint and asked: 'What's the craziest thing that's happened to you guys so far?'

Tony gave a very wry account of the December gig they'd done in the Gathering Hall on the Isle of Skye, part of a four-stop tour of the Highlands and Islands sponsored by Potter's Whisky. What had happened was four girls had accompanied the group back to their lodgings, to continue the ribaldry.

'I think we might have been hoping for certain favours to be extended to us, but it was by no means taken for granted. We just thought they were a laugh and we wanted to carry on drinking. Anyway, we got back to the B & B and Black Margaret was waiting up. Black Margaret was always shrouded in black like one of those New World Presbyterian birds and she was a complete fucking psycho. She owned the B & B, the post office, the harbour café and, as we were to find out, her influence was everywhere. She took one look at these girls and goes: "Lowlanders! Lowlander strumpets! Get off this island!" And her eyes actually went green and white, like the wicked queen in *Sleeping Beauty*. These girls just started laughing and one of them tells her to fuck off, just under her breath like, and the next thing the girl's choking. Honest to God, she can't breathe, she's asphyxiating in front of us all. Black Margaret sweeps off up the stairs, miles of black dress still on the bottom stair while she's up on the landing, and suddenly the girl can breathe again. Obviously a certain amount of fizz has gone out of the party, but we soldier on. I try to put on a Beach Boys cassette. The cassette snags. We go outside, determined to spite the old witch, and dance around the car stereo. The battery goes flat. We give up, but the good news is that the girls are cacking themselves. They don't want to be left alone. We all shack up with one each. Next morning everyone's bricking it. What happened is, I swear to God, right . . . all the girls had come on their period that night. Honest! It was *The Wicker Man*. All in all, quite the cookiest few days I can recall off the back of me hand . . .'

'Although . . .' interrupted Keva.

'Yes?' said Pat, eager.

Keva told of the time Cindy Hogan came to Blackpool to interview them and went away thinking Sensira were the Grams. He flashed a look at Hannah. She refused to catch his eye. It was a calculated risk, telling Pat this story, but one which Keva suspected might open up *Melody Maker* versus *NME* rivalries. He wanted to encourage Pat to pledge his troth to the Grams in counterpoint to Cindy's brazen championing of Sensira.

It worked. Pat McIntosh seemed to hate Sensira for the same reasons Keva found them so loathsome. For the next hour, with the interview seemingly indefinitely suspended, Pat regaled them with stories of Helmet's recently *bonkers* behaviour. A writer at *Select* had told him that he went into the kitchens of the Columbia Hotel a couple of weeks ago to see if there was any cold wine in the fridges. He stumbled upon a frenzied Helmet, force-feeding himself.

'Hello, thinks our man from *Select*. Bit of an eating disorder here. Poor old Helmet. Still, I'll keep it to myself. I'll sneak out before he knows I've seen him. Don't want to embarrass the poor love. So he goes back out into the main bar. Almost immediately, Helmet appears in the same bar, groaning, rolling his eyes around, saying mad things in Latin. Then he stops, looks at everyone in the bar as though he's just snapped out of a nightmare, smiles and vomits all over himself. His manager comes in and screams at everyone to fuck off out of there. But not before he approaches each journo individually, apologises, explains Helmet's really been overdoing things and he's going to get him away for a week or two, get him fit for Reading.'

Once the cackling had subsided, Beano asked: 'How come youse all still lap it up then? How come you write him up like a messiah when you know he's a phoney little shitehawk?'

'He's good copy.'

'You wha'?'

'Hang on, hang on, I don't subscribe to all that myself. In fact, there's an ever-growing gang of us who won't give him the time of day. But you know how it goes. He's big. He's getting bigger. Stick a microphone in front of him and you know you'll get something good. Stick him on the cover and you'll sell out. We're pretty needy at the moment, the music press. We have to take what we can get. We ain't had a banker like Helmet in years . . .'

'Merchant Banker, yeah!'

'I mean it. I don't like the little shyster, but you've got to hand it to him. He's an artist. He's a spin-doctor supreme. No offence, Hannah, but there's not a press officer in the world who could get him better PR than he gets himself. It's like he's read every guru's memoirs – from Malcolm McLaren to David Koresh– swallowed them whole and shat them out in his own colour scheme. He's a maniac.'

'He's not that interesting.'

Wheezer stood up again. It was a general address, but he was looking Hannah clean in the eye. How he wished he could get her out of his mind. She was out of his league, he knew . . .

'Final offer. I'll buy everyone fish and chips at the Atlantis if we go now. Resist the gravitational pull, tempting though it surely is, to stay put and have one more drink. Come home. Have a little kip. Be fresh, witty, lucid and dynamic. Impress guests with your white eyeballs and feisty quips. Anyone?'

Reluctantly, they got to their feet and spilt their way across Hardman Street, peckish through all the drink. As they traipsed, weary, wanting to be carried to the next interesting bit of their lives, into the Atlantis, the familiar stirring strains of 'Desert Rain' smoked up from the radio and filtered up and out to choke their soul, wipe their brow and anoint their tired feet. Keva, first inside with Hannah, was overcome. He was swamped. The hairs on his back and on his neck stood up sharp. Once again his face was twitching and falling apart, but this time it was a euphoria he could never rein in. A thunderous wave of joy, joy, joy, swept him away, turned his viscera inside out leaving him breathless, unable to speak. The man from *NME*, who was next through the door, said it all for him. He pointed, shocked, at the radio: 'Fuckinell! That's your fuckin song, man! Turn it up, mate! What you listening to? What channel's this, mate?'

'Er . . . Radio One, I think.'

'Fuckinell! Daytime Radio One! Jeezuz! This is his band! This is HIS BAND!'

Pat turned around to embrace them, his face a burning beacon of pride. Everyone grinned at each other. The man turned the radio up.

Keva was half aware of her slipping into bed next to him. He knew it was Hannah without turning round. She slid up against him and kissed his back and shoulders, tracing his spine with her finger. His heart beat hard and tight, but he couldn't let himself awaken. She draped her arm around his waist and left it to hang there, fingertips stroking his solar plexus as she drifted into sleep. Keva, gulping, lay wide awake now, waiting to be sure she was asleep. Rigid with fear and anticipation, gulping so hard he thought she'd hear him, he turned over and stroked her through her knickers, feeling the heat and the wet. He tugged them away from her with one hand and guided himself with the other. She bucked to let him in and sighed fully, smiling and frowning in her dreams as he humped, slow, then faster, full of anxiety.

There could not have been a more stunning anti-climax. Self-conscious, and stricken with an endless list of phobias and superstitions, they'd made no plans to meet. They'd celebrated so many stupid milestones and people and auspicious events in the last few months that the actual release of their first ever single seemed like just another part of the process.

It wasn't really a part they could get very involved in, either. The one group of people who could not barge into the Virgin Megastore at 9.01 a.m. demanding every copy of the Grams' super new single they had in stock, were those very Grams themselves. Release day, D-Day, albeit of their own debut disc, was an occasion for hoping and worrying and unalleviated waiting – but not for celebration. The record's destiny was now in the hands of the punters. Its physicality had long since been taken for granted by the band. They were already impatient for the next trick. They'd all held, cherished and fondled the finished thing weeks ago, when Guy turned up in Liverpool with a box of 'finished product', as he called it, the day after the party.

That had been a day worth getting born for. Keva, in particular, was on a high. He and Hannah had woken early, kissed with stale breath and stared into each other's faces.

'Come on,' said Keva, jumping out of bed, pulling snug cords over his tight girl's bottom.

'What?' laughed Hannah, far from joyed at the sudden activity. She was looking forward to a slow, languorous morning fuck to cement their love. He seemed to be denying it.

'Come on! It's lovely this time of morning . . .'

He led her out of bed by the hand, watched her dress and, impatient, ushered her downstairs, down Ivanhoe and through the Lark Lane gates. Sefton Park, in the misty haze of the very early morning, was full of whispered promises. They walked, holding hands, wetting their feet in the dewy grass. Sitting by the gently lapping lake, both wanted to talk about last night. Neither could.

'I saw the Bunnymen here. Right there, across the lake, last band on, *dead* dark, mad reflections on the water. Magical.' He caught her puzzled expression and blushed. 'I was only a kid, like. It was a big festival. Larks in the Park. There was loads of us come down . . .'

She hugged up to him. 'You must've been a very *little* kid . . .'

'Oh, aye . . . tiny. *That* big . . .'

She laughed lightly. 'Bet you were adorable.'

'I was.' He thought that now was probably as good a moment as any. 'Did we, er . . . last night?'

'Don't you remember?' She turned to meet him full on.

He smiled. 'Yeah.'

She nodded and looked away. 'Keva?'

'Madam?'

'Don't joke. It's, like . . . I don't do this.'

He put a finger over her lip. 'Don't.'

She sighed out loud. 'Fuck!'

He looked into her troubled little face. Her eyes filmed over. He stood up. 'Come on. I'll show you the Palm House.'

As the morning idled by, Hannah, tearful in the end, got it out in fits and starts. She'd met Keva at the wrong time. She'd been hurt badly by her last encounter. Men, any men, were not in her scheme of things at this point in her life. There were things she wanted to do for herself. As for Keva, he was about to take off and fly on his own wings. They'd still be close through work. Real close. She didn't believe a word of it, but Keva didn't argue as much as she wanted him to. She was always wanting him to do things, hoping he'd do them unprompted. He never did.

When they got back to the house, feeling desperately, hugely, tragically in love with each other, Guy was hopping around like a demented Santa Claus, knocking on bedroom doors and bursting in with finished copies of the 'Desert Rain' EP. The sleek red vinyl felt exotic. It looked beautiful – glossy, pouting, tempting – and it was theirs. Keva burst into tears. Hannah stroked his face.

'Come on, you selfish bastards!' shouted Guy. 'Get up! I've been driving since six this morning! I want to fucking party!'

Party they did. Everyone headed down to Keith's for a late lunch with gallons of red wine. Pat McIntosh and James, firm coke buddies, kept the restaurant amused with tuneless Bob Dylan and James Taylor renditions, while Wheezer stole the show with a gloriously drunken version of 'Where Do You Go to My Lovely?' The party carried on back at Ivanhoe, with Wylie, Jane Casey, McNabb, McCulloch, Cast, Hunkpapa, Gomez, Space and a never-ending stream of Liverpool luminaries beating a path to the door as word of the summer revelries got around.

Keva and Hannah danced closely in the cellar, holding each other tight like lovers. Wheezer observed the couple with a pleasure that took him by surprise. He was glad and greatly relieved that the Hannah infatuation could now be laid to rest, put out of mind for ever. He was glad it was Keva, too. He'd long worried that the singer needed a greater passion than music. His brooding melancholy was all part of the band's appeal, but Keva, he thought, was isolating himself. He was *too* remote. He watched them dance and smiled with a paternal, a matchmaker's satisfaction. They made a good-looking couple. And the Grams' press was going to be fantastic.

'One for the road?' smiled Hannah, leading Keva back upstairs. Even through the mellow fug of the wine, he couldn't ward off that recent panic. As he held her and thought of love, he thought instantly, too, of betrayal. He knew that he'd be left on the doorstep, crying. He knew he'd be left alone. He knew, he knew that this time with Hannah he'd be crippled once more. He put off the dread moment with skilfully flickering kisses and caresses, only whetting her desire to have him fully. But he couldn't. She held him and kissed his ear and told him he was the most beautiful boy in the world. Long after she slid into loving sleep he still wet her shoulders with tears.

Beano and Tony eventually decided to take a train to Warrington. There was a good Andy's Records, an HMV and an Our Price – and no one would recognise them. Getting off the train, they half expected to see posters everywhere, queues of people filing patiently towards the shops with one thing on their mind: 'Get "Desert Rain"! Get "Desert Rain" by Liverpool's the Grams! Must get "Desert Rain" . . .'

But Warrington was full of angry mums and hot kids and, when they couldn't spot their record out on the racks, Tony had tossed Beano to go up to the counter and ask for it. It wasn't in yet. Andy's had ordered it, but didn't expect the rep until later that afternoon. They decided to wait.

James felt conspicuous treading the vast floor of HMV's Church Street superstore, but even on a Monday he was able to lose himself in the throng of punters. He wasn't even going to buy the record. He just wanted to see it. Something he'd done, out there, out now, £3.99. He found the wall with all the new single releases, but his eye didn't immediately detect their sleeve. It didn't belatedly detect it either. It didn't detect it at all. Feeling his body heat rising, feeling the sweat prickle his top lip and behind his neck and ears, he scoured once more and left without enquiring. It wasn't there.

Trickling with perspiration, now, he called Wheezer from the Paradise Street boxes. ''Kinell, Wheeze! Sort it out! Fuck's goin' on?'

'Slow down, old boy. Say it again. You've been to HMV and they've *told* you the record isn't in stock?'

'They don't need to fucken *tell* me! I've *seen* it's not in stock! Listen – It! Is! Not! In! Fucken! Stock!' Wheezer resisted the temptation to add a clipped 'an' that'. 'They haven't got the fucken thing!'

'OK, chappie, leave it with me. I'll make some calls. Do us a favour, if you don't mind? Will you hop up to Probe and see what the score is there? Could just be a late delivery all round, but I doubt that the distributors'd balls up the account in the band's home town. Will you have a mosey and see how the land lies up there?'

'Probe! Ah-ray, Wheeze! I'm not going in there asking for me own record!'

'No. See what you mean. OK. I'll call them. I'll call all the shops. Go on home or pop into Crash and help Marty or something. Put it out of your mind. It'll probably take a while.'

'Nice one, Wheeze.'

He was starting to have more confidence in the asthmatic weirdo, these days. He seemed to be growing with the job. He wandered down Whitechapel and over to Crash.

Keva moped around his bedroom, picked up the Martin, put it down. He doubted he'd ever write anything any good again. He felt shit. He'd felt bad when he woke up, felt this overbearing sense of pointlessness on the morning of the release of his first single. It got worse when he turned on the radio. Somehow he'd hived himself off from all that outside world of pop. He'd absorbed himself in the small world of ReHab and the Grams. Now, on the wireless, Radio One were giving a rundown of yesterday's chart. The Purple were in at 19 with 'Bolero'. Hearing it again, it was OK in their completely dot-to-dot retro Byrds-wannabe rehash sort of way. Unremarkable. Hardly worthy of one of Radio One's cherished A-list places and, try as he might, Keva couldn't see what was in it for the fans. Bit of a tune. Not astonishingly moving words. Gravelly voice. All the bits were there, but they didn't amount . . . there was no *magic*.

Worse was to come. 'Beta-Blokka' had gone straight in at Number Three. Radio One loved it. What the fuck was up with all these people!? They were saying things like *out there* and *junkbeat*. What the hell did *that* mean? There was only one thing to say about 'Beta-Blokka'.

'Shite.'

It was going to be a bad, bad day.

*

Between Wheezer, Guy and Paul Parlour, they got to the bottom of it. Paul was massively apologetic. MSF should have seen this coming with an all-vinyl release, although, strictly, if it was anyone's fuck-up, it was ReHab's.

'It's not a distribution problem,' he explained to Guy. 'As you know, we've shipped the entire ten thousand and, with this sporadic Radio One support, we definitely expect to sell them through. All of them.'

'Cain't do that if the fuckin fuck ain't in the showapps,' said Guy in a suddenly bizarre, Texan accent.

'But the fuck *is* in the shops. It's just that they can't *rack* the fuck! Most stores don't have the capacity to rack vinyl now. Certainly not seven-inch. So most of the traffic is going through the Cartel and the indies – which is not to say that your high street multiples are not dealing with us. They've all taken it. But punters are going to have to do that little bit of extra work to get hold of this baby. They're gonna have to stride up to that counter and ask for this little beauty loud and clear! "Good day, my man, have you the new waxing by the Grams in stock, perchance?"'

Guy gave him no encouragement.

'Great record, by the way. I've taped it. Hope you don't mind. Play it in the car all the time . . .'

'Home taping is killing music, Paul. Probably gonna have to give your details to the piracy people . . .'

'Sure thing. No sweat.'

Guy relayed the news to Wheezer.

'Well, that's no problem, mucker. I can do a mailout to the list and word-of-mouth should take care of the rest. If I get on to it now and shoot them out first class, they'll get them tomorrow. Even the ones on the Isle of Skye'll get 'em Wednesday. Plenty of time! Can I bill you for the stamps? And we're gonna need reimbursing for the party, soon as, if you can . . .'

'End of month, as per. Er, Wheeze?'

'Ghee?'

'You on your tod up there still? Haven't you got someone to help you do all this?'

'Not necessary, mate. Really. I work so much better on my own . . .'

'Nonetheless, d'you have an inkling how busy you're gonna get?'

'Some.'

'Who's going to keep things oiled when you're away on tour, or in the States on business, or down here for conference? You've got to have, like, a secretary at least!'

'Maybe. We'll see.'

'Well, see to it soon, Wheeze! Yeah?'

Wheezer bristled at the criticism and returned to the planner he was devising on his computer. Guy was not wrong. His schedule was starting to look congested. But he didn't need that stuffed blouse to tell him.

If Monday was tinged with blue then Wednesday was proud, throbbing red. At last Keva could sit in his window seat at Keith's, reading the music papers, smarting with pride. Mr McIntosh had gone overboard. His spread on the group was almost embarrassingly laudatory. He loved them. They were the Stones, Love, the Who, Velvet Underground, Nirvana and . . . Charles Mingus! Even this last was justified in terms of Keva's simmering, foreboding relationship with his emotions, one minute up on top of the universe, polishing his reflection in the stars, then, next time you looked he was back down in the gutter, in agony. For a chap who'd spent most of that lost weekend with a rolled-up twenty shoved up his nose, Pat was an intuitive and perceptive judge. Everything Keva thought of as special about his songs, Pat had tuned into, in particular the melancholy lurking beneath even his most innocent lyrics. Pat McIntosh had sussed the whole deal out. He even cottoned on to things which weren't there. Some of his theories sounded great, but they were nothing to do with the Grams. As Keva sat reading this, so were thousands of others across the country. Across the world. To Whitehaven and Waterford and to Book Soup in Los Angeles the message was filtering out: The Grams Are Here.

And the photos – they made the Grams look like rebel rockers, with Keva the genius ruffian supreme. James, more angular now he'd lost a little weight, looked like the most misunderstood, most demented, freebase, freeform, free spirit guitarist in the world. His eyes were mad – glinting with cheek as always, but his drugging and staying out had sketched dirty, perverted shades of black in there and lurid charcoal lines underscored his lids with demonic kohl. He was the real thing.

Dave Amber, the *NME* snapper, had taken them out to the old disused airport in the south of the city. The enormous desolation of the site with its silent, magnificent towers and cracked, weed-ridden runways lent a grandeur to the pictures, which said everything about the tone and beauty of 'Desert Rain'. As a photograph, it was the best introduction to *NME* readers the group could have wished for. You felt you knew what they were about from this one shot. They were a serious band, worth your investment of time, devotion, curiosity and money. And Pat's write-up was terrifying:

This should have been the best weekend of Keva McCluskey's life. Forty-eight hours ago the lugubrious frontman of the Grams, the greatest new group in Liverpool – and the world – had just heard the band's debut single, the heart-draining 'Desert Rain', played on daytime Radio One for the first time. This signalled a weekend of wanton celebrations by the band, climaxing in a word-of-mouth gig in their own cellar which will come to be recognised as epochal. Yet by the end of Sunday, like each and every one of the great manic melancholics before him, from Mingus to Curtis, Keva was killing himself trying to get the point of it all.

The Grams, with their grand, universal tragedy and beauty, have made a world out of their Liverpool lives. They have something to say to everyone and, before this year is done, the world will known their gorgeous desolation. In our simplicity, we imagine that this is why a group is born and this is the dream that keeps them alive. To be able to speak the one universal language, and to make people want to listen, everywhere – this is why they do it, isn't it?

And the Grams are going to be one of the biggest. There is no other way it can be. Yet, when last I saw Keva McCluskey, on the last afternoon of their already legendary weekend-long party of which he was the gilded focus, he looked as though he had lost something for ever. He looked like someone, or something, had died.

Maybe it has. Perhaps it is that the moment he makes public his most private nightmares, he has sacrificed something of himself. But to come anywhere near to understanding the complexities of this important new band and their enigmatic frontman, it's necessary to go back a few years.

The Grams are the issue of the stellar collision, nearly four years ago, of two eternally oscillating forces: Keva McCluskey, poet-depressive, and James Love, optimist, fine, fine guitarist, and, well – lover. James is a lover. As will be seen.

The Grams knew from the very start that they were to walk among the chosen ones. Instantly great, their destiny was to reclaim a generation nurtured on beats, starved for years of songs, of songwriting. With the instant nirvana of dance and Ecstasy, who could need the tortured soul music of despair and self-hate which has been the hallmark of every true poet from Presley to Cobain to Lennon? Answer? Everybody. The Grams represent the reality we all wake up to, every one of us, day after day. They are the low, the high and the low, telling it out, giving it up, killing you softly. The Grams are what pain sounds like, and their tune is addictive.

From the first collusion of James Love's lascivious chords and Keva McCluskey's elegies, the path was clear. They had no doubt, through the years of playing to thirty game locals in every wretched outpost you've never heard of, that each step, each ballsy gig in Haverfordwest or Skye, was bringing them closer to their calling – to be, to their people, the most important messengers of their time.

There are four of them. One plays drums, one plays guitar, one plays bass and the other one sings. Yet their song is different to anything you will hear, in this time. The shattered hymns of R.E.M., Nirvana, Leonard Cohen, Radiohead and Joy Division give a hint of the bittersweet taste of the Grams. They are an intense new voice and they come at a time when we need them most.

Chance brought them together. There was no personal odyssey by Love or McCluskey to find the eternal foil for their talent. Chance is the unknown that makes great groups great. It's the intuition, the unspoken understanding that allows the Grams to sledge your spirit with devastating layers of joy and pain. Chance is what brought them together. All of our greats, from the Beatles to the Smiths, came to be because a mate knew a lad who was OK on the bass. It was the same with the Grams.

Keva, dying with a Smithsy angst-rock group that pity prevents him from naming, had sneaked to the bar at Crash Rehearsal Studios to call his neighbour, Joey Snow, for a lift back to Crosby with his Martin and his gear. He was not going back upstairs to that band, ever. That was it. He was done with bands. If he was going to carry on with music, it was going to be just him. Little did he know. In the van with Joey, along for the ride, was one James Love.

'That was it, really. We just got talking from there. Joey Snow turns up, gives us a lift. I'm rattling on about how all the groups in Liverpool are shite and how I'll never get a band together, now, and James just goes: "I'll be in a band with you." Then Joey says their kid Tony's all right on the bass and he's got a little band, like. That's the very glamorous story of how the Grams got started. I'd like to tell you there was a mission to Memphis to find some soul – but it was a bellyache in a transit van!'

As we sat at Liverpool's regenerated docks, overlooking centuries of culture and the same great warehouses a youthful John Lennon used to scour for rare R & B imports, James points to a moment when, he thinks, the Grams became a real group.

'We were all listening to the same stuff, an' that . . . Beefheart, the Turtles, Roky Eriksson, Tim Hardin – not for any fucken big mad pattern, like, but for certain things that we were all into. Me and Keva'd listen to Tim Hardin just to get into, like, a mood . . . to find a feel. So it's not like we were fighting each other. But in a sense, because of that, because Snowy and Beano were, like, really fucken young, knoworrimean, sixteen, seventeen, it was easy to treat it as a hobby. Two nights a week in Joey Snow's workshop. And this one night we're practising for half an hour and Keva goes: "That's it! This is shite! This is going nowhere! We're too fucken good for this! There's a big wide world for us out there, and we're titting about in a panel-beater's yard . . ." He was going mad. He said we all had to bring a tenner in next week, and from then on it was going to be a fiver a week subs and we were getting a room in Crash like a real band. We could only afford to practise once a week, but because of that we really used the time properly, like. It* became the pinnacle of the week. Keva would write the basic song on acoustic at his place and come round to mine to, like, flesh it out. But for that four hours every Tuesday night we were the fucken Who! No one could have taken it more seriously. And I don't think that that, like, you know – work ethic has deserted us. That may not sound, like, the most rock 'n' roll thing but, because we knew what we were trying to do, we didn't mind going out on the road all over the place. We loved playing. We didn't give a fuck whether there was anyone there. If there was a call from an alehouse in Oldham, we'd be there like a shot. It was a gig.'

Keva sums up that period with typically blunt immodesty. 'I think we all knew, from very early on, that we were going to do this. It seemed meant to be that we'd become, like, a dead important band.'

That feeling of pre-ordained greatness was not the only thing which kept them going. Out on the road, in the sticks, they found other like-minded bands, kids with guitars and aspirin and something to say. The comet-like success of two of their troupe, The Purple and Sensira, has been a source of twisted inspiration. Keva, in particular, is dominated by a startled sense of injustice over the acceptance of Sensira, a group he helped define. The band don't want to talk about other groups, but fans in Liverpool who've been with the Grams from the start tell of Helmet Horrocks's obsessive stalking of the group until his fledgling band Sensira were given a support slot.

There's much more to it than simple artistic jealousy, but Keva wants to acknowledge no problem, no bitterness. I cornered him after the Grams played a short set at their party – a set of songs which, really, took the breath away. I wanted him to define, as an artist, as a great, how it is when others seem to reap the acclaim you deserve. Still panting from the excesses of showmanship that ignited this Liverpool cellar, he flaps at the question with his hand. He wants to say, forget Helmet, this is about us. But he has too much in his heart to be able to just let it go.

'What can I say? All those people must see something in it. Maybe I can't separate the guy from the rest of it. The guy himself is such a . . . dickhead . . . d'you know what I'm saying. He's an idiot. *There's fuck all to him. How can he have anything to* tell *to anyone. He hasn't seen anything to tell us about. I don't get it . . .'*

Pushed about the same subject, James just shrugs and says, 'Whatever an' 'at, you know. Whatever. I'm too busy thinking about love. I want people to be blessed. That's what I want. I want to bless people.'

Over the course of the next few days, I try to understand what bonds these disparate songwriters together, what it is that the band feel they *have* to say. If anything, the complex, twisted Keva is easier to read than the implacable James. Two things stand out, one from each.

Keva, sodden with his own sweat at four a.m. after that stunning, powerful gig in their own packed basement, sits alone on a staircase, breathless. I approach him to congratulate him on the show. It was, genuinely, frightening. Keva smiles and tells me, 'That's the highest I can go. I'm already on my way down again the second the last song's over. I want to be back up there again. There isn't much point to the rest of it, is there?'

Keva smokes a little, but is generally anti-drugs. It was him, his psyche talking. He's saying that he was born to tell the world that we live a futile life. He succeeds. 'Desert Rain', a wrenching, drenchingly beautiful song, is the saddest thing you'll hear on your radio this summer. It seems to tell of McCluskey's abject failure to enjoy the things so many of us embrace. His song complains, bitterly, of the pointless, transient nature of 'good' things – love, sex, friendships. They are all perfectly glowing, shimmering, beautiful concepts to Keva, but ultimately they flatter to deceive. If not mirages, then they're the desert rain.

Much of the remainder of their work touches a similar chord. Listening to a compilation tape of tracks from the untitled forthcoming album, one was left shaking at the sheer sense of alienation in this music, which in itself is so beautiful. Tracks like 'Librium', 'From Now On' and 'Chimera' are at once brutal and beguiling. Let's say it one more time – they're the work of genius. I could not then and still can't get around the apparent clash of philosophies, the utter incompatability of James and Keva. James, walking through Sefton Park at first light, unable, unwilling to *sleep through pure exuberance, finds it hard to take himself, or the band too seriously.*

'Don't get me wrong, like. I do want recognition an' that. I'm a fucken great guitarist. People should know that. But I don't want them to . . . like, go all weird cos I'm in a band an' that. I just want to be accepted as someone who did something good. I want to be loved. Like Sinatra was. D'you knoworrimean? And I wanna give love back. I wanna bless people, everywhere, make them happy an' that, if I can . . .' He blinks at me in the pure new light of the day, his doughy face craving understanding. 'D'you knoworram saying?'

I think I do. And I think I understand the perverse science which makes this awesome new group so dangerous and so good. Nobody should dilly-dally over this, watching the situation to see how the group develop. You have to jump on them, now. They probably won't be around for ever. There will be only a limited quantity of the 'Desert Rain' EP in the shops. Beg, steal or borrow a copy of the most significant release this year.

It spanned a double page and was flagged with the banner 'Heavy Soul'. Keva felt faint. It was all bollocks, the romantic suppositions of a bad writer who wanted to be mates with a band, but fuck it. Here come the Grams! Keva was a rock star! Sensira and The Purple were welcome to their fucking A-lists. They were a fad. The Grams are for ever!

He ran to the payphone on Lark Lane and woke up James.

'Roky Eriksson me arse!'

James cackled. 'Just sounded good, like. Sounds like you're a serious group an' that, doesn't it?'

'Get down here and cop a look at it, la. It's too fucken much. In fact, no, I'll bring it round. I've just seen that tit from Crinolene going into Keith's, he'll tell all sorts of tall stories if he sees me in there reading me own press. See you in a sec, fat man!'

He hung up and flew to Ivanhoe on his own little fluffy cloud.

The day got better. Guy called with news from Gil that Radio One had C-listed the track. That didn't guarantee any more play than they'd already been getting – bits and pieces, here and there – but it sounded superb on the CV. The Story was taking shape.

Wheezer phoned five seconds after Guy, wanting to tell them the same news, miffed that Guy had gone to them direct. 'That's not on, that. It's just not on.'

'I agree with you,' said James.

Hannah was next on the vine. 'Hi, honey,' she crooned. Her voice was thick with love.

'Hello, publicity-type person.'

'Well?'

Keva wanted to talk about Pat's write-up, but sensed that she wanted something for herself.

'I'm missing you. I . . .'

'Fuck *that*, slush-queen! What about *NME*?'

Bitch!

'You're a superstar.'

'Well. You know. Always have been, haven't I?'

'Good, babe. That's more like it. And remember, no matter how strong the urge, resist, yeah?'

'I'm sure I don't know what you mean, madam,' quipped Keva, assuming that she meant masturbation.

'Pat McIntosh. Don't call him, yeah?'

The thought had not even crossed his mind, but he wondered, now, if it'd be polite, in spite of Hannah, to give him a quick tinkle. Did rock gods do things like that? He didn't need to worry about it. Pat, sounding unsure, called just before noon.

'Hi there, fella.'

'Greetings, scribe.'

'You OK?'

'Sure.'

'You didn't mind . . .'

'The write-up?'

'Well . . . Sensira. The stuff about Helmet?'

He did. He minded. He'd made it clear he wouldn't talk about other groups, but Pat had chased him down and squeezed out of him the comment he needed to make his bits and pieces fit. 'Fuck, no! We need the world to know, don't we? We have to save . . . The Kids!'

Pat laughed, feeling more sure of himself. 'You'd tell me, though, yeah?'

'Course.'

'It's just that you sound . . . you know . . .'

Keva chuckled kindly. 'I just don't want you psychoanalysing every fart and every scratch of me head, man!'

The telephone wires hummed with Pat's relief. He laughed, loudly. 'Sorry about that, mate. It's just . . . it's all a part of it, isn't it? The story . . .'

Keva wanted to tell him how much he liked the piece but, again, he knew it was best to hold back. The silence was uncomfortable. He found a good exit route. 'Listen. I think we're all coming down at the weekend. Might be having a little do on Sunday night. You know us. The everlasting toasters. Celebrate the sound engineer's dad's divorce anniversary, us lot. Give Hannah a shout on Friday. Be good to see you.'

It felt strange, the power surge that kicked in as Pat grovelled and thanked him and tried to keep him on the line. As Wheezer was forever saying, life is jolly strange. The Wheeze was back on again a few hours later, much happier, with tales from the frontline. MSF were inundated with reorders for stock they were unable to supply. The *NME* piece was having a direct effect. The EP was definitely going to sell out everywhere. 180 Degrees had a Wednesday midweek of 11. Keva relayed the news to James, whose whooping from the other end of the hall was audible to Wheezer.

'Ay, don't be such a pushover,' laughed Keva. 'We're not arsed about all this business stuff. We're . . . the most dangerous new group in the world today, ever!'

Keva and James cracked up. Wheezer shouted for attention. 'Hey, boys, seriously. This Wednesday midweek stuff, it's nothing, you know. It's just a strikeforce sample taken over the first two days. Two things you need to know about strikeforce midweeks. One, it's just an impression, quite accurate but a guestimate nonetheless, really nothing more than a feel the fleet gets – just feedback from the stores, really. Useful, though. Secondly, bands like us, anyone with a dedicated fanbase, always has an artificially inflated first couple of days. The fans all have to have the track as soon as it comes out but, even allowing for late delivery of stock, most of them have got the thing by Wednesday.

Friday we get a true midweek from CIN, real sales right up to end of play on Thursday. Then we can knock off another ten places for all the clubbers and teenyboppers who only buy on Saturdays. If we're still in the twenty on Friday I'd say we're in good shape . . . Keva? KEVA! . . .'

Keva had left the phone dangling and gone off for a little jig with James. The two of them waltzed around the echoing, mosaic-tiled hall, singing, to no particular tune: 'Oh! We are! The most dangerous group in the world, la!'

James picked up the phone. 'That you, Wheeze?'

'Who d'you think it is?'

'Nice one an' that!'

Wheezer smiled to himself. 'Listen. Jimbo. It's gonna be cursed hard work from here on in. This might actually be the last day of . . . you know . . . *normality* we ever spend ever again! I mean it! It's too late to jump off, now! Let's get Snowy and Beano and let's all go out and get hog-whimpering drunk. Let's be real pains in the backsides. We'll get away with it, cos no one knows what we know. It'll just be us, getting sloshed again as far as Liverpool's concerned. Except we'll *know*! Hahahah!! See if Marty's around. In fact, no, let's get Long Richard and Joey Snow and we'll all get absolutely blasted and rip the hell out of every other group in Liverpool. Shall we?'

'Not 'arf! 'Kinell, Wheeze, you're starting to find a bit of style in your old age. You'll be turning up in a black fashion polo-neck sweater next!'

'In this weather?'

'Forget it!'

Wheezer got off the train at Liverpool Central and took the Bold Street exit. He heaved his Tesco Bag for Life into the post office and, after queueing for a few minutes, humped a pile of cardboard mailers on to the counter. 'This lot to the US, please.'

Inside each mailer was one of Wheezer's personal supply of 'Desert Rain' promo-CDs, a photostat of Pat McIntosh's *NME* piece and a copy of What's On (the *NME* jukebox). There were thirty-nine of them, destined for alternative radio stations and journalists The Wheeze had contacted through the Internet in places like Sacramento, Austin, Grand Rapids, Toledo. He'd follow up with more e-mail messages to tell them to look out for the package. The word was spreading. As Wheezer hurried up Bold Street to meet the boys in the War Office, he found himself giggling furiously. He was beside himself with excitement.

There was no way of telling what time it was. One or other of the Lovely Girls was in bed with him. Keva couldn't tell which, not by Braille. He knew he hadn't shagged her, though. The drink, this time, was a perfectly plausible excuse. Drink had been consumed, over a thirteen-hour period, in monstrous quantities. His Taz digital alarm clock had said 6.10 a.m. when he and whichever Lovely Girl had tumbled on to his bed. They'd snogged and groped at each other furiously. Lights out would've followed at about 6.13, for both of them.

Keva hauled himself out from his pit and, finding no legs, collapsed in a heap on the bedroom floor. He lay there a while, getting it together. There were things to feel good about. Lots of them. But he felt leaden. He'd said bad things to so many people last night. He'd smoked lots and lots of cigarettes. He'd bought none. He had drunk an enormous ration of beer, wine and spirits. Cider, when offered, had been turned down with a volley of invective directed at the merry eco-warrior who'd passed the bottle. Keva'd been an arsehole. He'd given rock stars a bad name.

He dragged himself to his feet. The pulse in his temples and at the back of his neck lurched like a jackhammer, forcing him down on his knees again, gasping for breath. Now he could feel the wrenching nausea in his stomach. The pain was so real it couldn't ever get worse. He crawled to the bathroom, dragged himself there and managed to force his head up over the bath. He tried to breathe regularly, knowing there was no point in putting this off. He had no choice. It was this, or suffer for ever.

He jabbed two fingers savagely down his throat, choking drily, and heaved acidic burning bile into the tub. He slumped forward, his head lolling on his forearms, exhausted. He couldn't get his breath again in time for the next vomiting spasm. Heave! Heave! Gag-gag-gag-gag heave! Bleurrrgghhh! Nothing came out. It was agony. He lay on his back, panting. He could now smell his breath.

The stench of ciggies and ale and the bits of his lungs which were already rotting would hang, thick and rancid, for days. He coughed hard and produced a slim, black pat of sputum. He was toxic. Thick, noxious cream caked his lips. He scraped his palate with the nail of his index, scooping up a yellow-white residue of the big night out.

He was coming alive now. Head banging, stomach vaulting, innards fermenting, but he was standing on his own two feet again, propped against his basin, gasping. How did he end up smoking again? Fuck! He would never, ever, drink again.

He looked in the mirror. It was bad. He looked his age. Worse. His eyes bugged out like a frazzled gecko, wrinkled, pinched, distorted, while the dark circles around them bore testimony to high times. The shattered eyeballs were striated with a thousand bloody rivulets. Never again. Definitely. That's it. From now on starts from now on. At worst, if history was anything to go by, the Grams had eighteen months. The singles would achieve consecutively higher chart placings, the band would play bigger and bigger venues in more and more countries and then one of them would die, or go mad, or break up the group in some other stupid way. So – a year and a half. Keva intended to a) taste it and b) remember it.

He reached for his toothbrush, thinking he could start to scrub away the taste of yesterday's badness. Fuck it! They deserved it! One night of piggish self-gratification didn't change a thing. The boys were cool. They were the fucking Grams, for fuck's sake! Stop bleeding over it. He smiled at his devastated face in the mirror and stooped to scrub his teeth out. Just the feel of the brush inside his mouth had him dry-retching again, gagging violently, eyeballs pressing themselves full force, popping hard out of his head. A long string of phlegm hung from his mouth to the sink as he caught his breath in painful fits, gulping and gulping for air, gag-gag-gagging, then starting to breathe again. He stared at his puffy, exhausted face and made lots of decisions.

Waiting for the teaspoons to chill in the freezebox, Keva cut a couple of cucumber slices and watched the kettle boil. The house had never got around to buying an electric one, thinking the whistle on their old battered stove kettle characterful. For once, face smeared with yoghurt, eyes soothing under the cool of the cucumber, Keva was happy for it to take its time. He took the frozen spoons from the fridge and shocked the bags under his eyes with their icy stab. Holding one spoon to each eye, yoghurt beginning its thick droop on to his Sun Studios T-shirt, Keva was a little surprised to hear a chirpy, 'Hello, old thing! How's the head?'

Wheezer made no reference to the slurry of poultices drooling on Keva's face. He might as well have had his dick inside a jar of Rose's fine lime marmalade. The Heswall nut job, sitting on the big basket-chair in the corner, lowered the *Guardian*, smiled and said, 'A watched pot never boils! Good midweek, eh? 'Tween me and thee, I was half hoping for Top Ten. Still . . .'

He swiped the kettle off the flame with alacrity and poured the steaming water into Keva's crackled old china pot. You couldn't help but like him.

'Glad we didn't rope Richard and Joey in, in the end. Wouldn't't've worked out. Most likely've had words. Good blast, though, eh? Eloise gone?'

His rambling was just the tonic Keva needed. He sat back, closed his eyes and slurped at the piping hot tea. So now he knew. It was OK to sit and rap with Wheezer in a face pack.

James made his way up Canning Street's elegant cobbles. He was, for once, stunned. He didn't know how he felt about it. He felt nothing. He wanted only to get back to Ivanhoe and get to bed.

A couple of hours ago, high as a hawk, he'd gone back with Madeleine and he'd had her, skirt shoved up over her backside, kneeling against the couch in their front room. It was a good one, he was right into it, but something made him look around. It was her mother. Joy was standing in the doorway, watching. She was watching quietly – not angry, not appalled. Her hair was down and her eyes were dancing. She was alive. If James had been just routinely out of it he'd have stopped, mumbled something and shuffled out of there with his head down. But Paulie Hanlon and Billy the Brief had been serving him all night, good gear and masses of it. James knew that his time had come now Liverpool's dealers and touts wanted to make a fuss of him. They'd all been drinking champagne and he'd split an E with Maddy. He thought he could fucking fly.

He'd always thought there was something about Joy. She watched, watched everything like an outsider, an onlooker, but she seemed to watch that bit too intently. You'd catch her in the pub, just looking over. And she wouldn't look away if you caught her. Sometimes there'd be a rueful half-smile, a sort of self-sacrificing look, but if anyone was going to look away it'd have to be you. Sometimes he thought she was looking out for her girls. Sometimes he thought it was just him, the sensualist, making a fantasy figure of a handsome older woman. But last night, this morning, as Joy lingered in the doorway and watched him enjoying her daughter doggy-style, every prick of James's senses seemed to understand her. He held out a hand and she came over and knelt down next to him. Hot sunshine was already slanting into the room, channelling beams of dust through the scene of the crime. Joy wore nothing but a long, loose T-shirt. She hung her head, but James lifted her chin again with his finger, making her look at him, look properly into his eyes. In silence, trembling, only her quickening breath to be heard, she pulled off her top and knelt in front of him, pleading, wanting him not to turn away. Without a brassiere her big breasts weighed down to her ribs. He let go of Maddy and went to her.

When he was leaving, mother and daughter still held each other, stroking the other's hair. This disturbed James more than anything he could imagine. He had loved the sex. He'd been over-eager, ravishing them in turn, wanting them quickly. He didn't feel he had to be attentive to the two women. He knew that wasn't the thing for them, for any of them. Doing it to them, with the drugs and the booze and all the wrongness of it, felt, to James, fantastic. It was the best. But when he stopped there was nothing to say, nothing to linger over. He wasn't ashamed – but he couldn't stay. He wanted out. Seeing them there, so close like that just brought his low on bad.

Walking up through early-morning Canning, the rush of new thoughts bombarded each other. But this one thought he could not sack from his mind. Once he gave birth to it, he couldn't submerge the notion. It was Joy. Joy had sought this out. Joy had wanted this whole thing, now . . . because his band were getting played on Radio One. That was why. He knew it. The winged beast of Fame had come home to roost.

He stepped into Upper Parliament Street and sensed the whoosh of the wind before his perceptors had a chance to warn him. The horn bleated feebly and the tyres shrieked as the little courier van, going too fast, swerved violently to miss him, spinning almost a full circle and coming to a screeching standstill in the outside lane. James just stood there in the road. The driver shot out of the van and, seeing that James was unhurt, gave way to his own shock.

'You stupid cunt! You didn't even fucken look! What the fuck were you doing? You on fucken smack?'

James looked at him. Cars began a caterwaul of angry beeping. The driver backed away to his van. 'Fucken smacked-out gobshite! Get your head together!'

James stepped back on to the pavement. He spoke calmly to the driver, who was still pointing and cursing at him. 'You'll never see *half* the things I've seen.'

Back in his own bed, James tried to believe that his downer was just a natural post-binge, post-coital low. But still it ate away at him. He couldn't sleep. His closed eyes only called up nightmarish sexual fantasies, fantasies he knew could be real to him.

He went down to the kitchen and, finding nothing in, dressed and walked to the Eggy Vale. After two stunned, thought-dead mugs of sugary tea he consoled his hangover with a full, guilty fried breakfast and, dunking his toast in the delicious acid melange of tomato juices and egg yolk, he stopped looking for answers. He gave in to thinking back to the mother and daughter. He was bothered by the whole thing with Joy and Madeleine, but he was obsessed, too. Already he wanted more of the same, more and now. But what was he to do? Go back round there again? Do it always? Who knows anything. He could probably get away with anything, now. He didn't feel better, but it was a start. Still horny from the drugs and the drink he went back to Ivanhoe to wank himself off, so he could sleep.

They felt a little foolish all of them, squatting around the radio in

ReHab's offices. The drink, chilled champagne and cold lager, was helping, but somehow the sense of ceremony seemed out of kilter for an event which, at best, would see 'Desert Rain' hit the chart in the mid-twenties.

The rundown had got as far as 31. To Keva's immense joy The Purple, in spite of *Top of the Pops* and good coverage on *The Chart Show*, *Fresh Pop*, MTV and some of the kids' shows, had plummeted to 33. Gil and the MDF crew weren't even hovering by the system yet, so confident were they that the Grams would not be on for a good half hour or more. The 180 team were more edgy, worried that the lack of stock over Saturday would have hit them badly.

The Friday midweek had given a cosmetically rosy picture, with the EP hanging in at 17. But between 15 and 28 there were only fifty-four points separating the positions. A few hundred sales less and the Grams would've been number 23. Worse, stocks were selling out everywhere. While the plan had been to sell ten thousand records and fuck the chart position, everyone, Guy included, had been sucked in by the drama of the Top 40. They all wanted the highest possible entry. But with Saturday looming and nowhere near enough records out there to satisfy demand, it was clear that 'Desert Rain' would be overtaken by some of the records immediately below it. To make the picture even foggier, a lot of pop and dance acts would institutionally have eighty per cent of their sales on a Saturday alone, with weekend DJs and pocket-money buyers flocking to the shops. It wasn't unusual for a record to spend the entire week just off the 40 then see it rocket into the Top 10 or 20 on the strength of Saturday's activity alone. Johnny Barclay from 180 was half pleased to have got as far as 31 without hearing the record but was privately harbouring fears that they might have dropped right off the chart altogether.

Todd King came in, bringing champagne. His upper torso seemed madly out of proportion to his bottom half, a black polo T-shirt stretched to tearing point across his chest. He had a ridiculously worked-out physique and a sly, roving look, like a sneaky bastard brother of Joey off *Friends*. He worked the room, breaking everyone's knuckles, but he didn't really fit.

Mark Goodier finished running down numbers 40 to 31 and

trumpeted another new entry. Hearts sank all over the office. Wheezer squeezed his fists tight and shut his eyes, chanting: 'Notusnotusnotusnotusnotus!'

Johnny shouted back, eyes wide with warning. 'Ay! Thirty's bloody respectable is thirty!'

'No, mate. Thirty's fine. But twentyanything is what we want.'

It wasn't them. It was Sumatra, a catchy Eurocheese import from Tenerife which was massive in the clubs. Wheezer, Ticky, Hannah and Tony danced self-consciously to the track, trying to ease their nerves. James and Purvis gurned at each other. Purvis made a gesture towards the door and the two of them slipped out. Todd followed them. He was an unlikely cokehead, but he had a mission to be down with whatever was going on. He wanted to be the very thing he could never be – a character. He could imitate accents, remember jokes, hold down a funny story, but he had no personality.

Keva stood alone at the window and watched Todd scurry stockily to catch up with them. None of this was making any impact on the singer. He didn't give a fuck what number the record came in at. It was going to be lower than Sensira. If they hadn't fucked about playing clever bastards with the market – if they'd pressed up enough records to satisfy the sudden surge of interest in the group, 'Desert Rain' might well have gone right into the Top Ten. It certainly would've been a bigger debut than 'Noodledoodled'.

Keva glanced across at Guy and Beano making a big deal of talking to the distribution boys, the foot soldiers, the workers. He drifted off, arguing with himself. Was it better to be true to yourself, to be honest, to show *no interest whatsoever* in these moribund travelling salesmen? Or did it make you a better person, knowing how much these guys define their lives by the stars they meet, to make an effort with them? Surely that was worse. If you're not interested in someone . . .

Anyway, what the fuck? It was too late to save the record now. It sounded like a great plan when Guy first floated it and, in truth, everyone had gone for it. But it was clear now that it was nothing more than a clever-silly wheeze, a stupid, amateurish cock-up. A Rich Boy's cock-up, at that. No grafter would deliberately suppress the market, turn down sales for the sake of a neat idea. Fuck it. He actually didn't give a shit.

There was a buzz on the entryphone. Pat McIntosh came up, grinning, embarrassed, carrying four cans of Stella. Keva was surprised by how pleased he was to see the scruffy bastard. They slapped hands and feigned to hit each other.

'Haven't missed the fun, have I?'

'No. Haven't come on yet, mate. Unless we're number 41 and these twats aren't letting on!'

'Ha! No chance!' He immediately lowered his voice and eyeballed Keva. 'No, I mean, is there some, you know . . .' He jerked his head comically and rolled his eyes. Keva had never quite got why people like Pat hated to say the word. He gave no indication that he knew what the fuck Pat was on about and made him carry on with his jerking, wide-eyed routine. '. . . how's your father?'

'Pardon?'

Pat laughed nervously, not sure how much mateyness he could presume. 'Fuck off, Keva! Is Pedro here?'

He wouldn't have been surprised if he'd tapped the side of his nose and winked at him. Keva felt better for all of this. 'I think Mr Love's on the case. He was seen with a trusty batman heading off to uncharted territories . . . 'spect he'll be back soon, like.'

'SSSSHH! Shut up!'

They did. Goodier was on again. He was on to 29. *Another* new entry. It was them.

'WAAAAAARGGH! YES! YES! FUCKING, FUCKING YES!'

Everyone was screaming at once, hugging each other, pulling twisted-up, ecstatic faces, jumping up on to anything which would take their weight and shagging thin air like they'd just won the World Cup. The loudest, happiest, most deafeningly squealing voice was that of Keva McCluskey.

'TURN THAT FUCKING BEAUTY UP! FUCK ME! WHAT DOES THAT SOUND LIKE? IS THAT A FUCK-ING EPIC OR WHAT . . . ?'

He collapsed on the floor, beside himself, tears of happiness streaking down his face. Hannah crouched beside him, stroking his hair, her own eyes filling up. 'What can I tell you?' she smiled. 'You've done it.'

Keva looked into her, savouring her words. He pulled her down and kissed her, long and full. When they broke, Pat McIntosh was huddled in a corner, talking into a miniature Dictaphone.

Things started to go mad. Hannah was swamped with press enquiries, from the tittle-tattle bits-and-pieces demands of the tabloid columnists to substantial interview requests from the monthlies. *Mojo* offered her September's cover. She giggled richly. 'Oh, I getcha. Right, you're giving the cover to a completely unknown band who have, thus far, released a sum of, er, one single. Uh-huh. What's the sting, Will?'

'Easy. We want an exclusive . . .' She didn't answer. She couldn't answer. She didn't know what to say. 'Come on, Hannah! The fuckin *cover* for Chrissakes!' urged Will Williamson, the features editor. 'The cover of the world-famous *Mojo* magazine for a band that's released one bleedin' single! Yeah! I can see your conundrum, babe! Jeez!'

'But you can. Can't you?'

'No!'

'Don't be silly, Will . . .'

'Jeezuz, Hannah! The *cover*! Eight, ten, maybe twelve pages of feature inside. Loads of beautiful pics. Your band don't *need* any more coverage than that! This is, like . . . the biggest announcement of a new group, ever . . .'

'To *Mojo* readers.'

'Oh, please, I'm going to put this phone down in a minute!'

'You know what I mean, Will. It's fantastic. Of course it is. But I can't bar everyone else out from a brand-new group at this stage of their development. Yeah? I agree with you . . . it's unbelievable exposure for a new group. I could almost argue with you that it's *too* much, yeah? You know I don't like hype. But what I will tell you, for sure, right, is that there will be no exclusives on the Grams. I'd love you to have the band in *Mojo*. I'd *love* you to give us a cover. But I can't agree to any deals. Sorry, Will.'

'And that's that?'

'Yes.'

Long pause. Long, long pause, as though he thought she might cave in under the tension. After a half-minute of silence, he spoke again. 'Will you put me through to Purvis?'

'He'll tell you the same thing.'

'Put me through, anyway.'

Hannah put him through. She was irritated by his refusal to take her seriously, but there was no real malice in Will. He was a nice, cynical, worn-out old rocker, and he was typical of all the press community's most devout coke maniacs. Every simple thing hid a sinister agenda from him – conspiracies, insolent newcomers and backstabbing deals lurked around every corner. He probably had Hannah down as an overzealous clerk who thought she was protecting her boss. One of those officious new kids who tried to bite off more than they could chew. He might not like taking his medicine from girlies. Whatever, Purvis would put him right.

'Hello.'

'Hannah, it's me. Can you pop in for a minute?'

In her two years with Purvert, she'd never known Jeff to speak to a colleague on the phone. He was one for ambling over, or sticking his head round the door to dish out praise or good news or, very seldomly, rebukes. Even then he'd suffer instant remorse and guide the entire staff across the road for restorative bevvies. What the fuck did he want?

'Just had Will Williamson on there.'

'I know. I put him through to you.'

'D'you think it was wise to turn down the cover of *Mojo*?'

Wise. Sort of thing your headmaster might say. She'd never heard Purvis use a word like that.

'You don't, I take it?'

'I'm asking you. It's your baby. I'm just interested in your reasoning.'

'God, Jeff, where do I start? It's just so obviously the wrong thing to do. I mean . . . you are with me on this, aren't you?'

'I don't know.'

'What? Blimey, Jeff, I mean, like, I was raised at your knee, yeah? Things like this, right, I mean . . . *I am you*! That's what I do. I think, "What'd Purvis do, here?" And I always, like, *know* what you'd do. It gives me confidence to know that. I do it second nature now. I just know, OK – I know right from wrong.'

'The cover of *Mojo*, though . . .'

'The cover of *Mojo* is wrong. Three reasons. One, they want an exclusive. You cannot risk pissing off every other rag in the land because one very fine specialist magazine wants an exclusive. Two, it's completely out of kilter, yeah? The band was unknown a month ago. You do not build your best new talent like this. Boy bands, fine. Pop acts, fire away. Go for it. Ride that bronco for all it's worth, yeah? But if you think your band might be around for more than six weeks, y'know . . .' She tailed off, disconsolate, the question hanging in the air.

'And three?'

'Three? I like threes. There is no three.'

Purvis smiled. Hannah stood there, flushed, her gammy eye flashing at him in anger.

'You've gone over my head, haven't you? You've told him we'll do it.'

'If it was any other paper – *any other paper* – I'd tell them to fuck off . . .'

Hannah slumped down into the kitsch red bowl-seat, head in hands. 'And this is my baby, yeah? You just want to hear my reasoning?'

Purvis got up and went round to her, crouching so she could feel his stale breath. 'Look. This *is* your baby. Just . . . that thing with Cindy Hogan, right. I mean . . . fuck! Everyone gets it wrong sometimes!'

'You think that Cindy thing was down to *me*?'

Purvis kept calm. 'Yeah. You gotta look for the motive – all the time. Why's she gonna drop everything and come and have a drink with a bunch of nobodies? You got her wrong, Hannah darling.'

She looked up, eyes gleaming with angry tears. Through her anger, she still kept her voice even. 'No, mate. No. You've got it wrong, this time. Badly wrong.'

She walked out of the office and out of the building. She crossed Clerkenwell Road and walked blindly into Vine Hill, finding herself at the foot of the Rosebery Avenue steps. She ran up on to Rosebery and sat, bitterly dejected, unable to decide. She knew she should do nothing. She got up and walked towards King's Cross. She needed to talk to Ticky.

Every production company in London was vying to make the 'Beautiful' video. Ticky's fax machine spewed out treatments from the best – and the worst – directors in town. Up in Liverpool 60, Wheezer's e-mail clanged with more and more video scripts, most of which he and Guy discussed and dismissed by phone, without recourse to the group.

'Jings, Guy, I could do better myself. This is the cream of London's creative community?'

'Wankers, aren't they?'

'I mean, what does this one mean?' He read it out to Guy, emphasising the most pretentious moments.

In a drizzly black and white homage to the noir classics of the late forties, we pick up the band dressed in gangster-chic overcoats and Derby hats playing rummy in a speakeasy . . .

'I mean, how the heck do we know they're playing *rummy . . .*'

. . . A Jean-Harlow-type moll takes to the stage and starts to dance in achingly slow-motion . . .

'That's *achingly* slow-motion, Guy, by the way . . .'

The chiselled face of Keva McCluskey fixes upon the moll. He stares his tough-guy stare at her. She smiles back. He checks to see that his guys have not noticed and suddenly jumps up on stage. Everything is transformed into vibrant technicolour. The band smile as they play the double bass, the brush-drum and the trumpet. Keva, now a light-footed muse, dances sensuously, slowly, ingratiatingly around the beautiful moll. Her smile has lit up a world of violence and terror. All is now beautiful. Keva goes over to the vacant, old RCA-style microphone and sings to the girl. Everyone dances and smiles. End on a joyous scene of exultant humanity.

'Pile of cack, what?'

'Hear, hear. Wannabe film-makers, these guys. You need to tell 'em what you want, really.'

'I hate seeing bands in fancy dress. Don't you?'

'Utterly. So, then. What do we think? Is there *anything* we like?'

'I still think Adam Rice. I think he'll do it for us. I really do.'

Adam's treatment, hand-scrawled, had read:

Go to Ibiza. Have it bigstylee. Beautiful.

'Hmm. Maybe I'll get him in. He's a bit . . . you know. Bit barmy. Can you come down for the meeting?'

'When?'

'Try and fix it for tomorrow.'

'No probs. Try and make it later in the afternoon. I can get the cheap fare after nine forty-five. Do we still have Farm Place?'

'I'll ask Ticky . . . ay oop! Hannah's in with her. I'll call you back. Cheers.'

Phone-slamming race.

'Wheezer? It's Guy again. Hang on, fella, I'm going to put us on Conference. I've got Hannah Brown with me . . .'

Wheezer smiled at Guy's use of Hannah's full name, failing to distinguish between The Wheeze and the status-crazy Americans.

'Hi, Wheezer . . .'

'What's to do, chaps?'

'Hannah?'

'Wheezer, this is what's happened, yeah, and I've never done anything like this before, not with Purvis, I've usually just put up and got on with it if we didn't, like, totally agree before. But I'm about to, like, go sneak behind his back so, sorry about that – don't think too badly of me, OK?'

'No probs. Fire away.'

Hannah told him about *Mojo*. '. . . I mean, like, I do *utterly* understand Jeff's stance. *Mojo* stands for quality. The writing, the journalism, yeah, is spectacular. There can be no more meaningful seal of approval than the front cover of *Mojo*. And for a new band, well . . . it speaks volumes, as they say. The other plus is they don't, like, fuck around with bands. You're in there because they really, really think you're the tits, yeah? They don't get into any of this building up a band to knock them down. If you're in the mag, you're there on merit and you're there to stay . . .'

'Sounds OK so far.'

'Well, yeah, like *so far*. Because we can only go so far with *just one mag* behind us. That is very likely what's going to happen here. We already have *NME* massively behind us, *Select*, *Vox*, *Q* and *MM* have all been in touch, plus the supps, the style mags, the specialist press . . . *everyone*'s into this band, yeah?'

'And if we decide to go with this exclusive from *Mojo*, we risk alienating those publications?'

'Risk? No, it ain't a risk – it's a *guarantee*. And it's not just the publications, it's their *publishers*. IPC, Emap, we could blot out whole avenues of potential support. I just don't see any case for it. Sorry.'

'Can we get Purv on the phone?'

'I'd prefer that we didn't, Wheeze.' Hannah's voice sharpened. 'Anyway, can we not, like, take this decision ourselves? Do we have to refer everything back to the mighty one, or does our own little opinion count for something around here?'

'Hey, cool it,' soothed Guy. 'All Wheezer's saying is, like, is there something we might've missed here?'

'Oh, fuck off then! Call him! But don't call *me*!' Her receiver slammed down.

Wheezer spoke first. 'Listen. I'll speak to Purv. I think I know how to broach this one.'

'You sure, Wheeze?'

'Trust me.'

'Jeff, hi, man. Look, I know you're busy. I'll come straight to the point. In a roundabout sort of way. Look, you know we all have nothing but the highest regard . . .'

'*Mojo*?'

'. . . what?'

'You're calling me about *Mojo*.'

Pause.

'What d'you think?'

'Let me give you a couple of precedents. Both within our living memory, both Manchester bands. Inspiral Carpets. Press darlings when they started off. Could not put a foot wrong. Did all the mags, all the telly, *Smash Hits*, everything, mates with the journos, drinking buddies, all of that . . . fucking five-a-side, quiz nights, whatever you want. That should stand 'em in good stead. Fuck off! Don't want to know. Inspiral who? New album? Don't make me fucking laugh! Or Sleeper. That's even better! Zoë Ball playing guitar with Sleeper! You can fuckin *hear* the justification . . . guaranteed Breakfast Show playlist, blah-blah-blah . . . Sorry, Sleeper! End of the line, darlings!! End of, over and out! I could ramble on, but that's what's always going to happen to bands who do every fucking thing they're offered and appear on every cover and every show and get right on everyone's fucking tits! Think quality, Wheeze, not quantity. Hannah's trying to rationalise this like there's a loyalty card, some reward scheme for bands who play the game and . . .' He squeezed extra contempt into his voice. '. . . *give of* themselves. There fucking isn't! The press is looking to fuck you over. From the moment they've made you, the thing they're looking for is the cracks. All's you can do, all's the likes of me can do is delay the agony.'

'Cripes, Purv. Bad knee day or what?'

'You what?'

'Nothing. Who's the other band?'

'Stone Roses.'

'But the press murdered them.'

'They did. But the Roses murdered them first. Fucked them right off. Never, ever *played the game*. Would not give them a fucking light. Gave an exclusive to the *Big* bleeding *Issue*. Magnificent!'

'Sorry, Purv. I don't get you . . .'

'Compromise and pride. It's about pride. You've got a great band there. A truly fucking brilliant band. You don't need to toe the line. You don't need to sell your souls. I'm only telling you all this because I like you. I should tell you to fuck off. I don't like to justify myself . . .'

'But the Stone Roses . . . the name stands for shit.'

'That's what the music press have tried to make of it. But listen to those *songs*. Listen to those fucking songs, man. They're *pure*.

They're eternal and pure because they were never, ever bought with a pound of flesh. They're unsullied. And they'll last for ever because the Stone Roses never did no bargains with the fucking press.'

But you're a press agent, Wheezer wanted to say. Purvis anticipated it.

'I only deal with the cunts to help prevent my bands from castrating themselves. I chart the course around the rocks, knowing that, sooner or later, we'll hit one of the fuckers. I minimise the damage. They're animals, Wheezer. You'll find that out. And to be handed a chance, a golden, *golden* opportunity to work them over this early on . . . it's just fantastic. It's manna.'

'But . . .'

'There's no alternative. This is how it works. This is how it is. Get on it.'

He put the phone down bristling with inspiration. He felt honoured. Once again, he felt as though he was living, now, through the pages of the rock history of his time. He was going to do it. He was going to fuck the press off.

'Why didn't you come to us before just fucking going out there and blowing our career out the water?'

Career. What a word to hear from Keva. He was livid. He'd been venomously angry since Wheezer told them the news.

'You know why, guys. Things have gone crazy. For weeks, months now, we've just been getting on with it as we see best. We're not, like, trying to mess this up for you! You know . . . you've got to start *believing* in us, you know. You have to give me that licence. I *have* to know that, when I decide something – whether I'm saying you'll make a TV appearance or that you'll visit some poor waif in hospital – that it'll be absolute. I have to be allowed to *manage*!'

'But Hannah, Wheeze. Little Hannah. She's poured everything into this band. And now, what? She's as good as off the case.'

Beano cocked his thin head on to his shoulder, trying to sound sarcastic. 'It's business, Keva.'

Keva declined his support, staring intently at Wheezer. Wheezer was unflinching. 'It's not. It's the opposite. It's integrity.

It's longevity. Anyway, it's only for the duration of the next single.'

The band howled their disdainful laughter. 'A non-exclusive exclusive! Love it!'

'The press, I promise, will *not* desert you! They'll be desperate! Look, there's no cartel here! They're all chasing the same stories, all looking for different ways of dressing up the same basic tale. By knocking them back now, we're just making them more keen!'

The group were too stunned to laugh. 'Wheezer, mate – that's . . . *shite*,' stated Tony. 'You know it's shite. One minute we can't get an interview in *L-Scene*, the next we're knocking back *NME*? I don't think so.'

'I'm sure Pat McIntosh'll be terrifically understanding when I explain to him that I can't speak to him, on or off the record, because, like, regardless that he's the guy who gave us the first, biggest, greatest write-up we're ever gonna have, our manager has signed an exclusivity deal with another paper. Bollocks!'

'Well . . . actually, good point, because with *NME* doing such a big piece around "Desert Rain", they're not going to want another major piece until the album. Pat can still review you live . . .'

'Oh, fuck it, Wheeze!' shouted James. 'I've never heard such shite! Why does there always have to be a clever-clever little fucken angle with you and Ghee-de-Ghee? Why is it, like, limited edition an' that, limiting the press an' that, secret fucken gigs? Is Snowy right? Are we a secret band?! The Band That Never Was? Cos we fucken well will be if we carry on like this! If you want me in this fucken band, we act like a fucken band! We gig. We drink. We take drugs. We shag birds. And we do every fucken interview that comes our way. Am I right?'

'IS RIGHT 'N' THAT, HECTOR, LAR!'

Wheezer got up, shaking his head. 'Bluster, Hector. Blind, bullish bloody rhetoric!'

'Whoo!' He laughed and made eyes at Wheezer's resorting to swear words, but he looked harried.

Wheezer pinned in on him. 'You'll bump into the roadsweep on the way out and he'll tell you to physically *attack* journalists and release cassettes of chimpanzees regurgitating their cud, and you'll go . . .'

'I AGREE WITH YOU!'

The joke lightened things a little. Wheezer told them he was going to London and promised to hold off on a final decision until he'd spoken with Hannah again. He knew, he *knew* he shouldn't do it, but he stopped in the doorway of the rehearsal room anyway.

'Keva. Your dalliance with Ms Brown is not, maybe, guiding your loyalties in any way, is it?'

Their mouths, the rest of them, actually hung open. You could have placed chirpy parakeets on their lower lips.

'It's over, Wheeze,' he stated. 'It never even got started.'

Wheezer could have skipped to London whistling 'Happy Days Are Here Again'.

Wheezer jumped on the 73 outside Euston and, after a sprightly jog from the Angel was sitting inside the Peasant with Todd and Guy fifteen minutes later. Both were sipping bottles of Budvar but Wheezer, with a raging summer thirst and unaccountably nervous about this raft of tricky meetings, sank a large vodka, cranberry juice and lemonade immediately, then joined the boys on Budvar. Food was ordered and devoured – oysters to start, followed by a seafood platter of grilled mullet, crabcakes, crawfish, a steaming, lemony dish of moules and four different types of bread. Guy swapped his beer for a Colombard Sauvignon after the oysters, a good half of which was quaffed by the gradually effervescing Wheezer. All of this for under sixty rips in a St John Street pub. London kills you.

Todd handed Wheezer a copy of the tour itinerary he'd pencilled for October. It looked tremendous. College gigs in Dublin, Cork, Belfast, Aberdeen, Stirling, Preston, Bangor, Leicester, Cardiff and Norwich, and good-sized club dates in Derry, Glasgow, Dundee, Edinburgh, Newcastle, Leeds, Manchester, Birmingham, London and Liverpool.

'D'you not think it's a bit of a baptism of fire?' asked Guy.

'Why d'you say that?'

'Just, like, it's twenty dates with very few days off. They've never been out for more than a week at a time. Wouldn't it be better to do, say, ten in October, a select few at Christmas, then come out all guns blazing with the album in the New Year?'

'It's one way of looking at it, sure. To me – and of course I would say this – if a band can play live then they should be on the road all the time. It is just singly the best way of breaking a band humongous. If they can play. And from what I saw down at Mono, they can fucking play!'

'Oh, aye, they can play,' said Wheezer. 'They could probably do twenty dates on the bounce. The concern for me – and I'd have to throw myself at your mercy on this one – is burn-out. By the looks of things, we're going to have a fairly substantial success with the follow-up single . . .'

'. . . *a fairly substantial success* . . .'

Hot torrents of excitement flooded through his jugulars as he spoke. This was real. This was happening. He was taking part in a top-level meeting about a top-priority band, and his opinion was being sought and valued. Guy and Todd listened intently.

'. . . which will, we hope, lead to renewed interest from overseas. I'm just a bit concerned that we should use what time is available to the best possible effect. With all due respect to Bangor or Preston or wherever, I don't want to have to turn down promo in Tokyo because of prior commitments in Wyre Piddle.'

'. . . I *don't want to have to turn down* . . .' Me. The boss. *Wheezer Finlay.*

They guffawed generous laughter. Wheezer flushed with pleasure. He was a player.

'Utterly valid point, Wheeze. Thing with the college gigs is, like, fuck 'em! You know? We're doing them a favour. We book the gigs and if something better comes along, you know, the Ents Sec is not gonna come after your kneecaps with an Uzi . . .' He waited for them to acknowledge his witticism before continuing. '. . . so long as we fulfil the date at some other time or, as H3O, maybe we offer them another act at a tempting price . . . whatever. We can work around it. To me, the important thing is to get you guys out gigging. The more the better. If we need to rethink nearer the time, we can absolutely do that.'

Guy pondered. 'Your feeling is what, Wheeze? That the boys will relish a tour schedule like this? Or will they freak out?'

'You're kidding!' They'll *love* it. It makes them a real band. In fact, if we're doing it, we should go the whole hog. Acoustic sets in megastores. Interviews with local radio, maybe record unique sessions for syndication on the ILRs. We can get 180 Degrees on the case and really hammer the local promotion angle. Are these venues big enough, Todd? I can only see one hall above seven hundred capacity, and that's in London. We'll have seven hundred on the perishing *guest* list in London . . .'

Guy intervened. 'Yeah, that's usual, Wheeze. What we want is to build up a vibe, a hysteria if you like. The Grams have to be the ticket people will shag their granny for. We want them breaking down the doors with battering rams to get in to these shows, and the ones who missed out, who missed the legend when it came to town, will have to make fucking sure that they're first in the queue when the Grams come round again. We're after building a rep for the band . . .'

'Which means . . . ' continued Todd, '. . . we need to keep the Famous Grams Medicine Show well and truly on the road and in the public eye. People are talking about one track. We want them to talk about the live phenomenon too. We put them on the road and when they get back we pat 'em on the head, turn them back round and send them out again, more, bigger . . .'

Wheezer would have to allow that he now *hated* Todd King, almost saw him as an enemy, but he had to take his hat off to him. He was damn good.

'What did you have in mind?'

'Two things. London show immediately, like, within four weeks, August twenty-six, twenty-seven, word-of-mouth thing . . .' Wheezer was already planning how to break another word-of-mouth gig to the troops. Todd paused, looked away casually for effect then hit them with part two. '. . . then a headline slot at Reading.'

Wheezer was still on the London bit.

'What?' spluttered Guy, olive oil oozing down his chin. He mopped it with soda bread.

'Reading?' said Wheezer.

'Sure.'

'Reading's been on sale for ages. It was booked back in February, wasn't it?'

'Most of the main acts, sure. But we're H3O. We have ways and means. You didn't join the most happening agency in Europe just to get a showcase at the Borderline, did you?'

'Woulda killed for one not so long ago,' laughed Wheezer, slipping into Todd's easy transatlanticisms.

'Well, I'd love to be able to tell you that the mighty H3O was able to shift Sensira off the Saturday night, but, alas – this is the situation. Sidewalk have been offered an opening slot on the US leg of the Blackhole tour. Our advice is that they take it.' He opened his fox's eyes as wide as he could manage. Wheezer wanted to laugh. Todd nodded once, violently, as he continued. 'They'll take it.'

Beat. Drums fingers on table and grins.

'Means they'll have to vacate their Reading date . . .'

'You could always offer *us* the Blackhole slot,' grinned Wheezer. 'Believe me, you could get it.'

Wheezer blushed. He could barely breathe for fear of betraying his coltish excitement. The Grams were going to be big. The Grams were going to be big.

'KROQ and WXRT are already on "Desert Rain". FNX in Boston loves it. I understand there've been spins on Live 105, the Edge, the Zephyr and a whole host of P2s. Those guys are *on* this. Believe me.'

Wheezer nodded soberly. He was half pissed and faint with pride. He already knew these guys were *on* this. And he knew why. His mailout was working. Should he tell them that *he* was the tactical mastermind behind the slowly-building pattern of airplay in America? Not just yet.

'There's a nice little story emerging in the States and we aim to work with you on making the most of that situation. Obviously you're aware of the tentative link-up with Taurus? So we're in good shape over there before we've kicked a ball. We're all in the loop.'

Wheezer was getting a hard-on.

'No, the trick from now on is to completely solidify things here in Blighty. We've made the best of all possible starts and it's now a case of keeping the momentum going. Headlining the *NME* stage on the Friday night is just what the doctor ordered . . .'

Wheezer could feel himself droop in his seat. One minute they'd been discussing the Grams' imminent takeover of the USA, the next they were in a tent in a field in Berkshire.

'The *NME* tent?' repeated Guy, pausing slightly between each initial.

'Is there a problem with that?'

In a stroke Wheezer saw the anger and pride flash through Todd. He had obviously been pulling strings to wangle the slot and thought this was a proper result for the band. As quickly as he sensed out Todd's injury, he had the answer. 'God, no, Todd, there's no problem with the perishing *gig*. Blimey, a headline slot at *Reading*? You're kidding! No, no problem there. The opposite. But there might be . . . well it could be a little difficult with *NME* . . .'

Wheezer explained the potential problems which might be caused by their decision to give *Mojo* an exclusive. Todd leaned his chin on his fingertips, pensive, his sense of self fully restored. 'Is this set in stone?'

'No,' gabbled Wheezer. 'It's a movable feast. Er . . .' Guy shot him a look.

'I think we should look at it again,' said Todd. 'I mean . . . I see, I do see the case for going with *Mojo*. I mean, Christ, the cover, the fucking front cover for a band that's done, really, diddly squat . . . God, it makes you weep! I almost think we should say fuck the rest of it, let's have it! I mean, the cover of *Mojo*, thirty–forty dates, mm. Could be a better route . . .' He said it *rowt*. 'But then . . .'

They looked at him eagerly. Wheezer, again, was experiencing niggles of jealousy way down in the base of his pancreas, little naggings of anxiety that one as young as Todd should *know* so much. '. . . I dunno. I mean *can* we risk casting so much of our armoury aside for the sake of this one mighty thrust of the broadsword? Can we do that? I don't think we *need* to. I mean, let's look at it again . . .'

Within half an hour, after much looking at things again, Todd had convinced them. The gut-wrenching spleen and passion of Jeff Purvis was supplanted by the cool international acumen of Todd King. The Grams were doing Reading. Tent or no, it was a headline slot, a fuck of a headline slot and it would wed them to their new pals at *NME* for the run ahead. Guy volunteered to speak to Purvis, but Wheezer wanted to make the call. Purvis was cool.

'Whatever, Wheeze man. I don't think it's necessarily a bad decision you've taken. I'm probably . . . you know. It's just that I know how things work out, that's all. I know how it always ends up. And I know that the Grams are a band who can do it, do it all, on their own terms, without fucking pandering to anyone. I guess I'd just like to work with one band who were . . . *sacrosanct*, yeah? I think you know what I mean by that, eh, Wheezy? But fuck it. You only get one crack at this. You should go for it. No problem. D'you want to speak to Hannah or shall I?'

'Jings, Purvis – you nearly talked me into it all over again. You're a wicked, wicked man, d'you hear? You're Rasputin.'

They strolled up Amwell Street to Filthy's. The place was emptying now, they could talk freely, and three large Paddies seemed just the ticket to digest the afternoon's feast. Hannah walked in and cackled at the three of them. 'Good grief! It's, like, a scene out of Hogarth! Well, I'm glad to see that some of us are taking our rock 'n' roll traditions seriously . . .'

'Wotcher, Hannah. Welcome back on board the groovy train! You know Todd King, don't you?'

Todd held out a mitt. Hannah eyed it with suspicion. 'Course. Hi again, Todd. Hello, Weasel. What we all drinking? Paddies, hey? Same again, yeah?'

By six thirty, when Wheezer and Guy stumbled out to meet Adam Rice about the 'Beautiful' video, they'd agreed that Todd could book his tour and add one or two more dates in the Midlands and the west. After much divisive debate, too, Hannah won the day over the location of the Grams' word-of-mouth London show. Guy and Wheezer had been in favour of somewhere grimy, a rock 'n' roll dirtbox which would display the band's live credentials without any trimmings. Todd and Hannah argued that this was all *about* trimmings.

'We want loads of DJs, terrific party atmosphere, a real sense of occasion . . .'

'What? Like the Marigold do?'

'Like Marigold *should*'ve been, absolutely.'

She won. Promising minute collaboration with Todd over sound, lighting, special effects and overall production, Hannah and Ally Bland were going to put on a night to remember at the Hanover Grand, with an after-show party at the Diorama. They'd give away a hundred tickets to the beautiful and garrulous of London, the glow-worms who lit up every party, every opening, and whose presence assured the rank and file that this was an occasion to aspire to. By inviting them, the Grams could assume two things: that their show would be talked about like no other event in town that week, and that it would radiate glamour from the inside out. This was Hannah's contention. That rock 'n' roll did not need to be dirty. That it could learn from the sexy, sinuous sheen of dance music, weld that culture's purring, feral grace to the throbbing physicality of guitar music. She wanted beautiful rock 'n' roll. She was going to get it.

They'd decided to go with Adam Rice's Ibiza video. He hadn't given them much to go on, but both Guy and Wheezer had a good feeling about the carrot-topped nutter. The evening they'd met him, down in the Cross Bar, had been hilarious. Guy and Wheezer were both sloshed from their afternoon in Filthy's, but they were cherubims of sobriety next to Adam.

He made an indelible impression upon Guy. Spotting him and Wheezer, Adam had made his unsteady way across the floor, brutally spiked vermilion hair, eyes aflame, one hand holding the frontispiece of his garish, checked Edwardian coat closed, the other proferred in anticipation of a warm greeting as he neared touching distance. And then, just as his fingers interlocked with Guy's, he threw up. He vomited, a horizontal volley of purple spew, right in Guy's face.

'Fucking Pernod, man,' slurred Adam. 'Don't touch the stuff.' Wiping strands of sickly bile from Guy's horrified face he continued, unabashed. 'Thank fuck it never went on your dicky, eh? Paul Smiff, innit?'

A minute later Guy was shuddering with laughter, shaking Adam's hand and slapping his shoulders. If he'd have pitched them a storyline involving corpulent middle-management types on a splat-gun assertiveness training weekend he'd have still got the gig. But he didn't. He said: 'There's this really beautiful village called San Miguel. Lots of ex-hippies live there, been there since 1970, gorgeous kids. I mean, fantastic, *beautiful* . . . lots and lots of sex between various races, I think. I was out there in May. There's lemon groves and fields full of mad cactus and big, mad, wild flowers, flowers like you never seen before, explosions of colour. What I want to do, right, I hope to fuck she's still there . . . there's this girl called India . . . no, fuck, that's her muvva. What's she called? Air? Ocean? Fuck, I dunno – she's about seventeen, you have never seen a face like it, I swear to you, man, she is truly the most beautiful thing you have ever laid eyes on . . .'

They waited, nodded, liking the sound of it so far. For someone so stunningly drunk he was a vivid and compelling raconteur. They waited. Adam grinned and returned their nods. 'So. What d'ya think?'

Guy and Wheezer looked at each other. The Wheeze spoke first. 'Errm . . . is that it?'

Adam was crestfallen. 'Well, like, yeah. I mean . . .'

'No, I mean we like it, don't we, Guy, but . . . is there a, you know, a rough sort of *structure* . . . ?'

'What Wheezer's asking is – what's the story?'

'The *story*? Oh no, man, I don't do stories. If I hadna puked on your kite I'd be out of here. That's a fucking insult!'

'He-hey! Steady on, boys! I don't think we're miles apart here, you know,' soothed Wheezer. He liked Adam. He knew he'd come up with the right images for the song. 'Come on! Let's carry on talking. And drinking. What you having, Adam?'

And so it was that Wheezer collapsed into his dear old Farm Place pit after a night of chaotic carousing in the late-night dives of old London Town, as sure as he could be that Adam was going to deliver a sumptuous, poetic, beautiful video.

After Janey's call, Wheezer was even more pleased that they were going somewhere photogenic. Janey Heal was Acetate's Head of Televisual. She and her team of one were responsible for placing their acts on any number of television opportunities. It was their job to service videos to MTV, *The Chart Show*, VH1, *Fresh Pop*,

Exclusive, *the O-Zone* and all the other, ever-increasing outlets offering profile for clips. They also booked their bands on to whichever shows they considered appropriate, *Jack Docherty* for some, *TFI Friday* for others, and Saturday-morning kids' shows for others yet. Janey roused Wheezer from his slumber of the drunken dead with tremendous news about the show they all considered to be the jewel in the crown for serious bands. They'd got the green light for *e.p.* Wheezer dragged his head off the pillow, gripping the phone.

e.p. – Electronic Postcards – was the highest-rated 'youth' music programme in its TVR grouping. What that meant was that it was watched by more of the desired affluent young than any other music-specific programme. The format of *e.p.* had been so successful that its producers had sold it around the globe and were expanding the next series to an hour to include other types of celebrities apart from bands and musicians.

'That's fantastic news, Janey,' he croaked, trying to sound straight. 'The best!' He could feel her pleasure radiating back to him.

What they had to do was make a film about themselves. It could be either six minutes or twelve minutes in length. A half-hour edition of *e.p.* would contain two, three or four 'postcards' from bands, short films displaying an unknown or unique aspect of the group. The bands solicited by the production company would first submit a short synopsis of their proposed film, to be discussed by *e.p.*'s production team. If commissioned, however expensive, the filmed postcard would have to be paid for by their record company – who were happy to buy into the guaranteed prestige and exposure of the show. Some of *e.p.*'s best films had varied dramatically in the scale of their ambition and budget – from a night out in a Bradford curry house shot on Hi-8 video by glam-metal trio Banshee, to Medsin's famous Harley-Davidson face-off in the Nevada desert with a bunch of terrifying Hell's Angels, directed by Martyn Atkinson, the LA-based bike fanatic.

The Medsin treatment had upped the stakes. More and more bands were now vying for more and more extrovert ways of using their slot. Thirty-five and 70mm film epics from Damien Hirst and Blaise Drummond and other maverick directors were becoming the norm on *e.p.*, so it seemed an obvious step to Wheezer and Keva, both devout fans of the programme, to go the other way, go for more of a DIY feel. Guy was prepared to spend money and lobbied them hard to tie Adam into the process, but Keva was unflinching. This was to be his film.

He sent in an idea about the Grams going to Ibiza to find Syd, a legendary Liverpudlian hippie who had been Keva's guru, his childhood hero and who was responsible for his unquenchable thirst for music. Syd had lived a quasi-hippie existence in Ibiza since the late seventies. When it had finally dawned upon him through the pot fug that he wasn't going back to Liverpool, Syd sent a message back to his mum. He said that Keva, the music freak kid next door to whom he'd taught a few basic guitar chords, could look after his record collection while he was away. He never came back. So instead of cutting his teeth on ABC, Spandau Ballet, Depeche Mode and the rest of the synth-pop set of the early eighties, Keva was still working his way through box after box of Curved Air and Neil Young and PFM albums, separating the wheat from the chaff. He could still raise a semi for Sonja Kristina. Cream, Dylan, Leonard Cohen, Tim Hardin – these were the miasma of influences in Keva's young life. So this pilgrimage by the ascendant star to find his muse and talk rot about ballads in Ibiza was perfect for *e.p.* It was a real story, Keva was going to shoot and edit it himself on video and ReHab would be getting extra value from their Ibiza shoot.

'Janey,' slurred Wheezer. 'I love you.' He stared wonkily into the mouthpiece for added sincerity. 'I do.'

Kitty was late. Keva had arranged to meet her at six in the Carlisle. He'd killed time by walking down to Soho from Euston, dawdling and browsing in Waterstone's so that he wasn't there bang on six bells. He got there about ten past, but there was nobody fitting Kitty Trevelyan's description of herself: 'I've been described as a busty and ebullient hackette before now, darling. You'll know me when you see me. Later!'

Kitty was associate producer – basically a super-researcher – on *e.p.* and other programmes for Magic Number, the biggest independent producer of youth programming in the country. Magic Number were based out in Mile End for the extra warehouse and studio space your money could buy, so their production team always leapt at any half-chance of a meeting Up West. Keva was due to meet Kitty to run over final details of his Ibiza *e.p.* As six thirty beckoned and Keva was beginning to think he was in the wrong Carlisle, a breathless and indisputably bosomy Kitty candidate tottered in on Emma Hope heels.

'Fucking tubes!' she wailed, allowing a slightly lingering sibilant on the 's'. 'I'd have taken a cab but they're worse at this time of day – when they bloody turn up! Sorry! Hi! Kitty Trevelyan . . . you must be *famished*.'

For no real reason at all this set Keva to giggling and the more he tried to stop, the more 'what? what!' curious Kitty became, until she, too, was chuckling helplessly. They felt at home with each other and spent an infantile evening in dell'Ugo thinking up people who were uglier than Antony Worrall Thompson and making waiters pronounce things in Herbert Lom accents. It was a good night. Working on this *e.p.* thing was not going to give either of them a headache.

Walking down Dean Street, Kitty beseeched Keva to come into Groucho's for a nightcap. 'Come on, boy! What sort of a pop star are you? *La toute* Channel Four'll be there! And my boss – do you want to be blackballed from terrestrial TV before you've even had a *hit*?'

'Can't!'

'No such thing as can't. Why not?'

'Told you. Got to go up to Whitfield Street to hear this remix of the track. You're welcome . . .'

'A *recording studio*? Ugh! No thanks . . .' She pulled a card out of her dinky little Prada bag.

'. . . look. The Oaf is having a whole tribe of roistering pigs up to Durham at the weekend. One is simply duty-bound to respond in kind. I've invited a counter-cult of my most pretentious luvvies and homosexuals just to drive him mad. We'll take over the West Wing. If nothing else, it'll speed up the settlement. Can I count on your support? There'll be some gorgeous, gorgeous girls there. Thick ones, thin ones, you name it. Why, you may pleasure *me*, sir, if you're of a mind . . .'

Keva chortled, thinking of Ticky's birthday bash, so near and yet so very far away. 'How can I refuse?' he smiled, thinking desparately of ways out of this. Kitty puckered at him.

'Come on then. Kiss the birdie then fuck off!'

Instead of pecking at her, Keva swept her gallantly over his knee and smothered her neck with wet kisses. 'Madam! Durham cannot come a day too soon!'

Durham was impossibly dreary. That was his first impression. He'd slogged it overland from Liverpool on the laughably-named Sprinter train, only to wait forty-five minutes for a dumb subaltern to collect him in a 1943 Land Rover with oblong, gunmetal benches in the back. They bumped agonisingly along mile after mile of unadopted country scree track through endless reaches of conifer forest. By the time he alighted at Hamsterley, his arse was battered black and blue. He couldn't imagine wanting to sit for weeks. He stared up at the mansion, a black *Scooby Doo* haunted castle against the navy night sky. He'd managed to get it out of the driver, who smelt of lambshit and had an unbearable copse of sandy-coloured hair growing horizontally from a mouldering off-white wart on his neck, that Hamsterley was the ancient country seat of Lord Hamsterley, who owned much of County Durham. Young Lord Hamsterley, it could be presumed, was the Oaf.

The Wart carried Keva's single overnight bag to his room, lit a candle and left him to it. It was fabulous. Twigging, after a minute, that there was no electricity in this part of the old fortress, Keva took the candle and set about locating and firing other strategically placed beacons. The flickering tongues sent shadows and spectres to each cranny of the room. A solid, dark-black wood four-poster bed dominated, with a hearth big enough to stand up in at its foot. Embers from a small fire gave out enough strange light for Keva to spot the big wood basket, full to the top with logs, and rag-and-twig homemade firelighters. He chucked a couple on to the smouldering pile and stacked five or six hefty logs on top. Flames licked around the sides of the logs then engulfed them, sending up sparks of burning wood in a red, red fire. He lay back on the bed, grinning. This was wondrous. He loved it. He'd be happy just to lie there for the night, regardless.

A persistent and none-too-gentle knocking made him sit up sharply. Hard to know how long he'd nodded off for. He went to the door. The Wart was there.

'Sir. Lady Hamsterley calls from the Bull's Head. She wonders whether sir would care to join the party?'

'Lady Hamsterley . . .?' Keva wondered back, still not fully with it after the journey. His bum had all but seized up.

'Lady Hamsterley, sir.'

'Oh. Right. Is that Kitty? Sound. Tell her I'll be down. Er . . . sorry. Don't know what your name is.'

'Smith, sir.'

'Mr Smith. A'right, la.' He offered a hand which remained unshook. 'How do I get there, like? The Bull's Blood an' that?'

'I'd be happy to drive you down there, sir.'

Keva's face dropped. He grabbed his pillow to cushion the ride and followed the disapproving Smith.

Kitty was effusive in her greeting, enveloping Keva in hugs and introducing him to lots of people he hated on sight. After five minutes of parading her pop star around the twittering throng, Kitty left Keva to his own devices and returned to an argument about obligatory state euthanasia upon attainment of pensionable age.

Why had he come here? Why had he got himself into this crazy situation, surrounded by phonies and phantom intellectuals? Wankers. He knew why. Two reasons. He was starting to fall for this whole cult of his own personality thing. He was reading his own interviews, hearing himself on the radio and he wanted his life to change in tandem with his persona. He didn't want to remain the same person. He didn't want to stay ordinary. He should push himself, do things he might not ordinarily want to do, taste whatever's there to be sampled, just because. Because he could, now. Because he should. It was like James Bond. He'd let a beautiful woman show him into her sumptuous suite, well though he knew that danger lurked within the wardrobe. He should do the same. If doors were opening to him he should peek inside. But so far, so bad. This was less entertaining than Ye Cracke on a slow night.

There was another reason he'd made the journey too. That evening with Kitty, he'd found himself immediately attracted to her. There were no pauses, no conscious efforts to find a common ground. She was like Hannah. They were mates. But she was a Somebody, too, and maybe somewhere he thought that, as a star, he should have a suitably stellar girlfriend. It was not yet a clearly distilled notion, but he was here to find out more. Him and Hannah, it was too weird with them working together. They'd agreed on that. Every time they had sex. But here was an opportunity to go to the source, to, at very least, take in a new experience, and he would have despised his cowardly self if he hadn't taken up the chance. So here he was, hating it. Worse, now he didn't find Kitty so attractive here in her natural habitat. She seemed disappointed by him, too, on renewal. She was enraptured by a sickeningly self-satisfied couple as they relived a meal they'd recently enjoyed of which the main constituent was placenta. He had to get away from here.

He hastened to the phone on the wall, desperate for a taxi number. There was no card. His heart sank. He'd see this evening out, make the most of his pop star's right to moody isolationism and clear off first thing in the morning. He turned to re-enter the fray and came face to face with the most stunning – he actually sucked in his breath – the most amazing-looking woman he'd seen, ever. He wanted to look, to stare, to imbibe every part of her astonishing physique all at once – the flashing, slanted, coal-black eyes, the violent cheekbones, the unearthly thrust of the tits. Kitty saw his fascination and seemed happy to bridge the exit route.

'Keva, darling, I want you to make my friend giggle. She's terribly unhappy. She hates it here already, don't you, Evie, darling. You hate me and you hate all my disgusting friends. And who can blame you. God, Keva, isn't she gorgeous?'

Keva smiled his sympathy.

'I'm fine. Honest,' growled Evie, in a strangely manly voice. '*Faaan*'. There were traces of Yorkshire, traces of honey and traces of whisky in there. Her eyes, for all their soft-hard beauty, were glassy. Maybe she was bored, maybe she was half drunk.

'Can I get you something?'

She smiled for the first time, a mischievous, comely smile which betrayed all her knowledge of all her power over men. Keva had not known such an instant, intense attraction. He was burning up for her.

'Out of here'd do for starters.'

He laughed. 'Yeah. Me too. Let's go somewhere.'

Still her eyes flattered and belittled him. 'Where you gonna take me, darlin'? We gonna walk in the woods? Find a little cottage?'

Lickle. The way she said it made him love her. A big, massive love rocked him back out of nowhere. Her eyes stared wide, then her lips softened as her face broke into an enraptured, mocking grin. Keva was helpless. 'Well, fuck, I don't mind where we go. Let's just go . . .'

She observed him slowly, looked him over from head to toe. 'You the singer, yeah?'

'Sort of,' said Keva, looking down. 'I think I'm more the Turn.'

She smiled at him again. 'Come on. There's a pianner over there. Let's go an' bother 'em.' She paused and laughed silently at him. 'Mr Turn.'

He liked her too. His face conceded defeat. 'Don't be giving me any smoky fucking torch songs, though,' he whispered as they mounted the tiny joanna. 'First hint of Billie Holiday and I'm out of here. Clearing orff, that is!'

She cackled generously, doubling herself over so that Keva could see the fine curve of the spine rippling under her tight black skin. In homage to Wheezer, they led with 'Moon River' and 'High Hopes', then Keva brought the house down with 'My Kinda Town', changing 'Chicago' for 'Hamsterley'. Evie winked at him and began a theatrical warble. 'Thad ole-ah a-dev-ill call *luvvagen* . . .'

Keva groaned and grinned and pulled contorted faces of horror. She could sing. They sang until they were bored of it, earning a standing ovation from Kitty's friends and local curmudgeons alike. Their reward was a ride back to Hamsterley in the comfort of Kitty's Explorer.

*

He was only sleeping lightly when the knock came. He'd been up there an hour or so, thinking about Evie, thinking about Kitty, thinking about Hannah, frustrating himself. He took his mind away, wondering what Ibiza would be like, hoping he'd find Syd. He didn't think he could've done his relationship with Magic Number any harm by coming up here with Kitty, but perhaps he ought to be less approachable in future. You wouldn't just get Thom Yorke to come up for the weekend like that. He wondered if Syd'd have heard word of the Grams, hoping he'd be proud of his protégé. Things were good. He had things to look forward to. That, for now, was to be his definition of living – to always have a thing to look forward to.

He'd left the toffs and the luvvies downstairs playing whist and charades and backgammon. Evie seemed to forget him once they got back to the Hamsterley pile, immersing herself in a silly game of postman's knock. Keva felt a childish urge to join in but a more powerful one to exclude himself. He went up to bed unnoticed. He expected someone or other to come knocking at his door in the dead of night, and only hoped it would not be Smith, with the hammer.

It wasn't so much a knock, when it came, as someone trying the doorknob, repeatedly, shaking the door, unable or unwilling to twig that it was locked. He climbed down from the bed, a drop of some four feet, and went to the door. The big brass key gave a reassuring clunk as he unlocked. Evie stood shivering in red T-shirt and knickers looking tiny, scared and lovely.

'Come in. What's up?'

He went across to the fire and stoked up the remains, throwing a firelighter on top and holding a candle to the glow until it took. He passed the lit candle to Evie then rummaged in the wood basket for the biggest, driest logs, hurling them manfully on to the kindling. He could see the goose bumps on her shiny legs. 'There now. Come on. Sit down and tell me . . . What's the matter?'

She hesitated as Keva slumped down into the sumptuous couch, perching primly on the edge of the seat. Keva put his arms around her and drew her shaking, waiflike body to him. 'It's OK. I'll just hold you.' He pointed his pelvis away from her.

'Can you hear it?' murmured Evie.

'No. Hear what?'

Far away in the distance came a faint whooping, followed by a thwarted engine noise, like a car stuck tight in the mud, revving and roaring bluntly.

'That! Listen!'

He listened. There was a definite noise of the engine backfiring repeatedly, like gunshot. Worse, was the eerie sound which followed, a dismal, defeated, terrified wailing, like an animal drowning. It was hard to tell what it was, or where it came from. Keva pictured Kitty's crowd of funsters getting bogged down on a midnight streak, sinking hopelessly into the swamps of the forest as a lone jeep tried to tug them out.

'Owls.'

'That weren't fucking owls!'

'Well, something like that . . . It'll just be country sounds. Don't worry about it.'

'I don't like it. It don't sound right.'

'D'you want me to go and have a look?'

She stiffened. 'No! Don't leave me! Just stay here, with me.' She gazed up at him with white, freaked-out eyes. 'Please?'

Keva smiled down kindly at her. 'Sure.'

He stroked her head and blew on her neck and told her harmless ghost stories about lovelorn headless ladies who haunt the fields and graveyards at night, looking for their loved ones so that they can come at last to rest. She nestled into him, barely breathing at first, those extravagant cheekbones heightened by the weird glow from the hearth. Then she was snoring gently, her lovely head on his stomach, long, thin, shining legs draped over the edge of the couch. She was exquisite. He loved her.

He eased himself from underneath her and hobbled, numb in one leg, to turn back the sheets on the near side of the bed. He carried Evie, wisp light, to the bed and tucked her in. He sat awhile, wide awake now, and watched her sleep. His senses warred, the fond, loving, protective instinct flailing against the red impulsion of desire.

He brought candles from the bathroom and the window-sill and placed them on the cabinet beside the bed, lighting each from the twig he detached from a firelighter. The light anointed her

182

sleeping face. He kissed her forehead lightly and went around to the other side of the bed. He got in and faced away from her but, unable to rest, wrapped his arms around her and sighed deeply. She stirred a little and muttered something, troubled, now, in her repose. As quickly as the storm blew up, it subsided, and she wriggled against Keva, finding her comfort again.

He could find no ease, and lay there on his back, pondering and planning until his mind ached. Evie purred and gave a sharp, childish giggle. Keva smiled and leant up on one elbow. Her face, her brow tightened, the sighs becoming rhythmic, deep and wanting. She bit her bottom lip and lifted her hips, gasping with the incline. Keva groaned. No, no, no. He lifted the sheets back. A coin-sized signal of moisture betrayed the mound of her knickers. He put his hand there. He left it there, on top, tasting the tense dryness at his throat.

'Mmm.' Not even a word, but it swept all uncertainty, all misunderstanding from Keva's conflicting conscience. She was saying: 'Do it.'

He rolled the knickers down, sensitised, feeling every moment, every next caress. He wanted to be more gentle, to do this more slowly, but her fineness made him on fire. He couldn't stop. He had to do this. It was so wrong, he knew it . . . but he had to. He pulled her flimsy shirt over her head, kissing around the smooth, dark brown of the aureolas and, letting out a terrible groan of relief he pushed inside her, eyes wild, sucking, bucking, out of all control.

Keva lay there, trying to remain relaxed, keeping his eyes closed and his breathing rhythmical as she traced his vertebrae with her tongue. First light arrowed through the slit in the heavy drapes and drilled his flickering face. Her lips massaged the base of his spine, one hand cupping his balls, the other working his dick. He lay still, loving her touch, wanting to turn to her, afraid to. What had he done to this girl? He couldn't make himself think about what had happened there, hours ago. He lay tense, mortified, his dick dead.

She relented, the hiss of thwarted desire felling Keva lower. She squirmed and turned and tutted next to him, demanding his response. He made a big deal of coming round. He forced some expansive waking sounds, stretched and faced her, smiling. 'Hello, you. What *you* doing here.'

'Thought *you* could tell me,' she murmured, circling his nipple with a bony finger, lowering her eyelids and sliding the sole of a foot down his thigh. Released from the dread that he was her rapist, he appreciated her anew, reaching out to stroke her bony shoulders. Her smell, the sweat of sex rubbed into the musky perfume, fanned a distant stirring desire in him. She kissed him, her easy-burning sensuality transmitting itself, awakening him. They kissed deeply, Evie's strong tongue mastering Keva's as she fought to please him. He pulled away, aroused by her aggression, kissing down the supple muscle-board of her stomach and flicking at her hip bone. He felt her tense as he nuzzled the fragrant wisp of her bush.

'No! Not there . . .'

He stopped. She sighed and let her body relax again. She jumped out of the bed and dragged back the weight of the curtains.

'Sorry . . .'

He propped himself on his elbow, only more intoxicated, more curious for her.

'Come on! Let's get out of here before all the toffs get up. Let's go and explore!'

He responded to a childishness in her which he scarcely felt.

'Let's rob one of them Range Rovers and razz off into the countryside!'

'Come on then!' yelled Keva, clapping his hands, and rolling himself off the bed. They pulled on clothes and ran downstairs.

Finding a way out into the grounds through the kitchen and scullery, they were unprepared, utterly, for their findings. Defining a sparkling baize lawn was a mouldy stone balustrade with steps dissecting an incline into a wilder grassy paddock and woodland beyond. The furthest reaches of the paddock were churned to brown by savage tyre burns and it was in these deep ruts that a heap of gaping dead sheep lay. On the stomach of each of the slaughtered sheep was a daubed red Anarchy symbol, some made illegible by ruptured guts, blackened blood and the colonies of flies now congregated on the hardening offal. Their happy hunters had turned each victim on its side so the target, the capital A enclosed in an unsteady circle, could be seen by Kitty's guests. This was what they'd heard last night – the Oaf and his bloods out on a screaming drunk, using the stupid sheep as target practice, out to let Kitty know whose home she was squatting. They were in the company of the deranged noblesse.

Evie held her hand over her mouth, eyes boggling, unable to look away. She started to sob. Keva put an arm round her shoulder and pulled her tight into him.

'Come on,' he said. 'Let's get out of this sickhouse.'

'Nice car,' croaked Keva for the sixteenth time in a couple of hours. He gripped the seat between his legs, terrified. Yet again she hurtled towards the tailgate of the car in front at mind-curdling speed and lurched out to overtake at the last possible moment, without ever indicating, seemingly oblivious to traffic in the other lanes approaching from the rear at pace. He was starting to put all his trust in the car, a rip-snorting BMW Z3, which seemed impregnable. No matter how erratically Evie drove, the car seemed up to the task of delivering them safely through the ravages of the M1.

'*He* give it me,' she'd said.

'Who?' asked Keva. But that was twenty minutes ago. The CD, M-People's *Bizarre Fruit*, ended. He was thankful for little mercies. The voice of Heather Small from M-People was one of the handful that could propel him from his deathbed to turn off the radio. That self-consciously crazed-out range and the sound of her warbling through a mouthful of marbles made him mad. So senseless was he rendered by Evie's driving that he'd been barely aware of the extramural pain of M-People until the last track faded immodestly into the new afternoon. Nothing else came on in its place.

'Well – he didn't so much *give* it me, but he's never asked for it back.'

'Who?'

'I can use it whenever . . .' She put all the emphasis on the *can* and the *when*. 'Ah can youwse it when-ever.'

Keva decided not to pursue it. He'd made up his mind to get her to drop him outside Leeds, which was only another fifteen miles away. Another sign came up. Evie sighed wearily, her shoulders slumping with the exhalation. She looked at Keva, making up her mind.

'I used to go with this rich guy. I were right fond of him – we were really into each other. He wanted me to marry him an' that. His old man were dead set against it. Used to have me tailed all the time. Real lairy blokes with them fat blue noses, you know, like real boozers have. They started giving me money to stay away from him. Good money like, an' then he just fouckin disappeared anyway, so I were on money for nowt. I'll tell you now, I were on gear, all sorts, I needed it, like, the cash. His dad, like, this rich bloke's dad . . .' She stopped. Keva was expecting tears, but when he caught a look at Evie she was erect and clear-eyed. '. . . well . . . *he* started fuckin me for a while. Dirty old cunt. Said he'd look after me. He did, too. He were a fuckin randy old cunt, always used to just turn up with an 'ard on. Had me in a flat in Knightsbridge, only a cupboard of a place, like, but nice, porter in a uniform an' that . . .' She smiled to herself. '. . . had all his dirty old mates round, all getting into me, wanking themselves off and saying things an' stuff . . .'

Keva was all ears. Leeds came and went at high speed, his dick forced out at a right angle against the thick denim of his jeans.

'. . . I dunno if he got bored of me, or the heat were off with his lad or what, you know? He stopped coming up. The old fella. I didn't really know what to do. I were getting panicky, like. What if he ain't paying the rent? One of the others asked us to marry him, so I just thought, yeah, all right. He's not old, this one. I dunno if he's a poof or what, but I don't have to do owt. Drive round Gloucester in his cars, spend his money, turn up with him at the odd party in a nice frock. He fuckin worships me. Other blokes, like – they want to use me. He don't. Haven't seen him for six weeks . . .'

She started shrieking with laughter, shaking her head and laughing really hard. Keva joined in. 'Good marriage . . .'

'Oh, aye. Made in heaven.'

Keva eyed her sadly, this lonely, abused, unloved beauty and his heart went out to her. 'Aren't you . . . don't you get . . .'

'Bitter?'

'I was going to put it stronger than that. It's awful.'

'It's what I'm used to. I've never known nothing else.'

'Me neither.'

She turned to hold his look. 'Whatever you've been through, believe me, it's nothing.'

He wanted to argue with her, but she was right. He wanted to glamorise his pain, make her pity him and love him. She seemed to guess what it was with him, and she was hardened to him. She seemed to want to belittle his suffering. In the most singsong, matter-of-fact way, she told him her father had tried to circumcise her. Only half succeeded. She got away. Ran away.

'Jesus!' He felt sick. Not nauseous, but weak, empty, gutless. 'Where did you . . .'

'Down here. Ever since.' She bit down on her lip a little, but otherwise she showed no emotion.

'The bastard . . .!'

'No. I didn't understand at the time. It's almost . . . it's not that unusual in Somalia.'

'Fuck! You poor kid . . .' He looked at her with tears in his eyes. 'That's why you . . . this morning?'

She nodded. 'Men have been taking from me all my life.'

'No! Not all men are like that . . .!'

'You are.' She looked over at him, then back at the road ahead. Keva folded plans of getting out at all. His face was burning up.

'I . . . I was in love with you. I was feeling something for you. It's not the same.'

'No. You just took. It's the same.' She shook her head, no melodrama, chewing her bottom lip. 'It's all right. It's what I'm for, innit?'

He hung his head. 'I'm so sorry . . . I . . .'

Again the parakeet laugh. 'Don't fuckin shit yourself! I liked it! I'm just saying . . . that's life, like. You can't let things get to you. Don't fuck around feeling sorry for yourself. It's writ all over you.'

He shook his head in half-admiring, half-despairing disbelief. She couldn't alter the way he saw the world, the way he felt about

himself with one stern lecture, but he felt humbled by it. He had a
lot to feel good about. The remainder of the drive to London
flashed by with Evie's candid and witty replies to Keva's gently
prurient inquisition. She made her tragic, astonishing life sound
run-of-the-mill. She only faltered when she started into telling
him more about her father and her uncles – and she quickly
changed the subject. She stuck out her breasts as she drove and
laughed: 'These, right . . . without these I'd probably be dead.
Now that *would* be a shame, 'cos I'm having a ball . . .'

She was unconvincing. He didn't know if he was in love with
her. He was in awe of her. He didn't feel worthy. But the thought
of her leaving him later in the day, driving off to reprise her sham
marriage in the back of beyond was starting to hurt him. He was
going to Ibiza in two days. Maybe she'd stick around that long.
She'd be fantastic as a rock star's girl. Maybe he could show her
how it is to be loved by someone. Maybe he could find out
something about himself too – the self he was now. She eyed him,
weighing him up. 'Come on, then. There's somewhere I want to
show you.'

As the heat went out of the sun and the sky began to frazzle white
around the edges, they stood quiet on the Hornsey Lane bridge,
high above Archway, drinking in the heavenly aspect of London.
Canary Wharf glinted and shone with a melancholy unexpected
from such a proud, hard, modernity. The dome of St Paul's,
Tower Bridge, the Houses Of Parliament – all seemed close
enough to blow into the river, yet it seemed perverse, exhilarating
and at once completely odd, for these things, these adornments of
history, to be now in Keva's life. They were real. He had his own
relationship with them.

'I used to come up here all the time when I first come to
London. I used to have a bedsit in Tetherdown Road – just got on
first bus from King's Cross and got off when the tower blocks
stopped an' it were more trees an' that . . . nicer-looking place. I
found this card in the post office, like, advertising studio flat . . .'

She laughed. She'd transformed back into a frightened, hopeful
schoolgirl, some of her innocence still intact. He could see how she

must have been, back then. How could anyone do that to her? How could they do it to anyone?

'Studio flat! It were fuckin smaller than Barbie's house!' She broke off, staring out at the grand urban vista. 'It's fantastic, innit?'

Keva nodded. To his right was Highgate Cemetery. Every grave in there was more famous than he'd ever be. He was small, but he was feeling all right again.

'Makes you feel like you're *nowt*. Dunnit? It's like . . . you're *powder*.' Keva laughed and nodded. 'Definitely gives you a sense of yourself in the big scheme of things.'

He closed his eyes and nodded enthusiastically. 'Powder, eh? I think you're right. Ashes to ashes, powder to powder. That's what our guitarist says. You'd like him. He's as mad as you are . . .'

She stared straight ahead, straight on through the blood-melon sun, sucking it all in. 'I used to stand up here and . . . I can remember now exactly what I were thinking. I were thinking . . .' She checked herself to be sure that Keva was sympathetic. He inclined his head, encouraging her. '. . . if the right bloke were to come along, just a nice, ordinary bloke, nowt fancy . . . and just . . . *look after me* . . .' She turned and faced Keva, the haunting eyes searching all over his face. She seemed totally alone. To Keva, she seemed like she was still waiting to be born. He saw himself, sitting on the step outside the house.

Let me in!

He went to hold her, but she took a step back and gazed out over London again, lost to him.

'What?' said Keva.

She shook her head. He saw the trouble come back to her eyes and he knew he had not the strength to take it away for her. He had neither the strength nor, right now, the time. He had himself to consider, first. As he was realising this, she seemed to know it already. She straightened up from the railing and took a lusty draught of dirty north London air.

'Well, Mr Pop Star,' she smiled, not unkindly, looking him up and down. 'Ta for all that. Maybe I'll see you around . . .'

He didn't try to stop her as she made her way back to the parked car.

*

As soon as they stepped off the plane, the dazzling white heat rocked them back on their heels. The thin air, putrid with diesel, scalded their faces. Outside, the airport signs told out the polyglottal schizophrenia of the island – Ibiza. Eivissa. Ibica. The years and centuries of invasion and occupation by a dozen simmering cultures – Romans, Moors, Venetians, Carthaginians – left this Mediterranean paradise with two faces – Madness and Serenity – and one language: Hedonism. Tony could feel it the moment the Disco Bus nosed gingerly out of the airport.

It was a Disco Bus from the moment they boarded. Ostensibly a People Carrier, this Seat eight-seater was a glorified minibus. But its sound system rocked. Adam, already on the island two days for pre-shoot location recces, picked the group up from the milling arrivals hall and marched them out to the Seat, where Libby, his producer, had the engine running and the cassette deck thumping. Sash, David Morales, Stardust, Mousse-T – a seamless splice of whomping summer pre-releases had them bouncing in their seats, fists in the air, smiles on faces. Even Beano was grinning. The party was on.

'Fackin Eye-beef-ah!', giggled Adam, fucked. Everyone high-fived him and tweaked his nipples, trying to take in the dusty, surprisingly hilly terrain.

Libby got into fourth gear and dropped her head down to light a fag, nearly smacking into the back of a donkey and cart, ridden at lugubrious pace by an expressionless, black-clad *paysan*.

Adam gurned comically at the troops. 'Thing about Libby, yeah? She can't fucking drive. She fucking definitely can't produce! But she can you get into any club, anywhere in the world, eh, babe . . . ? And as for the drugs . . . don't even bother asking! She'll have 'em in your mitts before you've even finished thinking the thought . . . Eh? Libbs? Eh!'

She shook her head, patiently. 'Don't take any notice of this lunatic. In case you hadn't noticed he's been up all night, wallowing in foam. Very responsible . . .'

'*Clockwork Orange* party, man! Es Paradis. Too fucking much! Fuck! You wanna feel them foamy bubbles prickling and popping against the back of your neck when you're on a tablet, man! I must've come about thirteen times and I weren't even *wiv* no one . . .'

Libby rolled her eyes. She had a boyish crop, slim figure, dark eyes, pretty. It was impossible to know how old she was. She dressed young, but her voice was hacked deep from years of nicotine. 'It's my lucky lot to get a fucking broadcastable video out of these next three days, so ignore this dickhead. I'm here to make your lives hell! I want you all in bed by midnight, tonight? Wake-up call's eight o'clock for an eight thirty leave? Shoot starts at ten?'

Australian. Or New Zealand. Strident.

'If you want to be in your first-ever video, chaps, I'd advise you all to be good boys, tonight . . .' She allowed herself a sly titter and watched in the mirror as their faces fell. She couldn't keep it up. She and Adam bumped shoulders with each other and burst into stammering peals of hilarity.

'Cockney bastards!'

Adam turned round to face them all again. He was twatted. His eyes were on fire. 'Ain't she the fuckin tits? Ain't life fuckin' unbearable!' He starting rotating Libby's breasts with the palms of his hands, an activity she resisted politely and resolutely. 'Jesus God, what a fucking *honey*! I *lavvah*! Wait till you see her arse, Mr Love. The arse is fucking choice . . .'

Libby whacked him, quite hard, in the face, and pointed at him, warningly. James found himself willing the arrival of Santa Eulalia even more fervently, the better to arse-clock the gamine Libby.

It wasn't quite the Ibecinco idyll they'd been hoping for. It wasn't even a villa. But it wasn't bad. A collection of two-storey, cottage-style apartments gathered around a cute, figure-of-eight-shaped pool. The band and the video crew had colonised three adjoining apartments at the remotest point of the small complex.

Childishly excited, Beano was running around in his shorts, concave chest smeared with factor 25. 'Come 'ead. Let's hit the beach! Let's go in the pool! Let's explore . . .'

'Jesus! Give us a second, will you? I haven't even unpacked . . .' Tony Snow was a great unpacker and folder of clothing, no matter how short the stay.

'I'll see you down there!' shouted Beano, and ran down the short flight of steps, straight into the arms of the waiting Libby.

'Set a thief to catch a thief,' she laughed. 'Any more of you naughty boys planning to do a runner?'

'Er . . .'

The paella was lip-smackingly good. Made with fine noodles and charcoal-black squid's ink, the enormous cast-iron dish in the centre of the table was emptied by ravenous Grams and had to be refilled. Libby ran through the agenda, and gave them their options.

'What's left of the daytime is yours. The hippie market's on today over at Es Cana – it's only a ten-minute drive away. What Mr Rice wants to do, as I understand it, if he's capable of giving direction at the moment, is to follow you around with Super 8 and some time-lapse stock, flash guns, that sort of thing, and just squirt away *au naturel*. So, maybe if you want to hire mopeds, shoot off into the hills, that might be good. Whatever. As for this evening, I know I'm wasting my time telling you not to cane it too much . . . yes, James?'

'Why are all efficient people Aussies an' that?'

She rolled her eyes and continued. 'Because we like to *punish* naughty boys! May I . . . ? Good. As I was trying to say, tomorrow is such a mega important day. I'd *love* an early start. I'll settle for midday. I'll be really upset with you all if you lose it tonight? There'll be plenty of opportunity for madness . . . but tomorrow we want to break the back of this promo so that we *can* enjoy the next few days, yeah?'

Everyone nodded. Tony was falling for her. He just loved the way she talked down to them, liked a teacher.

'Now, I know that Keva and Mr Finlay are going to try and find his old long-lost mentor this evening. I've a feeling they may find him down the Café Del Mar round about sundown. Again, if we could get all of you down there, that'd be cool. There's some nice sunset shots to be had down there . . . whatever, I'd like you to check in with me regularly. I've given each of you a card with the mobile number on, so there's no excuse for going missing. So –

whatever you decide to do, meet back here at seven this evening, yeah? Cool. Thanks, guys.'

They immediately scattered in different directions. Beano and Tony simply legged it, before they were called back to perform any serious duties. James and Adam loped over to the moped hire.

'Anyone for the hippie market?' asked Libby.

Keva and Wheezer looked at each other. Keva really wanted to go. But he wanted to be talked into it.

'It's not, like, a market you know. It's cool. I'm only popping over to firm up tomorrow with a couple of the girls who live up in the hills. And to get some dope.'

Keva shrugged his consent. They jumped up into the Disco Bus and set off, bouncing to Faithless.

Adam kept a precarious grip around James's waist with one arm, while he stood on the flimsy stirrups and shot slo-mo footage of the staggering hills and ravines from the moped.

'Just a bit slower, mate. Sorry. It ain't like me to ask anyone to go slower, but I just want to get this . . . see how the sun keeps popping out from the side of the mountains, yeah? Always a different perspective, man. Gorgeous. Fucking gorgeous.'

It was, too. The sunlight was fluoride white up there in the mountains. It eluded them constantly, travelling always away from them at incomprehensible speed, hiding behind peaks then splintering out in fractious, blinding bolts.

'Wheeeeee!' gasped Adam. 'Fucking magic! Pure fucking magic!' He wrapped himself around James, doubling back to be certain of his shots. If he was a nutter, he was a nutter who loved his work.

When he finally ran out of stock, they pulled over for a smoke. Adam was breathless, euphoric. 'I'll tell you something, man. That light was fucking divine! It was religious! If that comes out how I hope and pray it's going to come out . . . oh, man – what a film this is gonna be . . .'

James lay back and toked on his full-strength, declining Adam's fat spliff. They were silent for a minute, no more, when Adam leapt up.

'Hey! D'you play backgammon?'

'I do, as a matter of fact,' smiled James. 'I happen to play backgammon superbly.'

'Fantastic! Come on, crank her up – we're gonna kill two birds with one stone, here. Hah! The Rock! Tablets and backgammon all under one roof. What more could a chap ask for? Giddy-up, James! The Rock Bar. And don't spare the horses!'

Wheezer couldn't stop staring at her. Her skin was clearer, more shimmering than the posh birds' at Ticky's party. It looked like caramel-brown silk, stretched fine across her delicate bones. And her smile. She sat there cross-legged on the ground with Libby, smiling and laughing, bare brown legs exposed as her sarong hitched back.

She'd been introduced to them as Lotte. Keva betrayed the depth of his attraction by filtering off on his own, pretending to be an untouchable. But Wheezer stayed on, browsing her stall, feigning interest. He couldn't excusably buy another length of purple cheesecloth. He'd already taken three pieces at exorbitant prices for non-existent relatives. These Ibiza hippies had replaced free love with the free market, it seemed, though Wheezer was happy to help finance Lotte's Balearic dream.

She was from Holland. She lived up in the village of San Miguel. 'Not the resort,' she kept laughing.

There was quite a community up there, she explained, people from all over the world sharing resources, skills, philosophies. Libby knew all that, but she let her carry on, nodding her encouragement. Lotte and her sister had been there three years, though her sister was on the mainland just now, buying material. Wonder what *she* looks like, mused The Wheeze.

'It's nice and mellow, you know? We don't bother nobody. We just . . . *live*.'

She tinkled her laugh again. Wheezer loved the sound of San Miguel already. Would they accept him? Could he fit in? Probably not. But it'd be nice to be part of a community. A family. Maybe he could offer an Internet service? But they'd already have one. Hippies are always the first to any new technology – anything that makes life less complicated, at least.

'Is everything OK, Visa?' she said, looking up at him with concern. He was still gawping at her.

'Mm? Oh, yes. Fine. Cool.'

She smiled beautifully at him. He'd been dribbling. 'Good.'

He slapped his hands together in embarrassment, like Basil Fawlty about to make another gaffe. 'Well!' he almost chanted. 'I suppose that wraps things up, for now. Libby?'

'Yep. I'm cool.'

'Grand!' he smiled. 'Well, erm, Lotte. Thanks . . .'

Then he did something he wished he had not. He took her hand and kissed it. She stood there, watching him do it, concern etched on her brow. Seeing her misapprehension, Wheezer reddened. 'Erm . . . well. I guess we'll see you tomorrow.'

He turned quickly and made off. He didn't see the smile between Lotte and Libby, he missed her making an 'aaah' face and mouthing the word 'sweet', and he didn't see her watching them walk away back to the Disco Bus.

'We can't just park here . . .'

'Course we can. This is Ibiza.'

Libby turned off the ignition and, with it, her much-requested Eurocheese compilation. Tony was besotted with that ecstatic keyboard hook on 'You're Not Alone', which Libby seemed to have, in a variety of mixes, on all of her tapes. She jumped out and, slowly, everyone else followed. Everyone else except James and the director, who had not returned.

They were parked right across the forecourt of a dirty, two-pump filling station in the chaotic backstreets of San Antonio. Libby headed off at a jaunty pace, with Wheezer struggling to keep up and the others happy just to keep them in sight.

As soon as they ambled down on to the balmy terrace of Café Del Mar, Tony fell in love with the chilled-down stasis of the place. He felt a warm, engulfing familiarity, an instant empathy with the slow-moving karma of it all. There were all kinds of people. A few of the hippyish, dreadlocked Balearics they'd seen around, dressed in outrageous striped or purple silk pantaloons, tied at the waist with a drawstring, sandals on filthy feet. Lissom Scandinavians in sarongs. Silent, well-dressed Spaniards in shades, next to stoned, happy British clubbers. Everyone was sitting back, talking, playing chess, browsing week-old newspapers, but most of all they watched. They just looked out to sea, dreaming or thinking nothing at all, seeing whatever they wanted to see.

He felt a lovely slow invasion of comfort, a general satiation as he sat down and said nothing and let his eyes accustom themselves to the spangling light slanting in off the sea. The crew headed over to the rocks to shoot scenic cutaways, while Beano waited to order drinks. Libby and Keva were at the far end of the bar, talking with a white-haired guy. Tony let his head drop down against the backrest as he slid low in the chair, legs stretched out, enjoying the healing glow of the late evening sun.

'Yiiiiss! Is right an' that! Mr Love cleans up again!'

Drowsy café society tilted their heads, lifted their shades, more curious than perturbed to know what would make a person shout in a place like this, on a night like this. Down below, spread out like salamanders on a flat rock in front of the café, Adam and James were crouched over a backgammon board. Tony closed his eyes, shutting them out, trying to regain his state of bliss. They'd all meet up soon enough. For now, the gently dappling sea and the slow infusion of sounds and senses was all he needed.

He heard the gritty grind of the beer bottle as Beano placed it before him, on to the sand-dusted table top. He pictured the cool droplets running down the icy glass bottleneck, the green glass still misty from the refrigerator. He wanted to stay in his dreamlike cocoon, but he could almost taste the beer. If there was a time and a place for fancy bottled lager, it was here and now. He blinked an eye open, to see Beano lifting a large frosted glass to his lips, see him sipping at a lurid pale orange concoction, see him smack his lips together and lick the remnant stains of juice.

'Fuck's that?'

'Mm? Peach juice. Delicious. Want to try some?'

'Noooo!' Tony sat up and held his bottle protectively. He eyed up Beano's glass again and laughed. ''Kinell, Al! We've only been here a few hours and you're drinking Wham cocktails! Club Tropicana!'

Beano laughed. 'Libby got it for us. You should try it. Fresh peach juice.'

'No voddy?'

'Nothing.'

'You surprise and dismay me.'

Beano drained the glass theatrically and winked. 'Ay! There's James and Adam! JAMES! ADAM!' He whistled shrilly. Tony could feel the lazy gaze of the terrace burning into the back of his neck.

'Leeverpool Seed? Of course! Hay-verry body know Leeverpool Seed. He here sometime now. I tell the lady another day. I no remember.'

A surge of terrorised anticipation shot through him. Breakthrough. They'd chatted up the erudite old phoney at the bar without joy. He was happy to tell them about his art collection, his influence on all the key town and country planning boards, his award-winning architecture and the nightclubs he'd designed in Ibiza, Majorca, Tenerife – but Syd? No. He didn't think he knew this guy.

Libby went off to quieten down the boys, while Keva got talking to the young lad collecting bottles and washing glasses. He knew Syd. The bloke with the white hair disappeared behind a huge green football newspaper, full of Spain's shame in the World Cup.

'OK, team. Synchronise watches for a nine o'clock drop, yeah?'

They all nodded. Tony had already made up his mind he was going to clench his in his fist and pretend to swallow it. He didn't fancy it. He sensed he didn't need it, here. He was happy with the Cruzcampo, which was going down a treat.

'It's five to. Let's stock up on water and that. Come on, Libs, you up for it?'

'I suppose so, if I must. But I'm only obeying orders, you understand . . .'

'We better neck these. Sunset in half an hour. OK, everybody?'

Keva nodded more enthusiastically than anybody. He had no

intention of doing a tablet. Not like this, anyway, in a big gang, under pressure to have a good time.

'We all havin' it? Niiiiiice one! OK ladies and gentlemen . . . five . . . four . . . three . . .' Adam was a hoot, but he was getting on Keva's tits already. He was like some garish Ebeneezer Goode, in your face the whole time, driving everybody on – on one, up for it, mad for it, top one. Heaven knows. He'd be having it large before the night was out. '. . . ONE-AH . . . AND . . .' He started whooping like a Canvey Island soulboy. Hands darted to mouths, heads went back throats gulped and adam's apples vaulted. People said 'aaah' and wiggled eyebrows at each other.

'Can I have another beer, please?' asked Tony.

The sunset was spellbinding. Great swathes of purple and orange and pink rent the horizon as the staggering red sun bled into the sheet-silver sea. Keva and Syd sat away from the café, on a rocky outcrop, silent for the first time since the shattering realisation of the reunion. They'd both long become accustomed to the Hi-8 video camera perched on the tripod in front of them.

'I still can't get my head round it.' Syd broke off to watch the last of the sun's demise, throwing his pungent, riotous dreads and sighing as though to acknowledge his insignificance. 'It beats me every time. How can this place, this calm, peaceful, fucking paradise, this Garden of Eden . . .' He looked Keva in the eye, '. . . be privy to such *madness*?' His face blistered slowly into a sulphurous grin. 'Whatcha think, kidder? Do you know anything, yet? Do you *know* anything?'

They sat and talked until it was too cold down there. They remembered funny little things. Keva recalled Syd's school rucksack, with a florid Yes logo painted one week, a louche ELP the next. His favourite was the Camel design. It always seemed remote and impossible to Keva, the key to a world he could never inhabit. Syd could remember how Keva would pick up his guitar, dwarfed by the sheer size of it, holding it left-handed at first.

'You could play anything, lar. It used to leave me stunned. I'd play you, like, something easy. "The Clap". "Tangerine". And you'd just have them down, just like that. So I'd give you something harder. I remember sticking on "Paint It Black" and you started playing along. Had it off perfect, lar. Uncanny. Started doing me 'ead in. I thought, like, I'll give him something impossible. "Rhayader". "The Gates Of Delirium". Stuff that wasn't wrote for the guitar. But you'd ignore the instrumentation, cut right through to the basic chords and – bang! You had it. You had it, man . . .'

He shook his head. Keva winked at his old hero. 'You had some shite records, Syd.'

They both laughed fully. 'I had some fucking epics too. Still have, I hope . . . ?'

Keva nodded. Syd put his hands into a praying position, flats of feet together in a sort of lotus, scooping out sand from between his legs. He looked up at Keva again.

'That's why I wanted you to have 'em, lar. I knew you could do it. I *knew* you had it. If only you'd *let* yourself do it. If only *they'd* let you . . .' He broke off. Keva felt an uneasy black stirring in his soul. It was something awful, so bad that he killed it back down before he would let himself know it.

'You cold, mate?'

He must've been shivering. 'Bit.'

'Come 'ead. We'll round up the others. Go to Café Mambo. Madonna's meant to be in tonight.'

Tony took another long slug of Cruzcampo. Was this really *lager*? He loved it. He absolutely loved the taste and the sensation of the icy golden tendrils gushing down his throat. He liked to have a lot of the beer in his mouth, a hefty gobful, so he could really taste it and swallow it hard, feel like he was *drinking*. He must have had, what? Twelve bottles? At least. And he was steel-eyed sober, lapping up the liberated frenzy of the club. Beano, Tony, Keva, Wheezer and Libby were standing in a group, only slightly aware of themselves, nodding their heads minutely to show that they appreciated the music. Adam bounced over, pie-eyed.

'Yeeeees! Yeeeees! Look at Mr Love!'

James was dancing with two girls, slim as silhouettes, gyrating their long, tanned limbs, twisting their arms and fluctuating their lithe midriffs like rain-dancers.

'Look at him go! Ain't these tablets the tits?'

'Mad!' agreed Tony, widening his eyes madly and gurning.

'Bonkers!' added Beano, nodding to the music more energetically.

'Milanos!' beamed Adam, pulling out another capsule. 'Fucking the tits! Can't get 'em any more . . .'

They exchanged puzzled glances.

'You still on one, boys?'

'Oh! Large!' spluttered Tony. 'Largein'.'

'Substantial!'

'Hefty!'

'Wih-kidd!' grinned Adam, making an impressive cicada-click with his fingers. He kissed each of them on both cheeks and danced off back towards James and the twig women. Keva made a face of relief at the others. 'Too much, him! How d'you put up with it, Libs?'

'Ah, he's just a baby! He's harmless.'

Tony swooned at her authoritarian dismissiveness. 'I can't imagine ever being that . . . *high*, like.' He turned to Keva. 'Are you er . . . is your tablet, like . . . is it working?'

'I never took mine.'

'Me neither.'

'Nor me.'

'I'm saving mine.'

'Stop! Libs! Stop now!'

She braked hard, sending the boys doubling into the backs and headrests of the seats in front. Adam grinned hugely.

'Ta.' He bounded out, eulogising. 'Yes! Yes! Oh, yes!'

He wandered over to a group of village urchins. It wasn't even a village. Just a few whitewashed, biblical dwellings and a small, shuttered grocer's. A gorgeous little girl, aged six or seven, masses of wild black hair, smiled into Adam's camera and held up her wrist.

'Look! Look!' gushed Beano, lurching towards the window.

'She's got something on her arm! It's a lizard! A little lizard!'

The kids performed like celluloid legends for Adam, holding hands, kissing, walking arm in arm.

'That's going to look great,' murmured Wheezer to himself, but loud enough to be heard.

'Bit gooey, isn't it?' said Libby.

Adam clambered back on board, elated. 'Got any change, anyone? Hundred coins? Two hundreds? Just something to give the kids, like . . .'

They collected eighteen hundred pesetas in all denominations of coin, including a five-hundred from James.

'They'll go mad on that,' he laughed. 'They'll be pinned on smack before we get the engine running!'

Wheezer, Lotte and Libby sat in the cool shade of Las Dalias, ladling piquant chilled gazpacho from painted ceramic bowls. Wheezer couldn't get enough of it. He added more croutons, more peppers, more onion from the quarterised wooden dish in the middle of the solid country table, slurping it keenly, peeping up belatedly to check whether anyone had noticed his gluttony. He hadn't left much for the others.

Only Keva was to be filmed. Beano and Tony had gone out to the cactus fields and lemon groves with them to watch. James was sitting outside with the best-looking kid in the commune, the Argentinian girl, Grass. Her eyes were an astonishing turquoise blue, her hair a wild, dirty blonde and every movement of her thirteen-year-old body was feral, fully aware of the impact she caused.

Grass was the girl Adam had seen when he was driving through, earlier in the year. It was she who inspired the concept for the video. Even now, dressed in a faded yellow sweatshirt and jeans, no cosmetics, streaks of dirt from her tears, she looked born to be a star. She was amazing to look at, and her parents knew the value of that. Mum India from San Diego and dad Juan from Buenos Aires had had her signed to a modelling agency for years. They wouldn't let her appear in the video for less than five thousand pounds. Adam had gone mad and told them to piss off back to hippie dreamland. The other girls and boys in the village were exquisite too. So Grass had to sit there, crying, with a priapic James trying to keep his mind civilised while her friends made movies in the hills.

'This sucks,' she moaned in that almost-American twang that all the kids out there seemed to have. 'D'you wanna have a ride with me?'

'Do what?'

She flashed him her scimitar smile, only half her lip curving upwards while the other glistened still.

'Wait there!' She jumped up and headed off up the dirt track to the side of the café, insouciant bottom forming two perfect cupolas in her Levis. James watched and watched, and ached when she was out of sight. She was back five minutes later, hair roaming free in the wind, ragging the clutch on her moped.

'Come on, Jaymssss!'

He hesitated, but for no time at all. Arms around her long waist, fingertips touching her smooth back he was immediately aroused, resting his head on her back to avoid the sting of the wind in his eyes. She sped hard into every bend, hitting each bump and crater with wilful force, jolting James's groin.

'Slow down!' he laughed, but his pleas were lost in the drag of the slipstream.

They stopped by a little copse, utterly in the middle of nowhere. She shook her hair at him and held out a hand. 'Come!'

They walked through the trees, under the thousand-volt siren of the crickets, to a reluctant stream. The most meagre spume bubbled over red rocks, coming to rest in a still pond below them, green from the sheltering trees. It was paradise. She peeled off her sweatshirt. Nothing underneath. A slender, delicate back and long brown arms. She didn't turn around, but he could see the coffee tips of her upturned breasts. She took her jeans off quickly and, wearing only brief white knickers, dived nimbly into the clear green lake, so neat as to hardly stir the surface. She emerged, breaking through the skin of the pond, breathless, smiling. 'Come on in! It's beautiful!'

It was. It was beautiful. Come what may, James determined that Adam would not leave the island without a slowed-down shot of this heavenly girl making that graceful dive into this limpid pool. It was the most beautiful place on earth.

'I can't swim an' that!'

'No! You lie!'

'Honest!'

She flashed such a lovable white smile that it made him want to hold her tight in his arms. Her smile mocked him. 'I'll teach you!'

She stepped out of the pool, wringing water from her hair. James summoned every resolve to keep his eyes locked into hers. She sussed it straight away.

'I'm beautiful. Look, if you want. It's normal.'

He blushed momentarily, but dropped his eyes and lingered over her. Tiny blonde hairs bristled on her thighs as the droplets dried off in the hot air. She stopped squeezing her hair.

'Do you like me?'

'You're . . . you're the most . . . I can't tell you how lovely you are.'

'So? Do you want me?'

'Oh, God, baby – do I want you? Fuck! I want to fucking eat you . . .!'

'So do it . . .'

He threw his hands up, letting his head drop, sighing out his dismay. 'You're . . . I can't. You know I can't!'

'Oh, right. Lolita. You can't have what you want. Look. I don't care. It's normal for us. If you want, fine. I'd love for us to be together. But, whatever you want . . .'

She fixed on him with those astonishing bright eyes. This girl, this woman was in front of him, all but naked, saying these things to him. His mind hurt with the passion he was pressing back. She was an adult. She knew her mind and her body. They were in a hidden place, a secret garden, miles from scornful, watchful eyes. No one would know. Nobody could ever find out.

He looked over the petulant upturn of her golden tits and turned away, back towards the moped, shaking his head.

They were lovely people. They were eager for money, for sure – too eager, perhaps, but no doubt they needed to rake it in while the sun was shining. The summer take would need to be eked out until next May.

But they were nice. Syd had assured Libby they'd have no trouble with them. He told them he was going to come up for the day, but there'd been no sign of him. Really, though, apart from the nonsense with India and Juan, they hadn't needed him. Adam was overjoyed with the footage he'd shot, though still sore about Grass.

They'd eaten a banquet in Las Dalias, all locally produced vegetables and cheeses and freshly-caught fish. Stuffed peppers and mixed rice and sardines grilled whole over charcoal sent magical aromas wafting into the purple night sky.

Juan reappeared, a slim, copper-toned gigolo in faded jeans and white cotton shirt. Every female eye followed him from the street to the café entrance. He had a decorous guitar slung over his back, which he placed on the table by Wheezer.

'Guys. I think maybe I made an ill-conceived judgement today,' he said, carefully. 'I made my little girl very unhappy and I regret that. I don't know if maybe you guys wish to come back again tomorrow . . .?' Much shrugging and consulting of faces and gradual affirmative nodding. '. . . maybe stay the night? Be our guests!'

Lotte and her friends began clapping. Wheezer, then James, then everyone clapped back.

'What we clapping for?' muttered Tony.

'Fuck knows!' Beano muttered back.

Juan sat down, rocked back the front two legs of his chair and picked up his guitar. He started picking the opening chords of 'Knockin' on Heaven's Door'. Just then, Grass made her entrance, this time Armani'd up to fuck. She wore a simple white cotton denim minidress with white ankle-strap sandals to devastating effect. James found himself clapping again as she walked in. She gave him her adorable, wonky smile and perched herself on the table corner, swinging a golden limb.

The singing was still going on after three. Keva had taught Juan the chords and the chorus to 'Beautiful', and the regulars at Las Dalias requested it time and again.

'It's so lovely,' he purred. 'To think I almost stopped my little girl being part of this.'

His little girl was feeling James under the table. 'Come on,' she whispered in his ear. 'You're hot for me . . . you can't stand it any longer!'

Wheezer saw them whispering and making eyes at each other without taking it in. He was trying to distract Lotte's attention away from Keva, who she'd been staring at all night.

'He seems so lonely,' she said at one point and, on a couple of occasions, 'So sad . . . so alone.'

'You're very intuitive,' murmured Wheezer, jealous, hoping his flattery would get her focus back.

'No,' she demurred. 'I just have too much time to think. I think too much, up here. I impose my little fantasies on to people.'

Wheezer found that concept immensely stirring. 'How do you cope out here, though? I mean, you're a sophisticated woman. I don't mean *sophisticated*, but you've come from a city. You're used to stimulation. You have needs, surely?'

'Sure. I need to eat. I can eat here,' she teased. 'I need to sleep. I need to feel safe. I live and sleep safely here. I'm happy. I'm totally, totally at peace. How many people do you know, in the city, in England, who feel safe? Hmm? They don't know it, but they're terrorised. They're scared. I can see it in *you*. You're hunched, coiled, waiting for the attack . . .'

Hippie bollocks, thought Wheezer, 'I see what you mean,' said Wheezer, straightening his back. 'I am pretty tense.' She hadn't looked at Keva for five minutes. 'That could just be stress, though. Comes with the job.'

'Comes with the city,' she persisted. 'I felt it slipping away, could feel that strain just floating away from my shoulders the day I first came out here. Don't you feel it?'

No.

'Yes. Yes I do. My asthma has hardly troubled me since we've been out here.'

'You see what I mean then? I knew then that I didn't want to live anywhere else.'

So why are you trying to push your ideology on everyone else, then? Because, you don't believe it. You're bored shitless out here and you're fleecing tourists with hippie shit because you can't face going back to Holland. You're *bloody* good-looking, though.

'Yes. I see that, now.'

She turned to face him fully. 'I've been out here all day, eating simple food, drinking, singing. I haven't even thought about my place. My place doesn't have no locks. Doesn't have no burglar alarms. I leave my possessions there, what I have, unlocked all day. I know it'll be fine when I go back. Can you say that?'

Wheezer felt a gnawing sensation of dread. Had he locked up before he left? Did he shut the office window? 'I don't worry about things like that. If it's going to happen, it'll happen.'

'Existentialist, huh?' she smiled. But she wasn't dismissive. She was interested. 'How come you're so tense, then?'

'I'm not.'

'Sure you are. It's not a criticism . . .'

Wheezer thought about it. This could clinch it. 'I think I'm still carrying a lot of un-reallocated grief from childhood.'

She leaned forward and massaged his taut brow with her thumbs. 'Wow! Yeah! I *feel* it . . .' She looked him over carefully. 'Listen, I mean, I usually charge for this but . . .' He could feel his eyes popping. '. . . why don't you come to my place with me . . .'

Yes! Yes!

'I do shiatsu. I think it could be of some real lasting benefit to you.'

Massage. Oh well. Better than nothing. He slipped out of Las Dalias with her and walked hand in hand, up the hilly track behind the café. The music below sounded magical, disembodied but eternal, as though there would always be this celebration if you passed by here again. The night was alive with bats and crickets and insects and noises, high up above in the hills. It was enchanted. They walked on and up until they could hear the singing and the merriment no more. Lotte stopped and turned to Wheezer and took hold of his face. 'You are a very attractive boy, Visa,' she said. 'I don't think you know this.'

And then she kissed him.

A similar feeling of suspended animation survived throughout the last day. Everybody was happy. Everyone was on a high. The spirit of Ibiza had infected even the most reluctant souls. A joyous moment came when, filming the diving shot with Grass out in the copse, a plodding, thrashing noise interrupted their concentration. It got nearer and nearer.

'Might be a wolf,' stammered Grass.

'D'you get 'em out here?' quibbled James, still unhappy that nine men were needed to watch the gymnastics of the love of his life. Before she could answer him, the loping figure of Syd peered out through the foliage.

'Thought you'd be here,' he grinned.

Keva and Syd finished off the sentimental journey they'd commenced on the first night, down by the sea at the Café Del Mar. Adam followed them past surreal, tree-high cacti and through groaning orchards of orange and lemon trees, firing off Super 8 from one hand and Hi-8 Video from the the other. He rotated his arms like the silhouette girls in Mambo, sweeping and panning the cameras. If this stuff came out, Keva's *e.p.* was going to be a sensation.

Back at Las Dalias, there was some debate about how their precious final evening was to be spent. Libby had to get the gear and the film back under lock and key. Adam, a lunatic genius, had worn himself out. He directed with a manic enthusiasm, losing all sense of time and place. His fair skin was tanned, stinging red, his orange hair a confusion of spikes and perspiration. He was quiet for the first time in days.

'I'll just chill here for an hour, I reckon. Just have a beer and a think.'

James just wanted to be with Grass. He could not remember feeling so strongly, so deeply for a girl. Last night he could hold out no longer and fell starving upon her, maddened with desire. He fucked her with an exaggerated, devouring lust, feeling every tremor of every scratch and thrust, but it was afterwards that his emotions precipitated this consuming, possessive need.

It was agreed that everybody would meet at the Mambo Café at ten bells. Syd had organised an *Ibiza Complet* for them. 'After Mambo it's Manumission – Madonna's coming down, apparently. Then all back to Bar M, then fun and frolics at Space. If that doesn't set you right then nothing will.'

Wheezer and Lotte went with Libby. Having stored all the equipment then driven straight on to the airport to freight all the exposed film direct to the lab for processing, they sat in the Disco Bus, checking watches aimlessly.

'We could do a tour of the island?' offered Libby. 'I've told the crew and anyone else who wants a lift that I'll pick 'em up back at base at nine. We've tons of time . . .'

Wheezer liked the sound of that.

'Have you seen Ibiza Town?'

Wheezer and Libby shrugged at each other, signalling 'why not?'

'Oh! You have to see the Old Town, Wheezer. It's nothing like anywhere else you've ever been . . .'

So they pottered around the side streets and barrios of Old Ibiza, lingering at the City Café for frozen lemon vodkas, before heading up to the ancient fort which stands guard over the port. Way down below they could make out a supple Rastafarian balanced on the furthest jut of the headland, facing the sun, enacting a poised, balletic t'ai-chi manoeuvre. He was completely naked. Even from there they could make out the substantial drop of his member.

'That's Tannit,' chuckled Lotte. 'The Sun King. He brings fertility to the island.'

'Single-handedly?'

They wandered back down past the touristic cafés of the cobbled fortress square, down tight alleyways and steep paths until Lotte ushered them down into an old bar hewn into the stone of the town. The Rock.

'This place has the best selection of vodkas in the world, man. I'm telling you. You like vodka? You won't want to leave this bar. Then we eat.'

The guy behind the bar greeted Lotte and disappeared through a tiny door with her. Wheezer found himself shot through with a suspicious malice. Libby necked her vodka and hopped down from the stool.

'Just hang on here, yeah? I'm going to just nip back up to that place we passed, buy some ceramics, yeah? I'll be twenty minutes at most.'

'No problem.'

He sat at the bar with his back to the counter, watching two suave old men playing backgammon, feeling he'd been left behind, somewhere. The old boys looked great. Crisp cotton shirts, chinos, no socks, loafers and, even indoors, raffish berets pulled low over their brow. Wheezer envied them. They'd done their bit, whatever it was they were expected to do, and now they were seeing out time in the loveliest, idlest way. Maybe Lotte was right. Maybe Ibiza would work for him. Dunno. Would he fit in? Was he cool enough? Anyway, too many things to do first.

He fiddled with the change in his jeans and came across a lump in his hip pocket. He traced round the smooth torpedo shape with his fingers and prised it out with difficulty. In the palm of his hand was the Ecstasy capsule Adam had doled out to him the other night. All he could remember was feeling peeved that such luxuries were, apparently, coming off the production budget. He didn't mind everybody eating well and staying in comfortable accommodation, but he could only think Adam was taking the piss by running up a drugs tab. He caressed the shiny pod and looked at the old-timers and wondered what they were like as young men. Where they cool and debonair and effortlessly attractive? Or did they worry about things?

Wherever it came from, an irrepressible urge came over Wheezer, beguiling him to break the mould, to stop being a manager, act out of type. It was ages since he'd done an E – certainly not this year. He fingered the tablet, thought of Las Dalias and the unique free spirit of their night in the hills and, pondering no more, he swallowed the capsule.

Nothing happened. He sat on his stool, vaguely aware of a kindling happiness, a generosity invading him. He smiled over at the old backgammon players, felt good about the work they'd done in Ibiza, felt fine about everything and then ZONK! It hit him.

The most powerful rush of shocking emotion whacked him sideways. It came on so strong and pure that he had to stand and catch his breath. One-two-three, one-two-three. The old boys smiled over at him. They were in on it. They were all in on it. The drug rush was overpowering him now. It was too intense. He was frightened.

He tried talking himself down from this heightening dread, but he could only transmit unhinged, indelible, panic-stricken thoughts. Lotte. She'd left him to it. She was in on it. Libby had left the way clear for them do it. Who? Do what?

He staggered out into the alleyway. It was still twilight. He couldn't compute what time it was. People were everywhere, milling about. He pushed abruptly through browsing, loitering, strolling shoppers attracting tuts and stares. He was a madman. People stepped aside as he lurched aggressively, looking up this street and that, searching for a way out.

A hag tried to sell him lucky charms. She terrified him. A little gypsy girl who had passed only moments ago, wearing a bright orange frock, ran back in front of him, nodding to a woman walking towards him. That was it! That was it! They were a pickpocket team! They'd singled Wheezer out and now they were following him, baiting him, waiting to pounce. Right. Keep calm. Keep calm. Keep going downhill, back towards the harbour, no – not the harbour, too many men, too violent, maybe . . . spotting a convertible with its canopy down he hopped into the back seat and curled up into a tight ball, willing sleep, or oblivion, or just that people would leave him alone.

'You very pretty boy.'

He'd only stepped out of the bar for a moment for fresh air, when this young lad, a Prince lookalike, even smaller, with bright red lipstick, had emerged from the shadows, pulling funny faces at him. He didn't want to be abrupt, but he didn't want to encourage him either.

'Thanks. Er . . . you're quite pretty yourself.' There. Nothing wrong a bit of civility. They were in Ibiza, after all.

'May I suck your cock?'

Keva ran back inside, burying himself deep into the crowd until he was certain he was safe.

When he came round he was still cowering in that same position. His mouth was rancid. The laughter and the noise woke him, but it was a more late-night, more evenly spaced atmosphere than the frantic mêlée of before. It felt like the end of the evening, like all but those with nothing to go home for were sloping away. There was nobody about. Although Libby and Lotte would be long gone, he was immediately and hugely relieved, happy, surprised. Still speeding, his mind was incisive and direct. Manumission. They were all going to Manumission. They'd passed the place every day, the old Ku club out on the highway between San Antonio and the town. He remembered everything Syd had told them. Privilege. The club's called Privilege. Ask for Anthony. Say you're a friend of Syd. Wheezer Finlay was not going to retire to bed, pleased just to be alive, licking his wounds. He had a story to tell. He was Mad, and the night had only just begun. He hopped out back into the street and set off down to the City Café to call a taxi.

'Frayn of Seed? MAYNEE frayn of Seed in this night!'

He probably would've let him in. He wanted that brief, sexual ritual, played out in front of the patient line of punters where, for a minute, all the power in the world, the yes and the no rests in his gift. But Keva wasn't playing. He'd hung back while the others got in, in ones and twos, and now he just wanted inside. He'd been certain, with nothing to hang it on, that the guy on the door would just wave him through without all this bollocksy 'Friend of Syd' palaver. It sounded like a benevolent society. He'd recognise something in Keva's walk, his swagger, that'd tell him just to let him through. He was a Star. It was written all over him.

He bypassed the waiting line and headed down the ramp towards the seductive entrance lobby, only for the guy to stroll up towards him, holding the billowing flaps of his jacket together, looking at the floor in that casual, menacing way of all violent men. He headed him off two-thirds of the way down the slope.

'Look, you'd better let me in pronto. I'm meeting Madonna . . .'

'No, my frayn. You not meeting nobody.'

'Eh . . .?' He glanced around the doorman's wide body, suddenly desperate, hoping he'd spot Syd, Adam, Libby, anyone. His mind was racing. What would he do? Where would he go? How would he get back to Santa Eulalia? He had a ludicrous conviction that this was a joke. Someone was having him on.

'Come 'ead, mate. I'm Keva McCluskey. The Grams. Don't you know me . . . ?'

'I don't know you. No one know you. You don't have no frayn in this night.' He hawked with amusement at his own wit and patted Keva on the shoulder, turning him around and pushing him firmly back up the ramp. One of his fingers gave Keva a sharp dig. This wasn't panning out to be his night. 'Good night, my frayn.'

Keva was boiling, a torrent of revenge plots fomenting in his head. Bastards! They were in there! Representing his band! *His* band . . . A taxi pulled up just down the hill. He ran to catch it, pleased and excited at least to have a means of getting back to the apartment. He lost his footing on some loose ground and flew headlong into Wheezer Finlay. He'd never been so pleased to see the loonbong in his life.

It was like a Brazilian carnival in there. Other-worldly transvestites fanned themselves with ostrich feathers, their white foundation melting into their stubbly cleavages. Old men in bikinis walked arm in arm with supermodels, smoking cigars. Dwarves and gargoyles patrolled the dance floor, handing out condoms and slices of freshly-peeled fruit. The club crackled with a turbo-charged sexual decadence. Everyone was dancing, those who were not were kissing, groping, prowling for erotic opportunities or snorting cocaine, MDMA and Viagra in the lavatories.

James, his head trilling with love and Ecstasy, had only an hour ago pledged his troth to Grass as he waved her farewell. Juan, mellow as he was, was not letting his little girl out to Manumission. She said she'd come down to the airport tomorrow, see him off. That was the next moment James would be alive again. For now he was treading water, heart and soul all of a flutter, wondering what he could do about it. He was cracked on a thirteen-year-old girl. She lived out here. It was hopeless.

He stood back and soaked in the liberation of the place. Punters were going for it with an end-of-the-world abandon. They didn't care. They were dancing feverishly, throwing their bodies like voodoo priests; boys, girls, men, women, both, neither – every soul was lasciviously sold to the devil. It was a spectacle.

'Anthony!'

He could hear the hard chill of the drugs in his own voice. Could this be him taking control of this situation?

'My client is contrite.' Keva nodded. 'He is humble. He only wishes to join our friends inside.'

Zing-zing-zing, his brain rushed ahead, full of brilliance. He licked his lips, chewed on them, face flickering, thinking himself the picture of reason. Anthony smirked, ready to send them both packing.

'I wish to make amends on his behalf . . .' He cleared his throat. '*Moooooooon riiiii-vah/Ah why-dah than a mile-ah . . .*'

Anthony keeled backwards, eyes startled. He beckoned them inside the club.

Tony and Beano stood to the side of the bar, waiting for Libby to come back with the drinks. She was horrified at the prices they'd paid. She made them promise to find her, wherever she was, to go to the bar for them in future. Tony was still mad on her. He loved her telling them what to do. He'd stopped taking Es two summers ago, when the dealers in Liverpool started taking the piss with worming tablets and zinc pills, but Manumission made him think again. He wanted to get out there with everybody, dancing. He wanted to dance with Libby. He was no dancer, though. But then, neither was James and he was the unstoppable groove machine the other night. Surreptitiously, he slipped the tablet into his mouth and slugged it. He looked over to the podiums. Sinuous club chicks moved hypnotically next to monstrous, painted mutants, a rhythmic current of sexual syncopation. They looked aloof, alien, closed to him. He could never go up there.

An English girl made direct eye contact with James as she passed to go to the ladies, drink in hand. He let the cool winds of Ecstasy breeze through him, fanning the flames. All day he'd been trying to get Grass on her own again. She'd been filmed and applauded and celebrated. She kept catching his eye with her phosphorescent gaze, a look which was only for him, but he couldn't get her alone. He was swamped with conflicting emotions, all swept away by the power of his lust. His every nerve end tingled with desire.

He watched the girl make her way inside the lavatories, that slow, exaggerated, overly-sexual walk. White skirt, deep-tanned, ultra-waxed legs, white halter-neck midriff top. Pure club babe fuck-me gear. He didn't hesitate longer. Feeling the confident warmth of his blood soothe through him, he was assured, calm, utterly definite about what would happen, how it would happen.

He went inside. Two girls applying cologne to their cleavages barely gave him a glance. The other girl was bent over the slab, snorting a long draft of powder. Her skirt rode right up, showing a slim filigree of G-string accentuated white against her taut bottom. He picked up her drink and took a provocative sip. Vodka tonic, weakened by the melting ice. He put the glass down and pressed himself up against her, staring over her shoulder into her dilated pupils in the mirror. She reached into her little purse, handing him a miniature Bergasol aftersun spray.

'Do my back?' She was as sure as he was. Her voice was well-to-do Home Counties. Not as distortedly posh as Ticky, but she was a well-bred girl. James sprayed a gossamer of aloe vera mist on to her spine.

'Mmm.'

She licked her lips in the mirror, dropping her head and scooping all her hair forward so that the cartilage in her nape tensed. Her legs were slightly apart, straightened at the knees as though she were about to touch her toes. She leaned towards the mirror, hugging her breasts together then letting them fall free, dry and salty brown from the beach, needing moisture. She watched his eyes drink in the contours of her flesh as he pushed his groin hard into her arse.

'Are you going to just fuck me?'

He was iron-hard, but the cool delay of the drug let him wait, let him grind into her and feel her tits and keep waiting. He took a crystal of ice from her drink and felt for the rim of her G-string, eyes fixed on her, hers on him. He stroked the cleft of her anus with his thumb, then slowly rubbed the ice around it, slipping the drooling sliver inside and pushing it right up her arsehole with his finger as far as he could go.

'Uhh.' She bit down on her lip, closed her eyes. 'What are you going to do to me?'

'Ssh.' He turned her round and pulled up the top roughly, sprayed her nipples with the Bergasol, felt the yield of her tits. She reached for his mouth with her tongue, but he held his head back, kept staring into her eyes, massaging her. She pushed free and ran to the cubicle, hiking up her skirt, panting hard. He followed, undoing his flies and letting his cock out.

Tony, shirt off, hands in the air, was rocking the podium with a tribe of trannies and coked-up Brits. Everyone was gorgeous. Libby looked on from the dance floor, laughing, happy for him. She'd get him later.

They didn't want to stop dancing, but they were too curious about the sex show. It was the talk of Ibiza. The bloke who ran Manumission was going to get up and screw his girlfriend for the delectation of the punters. The buzz of anticipation infusing the place announced that the deed was about to be done. Tony and Libby pushed to the periphery of the crowd, but couldn't see anything. *Bah-bom! Bah-bom!* He could feel the throb of his heartbeat. He could do anything – any thing he wanted.

They headed in a different direction, trying to get an elevated view. There was laughter and an air of eager prurience as hedonists of all sorts jostled and mingled and fondled, just for the hell of it. Frotteurs squeezed through the tightest-packed galleries, squirming with satisfaction. For a fleeting moment, Tony caught sight of the entwined couple, pawing each other with evident appetite. He lifted the elfin Libby to his side, letting his hands enclose her waist, his thumbs grazing her hips. They stopped to kiss deeply, pulling each other close. Noises of amused alarm from the audience disturbed them. They looked up. A naked, red-skinned and prominently aroused young man was attempting to join the couple in their lovemaking. As he stooped to insinuate himself in the act, seemingly intent on spearing any convenient hole with his hugely engorged penis, a jet of ultraviolet spew showered the startled lovers. The boy was grappled away, spluttering, one of his chaperones kindly and assiduously covering his bare penis with his own hand. He gave a jerk of recognition as he passed under Libby and Tony. It was Adam Rice.

The stark white lanes heading down and away from Privilege were thronged with the dawn flotsam, hitching, laughing, arguing over where to go. Girls and ladyboys, glittering divinities inside the club now looked like molten shit. But they were staying out. Everybody was up for it, everybody was going on somewhere else. The spirit had taken them over. That great syphilitic god Bacchus had pissed in the water supply and everyone had it bad.

Bar M then Space, they elected. Libby was going to drop them at Bar M, then she was driving Tony away at speed and that was that.

'Can we go to the top of the highest mountain?' he whispered to her.

'I heard that an' that!'

The happy mob in the back struck up a chorus of 'Love on a Mountain Top' while Libby and Tony swapped affectionate glances. But not for long. Right in front of them, two cars that'd been jousting for a couple of miles, changing lanes, roofs down, laughing and waving to each other, suddenly both accelerated and cut in on each other at the same time. The crash was horrific. The Disco Bus span round and round and round as Libby swerved and braked and clung on to the wheel, fighting to master it. Something rammed into them from behind, sending her head smashing against the steering wheel. Even in semi-consciousness she could feel the vicious burn of her seatbelt on her shoulders as she shot forwards in her seat. There was groaning everywhere. Out of the window, through blood-spattered eyes, James could see bodies staggering around, out of their minds. If he had to stay in hospital, he might see Grass again.

It was good to be back in the Duke of York. It seemed a life ago that Keva had last sat there, up on the raised platform, waiting for his turn to come. And if he had still not docked yet then land was definitely in sight. He sipped at a cool August lager and turned the pages of *NME* with relish. The Grams were an item. They were playing the *NME* tent at Reading. They mattered. He was news.

Today was his first proper press day. He and James were going to do it together, James objecting at the last minute to Tony, a non-songwriter, being ferried to London on a freebie while he was left to tune guitars with Marty. So James it was who made the trip. He, Guy, Wheezer, Todd and Hannah were lunching up the road in Moro, Hannah briefing them on the two days of interviews she had lined up, but Keva was happy to dispense with the preparation and take it all as it came. Rarely had he felt better suited to something, more comfortable that his time had come. He would probably let James throw in some anecdotes but this was to be *his* story. If his reunion with Syd had told him one thing it was that he was born to do this. He was a Star.

He turned again to the three pages of SJM concert adverts – the Manic Street Preachers, Catatonia, Fun Lovin' Criminals, bands of this calibre – and gazed with utter satisfaction at the Grams' strip-ad along the bottom quarter of the page advertising their autumn tour. 'New single "Beautiful" released 7 September on ReHab Records,' it said underneath. Fantastic. He looked up from the paper, wondering if the smattering of afternoon drinkers in the Duke knew who he was, yet. They would do, soon.

Guy was listening to Hannah's proud campaign, vaguely aware of enjoying forkfuls of flavoursome brik, but his mind was elsewhere. The ReHab cashflow was now a significant worry. The bills from Ibiza were coming in thick and fast, there was still the post-production of the video and Keva's *e.p.* to finance and they were about to go out on a substantial loss-leading tour. The office and the set-up of the single were eating up funds with mounting voracity, and now Todd had called him that morning to put him on notice of various opportunities coming up in Europe. There'd be a drizzle of income from 'Beautiful', but that'd barely cover the costs of putting it out unless it was a major, major hit. It'd have to be. Top Three here and a mainstay on MTV to get some publishing income rolling in. Maybe license out to a few compilations, too. But to do that, it was going to have to be a hit.

It was all looking good, no doubt about it – Hannah and Todd were ebullient, Wheezer and James surfing happily in their wake – but Guy deBurret was starting to feel distinctly exposed. He could cheerfully wave farewell to the family name and fortune and all the hang-ups that came with the seal, but the more he started to stare disaster in the face the more he realised how much he wanted ReHab to thrive. He wanted to give it a real chance, this ethic of his, the pilgrimage to do it right. *Right*. There had been times when he was sucked into the vortex of hard-dealing and backstabbing. Wheezer had felt the brunt of his paranoid lashing out, but he felt that they were all now finding their way. ReHab was a good company. It was fair. It was his. It was all he had, and he wanted it to work, badly. He wanted to show them what he could do. James tugged at a passing waiter. 'Excuse me? Are you sure these tomatoes are sun-dried?'

Guy wasn't sure whether he was taking the piss, or whether he was starting to take his new-found highlife a little too seriously – or whether he'd just lost it. That, most likely. His nose had been leaking intermittently throughout the meal. He watched the systematic trickles water the gack scabs around James's nostrils without judgement and listened to the others chattering and scheming for the remainder of the meal. He almost pulled his hand back when Todd tried to insist upon paying the bill, but he recovered quickly enough to chase them out into the warm afternoon while he settled up.

As he approached the smiling huddle, waiting for him on the corner of Farringdon Road, it was suddenly obvious from that comfortable distance how much Todd fancied Hannah. Had something happened that evening he and Wheezer'd left them in Filthy's? Hannah seemed oblivious, but Todd was gunning for her. He was standing right up close to her in an aggressively casual stance, legs wide apart, his head lolled to one side as he over-concentrated on her, eyes fixed upon hers, nodding self-assuredly every now and then, as though his concurrence would validate her point. Guy slowed his stride, narrowing his eyes behind his shades, watching Todd with detached amusement. He was glad to have him on his side, for sure – he was a winner, Todd. But he was a machine, a tennis-playing, treadmill-slogging, weightlifting, hyped-up, over-motivated, ultra-competitive, third-millennium shithead. He was the classic Corporate Man in the way he failed to differentiate between people and other things that he could have. The tip of his tongue touched his top lip as his gaze raked all over Hannah's face, summarising her worth, calculating what she could add to his standing. Guy was both amused and disappointed as he rejoined the gang. He ached for some humanity, some humanising thing in his wrong-way-round life. He wanted all this, yes – he wanted ReHab to thrive, thrive and grow into something of enduring value, but he had no *roots*. He didn't belong. He shook firmly with Todd, not allowing him to grip his knuckles.

'Nice one, Todd. This all sounds excellent. I feel a little jealous of you chaps, thrusting away on the front line. I find myself in a strangely, um, *clerical* role at the moment . . .'

'Don't be *silly*,' chided Hannah.

'Hey!' pumped Todd. 'You're doing fine! Just keep buying us those lunches!'

He could not have said a more fatuous thing. Wheezer put an arm around James. 'Come on, old Lovey, old thing. Better catch up with the muse and tell him who's coming to supper.'

Hannah shooed them away, saw Todd into a cab and idled back past the Italian church with Guy.

'Are you terribly frightened, baby?' she soothed. He came on mock-valiant.

'Me! The raffish and charismatic Guy deBurret? Frightened? With my reputation? . . .' He held her face between his palms and kissed her lightly. '. . . little bit, yes.'

He broke off and scrutinised the dried-up bouquets outside the church. 'I just have no control over the way I'm feeling. I can wake up and feel ready to carry the planet on my shoulders. It almost feels like I'm on smack again I feel so good. And then, an hour later . . . Oh, fuck it! I can't explain!'

Hannah took his hand and said nothing. They reached the Duke of York.

'Are you going to come in?'

'No.'

'There's no journos due for another half hour. Just say hello to Keva?'

Guy liked the sound of it. 'Yeah. Why not? Just for a mo.'

Keva was taken aback by how pleased he was to see Guy. He jumped up from his chair and said, 'Ye-esss! Ghee de Ghee! Fucken nice one! What's the boss doing down here in a common or garden drunkerie on a Wednesday afternoon? Don't tell me! This is Tough Love, isn't it? We all have to blank you!'

Guy's face crinkled with amusement and gave way to generous laughter. 'What the fuck is this lunatic on about, Wheezer? I come in here to buy you savages a drink and what? Insults and insolence! Barman! Eject this man!'

They hugged and sat down. James brought drinks over. 'A'right, Guy. Sorry. Hannah didn't tell us you was comin' an' that. What d'you want? I got you a Moscow Mule, Hannah, that right?'

'Suppose it'll give me Dutch courage. Thanks.'

'Guy?'

'Nothing, thanks, James. Glass of tap water, maybe. With ice.'

'Fuck off! Mr Love isn't asking for that! I'm a household name, mate! I'm *that* big, me!'

Guy chuckled and held up one hand, palm outwards. 'Nothing then, thanks. Honestly.'

James rolled his eyes. 'All right, then. Make me feel guilty an' that. I'll get you the water. But I'm pointing you out to Mick so's he can see who the weirdo is!'

He toddled off to the bar, made a big point of identifying Guy to the vociferous Australian barman and returned, grinning, with a glass of iced water. 'Gratis,' he smiled as he set the drink down.

'Thank you kindly, sir.'

They sat and passed half an hour, pleased with themselves for getting this far, this quickly. Guy's cab came. He got up, kissed Hannah and squeezed James's shoulder, looking at Keva.

'Well, chaps. This is it, I suppose. Your last few moments of mortality. Next week you're public property, eh? Those gorgeous mugshots are going to be all over W.H. Smith's . . .'

'Ugh!' winced Hannah. 'Maybe we should've stuck to *Mojo*, after all.'

'Seriously,' said Guy. 'You, gentlemen, are about to become . . . Big.' He winked at Wheezer. 'Good luck this afternoon, boys. Give 'em hell. Wheeze, if you want an office for the afternoon, you're welcome . . .' He held his stare long enough for Wheezer to realise he was being told off. Guy was right. It'd look stupid for the manager to sit in on all the interviews, very foolish, but he resented that being pointed out in front of everyone.

'Thanks, Guy, nice one. But no problem. I'll just pop over the road and use Hannah's billet. Nice and handy, sort of thing.'

Guy shrugged. 'Whatever. Give us a ring, later.'

'Definitely.'

Once Guy was gone, Wheezer finished up his Canadian Club, large, one cube of ice – his new drink – and wished them luck. He ambled over to Purvert and, finding no Jeff to rap with, installed himself at Hannah's desk and tried to think of people to ring. There was a pervading terror in his stomach which had clung and festered since they got back from Ibiza. This was the bigtime. This was not junior management, any more. He was being sent out into the front line, against major labels, big bands with Reputation managers. People with track record. There was no turning back.

He wanted to touch base with Snowy and Beano, but that would've meant having to speak to Marty. Marty! He was already ducking out of contact with him and they'd barely started. He'd better be good on the road! He called Todd, made an excuse about having to run for a meeting, and asked if he'd mind getting hold of Marty to run over technicalities for the Hanover Grand and Reading. Todd made no attempt to hide his surprise – and his displeasure – at the unorthodoxy of the request: 'This can't wait until you come out of your meeting?'

'He's waiting for get-in times, stage dimensions . . .'

'Woah! Hold it! *I* don't have that information . . .'

'But you can get it. Yes?'

'Sure, I can *get* it . . .'

Silence. Wheezer caved first. 'OK, Todd. Forget it. I'll get on to it when I get out of this legal meeting . . .' He was making the whole thing up. There was no legal meeting. Furthermore, he had fuck all to do all afternoon. Why was he spinning Todd a story like this? It was Wheezer's *job* to be on top of things like this. Why couldn't he be? He despised himself and, with his hatred, came another curtain of defence. '. . . don't even think that I thought of calling you, yeah?'

Todd found himself responding to the anger. 'Hey, Wheeze, look – if it's a problem, I'll do it, you know. Shazzan! No longer a problem . . .'

'No, mate. It's not a *problem*. I'm just short of time right now.'

Right now. He said that.

'You eschew the perfidious mobile, right?'

'Correct,' he said, testy.

'Cute.'

'Todd, I have to go. I'll call you last thing, whenever I get out. You'll still be there around seven, won't you?'

'Seven? You bet.'

'Thanks. Bye.'

Prick. Why did every little thing have to be a negotiation with him, a question of who was going to give ground? He exhaled, a slow, plaintive hiss, and grabbed up his jacket off the back of the chair. He bounded out of the building and walked, not certain of his plan, but finding himself cutting off Gray's Inn Road down Roger Street and Doughty Mews. He walked slowly around Mecklenburgh Square, aware of its grandeur but too sulky to thrill to it. He found a newsagent on Guildford Street and bought cigarettes and Cola.

He spent the remainder of the afternoon reading the *Standard* in Coram Fields, feeling wretched about the whole episode, dwelling in a well of desolation. Just as he was getting into his stride, he disabled himself. Two steps forward, one step back. He could dream and scheme with the best, but he was shying away from the men's work. He knew it. He had to crank himself up for the meekest confrontation. He'd always been like that. If he could fax his demands or file them down the Internet, no problem. But if he had to ask a promoter, face to face or on the phone, for an extra five pounds he'd almost throw up at the dread of it all. The group were always too busy, now, to notice things like that – but he was letting them down. He was. He was letting himself down. Here were the fastest, the best of times, and he wanted to hide away from the thick end of the action. He wasn't handling it. He couldn't handle it.

He walked down to the Lamb and Flag, a good pub he'd stumbled across in Lamb's Conduit Street and, finding no Canadian Club, had a large Jameson's – with one cube of ice – swigged it down and ordered another.

Purvis hung his head around the door.

'Wheezy! You on heat, mate?'

'Say 'gain?'

'Hannah's phoned about five times. They're finished over there.

They're gonna go out with Pat McIntosh and, whatzizname, the little snapper, nice fella, used to be in Fabulous . . . Shakey! I couldn't get you off the phone, mate! Anyway. I'm off over there myself. Wouldn't mind locking up, as it goes . . .'

It dawned over Wheezer, like coming out of a dream, that he'd been on Hannah's phone, non-stop, possessed, since half-five. He shouted back into the mouthpiece.

'Marty! Sorry, mate, got to go! That's all clear enough, though, yeah? Good man. I'm back Friday.' He slammed the phone down. 'Sorry, Jeff!' He felt great. Whisky-charged, but supercharged. He'd confronted every tricky call he had to deal with – Adam, Guy, Todd and now Marty. 'I'll make sure we pay for all these calls. What time is it?'

''Bout ten past eight?'

'Shit! I really am sorry! We must owe you a fortune . . .'

Purvis was laughing. 'Don't insult me! Anyway, it was worth it. On two counts. Hearing you rabbit on like a demented crackhead all evening . . . blimey! I know Adam Rice! He'll come round and glass you!'

Wheezer shrugged, grinning, pleased with himself. 'Him and Todd'll have to come mob-handed. The Wheeze is ready for 'em!' He tugged his jacket on as he walked with Purvis to the door.

'And you *swore*, Wheeze. I'll never forget it. It'll go down as one of those, where were you when Wheezer Finlay said "SHIT" moments. Fantastic! Say it again?'

'Shan't!'

'Go on! Just one more time!'

'Shit.'

They crossed the road in fits.

The Wheeze had been awake since six, pacing Farm Place, impatient for the day to start, but he was surprised when the phone rang just after eight. Kitty Trevelyan sounded disappointed. 'Oh, Wheezer. Hi, darling. Listen. Is Keva there?'

'Physically, yes. That I won't attempt to deny.'

'Oh.'

'D'you want me to wake him?'

'Oh no, no. Well, yes. Actually, I do. It's pretty exciting.'

I'm the manager, thought Wheezer. Speak to *me*. He made a decision. He placed the telephone on the little smoked-glass table and ran up the short flight of the stairs. He forced a slash, didn't flush and clumped back downstairs.

'Sorry, Kitty. The boy's not for waking. Out cold. Is there anything I can do?'

'Well. Yes. Tell him Kevin *loves* his postcard. He adores it. Says he was spellbound, thought it was beautifully told, imaginatively shot – everything *e.p.* wants to be. He's going to show the full twelve minutes the week the album comes out . . .'

'Oh, excellent! Fan*tas*tic! Nice one! Thanks . . .'

'Hold your horses, sweetie, that's not all. You know we make this frightful *Underground* series for Channel Bore? Well, the producer asked me last night if they can come along and film at soundcheck today, do a few interviews, maybe do something at the party? I said I didn't envisage any problems with publicity sluts like yourselves . . . joke, sweetie!'

Wheezer grinned to himself. The world wanted in on the Grams. 'Does Janey know any of this?'

'Why talk to the organ-grinder?'

'OK, look, Kitty – no problem with shooting at the venue. I'll call Janey on her mobile. But do me a favour, yeah? Let Janey liaise with *Underground*? It'll make my life easier . . .'

'As you wish, my liege. And you do me a favour. Tell that Keva trollop to call me. I need a guest list for tonight.'

'Sure thing, ma'am. Or if you want to just give *me* the names . . .'

'I'll fax them to ReHab. Have Keva buzz me. Ciao.'

So the *e.p.* had got a massive thumbs up. It deserved it. Keva had made a startling, revealing, deeply affecting film. There was stuff in there that none of the band knew about. He was a natural communicator, whatever the medium. And Guy would be relieved. He'd be pleased about *Underground*, too. The video for 'Beautiful' was taking time – Adam wouldn't let them see the finished thing until he was absolutely convinced it was as good as it could be – but the clip he'd supplied *The Chart Show* with for next week's Preview warned of a gorgeous piece of work. The time-lapse freeze-frames of Grass had a kind of naive beauty that fashion houses spent hundred of thousands to achieve. The diving footage, which he'd shot in black and white as well as grainy colour, came out like old 1920s Golden Age beach-belle shots. It was just a wonderful piece of work. He'd put everything into it.

Feedback from Hannah was that last week's interviews had gone spiffingly, and the first write-ups were due today, in *MM* and *G2*. They were getting some serious press, now, and Virgin had 'Beautiful' in heavy rotation. Radio One, while still not A-listing the track, were giving it more and more spins. The snowball had started rolling. The band floated into their soundcheck on cloud nine, shaking hands with the crew Marty had been assembling and hugging Marty himself like a homecoming brother. Wheezer clapped him on the back and headed off to spend the day at ReHab.

'Shit!' gasped Wheezer.

'What?' shouted Guy and Ticky, together.

'I forgot to tell Keva to call Kitty Trevelyan.'

'What for?' said Ticky.

'I dunno. Something about a guest list. She just wanted him to call her.'

'She'll just have to want, won't she? Keva's too busy to be bothering with things like that . . .'

'Things like what? Like keeping sweet with the producer of the most important music show on TV?'

'Associate producer. She's got no more influence over the content of that show than you or me. Janey Heal has more input.'

'Don't talk soft, Ticky. If we start messing around with people like that, we're going to get a reputation. Too big for our boots. We'll be over before we've even started.'

Guy chuckled plummily. 'I take your point, Wheeze, but Ticky's right. The likes of Kitty Trevelyan aren't out to damage Keva – even if she were able. Kitty's just a socialite. She wants to *hang* with Keva, that's all. She's got her claws into him and she's going to hang on for all she's worth. We don't need to aid and abet her . . .' Wheezer's face was twitching. Guy put an arm around him. '. . . In a year's time she'll have died of a smack overdose or she'll be living in the country with a rock star. Or his manager . . .'

Wheezer hung his head. 'I dunno. It seems too early in the game for us to start calling the shots.'

'On the contrary. It's exactly the time that we *ought* to be calling the shots. This is when we stand up and say what sort of band we are. Are we a band who takes every interview, every show, every opportunity. Or do we do what's good for *us*?'

'Both!'

'Nonsense!'

'I know!'

They all guffawed. Wheezer collected himself. 'Like, the *e.p.* hasn't even gone out yet. We should play ball.'

'You're right, but you're wrong. Kitty means nothing in all of this. Don't confuse who she is with what she does – she's a worker. If you want to be cold hard cynical about it, she's served her purpose. We'll put her on the guest list and make a fuss of her at the aftershow. That's her kickback. Everyone's happy.'

'You're mad. What if we want to get the band on *e.p.* again? Or if she gets promoted. What if she becomes a real big cheese . . . ?' Guy was shaking his head determinedly. '. . . or if ReHab signs another band they need to plug? Isn't it all filed under the general heading of Contacts? And don't we keep contacts sweet?'

'We're ReHab. The Grams' label. People'll come to us. Get used to it, Wheeze.'

Wheezer grinned. 'Whatever you say. But I think I'll call her, nonetheless.'

Five minutes later she'd browbeaten Wheezer to meet her in the Carlisle with four backstage passes which he didn't have.

In the short walk across Regent Street to Harry's, the band had found a whole list of things to be unhappy about. Catering could not get their ovens going, which meant no hot food, which was why Marty was walking them down Kingly Street for an early supper. But that was just the thin end of it for the newly-affronted, preciously piqued James Love.

'This can't happen again, Mart. I know it's not your fault, 'n' that, but we're making a leap in perception, here. You know what I'm saying, don't you? We're the Grams, now. We can't be having none of this amateurism no more. I thought we'd left cock-ups behind . . .' He was cut off by squeals of delight from Snowy and Beano.

'Ah, brilliant! Our first outbreak of additood! Hector's got additood! Brilliant!'

'Hector's always had additood,' muttered Keva.

'Too right!' blushed James. 'I'm a professional. All I'm asking is that everyone around me does their bit. That's how things work . . .' The others carried on giggling. Tony pointed to a cluster of fly-posters.

'Hey, Hector! How come The Purple've got more posters up than us? Our single's out a week on Monday and we've only got two posters up in . . .'

'Regent Street,' offered Beano.

'Ours'll all be out next week, won't they?'

'Seriously, though,' interrupted Marty, keen to shift the emphasis away from any perceived shortcomings of his own, 'you should have someone look into that. Posters don't have much more than a symbolic value − but that symbol is the status of a group. To look at that, now − that says to me that The Purple are bigger than the Grams. You should have Wheezer do something about that . . .'

Keva made a mental to do so, as soon as he got Wheezer on his own.

Wheezer eventually tracked them down to Harry's. They were arguing over the *Melody Maker* write-up. Wheezer had thought it was fine − a bit short, less gushing than some of the reports they'd come to expect, but fundamentally positive. You'd go and buy the single if you'd read the piece, for sure.

'Look at that!' spat James, stabbing his finger at a paragraph. 'I never said that!'

'You did, Jimbo,' said Keva, quietly.

'Well, I never meant it. Not like that!'

Wheezer walked through the door and caught James in full blustering flow. 'We should be protected from this, Wheeze! We're getting misquoted! You've got to pull your finger out, la! The press are having us off good style!'

Marty tried a sympathetic look. Wheezer decided the only way to work with him was to work against him. 'What seems to be the problem, Mr Love?' asked Wheezer, squeezing between Beano and Tony, ignoring Marty completely.

'That!' James thrust the article at Wheezer. 'You should make sure these sort of things don't get written! Fucking Hannah should be on to these twats – without us having to tell her!'

His round face was red, angry, utterly unreasonable. Keva looked away, suppressing a smile. 'Well, she got Cindy Hogan taken off the case, didn't she? Doesn't she deserve some credit for that?'

'Not if she's gonna get her replaced with someone worse,' he spluttered.

'I don't see anything *so* damaging,' started Wheezer. He was ready to fight James over Hannah's honour, but right now Kitty's guest list was his bugbear. 'What's your problem with it?'

'That! That!' screamed James, ramming his stubby finger into the middle of the page. Wheezer read it out.

It's all me arse this band saying they're bigger than that one . . . bigger than Jesus, bigger than God and all that. Shite. If Sensira are bigger than God then the Grams're bigger than Rod. WELL, bigger!

He broke off as James started to shake his head in frustration.

'I'm sorry, Jimbo,' said Wheezer, gravely. 'I see what you mean. You'd never say "and all that" . . .'

The cackling around the table sent him livid. 'Thank you. You've just fucken proved me whole fucken point 'n' that! I'm being patronised, aren't I? It's the amiable buffoon, isn't it! They refuse to treat me as a fucken musician! I said *loads* of things during that interview. I made some really good points and talked about, like, influences an' that. And what do they print? A throwaway stupid fucken gag that wasn't meant to be said anyway.'

'So don't say it,' murmured Keva.

'Anything to make me look a prick. You've got to get on to it, Wheeze!'

'I will, James. Don't worry. You just concentrate on the show. Enjoy it. Everything'll be fine . . .'

Keva decided to get it off his chest. 'Haven't seen any posters for the single, yet . . .'

'No. You won't do.'

'You what?'

'Waste of time. Waste of money. Posters don't lead to one record being sold.'

'Why've The Purple got 'em all over the fucken West End, then?'

'Because Mantra are a load of shithouses . . .' Everyone whooped at Wheezer's foul language. He'd been starting to become quite profane of late. He grinned gamely, but he was rattled. 'Look. Can this wait? I'm happy to explain everything . . .'

'Marty said posters are a good indicator of a band's status.'

Wheezer's eyelids flickered madly. He scratched his face. He made no eye contact with Marty, but spoke up, menacingly. 'Just remind me about all Marty's management experience. The Sobbing Bride, wasn't it, pride of fucking Dundalk . . .'

'Look, Wheezer . . .' pleaded Marty, getting up. Wheezer ignored him. Marty tried to catch James's eye as he left the café.

'I'll see you in a minute, Marty,' said Wheezer, without turning around.

'Wheeze?' grinned Tony, enjoying Wheezer's performance.

'Snowy?'

'Got any PDs?'

Back at the Hanover Grand's production office, the lines were going crazy. Wheezer's heart was bursting through his ribcage. Everyone wanted the guest list. Everyone wanted details of the aftershow. Magazines who'd done the group favours wanted favours of their own. Photographers wanted access front of stage. Magic Number had been on to him five or six times for the band's MU details. He'd hoped they'd just forget, but *Underground*'s producer, Seth Sneekes, would not turn over until confirmation had come through and when the fax eventually materialised it only confirmed that Snowy and James's memberships had lapsed. They owed about twenty-five pounds each. Wheezer paced around in circles.

'So, Seth, what you're saying is that this now can't go ahead?'

'That's what I'm saying,' said Seth, calmly.

Marty popped his head in. He was desperate to get back in favour with Wheezer. 'Why don't we send a bike round to the MU with the overdue subs? They'll have it, I know they will. They want money . . .'

Wheezer spent a quarter of an hour getting through to the right person and authorising it. His pulse was racing. He was talking faster and faster, almost barking, trying to get more done in the scant time available. He was cutting people dead, sweating, palpitating. Sort it, Wheezer, sort this, where're the band, Wheezer, did Zildjan bike those cymbals over . . . ? He was coping, he was coping, he was going to get this Musicians' Union shit sorted . . . Fuck! He had neither chequebook nor cash. He'd have to go to the cashpoint. Shit! They only had twenty minutes to get this together! Jellyfish-sized aureolas of sweat stung his armpits. He rushed towards the door. Marty blocked his path.

'Wheeze. Phone for you.'

'Tell 'em I'll call back! Fuck!' He stumbled on a cable and went sprawling on to the oily floor. He got up, hands blackened, befuddled. Marty applauded loudly and beckoned Wheezer back into the production office.

'Here y'are, Wheeze! Take your call! I'll sort out the MU.'

Twenty-five minutes later, filming started.

'Thanks, Marty,' said Wheezer, still breathless. ''Preciate it.' He'd have to confront him about the posters some other time.

'No problem. I just dipped into my float. You'll need to sign this chit when you get a mo . . .'

Wheezer signed, feeling dumb. He dragged on his inhaler, banging the doses, two, three, four hits of Ventolin, then lit up a cigarette.

'Listen. I need some passes.'

'All Areas?'

'Yep.'

'Who they for?'

Wheezer quickened at this impertinence.

'TV people.'

'I've already sorted their passes,' said Marty, pleasant but firm.

'Different crew.'

'Fine. Just bring them over to me when they get here. But Wheeze, man – in future, let me know about things like this. The group are very concerned as it is about the number of people wandering around . . .'

Oh, they are, are they? *My* group are very con*shorned*? And they talk to *you* about this? Fuck you! Give me the fucking passes and piss off back to Ireland! I'm paying you off, you sly, sneaky cunt!

Wheezer said nothing. He nodded humbly and blinked at the industry around him. The band, up on stage again, seemed born to it all. They dominated the room and cracked gags with the roadies. Wheezer went unnoticed. And unnoticed, he slipped out of the stage door and headed back into Soho.

A minute, no more, after Wheezer left the building, the production office phone rang again. It was Guy. The 'Beautiful' video was finished. Adam had invited the band and Wheezer down to the online suite. A quick check of the hall found no Wheezer Finlay.

'Actually,' piped up one of the catering crew, 'he was looking pretty bad. I have asthma myself. He was using the Ventolin a lot . . .'

'Hope he's OK. Maybe he's had an attack?' suggested Snowy.

'Probably stressed himself out,' said Keva.

'Fuck that!' said James. 'That's what he gets paid for! To get fucken overstressed! I'd be worried if he *weren't* over-fucken-stressed . . .' He grinned winningly. 'Come 'ead. Maybe he already knows. He might be down at Adam's, waiting on us . . .'

Nobody believed it, but they filed off stage and into the Renault Espace Marty had organised for them.

By the time Kitty showed, Wheezer had sunk four large Canadian Clubs and was feeling on top of the world. He was indescribably pleased to overhear a couple of trendy young kids speculating about the impossibility of getting tickets for tonight. How he'd have loved to just pull out a couple of passes and shock them. It was too weird. There was a whole wide world of the Grams going on out there, rocketing along under its own momentum, gathering more and more velocity as it prepared to go into orbit. Was anyone at the controls? Did anyone need to be? Or did you just haul the rock up to the peak and let it roll away until it could roll no more or had nowhere else to roll. He felt in control again, happy that all this was going on around him and that he was feeding the entire operation.

He was excited that people were excited about going to his show tonight. He was excited that more people wanted to get in than could physically be accommodated. He could scarcely wait to see twelve hundred people going shit-crazy for the Grams. Yet none of this got close to the gnawing wrench in his gut of a year ago, when he used to stand at the entrance of clubs and pubs in Dudley and Buckley and Gloucester, waiting for the crowd to arrive, unsure if anyone would come at all. That was excitement. The point where hope has given way to despair, where you're just about past caring, when you're on the verge of going back inside to tell the band that the promoter's cocked it up and suddenly you hear loud voices, not far off, laughter, boisterous shouting and a gang of ten or twelve kids all come round the corner together and *pay in*. They pay money, three or four quid, to see your band. They cough up as though it's normal to hand over money to see a band called the Grams. Then another five show. Then a few couples and a smattering of loners. You've got a crowd! People want to see the Grams! Forty-odd people have come out on a relentless, black, rain-sodden Tuesday night in Buckley to see *your* band! They've heard of you. They like you. Could he better that? Really? Wheezer waved to Kitty as she blustered in through the door and thought that he might well resign this evening.

Keva, for a long time – since leaving home, *home* – had been one to keep it all in. He didn't blubber any more, nothing made him. Even the talks with Syd and the memories that that undid made him numb and heroic and determined, not moved. But when the images Adam had made floated before him, in the darkened room, with its smell of violets and the hum of its air-conditioning, when he heard his song and saw what it was to one person and what it might come to mean to others, he sat down and wept. It had, all of this, come from within his own soul. Adam put his hand on his shoulder.

'That's what I did, too, man . . .' He pulled on his cigarette. '. . . and I'm a cunt.'

Tony and Beano hugged each other, while James just stood there, beaming. 'Can we see it again, like?'

'You can see it as many times as you fucking want, my son,' said Adam, his nervy jabbering mellowed out by the dope. 'Just so long as you don't tell me I'm a genius.'

'You're not, like.'

'What happened to an' that, you cunt? You was driving me to murders with that out there . . .'

Beano butted in, smiling, 'James isn't using the trademark an' that any more. He believes it's contributing to a generally negative perception of him as an artist . . .'

Adam looked at James closely, awaiting confirmation. He nodded. Adam screeched for joy. 'Facking 'ell! You *kants*! You little Scouse cunts! You're turning into fucking pop stars! Let's go an' get mortal, while I still know you!'

Wheezer burst into the dressing-room, wild-eyed. When they'd told him he'd find Marty in there he was hopeful of an audience to witness this show of power-management, but there was only Marty, restringing a guitar. He barely lifted his head. 'Oh, hoi there, Wheezer. Did you catch up with the band?'

'What? No. I did not. Would you put down what you're doing, Marty, please. Thanks. We need to talk.'

Marty was all attention now, his face tense. 'Is it about the passes, because if it is . . .'

'Passes, posters, whatever you want, Marty. It's about who you think you report to around here, who employs you and what the parameters of your job are . . .'

'Look, Wheezer, the thing about the posters – I just want to see the group do well, you know, I . . .'

Wheezer shouted him dead. 'Shut the fuck up! What I'm here to tell you is that if you in any way whatsoever try to undermine me again, you can pack your bags. I should fucking sack you now. D'you want the job?'

'Sure I want the job. I'm mad for it. I'm just a bit confused where all this is coming from . . .'

'No you're not, Marty. You know full well where this is coming from. Don't try and deceive people any more. You're not clever enough. Now, open up that fucking stupid . . . *roadie* belt and hand me six passes.'

He did. Wheezer's eyes stayed trained on him throughout. Marty couldn't look at him. 'Look, I'm sorry. I won't give you cause for complaint again. I . . . I'm still not sure . . . I mean, the MU. I sorted that out to *help* you, not to . . .' He looked up at Wheezer, eyes darting around desperately. 'The show'll be fantastic, tonight. You'll love it!'

Wheezer pocketed the passes and went to leave.

'Wheezer?'

He stopped.

'I'm really sorry, mate. I just . . . I thought you was into delegation, that's all. I'm sorry if I took on too much.'

He held his hand out to shake. Wheezer looked at it, looked at Marty, pleading, and shook his hand. He felt bad about all of this, now. Lord Turnbull's words of advice had been goading him on since he'd met Kitty. *Don't be a nice guy* . . . And he hadn't. He'd been vicious. He'd emasculated the poor twat, ripped him to shreds. Only now would Marty start to respect Wheezer. Why? Why were all these foot soldiers like that? Treat them well and they fuck you. Scream at them and slap them down and keep them down and their devotion is almost embarrassing.

He was already starting to regret some of the things he'd said. He should have had this out with Marty some other time, when he was sober and rational – not ninety minutes before the biggest show of the group's life. He walked out, and straight into the group, still yattering about the video. Beano was first to him.

'Ah, Wheeze, mate. You wanna see it! You wanna see it! Keva was in bits!'

Keva nodded. 'It's . . . it's everything we hoped it'd be. It's beautiful.'

'What is?'

'The video, Wheeze. We looked everywhere for you.'

Wheezer's face cracked into a huge grin. 'Magnificent!' he laughed. 'Magnificent! Is Guy pleased?'

'Shit! We were supposed to phone him as soon as we'd seen it!

He wanted us to see it first . . . Adam put the shits up him, didn't he, phoned him up at four in the morning, crying, saying it was too beautiful for television! Fucking Guy was too scared to come down to the viewing in case it was a heap . . . fuck! He'll be perched on Tower Bridge, now!'

Three hours later the Grams walked off stage, drenched, elated, shattered. The crowd bayed for more. Too high to want to be alone, the band left the dressing-room door open and welcomed in the hordes. Kitty, who'd spent the show hovering backstage, was first in, followed by Wheezer and Marty. Guy and Hannah hung back while Ticky, Ally Bland and Maxine pushed their way in, delving into the melting ice for beers. The *Underground* TV crew milled around, sticking the camera into Keva's face at a bizarre angle. Beano craned his head around the door, recognising a voice, trying to see who else was outside. There was a tumult of people, all talking, enthusing, edging towards the real object of their curiosity – the band. Andy Lachlan was there with his wife, Adam and Purvis were deeply ensconced with Paulie Hanlon while Paul Morrow was handing a wrap back to Billy the Brief. And then he spied her. Jumping off his bench, Beano went surging through the throng, ignoring the plaudits and attempts to shake his hand, his smile getting bigger as he got closer to her. She had her back to him, chatting to Janey. Beano tapped her on the shoulder.

'Celeste!'

She turned and must have surprised herself with the joy that overcame her. 'Baby! Oh!' She smothered him in kisses and pushed him back for a better look. 'Oh! Come here! Let me squeeze those little buns!'

They disappeared into the night, Beano still topless with only a towel around his neck. Keva ambled out to take communion and spotted a familiar figure off to one side, holding court with Dave Balfe, Pete Wylie, Rob Stringer and a glut of chuckling acolytes. He sidled up to Guy and nodded at the raconteur.

'Who's the storyteller?'

Guy smiled. 'That, m'boy is one of the surest signs yet that we're on to something here.'

'Tell me more, oh, master . . .'

235

'*That* – is Monseigneur Willard Weiss. If you want some barometer as to how you're doing, there's your man. His timing's uncanny. He just drifts in from nowhere, no foreplay, just as you're about to get hot. Not before, not after. He's beyond compare.'

'Doesn't sound like you're mad keen . . .'

'*Au contraire*, dear boy. I'm as flattered and as excited as you should be. He's not just here to be seen. He'll be here to do business. He'll try and sign us to Worldwide for the States. Tonight. And once he's got us . . .'

Worldwide! Now it clicked! Willard Weiss had been profiled in *Q* about a year ago. This was the guy who started his label with five hundred dollars and was almost single-handedly responsible for getting most of the dangerous avant-garde bands of the late seventies a release in the States. He'd taken tremendous risks with punk bands and experimental music, but he had an unfailing instinct for classic, commercial alternative pop. He was an extraordinarily charismatic figure, loved and detested by his bands and his staff, all of whom stayed with him until he tired of them. He'd had at least one wife, three boyfriends, two heart bypass operations, a major cocaine addiction and seven of the world's best-selling artists. He was a living legend and he was here, for them.

'Who're the blokes with him? The spooky-two, next to Wylie.'

'Bad news on both counts. The one next to Wylie is Tony Wolfe, one of the biggest music lawyers in the UK. The biggest, actually. And next to him is my dear old boss, Ronnie Lazarus, here with smiles and a zipper wallet. Between now and tomorrow the two of them will try to get me on my own and make me an offer I'll find terribly easy to refuse.' He turned to Keva, who was agog. 'I believe the video's something to behold?' Keva nodded, still staring at the three power-brokers. Guy grinned. 'Come 'ead,' he teased. 'I'll introduce you. Cover your neck up.'

Keva was still unsure how The Players had worked it, but he and Wheezer ended up being chauffered to the Diorama with Weiss and Wolfe, while Guy caught a cab with Ron Lazarus. It was a short ride, made shorter by their almost constant flow of praise for the Grams, and was only interrupted by Willard's heavy breathing and his pronouncements, punctuated with long, exhausted pauses which gave the impression of deep thinking but were more likely the respiratory tribulations of the bulky *bon viveur*.

'Now tell me. The Grams. That's a fantastic name. I love it. How, I mean . . . how did you come by that particular name?' He didn't listen to the answer, butting in to offer out his drugs. 'This is excellent coke. Excellent.' He chipped, squashed and chopped four short lines of crystalline powder on the pull-down leather tray in the back, and handed Wheezer a rolled-up dollar note. 'Mr Finlay?'

Wheezer nodded and sniffed up the first line. Keva declined, but did so in that elegant and non-judgemental way that served him so well in these situations. Wheezer lolled his head back against the seat, closed his eyes and gave a brief shudder. 'Nice,' he said.

'Good,' said Willard. 'We're getting along famously.'

The party was riotous. Ally Bland had conjured a carnal, animal, delirious atmosphere with a pumping garage soundtrack and a mirage of sophistication. Everybody was either beautiful or famous and awash with pills and powder. Everybody wanted to buttonhole the group, shake their hand, have a quick word – and no one was in greater demand than Keva. Each short trip to the bar or the bog took an eternity as he was stopped and congratulated by people he'd never met before. Was that Kylie Minogue who just smiled at him? Two Japanese girls shadowed him around the room, keeping a distance of three metres, content just to stare. They didn't even stare – they watched him. They looked.

He spotted James sitting with Willard Weiss, Wolfe and Ron Lazarus in a roped-off area which had been got up with gauze to look like a sultan's marquee. Keva joined them, resting his hand briefly on Weiss's shoulder. 'So, gentlemen, you've met Mr Love. Whatever could've brought you chaps together?'

James produced his chip-toothed grin and his silent laugh and made room for Keva to sit. 'Seriously, la, these boys've been telling me some very interesting things . . .'

'Oh?'

'. . . about publishing 'n' that.'

Keva blanched. He'd have to nail down this publishing thing before it all got out of hand. Tony Wolfe took over. His voice was almost a parody of the rapacious Dickensian attorney, all stiff smiles and fantastically formal speech patterns.

'I mean this is not the time or the place, but . . . if you'd like some proper advice . . .'

Pprrrrxogh-pah ad-veiss.

'. . . independent advice, in total confidence, I'd be happy to speak to you about anything at all. James was just telling me that publishing is a bit of a grey area . . .'

Ggchxrrrrrrayyy eeehhhggghhrr- eeee- ah.

Keva got up, weary. He felt curiously empowered, powerful that he was able to walk away from people more used to grovelling indulgence from their audiences. Something was willing him to relish that power, while he was there. He liked Willard Weiss, but he didn't feel like getting too friendly.

'Well, thanks. I'm quite happy with everything right now, myself. But thanks, anyway.'

Willard watched him go, impressed. He wasn't often or easily impressed. He was determined to get this band. Keva went off in search of Wheezer or Marty, anyone who could get him out of there with a minimum of fuss and back to Farm Place.

'Smart guy,' said Weiss, watching him go. Lazarus and Wolfe nodded. Weiss took out his pewter tin. 'Shall we?' James hovered over the powder like a vulture. 'So, you feel as though you're not enjoying the standard of living your celebrity status ought to offer . . .'

Marty found Wheezer chatting away to Jeff Purvis and Pat McIntosh. He pulled an apologetic face. 'Can I borrow you a sec? Sorry to butt in . . .'

Wheezer tried to look stern, but came to his side. He didn't want to let all that respect slip back into no man's land.

'Keva wants to get off. He's starting to feel a bit para. Shall I take him back?'

'D'you mind? I mean, tell me if you want to stay. You've got just as much right to stay and enjoy yourself as anyone. You worked darned hard to help pull this off. I can jump in a cab with Keva if you'd sooner stay.'

'Is this a test?'

Wheezer smiled at him. 'Honestly, no.'

'Well, in that case, there *is* one certain little lady that I'm trying to lure into my confidence. And I don't get to London so much these days . . .'

'Go for it,' said Wheezer. Marty gave him the thumbs-up and went to walk away.

'Hey!' he remembered. 'Who's the guy James is sat with?'

'The one with the white hair?'

Marty looked to check. 'That's him.'

'That's Willard Weiss. Head of Worldwide Records.'

Marty pulled a slightly wincing face, like he was cursing himself. 'Of *course* it is. Shit! Well, hey, anyway! That guy, Willard Weiss. I don't know if he's here to check the band out or what, but I should tell you . . .' Wheezer nodded him on. '. . . he come in halfway through the set, stood right by the mixing desk, nodded his head to "Librium" and fell asleep! I swear! He fell fast asleep standing up next to the mixing desk, just like that! Then, just as the band's going off, he wakes up and starts clapping! I promise you! So if he starts giving you any bullshit about how *awesome* the band were . . .'

Wheezer smiled. 'The legendary Mr Weiss, up to his antics, eh?' He glanced over at the huddle around James. 'Tell you what, though. I wouldn't mind knowing what *that* lot are talking about.'

Marty was all eyes. 'I can find out if you want!'

Wheezer was starting to feel uncomfortable with this new-found servility. He winked at Marty. 'Nah. You go and find your filly. Enjoy yourself. I'd better find Keva.'

Marty looked relieved. As Wheezer was turning away he tapped him on the shoulder. 'Here y'are . . .' It was a little plastic packet, with a couple of white pills inside. '. . . in case you get bored, later. Original formula Doves. Eighty mgs of MDMA,' he added proudly, and made off into the crowd. Wheezer stared after him. He knew he should have chased after him and given him back the tablets. No matter how well-meaning the motive, to accept Marty's gift was to take their relationship in a direction it had no need to go. He'd be acknowledging a familiarity which did not exist, but worse, he'd be in The Club. He had to decline, but he couldn't do it. He couldn't put Marty down again, so soon after they'd got things on to an even keel. And he'd never tried a proper Dove. He picked one out of the sachet and turned it over to check the embossed bird of peace. It looked more like a duck. He didn't know if he'd handle a whole one, with Ibiza still fresh in his memory. Still, it had had its compensations. When he met up with Lotte again that night, when the dwarf was chasing him round Manumission with those big, fluorescent stickers, he'd done something so out of character that he could not now fully credit himself with it. Dancing like a Fijian firewalker, dancing and dancing, swept away by the carnal, carnival atmosphere, he was overcome with love and a need to give pleasure. He went down on Lotte right there, in the thick of it, in the middle of the dance floor. Hardly anyone saw, and those who did looked at Lotte with envious appreciation. Afterwards, she bought him champagne, paying out of the stacks of notes she'd won playing backgammon against tourist hustlers in the Rock. That's where she'd gone, when they'd left him there drinking vodka. The more he thought about Lotte, the more he wanted that liberating Ecstasy buzz. He nibbled at the little pill, made a face and just necked it. He glugged some Evian and went in search of Keva.

Hannah found him sitting outside on a bench overlooking Regent's Park.

'Hello, handsome.'

Keva gave a mock shudder. 'Don't say that. Reminds me of someone I used to know.'

'Someone bad?'

'Someone OK from a bad previous life.'

'Is this one better?'

He turned to face her. 'I don't know.'

They sat in silence in the still, perfectly still petrol-blue light. Dawn was still an hour away. The only sounds were the distant rumble of the taxis' cumbersome diesel and the pulsating bass lines from the party. Hannah touched his cheek.

'You're so unhappy.'

'Not.'

'This should be, like, the best time of your life.'

'I'm loving it.'

She smiled sadly. 'Well, you're, like, the least happy pop star I've ever known.'

He pulled tongues at her and looked out into the blue.

'Can I be your girlfriend?'

'Yes.'

'No, really. I mean it. I fucking *love* you. I'm what you need.'

'I dunno if I'm what *you* need,' he sighed.

'What's up, baby?'

He levelled with her gaze. 'I'm just so . . . *tired* all the time. I can't get worked up about anything! I'm doing Reading at the weekend, I've got a single coming out, the best song I'll ever write, I've just played probably the best show I've ever done, I'm proud of the video, my *e.p.* gets shown in the next few weeks, everyone says it's the best *e.p.* ever, everyone tells me we're going to be huge, but . . . I don't give a toss, Hannah. It's not what I thought it'd be. I've *always* known my stuff was good – all that's different now is that lots of people agree with me . . . I thought my music would take me away from things. But it hasn't.'

She let all the 'I's and 'my's go without comment. 'You're not always like this?'

'Not always. Too often, though. It's like having the flu then you shake it off and the next day you catch it all over again. Like there's something out there, waiting to get you.'

'And is there . . . ?'

He didn't want to think about it. He pushed it all back down. He said nothing. She lowered her voice to a whisper. 'What you want is someone to look after you.'

'I like you.'

'Do you?'

'I do. I think we were mad to try and hide away from each other.' He leant his chin on her shoulder. 'Will *you* look after me?'

'I will.'

'You won't leave me?'

'No. Never.'

He kissed her gently, put his head on her lap and went to sleep.

*

Unable to find Keva, and with his tablet coming on quicker and more fiercely than he'd bargained for, Wheezer, reprising those familiar panic stations, had to get out of there. He paced towards a dimly-illuminated exit, changed his mind, headed to the bar and ordered a Becks, very conscious of his grinding, twitching mouth. He took a sip and went to sit with Willard Weiss's company but, getting closer, he heard their raucous laughter and saw them looking over at him. 'There's the manager!' he could imagine them laughing. 'Whacked out of his little nut! HAH-HAH-HAH-HAH-HAH!'

He turned smartly and walked back towards the exit, then decided against it, turned again and stalked back the way he'd just come. Everyone seemed to know he was out of it. They all seemed to make way for him, let him past. Everyone was looking at him, talking about him. He pushed on, breathing deep and slow, but every time he saw a person heading his way he turned, changed direction, changed his mind and turned around again, marching this way then that, until he found himself out by the exit again, heart pounding, trying to regulate his breathing. 'Come on, Wheeze,' he was telling himself. 'Hang in there. It's just a pill. You're just a bit twatted.'

'Car, sir?'

He nodded. So what if the bouncer was sending him into a trap? It was bound to happen sooner or later. It was best not to resist. Just let it happen. One of the curt ex-Scottish Highlander Guards Ally had hired to run the door guided Wheezer out and gave him a friendly hand up the ramp. He beckoned a cab over and helped Wheezer inside. 'You go easy now, sir.'

He gnawed and ground out the address. It hit him with a joyous insight that everything was OK. It was all going to be all right. Safe in the taxi, Wheezer's paranoia was replaced by an ever-stirring, continually building eroticism. He smiled to himself, knowing how he intended to use the solitude. Pulling over by the Coronet, Wheezer couldn't wait to get inside Farm Place and get his clothes off. He was almost clucking with anticipation as he fell inside the door and shut it with his back, sliding to the floor.

'You've got the whole place to yourself,' he said out loud in a husky voice. 'Why don't you come and fuck me?'

He stripped slowly, the brush of the nylon against his skin sending shivers of delight through him. Imagining that his was the most desirable torso of all, he lay naked in the middle of the floor, ears zinging, staring at the alabaster ceiling, stroking his nipples. His fingers grazed down his sides and massaged his hips and the muscles at the top of his buttocks. He groaned to himself and let his fingers stray to his inner thigh. His hairs stood stiff, each one a gently probing electric current. He licked his lips and tried to moisturise his tight throat. He reached for his penis. He was so sensitised that his fingers felt blunt, too warm and all-pervading for the precision he craved. He got up, madly erect, and tiptoed to the downstairs shower, pulses and currents still strumming his mind, each shimmering step taking an eternity. Without turning on the faucet, he traced the ice-cool black tiles with his lips and his tongue and the tip of his knob. It felt delicious. He kissed the cold tiles more sensuously, groaning to himself.

'Do you still want to fuck me?' he murmured.

'Yes,' came his own whispered response.

'Fuck me.'

'Yes.'

He licked the tiles and kissed them and moved his belly over their cold surface, standing on his tiptoes and stroking the chill steel of the soap-dish with his cock-end. A tingling breeze of euphoria eased through his limbs, burning his solar plexus with probing shortwaves. He was overcome by the invading riot of stimuli, eyes closed as he turned the cold water on himself.

'Is that how you like it?'

'Fuck! Yes! Yes!'

'Mm. Yes! Fuck, that's good!' gasped his female voice.

'YEAH-YEAH-YEAH-YEAH-YEAH-YEAH!' squealed his male voice as he squirted white juice on to the black tiles. He sat back in the shower, frozen jets strafing his mind and body, gasping painfully, gulping down the air.

'Oh, God,' he said in his own voice, shivering as he got to his feet. 'Where's it all going to end?'

He climbed out and towelled himself off, lingering between his thighs and buttocks, still getting the feeling. He chucked the towel into the washing basket and strode, naked, back into the main room where Beano was pole-axed with Celeste, sobbing with laughter. Only after an eternity could he sit up and speak. 'Come on, then,' gasped Beano. 'Aren't you going to introduce us?'

Reading was gloriously hot. It had become a standing joke among festival-goers that they'd pack the factor 30 for Glastonbury and their pac-a-macs for Reading – it always pissed down over the August bank holiday weekend. But not this year. It had started out sunny in April and, apart from rogue spells of precipitation lasting a couple of days at most, the England cricket team had been unable to resort to the weather as a means of reprieve. Even Beano, a notoriously uncomfortable sun-dweller, had been wearing a beige tinge to his pallor for most of the summer. It'd been roasting at ten in the morning, as they made their way down to the site for the midday soundcheck but now, sitting backstage sipping cool Becks, it was ninety-and-counting. Bands, journalists, promoters, agents and jetsam sat around in freaky shades, trying to look unflustered. The Grams, on best behaviour, had to try less hard than most as they stopped to pose for pictures and give mini-interviews to the tabloids' stringers and the fanzine kids who'd penetrated security.

The afternoon after the Hanover Grand show, Guy'd hit the roof with them. For the first time in the short period they'd been together he completely lost his faith. He'd been at his desk at ten thirty, the morning after the big party, and at eleven o'clock precisely the buzzer went. He opened up without checking, imagining Ticky to have mislaid her keys again. A beautiful, pale-skinned Japanese girl appeared at the top of the stairs, which opened directly on to ReHab's floor. She smiled and, with a trace of an American accent, said, 'Hi. I'm Coco. *Event* Mag.'

She shook hands with Guy and looked around, still smiling, and rocking on her toes, hunching her neck into her shoulders like she was expecting something else.

'Sorry,' said Guy, after he'd brought her some water from the bubble-tank. 'Hannah must've forgotten to tell me. Are you here to see me?'

'No. I have an appointment to interview the rest of the Grams. Not Keva. Hannah explained Keva is quite unlikely, but might come if he can make it. That's no problem. I totally appreciate her fixing up the rest of the guys for me.' Her head was passionately nodding her story along. 'Keva's been working very hard.'

She smiled again but didn't sit down. Guy telephoned Farm Place. James picked up. '*What* mag?' Guy told him. 'Never fucken heard of them!'

'James! You met them yesterday and they're here, now!'

'Not much I can do about that, then, is there?'

The line went dead. Guy phoned back immediately, but the engaged tone rang out. The little . . . *prick*!

He tried to hide his rancour from Coco, who was now sitting and still smiling. He called Hannah at Purvert.

'Hi, Hannah . . . good to know *someone*'s at work . . .'

'Uh-oh. Problem voice.'

''Fraid so.' He told her about James.

'The little shit! That's so evil of him! It was him who met the poor girl. *He* brought her over to *me*! He *assured* me he was up for this interview, otherwise I never would've . . . sorry, Guy. Leave it to me. Listen, give the girl some goodies, any rarities you can spare – I know you don't have time, but just keep her happy and I'll be up there in two shakes. I'll take her down to Farm Place and they can bloody well do the interview in bed, the bastards!'

She didn't like to mention that Keva was fast asleep back at her flat. She called him straight away and he picked up, sounding cheerful.

Guy gave Coco all his attention, filling a ReHab despatch bag with rare mixes and colour printouts of potential album sleeves.

'What you gonna call the album?'

'Undecided.'

'That's a good name,' she nodded, resolutely.

The buzzer went again. Again Guy let the caller in without checking, certain that it was Hannah. A young fellow appeared after an eternity, head hung low. It was an effort for him to shake hands with Guy and Coco. He couldn't look them in the eye.

'Manolis from Greece.'

From his hands you could make out the rich Aegean tan, though hardly from his face which was covered in furious boils. Wherever skin should traditionally have been was a welter of throbbing purple. It was understandable he should prefer to look at the floor.

'Do you also have an appointment with the band, Manolis?'

'Yes!' he beamed, tugging an A5-sized black-and-white stapled fanzine from his tucker bag. *Klash Kult*, it said on the front. 'I make time with James. I speak this with James while await soundcheck yesterday.' His eyes narrowed happily as he recalled the gig. 'Very good! *Very* hardrock!'

'Right,' smiled Guy. He dialled Farm Place again. Wheezer picked up, trying to sound bright. In the background he could hear Beano and Celeste shouting, 'Oh! Wheezer! Yes!' Wheezer silenced them, listened to Guy's threats, explained that he knew nothing about any interviews and would have had the group up long ago if it was in his schedule.

'Oh, right. You're an itinerary monkey, are you, now? I expected better of you, Wheeze!'

He slammed the phone down. He was about to apologise to the young journalists when the buzzer went once more – this time it was Hannah. The looks of disbelieving joy from Coco and Manolis when Keva loped into the room behind her made the previous hour's suffering almost worthwhile for Guy. Hannah winked at him. 'Thought these guys'd prefer the real thing.'

'Yes,' said Guy, shaking his head in admiration. 'I feel sure they do.'

So Keva, Hannah and the writers headed off to Highgate Cemetery, where he insisted the interviews had to be conducted and the pictures taken. As soon as Ticky showed at the office, Guy was off in the MGF, speeding angrily west.

Tony, Wheezer and Celeste were all apologies. Wheezer, in particular, took it badly. 'I've let you down. I know that,' he kept saying.

But Beano was infuriatingly militant, even though he hadn't been responsible – and James kept laughing. 'Who are they? Fuck 'em. It's not the end of the world an' that. I'm Mr Love. Mr Love can't be tied to schedules. Hah-hah-hah!'

'Shut it, Hector!' hissed Wheezer.

'Ah, shut ya face, you, poshwank!' he smirked back.

Guy stood up. He started calmly, but his voice quivered with the gradually increasing velocity. 'You're an imbecile. God knows how any creativity exists in you – you're a fucking lump. You have no sensitivity. No sensitivity. You think you're a musician. You think you're Mr Lover, but you're not. You're a joke. You're a fool. A fucking court jester. Let me tell you now. From today we're on opposite sides. I want to work with people who have passion. I want to know people who treat others as equals . . .'

'We blew out a fucking fanzine from Japan!' James giggled. 'Keep your hair on, mate . . .'

'What you just said is so stupid that I'm not going to hear it. Thank Christ for your singer is all I can say.'

James stood up, reddening. 'Oh aye. Into you for the publishing splits already, is he?' Guy was too surprised to answer. 'Well, let *me* tell *you*. I wrote half of all them songs and I'm not signing them to you.'

Guy was still stunned, answering on autopilot. 'You've signed them to me.'

'I was badly advised. That contract is not enforceable.'

Guy twigged. Tony Wolfe. Wheezer was up now. 'James. Sit down. I forbid you to say another word on this subject.'

It did the trick. James collapsed on the sofa, face contorted in silent laughter, looking up every few seconds to point at Wheezer. Just as it seemed that he'd be unable to breathe in again he sucked the air back in, shaking his reddening head helplessly. 'Didya hear what he just said? A-HAH-HAH-HAH-HAH-HAH-HAH!'

Wheezer looked at Guy. 'I'll sort this out, mate. I promise you, I'll sort it.'

Guy left the building without confidence.

Even James had had to admit that Wheezer handled the meeting well. They were sitting outside Filthy McNasty's, halfway house between Purvert and ReHab. Once Keva came out with the last of the drinks, Wheezer took a breath and said, 'So, you were telling us earlier, James, that basically you want to leave the group.'

They actually sat bolt upright. James, even by his standards, was bewildered. 'Wha'?' He took a deep breath. Everyone looked at him. 'I mean, like, were *you* telling *us* that *you're* jackin' it in?'

'Look. This is going to be a very long session if you respond to every point with a playground retort. We want resolution, not revolution . . .'

'You sound like William Hague.'

'. . . but by meeting with third parties and making your own commercial arrangements it seems that what you're telling us is that, basically, you're going your own way.'

'Is that what *you* want.'

'Me? Frankly, yes. I'm sick of you. But it's not what I want that's important here. I'm just a conduit and I now think it's time for some honest talking. I'm not saying we've been *dis*honest but, you know, we've all been working hard. We don't get so many opportunities to talk . . .'

'He's right, though,' said Snowy. 'I mean, blimey, where d'you start? Thing is, like – this has turned into a fucken *job*, hasn't it? I don't mean that's bad, like. But it takes getting used to. We're not used to being, like, *professional* about *music*. It seems mad.'

Wheezer nodded fully. 'Tell me about it. But if we're going forward with this, that's how we've got to be. All of us.'

'I don't mind doing most of the interviews,' said Keva. 'I quite like 'em. I think I can come across with stuff like that. Do you know what I mean? I think I can pull off that particular long-con pretty good. But you'll all have to watch my back. I don't wanna lose my voice doing too much gabbing. And I don't want to be knackered all the time. So, like – if we can just do a line-check sometimes instead of a full-blown soundcheck . . .'

James covered Amwell Street in a fog of Players smoke. 'Sound. No problems. But we haven't sorted this whole thing about the dough, royalties, publishing, whatever. I still don't fucken know what these things mean. And if this is a job, shouldn't we know, like, what we're getting paid?'

'Well, Jimbo, that's what Guy's been trying to stress from the start . . .'

He held up his hands, blew smoke and nodded in defeat. So Wheezer, using pie charts drawn in biro on mutilated beer mats explained how it would all work, how they'd be better off with Guy and how their arrangement was grounded, first and foremost, in morality. It was business ethics, not a get-rich formula. James was placated, if not wholly convinced. 'That Tony fella said he could get us a quarter-million advance on the publishing, like.'

'Pity he didn't offer it six months ago, hey? Where was Tony Phlegm when we needed a grand to record a demo?'

James nodded.

The band went up to see Guy and apologised – Keva, too, just for solidarity. James mumbled an assurance that he wouldn't be pursuing his own publishing deal and telephoned Tony Wolfe on the speakerphone to let him know. Tony, a pro, seemed to guess he was being overheard.

'Well, I appreciate the call, thank you . . .'

Appkxrchreeee-sheeyate.

'. . . you've probably made a very wise decision in the long run. Let me know if there's anything else I can do for you. Say hello to Guy. Adios!'

Keva stayed behind with Guy and Ticky to do a pre-recorded interview with Steve Lamacq to go out next Tuesday, while the rest of the boys and Wheezer headed off to Reading, feeling like a band.

After the Lamacq interview, in which Keva previewed tracks from the new album, Hannah picked him up to cook him supper, promising to get him to the hotel in Reading in plenty of time.

'Can we take a quick detour?' he asked.

'Where to?'

'Up where we were today?'

'You're the boss. You're not going to sacrifice me on Karl Marx's grave, are you?'

'Yes. I'm going to drink your blood and fuck your corpse.'

'Like it!'

'Or I might just sit there and look at you.'

She started the car. 'You're crackers,' she said, and drove.

When they got there he looked out over the monstrous city, shaking his head. 'Powder,' he said.

Things like that in him made her long to possess him.

When Keva had phoned to say that he'd be staying over in

London, Wheezer, enjoying a new surge of respect from the troops, cleared them all off to bed after one last nightcap.

'Yessir,' they all said, touching their foreheads as they bowed past him.

James, unable to sleep, tapped at Marty's door. Marty was momentarily embarrassed to see him. His room was crowded with girls from Rock-Cakes, the catering firm, and various crew types and sallow young men in Zildjan T-shirts.

'Join the party!' he announced, unsure. He knew all about the meeting they'd had and was unready to risk Wheezer's wrath again.

'Just an hour, right? Throw me out after an hour! You have my express permission, no – Mr Love *insists* – that you bodily hurl me into the corridor at . . . one fifteen ayem.'

'Here. Drink this.'

She placed a tumbler full of dark orange pulp juice in front of him. For fifteen minutes she'd been juicing ginger root, carrots, spinach and other menacing ingredients. He sipped it and pulled a face.

'Not bad, actually. What's in it?'

'I'm going to write it all down for you. And when you're on tour, yeah, Catering are gonna make this up for you every day. Every day, yeah, whatever shithole you're staying in? And you're gonna be a new man?'

She kissed him fondly. The night before, up on the Hornsey Lane bridge looking out over London, Keva had started kissing her with a fervour she hadn't known in him.

'Look after me,' he'd kept pleading, then he'd pulled down her zip and had her straddle him in the passenger's seat. It was sudden and fast, tongues buried deep inside each other's mouths, T-shirts tugged up above their shoulders so they were flesh on flesh. He came violently, bucking her so hard that her head hit the roof, continuing to pulsate and thrust while Hannah pushed on hard against him, hugging his head tight. She collapsed on to him, paralytic from the fury of her climax.

'God! I fucking *love* you!' she said. He didn't say it to her, but he was aglow.

They slept together, naked, and made love again. When the alarm went he reached for her and started to kiss her, but it was Hannah who pulled away.

'Come on, you!' she said, jumping out of bed. 'You need your energy. I'm not going to be held responsible for breaking up this band. No one's calling *me* Yoko Ono!'

She gave him cereal, toast and juice, and slipped a brown glass apothecary bottle across the table. 'Take two with your lunch, every day.'

'Er . . . what is it, like?'

'It's hypericum. Otherwise known as St John's Wort. As used by literary loonies and manic depressives for centuries. It's like a natural Prozac, I suppose. It's quite safe.'

'I dunno,' said Keva looking at the little bottle. 'I don't think I like potions. D'you know what I mean? If my character's depressive, then that's my character. I'm stuck with it. It's more a thing of getting to learn to live with it.'

She threw a tea towel at him. 'You little Luddite!' she laughed, her squiffy eye gleaming at him. 'I bet you're one of these zealots who won't take a fucking paracetamol if you've got a headache, yeah?'

'Well, actually . . .'

She hit him. He pushed her down on to the table but she wriggled free and went to the door. 'Come on. Show's over. The drugs don't work if you don't take 'em – it's up to you, honey. Come on. Get out the door. Let's go take Reading!'

She dropped him away from the hotel – her suggestion – so that nobody cottoned on to them. Flashing her pass proudly, Hannah ambled around the site, trembling at what was to come. She found herself smiling at gangs of grimy indie-kids. She was going out with the Grams' lead singer.

Marcy Playground were on when they saw him heading for them, smiling.

'Fuckinell! Knobhead's coming over!'

'He fucken wouldn't! He wouldn't have the nerve! Not after *NME* . . . Hey! Helmet! Il Duce! How's it going, la!'

Helmet seemed genuinely pleased to see them. 'Can't complain, guys, ha! Bonkers! Without whom none of which and all that, anyway! Nice one! Tops!'

They shrugged at each other, befuddled. 'Can you say that again, old boy?'

'Ha-hah! Same old Keva! Always taking the piss . . .' He was lost for words. 'Anyway! Great to see you guys!'

He gave Keva a gentle punch on the shoulder. It wasn't even a punch. He just placed his fist on to his shoulder and moved it slightly, and said, in a supremely sincere voice, 'Good to see you're doin' it, man. Tops.' He bounced away, stopped and shouted back: 'Hey! You're all coming to the party, right?'

'Try and stop us!' shouted Keva, beaming.

'Top one!' Helmet faded into the crowd.

'What party?' asked Beano.

'Fuck knows . . .'

'Is he real?'

'I don't think he is,' said Keva, slowly. He was still looking at the crowded bar area Helmet had melted into. 'But we're gonna blow the little twat off stage. He might think this festival's all about him. Let's see what the papers think next week. No more ale till after the show, lads. Come 'ead. Let's get back to the hotel and take it easy.'

Wheezer was twitchy. He'd just walked past a gaggle of roadies and he was certain he heard one of them shout: 'I forbid you to say another word!' followed by a brief pause and the craven guttural cackling of the pack. How could they have known about *that*? None of the boys would've ratted, surely? Not after their perestroika session. Over by the roadies, overconfident, rapping to Head of Security, was Al Meredith, Sensira's prematurely aged manager. He caught Wheezer's eye and waved over, winking sarcastically at the same time. No way! They wouldn't split a joke with the enemy! It just could not happen. But he couldn't quell the thought. Boiling with indignation, arguments already raging in his head, he went off to find Marty.

He found him with a security guy, leading the group away from backstage toward the artists' parking area. He jogged to catch up with them. 'Hey! Whoa! What's going on?'

Marty turned around. 'Oh, there y'are, Wheeze. Been looking everywhere for you . . .'

'Is there some sort of roadie's criticism lurking in there? Have I violated some little-used backline tech code of honour, somehow?'

Marty looked at the grass, rocked forward and back then looked up again. 'Not at all. The guys were just keen to get back to the hotel . . .'

'I thought we'd been *through* this!' He stepped forward and pointed violently at Marty. 'You do not answer to the fucking group!'

They all looked at each other, experiencing the embarrassed thrill of a classroom punishment. Wheezer Finlay was losing it.

'You go through ME!'

'I did try to . . .'

'What the fuck's *this* contraption for? And this?' He pulled out a pager and the mobile he'd reluctantly accepted from Guy. 'Just . . . stop using your fucking initiative, will you . . .'

Keva stepped forward. 'Wheeze. You're out of order, mate. Marty was just . . .'

'Shut the fuck up, you, you treacherous piece of shit! Try and have a think whose side you're on before you stick your fucking oar in! And suss out who's on *your* side, you idiot!'

There was a shocked silence, followed by Tony Snow: 'Are you not getting your full complement of sleep, Wheezer?' The others bit their lips. Wheezer glowered at Tony. 'Just, like – the old lingo's started getting a bit ripe of late . . .'

Wheezer shot him a look of undiluted contempt. 'Right!' he spat, ripping the walkie-talkie from his belt. 'Fuck you! Fuck the lot of you!' He flung it to the ground. 'That is IT!'

He stalked away, back towards the site.

'Come on,' said Keva. 'It'll all come out in the wash.'

'There's people getting carried out, out there!' croaked a perspiring Beano.

'Is that good, or bad?' asked Tony.

'It looks too full,' said Marty. 'The tent's only supposed to take a thousand. There's twice that in here. Easy.'

'So what do we do? Is it safe to go on?'

'Fuck it,' laughed Guy. 'Go and rock them. Send them out on a high!'

Wheezer had left a message on Guy's mobile saying he was fatigued. He was cracking up. He'd caught a train back to Liverpool. Guy, Todd, Hannah and Marty were backstage, helping to keep things calm. Keva, who had learnt to tame his stage-fright nausea by eating four hours before showtime, was sick with terror. There was a teeming multitude out there, delirious, almost out of control waiting for the best new band in the world. This was going to have to be good. It'd have to be the best show of their lives.

'Come 'ead!' said James. 'Let's go and fuck 'em up!'

'Yeesss!' hissed Tony between gritted teeth.

Guy gave them the thumbs-up, and they filed out on to the greasy stage. They were choked, physically, by the assault of noise and heat and bright white light. All they could see was a swelling mass, sweeping forwards and sideways, roaring, cheering and roaring, jumping up and down before a note had been played. A football-style rhythmic clapping started up from the back.

'1-2, 1-2-3, 1-2-3-4, the Grams!'

Tony looked across at Beano and grinned at him. Beano, terrified, cracked a smile. James wandered around the stage, making come-and-have-a-go gestures at the crowd and beaming at Keva, laughing his silent laugh. And then he started playing. The crowd went mental. As one they surged forward, bouncing, flailing, flinging themselves at each other and at the stage. Security were straight in there, pushing the crowd back from the barriers, helping up trampled revellers, passing the fainted ones back into no man's land between the barriers and the stage, where paramedics carried them outside for treatment.

'Is everybody OK out there?' shouted Keva between songs. The cheer was deafening. Keva couldn't keep the smile off his face. Many a Sefton Park evening had been whittled away by Keva and James arguing whether rock stars should smile. Tonight Keva was smiling. They took the usual breather after 'From Now On'.

'Good evening . . . *NME* Tent!'

Cacophonic applause. Keva waited.

'There's one thing and one thing alone you have to remember, *NME* tent-goers . . . and it's this. The *NME*'s a mast!'

Demented laughter. Sustained, rhythmical clapping and stomping. Keva was receiving frantic signals from Marty. He went to confer with him and returned to centre stage.

'We've been asked to request you beautiful people ease up out there a little bit.' He sprinkled the throng with Evian, to more raucous applause. 'But we're not going to! Because *we* . . . are the Grams . . .' He waited for their hoarse appreciation to soften. '. . . and people cannot be held responsible for their actions when they come under our spell! Let's have it! This one's called "Chimera"!'

The band tore into the track, seeming to ignite a thunderclap from the back of the tent. All the bodies jostling outside, trying to get in, seemed to become possessed by the energy of the track, launching a desperate charge on security, some managing to barge their way through and sending a knock-on cascading through to the front. By the end of the song there were clouds of steam coming off the crowd and more bodies being passed over the barriers than the paramedics could deal with. They paged the promoter, who was on site within minutes. They wanted him to pull the plug. He consulted Marty.

'Give me a second!'

He called Wheezer on the mobile and quickly summarised. Wheezer, while over-thanking him for calling and over-apologising for his outburst and over-explaining his exhaustion, was then similarly precise. 'Tell them to do "Beautiful". They can close the show with that. It'll slow them down a bit. At worst, the crowd'll sway a bit too much, but no one's in any danger. Marty – they *have* to do "Beautiful"!'

So they did. Keva led the band back on stage and picked up the microphone, carefully, gracefully, the whole time swivelling his flat stomach around his hips. 'This is from our new album . . .' He had to break off as the crowd's acclaim drowned him out. He waited, half laughing and beaming at Tony as he tried to get his words out. '. . . our new album . . . which shall be known as *Powder* . . . and which will be available at all reputable retailers presently. But you can get this one next week. It's called "Beautiful".'

Those watching Sensira on the other side of the site claimed you could hear the roar above the noise of the band. As Radio One's Andy Parfitt, who witnessed the performance, later said, it was probably the moment when the Grams became the biggest band in England.

They attended the Sensira party with their heads held high. Sensira, by all accounts, had been special. But those who'd scuttled between both shows, particularly the journalists charged with reporting the whole weekend, reckoned that the Grams were in a class of their own. They were the story that was sweeping Reading.

'Did you see the Grams? . . . Did you hear about the Grams show? . . . Fifty-seven had to be carried out . . . I believe they were fantastic . . . over a hundred taken out . . .'

This was the talk of the party, as must have been appreciated by Helmet, who was nowhere to be seen. Todd paraded the group, making sure he was conspicuously a big, visible part of this success story. He, Keva, James, Guy and Hannah made endless toasts, several to 'our demented manager'. Beano and Celeste sloped off, while Tony walked around smiling at people. When Guy found him, later, he was holding four bottles of Becks.

'Not for personal consumption, you understand. Just in case of emergency.'

Guy laughed. Tony wondered if now was the time to ask. Since Ibiza, since Libby had made him crushingly aware that their fling was just a bit of fun, his thoughts had returned to his one enduring love. He hadn't even kissed her. He decided to go for it. He'd start with something general.

'Hey, listen,' he said, in hushed tones. 'I didn't want to ask in front of everyone, but, like . . . is Ticky still on board?'

'Y-eeesss.'

'It's just that . . . no one's really seen her. We hardly saw her the other night and before that . . . I can't think when she was last with us.'

'Well, let me reassure you. She's very much with us and is working so hard that I think she's just buggered. She's never had a job, before, you know! Lazy cow . . .'

'I miss her. She should be here for things like this. It's her triumph as much as . . . or does that sound stupid?'

'I'm sure she'd be chuffed to bits to hear you say it. And I'm sure she would've loved to be here today but . . . you know. Bank holiday. *Big* week coming up. Offer of a long weekend on a yacht off Capri. You'd have to give it special consideration, wouldn't you?'

'You would indeed.' He wanted to ask him. He couldn't. He held up a bottle and passed another to Guy. 'Here's to her, then. Here's to the lovely Ms Turnbull.'

They clinked bottles. As he walked away to find the others, Tony cursed himself for not taking it further with Guy. He wanted to know, basically. He wanted to know if it was a complete joke for him to nurture thoughts of romance with Ticky Turnbull. Guy knew her better than anyone. He wanted to ask him if he reckoned there was *any* chance at all.

As Guy walked away to find his car he questioned himself about Ticky. She was becoming more and more remote. She was late for work. She seemed tired and withdrawn. He was generally aware of all of this, but in all the furore of the past few weeks he'd been unable to shift his focus. He just didn't have the time. He decided to call her on the yacht as soon as he got back to Dolphin Square.

Part Two
Losing It

'Ye-esss! A Norbert! D'yer see it! I promise you! A fucken Norbert!'

The blacked-out Mercedes tour bus grumbled along the A172. Last night, Middlesbrough Town Hall – another hastily-added date – had been carnage. Again. Everything had gone berserk since Reading. In the parlance of a dearly despised foe, the Grams' world had gone bonkers.

Burger smiled to himself as Tony scribbled down his latest score. Everyone but Tony, Wheezer and Marty had dropped out of the game, which comprised the spotting of various haulage trucks with points awarded for their relative scarcity. Eddie Stobart trucks, which were ubiquitous, scored one point while the prize 'spot', the flamboyantly-liveried Norbert Denstressangle juggernauts, were worth ten. Burger, a popular member since his appointment as Security, braced himself for the squabble.

'No way, Snowy! We wouldn't've missed that! How come you're the only who ever spots a Norbert?' whined Wheezer.

'Yeah! And how come it's always when we're looking out the other side?' added Marty.

Tony was outraged. 'Are you saying I'm cheating? Are you calling me a cheat? Cos if you are there's no point in carrying on the contest!'

'It's not a contest! It's a perishing game!'

'I gave you loads of warning! If you two are too dozy to turn your heads round in time to confirm the spot then that's your own problem!'

Burger and Keva squealed with laughter, clapping their hands.

'Fuckinell! Did I hear that right? Con-firm the fuckin spot!' Burger's mellow, mocking Leicester-Jamaican inflections made it sound as silly as it was.

261

Tony looked away, blushing. 'It's just something to do, isn't it?'

'Yeah. Takes his mind off that disco shite he keeps putting on,' muttered Beano. Since returning from Ibiza, Tony had become an unlikely and avid taper of Pete Tong and Danny Rampling's Radio One shows, playing his 'Anfems' at full blast on the Stardes bus. The band pretended to hate his compilation tapes with a passion, but only Beano was genuinely gutted by the soundtrack. For the sake of peace, Marty had to alternate uplifting club cuts and Euro classics with scratchy recordings of the Ruts and the UK Subs, Beano's current favourites.

'You should bounce along to it, Tone. Do some aerobics. Callisthenics, an' that. Keep on top of the weight thing . . .'

'Fuck off, eight-chins!'

The bus was barely tolerable. Mercifully, the journeys between venues weren't too long. The only task they relished were the personal appearances at record stores – a perfect opportunity to make blow-job assignations. They had slipped thoughtlessly into the easy relief of a daily stranger's mouth sucking their dicks. They just did it. It happened every single day, now. The routine, the circumstances never varied. It was life on the road. They'd turn up someplace, the hotel or the venue they were playing, meet that town's girls, and let them get their cocks out. Record shop PAs were a cert. They couldn't get enough of them. They were a band, touring, and this had become their normality, young mouths engulfing them in a strange but familiar precinct. Little wonder they could no longer stand each other. They hated themselves.

Keva did all the local radio stations, too, keeping the Heads of Programming sweet. They were all, more or less, getting on with the pulsating whirligig of star life. James had gone missing a couple of times, but Keva seemed to thrive on the demonic schedule. Ferocious arguments triggered by trivial events were liable to blow up at any point, but they were too busy and too tired to kill each other. It was murder, but it was paying off.

'Beautiful' was still Number Two. It had been Number Two for three weeks, unable to shift a mesmerisingly dull Hollywood blockbuster theme from the Number One slot. Surprisingly, though, sales were stronger in week three than they'd been in the previous two, suggesting that the track could stick around, like the rare handful of other modern classics, such as 'Missing', or 'Brimful of Asha', both of which stayed in the Top Ten, here and overseas, for months by virtue of their unique, pervasive appeal.

Paul Parlour from MSF cheapened the mystique when he turned up at the Wolverhampton show a few nights previously declaring chubbily that the track had 'legs'. Keva was horrified. It made his epic sound like a hardy ZZ Top standard.

The bonus in all of this was that it relaxed the pressure for a follow-up and allowed Guy to put back the release of *Powder* until the middle of October. America had woken up to the Grams with import play of 'Beautiful' storming several key modern rock stations with top three phones – called-in responses from listeners – and without Wheezer's prompting, this time. So while Willard Weiss was still ahead of the game and keen to close a deal, Guy and Wheezer had nonetheless decided to fly out and see what the other companies had to say. A synchronised release was going to be impossible, but by delaying the launch of the album these few weeks, ReHab were building up a fury of anticipation at home while minimising the flow of import CDs into America. They were co-operating.

Vulnerability to imports was a big issue in the States and this acknowledgement by ReHab of the problem would be appreciated by the eventual licensee, be that Sony, Geffen, Worldwide or someone else. It'd stand them in good stead.

The European picture was much clearer. Once Wheezer and Guy had decided they would avoid cross-collateralisation by signing licence deals with different labels in each territory, it was just a case of extracting the best terms from the leading companies. From the start they'd debated the pros and cons, but through September Wheezer met regularly with Tony Wolfe for sound and expensive advice. Signing for the whole of the European territory with, say, Polygram, would have advantages for a priority group like the Grams, not least its financial emoluments. A strong multinational would provide real marketing clout, an integrated, focused development plan, a substantial budget for tour deficits, video clips and promotion, plenty of well-connected local ground staff to make it all happen and a nice cash advance to show the group and their management how much they rated them.

The problem, Wolfe explained, was that big, powerful multinationals with marketing muscle will always see any such deal as just that – a deal. Once the contract's agreed, the group becomes a means of making money for the label and, more importantly, its parent company. If they sign the group for the world, the label want to recoup their outlay from the receipts of every record sale in every territory before the group see another penny. It can take a long time to recoup.

'It's the same principle if you decide to sign the band just for, say, Europe. Let's say it's Sony, yes? Sony might sink a million dollars into signing the Grams for Europe – advances against royalties, tour support and the cumulative costs of marketing and promoting the first album over a six- to twelve-month period and so on. The Grams might go on to enjoy substantial success in Spain – but it may also be that they have little real impact elsewhere. Are you with me?'

Wheezer nodded, fascinated. Since his breakdown at Reading he'd bounced back invigorated, composed and driven. He was on the wagon again, he'd given up the ciggies and he was ready for the scrap ahead.

'Let's say the Grams go platinum in Spain, OK, but they don't do a light in Germany, France or any of the other territories. Sony might be billing, what, a million give or take on your runaway success in Spain – but instead of ReHab seeing their percentage of those profits, the surfeit, your two hundred grand, say, goes towards wiping out losses in other territories. It's called cross-collateralisation. Remember those words. Cross-collateralisation. The chant of the devil! The multinationals *swear* by cross-collateralisation. Unless you get to be a monster-selling international act, those are words you'll come to know and despise! They'll come back to haunt you . . .'

He chuckled smokily and went on to precis an alternative. By signing individual licences with a different label in each country, the Grams and ReHab might stand a more realistic chance of seeing royalties, especially if they were to link up with one of the more powerful local independents. Companies like Intercord in Germany and Ginger in Spain had enjoyed great success with overseas acts. Advances and marketing resources might not be as rich, but the relationship – and the motivation – might be more personal, Tony argued. Above all, the group should be able to negotiate better royalty terms and would most likely see those royalties – the band's percentage of profits – much sooner than with a major.

'Don't commit to more than one album, if you can help it. Ninety-nine per cent of the deals I make, I'm pushing for a two, three-album commitment – but with this band, believe me, Wheezer, you can write your own prescription.'

He stood up, shaking Wheezer's hand. 'Tell Guy he needn't be shy if he wants me to help with any of this. He's too busy as it is. He looked shocking the last time I saw him.'

So between Guy and Wheezer they'd struck deals, some via e-mail, with labels in Europe, Japan, Australia, South America, South Africa, South-East Asia and the Middle East, with Tony Wolfe transforming their one-page deal memos into binding contracts. Ticky, fatigued, had brought in two assistants to help collate and ship out the 'parts' – mastered DATs of the album, artwork, calibrated masters of the 'Beautiful' video and various T-shirts, badges and other promotional merchandise. Europe and the rest of the world were nearly ready to go. The one big territory remaining was the US. Guy and Wheezer'd be flying out there the morning after the Ally Pally show to finalise a deal.

The bus laboured through the outskirts of Leeds. This was the last of the tumult of hysterical, sold-out regional gigs, with London's Alexandra Palace coming after tomorrow's travel day and a further day off. Todd had had to switch the London gig from the Forum after the venue was swamped with ticket applications. The group steadfastly refused to do more than one show in each town and equally vehemently refused to contemplate a stadium gig. Todd was getting frustrated with them. They could have sold out Earls Court but Keva laughed off the proposal: 'Too Oasis, Todd, man. Too fucking ELO.'

Alexandra Palace, with the ceiling set at eight thousand, was a nice compromise, though Todd hated letting all those thousands of fans go unsated – and unseated. He'd known right from that day at Mono that the Grams would be major ticket-sellers, but had not an inkling that it'd blow up to this enormitude, this quickly. They were bastards to have to deal with – contrary, illogical, belligerent bastards – but they were a licence to print. And they were his band.

James, ashen, puffy, nose leaking stagnant water, rolled his eyes at Burger. He sounded like a nicotine-stained Donald Duck as he rasped stuffily through bunged sinuses: 'Fuck off! The fucking Lizards are there! Have a word, Burger! How the fuck do they know where we're gonna be each time!'

What he wanted to say in reply was: 'Erm – difficult one. Unless they've read the tour dates in the music press. That could be *one* way . . .' but James was so unpredictable these days, he'd probably have him sacked. One day they were cocaine chums, swanking it up in the nightclubs and entertaining several women at a time on the bus or in the hotel, the next James'd be pressurising him to infringe the basic rights of punters. The Grams were stars. They had to get used, Burger reckoned, to fans pushing into their faces for an autograph, a kiss, a hello. Any sort of human contact. It was not a lot to ask for, or for the boys to give of. He watched him dab his snivelling nose with tissue, watched it turn dirty yellow from his output. James, of all the group, was the one who'd had the most difficulty adjusting. And Burger was just one of the many people he thought he'd acquired the rights to.

'You were glad enough to see them last night when they were all sucking your cock!' shouted Beano. He was developing an intense dislike of James. He'd always harboured these crass, boorish rock-star pretensions, but let off the leash at full force he was a fucking trial to be around. Wheezer had nicknamed James's behaviour Gangsta Tap.

'Well, what if I don't want them to suck me cock today? What if I want some other bitch to suck me off?'

'Jeez, Hector! Shut the fuck up, will you! What are you *talking* about? You're a bloody embarrassment!'

James grinned at Wheezer's crack-up and tried to make eye contact with Keva, who avoided his eyeline. Pat McIntosh, a note-scribbling, Dictaphone-carrying ever-present on the tour, continued staring out of the window, apparently oblivious to James's latest Tap outburst. Wheezer was still nervous about having a journalist, even an avowed and proven supporter, following their every move but Keva liked his spiel about chronicling rock 'n' roll history as it happens. He approached Burger, leaning over his shoulder rest.

'Sorry, Mac.'

'Fuck off, Wheeze! Why d'you have to call him that?' squealed James. 'Cos you're PC?'

He rasped helplessly at the mirth of his quip. Wheezer called their big minder Mac because Mac hated his given name. He was Everton McGregor. Most of his bands called him Big Mac. The Grams, out of affection, had given him their own pet name, but Wheezer was uncomfortable with it.

'Will you take care of this?'

'Not a problem, mate.'

So Burger had to hop off the bus ahead of anyone else and amble over to the three excited girls who'd shown up at most of the Northern dates, an odd combination of innocence and availability huddled together at the stage door of Leeds Town and Country Club, and tell them that the group were already at Radio Aire doing interviews. It saddened him, still, after all these years to see that hungry appreciation for any little bit of info, anything which set them apart from ordinary fans who knew nothing of their heroes' day-to-day minutiae – and the desperate alacrity with which they acted upon the crumbs they were thrown. A minute later they were in the distance, arms linked, heads bent slightly forward to get them quicker to their destination.

He watched them go, shaking his head. He knew their MO. He knew what they thought they were getting out of the deal. They felt as though they were *living* by doing this, following bands and providing a sexual outlet. They certainly didn't believe they were being used, deceived or humiliated. It was a laugh. It was better than real life and the sex was a mere facilitator. It was currency, cashed in with the backstage passes James called 'blow job vouchers'. Burger had the task of handing out the passes to the chosen ones, but he was not at ease with the routine.

The band got off the bus and went to press Vic for tea and butties while the load-in started.

This was as close as Keva could imagine coming to peace of mind.

He'd just had a fabulous nouvelle-Moroccan lunch with Hannah in Momo which he could only call singular, on the grounds that he'd never before been flirted with and pouted at by shoals of risibly camp same-sex Arabic-French waiters throughout the course of a meal. Hannah was all over him, but for how long? The novelty would pass, he knew it would, even if they became massive. She'd leave him. But not if he left her first. Not yet, though. Not yet.

He was now relaxing in the cool neutrality of Dickins and Jones's Grooming Studio, where the dextrous therapist was cleansing, toning and tightening every pore and every fine line on his face. He lay back in deep repose, letting the poultices get to work on his skin while he smiled at the thought of Alexandra Palace tonight and the queer notion of the ticketless multitudes who'd have to miss out. He could almost feel an empathy with Helmet Horrocks. It was, indeed, bonkers.

Hannah was trying to get to the heart of it. Keva was as beautiful and as pathetic as always, but, given she hadn't seen him for nearly a fortnight their reunion had been a let-down. They'd fucked last night, just the once, but that wasn't the thing. He might well have been sleeping with other chicks – she doubted it – but that wasn't the thing, either. What bothered her was that he seemed to . . . it was stupid, but he seemed already to be looking past her, looking to see what else lay beyond her. During lunch he talked enthusiastically about the tour, the crowd responses he'd been getting, even the way the waiters this afternoon were lining up to flutter their eyelids at him. He didn't ask much about her, he didn't want to know. She'd bloody well invigorated that jaded little fuck, got him up and running and full of himself again, and now he was cruising away from her. He'd never claimed to have loved her, never actually articulated the words, but she'd always sensed it. Right from the very start. She felt the need in him. Now she sensed nothing. The scent was cold. If he had needed her once, needed her then, he didn't seem to need anything now.

He flashed the purple SJM sticker at the security guard and crept to the side of the stage to ogle the crowd. Even now, a full hour before they were due on, the audience was packed tight at the front of the football-pitch-width stage and remained jammed all the way back to the sound desk. Only in the final third of the auditorium were people milling around, perusing merchandise and queueing for drinks. The atmosphere, though hushed, was supercharged. Keva felt a wave of giddy nausea rush through him as he started to imagine how that staggering mob would look and sound in an hour's time, when he paced across the boards to his mike. He went to find Dolphin, the spunky young London support band, to wish them luck in this terrifying, fantastic hometown gig.

James, loving the adulation, revelling, still, more than anything in that split moment of disbelief when the fans clocked him and twigged that it was really *him*, stood side stage, waving and grinning and scrawling his name in a giant, customised heart signature for them. Security was keeping them back and he knew he shouldn't be there, diverting attention away from Dolphin, but he couldn't help himself. This was what it was all about. This was stardom. He was a guiding light in a whole different constellation to these kids. He was an inspiration. He was, literally, someone they looked up to, just as they were doing now, hundreds of lost souls down there wanting to touch his robes and bathe in his incandescent glow.

More and more people were jostling to get close to him and security was having to forcibly heave them back now, but one little hand caught his eye, holding up a beer mat right at the side of the stage for James to sign. It was not so much a hand as a joint, with two withered stumps of flesh clamping the beer mat tight. Its owner was striking, her saucer-eyes and beautiful face seeming over-large for her tiny body. Everything else, her breasts, her lycra vest-top, her faded Levis seemed miniature, made-to-measure next to her large, pretty head. Her hands were deformed as with those of the victims of fertility drugs and her body was childlike. But James was entranced. Catching her eye and smiling, he instructed Burger to give her an aftershow sticker and vacated the stage, waving to his acolytes.

The heat, as they walked on stage, was stunning. They were

knocked back, momentarily, by the scalding, muffling heat – it was like the blast off the Ibiza tarmac – and the triumphant noise of the crowd. Fuck. They'd put out two singles in less than six months. Their debut album was still to come and they were being greeted like heroes at one of London's vastest and most prestigious venues. Standing there, soaking it in, promise seemed eternal to Keva. Life, *living*, could not be better than this – he was the leader of the most important band in the world and he was about to give his followers what they wanted. He soaked in the heat and the noise and the terror. It felt fantastic.

Hannah stood side stage watching the man she loved. Had loved. It was true, then. All men were the same. They were worth, they were worth . . . fuck all. Wonderstruck by that truth, calm but beginning to tingle with sadness, she found her way through the warren of passages and out into the still, still-light night. Wheezer saw her go and, torn, looking between the stage and the exit, band and Hannah, he ran after her.

'Hannah!'

She carried on walking, down the steps, down to the carpark. 'Hannah!'

He caught up with her and tugged on her sleeve. Her face was stained with tears. 'God! What's the matter?'

It crossed his mind for a second that she was devastated by the hugeness of the gig. She turned to him, chin crinkled into pathetic dimplets, lip quivering, and threw herself into his arms. He held her tight.

'Oh, Wheezer,' she cried, breaking free, half laughing at the spectacle of her and him, in the rain. 'You're too good for us all.'

She kissed him with real feeling, looked into his stunned face for a second, then ran.

'What song is it you wanna hear?' drawled Keva in a poor approximation of a Georgia accent. Syd was too right. This, now, this standing up above the gathering, on a platform, a stage, tantalising the throng, was his destiny. He was born to do this.

'What song is it you wanna hear?'

Ever since listening to Syd's *Lynyrd Skynyrd Live* album as a kid, he'd wanted to say that to a packed-out, jubilant crowd. The rest of the Skynyrd album smelt, but 'Freebird' – and more so the delirious chanting from the crowd leading into it – was a great moment. His own followers didn't disappoint him. Cigarette lighters, luminous bracelets and keyring torches flickered and spangled as thousands of hands and arms were raised in anticipation of the Anthem. A joyous, swaying knot down at the front struck up an off-key chorus, bellowing the words lovingly and hungrily. They wanted to hear *that* song. Keva and James laughed at each other as they waited for the din to die down. Keva stood still, mike dangling by his side, staring past and above the crowd, knowing that he would attain total silence. He waited. They watched. There was utter quiet for a few seconds. James began picking off the haunting intro, bent studiously over his guitar to get the perfect feel then, as recognition turned to elation, a gale of relief rose up from the overstoked multitudes.

This was the bit they'd been waiting for. Beano's drums kicked in with Tony's insidious bass and from nowhere, from underneath the blanket of sound, the lazy drag of James's guitar rose up like a scintillating valkyrie, soaring out above the song, elevating the crowd to a higher place. Keva watched the bulbous guitarist leaning back, eyes closed, shining face slick with sweat, working his spell inside out. He adored him. His posturing, his failings were all a part of this amazing, magical beast and Keva, just then, loved him passionately for all those peculiarities that made him. He felt the throes of a giggling attack, the impatient, hiccuping convulsions of the child who has twigged the way to crack a sum and wants to do it all by himself, now, without help. He gripped the mike hard to curb the surging hilarity and strolled forward to weave his own dark patterns, calming and regulating the spasms of his breathing and reaching out, his voice an aching chamber of want. For a still moment the crowd seemed suspended, held on pause while they drank in the husky, haunting words. The chorus crashed in, louder and more affecting than anything the tearful congregation could have hoped for and sent them spinning out of control. He found himself thinking that, come what might come, this was his deliverance.

*

They'd decided, Hannah included, that there was no point trying to repeat the razzmatazz of the Diorama party. That gathering had already gone down as a legend in London clubland's twisted history of Great Nights. They opted for a low-key all-nighter at Filthy's for the immediate clan, selected media pals and a very limited number of celebs and aspirants. Gerry opened up the cellar rooms so that more people could mill about, but by midnight Burger was having to keep people out of the front bar where the band and Wheezer were holding court. Guy, who still hadn't heard from Ticky, had left early to drive down to Balmerlawn.

Wheezer was in a corner with Marty, raking through figures on merchandising, which had exceeded three pounds per head throughout the tour. It was stunning business for a new group. As SJM had put their deal together on sell-outs there were hardly any percentages to settle out, so Marty was able to keep a careful eye on the three cheerful and unapologetic wide boys who ran Rope, the canny but brand-new swag outfit they'd appointed, against all advice, to handle merchandise. They came up trumps, actually *selling* their range to the punters instead of merely offering it for sale. They had a lot to prove and the Grams' tour was a dream ticket for them. Skimming the take would've been suicide and they handed over scrupulously audited thousands to Marty every night with the same jaunty sign-off: 'So that's lots of dosh for you and a little bit of money for old Rope.'

Wheezer was pleased with the way everything was shaping up. Marty was scared of him now, which still made him feel weird, but their working relationship was so much easier. Looking around, he had a good sense of paternal satisfaction. Keva and Pat McIntosh were rabbiting to Peter and Keith from Hunkpapa; Tony and Cerys from Catatonia were deep in a meaning-of-life conversation at the bar; Beano and Celeste were tottering down the steps to the cellars to play pool; Gil Acton and Terry were holding court with Shane MacGowan. *NME* was still a mast.

'Now then, Nina, my soubrette. Shall we just get you out of those things? I'm going to lick you. I'm going to lick you until you're wet all over. Everywhere.' She let out a whimper and looked away, eyes closed, nodding her head. 'And then . . .' He took out a chubby wrap of gack. '. . . I'm going to *cover* you in cocaine . . .'

'Mm . . .' She had her hands behind her head, elbows and hips writhing upwards, eyes still closed with the tip of her tongue spearing her lips apart.

'. . . and I'm going to snort you. I'm going to snort you all up and I'm going to dab my cock all over your tummy . . .' He touched her gently. She bit her lip. '. . . and I'm going to get coke on my cock and I'm going to put it right inside you . . .'

'Fucking Jesus!'

Her voice was deep for the girlish form, and urgent with desire. James pulled off one then the other of the built-up, cloglike shoes and massaged and kissed her malformed feet. She moved her hips up off the bed so he could tug her jeans down, pulling her tights away with them. Her skin was shiny alabaster white, marbled with a faint pink. She sat up and raised her arms for him to take off her vest, showing a faint coffee-brown furze in her armpits, and shook her long hair free so that it covered her shoulders and the straps of her doll-sized bra. She sat there and held out an ugly hand, eyes pleading, melting with trust.

James stood still, smiling past the hand, drinking in the slight mound under the tiny triangle of her panties and, eyes dancing, went to sit at her side. He kissed her, gently at first then more fiercely as her tongue darted inside his mouth and she pushed and struggled against him, working her wrist against his knob but getting nowhere with his buttons. James stood up and let it out for her but, as she moved to suck him, he pushed her back and began again to kiss her tenderly, letting three fingers of his hand prospect around the hot cotton of her knickers. She shuddered and exhaled hard, thighs clamped tight around his wrist as he stroked through the damp fabric, then she lay quiet as he unhooked her bra and reached out and sprinkled the gritty powder over her.

All Keva knew was that he hadn't been asleep long enough. Hannah hadn't shown up at the party, he'd ended up mortal in Gerry O'Boyle's office and someone was banging his head in. Urrrgh. Murder. James was snoring like a tramp, oblivious, dead to the world. Keva tried to hide under his pillow. The tour was over, today was a day off and fucking Marty or Wheezer was hammering at the door telling him to get up.

'Are you decent, Kee? I'm coming in. It's bad.'

Wheezer. Keva screwed his knuckles into his eye sockets hoping to fuck he hadn't left the Clarins Multi-Active Night Oxygen cream by the bedside. He groped for the dusty glass of water by the phone, popped a Ceramide complex capsule automatically and stumbled to the door, allowing Wheezer in while he fell back into bed.

'What the fuck is the matter, Wheeze?'

'Ticky.'

Keva grunted.

'She's gone.'

He dragged his head up off the pillow, ears ringing, knowing in a crushing sudden that this was going to be something dreadful.

'Where?'

'No, mate. She's dead. Topped herself.'

Keva felt his dry, scaly tongue plop out of his mouth. 'Fuck.'

'I know.'

They stared at each other, dumbstruck.

Guy was already there in the Upper Class lounge. Wheezer was surprised he'd wanted to continue with the trip, but Guy had informed him in a short call that he'd meet him at Heathrow as planned. Wheezer had gingerly asked about Ticky, and Guy promised to tell him more on the flight. He was definitely still going to Los Angeles. There was none of the usual 'it'd be what she wanted' cant, rather the opposite; Guy'd admitted that an escape before the funeral would suit him just fine.

He seemed cheerful. A red-liveried Virgin representative offered him drinks, snacks, conference facilities, computer terminals, massage and manicure, but Wheezer settled for a very spicy Bloody Mary. He was back in control, and a little soother to take his mind off the journey did not in itself mean that he was drinking again.

'Bad flyer,' he grimaced, more to Guy than the hostess. She smiled beautifully. 'Gosh!' said Wheezer, watching her go. 'What do the masseuses look like?'

*

274

Two hours into the flight and Guy had still said nothing about Ticky. He'd said very little about anything. Wheezer wanted to settle into his journey and plot the meetings ahead, but he couldn't risk saying the wrong thing. He couldn't say *any* bloody thing. He sipped at the flinty dry Chenin and mused that things could be, had been worse. This was his first big flight, his first trip over the Atlantic. As a boy he'd often stood in the overgrown garden at Parkwest, watching the mystical white trail of the jets in the blue sky above. He watched them all summer long, hand in salute over his blond young brow, shading his eyes from the sun as he tried to imagine what impossibly exotic motives took those people up into the sky, high above the world, to places far, far away. Now here was he, up above the tiny world and all its tiny lives, chasing the sun across the roof of the sky. He glanced at Guy, lost in time and space, gazing out of the porthole. He drained the wine and indicated to the hostess for another bottle.

Guy was still silent. Wheezer, tipsy, was trying to sit on top of a gradually fermenting anger. He stared straight ahead, trying to blank out the images from his mind.

'Did I ever tell you about my family?' mumbled Wheezer, knowing he had not.

Guy barely turned away from the window. 'What about them?'

'The crash?'

Guy looked Wheezer up and down. 'No. No you didn't.'

Wheezer sat back, a half smile giving his face a disembodied leer. 'Seems so long ago, now. Seems it never happened. But it happened.'

He shifted his weight in the roomy leather seat and turned to Guy. 'The details are only really of interest to me. Only me. In the whole world. Isn't that weird? But what matters is that they were wiped out in one little journey. All of them. I don't give two hoots about what happens to me. I really don't. You shouldn't either.'

'What do you mean?'

'You're doing that thing where people try to rationalise a tragedy. They cope with a loss by blaming themselves. It's pure vanity. It's a way of dealing with it, I suppose, but it elevates the bereaved to an equal or elevated status to the deceased. They're saying, like, he might be dead but it's *my* fault. *I've* got to carry on with my wretched, worthless life. You can forgive some people for needing to do that . . .' He fixed his birdish stare on Guy. '. . . not you, though, Guy. You know what it's all about.'

'And what *is* it all about, Wheeze?'

Wheezer gave this some considerable pause. 'It's all a load of crap.'

'Very profound.' Guy returned to his blue-black, eternal sky.

'It is. All this, life, the music business, the *music business*! . . .' He tailed off, shaking his head.

'Look, Wheezer, I had no idea about your family . . .'

'Forget it!'

'I mean it . . .'

Wheezer turned on him. 'I'm not a fool, Guy! Talk to me how you want, but try to remember this one thing – I'm not stupid!'

Guy exhaled hard, exasperated. Wheezer badgered on. 'If you want to paint some lonely, isolated tragedy for yourself, go ahead. But it's not like that. It's not. It's just another bloody fact. People die. Everything dies . . .'

Guy went to react, but sat back again. Wheezer slumped back in his seat. 'I'm sorry. I'm just . . . I'm trying to be of some use to you. Use me.'

Guy fixed on him and plunged in. 'Ticky seems to have killed herself because she was in love with me . . .' Wheezer swallowed and hung his head. '. . . she left a note – a rather confused, rambling note. She'd taken Ecstasy – all sorts of things, it seems – and thrown herself off the mountainside . . . There. Those are the facts.'

'Where was she?'

'Cairngorms. Loved it up there.'

'Christ. Sorry.'

Guy's face split into a huge grin. 'There we go! The great existentialist has feet of clay, after all! "Sorry!" That's the very best that any of us can do, isn't it? Sorry. No matter what, or who, or how, sorry is how it ends. It's just . . . pathetic, isn't it?'

Wheezer smiled. 'Pathetically inadequate, the whole grammar of grief. It's just people circling each other, really, fencing, trying to establish a proper hierarchy of bereavement. Who feels the greater loss. Who should tread most carefully.'

Guy eyed him with approval. 'Right! You're absolutely right!'

So he tried to set the record straight. Two things came out of Ticky's note. One, that she'd been in love with Guy for ever. He sort of knew but, then again, never took it seriously. She was George. His little mate. Working so close to him had made her own feelings more acute, but she was OK with it. She was fine. However, there was another thing. Something to do with Guy's father. She referred obliquely to 'this latest from your father'. Lord Philippe had been unable or unwilling to throw any light on that. That was all that had come from his visit to the Turnbulls'.

'Cripes! A real Agatha Christie. What d'you suppose?'

'Not got the foggiest, Wheeze. Honestly. He's a dirty old bastard, my father, but I couldn't see Ticky going for that . . .'

Wheezer shook his head with distaste as he spoke. 'What, a kind of shift of focus . . . love by association?'

'See what I mean?'

Wheezer sighed again. 'Poor kid.'

Guy was back looking out of the window, staring into the dark everlast. 'Get some kip if you're drunk, Wheeze. I'll wake you before we land. There's plenty of time to run through stuff.'

Keva was pleased to see her, but made the extra effort to be deferential. She looked too good to be true as she picked her way briskly down the steps and spotted him on a platform table. He grazed her cheeks with his lips, hoping it'd turn her on. A kiss from God.

'Hi. How are you?'

'Good. Certainly not as bad as I feel I should be.'

'I know. Sort of . . .'

'Don't be nice, Keva. I haven't come here to be nice.'

Keva felt the hot flush of foreboding. His armpits prickled anxiously. Hannah glanced over at the early lunchtime queue starting to build up at Cranks' Marshall Street café.

'Fuck it!' She checked her watch. 'I have to be in Hampshire for three.'

'It's not the funeral . . .?'

'No! Friday. No, I'm just going to stay with my folks for a few days. I think I should be down there, you know . . .' Her voice tailed off. She'd said 'you' and 'know' as separately enunciated words. There wasn't a trace of a trendy inflection or a nervous punctuation. She was in control.

'We're all coming . . .' Keva started. Hannah smiled, or rather she made her cheekbone muscles touch her temples.

'Thanks. The Turnbulls'll appreciate that. Look . . .' She groped for a cigarette. She lit it and exhaled. '. . . I'm going to get away for a bit after the funeral.'

''Course.' He tried to touch her wrist. She removed it. 'Maybe go to Goa or something. Zanzibar. Somewhere . . . haven't decided yet.'

His shoulders fell with his face. He couldn't say or do anything, other than carry on pointing his face at her. Her eyes were tear-filled. She turned sharply to him.

'Look, Keva. This whole thing. I feel completely . . .' She tailed off, dragging hard on the cigarette. He wanted so much to hold her hand. He nodded and attempted a sympathetic smile. She held his look for an uncomfortable moment then got up, gathering up her bag from the table.

'Right. That's what I came to say.' She grimaced again. Through all her dull, thickening grief, all she could think, just now, as she looked down on him was that this was the man she had introduced to Elizabeth Arden's Ceramide Complex capsules. She pitied him. She didn't want him. 'I'll see you all on Friday.'

He was shocked. She strode out and past the window, heading towards Broadwick Street.

One hour to landing. Wheezer had never felt more ready to take on a foe, which was how Guy was telling him to treat the record industry players of the US.

'These guys are arseholes, Wheezer, make no mistake. They'll put their arm around you. They'll show you pictures of their kids. They'll reveal incredibly inappropriate details about their personal lives. Their enthusiasm will dumbfound you. They'll do absolutely anything to make you feel like it's one big happy family pulling together. Do not be taken in by an iota of it – because once they've got you to sign up and join the marines it's just like the slogan says. It ain't what they can do for you any more, but the million things you should be doing for them. The slightest thing will be turned against you.' He affected a hurt, nasal, whine. '"Oh, you spoke with the radio station *yourself*."'

Wheezer smiled, dreading it all.

'Or the artist relations guys, the ones who liaise all the tour activities. They'll be: "Oh, you already discussed your lighting requirements *directly* with the venue?"'

Wheezer carried on grinning at Guy. Since he awoke, heavy-headed, it was as though Guy had cleansed his mind of its burdens, wiping the slate clean like an Etch-a-Sketch. He hadn't stopped psyching Wheezer up about the wiles of the perfidious Americans.

'Or, you know, one minute they'll be trying to ply you with cocaine, champagne, hookers. Next thing they're telling everyone you're out of control. You're a drugged-up English fuckhead. Don't forget the *English*, by the way – it can be used to imply any number of unprofessionalisms. Over here, religious cults are preferable to lack of professionalism. So don't give 'em the ammo. You know what I'm saying?'

He nodded, still laughing. 'Religious cults are mandatory, aren't they?'

Guy held up a hand. He was far from finished. 'Just try to remember that this is *your* group, man.'

Through it all, Wheezer sensed Guy's nervy anticipation of the days ahead. It was going to be a battle royal.

'Don't give any ground, yeah? Duck the charm offensive. There's one thing that never fails me in these meetings, it *never – fails*.' He looked at his ingenue, bolly-eyed. 'It's this – try to focus at all times upon the point in three, five, ten years – whatever. *One* year, that point when the group's all washed up and you want a little bit of belief and support and fucking *cash* for that make-or-break video or the back-to-basics tour. Don't forget this, now, right. *You will not be able to speak to those guys.* You won't get through to the lowliest foot soldier. Worse, you'll be despised for being the guy who's associated with these *failures*. Ugh!' He brushed an imaginary bug from his lapels. 'Even the secretaries'll patronise you. *The Grams*? You can, like, call us about this band? Without shame? So all I'm saying is, like, we haven't come here to make friends. We haven't come to make enemies. We're here on business. Yeah?'

Wheezer gave him an enthusiastic thumbs-up and engaged in a strange, rock-'n'-roll, back-clasp handshake. All the time he'd been talking and urging, Guy had been thinking: 'What the *hell* are these guys going to make of Wheezer?'

He'd seen it before. The English group from nowhere with their best mate as manager. He walks into a boardroom full of these horrific Ted Danson lookalikes, all fanatically smart-but-casual, all with tans and a not-necessary amount of buttons undone, all of whom have had sex in each other's company and, often, with each other – and these men are all thinking: 'THIS – is the *manager*?'

And then they'd set about tearing him apart. Little things at first. Commissioning a slight change to in-store artwork without prior sanction from the manager, just to see how he'd react. They'd chip away at him, systematically, overruling and undermining him over a period of time, until he could take no more. Maybe Wheezer'd find some way of beating them, but he doubted it. He pressed Print on his laptop and asked their hostess if she'd mind bringing over the finished sheets from the workstation.

He handed Wheezer his itinerary. They were here for three full days and would be seeing four record companies, three managers, a lawyer, an accountant and the Taurus team. Wheezer whistled, impressed. They were staying at the Bel Air Hotel. Even he'd heard of it. He couldn't wait to get going.

They gunned the hired Jaguar XK8, Guy's choice, down Riverside Drive, away from Burbank, towards the 101.

'That was cool, Wheezer,' laughed Guy, still in bits from his Kleenex routine. 'But maybe not so aggressive with the next lot?'

'You said to take no nonsense from them . . .'

'I didn't mean for you to call them heathens and assassins to their faces.'

'They loved it! They thought I was joking!'

'Sure – but let's not risk it next time.'

The meeting with Reprise, currently enjoying a good run of

form with a spunky roster of modern rock artists, had gone well. The team there knew their stuff and, in spite of Guy's forebodings, Wheezer had immediately warmed to them. He could see that they loved the band. Each one of them had gushed about the 'awesomeness' of the Grams. One blushing, passionate boy was 'floored' by what he'd heard. He'd tailed off, shaking his head, lost for further adjectives, unable to make eye contact. But they were music lovers, all of them. It was obvious. Howie Klein's still adolescent love of music was echoed by all his troops. Try as he might, Wheezer could not imagine any of them being beastly to him when the day came that the Grams would fall from grace. They were almost desperate to work with the band and, when Wheezer had pulled his Kleenex stunt, which took even Guy by surprise, Alicia MacNamara, the clear-eyed VP of Contemporary had yanked out a scrap of paper, giggling.

'Give this guy whatever he wants! Here y'are!' she said, pushing it over to Wheezer. 'Just write down what you want. Money. Dames. Anything! We'll do it!'

Everyone was laughing and getting on fine. Wheezer'd have been happy to get to work with them tomorrow. They were like a breath of fresh air – cool, young, motivated team players, unfucked by drugs or baggage, mad on music, ready to go in to bat for you. He loved it, loved the vibe – and he fancied Alicia – so tall, so pretend-tough – like mad. A couple of times he'd caught her staring right at him. She'd made no attempt to look away.

They hit the freeway.

'Why're they all VPs, anyway? Don't they have any . . . *Ps?*'

'Just the one. The rest of them are VPs and SVPs because they're completely fucked up on status and power.'

'Shame.' Wheezer mulled on it. 'So if they had a Really Senior Vice President . . . he'd be an RSVP!'

They chuckled about this and that, all the way along Sunset until they hit the Strip, where Worldwide had their LA offices. They were more of a New York company, anyway, but Willard had just got them out of their latest Major deal so they were off the Lot and into office space. It looked just fine to Wheezer. EMI and Book Soup were just down the road, with House of Blues and the *Spinal Tap*-legendary Riot Hyatt a walk the other way. You could almost spit on Hotel Mondrian from Willard's secretary Amy's window. They were having dinner with Willard and his LA chief Don Goodman later – but Guy wanted to grill the Contemporary Music team and, in particular, feel out their current standing with KROQ. He had an inkling that they'd still go with Worldwide, but Reprise, over the road from the all-powerful radio station, had made no bones about how much KROQ dug them at the moment. With an endorsement from KROQ, still the most influential radio station in the world, there was no limit to what a band like the Grams could achieve.

As Wheezer craned his head out of the window, looking down over Melrose and Century City beyond, Amy came back, apologetic. She'd been cheerfully solicitous from the moment she'd met them at the elevator – bright, chatty, but respectful. It was a good sign.

'He's still in there.'

'Hey! No problem! We're early.'

'He shouldn't be long. Can I get ya something to drink? Sprite? De-caff?'

Wheezer came back inside. 'An industrial-strength tea with just a sprinkle of sugar'd be good,' he said. She cackled her dirty laugh. Wheezer was liking America. The girls loved him.

'Nothing for me, thanks,' said Guy, studiously avoiding saying, 'I'm fine.' He thought 'I'm fine' was not a good thing to say, ever. Amy went off to make tea. Wheezer tried to peer into the corner office behind. According to Amy, Willard Weiss had turned up unannounced and scheduled a group meeting in his office. All the Contemporary Music crew were involved.

'It's all a stunt for our benefit, you know,' sighed Guy. 'I wish he wouldn't bother playing these games. I just want to get on with it.'

'Shall we walk out?'

'What?'

'You know – shift the balance of power. He's keeping us waiting in front of a team of people we might be working with in a few weeks' time. It's a bad precedent, isn't it, so early into a relationship. He's taking the piss. We're well within our rights to just do one . . .'

'What'd *that* achieve?'

'It tells him we've got other options. And we don't let people fuck us around.'

'No, man. Sit down. That's just rude. It's only just gone five past, now.'

'Sod 'em! Let's walk out!'

Wheezer's eyes were shining. Amy returned with his drink, a milky-brown concoction in a glass mug with the teabag still floating limply on the surface.

'You might wanna dunk another teabag in there – I ditten know how much milk . . .'

Wheezer laughed. 'Looks fine. Thanks, Amy.'

'You're welcome.'

Wheezer hesitated, still unsure whether they were having a laugh when they said that. He jerked his head at Amy. 'Listen. Tell The Man we're getting off to our next meeting at two forty-five. We don't mind sitting here until then, but we *are* leaving at two forty-five . . .'

Guy hung his head. Wheezer tipped the tea into the yucca pot while Amy went to interrupt Willard's think-tank.

Willard Weiss sat in on the meeting, breathing and cracking jokes. Guy and Wheezer let the team run through their plan for the band, which basically consisted of touring, touring and touring with a punishing schedule of interviews and promotion jammed in between dates.

'With an album as good as this and – don't take this wrong, but with one track as strong as "Beautiful", we can let the band spread the word live. Start the story slow and let it build organically.'

Wheezer looked at Guy, who jumped in before he could say anything. 'Sounds good, sounds good. It's certainly the way we saw the band developing over here. The band can play, for sure, and they're not scared of work, so this is clearly the way to go. Needless to say, we're looking for real commitment in that area from whichever label we decide to go with. Now – let me show you the video . . .'

He passed the cassette to a Lisa Loeb lookalike, who set the controls. There wasn't anyone, Willard included, who didn't shift in their seat and hunch forward. Adam's gorgeous, drenched images frazzled and flickered, in perfect harmony with the song. A couple of the Contemporary kids gulped and nodded to each other. Just on two minutes into the video, as the song approached its shimmering, coruscating, bleeding climax, Wheezer reached into his getting-famous briefcase, which he'd brought out to the States against Guy's counsel. He fished out a box of Kleenex, smiling, and tiptoed around the room, handing tissues to stricken World-wide employees. Guy looked down, trying to suppress his mirth. They smiled apologetically as they accepted the tissues, not knowing what to do with them. Only Willard played along, dabbing at his eyes theatrically and drooping his bottom lip.

'Excellent!' He clapped his hands and others followed suit. 'Excellent. Don't you think, Nancy?'

Nancy Spanke, VP, Creative Services, opened her eyes wide, searching for some indication from Weiss. He gave none. She cleared her throat. 'It's a beautiful video, no doubt,' she smiled. 'Kinda got shades of *Last Picture Show*, y'know, kinda that *Leaving Las Vegas* feel. Real filmic . . .'

'Mmmm . . .' everyone agreed.

'What on earth do you mean?' asked Wheezer. Guy, mortified, concentrated on a distant aeroplane.

'Well . . .'

'I think Nancy's trying to say it's too arty,' Willard interjected. 'Too arty for MTV, perhaps, do you think?'

'Well – not too *arty*, as such. But I think MTV may have a problem with it. It's very British.'

Wheezer made a face. 'Well, naturally. Did you expect it to be more Danish . . . ?'

Her face flushed slightly and she clenched her fists as though trying to quell some frightful tantrum. 'I'm not dismissing the video – I'm just telling you what I know . . .' She looked to Willard for help, unsure. A gentle smile flickered around Guy's mouth. '. . . I mean, we'll give it a shot, but you might wanna think about . . .'

The door flew open and a young Korean-looking kid burst in. 'Hey! Guys! We got it! *Buzz Bin* just added Marine . . .'

Guy rolled his eyes skywards. He'd seen the routine a dozen

times, always during key meetings when the record company was trying to press their Now credentials upon their guests. Some overheated company jock would come running in with spectacular good news, upon hearing which the entire crew would whoop and hi-five and 'all-rrrright!' each other. The room rose up and started whooping at each other. Guy rubbed his brow, half tickled, half depressed. Spotting it, Willard jettisoned the scam and turned it to his advantage.

'Thank you, Michael, neat timing. You were supposed to hit us with this when our illustrious guests first arrived!'

Everyone laughed nervously. Michael looked around, hurt at the injustice. 'But . . .'

Weiss held his hands up. 'But me no buts . . .' He stood, chortling and beckoning Guy and Wheezer to join him. 'Well. I'm sure you can't blame a dog for trying. Now, I know you have another meeting to get to, but . . . do you have a second to say hey to Bob Campione?'

'Bob?' said Guy, eager, knowing they had no other meeting until four. 'Of course we want to say hello to Bob! How an earth *is* the old dog . . .'

'Sorry, no, we got to go,' said Wheezer, wanting to play tough.

'Bob's Head of Promotion, Wheeze,' soothed Guy.

'I know,' said Wheezer, remembering where he'd heard the name. 'A legend as I live and breathe, but . . . he's coming tonight, isn't he?'

'He cancels, sadly,' said Willard. 'His boy is having rhinoplasty. He has to be with him.'

Wheezer accepted the truce. They popped their head around Bob's door. An affable-looking, big-handed man with Gene Wilder hair, Bob beckoned them in and continued screaming at his field staff through the tiny mouthpiece of his phone.

'Myra, that goes for you too! What the fuck's Sherman playing at with Boston? This is your call, Myra, but I swear to you, honey, I'm gonna come in there and piss all over your doorstep if that baby doesn't home today! So, you hear me, Sherman? You call me back in one hour and tell me Boston came through, or I'll call those assholes myself. They do not fuck us round like this! Three weeks in a row I sent that asshole shrimps . . .'

He disconnected, took off his headset and rose towards them, smiling, gesturing for them to sit. There was no resisting him.

'Heeeey! The Grams, right! Some tune! Some fuckin tune, man! I gotta tell you guys – you made a great, great record . . . I am blown away! I cannot wait to get to work on this. I am personally going to call ALL the key stations and get them ON this. It is going to be *sooooo* huge. It is going to be enormous. We are going to have SUCH a hit with this, excuse me . . .'

He made his speech and returned to his headset in less than twenty seconds, pulling an apologetic face over the mouthpiece and waving the boys farewell, thumbs-up. Willard, who'd remained by the doorframe throughout, gave him an elaborate bow and backed out of his office. Wheezer was gasping with excitement. 'Wow!' he laughed.

Willard chuckled with him. 'Now *that*, I have to tell you, was *not* an act! Il Campione tells you it's a hit – it's a solid gold certain hit!'

'We wanna solid gold platinum one!' grinned Wheezer, over-familiar.

Willard bowed his head graciously.

'Your wish is my command, my liege. Platinum it shall be!'

They reconfirmed Peppone for nine o'clock, said their farewells and hopped in the elevator, stabbing each other excitedly with their forefingers.

'So anyway – what's fucking rhinoplasty?' asked Wheezer. 'Some kind of fat removal or something?'

'Yes. It's a nose job.'

The Taurus offices were on Beverly Glen Boulevard, close to UCLA, so the boys had scheduled to drop in on their way back to the hotel. Bob Old, over from London, made the introductions. Tom Margolis, the CEO, gave them a tour of the company, dropping names carelessly, to impress upon on them that if they were to join up they'd be in good company – but if they decided against it, what the heck? Taurus was not short of clients. He was a hateful prick. Tom left them with Rudy Wexner, a pink-cheeked preppy who looked as rock 'n' roll as Ralph Malph. It was to be Rudy's job to sell Taurus to Guy and Wheezer.

He grinned and flipped a pencil over the backs of his fingers. It was difficult to tell whether he was blushing, or whether he was in excessively rude health. He started his pitch.

'Gaad!' he said, shaking his head in disbelief. He looked to Wheezer for help. 'I love my jaaab!' He groped for the killer superlative. '*Sooo* much.'

He looked up to smile his wonky Barbra Streisand smile and let them share in his luck. 'You know, I love my wife and I love my kids . . .'

Kids! . . . He's seventeen! thought Guy, smiling his assent.

'. . . but I'm gonna be here tonight, making the calls, e-mailing, dropping the faxes – I'll be here till nine, nine thirty – but I'll get home and I'll go kiss my kids and I'll tell my wife . . . Gaad! I'm so lucky!'

It was an oblique approach, in Wheezer's estimation. They left Rudy shaking his head, knocked sideways by the fortune through which he daily gambolled.

Back at the Bel Air, Willard Weiss had sent them a fax.

Dear Guy and Wheezer,

Thank you again so much for taking the time and trouble to come by the office this afternoon. I know you both are busy.

I know also we are not the only company in the running, but I do sincerely believe it is Worldwide who can achieve most for the Grams. I believe also that we have demonstrated our faith, through the patience and persistence we have shown in tracking this band. I know that you will not forget we were the first to show an interest.

After unanimously positive responses from my colleagues to Powder, *I now wish to advance the situation. I'd like us to try to reach an agreement this evening. To that end, Joely Masterson will join us for the latter part. I trust you share my desire to conclude business so that we can all get down to the real task in hand – that of breaking the finest new band in the world here in the United States.*

With my warmest personal regards

Yours

Willard Weiss

Wheezer couldn't settle. Every time he lay down on his bed, his head was full of the meeting this evening, the deal, the future. His brain ached hard. He read Willard's fax again and again. He nibbled the dark chocolates by his bedside then rolled off the bed, on to his feet. He wandered around the sweet, decadent-smelling grounds of the hotel and lingered by the steaming outdoor pool, inhaling the pungent orchids and delicate bougainvillea, trying to imagine what things, what stars this pool alone must have seen. He was shaken from his reverie by the spectacle of Pete Postlethwaite emerging through the mist, ploughing up and down the pool in a tight swimming cap. Wheezer Finlay found it hard to recall his recent, old, ordinary life. He wondered what Mum and Dad'd make of it, if they could see him now.

The first hint they had was that look in the doormen's eyes. They'd been getting used to the look, that glint of recognition replaced instantaneously with shock. Shock that it's *them*, shock that they're here, in real life, then panic about what they're going to do about it. Do they make a fuss? Do they think up something witty to say? Do they pretend not to have recognised the Grams or act as though it's not a big deal for stars to come ambling through the doors at L2. Do they make them pay? The boys had been getting used to the look, but they hadn't expected it here. They'd been coming to the L2 venue since it opened. They didn't know the doormen by name, as such, but they always exchanged 'a'right lad' greetings and shuffled inside without problems, whoever was playing.

Tonight it was Hunkpapa, sold out, big, edgy hometown gig and James had decided they should all go down there and have a Big One.

'Come 'ead! We haven't been out since we got back! Peter and Keith an' 'at'll be chocker if we don't go down!'

Keva, just back from London, was happy to go anywhere to take his mind off Hannah. He shrugged his support. Snowy looked gloomy. 'Peter and Keith an' 'at don't get . . . *bothered* by ample young men wherever they go!'

They guffawed and chubbled his cheeks. 'Come 'ead! They love you! You're a role model, aren't you? A tubby's hero . . .'

The doormen, after the initial shock of recognition, ushered the group straight through with a minimum of quips and offers to provide security. They'd barely got inside the bar when the mayhem was unleashed. A couple of young girls in Grams sweatshirts asked Keva to autograph them. A buzz went up and around the bar and before he'd finished signing the first shirt, the group was being greeted, cheered, jostled, pinched (bottoms, testicles), handshaken, touched, sworn at (twice – both Keva) and ogled. They had their cocks felt through their jeans by boys and girls. Tony was first to scream. 'Ay! Fuck off! We've come to see the band too, you know! We don't want this!'

Keva was shocked, agog, just letting it happen.

'Fucken sex, lar! You're pure fucken sex!' It was a girl's voice, just. He was only faintly aware of a hand groping his dick through his pocket before he was being carried out, shoulder-high above the insurrection.

'Sorry about that, boys,' grinned the biggest doorman, setting Keva down. 'You should think about getting someone in to look after youse, you know. This is how it's gonna be . . .'

Alone outside, they stared at each other before squatting on the floor, convulsing with the powerful laughter of freedom and shared insight. James groped for breath.

'Fuckinell, lar! Is it safe to say that, as of . . .' He grabbed Beano's wrist. '. . . nine forty-seven, Tuesday twenty-ninth September, we four boys can do WHAT THE FUCK WE WANT!'

More heartfelt, generous laughter.

'Is fucken right an' 'at, Hector, lar!' gasped Tony. They strolled down London Road, arms around each other, ready to take the world.

More than ever, they felt as though they were going through the motions. The remaining appointments were now courtesy calls. Willard Weiss had put forward a passionate case for signing ReHab and the Grams to Worldwide Records and they had last night shaken hands on a very substantial deal. Wheezer was on cloud ten. Steaming out the toxins in the sauna after breakfast, they'd decided to be cynical. They'd go through with the final two days of the trip as a fact-finding exercise, glean what they could from the rest of the record companies then concentrate on appointing the right partner to co-manage the group in the States with Wheezer.

They pulled into the Disney lot. They were going to see the new team at the revamped Hollywood Records. It wasn't the first label you'd turn to, for dark, melancholy new rock, but Guy had justified the potential match on the grounds that Hollywood needed credibility, might be prepared to go beyond the asking price to secure the right band and, given their current lack of competing modern rock repertoire, would be able to devote their resource pool wholly to the Grams. It was worth hearing what they had to say, at least.

Exposed and sweltering in the white heat of the vast parking lot, they wandered towards the first pathway looking this way and that for clues. A svelte, happy, blonde sashayed jauntily towards them. She looked beautiful dressed down in jeans and a loose white T-shirt. Nothing could take from the aura of natural, radiant, lightly-tanned goodness – this girl was born to be nice.

'Excuse me . . .'

'Hi-ya!' she beamed.

'We're here to see Fran Fraternity – could you direct us to his office?'

'No PRAB-*lem*!' she almost sang. 'OK, guys. What you want to *do* . . . is go straight ahead and make a right on Goofy. Follow Goofy 'til you hit Minnie, second right from the end. OK, now make a right into Minnie, first left into Mickey and Hollywood is right there in front of you. Reception'll take care of you guys from there. OK? You guys take care, now!'

This last was delivered with a cute incline of the head, a hint of a curtsey and another devastating smile.

'Thanks,' smiled Guy.

'You're welcome.'

'Thank you,' murmured Wheezer, transfixed.

'A-ha.'

And off she bobbed, without a care in the world. Wheezer watched her go, then walked over to study a road sign, gently incanting, 'GoofyGoofyGoofyGoo-fy . . .'

'Er, Wheeze . . .,' Guy shouted after him.

Wheezer, who had located Goofy Boulevard on the streetfinder, turned back to a wan-looking Guy.

'Let's leave it, huh?'

'Do I *have* to meet him, Guy. I mean, fuck it! I don't *need* help! I've got you. We can manage all this on our own, can't we?'

'Nope. Not the States. GOT to have a US representative. Anyway, I told you, Mel's not a manager, as such. He might just be exactly what we're looking for . . .'

'What *you're* looking for . . .'

'Wheeze, honestly . . .'

'I know, I know. All right! I'll see the lantern-jawed bastard!'

Guy chuckled. They'd spent the afternoon speaking to managers. Guy was starting to share Wheezer's disillusionment. Of the three they'd seen, all had boasted lasciviously about their cosy, go-back-*years*-together relationships with Heads of Programming at radio stations and television producers while only one, Mike Brietling, mentioned the record. He thought the band were from Manchester, Ireland, which was not a problem, but had a curly perm, which was. Mike was five foot three, wore a black silk shirt tucked into tight black slacks and shiny, shiny dress shoes. His perm was cut straight across his ears and bushed out defiantly over his collar. His teeth were scintillatingly white except, Wheezer noticed, the ones right at the side of his head, which you could only see when he threw his face back to laugh at a gag. Those teeth were brown. Wheezer just couldn't see the boys taking this chap seriously and it amazed him, thoroughly shocked him, on each of the three occasions during their poolside meeting that *Baywatch*-pretty girls had come over to the table to greet him. One of the girls, a lithe, aerobicised Barbie-babe was still ploughing up and down the pool, long after Mike Brietling had gone. Sucking on a cranbery vodka, Wheezer watched her wistfully.

'How come, Guy, how come you rate these arseholes so high?

What makes you think they can manage my band better than I can?'

'I don't. I just know how it works here. The boss of, like, Shitcake Radio in Idaho would like nothing better than to get a call from Mike Brietling, rap on about their families, their wives' breast jobs, talk about getting together at Christmas, not really mean it, then snap into business. I really do doubt that, with all the respect in the world, Wheeze, a call from you is going to have the same impact.'

'Like fuck! The Grams're the best new band in the world. We're gonna be huge! If people don't want to be part of that, fuck 'em! I'm handing the boys over to some cap-toothed chimpanzee for the sake of a couple of extra plays in fucking Fargo?'

Guy shook his head. 'I wish it were that simple. I do. Just trust me, right. Mel's a good guy. He's not like the fellas you've just met. He's not a *manager* . . .'

'Don't tell me. He's a real music guy, right?'

Guy laughed. 'Just *meet* him, OK?'

Wheezer was glad he acquiesced. After the least promising of starts – Mel, too, had a laughable floss of extra-dyed, jet-black, big at the back, receding at the front, Michael Bolton hair and a *beard* – Mel Parmese proved himself to be a wry and sensitive observer and an honest analyst.

'Your band may well be the hottest thing on eight legs in England, Wheezer, but, boringly, it doesn't mean shit pie here in the States. The situation here is that we have to want you and, just as important, you have to want us. *Really* want us. If we can rely on these givens then, certainly, Automatic can help you.'

Mel ran through the ways in which Automatic differed from an orthodox management company. It sounded good. They were geared towards marketing, promotion and tour support, with a full back-up staff to service each of these areas. They had three girls devoted to college and alternative radio promotion, and the company worked no more than three projects per quarter. Best of all, potentially, was that they didn't work on commission. The other candidates Wheezer had spoken to expected ten or twelve and a half per cent of all advances, fees and earnings, *before* deductions. 'Off the top,' they'd spit, with a flinty stare and a half smile. Mel's firm, Automatic, charged a one-off 'life of project' fee to work an album, no matter if it lasted for four singles and nine months or it was burnt out after six weeks. They had a performance-related bonus structure, with extra money payable on each increment of 250,000 albums sold. The only other cost was a monthly levy for expenses – bikes, long-distance calls, line-of-action expenses. Financially, it was quite a commitment upfront, but if *Powder* were to break through the 250,000 mark and really start to sell through, employing Automatic would be money well invested.

'Big question, Wheezer. Do the band *like* to tour?'

'God aye! Try and stop 'em! They'll do as many dates as you can chuck at 'em!'

He looked unconvinced. 'Mm, I'm sure, but what I'm saying is, you know – do they *enjoy* that side of it? Long, monotonous bus journeys, that sense of travelling without seeing anywhere, no sleep, interviews, soundchecks, interviews, motel rooms, rootlessness . . .'

'Well, you know, put like *that* . . . they LOVE it!'

He wasn't laughing. 'Good. I hope so. Not many bands really *like* touring, when it comes down to it. A real, genuine work ethic is the surest route of any to breaking bigtime in the States. Take Medsin . . .'

Guy nodded. Mel Parmese went on to explain how Medsin had written off six months of their lives to tour the various 'markets' of Middle America. In Mel's world of promotion and exposure, towns and cities ceased to be places. They were markets. There were Primary markets, massive conurbations like New York, San Francisco, Chicago and Los Angeles. These would be the first places you'd look to crack. In some ways, too, they'd be the easiest because of the abundant radio stations, cable channels, television opportunities, press, magazines, fanzines – each looking for product, each one in search of a developing story. These areas were served by the big, key, major radio stations, the P1s, still the surest medium for turning a promising tune into a hit.

Then Medsin had weaved their way back and forth through the Secondary markets, served by P2 radio stations, often huge populaces again but without the big-name glamour of their historic neighbours. Spokane, Salt Lake City, Orlando, Sacramento, Birmingham – places like these had huge catchment areas and were worthy of the attention of a conscientious band.

'Most Brit bands think they've had a hard tour if they do, you know, the forty-date hike around the Primaries and a coupla the P2s. They're ready to go home. They're fucked. They wanna see mom, wife, fuckin boyfriend. This can be the difference between a gold record and a mult-eye fuckin platinum monster!'

His eyes fired up. 'If you boys really wanna do it, OK . . . ?' Everyone was nodding, Mel included. '. . . if you can dig deep and stay an extra eight, ten weeks and really go out there, reach out to Lincoln fuckin Nebraska and Louisville fuckin Kentucky and fuckin I dunno . . . fuckin Augusta, fuckin crazy places where they're *wild* for rock 'n' roll and no band ever goes near there, those places will *worship* you if you go play to them . . .' He was still nodding, eyes still aflame. '. . . they will stay with you for ever.' Wheezer felt like crying. 'You make a pledge to the Tertiaries and they're with you for life.'

Mel went on to outline the ways in which Automatic could co-ordinate the whole fantastic roadshow and keep the thing moving smoothly. He stressed and stressed again that the band would have to be willing, zealously enthusiastic contributors to the whole process.

'I'll tell you straight up, Wheezer, they'll fuckin *love* it for a week. Ten days. Cute little valley girls sucking their cock and telling them "I love your accent!" Then the monotony kicks in. I guarantee you, there is no monotony like the endless fuckin . . . *endlessness* of an American tour. A *real* tour, right? Do you hear me?'

Wheezer nodded, dumbstruck.

Mel's voice softened. 'But if they can hack it, yeah? If they can ride this fuckin twister out for four, five, six months and do their job, right? Win friends, press palm, get around and play a *mighty* fuckin show every night . . .'

Not for the first time since the madness started back in spring did Wheezer find himself having to suppress those quickening, breathless giggles.

'. . . then those boys will go home millionaires. That's the difference it makes. That's the sort of commitment the USA is looking for from a band.'

He eyeballed Guy and Wheezer. Millionairesmillionairesmillionaires. Twenty per cent of four millionaires almost makes another one. Wheezer felt faint.

'Think they're up to it?'

Guy nodded and cleared his throat. 'Oh, very much so, I think. And, I dunno, I think you make it all sound a lot worse than it is . . . I mean, no offence, I know why you're doing that, but . . . I went along with Medsin on huge chunks of those tours and I reckon . . . well, I don't think it'll give our boys too many problems, anyway. What d'ya think, Wheeze?'

'They'll do it.'

Guy spent the remainder of the day faxing short, charming rejections to the disappointed parties and short, businesslike confirmations to Mel at Automatic and to Willard Weiss at Worldwide. The headlines included a $200,000 advance, with a minimum tour support fund of $150,000 and a marketing and promotional spend of another $150,000 to cover Automatic's fee, independent radio promotion and advertisement. That Indie money would, in theory, give ReHab an element of autonomy in shaping the band's progress in the US. If Worldwide, for example, were to give the Grams six weeks of priority promotion before moving on to another band, Guy could hire an independent radio plugger without upsetting Bob Campione's sense of pride. It was a handy safety net to have.

Furthermore, if Worldwide needed to remake videos or remix tracks for the American market, it was to be at their own, non-recoupable expense and only after ReHab approval. Similarly, if the band were to embark upon a short promotional tour of no more than five cities, this would be financed by Worldwide separately from the band's tour fund and would not be recoupable from record sales. It was a healthy deal for Guy, proving Willard's esteem for the band. He biked the album parts over to Mel, with instructions to catapult Worldwide into production the moment the Heads of Agreement was signed. As a gesture of goodwill, they could go right ahead and begin mastering the album immediately.

At six thirty, unable to temper his impatience, Wheezer called James and Keva, getting them out of bed to pass on the news.

'Are we getting a bonus?' said James, yawning.

'Is that all you've got to say?' clipped Wheezer, trying to curb the irritation he felt.

"Bout time we saw the money an' that . . .'

'I thought you'd stopped saying that an' that,' laughed Wheezer.

'I have an' that. Just when I'm dead, dead, dead excited an' that, you know,' he yawned. 'Sort the loot out, Wheeze. I'll just get the singer.'

Wheezer and Keva stayed on the phone prattling about plans, news, details until Guy came knocking at his door to go to dinner. They were meeting Martyn Atkins for a quiet supper in Santa Monica and catching a midday flight back home next day, in time for the funeral on Friday.

Wheezer dragged his head from the pillow. If this was consciousness, then it was a lumpen, throbbing, dull, deadly consciousness he was waking into. He knew who he was and he knew two other things. The telephone was still ringing and Alicia MacNamara was no longer in bed with him. He smiled. He felt OK. The recollections came gushing back, now, suggesting themselves to him, curling him up with mirth and pleasure. He picked up the phone. Guy.

'Fuckinell, Wheeze! We should've left twenty minutes ago! I've been hammering on your door for ages . . .' He paused. 'Are you all right?'

'Smashing. Seldom better.'

'Good. Tell me about it later. I've checked us out. Meet me in the car soon as. I mean it Wheeze, you've got ten minutes then I'm off to the airport. I'm not missing that plane.'

In a thudding haze of surreality, Wheezer staggered around the room, looking for things he'd already packed, remembering to do things he'd already done, trying to find tickets he'd placed in his inside pocket a moment before. He was moving more slowly than time. He could not crank himself up that little bit extra. Each search for a sock, a passport, a magazine, took him down avenues and tributary conduits of reverie and recall. Standing in the bathroom, brushing his teeth, he found himself staring at himself in the mirror with no hint of how he'd got there or how long he'd been daydreaming. Forcibly, now, he made himself shrug off the past and race once more towards his beckoning, enticing future. He jammed every lazy item into his suitcase, every business card, taxi receipt and magazine. He rummaged around one last time for any priceless memento he might have overlooked and called the concierge to send someone for his luggage. He groped inside his jacket pocket, his new, obviously-pricey Bonneville leather jacket which he'd bought the day before they'd left for LA. Shit!

He stared at the note from Alicia, starting to sense that something was wrong. It wasn't Alicia. Her note, as pert and witty as every single thing about her, said: 'Fanx. Ta-ra!'

Allowing himself half a second to quiver with pride, Wheezer gave in, instead, to the stronger emotion which came up yelling from behind. It was a cloying, access-all-areas dread, a general, thudding downer, a notice that *something* was wrong. He knew what. He had no small notes to tip the luggage boy. He knew that he had last night cheerily, tipsily tried to hand the taxi driver one hundred dollars for a twelve-dollar ride back from outside the Mondrian with Alicia. The driver had refused such a vulgar tip and helped Wheezer and his equally squiffy mate (God! What a *lion* he'd been! Huzzah for King Harry!) find the fare in small notes and change. He sat on the bed. He knew that, when he checked his pocket now, there'd be one one-hundred dollar note and fuck all else. The car was parked at the front of the hotel, a good ten-minute walk without the luggage trolley to take the strain. There was no way the luggage boy was getting a ton for carrying his bag, heavy though it now certainly was. He couldn't ask him for change. Shit! Fuck! Fiddlesticks! Guy'd be going mad. He'd be leaving in two minutes! The bellboy would be on his way!

Wheezer dived outside his bungalow-bedroom, dragging the suitcase behind him. Stuffed full of all the free CDs and goodies from Reprise, Sony, Universal and Worldwide he'd greedily accumulated and the two reams of copy paper and two hundred envelopes he'd inexplicably snaffled from the unoccupied hotel reception last night, Wheezer's bag was almost immovable. He could hear the bellboy now, sounding only feet away, occluded by bushes, reporting to some, momentarily invisible, bellhopping superpower.

'Sure. No prab-lemm. Lemme just do this guy, first, Finlay, right? He needs to leave, like, yesterday – then I'll get right back to Mr Postlethwaite. Sure. A-ha. You got it.'

Wheezer dived into the bushes and pushed his way through the undergrowth. Straight ahead, through the putrid orchids and overpowering bougainvillea, he could see the paint and metal of delivery lorries. That must be the carpark. Surely it must. He struggled on, the woven leather strips of the suitcase handle biting into his palms, for two minutes, tripping over roots and vines, breathing hard, praying that Guy'd wait. The voice came again. He stood shock still. It had come from right in front of him.

'Hey! Andy! Listen, no sign of Finlay! Room already vacant on arrival! No! No way, man! What? Like, five minutes ago, you know! He cuddint have! No way!' There was a pause while they conferred via walkie-talkie. 'Well, I think I woulda seen him? You want me to go after him? Sure. Sure. I'm on it. Still want me to go do Mr Postlethwaite?'

He still had a hundred dollars. He could get a cab to LAX in no time at all. Cripes! What a session with Alicia! And fancy bumping into Willard Weiss and Don Goodman like that! What a hoot they'd all had in the Sky Bar – Willard and Don had stood up on the bunk behind the pool, right up against the balcony with a three-hundred-foot drop below them, and started doing punk songs, these two sixty-year-old men, pogoing and spitting at the Sky Bar's glitterati! Fantastic! And everyone in there, people he'd never even spoken to before, were congratulating him about the Grams and the deal and sending over bottles of champagne and inviting him down to parties at Bourgeois Pig in Silverlake. Alicia had walked in with some steroid-head, but she'd soon chased him when she spotted the Wheeze. Jings! He hadn't even told her he was going home today. What a cad!

He spotted the carpark up ahead. And – glory! Hallelujah! – there was Guy, still sitting in the Jag, sunglasses on, looking cool, just waiting. He quickened his pace as he gained the outer reaches of the sandy, rusty-soil parking area.

'Ah! Mr Finlay! *There* you are!'

He was within lassooing distance of the XK8 when the bellboy pounced, heading him off between two Landcruisers with a sadistic smile. Wheezer was panic-struck. He could feel his face, nicely tanned after three days in the sun, turn gruel grey.

'I'VE GOT NO BLOODY MONEY!' he shrieked. He felt like he was going to cry. Hotel customers, previously inconspicuous as they chatted to parking attendants and pottered around their vehicles, came forward to stare. Wheezer was rooted to the spot, clinging on to his suitcase as though it concealed a mutilated dead body.

'Hey! No prab-lem! Like, I take Diners Card. I'm only kidding! Here . . .'

He went to take the bag. Perspiring, agitated, overheated, Wheezer, knowing he was being humiliated, let the Nordic youth carry his case the five yards to the Jag. The boot opened. Wheezer got in next to Guy, who, staring dead ahead, waved the staff farewell through the window and, as soon as the boot clunked shut, boomed out on to Stone Canyon Road. He draped his left forearm out of the open window and continued concentrating hard on the bends of the road. Nothing was said for a long five minutes, until Guy, unable to keep his act going, gave in to convulsions of shuddering, powerful laughter. He had to pull off the road. Wheezer, greatly relieved and generally, vaguely high from the non-stop of his LA experience, spluttered merrily too. Guy put his free hand on Wheezer's shoulder for support, catching his breath.

'You, m'lud, are fucking priceless. Fucking, bloody priceless!'

He stared at the page again. Since Wheezer had joined them in Rotterdam that afternoon, bringing news from around the world, more proof of the Grams' brilliance and magnitude, and the latest music press, Keva had been content to stow himself away in the back lounge of the tour bus and revel in the hard facts. Wheezer seemed to sense out his need for assurances, and since his return from the States he'd copied him on all the good stuff. Keva still had, folded and folded inside the little pop pocket of his heavy

Chevignon, the photostat of Paul Parlour's fax, with the first midweek reactions to *Powder*. He patted it for safety and, feeling its chunky square stack, got it out once more and unfolded the shiny paper with still-trembling pleasure.

Nth Ireland – Excellent stock, reactions. Flying out in all stores. Grams mania here! Prediction – 1

Scotland – Good stock and reactions. Number One in most stores. Prediction – 1

North East – Excellent stock levels, flying out on all formats. Prediction – 1

Lancs. – Biggest album of '98! Absolutely flying out! Prediction – 1

Yorks/E. Mids – Huge sales. Must go in at Number One! Prediction – 1

Midlands – Excellent stock found. Flying out. Strong reorders. Prediction – 1

London – Good stock, good reactions. Further increase expected next week. Prediction – 1

Central London – No stock problems, all stores well behind it, massive sales – will continue through to Christmas, at least. Everyone loves it! Prediction – 1

South Coast – Many shops selling out already. Huge sales and demand. Prediction – 1

Wales & West – Great stock but mixed reactions. Still expected to go in at Number One. Prediction – 1

East Anglia – Excellent, great reactions – massive! Prediction – 1

AVERAGE 1

What a nerve-shattering thrill that had given him, when Wheezer first faxed it through. He still liked to read it all the time. All those Number Ones. All those 'massives'. He tucked it away and settled down with *Music Week*. Smiling at the centrefold, he felt cold and remote and powerful. It was a good, constant sensation, a feeling of control, of general well-being. Not quite the same as the dizzying headspin of a few months ago when they'd heard 'Desert Rain' in the chip shop, or the numbing blow-back of walking on stage at Alexandra Palace, but good, anyway.

This latest, the platinum album, was expected. It was only a matter of how long it would all take. If it were to be the case, now, that the thrill of the new would inevitably gradually dull, then there were fine and tangible, earthly consolations. The sight of the centre page of *Music Week*, for now, was aphrodisiac enough for Keva McCluskey. After the look of the page, the words themselves had ceased to be just print and disseminated a meaning to him, he sat and glinted at the little black star. Next to the Number One album, *Powder* by the Grams, which was Number One for a third week, was a little black star which signalled that the record had now shipped in excess of 300,000 copies. It was a platinum record. Keva was a fucking crucial new voice. It said so here in *Music Week*. And now, to keep it all wonderful, he was going to just go out there, like a prophet, and spread the word further and wider. He was going to do every bit of nonsense Wheezer laid before him. He was up for it. Fuck the myths and the madness of rock 'n' roll music. Keva wanted his songs to be heard and known and loved all over the world. Everywhere. And he was going to blow Helmet off stage again.

Wheezer sat with Marty in the empty arena, catching up with figures and news. The tour was going well. They'd concentrated on Germany, where 'Beautiful' was threatening to become an enormous hit, and France, where it was starting to take off, fitting in Vienna, Zurich and Brussels, too. They had the Mars Awards live on satellite tonight in Rotterdam, then Amsterdam tomorrow and back to Liverpool to regroup before the US promotional tour.

Things were moving in the States. The album was already out, to mop up demand from kids who'd got into the Grams through their local college and alternative stations and through the music press and the Internet. Automatic were now liaising well with Steve Knopf, VP of Contemporary at Worldwide, in trying to regulate all the pirate play and bring the radio stations into line for the big push. Some, like KROQ in LA and New York, and

WDRE in Long Island had been playing the Grams for months. It was hard to persuade them to perservere with one track, 'Beautiful', while other stations played catch-up. KROQ and the other big giants of modern rock prided themselves on getting to the next track while the competition were still deliberating over the first single, but they were not unreasonable. It wasn't as though they had to ask permission, but they'd agreed with Knopf that they'd keep 'Beautiful' in rotation if they could add 'Chimera' to their night-time shows. These were good problems to have, though. In two weeks, without a video or any sort of push to radio, Worldwide had shipped 65,000 copies of *Powder*. It was all looking good for the promotional tour next month.

Sensira, headlining the show tonight, came out to soundcheck. Feedback squalled and monitors fizzed. Wheezer made a face and went to find Janey Heal.

'I'll catch you later, Marty. Thanks. Nice one.'

Janey was having a problem with MarsChannel. They were perfectly happy to interview Tony, James and Beano, but they wouldn't contemplate *any* interview without Keva. Janey had flown out with Wheezer, especially to ensure this all went to plan. MarsChannel, a dedicated youth culture and music station, had fifteen million viewers across Europe. It was a big deal getting the Grams on the show at such a late stage and Janey was rightly pleased with herself. Keva, when last she saw him, had decided that he'd done more than enough interviews for one tour. He felt that his voice was about to go. He wanted to try and preserve it for the show itself.

'I'll see if I can have a word,' said Wheezer.

He found Keva asleep in the back of the tour bus, *Music Week* at his side. Wheezer shook him gently, gurning at the singer as he came around. 'Hey! We're in Amsterdam! You've slept for two days!'

Keva smiled weakly and stretched. 'What time we on? When we eating? Fucken starving!'

'Yes, m'lud. All in good time. Just the small matter of one little interview for millions of eager viewers dotted all over Europe's benighted wastelands . . .'

'Ah, fuck, Wheeze . . .' Wheezer wiggled his eyebrows. 'I've *told*

Janey . . .' Keva pulled his hurtest sick-dog face. He looked like a kid trying to skive off school. Wheezer started tickling him.

'Come on! You know you're gonna have to do it! I'll just start harping on about the bad old days, otherwise.'

Keva grimaced. Wheezer's good humour was rubbing off on him. He put on a *Monty Python* voice and started stabbing Wheezer with his index finger. 'In th'old days we'd eat pigeon's testicles and be glad of it. How we hoped and prayed that one day Mam'd be able to afford tripe!'

'Come on! The others are waiting. Let's get it over with . . .'

They hopped out of the bus and braced themselves against the icy blast of the Rotterdam wind. Keva grinned to himself. Fifteen million viewers, Janey had said. Of course he was going to do the bloody interview. They just needed to plead a bit more – that's all.

Guy watched the awards show at home, seeing the boys' interview but hardly taking it in, only generally aware that they were on good form. Keva, in particular, looked fresh and sparky.

Since the funeral, Guy had been unable to shake himself free from that same leaden pall of despair that had blighted him in the summer. Again it struck at a time when promise and hope flowered comely. As Wheezer and the boys took off, unable to rein in their rampant, fulsome pleasure at it all, Guy withdrew and hid away behind paperwork, procedure, documentation. It was true – all those international licence deals had created a slough of correspondence and contracts – but these were not things that would ordinarily concern Guy. He could not shrug himself free of it. Everything, once again, seemed futile. His life was tasteless. He felt he had no dignity, no masculinity, no reason, no role. He sat at length with Dr Zwimmer, and with increasing regularity, each new consultation bringing him closer to the eye of his agony. There was no point in putting it off. He needed to see his father.

Wheezer found himself breathing harder, faster, willing the song forwards, urging the band to push themselves through this crisis. It wasn't happening. This overblown awards festival, the whole thing was made for the Grams. It was perfect. Their time had come, they were *right now* and the crowd, 12,000 alcopop-crazed teenagers, were mad for them. They'd sauntered out on stage almost too confident, too sexy, applauding back to the screaming, steaming audience. Wheezer, who'd been getting used to big occasions and stoked-up crowds, was once again sick with nervous anticipation. Keva stopped still, centre stage, and said, 'Hello. We're the Grams. This one's called "Desert Rain".'

That was it. The crowd went wild from Beano's first drum-kick, bodysurfing and hugging and jumping on each other. But the band seemed miles away. The sound was distant and thin. Keva sounded reedy and looked bizarre, throwing himself into a song that no one could hear. The diesel chug of Tony's bass spluttered in and out. It was a mess. The crowd gave a warm response, but Wheezer knew his band were committing suicide. He flashed his ID and pushed his way to the vast mixing consoles for sound and light. Marty was already there.

'Bastards! They've got limiters on!'

'What?'

'Sensira! They've got limiters on the sound! How the fuck did we agree to that? Where's Todd?'

Sensing Wheezer's befuddlement, Marty led him away from the mixing desks. 'Look. Sensira must have a clause in their contract that, as headliners, they have the right to turn up the volume when they come on. Or turn down the bands who're on before them, so's the crowd gets a sense of who they've really come to see, you know? Real, phoney, top-of-the-bill stuff, you know? No bastard does it any more!'

'We never agreed to that!'

'Are you certain? We *have* to speak with Todd. If he stipulated no limiters in the contract, we can pull the band off. No comebacks. In fact, we can probably sue the promoters . . .'

Wheezer gulped hard. He'd left his mobile on the tour bus, didn't want it tempting him during a live show. And Todd was almost the last person he wanted to speak to, after the band's humiliating treatment of him before the show. Todd had contributed to his own abuse, but only by virtue of being Todd.

He'd appeared, ample of tooth, on the tour bus that afternoon as though he were the most beloved, most welcome sight the boys could hope for. He'd flown over from London for the show, checked into his hotel and taken a taxi straight over to the arena, where the bus was parked. He waved like a boxer entering the ring as he pulled himself up into the little front lounge of the bus. There were the usual half-hearted greetings, James's 'A'right, Toddy lar' being the most effusive. Impervious to their ambivalence, Todd plonked himself down next to James, snapped open his folder and, grinning uncontrollably, whipped out a sheaf of fax paper.

'This, gents,' he beamed, waving the papers, 'sets you firmly on the road to being the biggest live band in the world this time next year.'

He was nodding as he said it, willing his act to be as slick and convincing as he wanted it to be. He passed the papers not to Wheezer, but to James. James scan-read the document as Todd stared straight ahead, smiling horribly to himself. He believed that the group were now taking in the best possible news they could ever conceive of. He was thinking that he was the smartest kid in the world for setting this up. He was thinking how the blurb in *Billboard* would read and he was thinking that the Grams would love him even more for this. He thought that one day, soon, he'd be their manager. James snorted, choked on his laughter and passed the papers to Keva.

'What is it?' asked Wheezer calmly, trying not to raise his eyebrows. Todd's pleasure in himself was more pitiable than offensive.

'Only an offer to open on the biggest European tour this winter. Rome, Barcelona, Lisbon, Stockholm, Munich . . .'

'Who is it?'

'. . . Paris, Amsterdam, Prague, Brussels, Berlin . . .'

'Who's the band?'

Keva and Todd both said the name at the same time, both putting the word 'fucking' before the band's name, both meaning inversely different things.

'Fucken *Black*hole,' winced Keva, disbelieving.

He turned to Todd. He was alight with pride, nodding his euphoric disbelief.

'I know . . . !'

'You're fucken joking, aren't you?'

The debate lasted less than a minute. The Grams, they told Todd, didn't support *no* fucker, let alone some grungy bunch of doom-angst merchants from Arkansas. Fuck them. The fax was ripped up in his face. Wheezer didn't feel inclined to rise to Todd's defence. If he was going to carry on this irritating ploy of bypassing management he'd have to take his medicine. Todd stormed off the coach, pausing only to tell Wheezer, with an uneasy stoicism, where he was staying.

Wheezer patted Marty on his way. 'You carry on trying to sort the sound out. I'll get hold of Todd.'

He raced back to the bus and snatched up his phone. Two messages. Todd. And . . . Todd. He called him back. He was in a cab.

'Phew, Wheezee, am I glad to hear your voice, man. I already . . .' He was unreal. He was a robot.

'Todd. Look . . .'

'Ah, forget it. I'd prefer they'd handled it differently but whatever, you know. We aim to please, but . . . their artistic and career choices need to be their own. Sometimes . . .'

Wheezer found himself laughing, largely through relief.

'Right. OK. Look – we didn't agree to limiters, right?'

Todd gave a hollow laugh. 'Like, er, *please*, Mr Wheezer. No way. Wheeze . . . no way. Let me be categoric here. No. Fucking. Way. H3O would not sanction sound limiters for our most *lowly* band. We don't hold with it, period. As a company . . .'

'What do we do then? They're killing themselves every second they're on, up there!' He tried to sound matter-of-fact.

'OK. Spoken already with Jaap Heindricksen, the promoter. He's *shitting* himself we're going to pull the band and sue his butt off. He's gone to find Sensira's management to clear it with them that we reinstate full sound.'

'Does it sound crap on TV?'

Todd's voice dropped to a conspiratorial whisper. He was enjoying the drama. 'You can hardly tell on TV. That's the good news. Different sound channels and all that. An ordinary punter wouldn't notice anything untoward at all. But if we carry on like this another two, three songs . . . the crowd stops dancing . . . people get agitated . . . we don't even wanna think about that stuff.

What you need to do is go right now and find Jaap, yeah, and give him thirty seconds to throw the sound back on. If he doesn't, pull the band off of that stage. Go for it! I'm on my way!'

Wheezer felt puny as he cleared his throat, blushing, and informed the promoter, who looked like a porno star, that he had to make a decision now. The promoter looked him over and decided that Wheezer was someone he could fuck with. He put a patronising arm around him, squeezing him close.

'No problem, my friend. This is getting sorted right out, right now. You watch. Five minutes that sound is bursting your ear eggs!'

Wheezer pushed himself through the pain barrier. 'You don't have five minutes. You don't have one minute. Do it now!'

The big promoter moistened his wiry, tobacco-stained moustache with his tongue and studied Wheezer's face for signs of bluff. He stuck a fat fist in his pocket and locked a tough-guy stare into Wheezer's head. Wheezer was over his stage fright. He was fine.

'I'm walking back to the mixing desks. If the sound isn't fully restored by the time I get there . . .'

He made a cut across his throat with his finger. He backed out of the production office, watching Jaap Heindricksen all the way. The promoter picked up his walkie-talkie. In a flash, Wheezer divined it. Jaap was not ordering his sound men to pump up the volume. He was ordering security to intercept Wheezer at the console and apprehend him until the Grams had finished their set. He could see the big grocks down below now, looking for him. They wouldn't know who the fuck he was until he presented himself and his ID at the barrier. So he wouldn't go to the barrier.

The band were halfway through 'Chimera', the third song of a scheduled six. It sounded weak and miserly, but nowhere near as bad as 'Desert Rain'. This was now damage limitation. Wheezer pushed right down the far left side of the audience and called Marty on his walkie-talkie. Fuzz and interference. The shortwaves had been scrambled. Bastards! He jerked his head around, frantic, looking for Marty. Security guards were now surrounding the mixing console. The two guards at front right of the stage were distracted, one of them talking into his radio. Wheezer got right down to the front and started jumping up and down, waving madly, trying to get James to look down. He spotted him and cracked a delighted, disbelieving smile. Wheezer shook his head manically, nonononono! waving his hands across each other, palms out, slicing his throat with his finger. James waved back and shook his own head vigorously. He tugged Keva by the sleeve and pointed out their nutty manager, pogoing and having a great time down the front. Keva caught Wheezer's eye. There could be no ambiguity. Wheezer pointed side stage, brushing non-existent fluff away with the back of one hand and pointing straight, sending them off for foul play with the other. Keva stooped and held his finger across his throat. Wheezer nodded. The band were off.

Shrill whistles, boos and catcalls rent the air as Keva, forcing his way past two security guards, took to the stage with a megaphone. The noise abated a little, enough for him to be heard.

'We're sorry! We genuinely are! We want to give you the best! Nothing but the best . . . Some joker's been messing with the sound . . . if you can't hear us, there's no point us making twats of ourselves! Do you agree?'

Mixed response. More boos than applause, then a rhythmical clapping, like a locomotive gradually gaining a head of steam. The whole arena was up, stomping in thunderous unison.

'We want Grams!! We want Grams!'

Wheezer pushed past the guards to consult with Keva.

'Fuck it! Let's go back on!' gasped Keva. 'They fucken love us!'

Wheezer was adamant. 'No way! This is better! Look at it! How could you *get* better publicity? If Sensira are behind this, then FUCK THEM! It's blown up in their faces! *We* are the story! *We* are the fucking news! The Grams blow Mars out!'

'I dunno . . .'

'I bloody do! Come on! Let's find Janey.'

As Guy watched with increasing relish, he forgot his woes. This was theatre. First the band, *his* band had put on a competent stadium-rock show. Nothing miraculous, a bit subdued and the crowd had responded half-heartedly. Seemingly angered by the sterility of the occasion, the Grams had walked off halfway through the show. The promoter, a ridiculous-looking cowboy in a tight leather coat had come on stage to try and reassure the crowd that the band would be back. Then Keva had barged his way on, furious, claiming through a loud hailer that the band's sound had been sabotaged. He was either telling the truth, or the band had developed a huge, paranoid drug tendency over the last few months' touring.

He was telling the truth. Sensira took to the stage with a cacophonous fanfare of intro music, hyping the crowd up to a psyched-out dementia. Their backline and sample DATs boiled and bubbled and, without words, Sensira launched into a loud, deranged, utterly spellbinding version of 'Noodledoodled'. It was even loud on television. Helmet Horrocks, exhausted, thin and sickly-looking, took the deafening acclaim with a slight bow.

'Thank you kindly,' he gasped, holding his side. 'Phew! Bonkers!'

The crowd yelled louder.

'This is rock 'n' roll! We ARE rock 'n' roll! Accept nothing less!'

Syncopated stomping from the crowd. Helmet leered out at them. 'Our apologies to you for the technical problems. Is the sound all right out there?!'

A deafening affirmation. Helmet grinned slyly. 'So let's have it, Europe! Let's have it! Sensira's gonna rock you!'

Guy found himself laughing out loud. Flicking channels, later, he found Keva on MTV, headline news, explaining why the Grams had felt compelled to walk off stage. He handled it well. At no stage did he rubbish or accuse Sensira. Good. Guy would get his teeth into this first thing tomorrow.

The bus parked at the Vondelpark end of PC Hoofstraat at around three a.m. They weren't due to be checking into the day-rooms until eight. Only Keva and Wheezer were still awake and neither felt passionately that a recce round Amsterdam could not wait until morning.

'Come 'ead, Kee, get some kip. Off to the land of nod with you!'

'Wish I could, mate. Can't get that little twat out of my mind. I can just see him there, smirking, the horrible little no-mark!'

'Forget about him. He's nothing. He's desperate . . .'

'That crowd didn't seem to think so tonight.'

Wheezer sighed out loud and got up, resting his hand on Keva's shoulder. 'Look. If Sensira are still with us twelve months from now . . . I'll eat your socks! All right?'

Keva forced a weak laugh. Wheezer gave his shoulder a little squeeze. 'I mean it. They're nothing.'

He patted him on the shoulder and went off to his bunk. Keva stayed in the lounge, thinking.

'Come 'ead, singer!' chirruped James, shaking him roughly. 'Amsterdam!'

Keva forced a tightly-glued eyelid open and frowned hideously at the beaming axemeister. He focused on James's dimpled smile, groaned and pulled his sheets back over his head.

'We'll leave a note on the table for you!' grinned James. 'We're gonna do a few galleries, go up the tower at the Westekerk, have a trawl round the Jordaan, check out the thrift shops then maybe have some lunch . . .'

'Like fuck!' croaked the voice from under the pillow.

'Hah! See you in the Jolly Sailor an' 'at!'

'No, hang on!' Snowy interjected. 'De Hoogte's better. Let's meet there.'

'Fuck that! There's better blimps from the Sailor! All the blondes, innit? The Scandinavian alleyway . . .!'

'De Hoogte it is then.'

Snowy scribbled a note giving directions to the famous music den in Nieuwe Hoogstraat and left it on the table in the front lounge. Spotting Wheezer and Marty loitering by the hotel entrance, the three of them took off down PC Hoofstraat before anyone had a chance to ask them to do a short fanzine interview or visit a campus radio station. Ten minutes later they were jumping off the tram at Voorburgwal and burrowing into the centre of old Amsterdam's red-light district.

Keva wasn't knocked out by the hotel.

'What more d'you want?' moaned Marty. 'It's clean, it's handy . . .'

'It's cheap.'

'. . . they don't mind pop groups . . .'

310

'It's cheap.'

'. . . it's *extremely* close to the venue . . .'

'So's the American. Closer. I bet you anything fucken Helmet stays there when his shitehawks play here tomorrow. The *rock 'n' roll* hotel! Bollocks! We're here cos it's cheap, aren't we?'

'They were happy to offer a day rate, certainly . . .'

Keva laughed generously and gave Marty a little punch. 'What time's soundcheck?'

'Gotta sort it out with The Purple. Meet back here at five.'

'Sound. I'll just brush me gnashers and then I'm off to see some Van Gogh. Where's Wheezer?'

Wheezer was already down at the Melkweg, arguing with Peter – no surname – one of the promoter's reps. After the shambles in Rotterdam he was doubly worried about the potential for trouble here. The Grams and The Purple were doing a double-header at the Melkweg. There was no question, when the idea had first come up, that one band was 'supporting' the other at the legendary club. This was just a nice opportunity for the Melkweg's promoters to give their regulars an incredible, value-for-money ticket. A night to remember. For the bands, too, it was the best way to play their debut Amsterdam gig – a combustible, sold-out, hottest-show-in-town major club gig.

'We can't support The fucking Purple!' laughed Wheezer. He put an arm around Peter. 'Whichever way you dress it up, the band who comes off stage last is the main attraction! Yes?'

'I suppose. I just wish you'd said something earlier about this. I only confirmed The Purple could close the show three days ago. And only then because I don't heard nothing from you guys.'

Wheezer sighed deeply. He really didn't like having to do this stuff.

'Well, look old boy. I can see the position you're in. I honestly can. And if – maybe if Rotterdam hadn't gone so horribly wrong last night – the boys'd be more, you know – more willing to share and share alike. But they know, now, don't they? They know that doesn't work in real life. So we need to work together to head off any trouble.'

Peter gave him a clear, steely stare. 'I GAVE The Purple my word! That's that!'

Wheezer met his stare. 'Then we have a problem, Peter.'

Keva, frustrated now, yanked the lampshade off the sidelight. Seizing the privacy of having the hotel room to himself, he'd set about steaming and exfoliating his face for the first time in days and was now removing a couple of ingrowing hairs from his nose with tweezers. He'd eased the main offender out without trouble, but was now tackling a stubborn, blunt, coarse black hair, only a centimetre long but right in the middle of his nose. He couldn't grip the hair properly with the tweezers. Each time he thought he had a winning hold on it, stern enough to extract the root, it'd slip free again. As his impatience mounted, Keva tugged at the hair without lining it up properly and succeeded only in snapping its end off. Now he had only a stump to try and grip and remove. He was going to get this bastard!

He held the naked yellow light of the sidelamp hard up to his face with one hand and manoeuvred the pincers with the other. Jesus! Few wrinkles and lines threatening to break loose there. Must consult with surgeon as soon as first big wonga cheque arrives. Soon. Keva pressed his face right up to the mirror. He could see the little growth of hair clearly, now, and, certain that there was enough of a follicle to get a good hold with the tweezers, he slowly edged the prongs over either side and clasped the root tight. He definitely had it. Now, rather than tugging the hair sharply, he eased the pincers slowly to one side, feeling the quick sharp bite as the hair was pulled from its foothold. He held it up against the light bulb, one whole centimetre of vicious black hair root. He was impossibly pleased.

Wheezer bumped into Marty coming over the bridge into the Melkweg as he was on his way out. He explained the situation.

'I don't reckon The Purple'd have a problem with us closing the show, you know,' mused Marty. 'It all depends on what the venue have said to them. They might've told them that we *insist* on going on first. I know Davey and Declan. I'll have a word. I can but try!'

'Cheers, mate. Do your best. I won't say anything to the lads, yet.'

Marty headed off towards the Leidseplein, while Wheezer, starving, went in search of sustenance.

Tony sat naked on the little bed, his fat little penis asleep between his legs, stroking the lustrous black hair of the Thai girl. 'You've got lovely hair . . .'

She shrugged his hand off. 'You can't do dat, neider! Dat fifty guilder more!'

Tony huffed and puffed. 'Well, what *can* I do?'

She pointed again to the menu. Nothing was less than fifty guilders. She tried her throaty voice again, running her fingers through his curly chest hair. 'Come on. You donn wonna fuck me? Come on. You wonna fuck me.'

His dick was responding, but it wasn't right. He was in a booth in the middle of Stoofstraat, about to pay for sex with a girl who wouldn't let him kiss her. He couldn't do it without at least a little petting. It wasn't right. She knelt down right next to him. He could feel her warm breath on his balls.

'You wonn I suck your cock. Very deep. Very beautiful.'

'Can we just talk?'

She rolled her eyes and, for the first time, flashed a white smile. She was lovely. She took an aerosol canister from under the bunk and inserted the plastic tube, attached to the nozzle, into her vagina. Greasy foam oozed back down her inner thigh. Tony, all eyes, was horrified.

'Er, don't do that. Please.'

His dick was sagging. She walked towards him.

'Come on, huh? Let's get it on.' Her tits were perfect.

'No. I, er . . . where are you from then?'

She laughed.

'It's up to you. Fifty guilder if we talk or fuck.'

Fuck it, thought Tony, eyeing her slick, shiny hair. Just a little feel won't do any harm.

Keva, having bought a splendid, battered suede jacket from the Albert Cuypmarkt and drunk a large cognac standing up at a busy traders' bar, felt an incurable urge for a smoke. Nothing too heavy, just a couple of nice pure-grass rollies to set him right. He left the market at the old brewery end and, just on the corner of Ferdinand Bolstraat, spotted a little weed café, unnamed, with a Jamaican flag painted on to the window.

Inside, behind the bar, was a tall, bony, strikingly attractive, yet grimy-looking redhead. She wore a hint of kohl under dirty blue, dazzling eyes, but no other make-up on the intelligent face. Her top lip was pinched and, only slightly, overhung the lower, like Thom Yorke's. She was grubby, hippyish and immediately sexual, showing pointed, death-white breasts each time she leant forward. Her boyfriend, if the bearded, handsome, mountain climber seated at the very end of the bar was her boyfriend, smiled at Keva and threw his head back, billowing green smoke at the ceiling.

'Hi.'

'Hi there. Can I get, um . . . a small beer, please.'

'Sure. Something to smoke?'

'Mm. What's good? What're you two smoking?'

The boyfriend tittered. 'Porn weed, man. Porn weed.'

She jerked her head in a take-no-notice way and pulled out various little plastic sachets of grass, all with hand inscribed price tags attached, all marvellously cheap.

'Porn weed, huh? Mmmmm. Sounds just the ticket.'

'Get you rutting like a fucking hot bull, man!' He threw back his shaggy mane again and laughed at the thought. 'It's like, you know, it's like smoking pure fuckin MDMA, man! Horny grass! Pure fuckin porn!'

He cracked up laughing again. The girl smiled, embarrassed. 'You can try some, if you like to?'

She rolled him a lithe one-skinner and watched with satisfaction as Keva enjoyed the grass. On his way out she shrugged beautifully: 'We tried to get tickets for your show tonight. It was totally sold out.'

Keva came back into the bar. 'Well, then. Write your names down and I'll put you on the guest list. I can't have my royal-appointment purveyors of horny weed locked out of their home-town show, can I?'

The love weed was starting to take effect.

*

Wheezer looked right and left and checked surreptitiously behind, before disappearing into the shop on Spuistraat. This was the place he received half his porn from, monthly, through the post, though they knew him better as Mr Lovett. The last brochure had offered lots of great-sounding videos for knockdown prices – he was determined to go home with some new fodder.

James persuaded the huge Surinamese bouncer not to damage Tony's face.

'Look, just kick him up the ass instead. He knows you've got to punish him, but not his face, yeah? Not just before a show.'

'What show?'

Bingo. He knew it'd work. There isn't a doorman in the world who isn't a starfucker.

'Are you guys famous?'

A little crowd gathered. Beano stood by, fists clenched tight. It was too weird to be brawling with grocks in the middle of Amsterdam in the middle of a Friday afternoon, with their Dutch tormentors swearing at them in English. Tony stood back, breathless, straightening his jacket. The Thai girl, Elena, had pushed the panic button when he'd leaned forward and started stroking her hair and kissing her neck.

'No! Hey, madman! No kiss! No kiss!'

The bouncers arrived almost immediately, forced him to dress, painfully coercing jeans over now tumescent penis and, having extracted one hundred guilders from him, kicked him out into the street where one of them slapped him in the face a couple of times. The other guy seemed prepared to leave it, glancing around him all the time for coppers, but the big Ruud Gullit lookalike wanted his fun.

'We're pretty well known, yeah. We're a pop group. The Grams?'

'Never fuckin hearda yah. Sing one-ah yah records.'

A voice from the now-sizeable gathering of onlookers shouted out in a Texan accent. 'Hey, y'all, look! It's the Grams, man. No way! It's the fuckin Grams!'

Most in the crowd stood still and watched, dumb, but the young

American kid and two goofy-looking pals pushed towards them. The big bouncer turned to Tony. 'You want privacy?'

Tony didn't have an idea what he was talking about. 'Er, yeah . . .'

'Where you playing? Milky Way?'

'Er, yeah . . .'

'Tonight?'

'Yes. Tonight.'

'You leave two tickets on the door for Tony Maeskeens.'

He spelt it. Then he picked up the amiable Texan by the front of his Puffa jacket and carried him back to the crowd, dumping him on the floor by the side of the canal.

'My friends need privacy!'

The young lad brushed himself down, eyeing Tony and the boys with disdain. 'They can have it! Fucking rock stars!'

The delighted threesome jogged all the way to Bar Hoogte, where they swapped stories about prostitutes who wouldn't be kissed.

Keva was tingling with erotic frustration as he opened up the hotel room. He'd thought about the girl Marisa all the way back, stopping twice, determined to go back there, sure that she'd be ready to share with him her long, white body. He could see her and taste her. It was going to be hard to make it until this evening.

He slipped into the hotel lavatories to buy condoms and hopped up the stairs, three at a time. He'd have an hour's sleep, meet the guys at the bar they'd told him and then it'd be time for soundcheck. He flipped off his suedies and got under the sheets, still dressed. He could hear a mouse scurrying and scratching in the wardrobe, but he couldn't make himself get out of bed again.

His hand flopped out on to his groin. He turned on his side to fend off easy thoughts of masturbation, but the caressing buzz of the grass continued to stroke his spine and gird his solar plexus, coaxing and engorging him with thoughts of the lissom Marisa, her pale skin, her sharp, perky breasts.

His cock gouged hard into his stomach. He'd have to let it out, let it breathe, just to stop it digging into him. He unbuttoned the flies and felt the rigid muscle, still pushed tight against him by the taut elasticity of his shorts. Defeated, he sighed and pulled his shorts off, lying there for a moment, watching the thing twitch in the hotel twilight. He didn't want to start handling it. It was for her, for later. He vaulted out of the bed and padded over to the sink, the hungry knob oscillating robustly with the tremors of his footsteps. He looked in the mirror. His eyes were hugely dilated, pleading with him: 'Have a wank! Do it! Toss yourself off!!'

He was going to resist. He turned on the cold tap and, limboing down to sink level, he shoved his erection under the jet and waited until he could take it no more. The mouse in the wardrobe scurried louder.

It made no difference. Emerging through the shock of the cold was the insidious strum of desire, heightened and whetted by the sensimillia. Porn weed, indeed. There was no choice. If he was not to turn up at the bar to meet the chaps with a prominent, painful stiffy he was going to have to take redemptive action. He reached for the condoms. A posh wank would put the world to rights.

Guy, still elated by the way he and Tony Wolfe had crushed MarsChannel into submission, decided to nail his father while he was still on a high. Parking at a meter in Duke Street he cut through to Lord Philippe's club, hidden from the world in Blue Ball Yard.

He was glad his father had agreed so readily to the meeting. Readily for Lord Phil, at least. He was, as usual, mannered and remote on the telephone, punctuating each clipped remark with endless, claustrophobic pauses. But they were going to meet and talk. Today.

A commissionaire, younger than Guy had imagined would inhabit such a place in such a world, showed him into the small, immediately cosy library where Philippe was reading the *Spectator*. He smiled at his son, but didn't get up, indicating the battered Queen Anne chair next to him. They shook hands stiffly. They did not hug. Philippe looked at Guy with something akin to affection, the large, rheumy eyes watering and the long face trying to approximate or suppress a smile.

'So, m'boy,' he coughed. 'How goes it?'

*

Keva was only now letting the funny side of it in. Wheezer, still quaking and shuddering at the thought of what had taken place, put his arm around Keva again as they walked to the tram stop, taut against the wind.

'Don't beat yourself up over it, man!' he laughed. 'Don't!' Keva lowered his head, mortified. Wheezer stopped and held him by the shoulders. 'Jesus, man! It could've been any one of us! I mean, Jesus! A second later and it would've been ME!'

What had happened was that Keva, priapic and almost demented with lust, had rolled a rubber over his peeling erection, backed on to the bed and set about diffusion with great velocity. He was into a satisfying stroke, pictures of the wanton Marisa dancing, bare-breasted in front of him, calling his name, calling him such a lover, when the wardrobe door burst open.

'NO! NO! STOP IT!'

It was Wheezer Finlay, quite naked, covering his genitals with one hand and halting a non-existent bus with the other. He stooped at the end of the bed to pick up his underwear and the remainder of his clothes, which lay in a bundle and which he carried, bent double, to the little bathroom.

Sitting on the tram, watching the huddles of humanity scurrying towards their futures, Keva was overcome with a great, tickling euphoria. Images of Wheezer, about to succumb to self-abuse in identical circumstances when he'd heard the key grating in the door, were too vivid, too risible to shut out. Careless of his surroundings he gave in to a long, cathartic chuckling, getting louder and more agonised, more convulsive, until he was almost in fits. They got off the tram early, at Leidsestraat, and guffawed their way through the warren of streets and bridges to De Hoogte.

How he wished he had not gone there. His father had told him something so awful that, although it was just a fact, a thing that was so and could not be made otherwise, he was consumed by a cloying, unsighted hatefulness.

He drove without thought, finding himself on the Embankment heading for Blackfriars. His head was in a maelstrom. He pulled suddenly into the left cut on to Temple Avenue and parked off Carmelite Street, walking back towards the bridge.

Sitting on the hewn stone bench, watching the muddy tumult of the Thames below, he tried to order the slew of facts his dad had imparted.

'Always wanted a girl.'

The way he'd said it, head cocked sideways as though he were trying out an idea on himself to see if it fitted, made him, momentarily, human. He seemed frail. But then he turned to Guy and casually told him some of the facts of his life. He just listed the facts. He was surprised when Maria fell pregnant with Guy. The marriage was over long before Guy was conceived. They were not having sex. It was a difficult period for them all. Yes, he was surprised when Maria told him she was pregnant again.

Lord Philippe insisted that he had, no matter that he didn't want this child, always tried to give equally of his time and his favours to all three sons. It tasted bitter on the palate – but it was nothing to the shock, the pure, unexpected shock of his parting shot. For this he stood up and, fiddling with his fob-watch, rasping infirmly, he looked at his glinting black shoes and told Guy that he was the father of Victoria Turnbull. Guy and Ticky had been half-brethren. Guy didn't know what he was looking at because he couldn't see anything. He became aware of his father standing over him and, so briefly, for less than a moment, placing a bony hand on his shoulder then withdrawing it in one tremulous movement.

The turbulent river was restful, returning him slowly to a point of cognisance. It was sinking in but its implications were, really, tragic. Lord Philippe, torn for so long, wanting to make his daughter a part of his life, had made over an endowment to her. She had had no inkling of her circumstances until the trust made contact after her twenty-first birthday. The rest was now all too horribly, glaringly apparent. In love, she believed, with her own brother, forced to work so closely with him, sadness at every turn of the day. She was not somebody who'd assume other people would want to know about her unhappiness. She had tried to keep it to herself but, looking at it now, the signs were everywhere to be seen. He could have helped. They could all have helped. Knowing Wheezer's blame syndrome, he could still not prevent that emptying freefall of his spirits. Guy's shoulders, his chest, his heart slumped way down low.

They were crowded into the side window of the Jolly Sailor, looking out on to the alleyway. There were no more than eight windows, eight functional cubicles, but the spectacle was worth the viewing. All the girls were young and blonde with fantastic figures. They were dancing hypnotically, tranced out on downers, beckoning to the boys as they pointed and giggled. They were doing their utmost to look sultry, but a swim in the canal would be more enticing. They were fucked. Properly fucked, going through the motions, no more animated than a blow-up doll.

'So this is Quality Street, hey? God help the rest of them . . .'

A squeal of laughter split the café's atoms. The one occupied booth pulled back its curtains to let the client out again. It was Todd King.

Marty hauled himself up on to the bus, looking pleased. 'Well, gentlemen. You'll be pleased to know that a practical, civilised solution has been arrived at . . .'

He sat at the table, budging Beano along in the process. 'The Purple, as you know, are a rhythmic, tuneful three-piece. They use few effects pedals, no keyboards, nor any other kind of pro-grammed or DAT-centric equipment, no grandiose intro music. It seems ludicrous for us to ask the audience to be patient as we strip down our gear before The Purple can go on. Equally, it's invidious, especially in the circumstances, to ask us to wait until The Purple's show is over before we're able to load out – so, out of logistical common sense comes compromise. The Grams will close this evening's show at Amsterdam's famous Milky Way – on the grounds, simply, that it makes sense!'

'Hurrah for that!' clapped Keva.

'Yeah, well done, Marty! Nice one!' smiled Wheezer, more mightily relieved than he had accounted for. Marty blushed with self-esteem.

After a fine, sweaty set which had, eventually, overpowered a tightly-packed Melkweg crowd, the Grams celebrated the end of their first European tour in their dressing-room with Amstel beer, Absolut vodka and the magnum of champagne Wheezer had given to Marty. Peter the promoter and Tony the bouncer congratulated them individually with crunching bear-hugs and clenched-fist handshakes, while The Purple sat with James, smoking grass and harmonising Dylan songs on acoustic guitars. Nobody missed Keva as he led Marisa out by the hand.

She was as tall as him, and took the initiative, kissing him deeply, scraping his lips with her teeth as she worked her tongue, leaving his mouth deliciously numb. Aroused and breathing hard, trying to quell his anxiety just to be thrusting inside her, Keva pulled the strap of her vest down over her shoulder, kissing her collarbone, licking and nibbling her long neck. Her hand felt for him. She unbuttoned him and sat on the bunk, taking his dick out carefully and pulling his jeans down and away from his thighs. Keva closed his eyes, fingertips rotating on her shoulders.

A determined but not aggressive thudding slapped at the window. She looked up at him with one eye then back to the inch of him that was not in her mouth. Slap-slap-slap! A voice this time. A drunk-sounding, dopey sort of voice. 'Heeeey, you guys!'

Keva felt his hardness start to fail. He pulled back one curtain, seeing nothing in the darkness of the Amsterdam night but his own strange reflection, jeans pulled down to his knees, buttocks exposed and a good-looking girl licking his balls. He screwed up his eyes and put his face closer to the window. There was a vague shape out there. Keva pressed his face to the glass and recoiled in fright as the depraved, hairy face of Marisa's boyfriend leered back at him.

'Come on, guys! I've got good smoke, here! Let me come in and watch!'

Marisa shrugged her permission as though it was no big deal, but Keva could at that moment think of nothing he'd less like to do than perform an indecent act for the leftish pleasure of an hirsute Dutch hippie. He touched either temple with his finger-tips.

'Erm, actually you know, I should get back to the others. It's supposed to be a bit of a party for us in there. Erm, it'd be wrong . . . you're both more than welcome . . .'

'But you haven't come yet!'

'That really doesn't matter. Honestly.'

'But the tickets . . .'

'Really. It was my, er, you know . . .' He edged to the door, pulling up his kecks, hoping she'd follow.

'I could give you a very nice hand job.'

He just stared at her. He was starting to think that life was very strange.

It was the oddest of all possible Wednesday mornings – the heart-stopping joy of the faxes and messages offset by the gnawing injustice, the *wrongness* of the music press.

Wheezer'd fallen asleep on the chesterfield with MTV on. Tuesday was the first day Worldwide had officially been going for modern rock adds – playlistings – on 'Beautiful'. The plan was to consolidate the track at alternative radio. This meant persuading those stations who were already on it to carry on playing it, at least for a few more weeks and to get the remainder spinning the track immediately. A good cross-section of hip, alternative, modern rock stations simultaneously supporting a band would be the perfect start for the Grams. With a nationwide pattern reaching beyond the hipster conurbations, a pattern of escalating radio play, phone reactions, sales and reorders, it would be possible to take the band's story to MTV and pop radio within a couple of months. Germane to the success of the plan would be the quick-hit pro-motional tour of four cities which was starting next week, but a good crop of alternative radio adds in the first week was just as important.

Wheezer had sat in the office, waiting for the fax to jerk into action, the phone to ring, fanatically trying to imagine what was happening, now, all those thousands of miles away. He fired off a few e-mail hits to friends in Denver, Sioux City and Buffalo, but their replies were instant and identical. Too early to know yet. His watched fax didn't boil and he went up to the attic to take his mind off things, flicking between MTV and VH1 to see which would be next to show 'Beautiful'. Time for a new single, he was thinking. He hit button 8 for Bravo and reached for his knob. And then it was daylight.

*

'WHADDA FUCK!'

Keva lurched out of his bed and groped, terrorised, for the light switch. Even before he located it he knew where he was again, that it was fine. He did it all the time.

'Aren't you gonna get that?'

'You're nearest,' moaned James.

'It's never for me!'

James rolled his eyes and, after rocking himself forwards three times, jettisoned himself from his bursting television chair and padded to the phone. It was Pat McIntosh. For Keva.

'It's Pat. For you.'

Keva tried to signal that he wasn't in – he just didn't feel like talking, he was well settled into an evening watching tapes of all the *King of the Hill* episodes they'd missed on tour – but James blew it in supreme style. Impatient, he shouted, 'I've already told him you're in, bollocks!'

Keva punched him in the gut as he took the phone and tried to sound pleased. 'Pat? Is that you, mate?'

Pat sounded jaded and downbeat, as ever. 'A'right, man.'

'How come you never came to Amsterdam? We was expecting you. Our scribe-by-appointment missed a bit of a night . . .'

'Well, that's partly what I'm calling about . . . I mean . . .' He stopped.

'Go 'ead . . .'

A deep sigh down the phone line. His accent, made heavier by a cold anyway, sounded more Essexy – Colchester or Southend – than London. He sounded worse than bored. He was defeated. 'Listen, man. If I'm getting in the way with this book, y'know . . .'

While his brain was skeetering through its reference library of recently-opined negatives on Pat, his voice carried on the dissemblance. 'What you on about, cockney-type man!'

'Just, like, I heard . . .'

'Then it's a lie, then, innit?'

'Be serious, Keva.'

Keva snorted and pitched his tone blacker. 'I'm never anything but. So, seriously, Pat, if you've got something to say to me, let's have it.'

'I thought you better know about what some people down here are saying. You're not gonna like it.'

Wheezer threw himself downstairs, opened up the little box-room office, ceremonially touched the Rand McNally wall map of the USA and stood rooted, comically turning to the flickering voice-mail then the fax then back to the ansaphone. He padded over to the fax, an antiquated, single-sheet job which couldn't guillotine incoming pages. One serpentine sheet had doubled over and over on itself, slithering halfway across the floor. He was guilt-stricken at sleeping through all this and mortified when he saw the glaring red stripes at one end of the fax sheet, taunting him that he was out of fax roll. What if he'd missed anything important? What'd the Americans think of a manager who allows his fax to run out of paper? He snatched it up hungrily, winding it over his wrists, and ripped it from the teeth of the machine, scanning the names, clocking the print-oceans of exclamation marks. Steve Knopf had faxed him. Mel Parmese. Sandy Santino at Automatic. Todd, of course, had stayed up through the night to get the news. There were requests for interviews when the band hit the States next week. Offers of live dates. Catering services. Rudy Wexner at Taurus had sent a fax illustrated with Smiley faces, with a hand-written enquiry at the bottom. Had Wheezer yet made a situation agent-wise in the States? No he flipping well hadn't and he flipping well wouldn't be using Puppy Fatner when the time came! There were faxes from Mike Brietling. Several indies. Willard Weiss. Alicia MacNamara. Alicia MacNamara! Hard-on Central! People wanted to know him. They wanted to congratulate him. Wheezer flipping Finlay was in demand!

There were pages and pages of statistics, radio stations' call-signs and initials, five-day and ten-day sales figures. In the short time they'd been back from Europe, rehearsing in Crash for the US dates, the album had put on another 10,000 units. It had done just over 75,000. It was going steadily, and with all this radio play about to kick in it was about to zoom into overdrive.

He sat down to study all the data in depth. They'd picked up good radio stations all over the country, from Seattle and Portland down to San Diego, through Phoenix, Las Vegas, Salt Lake City,

Denver, Austin, Houston, New Orleans, Memphis, St Louis, Minneapolis, Detroit, Philadelphia, Baltimore, Washington, Norfolk, Orlando, Atlanta. They had twenty-one confirmed adds as well as continued spins from Los Angeles, New York, Chicago, Boston and San Francisco, who were all staying with the record for now. It was a phenomenal start, even better than hoped for, and there was a second fax from Steve Knopf, right at the end of the red-striped fax roll, saying that there were another three unconfirmed reports from Dallas, Pittsburgh and Atlantic City which could not be converted by close of play. Wheezer's heart was thumping through his ribcage. They were going to make it. It was going to happen for them. It was the best feeling. The best.

He sat back in his swivel chair, catching his breath and clicked on the message playback. It was mostly the same people who'd faxed. Willard, conveying his satisfaction and reminding Wheezer why he'd showed the faith and commitment to pay so much for the band. There was only one message left. Todd King. Phoning from the office at 2.32 a.m., which even in Los Angeles is 6.32 p.m. After Work, whichever country you're in: 'Hey, Wheezy!'

Still made him panic. Made him feel he was being found out.

'Just want you to know, man – Dallas is now a *confirmed* P1 R&R and Gavin add. It's not a *Billboard* station any more, but it's a fucking good add! Good day to you. Good day, indeed! Wow! Over.'

Why did Wheezer think the man was a wanker for staying up all night to find this out and pass it on to him? Because he was.

Wheezer went downstairs to get his mail. Great! Wednesday! Music press! He'd forgotten, in his add-fixated bloodrush. Without Hannah, there was nobody pouncing on the breaking stories when the music papers hit London on a Tuesday. Guy was being Guy – moody and morose one minute, high as a hawk the next. That'd have to be the next thing. He'd have to get Purvis to take over the press. The requests were still coming in thick and fast, but it all needed regulating. He bounced to his doormat to get to the papers quicker. Maybe Pat's Amsterdam review'd be in – although he couldn't, now, recall actually *seeing* Pat in the Milkweg. There was too much going on. They were all, all of them, living life in furious anticipation and anxious retrospect. They needed to focus on now a little, too.

He swiped up the *Maker* and *NME* and idled through to the kitchen, swishing the kettle to check it for water and lighting the gas ring. He hadn't got as far as the kitchen table when he saw the headline.

GRAMS STORM OUT OF AWARDS CEREMONY

Organisers were left counting the cost after the Grams walked off stage only three songs into their set during the prestigious MarsChannel Awards in Rotterdam. Fans broke seats and demanded refunds after receiving no explanation for the band's behaviour. Sensira quelled some of the unrest with a powerful headlining performance, but many fans were left bemused by the Grams' walkout. Sensira's press officer, Cinday Hogan, said: 'It's a shame. The crowd were really up for the Grams but the band seemed really vague all day. They seemed to just lose interest. They looked fatigued, really.'

Bitch! Fucking bitch! She wasn't even there! Wheezer didn't see her, for sure . . .

Promoter Jaap Heindricksen said: 'I don't want to say too much about the Grams. They seem to thrive on this sort of notoriety. I'd like to focus on another great show from Sensira which, for sure, proves that fashion is temporary while class lasts for ever.'

The Grams were not available for comment.

Wheezer was blushing furiously. The bastards! This was so *wrong*! There was a footnote.

At press, reports were emerging of more problems for the Grams, who were supporting The Purple in Amsterdam. Full story next week.

The kettle was boiling. Wheezer ignored it as he read the story again. He snatched up the *Melody Maker*. Nothing on pages two, three, four, five but there, on page six was a tiny newsflash. It simply stated that the Grams had walked off stage in Rotterdam after an alleged argument with promoters. Wheezer walked over to the solid old stove, turning off the gas, tossing it all over in his mind. *Class lasts for ever*.

Big mercenary Dutch dickhead. He didn't mind that side of it so much. It was the apparent conspiracy of *NME* in all this. *Supporting The Purple*. They weren't! Everyone knew that . . .

NME had decided to run this non-story. Why? *Melody Maker* had virtually ignored it. Why? He poured the steaming water over three bags of Darjeeling in the stone pot – enough to see him through the next hour. He stopped dead. Cindy Hogan. Obviously. She'd left *Melody Maker* to become Sensira's Director of Public Relations – that was the actual wording of her business card. It was Cindy who'd farmed out this Rotterdam story. It had to be. He bounded upstairs to call Guy.

The Virgin steward was two rows ahead, taking dinner orders from Marty, Pat McIntosh, James and Rory, the backline technician. Wheezer stuck the *NME* in the elasticated magazine holder on the seat in front and with it tried to shelve all thoughts of the nonsense back home. It was probably best to let the dust settle. Pat was here to continue the reconciliation with the press, but all in all it was good that they were to be removed from the public eye for the next couple of weeks.

The situation wasn't irreparable. His letter had been witty and conciliatory. On the morning of the *NME* attack, Wheezer had tried everywhere he knew to locate Guy, to no avail. He left a message on the answering service of the only number he had, a mobile, for his mother, who'd called back that evening. Guy was not well. She wouldn't go into details, but it wasn't serious. He needed a complete rest. Maria told Wheezer not to expect to see Guy for a week or so, at least.

The next few days were a nightmare. Tony Wolfe advised him not to pursue the *NME*. They hadn't broken any laws. Defamation was difficult to prove in any case, but in the case of rock stars, who openly courted controversy . . . it was going to be very difficult and not the best use of his time and energy. They'd draft a letter together, putting *NME* straight on a couple of points, and leave it at that. Wheezer was relieved. He couldn't afford to fall out with the music press, least of all the *NME*. How they missed Hannah. Purvis, obviously, was unwilling to take the thing on now, second-hand, after they'd all gone against him over the *Mojo* cover. In turning the gig down, charmingly and as though it were the only sensible way ahead, Purv had told Wheezer he saw the whole thing coming with Hannah and Keva, saw it ages ago, that night in the Duke of York. He'd wanted to obstruct the relationship back then, for all the best reasons, but realised he couldn't interfere. It was just a shame they'd gone from start to finish so quickly. He gave Wheezer a couple of names to follow up, which he filed.

Of more pressing concern was the situation at ReHab. With Ticky gone and Guy absent, the company was being staffed by kids barely out of college. They were bright and able, but ReHab, at this most important passage in its short existence, was rudderless. Nobody had the authority to sign cheques, nobody could take key decisions. Everything was being referred back to The Wheeze. He had no choice.

For those five days he lived at the Caledonian Road HQ, planning ahead for the period he'd be in the States and beyond, clearing the workload so that only routine tasks were left to the kids, and leaving ever more desperate messages on Guy's mobile. He surprised and pleased himself with his capacity and easy ability to get through this stuff. Once again, he started to feel as though maybe, just maybe, Wheezer Finlay was the latest in a rich tradition of charismatic, individualistic character-managers. Kit Lambert. Peter Grant. Chas Chandler. Malcolm McLaren. Wheezer Finlay. He was considering the merits of cutting short his own participation in the promo tour to weave more miracles back home when, just like that, Guy called him, not unduly apologetic for leaving him in the shit, but ready now to come back and take up the reins again.

'Good. There's about sixteen grand's-worth of bills to be paid. You're lucky I'm such a smooth liar.'

'Welcome back, hey, Guy? Just what I need to ease me back in . . .'

Wheezer held his tongue a split moment, but he couldn't let it go. 'Fuck off, Guy! Welcome home! It's *your* fucking company! You may have the time and the money to piss off without even locking the door behind you, but I . . .'

'I'm sorry, Wheeze. I really am. And I'm appreciative of all you've done . . .' He sounded disembodied. He was almost whispering. 'I need some sleep. But I'll be in tomorrow. First thing. Back to normal. Business as usual.'

Wheezer hadn't heard a less convincing pitch since Rudy Wexner, but true to his word, Guy's key was scraping in the lock at 8.18 the next morning. Wheezer was free to manage his pop group again. He met with Tony Wolfe to agree tiny changes to the letter of rebuttal to the *NME*, then jumped on a train back to Liverpool for a meeting with the group to run through the itinerary for America – starting with the flight to New York.

The promo tour was routed from New York to Boston to San Francisco to Los Angeles, with a devilish crop of activity already slated for each city. He watched with affection as James, a true rock god, flirted with the stewardesses, obviously promising guest lists, freebies, the world. He ordered his food, prodded the slumbering Keva to see if he wanted anything and, getting no response, stared out at the gold flaring sun burning high behind his shoulder. Everything was going to be fine.

Guy laughed out loud a couple of times, but he felt like a jealous onlooker. He chucked the *NME* on his desk and sighed heavily. Wheezer was speaking for the band, now, developing a persona, becoming one of the handful of managers with a rep for himself. He'd managed to run ReHab while Guy had been wallowing in flotation tanks, going into regression, searching for himself. He was going to have to shake himself up. Wheezer was running the show, here, while Guy was farting round in alternative medicine purgatory, getting worse.

If it'd been tough getting them all through immigration, checking them into the St Moritz was murder. Landing at JFK, James chose the walk-up to Passport Control to ask Wheezer if possession of three Ecstasy tablets constituted a felony.

'You what! You fucking lunatic! Throw them away! LOSE

them ... no, DON'T! We're being watched! We're being watched ...'

James cracked his annoying, superficial cackle. 'Div-bong! Not NOW ... I mean that time I got nicked in Northampton with three Es? Do I have to, like, declare it an' 'at?'

'You gave a jarg name, didn't you?' Keva butted in.

'Think so, yeah ...'

'So, er ... *pa problemo, n'est ce pas?*'

James shrugged. Wheezer, still reeling from the shock, saw Rory and Crapston, the sound engineer, wandering off towards the Virgin rep.

'Where the *hell* are they going, now!', shrieked Wheezer. 'Marty! What the fuck's going on ... ?'

'Cool it, Wheezer, they're only ...'

'Don't move! No one move from this spot!'

He could feel the hot sweat of fear prickling his armpits, the back of his knees, his top lip. They were in John Fucking Kennedy airport, the toughest in the world for *normal* people, let alone a rock group. To immigration – especially the square-headed, humourless, US Immigration personnel, accustomed to knocking back all manner of infiltrators on a daily basis – to these people, rock groups meant one thing. Drugs. They could take all the time in the world, if they felt like it, sifting through the flight cases and racks, pulling everything apart until they were satisfied you were clean. Mel Parmese had been painstaking in his instructions. Don't give them an excuse, he'd stressed. Don't look at them, don't joke with them, don't even catch their eye. Just have your documentation ready, answer their questions, politely – and get the fuck out of there.

So what was the group doing? James and Beano were loudly chatting up two girls in the queue, attracting maximum attention to who they were and what they were doing in New York. Jesus! Did they have to be recognised and praised and adulated by every semi-shaggable long-legged chick they came across? Marty had suddenly split the queue, kneeling down, foraging frantically through his hand luggage for some vital piece of bureaucracy. And Wheezer was having to march over to the other side of the hall to reclaim two of the crew, who'd decided to go and invite some stewardesses to the show.

'Rory, what the fuck . . .' Rory didn't even turn around. He was bent over sheaves of paperwork with one male JFK rep and a female Virgin rep. Wheezer strode up, angry. 'Rory!'

He couldn't bring himself to shout the word 'Crapston'. Crapston turned, happy, as always.

'Just zapping the hardware through,' he explained in that dozy Stourbridge lilt of his. He supported Villa. Everyone called him Crapston. He was a wizard with live sound. Wheezer didn't want to ask what was meant by zapping hardware, but, now he was here, it looked to Wheezer as if Rory was in control. Far from dicking about with Virgin girls, he and Crapston were smoothing the way for the band's equipment to clear customs.

A JFK guy, who looked like Morgan Freeman, was perusing the documentation from Rockit Cargo. Everything had been properly listed and cleared and paid for, way in advance. Wheezer was out of his depth, making a cunt of himself.

'How many pieces in all, sir?' said the airport rep.

'Twelve, mate. Yeah. Twelve.'

'No problem. You just want to follow me and ID the pieces then we can get you guys some help and walk those babies right on out of here. OK?'

'Thanks, mate.'

'You're very welcome.'

Rory turned to thank the Virgin rep then followed Morgan.

'What about . . .' Wheezer thought better of it. By the time he got back in line the rest of the group had cleared passport control and immigration. To compound it, Wheezer, who couldn't make his mind up quickly enough whether he was visiting the States on business or for pleasure, was the only one in the party to be grilled.

'What's the nature of your business, sir?'

'Management.'

The Afrikaans-looking passport controller continued scrutinising Wheezer's passport, flicking contemptuously through its unsullied pages as though expecting a confession to come tumbling from the visa page any second. 'It's true, sir! My owner has a kilo of heroin concealed in his sock!'

The passport guy didn't look up. 'What sort of management?' he asked, still flicking. Now he looked up. He looked right into Wheezer's soul. Wheezer struggled to regulate his breathing.

'I manage a band.'

'A *band*?' He managed to make the word mean Hairless Boy Bottom Fondling Society. He managed to get the letter 'y' into the word. 'What *kind* of *by-and*?'

Now that Wheezer could despise him instead of fear him, it was OK. He wasn't in front of the headmaster any more. He could answer his questions curtly and factually, without giving the operative any satisfaction. He could keep this game going for as long as the jerk wanted to play. The entrymeister fixed his evil glare into Wheezer one more eternal time and scrawled something on his waiver form, beckoning him to proceed. The something he scrawled directed the second wave of welcomers, customs this time, to tear his bags apart.

Eventually, Wheezer and Marty found everyone scattered around the arrivals area, making phone calls, buying postcards, happily having their picture taken with new friends. They were happy. They were excited. They were Here. It was like trying to cup water in your hands, keeping them all in one place. From landing to check-in at the St Moritz Hotel, Central Park South, took five hours.

James, who always became louder and more audibly Liverpudlian in new places, excelled himself. Starved of the limelight for an entire hour while their convoy breached Manhattan, he made up for lost time by purchasing a particularly stupid jester's hat, without bells, from the hotel shop and roaming the bar and lobby area introducing himself to people. Wheezer couldn't check him into the hotel without James himself signing his registration card. By the time he was located and brought back to hotel reception, they'd lost their place and had to queue again. Marty pleaded with everyone to stay in one area so that they could run through itineraries, but Keva, excited to taste New York, knowing that now represented his best, his only chance of seeing the city, slipped out of a terrace door. Tony and Beano dumped their bags in their bedroom and ran downstairs, laughing and laughing, out on to Fifth Avenue, flailing at a yellow cab. The band meeting could fucking well wait.

Keva found himself brushing his teeth extra fast, willing himself to get to the next exciting bit of this ridiculous ride that little bit quicker. He'd got back to the room last night after a trawl of the Village to find James snoring and a scribbled note saying: 'Play messages. Weird.'

There were two messages, the first a giggly, pause-strewn affair from two or three very young-sounding girls which effectively thanked them for rescuing them from their mundane lives, for writing 'Beautiful' (one of them started crying at this point, but stayed on the line, sobbing – he couldn't hang up because he wanted to hear message two and, besides, he found he could stand the sound of young girls crying down the phone), for coming to New York and for being the Grams. They wouldn't regret it. The girls would be offering personal thanks. The youngest-sounding girl then went into a very detailed account of the many and varied ways in which she intended to thank Keva.

The second message could not have been more contrasting – unless it had been from a man, perhaps, and didn't contain the promise of New York sex: 'Hi. This is Katie Chick. The Chicks're gonna rock ya! Call ya tomorra!'

She had a deep, businesslike voice. He knew straightaway who it was – at least he'd heard tell of the Chicks, a group of wanton native New Yorker femmes fatales who lived on the blood of feckless English rock stars. James had rightly assessed it. *Weird*. There were also a couple of notes from the hotel, advising Keva of items waiting to be collected at reception. Unable to sleep, he called down and asked in his politest John Steed voice if it wouldn't be too much trouble to have the goods brought up. Nothing was too much trouble, if there was a tip involved, and five dollars later Keva was staring at a forlorn teddy bear. A red X marked out with plastic tape concealed his fluffy genitalia, and a gift card was stuck to his wrist. It said: 'I'm gonna suk your cok – Annie X.'

The other gifts were merely a routine selection of nipple clamps, penis suction pumps and Keva's own lyrics written in the sender's own blood. He slept like a baby.

This morning Keva was heading out to Long Island with Sandy Santino, Mel's Head of Alternative at Automatic, for a pre-record with WDRE. Since KROQ had started broadcasting in the New York conurbation, WDRE's unique relationship with adolescent New Yorkers was less binding, but Sandy had a great affection for the station, and a great respect for its influence, dating back years. She reasoned with Keva that he should make the effort to journey out there – which was no effort at all, to him. He was loving every little bit of the adventure, and found himself on a permanent Up. Not even the ever-present signs that Sensira had been, or were about to be, in town could bring him down.

After WDRE they had to get back for a lunch interview with *Details* magazine then meet up with the boys for a photo shoot with *Spin*. After a few hours off for sleeping, shopping, swimming, hiding from determined fans, general taking-it-easy and recovering from jetlag, they were due to have their first big Meet 'n' Greet. This was to be an informal dinner for thirty, being the group and management (which included Marty but not the crew), some of the Automatic team, most of Worldwide's New York staff and some cherry-picked guests from the media. MTV were supposed to be turning up, and KROQ had confirmed. After the mass dash for freedom on check-in last night, everyone had been on best behaviour.

'I love your accent; *coooool* hairdo; you have George Harrison eyes . . .'

The interview and playback with WDRE had gone superbly well. He was nervous, as nervous as he'd been at Marigold, but the two guys, Jimmy and Chuck, who did the *Alternation* show were witty, well-informed and great company. Bit by bit Keva relaxed and got into his stride, moving away from the anecdotal and talking passionately about Guy's favourite subject, the Emotion Signal.

'Like, I'm only interested in two emotions when it comes to music – joy and pain. Too much that you hear today is too, you know, too *jaunty*. There's only really Radiohead who are exploring the dark side; them, The Verve, the Bluetones and a couple of others. Mark Morriss, the guy from the Bluetones, has got the most gorgeous, you know – the saddest voice. "Sleazy Bedroom Song", man – it's just devastating. But, yeah – I'm not saying that the Grams are, like, angstmongers, far from it, but we understand both sides of the Emotion Signal. You can get a high from a low, if you know what I mean . . .'

Jimmy and Chuck nodded. Later they told Keva it was rare for them to let a guest 'steal' the show – the two of them *were* the show. But it was rare, also, to find a guest who was willing to delve beyond the promotional, get past the plug for the album, the gig, whatever and really talk, *reveal* something. Keva was pleased with himself. He felt as though it was right that he should be here, doing this. He had every right. He was a natural.

The two DJs told him things he didn't know, as well. Things about Helmet. For all that he was surfing high on the mad screaming roller coaster of the Grams, Keva still found it difficult to give praise to any of his peers in public. But rather than offering nothing back to interviewers who pumped him he'd learned to pick safer targets for his disdain – Jamiroquai and the Lighthouse Family were his current pet hates. When it came to Sensira or Macrobe or The Purple or any other of his vague contemporaries he played out a tactful goalless draw, giving no real opinion.

He didn't need to. Jimmy, who made no secret of revelling in intergroup gossip and rivalry, told him that Sensira were trying to fill venues which were too big for them and that word of mouth on their shows, which had started last week in San Francisco, was poor. Helmet was fucking up on drugs. Keva couldn't hold back.

'Is he fuck! He's never taken anything stronger than Panadol in his life . . .'

'That's what we're hearing from the people out West. The guy's fucking up big time.' He paused to let Keva know this was for real. 'Horse. That's what they're telling us. 'Course many a great artist has found, uh, a rich vein of inspiration . . .'

He didn't get any further. Again, Jimmy and Chuck were doubled over at the silliest quip. But the message had reached him loud and clear. Helmet Horrocks was on smack. When had *that* started? Could it be true? Even now, wanting so badly to think so badly of this boy he despised so avidly, he couldn't reckon it to be so. He couldn't even give him the credit for being a smackhead. Not Helmet. He liked to watch.

But it wasn't thoughts of Helmet, or relief at the good impression he'd made at such a key station, that occupied Keva as he trundled back to Manhattan on the overground with Sandy. While she disseminated news of their cracking good start to the promotional trail through endless barked exchanges on her mobile, Keva was thinking back to the reaction of the girls in the radio station as he walked through the building. He was starting to get used to the extremities of his sudden new life, but this, although suppressed, mannered, was like nothing he had experienced before. He imagined it was like strutting a Bangkok catwalk, but here in the States, nobody was allowed to slobber. Still, they made no bones about it. It was like . . . it was like Jesus had decided to start his Second Coming Walkabout Tour here in Long Island, and each separate employee had this *one chance* to make their impression before he walked past them, for ever. This was sex, sexuality at its rudest and most naked. Girls, women, *every* female in that place had made, no matter how covert, a sexual remark or advance to him. Direct comments, flattering remarks, but always, *always* about some aspect of his physicality, his demeanour, his outside.

'I *love* your accent! *Coool* hairdo! You have George Harrison eyes!'

They'd hold his look just that little bit too long or put an extra bump and grind into their walk if they were up ahead of him. He was not imagining it. All around him, people were giving him head while losing theirs. It was great. He was a God. He trundled into Grand Central musing on the marvellous shock that was in store for the group.

The *Details* interview was the first of three, spanning the group's first few days in the States. The writer, Randy Barbarossa, would track them discreetly, giving a documentary feel to the piece. Again, Keva warmed to the camp scribe and was quickly at his ease, giving up some wonderful quotes.

336

Thankfully, James was not there. Scurrying back to the St Moritz hotel lobby to meet everyone for the *Spin* shoot, Keva walked into a great kerfuffle outside the ground-floor bar.

'He can fuck off, the fucken fag! How come every fucken cunt in this city's a fag, anyway? He can fuck off! I never ordered all that . . .'

Wheezer stood by, wincing, trying to conciliate the pair. Keva didn't have to guess. It happened everywhere. Unless James was paying with hard cash he'd run up fantastic lines of credit – bar bills, room service, long-distance calls, meals for complete strangers he'd met in the elevator. No doubt he and Pat McIntosh, at home where the coke was, had sat in the bar all afternoon, regaling grateful drinkers with tales of debauchery on the road and insisting that all and sundry be James's personal guest. Until the bill came.

Wheezer had hammered home two things before they'd left. One was to assume that every man they met was gay and every passing stranger who could overhear them was his closest friend. This way they could avoid clumsy in-jokes which might be hurtful to casual eavesdroppers but, potentially, ruinous to the group's ambitions. Wheezer knew there were no nasties lurking in the gang, no racists or homophobes – but he knew, too, they liked sometimes to call upon a playful slang they often did not mean. How many times had Beano called him a 'hom'? It was nothing, but to an uninformed passer-by, it was virulent. Big stories can blow up out of casual little remarks, Wheezer told them: just don't even *think* it, let alone say it. Be nice.

The other thing Wheezer had stressed was that they shouldn't run up tabs – especially not at hotel bars. They were a touring group in a strange land and their budget was painfully tight. They couldn't go running to Guy or the bank to bail them out. Unless they'd brought cash or credit cards of their own, they'd have to work within their limit of thirty dollars a day. It wasn't much, but it was comfortably enough in this land of hospitality for mind and body. Wheezer had faxed each of the hotels they were due to stay at, forbidding any credit on the main group account. It was a worry – and a darned nuisance – that James had found a way through.

'Just pay it, knobhead!' spat Keva as he caught up with them. 'How much is it?'

'Two hundred and twelve fucken dollars for three fucken Michelobs! He's trying to have me kecks off, here!'

'Sir, I'll have to ask you again to moderate your language. There are other guests here who don't appreciate that kind of talk . . .' He was strident, self-assured and overtly gay.

'Ah, fuck off, you, you arsebandit!'

Nobody, when they went over the incident later, could remember exactly what had happened next, but James was on the floor, hat askew, with a cut lip *and* being apprehended by hotel security at the same time, while the little barman rifled his pockets for cash.

'I apologise to you all,' the barman gasped when it was all over, 'but I will not be violated in that manner by anybody. Guest or not.'

It took Wheezer, Pat and Marty ninety minutes, many apologies and a personal invitation to the show from Keva to persuade the young barman to forget about the whole thing. It could've been gelignite, a fast-track self-destruct to a new group trying to make its mark. Keva shuddered with real anger whenever he thought about it. He didn't mind doing all the work. He didn't mind writing the songs and the melodies and going out all over the place to explain it all to the world while the rest of the group got pissed and *saw* the world. They'd been to Staten Island on the ferry and up the Empire State Building while he was working today. Tomorrow they were going out in a helicopter. Keva didn't mind any of it, so long as they were . . . *grateful*. It was true. Fuck it, he wanted some gratitude from the bastards! And he didn't want them undoing all his good work by going around brawling like a gang of bricklayers on holiday and insulting ordinary, hard-working people. Keva had stayed with Wheezer and Marty for ten minutes, apologising to the barman and signing CDs for him and his pals, before he had to scamper off and join the photo shoot. He wanted to savour this little tour. Savour it and enjoy it. But the group had already forgotten their part of the bargain. As soon as this photo session was through he'd get back and have a word with Wheezer. This publishing thing needed to be sorted right now.

*

338

The group's inaugural Meet 'n' Greet, held at Frankie's, a homely Lower East Side Italian café, went smoothly enough. Mel Parmese had hosted a pre-meet in a lively SoHo bar, The Ludlow, to run through protocol.

'One thing you *can't* do, guys – you can't fuck the record company girls.'

There were choruses of relieved laughter. Mel held up his hands. 'Seriously, boys, you just don't do it. There are some fuckin *amazing*-looking chicks at that company. As there are at every record company. As there are all over the fuckin States, as you will shortly see. Which is my point. *Please* don't fuck things up by having any of the Worldwide girls fall for you. I guarantee you this – as much as you want to fuck 'em tonight . . .' He paused for dramatic impact. '. . . tomorrow night, at the gig, Coney Island High, man, coolest place in the Village, coolest chicks you ever see'd, yeah? Whatcha gonna do then? When there's two hundred chicks chasing your English asses, every fucking one of them is a *honey* . . . you will not want to know these little cuties you'll be meeting tonight. You won't have time for them. They'll be old news.'

He held a hand up to make sure they were still listening. 'But, as much as they may be history as far as you and your *cocks* . . .' He vomited the word. '. . . are concerned, those kids are still gonna be working this record. And you gotta ask yourself just how far they're gonna go, how pumped they're gonna be about a band who fucked 'em and left 'em.'

He gave them a second for the message to filter home. James looked up. 'Ay, Mel – your daughter doesn't work for Worldwide, does she?'

So they were on good form at Frankie's, if restrained. There were enough gorgeous women there for James to keep interested, but even he kept his flirting clean. Of all of them, though, out of the entire group, the one who then proceeded to sacrifice his duties on an altar of personal need was the supposed fulcrum, Wheezer Finlay. He'd started off as the perfect English eccentric host, working the room, always moving, smiling, introducing, enabling, laughing, and crookedly charming the room. Then he spotted

Myra Sweeney, alone at her table, drinking wine, the only person in the room who was not standing at this pre-meal stage.

Myra was Head of Promotion in the East Coast office. She reported to Campione although, in practice, they divided the country from Chicago down. She was a massively powerful woman, one of the most powerful in music. Myra was a person who could, realistically, make or break a group's career. Wheezer had spent an hour with her that afternoon, making plans. He'd left that meeting a little anxious. Not because of anything specific, but he'd found Myra difficult to get at. She was sharp and focused and tuned in to the minutiae, but she was remote too. Seeing her slumped in her chair, plainly drunk, seemed impossible – it was other-worldly, when he thought of the cool, impenetrable woman of a few hours before. Wheezer pulled up a chair.

It was hard work. Gone was the cunning strategist. In her place was a maudlin, resentful soak, cursing her ex-husband for his infidelity and bemoaning the scarcity of viable, heterosexual men in New York City.

'My mother was right. I never shoulda married a goddamn Paddy! God, I'm sorry . . . Finlay! You must be Irish yourself . . .'

Wheezer sparkled back at her. 'Oh, I'm deeply, personally offended. I'll be taking it up with the highest authorities first thing tomorrow. My family are related to Mayor Giuliani . . .'

Even through the drink, she picked up on his tone. 'You mustn't tease me,' she slurred. 'I'm experiencing some bad times right now . . .'

Instinctively, Wheezer put his hand over hers. She was a woman you'd say was handsome before you'd call her beautiful. She had good features and fierce eyes, but she'd contrived to make herself plain. Her clothes, possibly Nicole Farhi, definitely expensive, looked dowdy.

Wheezer smiled at her. 'I wouldn't dream of goading a tiger. You'd eat me alive. But, erm . . . if it's not presumptious of me . . .' He'd been finding that his childhood stutter, hardly an issue at all today, was thought to be delightful in the States. He was using it more and more. She took her hand away from his and looked towards to the exit. '. . . you seem like . . .' She looked back, sharply. 'Right. Don't take this the wrong way. I'm trying, right, to be nice . . .'

She laughed sharply and drained her glass. 'Fuckin men! Assholes!'

He'd been on the verge of suggesting, politely, that the drink was making her hurt and maybe she needed nothing more than a good night's sleep, but this, clearly, would have been futile. Myra was set fair for an evening's vicious drinking. So Wheezer was left with no choice now but to ignore Mel's rally-call for abstinence. He sat and talked to Myra all evening, then, having talked himself beyond the point of sociability and into the realm of intimacy, unable to back-pedal and at a loss to convince her with words that she was still attractive to men, he found he'd closed out all his own escape routes. He was going to have to jolly well, erm, make love to the woman.

Working the office next day, popping his head around doors, reminding folk to get to Coney Island High in good time, Wheezer found himself face to face with Myra. He felt horrible. He didn't feel horrible because he regretted anything which had passed between them – that'd been very nice. He felt bad, now, because Myra was behaving in a way which was wrong for her. He liked her how she'd been yesterday afternoon. Aloof. He didn't want anything to do with why she was like this, today. He felt bad, for a start, because she'd put on a lot of make-up. She was, also, acting a little bit coquettishly with him. He was half-expecting Myra to ignore him completely. Far from denying their intimacy, though, she revelled in it. She wanted people to know, to notice. He, too, was pathetically coy, waving 'see you later' at her window and thinking: 'Fuck! How do I get myself out of this?'

He glanced down the guest list. A few of the names were familiar or vaguely familiar people from MTV, *Spin*, *Details* and others James'd heard Wheezer calling 'key'. It always cheered him up when Wheezer went all American. He didn't even know he was doing it. And he certainly didn't know how much pleasure his performances gave the band. He'd probabaly resign again if he ever heard some of the piss-taking and imitations: 'Hey, Mel! What's happening, man! Are we in good shape?'

He smiled and ran his eye over the last few names. Coney Island High was not a gigantic venue. A cool, ambient Village hang-out, ideal for the Grams, but there were close on a hundred names on the list, here. Who the fuck was paying for them all? Whenever he thought about it, which he tried not to, often, James was angered by the seemingly endless free ride his band were giving to any old cunt who wanted to hop on board. Everyone was having a great time. *He* was having a great time. But he was still skint. When he got back, he was going to go and see Wolfe again and sort something out. He was the fucking main man, here. Indispensable. Without him . . . Like, he wrote the music. The hooks. The fucking tunes! He wanted some recognition for that. He wanted his share.

He went to put the guest list down and only then did he spot it. Top right of the page. Madonna's List. *Madonna*'s list. Fucking *what*? He ran to find the others.

Wheezer loved them. Most of the time he couldn't think of them as sensitive, thinking, living things – they were a mass which he had to make malleable, mould in a certain way. This way today, that way tomorrow. But right now, looking at the shattered eyes and grey complexions trying to eat various combinations of eggs and potatoes, he loved them.

Last night they had filled him up with a feeling, a pride, he never would have imagined for himself. So many things went into making Wheezer feel this way, not the slightest of which was his mute, tearful satisfaction at another crowd of individuals in another strange place being made into a brief, spiritual wholeness by the music and the presence of the Grams. Wheezer felt blessed.

But it was their togetherness, too. After the show, when they came out into the fray for the latest Meet 'n' Greet – this time an opportunity for the foot soldiers at Worldwide to meet the group, everyone from sales and distribution people to art department, local promotion and advertising executives – the group had been radiant. They'd been an entity. In addition, there were more MTV representatives, radio producers, publishers, record retailers, club runners, DJs, fanzine editors, stalkers, journalists and scene-makers, all bustling around a narrow balcony area to say hello to the group. They were still full of energy, full of humour, still performing. They connected with people in such a direct, affecting way. Wheezer stood back and watched them at work – and they were at *work*. Each one of them was captivating. They looked people in the eye, they asked their name, they showed a real interest. Maybe they were still high from the show, but this, if anything, was a yet more impressive performance. The greeted were charmed. It was only after three-quarters of an hour, when James started to become distracted by the increasing numbers of female fans who'd made it up into this VIP area, that the Meet 'n' Greet started to break up. By then, three days into their tour, New York Loved The Grams.

Madonna didn't show.

After the Meet 'n' Greet, a less dignified scramble took over. It was open season, now, to bag a Gram, and each was surrounded by a scrum of women and a little knot of boys, all pushing for attention. Mel, after a shock-headed Wheezer had confided in him about Myra, was keeping her occupied at the bar, while the group, submerged by well-wishers and scalp hunters, tried to make their way out of the club. They were missing Burger, too luxurious an item for the tour budget. In his place, the unlikely trio of Rory, Crapston and Marty tried to push back the crowd.

'We're fine an' 'at,' beamed James, ridiculous in his jester's hat, arms around a posse of girls. A tall, raven-haired creature with much alabaster make-up and red, red lipstick, sidled over to Wheezer. She was wearing a basque which forced her breasts up so abruptly that they almost touched her chin. Wheezer had a quick look. Great body, but the girl looked insane. She eyed him slyly.

'So. Mr Finlay. We meet at last . . .'

'Er . . .'

She held out a hand which Wheezer shook, befuddled. He glanced back round. Myra was railing drunkenly at a barman. She had no idea Wheezer was even in the building.

'I'm Katie Chick. You wrote me a coupla times.' Katie Chick-

343

Katie Chick-Katie Chick . . . Her voice was almost manly. 'You e-mailed me about the Grams. I'm their number one fan.'

She cracked a sharp smile, but she was intent too. She was expectant.

Wheezer gulped. He was on trial. He was representing England in the Legendary Managers Who Drink and Drug and Screw stakes. What if word went around that Wheezer couldn't *party*? What if Al Meredith got to hear that he'd passed over a night with the Chicks? He eyed the tall, slender, painted gargoyle and swallowed hard, geeing himself up. 'Good. Well. Let's . . . get it on!'

She laughed shrilly and slapped him hard on the bottom. 'Ahh, Wheezy! You're the best! Come on, man – I'm gonna blow your tiny mind!'

So he just let her drag him out of the venue, out of Coney Island High, out into St Marks Place, out into New York's delirious afterworld. He just let it happen. He hardly said a thing, only the involuntary spluttering of the words 'oh' and 'no' when he twigged that they were to travel by hearse. 'Oh . . . no.'

He didn't even shout. He just said it. But he didn't have to say – or do – much else. She drove him, past movie-set steaming gutters, past cursing cab drivers and wretched down-and-outs, down to her cave on Horatio Street. And it was a *cave*, painted black and decorated with silver pentangles and ghoulish luminous hieroglyphics. In one corner was a bed, or more properly a stern, iron bedstead bathed from above with celestial blue light. There was a plain black sheet, but no other bedclothes of immediate evidence. There was certainly nothing to get under. This was not a bed for lovers. It was somewhere for a show to unfold. Above the headboard, manacles were set into the wall and to the right, as Wheezer looked, agog, was a neat dressing-table laid out with the tools and implements of torture. He didn't feel as bad as he had done in the club. A portion of him – a small part – was nervously excited.

'You'll have to go easy on me . . .'

She smiled, not unsympathetically, and kissed him slowly, slipping her tongue languorously inside his mouth. Then she pushed him on to the bed and, with his subservient compliance, she clamped him in irons.

'Now you're mine,' she smiled.

Wheezer ordered another bowl of The Carnegie Deli's famous soup. This thin chicken broth, with pasta parcels and spicy ham bits, was just the ticket. He'd loved New York, really loved it, but he'd be glad to be away on the plane to Boston later in the afternoon. He'd feel better with New York – Myra, Katie, madness – behind him. The others were still tittering about their experiences the night before. Beano had had the most bizarre encounter.

'So, like, after she's finished, she sort of sits back and licks her lips, looking up at the ceiling as though she's trying to remember something, then she nods her head and just goes, like . . . mmmm.'

James started giggling. 'Fuck off!'

Beano – still drunk, high, speeding, everything – was wide-eyed, impatient to tell them. 'Wait, will you! This is nothing! I mean this is properly weird, la . . . she licks her lips then goes into her little handbag and pulls out a notebook. A *notebook*, right? A real, actual little black book and she writes something down. I'm telling you, la! Just a little bit of scribble. So obviously I'm, y'know . . . what's that, like? And she just looks at me. Pink cheeks, looks about fucken ten without her make-up on, and . . .'

He started giggling to himself. Wheezer nudged him. 'Come on! You can't just start and not finish!'

'Honest! This is *weird*! This'll kill youse . . .' Keva held out a hand for him to continue. '. . . she goes . . .' Beano put on a squeaky, adolescent, girl-in-high-school-movie voice. 'Mmmm. Salty. Saltier than the drummer in Sensira, though not as salty as the singer in Macrobe. He was *very* salty. The drummer in Sensira was quite runny. You had more sperm than both of them. You were thicker, too. Thick and salty. The thickest, I'd say . . .'

The laughter was so strong and so sustained that everyone forgot to put the bite on Wheezer for *his* story.

'Jesus! What a twat! What a fucken twat! I deserve shootin'! Jeeze!

345

I've gotta speak to her again! I'll have to phone her as soon as we get to the hotel . . .'

Boston looked bleak to Beano, sobering up in the Landcruiser. After three days of almost constant partying, he was plunging head first into a mammoth Low. Chief among his symptoms was this overpowering guilt, not just at his first – and spectacular – betrayal of Celeste, but his complicity, too, in the macho bean-spilling ceremony which followed. He'd called Celeste moments after the Manhattan spunk-teller had left his room but, of course, she was at work and couldn't stay on the line. So pulverised by shame was he on hearing her voice again that he'd got dressed, gone to brunch with the team, laughed at their sexist stories then brought the house down with his own hilarious account of the Gotham Gobbler. He hated himself. Wheezer was making it worse. He seemed to revel in this side of touring. The twat never had a hangover, always seemed bright and chirpy and always had that fucking tape on first thing in the morning, when the rest of them were wallowing in self-loathing. 'Suzanne' by Leonard Cohen. 'This Is Low' by Blur. 'Decades' by Joy Division. Classic suicide tracks, sure to make them feel wretched about themselves. Celeste. Fuck. What a gobshite he was. He would never, ever do anything like that again. Never. He was going to call Celeste when he got to Boston, tell her everything, face the music and, if she blew him out, it would be no less than he deserved. But if she forgave him, by Harry, he was going to repay that faith. No. He'd never do anything like that again.

'But he *asked* to do the interviews!' whined Tony. He put down his Gameboy Pocket and concentrated fully on them. The meeting was not going well. Keva sat in silence, supping lukewarm tea in the cavernous lobby lounge of the Boston Omni while Wheezer tried to make his case.

'He *demanded* to do the interviews,' blustered James. 'It was his own fucken decision, wasn't it? So what's he saying? We've got to stay in and be good while he's out working?'

'I'm not saying that . . .' Wheezer started.

Keva felt it was time to intervene. 'I think you're all getting this bent out of proportion. What I'm trying to tell you . . .' Suddenly all eyes were on him. The rest of the group were looking at him as though he was someone new. Or someone they didn't know well. He paused. '. . . I'm just asking for . . . I dunno. It's not as easy as it looks. It's quite draining, like, you know, answering the same questions and trying to make the interviewer feel as though he's the only one who's asked it . . . D'you know what I mean?'

They shrugged. Keva tried to play it for laughs. '*So*, why the *Grams*? Are you all, like, major Gram Parsons fans or is there, like, a, um, *Powder* reference in there somewhere . . .'

No one laughed.

'Fuck it! It gets to be a pain, all that, you know!'

Tony piped up. 'Look, mate, we're not blind to all this. Really. We're made up that you're doing all this. Ta. Seriously. I'd rather you than me. But, like . . . wasn't that what you wanted? I don't see what any of this has got to do with us.'

Keva's shoulders slumped. He sighed out loud. 'OK. I'll give it to you, then. I think you're letting the side down. Not any one of you, personally. But I don't think there's any . . . collective responsibility . . .'

James got up, shaking his head. 'I've had enough of this shite! I'm going up to me room. Tune me guitar or something . . .'

Keva was up on his feet, blocking his way. 'Don't you fucking walk out on me, you fat, useless cunt!'

The sudden intake of breath from the others was almost audible. Keva and James had last had a fight over two years ago. Keva was a martyr, a moaner, a moody cunt, but he hardly ever lost his temper. He battered James that last time, too. James stood there, shocked, scared-looking. Keva jabbed him hard in the guts.

'I'm trying to tell you nicely, you cunt! You're a fucking liability! You don't give a fucking shit! Look at you! What's happening to you . . .'

Tony jumped up between them. 'Come 'ead, Keva! What's this all about? You're just stressed, eh, man!'

'I AM NOT FUCKING STRESSED!' He looked around at their dazed expressions, but he couldn't stop himself. He didn't want to stop himself. 'I just want some fucking respect! If I'm going to spend each day, every fucking day, talking this fucking band up, telling how we're the last of the fucking . . . *mystics*, I don't want some fat cunt in a HAT . . . running round . . . *farting*! And grinning! Always . . . bloody . . . *grinning*! All right?'

He collapsed back into his chair, head in hands. Wheezer wanted to rush over to him, but right now too much partiality would be a bad thing. The silence was excruciating. Nobody made eye contact. The tiled floor of the hotel lounge took on new complexities as five young men studied it fanatically.

'Fuckinell!' said James. He grinned at Keva. 'Say what you mean, why don't you?'

Their laughter was hungry, desperate and unanimous and, even after the last reprises and half-chuckles, Keva was still sobbing passionately.

The illuminated wall-clock said 2.37 when the phone went. 2.37 a.m.

'Heeey! Mr Pump-Action!'

Wheezer knew the voice straight away. He cleared his throat. 'Myra. Er . . .'

'So how're those gloots of yours doin'? Are they good and hard right now?'

Wheezer actually started to run his free hand over his bottom to check. 'Erm, Myra . . . er . . .'

'Oh, you little fuckin honey! You sound just like Hugh Grant! Stay right there! I'm comin' down . . .'

The line went dead. Coming *down*? What the fuck . . . Shit! She was here. She was in Boston. In this bloody hotel, coming to get him any minute now!

He jumped out of bed and ran to the wardrobe. Too obvious. Shades of Amsterdam, anyway. Shit-shit-shit! He turned round and round, chasing his tail, looking for somewhere to hide before it dawned on him. She already knew he was in there. Of course she did, she'd just spoken to him.

So he had a choice. He could just refuse to open up. Do it nice and innocent, blame jet lag, stress, big day tomorrow, I've been thinking – we should keep this thing professional before our feelings for each other get out of control – that sort of thing. Or he could let her in and succumb to sex once again. There was nothing to weigh up. He could not let that woman past the door. If he gave in, he was in trouble. He had to be strong. If he let Myra in now, he would never, ever get rid of her.

Knock at the door. Wheezer padded over.

'Myra! Wow! Come in!'

'Oh Gad!! Oh my Gad! You bastard! You fucking bastard! Fuck me! Fuck me with your big hard cock! Fuck me, you bastard!'

'Mmmm', offered Wheezer, out of politeness.

'Fuck me! Oh you bastard . . . you bad bastard! Fuck me!'

'I AM DOING!'

They were in the Spacevan, travelling to the venue from WFNX Radio where everyone had gone with Keva to lend some moral support. El Niño, as they'd taken to calling him, found that he didn't want them around, after all. Part of it was that they cramped his style, prevented his pretentious excesses just by being there but, worst of all, they detracted from the sense that *he* was the star and the Grams were *his* band. He powerfully wished he'd never spoken out about the workload. He didn't *want* it to be fair. He wanted to be a saint.

The interview had been cool, but Keva was laid low by the guy's obvious love of Sensira. This time it got to him, bigtime. He couldn't be sure whether the DJ was winding him up, smiling all the time, *huge*, fluorescent white square-shaped teeth taunting him with news of Sensira's impending megastardom in the USA. What about Chuck and Jimmy's stories? Who was telling the truth? He managed to stay buttoned up, but he was desperately down about Helmet. Simply, he didn't deserve to be big. Keva found, as he thought about it, that he didn't just want be big himself. He wanted to be huge. The biggest for ages. Ever. Way bigger than Helmet, for sure. No. That wouldn't be enough. He wanted Helmet to fail.

They cheered as they trundled past Cheers, but it was brief respite. There was another big Sensira poster by the bridge.

'Fucken look at them! The twats're everywhere! You've got to sort it out, Wheeze! We've got to start doing things properly . . .'

'Doing things properly' was James's latest rant. Wherever they stayed, you could guarantee that his hotel room was too small, too

349

noisy, too big, too cold. Other bands wouldn't put up with it. Catering was never on time. No one was looking after them. They had no idea how well or how badly they were doing. No one told them anything. Sensira were everywhere. They were Big News. Much bigger than the Grams. James wanted to be kept informed. He wanted things to be done properly. Wheezer was inclined just to tell James to fuck off – but it'd cause more problems than it'd solve.

'Look, Jimbo, I've told you I'll happily type you an update at the end of every day, but, you know – will you read the fucking thing? This particular fetish of yours'll have passed by tonight, won't it? You'll be off chasing schoolgirls again . . .'

'Fuck off, will you! I wanna know what's being done with me career! I wanna be totally in the picture, at all times . . .'

Tony was guffawing.

'What?'

'Did you really say that?'

'What?'

'Me *career*! Is that what being in a band is?'

'Ah, shut it, fatso!'

'Mr Kettle, I'd like you to meet Master Black.'

'I'm glad you're taking this so seriously, Tone . . .'

Tony carried on chuckling. 'Me career! He plays so loud no cunt can hear themselves on stage then fucks off with the first slapper who makes eye contact! You're a fuckin pro, Jimmy!'

'Will you all shut the fuck up!' shouted Keva. The group made hurricane noises and rounded on the retreating singer, blowing in his face.

'Niño! Niño!' they chanted. Keva looked away, bored.

Wheezer stared out of the window as they pulled up outside the Paradise, hoping and praying that Myra would, by now, be well on her way back to New York.

'You gotta keep on humpin' her.' Mel's voice rasped down the line. 'I told you already, kid – the worst thing you can do is hump a record company chick. But the *worst* thing you can do is to *stop* humpin' her. Yeah? Leastways wait until we get this band established before you start making waves. We're close on 100,000 units, we make a new clip for MTV tomorrow, adds are rolling in and things are panning out – you don't need to put that process into turnaround, huh?'

Wheezer, on the other end of the line, shook his head.

Mel plugged on. 'I mean, shoot, it's not a life sentence, hah-hah! I mean Myra Sweeney, man! She has *great* tits! Couple more days you're outta here, right? Game, set and match!'

Wheezer said nothing.

Mel tried his softball approach. 'Look, Wheeze. What's the reality here? You're balling a kooky chick, right? A not-bad-looking kooky chick. It's not the end of the world. She has her job to do in NYC. You have yours which takes you all over the world. So never the twain shall meet, right? You're probably gonna have to hump the kid, what? Four, five more times. Just until we go gold. A *month*. Two. Take her calls. Send her flowers. Slip her the snake when you gotta. I tell you, this could work out to be a blessing in disguise. This could be the deal that breaks this band wide open . . .'

'You cynical Yankee cunt . . .'

'That's my boy!'

He plopped the receiver down and dug out *Billboard* just to check. He was right. Gold. 500,000 sales. That could take months. He was doomed.

Another stupefyingly fine gig drove all the tension back from whence it came. The band were superb. The Paradise, packed to melting-point with hundreds of stoked Bostonians, took to the Grams from the moment they strolled on stage. Keva turned his back to the crowd, watched smiling while Beano counted the band in – one, two, three, four – then, BOOM! He leapt in the air, scissor-kicked his microphone and with a scream of 'Let's have it!' burnt into the new set-starter, 'Librium'.

They loved it. They went mental. It was one of those gigs which ignites, everything comes together, every single person is into it and nobody gives a fuck. The Boston kids gave the Grams a night to remember, and the band repaid the favour. Halfway through the set Wheezer abandoned his usual spec by the mixing desk and, spotting Pat McIntosh down the front, frugging with a gang of Alternate kids, went to join the scrummage. James, having the time of his life, almost blew 'Desert Rain' when he looked down to see Wheezer, perched on Pat's shoulders, laughing dementedly and singing every word. It was one of their greatest nights, ever.

Afterwards, a turbulence of eager fans packed into the dressing-room, still telling the boys they were the coolest, but less reverential than the New Yorkers, more matey, more wanting to show them their city.

'Let's all go to Axis, man!'

'No way, man! These guys'll hate it! Too much techno!'

'I don't mind a bit of techno an' that!' grinned James, eyeing every single girl in turn, and at once.

'Club 3!'

'The Loke, man! Local 186! Somewhere we'll all get in!'

They spent the rest of the night in the Cantab, a groovy good-time bar where Wheezer Finlay entertained the troops with a terrifying rendition of 'Moon River'. Crapston got up to join him for 'Somethin' Stupid'. Everybody – band, crew and management – was best friends with everyone else. They were the best pals in all the world. Everything was working out. Just so long as Myra Sweeney would stay put.

Wheezer, skipping into his room, light as a feather and drunk as a lord, stepped on an envelope. He whisked it up, knowing, just knowing that it was more good news. It had been such a great, great day. If it'd been a bad day, this would be a hotel fax from Myra, saying: 'Where da fuck are ya? I'm in Room 213.' But, because today was a good day, this slim envelope would disclose only nutrition. And it did. It was from Mel. A brief message: 'My Esteemed Wheezer – No Need To Ball Looney. See Enclosed.'

Attached was a list of new station adds, along with the moves up the airplay charts of those stations already spinning the track. It was just a list of radio station call signs and statistics, but Wheezer had never read anything so hungrily since stumbling across a sun-dried bundle of *Knaves* in the Riverbank Road carpark when he was eleven.

RADIO AND TRADES

Billboard Modern Rock:	Debut at 30*
R&R New Rock:	10* from 14
Gavin Alternative:	9* from 12
HITS Post Modern:	16* from 20
Album Network Expando (Radio):	7* from 8
Album Network Expando (Retail):	17 from 22
Hard Alternative:	9* from 11
FMQB Modern:	8* from 10
Rockpool College:	3* from 6
CMJ Top Radio:	5* from 9

* = Bullet. You have made a gain in reports which is at least 50% more than last week's. You're on the up, OK!

SALES

	1-day	5-day	10-day	Total
Powder – US	645	2616	4723	97,825

RADIO – COMMERCIAL ALTERNATIVE/MODERN ROCK

Adds –	Canada	CIMX, Windsor, Ontario
	Far West	91X, San Diego, CA
		KBCO, Boulder, CO
	KJQ	Ogden, UT
	KTAO	Taos, NM
	KTCL	Fort Collins, CO
	KUKQ	Tempe, AZ
	KUNV	Las Vegas, NV
Midwest	WAPS	Akron, OH
	KJJO	Eden Prairie, MN
	KRCK	Omaha, NE
	WOXY	Oxford, OH
	WWCD	Colombus, OH
Eastern	WBER	Penfield, NY
	WBNY	Buffalo, NY
	WBRU	Providence, RI
	WCDB	Albany, NY
	WDST	Woodstock, NY

	WHFS	*Landover, MD*
	WHTG	*Asbury Park, NJ*
	WMDK	*Peterborough, NH*
	WNCS	*Montpelier, VT*
	WXVX	*Monroeville, PA*
South/South East	*KACV*	*Amarillo, TX*
	KBAC	*Santa Fe, NM*
	KDGE*	*Irving, TX*
	WFIT	*Melbourne, FL*
	WRAS	*Atlanta, GA*
	KTOW	*Sandsprings, OK*

* V. Important add. The Edge is crucial to us in this region – and it was the last of the huge commercial modern rock stations to hold out.

Analysis

Sales are extremely encouraging. The underlying pattern is increase, increase, increase! We will reach 100,000 by the time you hit LA – a major, major achievement in this short time. Radio is unbelievable. This track is lighting up everywhere. Knopf has really done his shit. This is a superb job. There is hardly a significant add in this format that we don't have. All key stations now in line. If we can hold them for three more weeks, especially keep KROQ away from a new track, get a sense from MTV, keep those sales ticking, keep the bullets moving upwards . . . then, my friend, we have a Story. Will fax Guy. Don't go too crazy. Keep yourself nice for LA! All systems go. Onward and upward.

Best of everything

Yours

Mel

Wheezer sat there, a big, daft smile holding up his sleepy face. He stared at Mel's fax, read it again, read it one more time then jumped to his holdall, tearing out his Rand McNally US Road Atlas, checking out all these places the boys were getting airplay. It was all too perfect. He lay there on his bed, kicking his legs, staring at the map. His band were being heard in Eden blooming Prairie, Minnesota!

He run his finger down the list. Asbury Park! Too much! Bloody, bloody . . . The fucking *Boss*, that's all! And the Grams! Asbury bloody Park! Southside Johnny and the Asbury Dukes! And what about Monroeville, Philadelphia? Was Marilyn born there? It sounded like a fantasy town, somewhere where David Lynch would have long-headed recluses filing dead insects in alphabetical order. His eyelids couldn't stay with it. His eyes and his mind were still lapping it all up, all these mythical towns and songs. Santa Fe. Amarillo. He was still hugging his pillow when first light and a cricked neck woke him again a few hours later.

James was operating in his own little time chamber, now. He knew he'd had two alarm calls, and two from Wheezer. He knew everyone was down in reception, packed, ready to leave. He knew there was a flight to catch. But there was nothing he could do. He was fucked. He lay in the bath, where he'd lain for twenty minutes, unable to hurry himself. Every half-minute his nose leaked another involuntary cascade of sinus water. He rarely bothered dabbing it now. Every now and then he'd jerk out of his stupor, realise he had to wash, dry, pack, vacate, settle, leave in one minute flat, then the soothing cocoon of the warm water would lap around his shoulders, protecting him from duty, from have-to and must and now, and he slumped back into his daydreams. James Love. Hector Lovett. Guitar Hero. King of the States. He could hear the phone trilling again. Wheezer. He'd have to get a move on. He really would.

Last night, Beano had just given in. It was easier just to get on with it, give them what they want, get it over with, get some kip. All round, it was less painful. Tony had stumbled into the room, tittering, in the small hours, snapping on every light and yanking the sheets off Beano's bed.

'Look what pappa's brought home for *you*!'

With Tony were the three most striking girls from the Paradise, all of, perhaps, Korean or Vietnamese ancestry, all shrilly excited.

'This is *awesome*!'

'The *awesomest*!'

'Toe-dally rad!'

One of girls had dangling, copper-brown breasts, hanging loose in a denim dress. She wore the dress, a little backpack and a pair of Dr Martens with white ankle socks, nothing else, in frozen November. She was huge, large – but not at all fat. Everything was enormously outsize, yet in perfect proportion. She was a Big Girl. The other two were petite, possibly sisters, padded up in bubble jackets and leggings. They started massaging Tony's head, giggling and reaching for his flies. Beano sat on the bed with his sheets pulled tight around him.

'Who shall *I* fuck?' shouted the tallest girl.

'Not me!' croaked Beano, diving back into bed and bandaging himself in bedclothes. One hand flapped at Tony and a muffled, indignant voice wailed: 'Go and bother '*im*!'

She lolled her head on to her shoulder and looked him over, smiling, then went over to his bedside, kneeling so that her face was by his hidden head.

'Hey, bashful,' she soothed. 'Come on. I like skinny. Skinny for me works!' She put a hand under the sheets. 'Mmmm. Neat buns!'

This was all the encouragement she needed. Undressing quickly, she forced her way in next to Beano and dragged the sheets from around him, pushing him down and taking a nipple and half of his chest into her mouth.

'Mmmm! Cool! This for me is awesome!'

I wish she'd shut up, thought Beano, lying there, letting the girl seek him and mount him. She wiggled one way, then another then, seeming to find a place she liked, put Beano under starters orders: 'OK! Let's fuck!'

He could hear Wheezer knocking at the door. Someone else, too. Several people. He felt as though he'd only just got off to sleep. The girl had kept him awake all night, mauling him and inserting fingers into his orifices, talking non-stop. Wheezer was shouting. 'Beano! Come on, man! We've got a bloomin' video to shoot! We've all checked out!'

He forced his eyes open. Tony's bed was vacant. Shit! He sat up.

'Beano! I'm coming in, right? I wanna make sure you're OK,

mate. If you have company, my apologies, but I have to come in there. I'm coming in . . . NOW.'

Shit. Only yesterday he'd renounced corporeal sin. He couldn't let them find him like this. He could hear Tony's voice. Fuck. They were all out there. They thought he was dead. He looked at the slumbering giant next to him and hatched a cunning plan.

Wheezer came into the room alone.

'Stay there, lads! Come 'ead! You wouldn't like it if it was you.'

He could hear giggling and more silly shouts from the band. Everyone was hyped up, still speeding from the show and Wheezer's fantastic news over breakfast. Wheezer hurried over to the bed. The big girl Tony had warned him about was there, but no sign of Beano. There was a bit of an ungainly lump to one side. What if . . . no. But yes! What if she'd *crushed* him to death! He'd have to check it out. He'd have to!

Carefully, he peeled back the top sheet. The girl twitched slightly, but carried on snoring. Each gigantic breast looked as though it weighed thirty pounds or more. Certainly two hands would be needed to tackle such a breast. Wheezer looked her over a second longer, aroused now. She was magnificent. The nipples, so fat and dark, were a fascination to him. Everything was going his way, just now – would it be so bad of he were just to . . . She shifted, an angry impatience furrowing her brow as though guessing. Wheezer stepped back.

Lying there, slightly raised, snoring powerfully, the brown girl's brown breasts slipped either side of her ribcage, still round and robust, like newly-baked loaves. And it was just underneath one such breast, just as he was about to turn back and declare Beano missing that Wheezer spotted the stray tuft of peroxide-white hair. Beano was underneath the girl, perfectly occluded, hiding. Gingerly, Wheezer lifted the nearest breast to one side, taking special care not to move too suddenly. Beano peered out from underneath.

'Morning, Wheeze . . .'

'Turned out nice again . . .' smiled Wheezer.

'I will *never*, EVER, do anything like this again . . .'

'I'm not doin' that!'

Perry Martinez ignored him, looked straight past him and

beckoned Nancy Spanke over. Nancy, nervously obliging as always, hastened to Perry's side.

'*So*, what we have right now is a band who have commissioned me to make a clip for them who do not, as a matter of fact, want me to make a clip for them. How d'you suggest we resolve that issue, Nancy?'

'Like, what's the specific here? What aspect will they not deal with?'

James stuck his face down into his Puffa jacket to hide his smirk. It was freezing. They were in Golden Gate Park with a horde of children and a limitless supply of polystyrene snow and a lunatic egomaniac director. It did not feel at all Beautiful.

'I've asked him, the jolly one – the one I *thought* was nice – to pick up the children, one by one, black, white, purple and yeh-lew, and give them a little kiss on the cheek. That's all!'

'I'm not fucken Michael Jackson!' muttered James. Keva, red nose dripping, hustled over, swinging his arms to keep warm.

'Look, guys . . . this is nothing to do with what we will or won't do . . . it's like . . . This isn't the idea you sent us! We didn't agree to any of this!'

Nancy whipped her mobile out of her pocket. 'Hi, Paul! Could you fax over Perry's original treatment? Grams. Grams. Yah. No, I have my Siemens. Yah. Bye.'

Wheezer was with them, now, cradling hot soup in a plastic cup. 'Look, boys – can't we just get this done? We're due at Gavin at three. At this rate . . .'

Keva shook his head. 'Wheeze, mate, this is not a matter of fuckin scheduling. They've changed the whole fuckin concept of the video. It's gone from being, like, multiracial San Francisco in gorgeous, contemplative slo-mo to a gang of suspect Englishman hanging round a group of kids in a park!' He raised his eyebrows ironically, imitating Perry. 'I think that throws up some major artistic issues. Don't you?'

Wheezer shook his head. 'Frankly, matey, I'd rather keep my powder dry. I'm beat on this one. I've had longer than you to get used to it, but from the moment they told me our video was, erm, too *English* I was bracing myself for this.' He affected a tranced-out, mellow surfer voice. 'Just let it happen, man. Everything's working out so well. These guys, trust me – they know their shit. Be like me. Go with the flow one time. Be a corporate lackey whore, sit back, reap the rewards . . .'

Keva laughed. Perry was in a fevered pique, yelling at the make-up boy. 'Alfonse! You *dick*! That child has . . . SNOT! *Rivers* of snot *cascading* from its neowse! Wipe it! Wipe its fucking neowse! Not you, asshole! You're even more of an imbecile than Alfie . . .'

Keva waved over to James. 'Jimbo! Just kiss the kid!'

From the windows of Live 105 Radio, high above San Francisco, they could see the queue snaking away from Slim's, a hundred feet below. Since the interview, only half an hour ago, the numbers had started to trickle along to Slim's, little pockets of fans flapping around outside, trying to keep warm, trying to suss whether the band was inside the club. The gigs in New York and Boston had been fantastic, but this, even now, felt epic. In the silent twilight, way down there, a hundred or more kids were already lining up, three hours before doors. Keva watched, and felt enormous. I am a God, he thought.

He put his arm around Tony. 'Been a long journey, hey?'

Tony carried on staring down at the club. He smiled. 'Are we there yet?'

Keva's eyes became distant again. 'I dunno, mate. I don't think I'll ever get there . . .'

Tony snapped out of his reverie, turning to face Keva. 'What d'you mean? We've cracked America! We're going to be huge . . .'

Keva carried on staring past him, out into the half-lit sky. He looked back at Tony. 'I don't know.' He pulled himself away from the window. 'I mean, there's no finishing line, is there? You just go on and on. You want a Top 40 single. Then Top Ten. *Top of the Pops*. Number One. Straight in at Number One. *Another* Number One. More Number Ones than Sensira. More Number Ones than the bleedin' Beatles! Gold in the States. Platinum in the States . . . It's self-perpetuating, isn't it? I mean . . . it should be like climbing Everest. You know what you're striving for. You know where the peak is. It's up there! But there's little stations, little camps all the way up. Loads of 'em. So you can pick 'em off, take your time, get there bit by bit, eh?'

Tony stared at him mischievously. 'Have you gone mad?'

Keva shook his head, serious, still distant. 'See? That's why I never tell anyone nothing. You just take the piss . . .'

Tony put his hand on Keva's shoulder. 'I'm sorry, mate. I didn't mean to . . . I'm just saying, like. Look at that!' He pointed to the ever-growing crowd outside Slim's. 'That's for *us*! It's great!'

Keva peeped out again. This time, much to Tony's distress, he held his hand. 'It is, isn't it? It's fucking unbelievable!'

At the first opportunity, but not so soon as to be abrupt, Tony slipped his hand out of Keva's and continued staring out at the San Francisco night.

They'd never seen Pat McIntosh so drunk before. He'd left the band to their soundchecks and their relentless bloody promotion and met up with an old *NME* pal, Ken Wall, now running a specialist import indie shop in San Jose. The two of them had made up for a lot of lost time together, and Pat turned up at the Phoenix Hotel just after six, arseholed. He barged into Keva and James's room slobbering about genius – his own – and collapsed on James's bed. Sensira's video was on MTV with the sound turned down,

'Washish fukn shit onfah?'

'We. Don't. Know. Pat,' said James, enunciating every word as though he were a simpleton. 'Perhaps. Emteevee. Like. Shite?'

Pat laughed nastily and fell fast asleep. He was immovable. Here was one man who would not be making it to Slim's that night. James worked his fingers inside his hip pocket, knowing there'd be a bonanza, and was not disappointed. There was enough in the wrap for him to take half and still return a pile to the snoring scribe. But he didn't. James Love, chuckling to himself, swiped the lot. Pat wouldn't have a clue.

'IDIOTS! FUCKING DICKHEADS!'

Wheezer stormed out, face furious red, slamming the door so hard that the beer bottles shifted in their crate. The band sat there in silence, studying the dressing-room floor.

'It's up to you guys,' Sandy glowed. 'But KITS will not play your music again if you stiff them on this. Live 105 do not give out second chances.'

The threat seemed to trouble Keva more than the others.

'No. Fucking. Chance,' James intoned. 'I'm sorry, San. Honest. I don't want to embarrass you. But we have to draw the line somewhere. Are we a serious band or a sideshow? Do we have to *deal* like this all the time? You know, I'll play your record. I'll promote your gig. But my kid has to meet you backstage. Maybe he gets up and dances with you guys during the encore . . . it's . . . *bollocks*!'

He shrugged his shoulders as though that were the end of the matter. Sandy tried to stay calm. 'It's the way we do things here. It's what works.'

She carried on nodding after she'd finished, willing her truth to find its target. Beano joined in, paraphrasing James: 'It's a point of principle, Sandy. We're all for promoting the album . . . but in the right way, you know? Jimbo's right. We don't want the *Hard Report*'s Advertising Manager bringing his kid backstage to tell us we're awesome before the gig. Is that what works? Cos we don't *want* that shit . . .'

Sandy laughed bitterly. 'Cool. Another British band who don't wanna work. Makes a change. Like I say, guys, it's your party. It's this simple. Play the game and win. Drop out and lose. Over to you. I don't *give* a shit.'

Her fury glowed out under the flawless Mediterranean skin. She gave a shit.

'Just give me some warning, though, huh? No – tell me *now*. Am I calling up Steve Knopf and Jeff Silver and telling them the band ain't playing no more? Do I tell Live 105 to put out an APB for their prize winners to turn around and go home? Just tell me.'

Silence.

'I'll do it,' said Keva, head bowed.

She looked at him with pleasure and surprise and gratitude. She looked at him for ages, until he felt uncomfortable.

'Hey!' he laughed. 'I said yeah! Yeah?'

She hugged him and kissed him on the cheek. 'Thank you.'

'You got it!', he teased.

*

The crowd at Slim's were mental. Better even than Boston. More berserk from first sight of the band than anything they'd known since the *NME* tent at Reading. It was that combination of restricted space, anticipation, impossible expectations coming to life and that inimitable, unrepeatable frisson of a definitive moment happening *now*. Everyone knew it. It was unhinged. The band didn't want to stop.

Wheezer Finlay, creeping in sheepishly after a pointless hike around Union Square, stood at the back of the long room and watched his band carving out a little bit of history for themselves. They were twats. He hated them. But they were fantastic. On stage, they could do whatever they wanted.

Beano and James hit the big hipsters' bar down the block while Keva and Tony met and greeted and fretted. Only when there was no more cold pizza, no plaudits to field, no more modesty to feign did the entourage move down the road to the DNA. James and Beano were unmissable in there. James, just in case he should not be recognised in his civvies, had kept on his fool's hat. The prongs of the hat were the only thing visible above a throng of lusty teenagers, fighting, actually trading blows to get close to the two of them.

'You prefer to speak to *her?*' spat one rouge-streaked Bay Doll. She was not old enough to be in the bar. She was on heels under jeans, two wild gashes of lipstick goring her cheekbones, lending her face the very air of gauche immaturity that she was trying to hide.

'Check her tits out! No way do they pass the pencil test, man! Feel mine!'

'Devil's Haircut' came on, loud. The band surrounded Wheezer, patting his head and jostling him happily. Wheezer laughed bronchially, throwing his head back, rasping out his crusty, coughing, chuckling laugh, showing his teeth, blue-violet in the strobe light and shaking his head to Beck. James, still smarting from the row, came over to make friends. He crouched down behind Wheezer and, in a swoop, ducked his head between the manager's legs and hoisted him up high on his shoulders, just like Pat in Boston. The thrust of the manoeuvre knocked James's hat backwards and, as he groped to pull it back straight, he sent it tumbling to the floor. A brief, brief pause – then a stampede, as dozens of boys and girls charged for the prize. They banged past James, felling him, and Wheezer, hard to the floor as they fought for the jester's hat.

Wheezer, the nearest to the ruckus as he got to his knees, saw the most preposterous scene developing. A boy and a girl had hold of one end each of James's hat and, with their free hands, were belting each other rhythmically about the head and earholes. Grams mania was breaking out. Wheezer got up, turned on his heel and headed straight back out of the club.

'I'll get a cab. Might have a drink with the crew. Ta-ra!'

He turned to wink at Keva, who thumbs-upped him.

Tony had agreed to go with the two girls because they seemed nice. Sisters, clearly, both lightly tanned, brimful of good health and cheer, they'd been standing at the periphery of the DNA Lounge frenzy, smiling and seeming removed from the madness. Tony extricated himself from the mauling gaggle and approached the girls, apologetic. 'Hello.'

'Hi,' smiled both girls, at once. The older, more dominant one stood in front of her sister without meaning to. It must have been something she did all the time.

'How're you enjoying your fame?'

He pulled a comical face. 'Only really sticking around to give Beano some moral support . . .'

All three of them looked across the bar, to see Beano conscientiously testing a variety of teenage breasts.

'Welcome to California,' said the older sister distantly, glancing past Tony, who she towered over, leaving a deliberating pause between each word. She was trying to project a cultured ennui, but Tony didn't dislike her for it. He carried on chuckling. 'Quite like it, actually. Who the fuck are you, anyway?'

The tall sister bowed. 'Jenny Ortega, at your service. And this is Billie.'

Billie smiled. She hadn't said a word. She was lovely.

'How'd you like to get out of this place? Maybe see some of the actual city? You like Chinese?'

'Do I like it!' He was almost licking his lips. 'I *love* it!'

But somehow, as they trawled up 17th Street, past the Bottom of the Hill club, the plan changed. Jenny kept the engine running while Tony and Billie ran into an all-night, picked up a twelve-pack of Miller and a huge bag of popcorn, then headed off to the beach.

Beano let the girl in, checked Tony's bed to be sure that he hadn't miraculously lapped them and got back to the hotel first, and pulled the skinny Hispanic teenager towards him.

'I'm in love with someone back home, right. You can only suck me off.'

'No *praab-lem*!' yelped the girl, kneeling with alacrity to her work.

'I've got a better one,' laughed James. They'd been warned not to venture out into the streets around the Phoenix after dark, but there was a gang of them, they were young and they didn't give a fuck. They ruled the fucking place. 'Romo slapper!' he grinned.

'Say what?' said the girl with the limp.

'That Seahorses song? She was a rum old slapper an' that? I thought, like, he was saying she was into Earl Brutus. Romo slapper.'

The young Americans giggled with admirable abandon.

'It's gorgeous,' Tony swooned, gazing off over the endless Pacific.

'Come on, you English sap! Move your ass!'

He trotted to catch up with the girls. They'd disappeared into a grotto up ahead. Down below, maybe thirty, forty feet down, waves crashed up and spiralled in on themselves, making an echo chamber of pluming surf. He couldn't see a thing.

'Hey!' he urged. 'Where are you?'

Sticking close to the wall of the cave he inched his way along the path. He bumped into something.

'Hiya.'

It was Billie. She put her hand between his legs and massaged his dick.

'Er . . .'

*

364

It was only as they sat around the side of the Phoenix Hotel's pool, loads of them, drinking and laughing hard each time the famous toy frogs croaked out from the bushes that James noticed she had only one leg. She was swinging her remaining one insouciantly. He moved to sit by her immediately. Pat McIntosh, awake now, and back on the trail, leant forward in his chair, still part of the Kurt Cobain conspiracy debate, but more wanting to tune into James.

'I wondered if you'd notice me,' gasped the girl.

'I noticed,' grinned James.

'Thanks,' she said, looking down at her still-swinging leg.

'What's your name?'

'Andi.'

'Hi Andi.' He held out a hand. 'Mr Love.'

'I know.' She seemed to ponder on whether to continue, and seemed also to nod her own affirmation to herself. 'I've been talking to some people on the Internet,' she said, trying to sound teasing. 'They been telling me all about *you*.'

She said it with a prod to his chest and a funny little face. James wasn't sure about the false familiarity and the coy act, but he was certain about the tumult in his pants. He looked at Andi with all the sincerity he could muster. 'Shall Mr Love lick your stump, Andi?'

'Sure,' she said, as though he were asking directions.

'Don't stop!' spluttered Tony.

Eyes more accustomed to the dark of the cavern, he reached out to guide Billie's hand back to his cock.

'I want to make you come,' she stated. 'I do. But Jen'd get mad at me.'

'What?'

'She's up ahead. She's waiting for you.'

'Fucking hell!'

Wheezer, eager for more information, more statistics, as soon as he got his door open, hastened to the laptop, slipping on two or three envelopes on which his room number was written. More faxes bringing more tidings from the big bad world of rock 'n' roll. A world in which, at this very moment in time, he was News. He reckoned he'd find the porn channel and have a celebratory wank about that.

He pressed the handset to confirm *Hot Latino* and lay back, jeans pulled down over bottom and hips, ready to go to work. There didn't seem to be many women in the film, so far. There didn't seem to be *any* women. Maybe it was a San Francisco thing. There was a knock at the window. A silhouette pressed flat against the glass, trying to peer past the muslin inner curtains.

'Wheezy? Wheezy!'

Myra. Fuck.

'Hey, Wheezer, man! Don't fuck wit me! You in there?'

He didn't move. Her voice softened to a seductive croak.

'Come on, honey. I gotta meeting in LA tomorrow. I'm gonna be saying all sortsa wonderful things about you. I took this detour to be with you, honey? Please open up if you're in there. I'm bushed.'

He almost relented. Somehow, though, it was easier to lie there, motionless.

'Hey, asshole! Get your ass to this door!'

No answer. No movement. Surely she couldn't *know* he was in there? Surely she'd go any minute now.

'Have you gotta chick in there, you shit! You fuckin shit! I swear to you, Wheezer fuckin Finlay, if you have got one single piece of ass in there, your fuckin ass is toast! Period! I will personally fuck you and your fuckin group wide open! Startin' tomorrow!'

Shit! thought Wheezer. Better let the girl in . . .

In a movement he flicked off the gay love channel, pulled down his jeans, prised off his socks with each big toe and stumbled to the door, wiping sleep from his eyes.

'Who's there?' he groaned through the security chain. Her voice was pure delight.

'It's *me* silly! Open up. I can't wait to see ya!'

He rolled his eyes at an imaginary heaven, grinned fatalistically at an imaginary camera and swung the door open.

'Myra! Baby!'

'Mmmm! Gaaaad! Yes! Oh fuck! Oh fuckin yes!'

He couldn't keep it going much longer. It was hard enough

getting any kind of rhythm together standing up on this narrow path, but she was so tall as well. His thighs were murdering him. The waves crashed majestically all that way down below. Her nails gripped his arse.

'Fuck! Oh fuck, yes!'

She rolled her head from side to side, crouching lower to aid Tony's thrusting. She leant the small of her back into the cliff face, legs wide apart.

'Deeper! God! Fuck!'

This was great. Little Tony Snow was a stud. He eased back a step to give himself that bit of extra purchase and, jeans around his ankles, unable to steady himself, plunged forty feet backwards into the surf, cracking his head on an outcrop.

James lavished the stump with flickering kisses. Andi worked conscientiously on his dick, looking up every now and then to check that he was happy. Altogether it was the queerest sixty-nine Hector Lovett had ever known.

'Where am I?'

'You're fine.'

It was Billie, the wanker, who was holding his hand. Monged-out winos and shot-eyed psychopaths roamed around, muttering and screaming. A security guy came in with a truncheon.

'Come on, you bums! Get the fuck out!'

Tony tried to sit up, but Billie pushed him back down, gently but very firm.

'Where the fuck am I, man!'

'San Francisco General. You lost some blood. You're fine!'

San Francisco General. *San Francisco* General. He shot bolt upright. 'Don't let 'em mess with me blood! No transfusion, right?'

A look of sheer puzzlement invaded her flawless young face. Tony grimaced. 'Sorry.'

Pat woke up with a throbbing, pulsating head. His head was actually splitting right down the middle and he had to press a flat hand to either temple to keep it all together. He felt utterly, utterly wretched. He was in such pain that the physical act of vomiting would kill him. But through it all, he remembered everything.

He'd had a laugh by the poolside with Keva and the stunning young girl he'd brought back to the Phoenix. Pat had felt uneasy about blagging the floor – James was already in there with the one-legged brunette he'd been snuggling up to – but none of the roadies had come to his rescue, reception was closed, he was skint and he had no coke. There was no other choice in the matter. He was going to have to bed down under the bathroom towel while Keva ravished his latest admirer. Bastard. Pat was gagging to get his end away. Girls, as a rule, didn't go for him – but he generally did OK in the States. Especially when he had cocaine.

Keva had lolled his head back behind his deckchair, his voice becoming yawny. He eyed up the dormant hotel reception: 'Haven't got much style, you cockneys, have you?' The accent was harsher, less artful than usual. 'Watch and learn . . .'

He'd bounded over to reception with long strides and returned, only moments later, dangling a key. He produced his own key from his pocket and tossed it to Pat. 'We'll have the Loveless pad. Enjoy.'

Arms around each other like besotted lovers, the two of them had headed off to find their room. Quietly, Pat had let himself into James and Keva's suite, hoping he hadn't missed all the action. He'd quite like to have sat back and watched James walloping this monopede, but a nice line of charlie'd do instead, at this stage.

Disappointingly, James had been fast asleep, with Andi entwined around him, purring softly. Hammered though he was, the journalist in Pat got the better of him and he stole across to the bedside for a little forage. He wanted to see how many discarded Durexes lay complacent on the floor – and he hoped he'd find the remnants of a mal-snorted line or two. He had been shocked first, then angered, bitterly, by what he found.

On the crowded little bedside table sat a proud mound of powder. Not even James had been able to work his way through the lot. Immediately, Pat recognised the orange flyer it had been wrapped in and now lay upon. Reaction Records of San Jose.

Ken's shop. James had zapped his fucking drugs while he'd been out of it. Even among thieves, that ranked among the lowest of the low. Between drug buddies – Friends of Pedro – it was unforgivable.

'Shit, Wheeze, sorry, I . . .'

'What happened to *you*?'

Tony Snow, head bandaged like a cross-channel swimmer's skullcap, stood just inside Wheezer's bedroom door. Wheezer stared at him, aghast. Tony stared at Myra Sweeney, aghast. Fuck. The fucking manager was knobbing the big cheese from the record company. Nice tits.

'Snowy? What happened?'

'Are we insured?'

That had been the main thing the hospital had wanted to know. Before they'd even apply a cold compress to stem his bleeding, it was: 'Sir. Do you have your insurance details?'

'Of course not . . .'

'Please try to recall those details, sir.'

'Look. I've just fallen down a sheer fucking cliff face. I've split me head open on a big fucking . . . *rock*. If it wasn't for the Spitz sisters I'd have drowned before I bled to death. I'm most distressed. I cannot remember my surname, let alone the policy number of the band's insurance. Will you please stitch me up before I faint?'

'You're in a *band*? Which band?'

Keva set off up Eddy Street, just walking, grinning to himself, no particular place to go. Heading left into Polk, he spotted a tiny, old-style grill, the Sun Café. It looked great. He stepped inside, beamed hugely at the bemused oriental grill-chef and ordered bacon, potatoes, peppers, eggs over-easy, a side order of chipolatas and French toast. A half-pint of fresh orange juice and a vast mug of coffee made up the perfect breakfast in a perfect place. Just then he was happy, Keva.

'Eeee-yeuch!'

James returned from the bog, sniffing, snuffling, blinking. 'I can hardly shit. Just pips an' shaves an' that!'

They were all in the Phoenix bar waiting for Sandy to drive them to the airport, regaling each other with tour madness. Crapston had been seduced by a cross-dresser who tied him to her bed with a feather boa and shaved his buttocks. He couldn't sit down. Rory had sprinkled cologne inside his boxers. Everyone was drinking and scooping out vodka jello-shots, swapping tales, sharing the impossible hilarity of this unreal life they were living, having a ball. Except Pat. Pat wasn't laughing. He wasn't drinking. He sat to one side of the big group, feet up on his bag, watching James.

'Not even farting properly! Just proots an' blits an' that . . .'

Pat called him over and beckoned him down closer, conspiratorial. 'You haven't got a wee livener, have you?'

A look of sudden startlement came over the twitching guitarist. 'Shit!' He pulled out all the money in his pockets. 'I must owe you about a ton. More.' He straightened out the dishevelled notes. 'This fucken money. Can't tell a dollar from a fucken ton.'

Pat placed his hand on James's wrist. 'Hey. Wassup, man? What's happening?'

'I zapped your yaoh last night. You was out of it, lar. Couldn't wake you. Clean forgot. Anyway. Serves you right. That was for Riott Grrrl!'

It was something. It was an acknowledgement, but Pat could still not like him. To steal drugs from a slumbering user . . . it was heresy. He couldn't see the guy in a good light any more. Still, best to make the most of it.

'Is there any left, anyway, you lairy cunt?'

Wheezer bowed theatrically while the party applauded, cackled and pointed at the ridiculous stretch limousine. It was white, thirty-five feet long with blacked windows and Music Express on the side. James clapped his blushing manager on the back.

'Nice one an' that, Wheeze! Fuckin' nice one!'

'Well, you know . . . first time in LA and all that . . . Couldn't let you show up at the Riot Hyatt in a yellow cab, could I?'

Everyone piled in. The boys didn't need to know, but the stretch was great value for money. It took the whole mob comfortably and worked out less expensive than two cabs from LAX. That was before James discovered the drinks cabinet.

Laughing shrilly, screaming 'Rock 'n' roll 'n' that!', he prised out a bottle of Absolut and set about it with enthusiasm. Pulling down the walnut table top he nudged Pat, chopped out two fat lines and descended like a craven vampire. The two of them were still giggling like dickheads, shouting out of the windows at passers-by and tickling each other as the grand vehicle smoothed up La Cienega and turned right on to Sunset. The coke buddies seemed to have put their differences behind them.

Sandy handed out the itineraries gravely. Wheezer, exhausted, fucked from the vodka jellies and with half an eye on the dreaded, inevitable arrival of Myra, was happy to let her do the talking.

'Tomorrow's a real important day, guys. I know you ain't gonna stay in and act sensible on your first night in LA, right, but please be mindful that you start tomorrow at ten sharp and there ain't gonna be no let-up till we fly your asses back to England. Cool?'

They nodded dumbly. James and Pat smirked at each other.

'So . . . let's have a little look what's in store next few days. Any questions just shout out. You don't need to . . .'

'Why don't they just call it L?'

James.

'I beg your pardon?'

'I mean, if you want to call a big fucken city by two letters, like, to shorten it, d'you know what I mean? It's daft like, isn't it, calling it two letters. Why not just be done with it? L!'

She watched him carefully. 'Are you done, Mr Love?'

He glowered furious crimson at her and nodded. He was going to march out, that's what his scorching soul was telling him to do, but tensions between him and the boys were bad enough already. And Sandy was going to tell them the good bars to go to. So he sat through it all.

It didn't sound so bad. Looking at his itinerary, there was plenty of free time for everyone except Wheezer and Keva.

Tuesday

09.30 a.m.	– *Meet Sandy in hotel lobby (that's reception to you guys! No latecomers. No hangovers. No excuses.)*
10.00 a.m.	– *Worldwide Records. Tour of building, meet the crew.*
10.45 a.m.	– *Cab to Clerk Derek's studio, Santa Monica.*
11.30 a.m.	– *Photo session with Clerk for* Venice *magazine.*
01.00 p.m.	– *Lunch and pool at 14 Below, Santa Monica. Keva with Randy Barbarossa (final interview for* Details *piece).*
02.30 p.m.	– *Cabs back to Worldwide.*
03.00 p.m.	– *i) Keva and Wheezer with Jeff Silver* *ii) Sandy, Snowy, Beano and James record radio idents with Paul Beringer.*
05.00 p.m.	– *At leisure.*
06.00 p.m.	– *Keva to KROQ.*
07.45 p.m.	– *Rest of band assemble in lobby.*
08.00 p.m.	– *All to Rainbow Grill for radio and retail Meet 'n' Greet. VERY IMPORTANT!*

Wednesday

10.00 a.m.	– *Press and cable promo morning for Keva (see separate schedule. All appointments here at the Hyatt). Rest of band at leisure. See me for tours, Hollywood, guitar shops, etc.*
01.00 p.m.	– *All band assemble in lobby. Cabs to Triptic Editions.*
01.30 p.m.	– *Meet Nancy Spanke at Triptic. Rough-cut of 'Beautiful' clip.*
02.30 p.m.	– *Taxis to Roxy.*
03.00 p.m.	– *Soundcheck.*
04.45 p.m.	– *Cabs to Mondrian or walk.*
05.00 p.m.	– *Light supper at Sky Bar with Willard Weiss/ Bob Campione*
07.00 p.m.	– *Back to hotel. Snooze. Showers, etc.*

09.00 p.m.   – *First show, Roxy*
11.00 p.m.   – *Second show, Roxy*

Thursday

01.00 a.m.   – *(Er, just after the Roxy, guys!) Acoustic show at the Viper Room. (Just across the street from the Roxy.)*

They didn't get any further into Thursday. Everybody, Wheezer included, was talking at once, questioning, complaining, gesticulating.

'The Roxy? I thought we was playing the Troubador?'

'Thought it was the Dragonfly!'

'Thought it was meant to be Hollywood Athletic Club! It's meant to be sound an' that, that place. Fulla tott an' that!'

James blinked at his itinerary, full of courage now that everyone was getting at her.

'What's with this two fucken shows an' all?'

'This is a very *busy* schedule, Sandy! Keva's not going to have a moment to himself . . .'

'Excuse me!' she flashed at him. 'I didn't hear the bit where this went from being a promo tour into a fucking vacation!'

'I'm not criticising you, it's just . . .'

She held up her hands for silence. 'Look. Will you shut the fuck up and let me speak!'

They did.

'I don't wanna go through this every time you have to put your asses out a little. Let me tell you, guys – I can do without this shit! This shit I can do without most easily . . .'

Visibly, she calmed herself, breathing deep and fighting to look her most solemn. 'OK. Just get this. I do NOT wake up in the fucking morning and think . . . Mm. How can I put their asses out of line today? How can I make this life insufferable for them? I'm FUCKING DEDICATED to you, you shits! I do things, I make decisions, because I'm fucking good at my job and I KNOW WHAT'S FUCKING BEST! I can't check and double-check every fucking decision with you assholes!'

Wheezer was nodding in sympathy now, sorry he'd taken

against her. James was triumphant, trying not to make eye contact. He was fighting a giggling fit.

Sandy raged on. 'Fuck it! Yes! It's two sets at the Roxy. It's two sets at the Roxy because they can't cope with ticket demand! Do you know what a vibe that sends around the city about you guys? You can't *buy* that!' She had them now. One by one they were dropping their heads, embarrassed.

'And you're telling me it's a problem when the Viper Room ask you round for an acoustic set? It's a fucking *honour*! You will be seen, in that one little room, by more scene-makers and media players than your tiny minds could dream of . . .' Her voice was softening. 'It was a feat of supreme organisational brilliance – by me, by the way – to reschedule the gigs, put it all together, make sure all previous tickets were valid for either show . . . Two shows is a *privilege*! That you can do that, here, already . . . it's just so exciting for you! But you don't get it, do you . . .' She tailed off. Her cheeks were wet. Again, she searched Keva's soul with her eyes. No one spoke for a whole, humble minute – and then it had to be James.

'All that tittin' around just so's David Geffen can see us play acoustic in the Serpent's Tail? Fuck that!'

She looked relieved. 'OK, guys, right. I'm out of here. I'm back to New York. I, er . . .' She looked down at the ground. 'I have to tell you boys. You are one fucking incredible band. But I've worked with some shits before and you chaps really are up there with the assholes. Good luck.'

She hurried out of the room, head down.

They turned to face each other, sharing the guilt, actually speechless.

'Time of month,' grinned James. 'Come 'ead. Let's get wasted.'

If the world looked well enough to Keva as he let himself into the hotel room, it would look a blacker place by the time he re-emerged. A blacker, whiter place. He dumped the bags and went straight into the bathroom to make the most of James's excursion out to Silverlake with the crew. They'd said they were going to walk down to the guitar shop district a few blocks further east along Sunset, but Keva overheard Rory and Marty excitedly

374

calling up old roadie pals who now lived out in the creative community on the verges of east LA. They were all going to Silverlake, the whole mob, James, Pat, Crapston – everyone. They were going to get bladdered. James wouldn't be back, now, until three or four in the morning – if he made it back at all. Keva suffered a short, sharp pang of envy that everyone was out, out there right now, living it, doing their thing. But the emptiness didn't last. He didn't envy them their carefree time at all. He wanted to be him, not them. And he wanted to pluck his nose.

These American hotel bathrooms were the best. The stunning fluorescent light of the bright white tubes and the crystalline veracity of the clean, sharp mirrors gave no respite. Each and every blemish, every blackhead, every fine line and wrinkle was told out loud. Keva loved it. He could do this for hours. Steaming his face over the in-room kettle; squeezing, easing, coaxing out the plugs and impurities; plucking and tweezing the ingrowing follicles from his nose and cheekbones; drawing out any remaining badness with a clay or kaolin treatment, then lying back with a soothing mint and yoghurt mask slaking his face, toning and stretching and nourishing, feeding back the youth and elasticity he daily lost to his toil. Finally, he would spread wheatgerm oil around his mouth and eyes, and sit and read while it soaked its slow succour into his skin. This was paradise to Keva. That he could have time and opportunity to replenish like this was luxury now. As he sat and anointed himself with vitamin-E emollients, he browsed through the services offered by the hotel, his home for four days, and even allowed that he might visit the fitness suite.

The idea of institutionalised, regular exercise was heathen to Keva, but he had an eye, once again, on the end of the year. A session in the gym could not do harm. Blessed with the lithe physique and smooth-toned limbs of a gymnast, Keva had walked like a pimp and danced like a witch doctor for years. Girls would still pinch his arse in bars and clubs and give him a direct-line come-on if he turned to take it up. He could not put on weight. Since twelve, since pubic onslaught, fine muscle tone glowed out from beneath the surface of his skin. The narrow stomach, scratched slightly into six; the powerful shoulders and the slender, rippling back were all his, without effort. He'd come to love every bit of this self that was him, and wanted to stay the same way, for ever. He was a great, rock 'n' roll shape. He was that very thing – walking sex.

He sauntered back to the bathroom, powerfully satisfied with it all, throwing his arse into a rhythmic swagger, all dick, all hips, all bone-on. He leant his groin against the sink and arched forward to run the cold water and gently swill away the clay mask. That was when he saw it. He saw it, but completely could not register it. It was *frightening*. It took an age of realisation. He had to actually separate it out, pull it upward and snap it out between thumb and finger. He held it up to the harsh light, fascinated, disgusted to the pits of his sinking, querulous stomach. He was shocked. He was scared. He was holding a white hair.

He couldn't rationalise, but he was sore. Wheezer was stung. He would have wanted to believe it was just Todd, but it wasn't. It was Guy. The fax was short and upbeat:

> *Everything tickety-boo on the home front. Flying out for the Big One – Mack and Todd also. Will liaise with Willard.*
>
> *Your liege*
>
> *GdB*
>
> *PS A hundred hundred congratulations. Good work, fella!*

Every single thing about the short message upset him. Guy was riding roughshod over protocol. It was the worst of both worlds. He was embarrassed because he'd had *nothing* to do with this tour, this whole US success, but, worse, he was going to hive off that embarrassment and come riding into town as though nothing was wrong. Not only was nothing wrong but everything was fantastic and he was part of it, he was the biggest part – and he was now going to wave to the gallery and take his acclaim. It wasn't right.

It wasn't right, either, that Mack and Todd were coming over. Mack was a phoney. Yes, he could pick a band. This much he had proved, over and over, with stunning prescience. But he did it all wrong after that. As if he were unable to trust his own judgement he would then sit back and wait and see how the thing unfolded.

He'd allocate a menial to look after the band and leave them to their own devices. If they came up again, if they came out the other side, then he was there, waiting to jump on their backs and ride the parade.

Wheezer had had nothing but antagonism from Taurus since they'd started putting this promo tour together. Clearly, it was small beer to them. They'd sat back and let Automatic do all the graft. It wasn't a 'real' tour to them. That Wheezer avoided Rudy Wexner did not enhance the relationship, but Mack, even Todd, could have sorted it all out with one call. They wouldn't do that. They wouldn't get involved in Taurus matters, on Taurus territory. They'd left the band to their own devices. Had it not been for Mel Parmese and Sandy, and had not the Grams been riding an unstoppable rocket to the stars, they would've been fucked. But there was a will – from the venues, from radio, from the fans – there was a will for the Grams to do this, so there was a way, too. No thanks to fucking Taurus. No thanks to Mack Hansen and Todd 'Iron Shake' King.

Wheezer could foresee the two of them barging into the dressing-room with fucking Rudy and that arsehole Tom Margolis, his boss, with champagne, walking right past him, hardly acknowledging Snowy either, or Beano, marching straight up to James and Keva like they were the best of best friends and hugging, dancing round in circles, covering them in bubbly and regard. Well, fuck them. He was the manager. He wasn't going to let it happen.

And why was Guy going to 'liaise with Willard'? Why could he not 'liaise with Wheezer'? Was this a record company chief thing? Was Wheezer not a suitable person to celebrate with? Did this have to be between the two big guys? Well, fuck them too. Fuck them, fuck them, fuck them. None of this could have happened without The Wheeze. He'd done it all almost single-handed. From the ingenuity of pressing up another whole slew of promos to send out to hip little American scene-makers and influential college stations and alternative radio programmers right through to his hands-on, broken-nail, stressed-out handling of every last aspect of this little tour, Wheezer had been the dominant presence in this unlikely success. Where had Willard Weiss been, when the group were trying to shoot themselves in the foot in New York, and San Francisco, again and again and again? Where was the peerless benefit of his knowledge and experience in all of this? Where'd he been, hey? He'd been chasing some new band out in Iceland, just like he'd chased the Grams before them. Coveting them from afar, moving closer, soliciting, desiring, them, making overtures and, having had his quarry valued, slapping a sold sign on them. He treated his bands like the antiques he collected. They were of beguiling interest to him until they were his. As soon as he owned a piece he was already looking out beyond that, for his next. Only if an acquisition started to increase in value would he go back to it, polish it, perhaps move it into a more prominent position in his home or his office. The Grams were showing signs of becoming a most prudent investment. Wheezer didn't give a fuck. Willard and Guy were welcome to spunk up all over them, and each other.

The phone went. It was the nutter again.

'Hi.' The voice was almost comically effeminate. What stopped it being comical was that it was also chillingly matter-of-fact. 'I've checked in. I'm in a real nice room. Right above Keva, actually.'

'Fuck off, dickbong!' snarled The Wheeze. The line went dead. Wheezer actually looked at the handset and grimaced before replacing it. He'd better tell Keva about this knob. He was becoming a mite too persistent.

But Wheezer didn't have to tell Keva. Keva already knew. In a good, good year, this had been the worst twenty seconds, without exception. He was standing in front of the bathroom mirror stock still, petrified, holding up a strand of his own hair. Just holding it out, not looking at it, staring, rather, at his own frightened eyes. The telephone on the bathroom wall, by the door, vibrated. He picked it up slowly but automatically.

'Yeah?' he drawled, switching on his rock-star croak, just in case. No word. 'Hello? Would somebody care to say something to me?'

Nothing for five whole seconds, then: 'Keva. Your voice is just how I imagined it. I'm sitting right above your head, right now. I could piss for you in my latrine, if you wanted, so you could hear it, then flush it right on down to you.'

The handset was stuck to his ear. He couldn't put it down. 'Who is this?'

He asked it courteously, with curiosity and a little fear. A scraping, scratchy laugh, then: 'Who are *you*? Jesus or Satan?'

And the line went dead. Twenty seconds. Twenty seconds ago life had been so different. He'd pimp-rolled into that bathroom like a boxer, dry-humping the very atmosphere he drifted through. Now things had changed. He knew some new things. He didn't like them. But he stayed calm and looked it all in the eye. For a start he'd need to get out of that room. Perhaps get out of the hotel. That was first. Then he could take another look at his hair. He dialled Wheezer's room.

They sat in the lobby, talking dispassionately but with great feeling between them. What Keva knew from their talk was that Wheezer cared about him, very much. Maybe he knew that before. But right now it made him feel better.

'I mean, don't totally disregard this,' said Wheezer quietly, always thoughtful, always thinking the whole thing through on his feet. 'There's no need to be blasé, but by the same token, don't give the cunt too much respect . . .'

Keva laughed, partly out of relief. Wheezer feigned confusion. 'What?'

'You.' He grinned at his hunched, tense, deliberating manager. 'Never, *ever* thought I would've heard you talk like that . . .'

He laughed and tossed thick sprays of chestnut hair back from his eyes. Wheezer straightened up and stretched out his legs, yawning.

'Guess we've all changed. Whatever, eh? But this loonbong, I mean, fuck him! Wreck his head! Move into my room, I'll shift into yours, put Jimbo in with Marty – we can do what we want . . .' He reached for his hot chocolate. 'I mean, I wouldn't give him too much credence. These divs, like, they're not usually any kind of menace. It's almost an honour, having your own personal loony. It's a mark of esteem. Just about everyone you'd call, erm, famous has had a stalker, old thing. And I don't think any of them has come to any harm. Often, they're trying to help you get them arrested. That's why he called me, too. Easy for me to say and all

379

that, but I'd just forget about him. But, you know, if you want, swap rooms and throw the twat off the scent . . .'

Keva, clasped hands between his knees, looked down at the floor. Not laughing, this time, not at all amused by anything, he faced up to Wheezer as though he was facing up to a terrible, unavoidable journey. 'Nah, mate – you're right. Fuck 'im.'

They chinked mugs and pulled sympathetic faces at each other. Just as Wheezer was about to get existential and question the point of it all, a very earthly reality appeared, besotted, through the fronds of the overlapping cheese plant.

'You avoiding me, Mr Wheezer Finlay?'

'Myra! We were just talking about stalk . . . er, Worldwide. Come and sit down! What can I get you? Keva, I don't believe you've really met Myra Sweeney . . .'

He was determined, especially in light of Keva's trials, that tonight was the time to be strong. Tonight was the time to set the agenda for the future – for the start of the rest of his life. This woman would not be sleeping in his bed tonight.

'Hey!'

He rolled away from her. Myra persisted in scraping her nail extensions down his spine.

'Tigerrrrrrrrrrrr!'

She kissed his neck. She nibbled his ear lobe. She licked down his neck, and nipped at his shoulder blades, plying his nipples, grinding her mound into him. 'C'mon, honey!' she croaked. 'Myra's gotta go . . .'

She teased a fingertip around his arsehole, scratching his neck with her teeth. 'Fuck!' she croaked. 'Come on . . . one more fuckin ride for Myra, hmm . . .?'

Keva, aroused again, turned on to his back and pulled her on top of him.

He felt good about the sex. It was just the release he must have needed. He felt great. Teasing himself in the shower, deluging his numb bell-end with the scalding needles, holding the japseye up under the jet until the pain was too much to take, he was ready to go again. He was ready to give it to America. Three more days. He could give it everything. Easy. He'd take the place apart. Was this not, after all, what he wanted, where he wanted to be? Was this not what he fantasised for, every day, every day of his teens and twenties? It was. He was here. He was here in America and there were people who wanted him here. More each day. So, for three days, he was going to be the living black soul of rock 'n' roll.

And when he got home there'd be no stopping him. The others were all talking about holidays, getting off to Tenerife, St Lucia, anywhere. Tony wanted to go back to Ibiza, just chill, even in December. Good. Let them piss off and leave him to it. That was the way things were going now, and he really didn't mind the autonomy and the freedom. There were songs, some ideas which had been suggesting themselves for months which were starting to take on form inside his head. There was one which would not let go. It was a diseased, cancerous squall, just decadent noise at the moment, but it came to him every hour, every day and every time it sounded the same. He knew it by heart. He knew he could play it from start to finish, any time. He knew how and where the drums would kick in, where the bass would ply its necromancy and he knew all the bridges and middle-eights. All he needed was the words. This dark, frightened song had no name, no theme, nothing. It was taking him over. If he could keep it burning for three more days, he'd get it back to Ivanhoe and lock himself up with the Martin and sculpt it into his greatest song ever. Forget 'Beautiful'. Lovely. Optimistic. Twee. This bad seed was going to grow into one of rock's everlasting moments.

It made him smirk to think that Tony was starting to position himself as a co-writer. On the UK tour he'd often sit in the back lounge with his little Casio, working out basic drum patterns and hooks. Before Leicester he'd proudly handed Keva a cassette and made him promise to listen to it alone, maybe after the tour was over, whenever he had some time to himself. Keva had shoved it on the Walkman half an hour later, sat in the bogs backstage at the De Montfort Hall. The track sounded like Whigfield. He'd sat on the toilet, crying with laughter. He'd stayed for ages, scared to go back outside in case Snowy guessed. The subject of Tony's song had never, ever been raised since. It was just convenient for them both to forget about it. The closest they'd come, weirdly, had been during the riotous night out in Boston, when Wheezer took to the karaoke machine. The girl before had done 'Saturday Night' by Whigfield. Keva, drunk and full of love for his band and his fellow man, felt that this was the moment to put his arm around his loyal bass player and say, 'Sounds like your tune, Tone.'

But before he had chance, as though reading his mind, Tony put his arm around Keva and gasped, 'Classic track! Misunderstood genius! The genius of this track, la, is that it's "Spanish Bombs" by the Clash. Classic!'

And he was right. As Keva stood and laughed and listened to the girl belting out her cover, it was clear. 'Saturday Night' by Whigfield is 'Spanish Bombs' by the Clash.

Keva, torn between phoning Wheezer for a breakfast date and going for a mad walk down Sunset, decided to hit the gym. Slipping a note under Wheezer's door on the way past, he rode the elevator to the fitness suite, deadly self-conscious about his gym wear – a jaded Sun Studios T-shirt, a pair of disgraceful old Ocean Pacific shorts and the most battered red suede Reeboks still to keep out water.

The fitness manager had his back to Keva, filing cards. He slipped past him unseen, happy to avoid any interview. He'd seen enough of these sort of places on *Baywatch* and *Home and Away* to know how the basics worked. And all the machines carried instructions. It wasn't like he was going to become a life member. He'd just watch what everyone else was doing and give it a go himself.

A portly man in his fifties had just left some sort of chest exerciser, which had involved him sitting down and pushing two large pads together with the flats of his palms. Piece of piss. Keva hopped up on to the seat. Opposite, an octogenarian lady, snow-white hair and decrepit face but otherwise actually in good nick, was working her thighs. Keva made the mistake of looking up and catching her eye. She smiled. He smiled back and wished he hadn't. What she was doing was, she had her knees inside these two vinyl pads and she was pushing outwards, heaving her legs wide open against the weight then letting it back down, gradually, slowly closing her legs. She was sitting directly opposite him, opening and closing her legs, smiling at him, while he struggled to make sense of the Pectogram. He sat there, just like the old boy before had done, palms flat up against the pushing pads. But they didn't move. He tried not to heave. He knew this stuff was supposed to be pretty fluent, but as much as he threw his taut-necked might into the apparatus, the thing stayed still. He hopped off, careless, and checked the weight. Fifty kilograms. Didn't seem like a lot. If that little old fat guy could work with it . . . Nonchalant, he notched the pin down to forty, just to be on the safe side. Now, and only with furious effort, he could move the two plates together in front of his adam's apple and, with tortuous concentration, let them back to the starting position without crashing.

Again he forced the weight, but again he caught sight of the old lady opposite, squeezing her thighs out and together, out and together. He couldn't help himself. He found himself sitting there, quite still, wondering if her pubic hair was white. From there, he couldn't stop himself. He imagined he could see inside her tight lycra gym suit, see the spittle-moist blue lips of her vagina working with the machine, open, closed, open, closed. He wondered if she would still lubricate. If, perhaps, she was looking at him now and guessing what he was thinking and imagining him, lithe and febrile, guiding himself inside her. She continued to work her thighs, slowly, while Keva decided it was best he went to the other end of the room.

'Hello, sir! How're you doing today?'

'Just fine, thanks.'

'Did you hand me your membership card, sir?'

The gigantic lifeguard smiled down on him. He was unreal. He could appreciate what so many girls meant when they claimed to be repelled by excessively muscular men. This bloke was a freak. Even his jaw had muscles. His gums had muscles.

'Er, no . . . I don't, er . . .' Keva darted frenzied looks at the door to his escape.

'No problem, sir. Are you a guest of the hotel?'

'Er, yes. I . . .'

'Good. So, you could hand me your room key then?'

Keva, on gawping dumb autopilot, complied.

'Now, just take a seat with me for a moment.'

Shit. They went and sat on a small couch, the fitness instructor taking up four-fifths of its capacity.

'OK, sir. So what is your motivation this morning?' He hit him with a truly dazzling, bright-white smile. Each square tooth was the size of a paperback book.

To get the fuck out of here, Keva wished he could say. 'My *what*?'

The guy just grinned at him stronger. 'What do you aim to achieve this morning.'

Keva said nothing because he did not know what to say. He hadn't a clue what was being asked of him.

'Sir? Muscle tone? Definition? Cardiovascular wellness? Er . . . just a basic level of general fitness, perhaps? Overall wellness?'

'Yes! Yes! That!'

'Sir?'

'That one!'

'The wellness, sir?'

'General . . . or basic, you know, low-level fitness. Wellness. Yeah.'

'Aha . . .'

And so it was that Keva allowed himself to be walked all round the fitness suite, trying out Vertical Traction machines, Pectoral Presses and Ercolinas. He felt fucked. But it wasn't over. The big guy had him sitting on a sort of bike called a Recline XT.

'Now then . . . we just need some basic information here . . .' He stood over the key pad attached to the machine. 'Let's see . . . we'll go for the, ah, six-minute programme. That should give you no problems. So . . . Age?'

Fuck. 'Twenty-three.'

He gave Keva a quick glance over, but didn't seem to doubt him.

'Weight?'

'Ten stone.'

'Ten *what*?'

Half an hour later Keva was quite enjoying all this nonsense. He toddled over to the stepping machine and went to programme it himself. Age? He looked around to check if anyone could see over his shoulder. Twenty-three had been a bit hard-going for a chap of his age. No one could see the screen, but just to be on his guard, he had the fingers ready and in position to get straight on to Weight as soon as he'd tapped in the dreaded numbers. Age. 29. Quick, quick, quick . . . Shit! It was stuck! It was stuck there, big yellow lights blaring out those fucking numbers! 29! 29! Keva McCluskey, singer with the Grams is almost in his thirties!! He ogled the machine frantically, before remembering the Enter button. Relieved, massively, and still checking round to ensure that no one was sussing this deeply personal info, he entered and moved on to Weight. 65kg. Time. Six minutes. No. Eight minutes. Eight minutes of concentrated buttock toning. Let Los Angeles pant after his tiny arse tomorrow night!

He started to grind out a stepping rhythm, building up a momentum, pace by pace. Wellness. What the fuck is *that* all about? It was all over the gym. Posters advertising the way to wellness. Leaflets inviting folk to a private consultation about their own best way to wellness. Wellness. Wellness, wellness, wellness. And then it came to him. He stopped stepping as a huge, twisted smile took over his face. He looked over at the sprightly old dame, operating the tit machine, labouring to keep her breasts alive. Wellness.

Every word of the song fell into place, one after another, perfectly. It was heaven-sent. He knew it now. Something, some spirit, something had sent him into this place, a place he never would have even set foot inside, to finish off the song that would be, for evil, malevolent beauty, better than 'Sympathy For the Devil' by the time he'd finished it off. 'Wellness'. He scrambled back to his room to get the words down on paper.

Sat there in the Book Soup Bistro, Keva could not have been happier. He'd just waved farewell to Randy Barbarossa – thoroughly nice guy, genuinely into the band, bit *intense* – who had phoned Clerk's studio, all apologies, running very late up at Universal, asking if Keva could perhaps get a cab up to the Strip. It really would make his life that bit easier. Both Wheezer and Keva knew well that this was one last negotiation. That chapter in the life and history of the Grams when, for a week, they'd been within Randy's gift, was coming to a close. Today's was his last one-on-one interview with Keva. He'd done a long one in New York, then, in Boston, taken a back seat and observed. In San Francisco they'd had a lovely, emotional brunch in the Castro, Keva opening up about his lifelong dream to play at the Filmore and his surprise and sheer pleasure at the extent of his band's popularity over here. If Randy had had anything of a mind to stitch them up, he couldn't possibly after San Francisco. Keva was just a wide-eyed fan. Randy loved him.

So today, in LA, he knew that his week of power was just about over. The Grams were going to be huge, come what may – everyone knew that now. But they weren't there yet. The *Details* spread was part of that whole process, one of the big shaping influences that would give the band their green light. So if he wanted to fuck them up, nicely, by calling them up at the last minute to change the venue for their final taped chat, neither Wheezer nor his client was going to find a problem with that.

'Is it far?' asked Keva. 'Can I get there for one o'clock from here? OK, I'm on my way. But don't beat me up if I'm a wee bit late, yeah? I'm in the hands of whichever friendly local cabbie takes the fare . . .'

Wheezer stayed on at the photo shoot to have lunch with Clerk and the band. Keva headed off to meet Randy. And it'd been fine. An honest, relaxed, friendly chat about the struggle to find real life amid this new, frantic pop scene he now inhabited so luminously.

'So, to sum up, Keva. What means more to you? Success here in the States or back home in England?'

He slurped at his cranberry juice and thought about it. He was still examining the glass for hidden traces of juice as he started to answer the question thoughtfully, carefully.

'Well – I don't think we've ever consciously done anything to get success, not as an end in itself. You know, when you write a song and you know it's good, you *know* . . .' Only now did he look up and meet Randy's gaze. '. . . then, you go out and play it live and, like . . . when people start to *get* it, you know, like you hoped and dreamed they would, like you *knew* they would . . .' He looked down again, lowering his tone. '. . . then it really doesn't matter whether you're in Carlisle or Cincinnati, you know. Really.'

Randy grinned. 'Fair enough,' he laughed. 'I'm going to allow that terrible fudge.'

'Seriously,' Keva persisted. 'Like, I've just written the best thing I've ever done. It's so fucking good I can't believe I've done it . . .'

Randy's eyes danced at this hint of something exclusive.

'. . . I only completed it this morning. The whole thing was written in America. It's made in America and I can't wait to play it to US crowds because this, in a way, is the first thing that's, like, reflected our American experience . . .'

'What's it like? What's it called?' gabbled Randy.

'It's called "Wellness". I swear to you, Randy, nobody else in the *world* knows about this . . .' He started laughing at the goodness of it all. He was excited again. '. . . but this song is the best thing I ever wrote. Honest.'

And it was true. It was true right now, at least. Sitting there, sipping ice-cold 7-Up twenty minutes after Randy had scrambled away to file his suddenly hot copy, Keva was aglow at the brilliance of his situation. And keeping that glow burning was the knowledge that 'Wellness' was waiting for him. He couldn't wait to tell Wheezer. He hadn't had a chance through all the hurly-burly of the day so far.

This was as close as he could imagine himself getting to real calm, true peace of mind. He felt strong. He was ready for each new step, the next step first, then the one after that – he could deal with all of it. He'd be meeting Wheezer at Worldwide in a quarter of an hour to go through advertising ideas, artwork, merchandising, all of that with Jeff Silver. And then after that it was the biggie. KROQ. Live.

He flicked at the endless free papers. *Entertainment Today*. *LA Weekly*. *Barely Legal*. *Colors*. Some of the stuff was pretty close to the edge. *Colors* seemed to be dedicated to an admiration of fat women. *Barely Legal* was barely legal. The advertisements in even the most conventional of freesheets majored in fetishism, self-humiliation and scant-disguised prostitution services, some of which were all too tempting. Those ads which did not, in some way, offer sex for sale, offered various means of acquiring or prolonging sex. Whiter teeth. Thicker penis.

'*Laser Vaginal Rejuvenation – you won't believe how good sex can be.*'

He thought again of the old lady from the health club and thanked her silently for inspiration. He flicked the page, avidly uninterested in it all.

'*Are you tired of those love handles? Dr Norman can safely sculpt any body area to create a more shapely and attractive contour.*'

'Waste of an ad,' he thought. 'Shapely means fat, doesn't it?'

And then, just about to leave, strumming the pages backwards just to show anyone who might have been watching him that he really was just dipping in and out of these freebies, he spotted a face which made him sit up straight. Helmet. A full page and another half about fucking Sensira. The paper loved them. He grabbed another freesheet and looked up the music page. Not such a delirious write-up, but another good plug for their gigs and the album. Where's the fucking Palladium? How big is it?? How come *we're* not in all these papers? Surely they're even more important than all these fucking style bibles? They're *free*, for fuck's sake. The arguments raged in his skull. Gone, at a stroke, was the beatific philanthropist of a minute ago. Gone was his wellness. He crunched his ice cube and headed off to Worldwide to ask a few questions.

Wheezer was late. This was expected at home, but here . . . it was unforgivable. Wheezer had been preaching time and motion to them, almost driving them insane with his relentless nagging that this was not a holiday, this was *work*. So where the fuck *was* the nutter. It was two thirty-five already, Jeff Silver's door had suddenly closed tight, bang on two thirty, and there was still no sign of The Wheeze.

Keva sauntered over to Mikey, Jeff's assistant, to ask him another dumb question. 'Erm, Mike, Mikey – d'you think maybe I should go in and start the meeting myself? I mean, I can approve some of this stuff without Wheezer. It'd be down to me with the artwork an' that, anyway.'

Mikey rolled a pencil between thumb and forefinger and looked uncomfortable. He looked at his desk. 'Um, uh, I guess Jeff'd prefer to have the pair of you do this. It'd be more usual.'

Keva stared at his head and paced back to his seat. He was breathing hard, heart beating madly. Where the fuck was Wheezer? And why were Sensira so big in the States?

When Wheezer finally came gushing out of the lift doors it was two forty-two and he looked crazed.

'Fucking taxi drivers! How the fuck can you get a licence to drive a cab if you don't know where anywhere is? He didn't even know Sunset fucking Strip! He couldn't speak English! I had to write it all down for the twat!' He started an impression of a troubled Armenian. '"Mon-rhee-yan? Where is Mon-rhee-yan o-tell?? Is near Beverr-lee Will-shy?" I should've just fucking jumped out! Shit! Right . . . let's get this meeting started!'

Again, Mikey looked discomfited. 'Uh, I guess I'll just check Jeff's schedule with him.'

He *guesses*! raged Wheezer to himself. He was seething inside. Why did he *guess*? Wheezer didn't need to guess. He knew. All of a crashing sudden he knew too well what was happening here. Jeff Silver was being a shithead power freak. The meeting was for two thirty. The moment the boys were a minute late he'd shut up the door to his office. He couldn't take it. In his screwy mind, these two English kids were fucking with him by trying to turn up late at his door. Well, FUCK THEM! NOBODY FUCKS WITH JEFF FUCKING SILVER! *NOBODY* dares be one fucking minute late for Jeff. And if they are, well – fuck 'em! They won't do *that* again. Not to Jeff.

'Tell him he's a shithead!'

How Wheezer wished he had said that. A whole hour later, trying to relax with a vodka cocktail, still insane with anger, Wheezer was wishing he'd booted the cunt's door in. It would've been worth getting dropped from the label for. Jeff Purvis would've loved it. And they wouldn't have been dropped, anyway. They were making too much money for Worldwide. Maybe a studio label would've dropped them, but not Willard. He would more likely have sacked Jeff Silver. But instead of saying anything bold or true, instead of doing anything which even resembled honesty, Wheezer had explained to Mikey all about the taxi driver who'd driven him, in silence, all around Los Angeles before it dawned on The Wheeze that he was waiting for directions. If Wheezer had not spoken up, he would have driven on, all day, waiting for the moment of conflict. He told Mikey all this, making it into a big joke, and scribbled Jeff a witty, sorry, conciliatory note.

He sat up with Keva by the Hyatt's rooftop pool, the notorious, world famous, *Spinal Tap* pool, full of dread. Jeff Silver. Myra Sweeney. Todd King. Keva's barmy stalker. Guy, even. These were all people who were weighing his life down. The ice cubes spat and splintered in his vodka cranberry, as he poured out his woes to the singer.

'You'll just have to trust me, Kee. It's gonna be a fucking grind. We'll have some fucking royal battles. But we'll beat fucking Sensira into a cocked hat, so help me. We will. I won't stop until they're . . . a *microdot* in the rear-view mirror!'

'They're doing my head in, you know. They're taking me over. It seems like . . . whatever we do, they've already been there. And bigger . . .'

'They're shite. Never forget that. It's all that counts.'

'Fuck it all, anyway,' laughed Keva.

He dragged hard on his joint and looked down at the city of angels and devils, the city of legends below him. It was weird to know, now, that he had his own little part of this theatre of dreams. Years ago, *years* ago, people had come here, to this place, to harness its light and turn it into silver dreams. Could they have known the great awfulness it would spawn? The genius of creation and the price that came with it? He was a part of that now. Only he knew it just yet, but Keva McCluskey was now a Tinseltown legend. It made him feel tiny, and huge, all at once. He smiled over at his troubled friend.

'I've just written the greatest song ever, you know.'

Kevin from KROQ came in person to thank Keva for the interview and assure him he'd be at the Roxy gig tomorrow night.

'Which show you coming to?' asked Wheezer.

'Oh, the late one, most definitely. That's the one everyone's going to. Have you guys seen your guest list?'

'Er, looked like Mark O'Toole and Lemmy last time I looked.'

Kevin shook his head resolutely as he guided the boys to the KROQ elevator. 'Uh-uh. How about Kate Moss? Leonardo . . . Keanu . . . Chelsea Clinton . . . The Beasties are coming along with James Brown . . .'

'*The* James Brown?'

'The very same . . .'

'Wow!'

They made eyes at each other. *GQ*'s editor was in town.

'There's such a buzz about you guys. You coulda sold out the Palladium, no problem. *Everyone* wants to see the show. Andre Agassi is coming down . . . Michael Stipe is bringing Madonna . . .'

Keva collapsed to his knees. Wheezer pushed him over, slapping the air helplessly. They were in fits. Kevin looked on, alarmed.

'What'd I say?' said the affable Programming Director.

'Nothing,' gasped Wheezer. 'It's just that, like, Madonna has a special sort of, uh . . . *symbolic* resonance to the Grams.'

'Oh. Right. So long as it's not a Michael thing . . .'

They brushed themselves down and affected embarrassed coughs, Keva occasionally breaking off into little giggles again.

'Sorry.'

'You got it.'

'It's amazing all those people have heard of our band.'

'Oh, they all listen to KROQ.' He said it Kayarro-queue. Everyone else had called it Kay Rock.

'That true what you said about the Palladium?'

'Sure.'

They both waited for each other to go first. Wheezer did the deed.

'So . . . how's the Sensira show been selling?'

Kevin jiggled an invisible string puppet with the fingers of his right hand. 'Weeell . . . I wouldn't wanna say it's stiffing . . . but it ain't gonna sell out. They would've been better doing what you guys are doing.'

De Niro himself would have admired the way they kept their faces grave. Wheezer even managed a conciliatory shrug, as though Kevin from KROQ was Sensira's drummer.

'That's too bad.'

The elevator came. Wheezer smiled at Kevin and shook hands warmly. 'Thanks again, matey.'

'My pleasure.'

He paused and thought about it. 'Chelsea Clinton isn't *really* into the Grams, is she?'

'You betcha!' Kevin grinned at the freaky English crackpot as he backed into the elevator. He couldn't help liking him.

'Down, gentlemen?'

The moment the sliding doors closed on them, Keva and Wheezer were in each other's arms, dancing a jig of joy.

'Us . . . up. Them . . . downdowndown! Hah-hah!'

'Thanks.'

'You're very welcome. Warm tea with milk, sir?'

Beano cleared a space in front of him and the elderly waitress deposited the little porcelain cup with the trailing tea bag thread with the proud Liptons flag, sogging wet. He knew before he put it anywhere near his lips that it'd taste disgusting. It wasn't worth asking for tea. Next time, next tour, he was going to bring a big tin of Yorkshire tea bags and a kettle. That'd be the way to start the day.

'Thank you,' he smiled.

'Ah hah.' She busied herself off to another table.

Tony whipped out the St Moritz notepad. 'How many's that?'

'I think we can start a separate category for "you're very welcomes". It's, like, you're welcome with bells on, isn't it?'

'I agree. Five points for "very welcomes", and just the three for an ordinary "you're welcome". So what's that make it?'

'Let's see. You've got eleven you're welcomes. Four very welcomes. Four ah hahs. Three it's a pleasures. Three you got its. And only two no problems. That's . . . sixty-five points.

They made faces at their drinks and restarted their favourite game. Talking about what they were going to do when they got home, where they were going to go over Christmas – and how they were going to spend all their money.

Again, James awoke with a numb, pulsating head. He could feel each throbbing blow of his pulse in his brain. He could not breathe, except through his mouth. He knew the routine now. Pointless to attempt to drag air up through his nose. It was blocked, bunged tight. Sometime today, maybe this afternoon, maybe later, he'd sniff down a palate-sized lump of crud, a whole dirty plug of mucus which'd cling like a baby squid to whichever surface he gobbed it on. Then the trickles'd start. He could stick whole bog rolls up his nose, but the snotholes would leak like sluices – all day, all night. That was why he did it now. He carried on snorting, from noon to last thing at night, to stave off the drips. It worked. For James, the drugs worked.

Myra was long gone. They hadn't fucked. He hadn't been able after the way they'd caned his coke and the mini-bar. She told him everything. How she knew she was going to get sacked soon. She guessed as much when Knopf had told her she might want to think about getting some help before this got out of hand. But she was getting all the help she needed from her saviours – the Grams. She turned herself on thinking about having a line-up with them. She fantasised about being gang-banged by the whole tribe, roadies and all, one after another and all at once. Hearing her talk like that made James reach over for her, but when they got undressed he couldn't get it up.

'I seem temporarily indisposed to a state of erectitude,' he twinkled, careless.

'Come here,' growled Myra, swooping down and taking him fully in her mouth. She sucked and slobbered and, every now and then, had a little peep to check how she was doing with him.

'Would you mind not looking up at me when you're doing that?' he'd said. 'It really does interfere with me sense of fantasy an' that . . .'

He lay there now, feeling dull, dead, deadly dull. Somehow he knew that Myra was messing things up. She was calling up stations and punting the Grams ahead of schedule, out of sync, out of all proportion. She'd told him what a big number she was doing on the band, and it seemed unwieldly, even to Jimbo. He would've told Wheezer, if he could be arsed. But he couldn't. Mr Love didn't give a fuck.

It seemed impossible that Perry – queenly, vituperative, nasty

Perry – could have had the sensitivity to produce a film like this. The clip he'd made for 'Beautiful' was no mere video, it was a short film. It was gorgeous. Keva, inoculated against the emotional saturations of his ballad by nightly re-creations and renditions, was once more moved to gulping, quivering, silent tears as he stood at the back and watched, amazed.

'It's . . . it's just perfect, Perry.'

The lads nodded. Wheezer beamed. Nancy Spanke looked immensely relieved. Keva came over and hugged Perry.

'Thank you. So much.'

And then Perry was crying too.

As the Spacevan pulled up in the little parking lot behind the Roxy, everyone turned on James.

'You're goin' first, lar!' spat Beano. 'No way am I setting foot out there until that lot have gone!'

'Hear, hear!' laughed Keva. He didn't feel like laughing. Propping the Tryptic lavatory door shut with a bin so no one could interrupt, he'd snapped out three white hairs he spotted after a rudimentary slash. They were getting everywhere. They were taking over. He was going to look at this properly when he got home.

It was Tony who spotted the freakshow as the van pulled into the Roxy's parking lot.

'Fuckinell! Fans! What time is it?'

'And what planet are they from?' gasped Wheezer, scrutinising the line of people more closely. There were three girls in wheelchairs. One in a leg brace. There was a magnificently masculine transvestite with melting mascara. A woman of at least eighty-five years of age, probably older, was almost bent double with a hideous stoop as though searching for a dropped penny. She was wearing a Grams T-shirt. And there was one young man who was actually wider than he was tall. He looked like a dumpster. He was, possibly, five foot six or seven, but he was immense. It seemed likeliest that he was waiting there for the stage doors to open for ease of entry. No way would he get through the front entrance.

'Fuckinell, Jimbo! What've you got us into, here?'

'What's it got to do with me?'

'Fuck off! It's like the Cretin Hop!'

Everyone cackled, except James. 'You're warped, you lot.'

Tony started singing in a vocoder voice. 'The woodwork creaks – and out come the freaks!'

A familiar face leered into the van, making faces.

'Take up thy bed and walk!' he slobbered. Billy the Brief, grinning massively, clicking his fingers together at the thrill of it all. Paulie Hanlon appeared at his side, jerking his head back towards the sidewalk. 'Have you seen that, lar! Fuck's going on! Is it fetish night or something?'

They pushed James out of the van. 'Go 'ead, Hector! Go and meet your public.'

'Fuck off!'

But he went, feeling his penis raging again. A moment later he was back, smirking. 'Coupla very nice chaps wishing to make the acquaintance of Mr McCluskey . . .'

Keva felt his shoulders sag. 'Ah, fuck that! Let's go straight in and soundcheck, eh? I'm not in the mood . . .'

'They're most insistent that they meet you.'

'Well . . . hard luck! I'm not . . . fucking public property!'

He was almost felled by the winds of laughter. Pat McIntosh laughed hardest of all. This only made Keva more determined. Red-necked, he stalked off to the stage entrance, tried to barge it open with his shoulder and fell to the floor, flattened by the stubborn – and locked – iron doors. 'Bastard!' he cursed, massaging the bruised shoulder.

'Heeey! The Grams!'

A likeable, open-faced indie-kid with shoulder-length hair and a well-kept goatee approached them, smiling. His shorts were never-ending. They were longs.

'Heeeey! How's it going, you guys?' He nodded to Billie and Paulie. 'You found the guys, huh, guys? Cool. You wanna walk this way, everyone?' He extended his hand to Wheezer, who'd stepped up to intercept him. 'Hi, man. Jimmy G.'

'Wheezer. Wheezer Finlay.'

'The legendary Mr Finlay, huh? It's a real pleasure, dude.'

No one could know how much satisfaction this gave The

Wheeze. If someone would call him The Legendary every single day he'd be very, very happy indeed. Close up, the kid's goatee was more of a stubble job-creation scheme. His beard consisted of some dozen hairs, evenly dispersed at centimetre intervals around his chin. Everything about his even, untroubled, brown-eyed good looks told out an even, untroubled life. He was cool with everything and cool with who he was. He liked being Jimmy G of Roxy fame.

'Well – I guess we're gonna give you guys something to eat and drink while I find the keys and open up back again. Is there more stuff to come in?'

'No man, nothing. Have the guys finished the load-in?'

'Oh! Like . . .' He checked his watch, smiling. 'Three hours ago? Those dudes *work*, man!'

The sun seemed temporarily to be blotted out.

'Hey! McCluskey! Sign this, man!' The human dumpster blocked his way.

'Please! smiled Keva, amused.

'Fuck you, man! I bought your fuckin record! I play it every day! I was the second person to buy tickets for these shows, man! I've been standing here waiting for you since ten this morning – you're fucking signing it!' He shoved the CD at Keva again.

'*I'm* happy to wait,' simpered a voice they knew on impact. A sly, cunning voice. A male voice, just. A male voice in a dress. Wheezer and Keva looked at each other. The Stalker. He was a terrifying, painted, hag-thin marionette. Every bone rattled as he spoke. He made Michael Caine's psycho-tranny in *Dressed to Kill* sound cuddly.

'Oh . . . fuck.'

'Look. What do you want?'

The tranny seemed pleased at their fearful faces. 'I want *him* . . .' A bony finger picked out Keva. '. . . to be nice to me.'

And that was as far as the introductions got. A police car mounted the kerb with screeching wheels and, as two burly officers struggled out of the doors, the tranny picked up his skirt and legged it, stopping only to pull off his stilettos.

'Fucking . . . hell,' muttered Keva, watching the coppers give chase and rugby-tackle the squealing bitch. 'That girl can move . . .'

'Sorry about that,' grinned Jimmy G. 'I saw her in the line. She's just a nuisance. But I can't actually call in the cops until she, sort of, harasses someone. Sorry. I *was* waiting, guys, phone in hand, waiting to pounce . . .'

They all laughed. Keva signed the dumpster's CD without making eye contact. He was learning.

Soundcheck was all but through when the girl from MTV came in. They all stopped and looked at her because she was, truly, spectacular. Close to six feet tall, lithe in her loose dress, hair cropped butch, toned, marble-smooth pale arms, she would have been dykish but for the innocent, instantly lovable Patricia Arquette eyes and smile. Each and every one of them stood and gawped at her. She was the right person for this little job – Wheezer would've eaten out of her hand. Jimmy brought her over to meet The Wheeze.

'Hi, there. I'm Marta Barkin, with MTV.'

She had a slight Southern lilt. He couldn't tell where from. What she went on to tell Wheezer, and to ask him, was music to his puckish ears. Sensira had utterly fucked up a big MTV opportunity down at the Palladium. MTV news was due to film the band in soundcheck and Helmet was scheduled to give them some words of wisdom. But Helmet had not showed up for soundcheck. Worse, he was wanting to blow the gig and go home. Ticket sales had been slow, but the promoters expected a good walk-up. Helmet Horrocks, though, entering the middle phase of a month-long tour, had seemingly had enough.

Pat McIntosh had been detailed to interview him during his time in LA, and the pair of them ended up getting wrecked on speedballs. It'd irked Keva that Pat came back saying that Helmet was all right. He didn't give a fuck about anything. That, to Pat, was the ultimate accolade. Nobody had realised how deep in Helmet had got himself.

'D'you think you can help us out? I know it's very, very short notice. And Richard wants you guys to know that you are not in

397

any way to feel beholden, here. If this is bad for you guys, just say. It doesn't effect MTV's decision about your clip . . .'

Wheezer wanted to hug her. He looked for Marty. 'One moment, Marta. I won't keep you a second . . .'

Willard Weiss was a very amusing raconteur. He'd struck up an unlikely rapport with Billy the Brief, whose tales of ticket-touting triumphs at the Winter Olympics in Japan and backstage derring-do with the Rolling Stones and Rod Stewart tickled him no end.

'They all know me kite, like, those fellas, but they haven't got a fucken clue who I am. They all probably think I'm one of their roadies. Oh, look, there's that little Scouser snorting all our cocaine again. Who *is* he, by the way?'

Willard and Campione laughed generously. Bob told a tale, apropos of nothing at all, about a young English manager who'd tried to buy his favour with drugs and hookers. He'd made sure the guy's band sank without trace. Everyone glanced skittishly at each other, before a rumpus over by the lavatories drew the sting. It was an unbelievable – and unforgettable – spectacle. Immaculately tailored Michael, possibly the most powerful man in Hollywood with his capability to turn away Bruce Willis from the Sky Bar if the fancy seized him, was clinging to the leg of Todd King. Todd, wild-eyed, jugulars bulging manically as he fought and kicked to get Michael off him, was screeching immortal words in an unworldly, butane-fuelled Mickey Mouse voice: 'Geddoff me! Geddoff me, you cunt! Don't you know who I am?'

The most ludicrous words a man can ever say were rendered high comedy by his hoarse squeaking. He spotted Willard. 'Hey! Willard! Hi!'

He pushed Michael away, who was on his feet by now and actually taking hold of him by the collar. 'Would you mind telling this jerk who I am, for fuck's sake, before I knock him out!'

Willard pulled a sly face at the boys. 'I'm most awfully sorry, sir . . .' he started. 'There must be a mistake. I don't think I . . .'

'OH, COME OFF IT, WILL YOU!'

The band started giggling. Todd lowered his voice again and tried to laugh along with them, blushing fiercely. 'Willard, man.

Joke's over. I've flown a long way to be with you guys on this night . . .'

Nobody flinched. He was getting desperate.

'Come on.' He flicked a gold card out of his pocket. 'Guy'll be up in a minute. Let me fire the shampoo in . . .'

Tony and Beano mouthed the word 'shampoo' at each other and grimaced. Michael stepped forward, straightening out his jacket. He addressed Keva, only: 'Is this gentleman known to you, Mr McCluskey?'

Keva beamed broadly. 'Never seen him in my life,' he smiled.

Todd dropped to his knees, exhausted. 'Why?' he moaned. 'Why does everyone hate me so much?'

He began to sob. Wheezer, standing closest, saw big Bambi tears splash on to the poolside. 'Ah, come on, everyone,' he sighed, stepping forward.

Todd looked up, hopeful, tears shut off immediately.

'Let the boy buy us all a drink. Thanks, Mike. Sorry about that, mate.'

'It's Michael,' he huffed, striding away.

This was the moment, then. Willard, Bob, Todd and Guy had gone ahead in the first cab, while Wheezer made sure the boys were fine. He was about to make his grand entrance into the club. He knew Worldwide had bought out most of the tables. They'd all be sitting there as he came through from backstage. They'd all see him, straight away, and there'd be that little buzz of recognition as they all nudged each other and said: 'There he is. That's him. Wheezer Finlay. The Manager.'

He sucked down on the last millimetre of nicotine and stubbed the dock end, flicking it high past the Spacevan. Right, then. Time for action. He walked slowly, hands behind his back, trying to regulate his breathing. He felt that if his breath ran away from him then so would all this. In. Out. In. Out. There, now. Stay in control. Walk slow. Everything's fine. Nothing can go wrong. You're on top, man. You're The Boy.

'Bob Campione! Heeeey! Possibly the most handsome man in the world! Get down, Willard, you dog! Wotcha, Guy, mate!

They're sound. Except for Jimbo – he's gone missing. I'm only joking! Room for a small one up there?'

Tony glanced over at Keva. He wanted to shag him, sometimes, he was so fucking cool. There he was now, knowing that each deliberate slide of his hips was making the girls wet, knowing he could take this packed little crowd whichever way he wanted. But this, coming up now, was Tony's moment. This was what he thought about every morning when he got up. It was the break in the middle of 'Chimera', where everything drops out and the song grinds down almost to a silence, only his minimal bass thrumming under the dimmed lights. Then it builds again, louder and louder, the audience coming with him, bobbing expectantly, waiting for the moment. Everything stops sudden dead for a still moment then CRASH! Beano and Tony smash back in together, throwing the room into a frenzy. Every night. Every city. They go crazy for that moment. It was like Tony was plugged right into them, slowly increasing the dose, pumping up the electric shock until FRAZZ – he whacked the voltage right up as high as it could go, and they were smoking. He could never tire of that – the crowd, the madness, the power.

More people crowded into the little dressing-room and thronged the narrow corridor outside, backing up all the way downstairs. Bob Campione gripped the shoulders of Wheezer and Mel Parmese with his huge left hand and his huge right hand. 'Awesome, guys! Totally awesome! The last time I saw anything that kicked ass like that was when U fuckin 2 first came to LA. You saw that gig, right, Mel?'

'Sure. Unbelievable.'

'Totally unbelievable. You guys kicked ass tonight.' He reached out, spotting the back of Steve Knopf, and dragged him into the triangle. 'Was that awesome, Stevie, or was that the best rock 'n' roll show you ever saw?'

'It was totally cool, Bob. Wheezer, you should be proud, man.'

And Wheezer was proud. His boys had been sorcerers out there tonight, particularly with the second show. Keva was a higher being, he was magical – but it was James who transfixed him. How could he be that same person who dredged the lower levels of humanity? He'd fart in public and curse disgustingly at hotel receptionists. How could the same animus weave such beauty and intensity from guitar strings. He was fantastic. Tonight, Wheezer had stood at the back, leaned back against the wall and just closed his eyes. The band, James, everything, blew him away. He loved them absolutely. If he had spoken just then he would have burst into tears. He looked around the room at all the faces, all lit up, their mutually insignificant lives briefly intertwined for the sake of the manic elegies of this untouchable group – and the sense of self which coursed through his arteries was crushing. All he wanted to do was to go into a little corner and sob.

James was surrounded by the famous and the beautiful. They all seemed to gravitate to his smiling face, while plucking up the nerve to approach Keva. James Brown and Dave Beer rifled his pockets while he tried to keep his eye on a dozen beauties.

'Ay! Lemmy! What did you think? Giz a go on your wart an' that!'

All three gigs were good, in differing ways, but this acoustic set in the Viper had given him the most pleasure. He'd more or less done it solo. Done it on his own in front of that terrifying crowd. Every other face had been a household name. Every pair of eyes had been trained on him and him alone.

As they were, still. Sitting in the deep chair, drinks and snacks being ferried to him by folk he'd never met, Keva was starting to feel unnerved. He wanted Wheezer. He wanted the reassurance of his barmy head, bobbing around, busying himself. All he could see was faces, desperate female faces crowding in on him, crowding round the chair, looking down on him. It was like the scene from *Rosemary's Baby*.

'Keeeevrrr!'

'Heeeey! Mr Grams! You rocked tonight!'

'Keeeevrrrr!'

Hands were reaching down and touching him, feeling him all over.

'You have *great* abs.'

'You want some X, beautiful?'

'You need another beer there?'

'You wanna go some place?'

'I've written a poem for you. It's about you.'

'You have the cutest little ass.'

'Keeeeevrrrrr!'

'You're so . . . *poetic*.'

'I love you.'

'Why are you sad? You seem so sad?'

'Are you hot? How about I fan you with this?'

'Heeeey! *Awe*-some, man! Too, too awesome!'

'Keeeeeeevrrrrr!'

His heart was bursting through his bones. Bah-BOOM! Bah-BOOM! Bah-BOOM! They weren't looking at him. They were looking through him. They were seeing some mad other spectacle, something not all to do with him. Whatever it was, it wasn't him, Keva, they were seeing. They were just staring, gawping, ogling. If they were looking they would have seen the terrified eyes, the blank expression, the wanting to escape.

'Wheezer!'

He almost tugged his arm out of its socket in relief and, remembering only then who he was, who he was supposed to be, he introduced Wheezer to his acolytes.

'Howdy, Steve. Enjoy it?'

'Cool. Totally out there . . .'

'No Madonna, hey?'

Knopf grinned at Wheezer, prickled. 'I was kinda hoping this'd be ourselves, Guy and Keva, also.'

'You want me to go find them?'

Knopf seemed irritated that Wheezer was not insulted by the inference that The Wheeze did not have the authority to deal with this alone.

'Uh, no – I guess you and Keva can discuss this privately.'

'Sure. Is it something bad?'

'No!' His eyes sparkled. 'Least ways. I don't expect so. I don't anticipate you guys having a problem with this at all.' He handed Wheezer the cassette.

'This is a mix of the track done by a coupla the guys at the Edge. Well – it's not a mix, *purrsay*. More of an edit. Just gets us into the meat of the song earlier. Personally, I think they did a fantastic job here. I anticipate you liking this as much as I do.'

Wheezer bristled on his clients' behalf. But he saw through the whole thing, too. He knew that Knopf had already sanctioned this edit. He knew it was futile to fight it, pointless trying to reverse it. If the station was playing their own, exclusive mix of the track and they were happier with that version and it was selling albums for the band in that part of Texas, then why not just go with the flow? Who the fuck would know the difference in a place that vast? It'd only fuck them off if they stopped the thing now. Knopf should have liaised with the band at every step of this experiment, but now it was done . . .

'I can't wait to hear it.'

'Cool.'

'And I'll play it to Keva as soon as possible. And Guy.'

'Oh.'

'When do you need a response?'

'Like, yesterday. But whenever. I'm sure you guys have more important stuff to do, huh?'

'Can't think of anything that *could* be more important right now, Steve.' Wheezer's eyes darted around the club. 'And Steve . . . I don't want to embarrass you, but – I just want you to know that we all really appreciate the effort you've put into this. I'm sure all the boys will find time to thank you in their own way, and if they don't it's only because they're uncomfortable with outward gestures of gratitude like that. But let me assure you. You are a hero to those kids. They truly appreciate all you've been doing for them.'

Knopf blushed in the shadows. The bastard! Why did he have to be *nice*? He glanced around, anxious that the band should not come across and be nice too. That would make it very difficult for him to fuck them. Because he could. He could fuck any of these paltry English bands whenever he wanted to. Five foot three in stature, but fuck! Did he carry a big stick!

'That's very sweet, Wheezer. I appreciate those sentiments.'

*

Absolutely jiggered from the flight and the non-stop partying, Billy let himself in with the key James had slipped him. The bed looked sumptuous, but he couldn't take advantage. He'd be in the Land of Nod in seconds, anyway. He pulled a towel out from the bathroom and snuggled down on the floor at the foot of the bed.

When all the girls finally twigged that Keva wasn't sleeping with any of them; when Paulie Hanlon's drug mountain was decimated; when rumours of an all-night party over at Spaceland cleared out the last of the stragglers, there was only Guy and Keva left up by the poolside.

They sat in silence for ages, at peace, just watching Los Angeles at night. Keva could have sat there until dawn.

'Is it how you wanted it to be?' asked Guy, suddenly.

'Nothing like,' said Keva, without hesitation.

Guy smiled at him.

'Sometimes it's so, so much better. So far beyond anything you could ever just dream up, you know? But sometimes it's just . . . awful.'

Guy nodded. 'I love your songs you know, man. More now than ever.'

'Thanks.'

Neither of them was drunk, but Keva felt a speedy, powerful high.

'I mean it. Your stuff is so . . . it's so desperately sad, man. Sometimes I'd love to know why. But I don't want to find out.'

Keva laughed. 'Me too.'

He passed Guy the joint. 'D'you believe in love?'

Guy exhaled, coughing and wafting the sweet smoke with the back of his hand. 'Not sure. I want to. Why?'

'Just wondering. I think we're quite similar, sometimes. Nothing turns you on, does it? None of this is . . . do you get excited?'

'I do sometimes, you know. I do.' He pushed his head right back and looked up at the blue-black sky. 'I was definitely in love, once. If love is what I think it is, then it happened to me with this very . . . unusual girl. I didn't believe in fate until we found each other. Now I believe in nothing but . . . everything, *everything* is gonna either happen . . .' He blew smoke out high into the night. '. . . or it's not.'

He told Keva the story. And the more he told him, the more Keva became certain that he could help Guy find this love of his life. If he chose to.

Spaceland was rocking. Belching hardcore electronica stoked a heaving, stinking, bacchanal. Every single person was dancing – except for James and his coterie. He was trying to lend all three of them his attention, but he was captivated by the girl with burns. Half of her face had, really, melted away. The other half was beautiful. Even in club light, her clear grey eyes sparkled with knowledge. She spoke, through a voice box, with a scrambled, manly voice.

'I get it totally, James. I want you to know that I'm totally comfortable with that. You're here for forty-eight hours. You don't give a fuck about getting to know me. You want to fuck me. You want to know how bad my tits are burned. You want to know what it's like to fuck a girl with a voice box . . .'

'Nope . . .'

The girl with callipers sat up, suddenly surprised. The girl in the wheelchair just straightened a bit.

'Oh?'

'You see, I *don't* want to know, really, what it's like to shag someone with a voice box. That'd be to defeat the real object, wouldn't it?'

'Er . . .'

The three girls looked at each other, waiting for some unexpected revelation of humanity from the self-satisfied guitarist.

'No. I wanna know if it gets clogged up when you swallow . . .'

'It was great. Sound. We could've played a much bigger place, like. I think Sensira only got about five hundred to their gig. Three thousand . . . yeah. Oh aye. MTV are well pissed off with 'em . . . Mm. Have you missed me, anyway? Well, you could sound like you fucken mean it! I've given up the big end-of-tour party to come back to this hotel and speak to you! Ah . . . fuck off! FUCK OFF!'

*

He wasn't certain whether it was the sudden release that came with the knowledge that his part of the tour was over, or whether it was the music – but Tony Snow had not stopped dancing. He was with a nice crew of college kids. All the girls had squeaky voices, all the boys had spots. They were all right. They were made up just to have Tony, Tony Snow from the Grams, hanging with them, having a drink, having a laugh. And the music was sound. He'd only recognised Sabres of Paradise amid the eclectic throb, but just as it seemed that the tracklisting was getting too obscure they'd throw in Jason Nevins or the Beastie Boys and the whole place went up. The kids grinned at him, grinned so hard that their smiles were drilling a hole in him. He supposed the girls would be starting to wonder if he'd make a move for one of them. The boys were wondering when he'd spirit away one of their girlfriends. But more than anything, they were having fun.

'Fuckinell! Yeeeees! I don't believe it! Come 'ead, gang!'

For no apparent reason, 'Bizarre Love Triangle' had come on. And Tony was off.

The security guy explained it all as civilly as he was able, in the circumstances. The elevators were out of service due to a fire-extinguisher fight between the rival road crews of three bands currently staying in the hotel. This left James Love, not the most athletic hedonist slacker, with something of a quandary. He crouched down by the side of the wheelchair.

'Come 'ead.'

She toppled herself on to his back. She was heavy.

He got up the first few flights with relative ease, stopping for breathers then putting his back into it again. He could feel every stair working against his thighs and calves. Each step was mechanical. By the time he got to his floor he was bent double, and she was hanging on to his shoulders through her own body strength. He looked down the long corridor. Their room was right at the far end, opposite Marty's. He had an idea. He laid her down on her back.

'You don't mind, do you?' he gasped as he dragged her by the ankles down the passageway. 'Bit unladylike, like, but it's so much easier . . .'

Her head jolted over every carpet strut. 'Ow! Careful!'

James staggered right past the discarded bath towels on the floor and collapsed on to Keva's bed, panting, leaving her on the floor, looking up at him, waiting.

'You need to take some excercise, young man!' she smiled.

'Oh, I intend to,' he flashed back. He looked at her useless legs, pointlessly clad in tailored black 501s. He felt for her. He really did. 'Now then. How would you like to go about this?'

Billy the Brief, fast asleep, turned over and pulled the towel tighter around him, his senses just aware of a male voice nearby. James propped the girl against the bed, arms and face on the mattress, kneeling unsteadily.

'Just 'ang on a mo,' he said, ciggy in mouth, trying to tug down her jeans with one hand and keep her stationary with the other, his knee in the small of her back. He gave up and hustled her up on to the bed, pulling her jeans down and off with greater ease. A perfect peach bottom lay there, awaiting his caresses.

'Oh, baby! Oh, my dear, dear darling – that is beautiful!' he gasped, stroking her bum, amazed by its supple resistance. He wasted no time in wrenching off his own Levis and producing himself to full erection.

'All thy pleasures shall be backwards!' he whispered, pushing and driving down until he was in.

Keva tossed and turned but he could not settle. Images of Evie, lovely Evie, haunted him. What to do about her? Could he really just turn her over to Guy, just like that? No. No way.

'Oh, Gad! Oh, fuck yes! Yes! Oooooooooh yes! Oooooooooh! He's got his cock in my ass . . . oh, my Gad! Myyyyyyyyy Gad! He's fucking my ass! He's got his fucking cock in my ass!'

'So I have,' noted James with satisfaction.

It was rare for them all to be at breakfast together, but maybe some inward mechanism told them all. Last day. Day off, even for Keva. Pick up at three thirty from the hotel. Fly out of LAX at six thirty. By tomorrow afternoon, Keva and James'd be scrapping over the fresh orange juice in Ivanhoe Road. For all that they were glad to be going home, today was a day to be enjoyed. James, still crackling with cocaine electricity, was being skilfully baited by Marty for the general enjoyment of all present.

'Well, I'm *good* . . . in fact I *am* fucking *great*. But I don't know if I'd go along with the fucken greatest guitarist in the world, an' that. I mean . . . it's a bit of a fucken statement, isn't it?'

The breakfast room had an air of liberation about it. Everyone was sat at nearby tables, mixing outside the security of their regular collaborators. Tony was sitting with Crapston and Billie the Brief, laughing about last night.

'I thought he was bumming Keva! Honest to God! I hears this mad moaning, more like someone saying their prayers, just mad talking really . . . Oh, my God! You've got your cock up me . . . fuck my butt, you bastard! . . . But it sounds like . . . it's not a bird's voice, know what I mean . . . and it's Keva's fucking bed!'

Crapston was guffawing and slapping the table, Tony willing him on.

'So, like, I'm dead to the world and I just, sort of, pops me head up to see what's going on and all I can see is Mr Love's big shitty arse smiling at me, hammering away ten to the dozen, *walloping* the living daylights out of some poor bastard! I mean . . . what was I *supposed* to think?'

James wandered over to their table, smoking and smiling at the same time. 'Tell you what . . . I'd think twice before getting on that particular fairground ride again, lar. Fuckinell! The stench! When I first got it in there an' that . . . I'm telling you, man, I had to fucken *whop* it in, tight as fuck like, but I thought I'd burst a bag of farts when I fucken got it up there! Waft! It was like a blowback from a methane tank! I had to keep me 'ead back over me shoulder while I was, like, obliging her . . .'

'You're sick,' muttered Tony. 'You're a very sick boy, Hector.'

This was supposed to be a Big Deal for Wheezer, but he wanted to just get it over with and get out. He'd be fine. He'd do a good job, hype them all up, and get off home. It'd all look rosy again when he was reading the next batch of news from a fax on his bruised old chesterfield.

Knopf was first to greet him. 'You run that mix by Guy, yet?'

Guy's sayso does not matter a fuck, he wanted to tell him. But he didn't. Not in so many words. 'Keva's still sleeping. I'll have a response for you before we head out of town . . .' Why was he talking in that bogus, slangy Hollywoodese?

Mel Parmese emerged from the elevator. 'Hey! Wheezy!' he laughed, triumphant. 'How ya feelin?'

'Good, man. Good,' he nodded, trying to exude a confident control which he did not in any way feel.

'Guy comin'?'

'Doubt it. Think he's doing lunch with Willard later.'

'Cool. That covers all our bases. We have to capitalise on all this . . . *goodness*, right now. Everyone loves the boys. Everyone wants it. We have to convert MTV's goodwill immediately and push for a pop release straight away. You cool with that?'

They'd been given the great honour of being invited to listen in on the field-call to the troops. Every one of Worldwide's promotional staff tuned in for this weekly conference call in which everyone was asked for their opinion, their ideas, their feedback before Campione spelt out the current priorities. Wheezer and Mel had been asked to listen in because they were going to hear only marvellous things. Maybe at the end, during winding-up, Wheezer might want to say a few words of thanks and encouragement. The lowliest rep in Minnesota was pulling in $50,000 – but they still needed to be thanked for doing their job.

'Makes nothing but sense to me, oh master!'

Mel punched his arm affectionately. 'You're the best, man!'

Keva and Marty were chuckling over the adverts in *LA Weekly*.

A sexy smile is yours for the asking.
Catering to fearful people, Dr Theo Katz offers all-round oral wellness.
Stereo headphones and nitrous oxide.
Teeth whitening $250 (per arch).

Keva grinned up from the paper. 'Wellness, man, I'm telling you. It's where it's at. It's the future.'

Wheezer caught his eye and beckoned him over. 'Sorry, dude.

Just need you to listen to something, quickly. Don't want everyone throwing their oar in. Have you got a sec?'

'Sure.'

'Here y'are, then.' He stepped back, anxious, while Keva slipped on the Walkman. His face, within seconds, looked as though his food had been drenched in vinegar. He jerked off the headphones.

'What the fuck is this?'

'Nothing! It's just an idea from some of the kids at one of the radio stations. They're big fans of the group. I think they're after a remixing gig, should we ever decide to go down that route . . .'

'Well, they can fuck off! This is shite!'

'You don't like it?'

He threw down the headset. 'I. Fucking. Hate. It. Yeah?'

'Steve? He loves it! Green light! No problem, man. Later!'

The more drunk they all got on the gratis Virgin tipples, the more Keva wanted nothing to do with it all. Two rows behind, Tony and Beano were excitedly chittering with Rory and Crapston, planning what they were going to do with their time off.

'It's just a game to them,' he thought. 'A hobby. Can't blame them.'

He wished he could feel so carefree himself, but he didn't. Something was niggling away at him. Something big. And he didn't want to think about it, whatever it was. He wanted just to push it away, for now. But it was doing him no good listening to the kids banging on with their foolish fantasies – Sandy Lane was Tony's latest plan. Beano and Celeste were buying a cottage in the Cotswolds, just like Kate Radlett's. Guy was having the wrong kind of influence over them, now he was starting to revel in being a toff again. He was telling them things they didn't need to know. Keva felt like stopping them. Just walking down there, resting his head on his forearms on top of Tony's headrest and saying: 'No. No you're not. I'm stopping you.'

He eyed them with detachment. Beano was almost jumping up and down with excitement.

'An' I'm getting a fucken moped! A proper fucken sit-up-an'-beg moped, 49cc, to get me round town. Fucken rock 'n' roll, lar!'

Guy was off up in First Class with Mack Hansen, having a massage. There'd been a flash of discomfort when he was whisked through the priority check-in at LAX, a singe of embarrassment masked by his attempts to laugh off the disparity with boss and workforce jokes. Keva didn't begrudge him any of it. From the start, from way back at Ticky's party, Keva had admired Guy, envied his cool, easy elegance, his ease with people and problems. You didn't want your record company boss slumming it with the paupers. He *should* be fed grapes by nubiles – he should just maybe be a little bit more wary about sharing his world with the likes of Beano and Tony. His was a world they could never know. Not in the way Guy knew it. Keva coveted none of it – except perhaps the girl he loved. And she was from *his* world.

He moved up to sit with Wheezer, who was immersed in *There's Something About Mary*, guffawing like a teenager. It was odd how he'd got to like The Wheeze so well. Before America, it'd been Keva and James, the flatmates, the public face of the Grams, ready to take on the States and the world. Tony and Beano, Rory and Crapston, Marty and Pat McIntosh, swopping Jerky Boys sketches and coke marathon tales. Wheezer was the loner, the teacher, the one who had to keep them all in line. Yet he'd turned into someone Keva could spend time with. He was more sensitive, more feeling than any of them. Looking back, now, at their reddening, tipsy, ecstatic faces, he knew that the Grams would never be same again. Whatever they used to be, they were no longer it and would never be that thing any more. They'd gone through the sound barrier. Keeping it all together now – keeping it contained, galvanised, controllable – it was like keeping salt in a sieve. Whatever came next he was going to have to adjust and learn to enjoy himself.

'What're you going to do today, then?'

'Dunno. What about you?'

'Dunno. Think I'll take myself off down the Eggy Vale, indulge myself in a big, sloppy greasy breckie. With hot tea and milk.'

Keva didn't laugh. 'It's closed.'

'It's Friday!'

'No. It's closed. Closed down, like. I seen it last night as we went past in the cab. You were snoring your fat head off. Boarded up, like. Closed.'

'Fuck . . .' James was properly heartbroken. 'Feels like I've lost a friend . . .'

'There's always Keith's'

'Nice one! Yeah, sound an' that. Keith's! Come 'ead . . .'

Keva showed him the flats of his palms. 'Ah, no – not now. Maybe a bit later. I'm still lagged. I'm just gonna doss for a day or two.'

James looked frantic. 'You can't doss. It's Christmas!'

'It is not Christmas. It's the second of December.'

'Yeah, but . . . we're the Grams, like. We should be out there. Meeting our public . . .'

'Sure. In a day or two, hey?'

'Fuckinell . . .' He stared around the flat, trapped. 'Wanna work on any stuff?'

'Nah, mate. Fucked. Leave it a while, eh?'

'I've had a few ideas, like, while we been away . . .'

'That's sound. We should start thinking about new stuff . . .'

This seemed to satisfy the antsy hedonist. 'Think I'll go into town. See if Marty needs help sorting the gear.'

'Think he goes back to Ireland today. He's doing the Divine Comedy, isn't he?'

'I should catch him . . .'

Keva smiled as James bustled out of the door, still wilding on drink, drugs and whatever supernatural hormonal imbalance kept him so constantly craving. He loped up to his room and, reverentially, picked up the Martin from its stand. He kissed it, gently, as he always did when he was returning to it with a well of creativity, and went to sit. Perched on the corner of his bed he closed his eyes and went to strum the now familiar opening bars of 'Wellness'. He could hear it all right, hear how it should be – but it wasn't the same. It didn't sound how it sounded in his head. It didn't work. He tried to summon up those tracks which had suggested themselves when he was first giving birth to the song. Shades of 'Stripper Vicar' by Mansun; a hint of the intro, just the first ten or fifteen seconds of 'I Hear the Sound of Drums' by Kula Shaker; and the downbeat mood of 'Sleazy Bedroom Song' by the Bluetones. He sang them all in his head, but he couldn't get it. It wasn't there any more.

Wheezer didn't know where to turn his attentions first. He'd put all the faxes and letters and e-mail and telephone messages into chronological order. In spite of his having left a phone message asking callers to try again on his return rather than clogging up the tape, they were too vain to fall in line with other, humdrum associates with their non-essential queries. The last message was taken three days ago, when the ansaphone had run out of recording space.

He reckoned he'd deal with the backlog in order of time zones – first come, first served. So it was dear old Blighty to receive The Wheeze's unblemished attention, then Europe, then the US, Japan, Australia and New Zealand. He glanced at his little stack of unread magazines – *Music Week*, *Billboard Monitor (Modern Rock)*, *Select*, *NME*s galore, *The Face* and the new *Offshore*, catalogue for lovers of erotic video. But, apart from the tempting new availability of Dutch porn, he'd been updated daily on the key stuff by the ReHab office while he was in the States. *Powder* was still number three and showing no signs of ageing. Things were pootling along nicely.

He flicked at the covers. Keva, looking fantastically remote on the end-of-year issue of *The Face*. 'The Grams Rule Rock', ran the strapline. *Select* had 'Keva's Glorious Melancholy'. The boys were cover stars, but where was the thrill? It seemed if not mundane then a far, far cry from the nirvana of their first review. It seemed normal to him. He doubted if he'd even get to read the things, not in any hurry, at least. Like the addict cranking up his dose his head was already racing on to the *Billboard* charts, the platinum discs, the Number Ones. *That* would give him a buzz.

But it was good to be back, dealing with this shit. Offers of live dates and festivals next year, some of which Todd had briefed him about in LA; requests from megastores for the band to do in-stores, stock signings, acoustic sets – bloody Meet 'n' Greets, all but; there were enquiries from papers and magazines and TV shows about their Christmas specials – among them a possible *Smash Hits* Award for Best Indie Band which seemed to depend upon their willingness to perform live for the cameras at the awards ceremony; lots of fan mail – fuck knows where they'd got hold of this address; *loads* of approaches from charities, great and small, the obviously bogus along with the very, very established. The first of them, asking would the Grams play at a church hall in Malpas for the Susie Blake Appeal, set the general tone. Some were asking for donations but most were nebulous enquiries from folk who, really, expected to be turned down but lived in hope and, come what may, could tell their committee that they'd been in touch with the Grams and that the current status was wait-and-see. Wheezer would, in the next few days, reply diligently to each and every one of them.

He contacted the big HMV in Liverpool to find out more about the in-store appearance, charmingly declining similar offers from Newcastle and Leeds on the basis of schedule congestion. He got on to Janey Heal about *The Smash Hits Awards* show:

'Listen!' she gushed. 'There's loads going on . . . the Christmas *TOTP* Special is almost confirmed. The lads aren't running off anywhere, are they? Shall we just hammer it? Shall we just say yes to fucking everything then go into hiding in the New Year?'

'Erm . . .'

'Wheezer?'

'I think some of the boys might be planning on taking a little break.'

'Well, stop them! This is the chance of a lifetime, Wheezer! They can have lots of little breaks when nobody's interested in them any more . . . Tell them they *can't* go on holiday. They're not big enough. Not yet . . .'

They both burst out laughing.

'OK.'

Wheezer, bumped out of his solitary confinement by Janey's admonishments, decided to make the call he'd been postponing. He needed to speak to Guy. About money.

He dialled the ReHab number but slammed down the phone on its second ring. He didn't know what he was going to say. He had no idea how to broach this. All he knew was that if he was going to call up the boys and cancel their time off, he was going to have to have something to trade with. He was going to have to bribe them.

He turned to his WP for inspiration, trying out a fax message for size:

> Dear Guy,
> I've tried to reach you by phone without success. Could you call me for a general chat/debriefing about America, finances, the short and long-term future . . .

No! Fuck it! Too cowardly. Too disingenuous. He hadn't tried to get hold of Guy at all, and any note which starts like that makes it transparently obvious that the sender would rather avoid confrontation. And what about that snidey way he'd tried to slip in the subject of money, the true motive for this contact, between other more general headings? Fuck it! Guy, now of all times, would respond to something direct and honest:

> Dear Guy,
> If you, like I, are taking the first six-month accounting period as March–September, we are due a statement on 10 December. Let me know if that's a problem – though, with sales like we've experienced, I don't anticipate it being so . . .

No! NO! Too abrupt. Too impersonal. He and Guy had drifted far, far away from each other – they didn't even fight any more – but they'd been through a lot in that short time.

The solution came to him out of nowhere. He jumped up from his desk, gambolled downstairs, grabbed his ancient boneshaker and pedalled up Parkwest, along the taxing gradual incline of Davenport Road and up the Lydiate, hurling his bike down outside the Village Stores. He grabbed a couple of local postcards – ferries across the Mersey, the Liver Building – dashed over the road for stamps then freewheeled it all the way back home.

> Dear Guy,
> Desperately embarrassing hence cowardly avoidnik postcard. I make us due for our first account on 10 December. Has the time

It'd have to do. It was a bit jaunty, a bit too cringing. But it'd get
things moving. He hopped back on the old cycle and dropped the
card – along with a freshly completed *Offshore* order form – into
the tiny postbox at the bottom of Station Road.

Back in his little study, still soaring, mad with energy – he
waded through the e-mails and faxes from the States. Most of it
was messages from the various cogwheels of Worldwide thanking
Wheezer and the boys for a great promo tour, looking forward to
having them all back in the New Year, and updating him on the
record. More screed from Mel Parmese and Sandy Santino
replicated all the info. They were Number Four in the *Billboard*
Modern Rock chart, while the five-day sale was over 8,500 with a
ten-day of nearly 15,000 and a total of 125,000 albums sold to date.
They hadn't even gone to Pop, yet – and they'd be hearing about
MTV any day now. The pattern was up, up and away.

Mel mentioned in passing that Myra Sweeney had collapsed at
work in New York and was now taking an extended period of leave
due to nervous exhaustion. He signed off by saying that it was all
systems go to attack Contemporary Hit Radio, Pop, the big guns,
first thing in the New Year. And Sandy Santino added a
handwritten note to Wheezer apologising for being 'a asshole'.
Wheezer smiled and updated all his files, figures and accounts.
This was what he'd always wanted. He was doing it. He reckoned
he deserved fifteen minutes of *Tittentraume* before bringing his
attention back to the Far East and Down Under.

Guy's faxed response was brief to the point of being curt.

Therefore:
3) I'm happy to advance an interim payment on account and will
settle balance on signature.
Yours faithfully,

Yours faithfully! Who was the fucking bleeding toff talking to?
Wheezer snatched up the phone.

Tony watched Beano and Celeste idle their way out of Euston
Station, entwined and totally enraptured with one another. He felt
an acute isolation, made worse by his standing like an anxious
parent, waiting for them to turn and wave to him, which they
failed to do. He smiled to himself. He was envious, he wanted it
for himself, but he wished them well.

The pager Wheezer had bought for each of them and insisted
they carry at all times bleeped insinuatingly. It was him. Again.
Phone back immediately. Urgent. He knew he'd regret it if he did.
He stuffed the pager into the vast inner pocket of his Schott
leather – a New York bargain buy – and headed down into the
bowels of the London Underground for the short hop to Waterloo,
then onwards to Hampshire.

Keva had always liked the sensation of his breath cooling on the
chill December air. As a kid it intensified the mania of Christmas
and birthdays – his, Dad's – and made everything mystical and
exciting to him. That was then, and soon, soon he knew – he'd
have to go back and face all that. But now he hurried on, head bent
into the stinging wind, back to Ivanhoe with his *NME*.

James was still on the phone to Wheezer, getting nowhere. It all
seemed straightforward, but Hector wanted to go over it all again
and again and again. Guy was sending them some money. It
wouldn't be the full amount but it'd be heaps, nonetheless –
enough to make for a storming Christmas. The band needed to
meet for a state-of-the-nation discussion before anything could be
done about anything – and after that they'd all have to go to
London. Any chance of taking time out was now gone with the
Sefton Park wind. Keva didn't give a fuck. He was willing to carry
on flogging himself. He wanted to. Maybe that fucking song would

come back to him if he did. Maybe his mind needed to be in a flux to throw up whatever chemical disharmony it took to create these contorted masterpieces. This one, for now, was stillborn.

He spread out *NME* on the kitchen table. The cover was disappointing. It was them all right, the Grams on the *NME* cover, but it had been defiled by a not-insubstantial box-pic of Sensira. They seemed to be sharing top billing with the Grams. It wasn't a proper cover.

'FEAR AND LOATHING IN LA – THE GRAMS AND SENSIRA ROCK UNCLE SAM.'

Fucking Sensira! They had a way of blighting every Grams dalliance with the *NME*. Sensira had already had another cover around the release of 'Beta-Blokka' – there was no need and no justification for their mugs butting in on the Grams' big story. He felt wearied of it all. He braced himself for Pat's write-up.

Half an hour later he was still angry, but trying to find perspective. He read the two pieces through a fan's eye – and the Grams piece was definitely the more tempting. It was all right, but he was taking liberties with them. First and foremost he remained a besotted fan, describing the disconsolate beauty of the songs and the raw power of the live shows with pungent vivacity. He wanted the reader to feel it, and he made the band sound amazing.

But he was assuming too much, too. He was adopting the stance of a best friend who's trying to keep your feet on the floor before you run away with yourself. *Him*! Lord Charlie fucking Cokehead The Third! He'd charted the drug-addled decline of James Love as though he'd been watching Jimi Hendrix waste himself in front of his very eyes – and it wasn't glamorised, either. He made James out to be a technicolour clown. There was some good, funny rock 'n' roll stuff – Tony hospitalising himself in San Francisco, the fat guy in LA who'd ordered Keva to sign his CD. There was also the ubiquitous Myra Sweeney, turned into a frightening, avaricious symbol of corporate America for the purposes of Pat's article. But his assumptions about Keva were infuriating. Keva, to Pat McIntosh, was killing himself, pondering too hard on the meaning of life when, perhaps now more than ever, he should be living it and enjoying it. Maybe then he'd find the answers. Cunt! He *knew* that Keva hadn't had the luxury of letting himself go . . . they'd talked about it, often, how Keva was starting to feel isolated from the rest of the band.

But the most aggravating bit came with his piece on Sensira. The overview was that the *NME* didn't take sides – Keva knew all that – they existed to tell you what was going on, what mattered in music. But what mattered today was that the Grams were ripping the joint apart – they were taking the world by storm, for real – while Sensira were starting to sag. They didn't have the puff to get to the top of the hill. Now, *that's* interesting, Keva seethed. That's a story. Two bands who everyone knows hate each other's guts, pitching up at the same time at the biggest racetrack of all, one of them with a slight start on the other but both expected to show well. The Grams versus Sensira in the States. What a fucking story! And *NME* had ducked it. They'd bottled it. They'd printed the stuff about Rotterdam last month, they'd run Wheezer's letter giving the real story about the sound limiters – and now they had the chance to put the two warring factions head-to-head. But they shit it.

The only reference to the enmity between Keva and Helmet came in Pat's write-up about his binge with Helmet. This irritated the hell out of Keva. Not just because he was casting Helmet, now, as a magnificent waster. James was a funky fool but Helmet, that dickhead, the flailing wannabe Pat had joked about so savagely a few months ago, was now a tragic, fallible, heroic figure. That was sickening, but it wasn't the thing which had infuriated Keva. It was that Pat had used his interview with Helmet to send messages to him.

'Don't get too big for your boots, old matey,' he was saying. 'I'm only telling you for your own good. I've been there from the start, don't forget. Someone's got to say something to you. You think you're the biggest thing since The Verve – well, it ain't happened yet. And it won't happen without ME! So don't go thinking you can just drop people. You can't.'

He was saying all that, he really was, by allowing just one bitchy retort from Helmet. Pat had been there at the radio stations. He'd seen the phones light up whenever the Grams went on air – whenever *Keva* went on air. He'd seen the crowd reactions. He'd seen the MTV girl come round when Sensira couldn't face the truth – that no cunt on earth was interested in them any more. *That* was Pat's fucking story! That Helmet was fucking up on drugs because it was all over for him, already – and how well he knew it . . . The Grams had won. They were going to be the biggest band in the world, and Pat McIntosh had seen it all. So what, of all this, of all that he'd seen of the two rival bands did he choose to write? This:

> *'You must be aware, though – you must sense the excitement everywhere about the Grams? I know they're very aware of Sensira's impact over here.'*
>
> *'I'm glad it's happening for them. I mean that. But, you know . . .' He laughs that silent, never-ending, twisted laugh of his and shakes his head. '. . . I mean. I hope it all works out for them. I hope it doesn't freak them out when they start to move up to a bigger level. I mean, it's great when you're playing these vibey little club gigs. You can get carried away with yourselves and let yourself believe that this is it, for ever and ever. But they've never played to more than a few hundred people – except when they've supported us.'*

Bastard! He let the twat get away with all that! Cunt! Vibey little club gigs! What about fucking Ally Pally? *Vibey*! And what about Pat snitching to fucking Helmet fucking Horrocks . . . what'd he said?

> *'I know they're very aware of Sensira's impact over here.'*

Twat!

That was his first reaction. And then as he read it again, he felt a tingling prickle of admiration for Helmet – he'd got him good, really got him climbing the walls by his fingernails. Then he twigged what Pat was doing, here. Shit. If he could just drop him, just lose the cunt, he would do, without a second thought. It wasn't that the guy had served his purpose. More that the more Keva got to know him, the more he scared him. He was a fucking nutter. He wanted some part of Keva, wanted some say in all of this. He was going to have to treat Pat McIntosh with extreme caution from now on.

James didn't know what to do next. It was all right doing the bars, getting bought drinks, talking about himself, telling his tall stories about the States. There were new bars opening in Liverpool every five seconds, and each new bar wanted a James Love sat up there on the platform, like a firefly, drawing people in. But everyone seemed to go home, eventually. They'd go home when they could still be out, leaving him to talk to the bar staff as they brushed up. A few times, now, he'd found himself out on the street at four or five in the morning, knowing he wouldn't get to sleep for hours, yet.

Guy was as surprised to see Tony Snow as Tony'd been to find his dapper record company boss lounging with the Turnbulls, taking tea. But while Tony felt awkward, Guy radiated pleasure at his utterly unexpected arrival.

Driving him back up to London, later, he reiterated his demand that Tony should stop the night at Dolphin Square.

'They're all coming down tomorrow, anyway. Didn't Wheezer tell you?'

Tony shrugged. 'I haven't, like, been making myself that widely available.'

Guy laughed. 'Well, stay over, anyway. I promise that if I molest you, I'll do it gently.'

So he did. They took a cab to the Anglesey Arms in South Kensington and sat in a droopy two-seater next to the warming hearth, swigging IPA.

'I'm supposed to be on a diet,' laughed Tony. 'I never told no one, like, just in case . . .'

The two of them were immediately at ease with each other and slipped comfortably into a spiralling, eager conversation, taking them out to all the vantage points of life and back to themselves, their own take on it all.

'I used to want to be in bands, you know,' mused Guy. 'Anything to get attention . . .'

Tony smiled indulgently. 'You'd've been good at it. You'd make a very fine star . . .'

'I fucking well would, too.' Guy laughed. 'This is as close as I ever got, though. Never had the bottle to see it through.'

Tony took a hearty swig of his ale, shaking his head as he swallowed. 'Dunno. I've never really thought of meself as, like, a boss bassist. It's not a calling with me. I'm not like Keva, like. I'm not on a mission. I joined the band cos Hector asked us – and to see if I could shag a few girls . . . it's a job, now, isn't it? Beats a stint down at Crawfords though, eh?'

He went to polish off his pint but, seeing that Guy still had over half a glass full, sipped at it and gesticulated back at Guy. 'But, I mean, when we first come to see you, you was saying that, sort of, music *is* your world. I hope we haven't ruined it all for you . . . have we?'

Guy laughed and immediately went serious. 'I mean, what I've found is that those moments – you know when you hear a track for the first time and it's *magic*? Well, that happens so rarely, for me.'

He took another slug of the ale. God, it was going down well. It actually felt like Christmas to him. A warm pub, a cheering pint, good company. Life didn't have to be turmoil all the time. It wasn't so difficult to get the hang of it.

'But for that moment – the moment when I take the new song away and put on my headphones or slip it into the cassette deck in the car, whatever – I've got a year's worth of shit with accounts and contracts and invoices and worries, cares, distractions. It's not me, I'm afraid. It's not me.'

Tony nodded his head thoughtfully. 'Might find it's a good way of going forward, though, you know. If you really don't give a fuck any more, that's the best possible way to approach your job. There's no fear. You're not fucking dependent on it, not dependent on success, nothing. You don't have to smile at any cunt, if you don't feel like it.'

Guy smiled, sadly. 'I think you may have a point, Antoine. I think you're only bloody right, you know . . .'

All of a sudden they both guffawed and slapped the table self-consciously, signalling that it was time to change the subject. Tony went to get the drinks in.

'I *love* you.'

'You're pretty adorable yourself.'

He sat in bed, leaning earnestly on one elbow, thinner yet than the pale and slender Celeste. 'No, I mean it. I've never said that to no one before. You're all I fucken think about. You drive me crazy. I just want to be with you all the time . . .'

'Blimey!' she giggled, tapping him on the nose. 'Ten rock clichés in one short sentence! How on earth am I going to better that?'

'Just come 'ere, you, you posh, filthy, gorgeous . . .'

Downstairs the phone rang. And rang.

They read Wheezer's itineraries in silence as the train raced through the Staffordshire countryside. It all looked fine to James Love, guitarist. Bit of time off over Christmas and New Year, then more again just after Easter – but James couldn't think of anything he'd rather do than tour. If Wheezer'd put a three-hundred-date tour itinerary in front of them he'd have squealed like a pig, of course – but he'd have loved it to death, really, a tour like that.

There was the usual mad preamble from Wheezer, explaining how sorry he was that their schedule was so rammed but that this was the only way forward, for now, and they're all in it together and all that shit. And then there were the dates. They weren't that bad:

December

10   *Meet at Costa, Lime Street Station @ 9.30 for 9.45 train.*
      Meetings at ReHab offices: 2 p.m. Guy deBurret, 4 p.m.
      Todd King
      Evening – MTV Europe Christmas Party

11   *2 p.m. – Record session for John Peel @ Maida Vale*
      Time TBA – photo shoot for Q *with Steve Double*

12   Smash Hits Awards – *rehearsals @ Earls Court, London*

13   Smash Hits Awards, *live from Earls Court*

14	Train London Euston–Liverpool Lime Street @ 1.05 p.m. Telephone interviews, Japan and Australia*
15	Telephone interviews, US (East Coast)*
16	Telephone interviews, US (South and Midwest)*
17	Telephone interviews, US (West Coast)*
18	Granada Tonight special @ Granada Studios, Quay Street, Manchester
19	In-store appearance @ Records, Church Street, Liverpool, 3–5 p.m.
21	Meet 9.30 @ Lime Street Station for 9.45 train. 2.00 p.m. Record Lamacq session @ Maida Vale
22	Record Jools Holland New Year's Eve Special @ LWT Studios, Upper Ground, South Bank, London SE1
23	Record TOTP Xmas Special @ BBC Elstree

Accommodation in London 10–14 & 21–24 December is @ The Gore Hotel, Queen's Gate, London SW7.

Transport back to Liverpool 24 December will be by private charter plane from Northolt Aerodrome to Liverpool Airport. Taxi to Northolt leaves Gore at 11.00 sharp. Flight is at 12.30.

January

5	Fly London Heathrow to Tokyo
6	Promo day in Tokyo. Reception with record company
7	Gig, Tokyo
8	Fly to Nagoya. Gig, Nagoya
9	Fly to Osaka. Gig, Osaka
10	Fly to Sydney
11	Day off
12	Gig, Sydney
13	Promo day, Sydney. Fly to Melbourne
14	Gig, Melbourne
15	Fly to Adelaide. Gig Adelaide.
16	Day off
17	Fly to San Francisco

Final itinerary of US tour subject to confirmation with Todd King and Rudy Wexner. Dates 19 January to end in Florida 5 April.

Week off in Florida or at leisure, then return flight to UK from Orlando on 14 April.

UK and Ireland dates

April

18	*Aberdeen*
19	*Edinburgh*
20	*Glasgow*
21	*Off*
22	*Newcastle*
23	*Sheffield*
24	*Manchester*
25	*Birmingham*
26	*Cardiff*
27	*Off*
28	*London*
29	*London*
30	*St Austell*

May

1	*Dublin*
2	*Belfast*
3	*Derry*
4	*Travel*
5	*Liverpool*

Then, some time off!

Festival season starts in June: we've booked headline slots going right through summer in Ireland, Spain, Italy, Holland, Germany, Denmark and Sweden, and will confirm one or more of the big UK festies. Glastonbury looks extremely likely. Will rationalise some of the European festivals with additional live dates around the festival appearance in each country, plus will book France, Belgium, etc.

Stress that this is a working document to give you a feel for the weeks' and months ahead. As you all know well, this will require total belief in the band and total commitment to our mutual aims.

More bands have foundered on the rocks of their first big tour than you'd care to shake a stick at. You're going to have to find the strength to keep it all going, from your deepest reservoirs of Grams spinach. You should also know, of course, that all of this is liable to change, without notice, at any time! Good luck and God Bless You, one and all.

Wheezer

* Keva only. See separate itinerary.

Wheezer watched intently, worried, watched them scanning the brief, waiting for the first complaints. He'd allowed nearly three months for the US tour. He and Mel had asked Todd and Rudy to devise a routing that'd cover the entire continent. They wanted to go everywhere.

Keva and James browsed through it all, nodding, pausing to giggle at the private jet, complain that it should be a limo instead of a taxi, howl at his use of *festies*, ask why none of the other times given in the itinerary were *sharp* and insist that under no circumstances would they perform at *The Smash Hits Awards* – but, by and large, they seemed fine with it all. They didn't mention the USA aspect of it, at all.

'Has Beano seen it?' chuckled James.

'Can't get hold of him. Tony said he'll track him down. They'll both be there later on.'

Keva gazed out of the window for dramatic effect, perfecting his wistful, lost-in-thought demeanour. Without turning back to James and Wheezer he said, 'Doesn't give us much time to record, does it? Or if we want to bung another single out. Make a video. *Top of the Pops* and all that . . .'

'No, but . . .'

'Other groups manage,' blustered James. 'I agree with Wheezer.'

'He hasn't said anything yet,' smiled Keva, chillingly.

They both looked at The Wheeze.

'I think it's messy to get into thinking about Record Two while we're still busy on Record One. I know people do it, sort of throw out a taster to keep the dogs quiet for a bit . . .'

'A pacifier,' James interjected, deadly serious. They both looked at him, unsure.

'Yes. But we won't do that. We'll keep people concentrated on *Powder*. We've done well with it in this country, but we've only just pricked the surface. Plus, our friends in Americaland are only just getting into sync with us. You know what an immense market that is . . .'

James tittered at his use of 'market', like a real manager. Wheezer didn't even frown at him, this time, just waited for it to go quiet again.

'Yeah . . . I say it's best all round if we choose a third single and use that time between Christmas and New Year making a clip for it. If we're cute about it we can have the record and the tour details, the concert ticket sales keeping our name alive back here while we're on the other side of the world, being *enormous* . . .'

'Like it!' beamed James. Keva said nothing.

'What d'you reckon, Kee?'

'Makes sense,' he allowed, eventually. 'So long as we're not flogging a dead horse – so to speak.' His tone was morose, uninterested.

'There's *loads* of cum left in *Powder*, yet. Wads an' that.'

'What'd be the next single?' gushed Wheezer.

Wheezer and James leaned their heads forward at once, full of self-importance. Keva returned his attentions to the lolloping countryside.

'I'm not fucken doing it! It's *that* simple!' raged Beano, screwing up his itinerary and hurling it at the pub window. He'd been simmering since Tony had met him at Paddington, had sat in silence throughout the planning and financial meeting with Guy and, realising for the first time in the pub that all of this started *now*, he exploded.

'Celeste is waiting for me, right now, a hundred miles away . . .' He paused and eyed Wheezer. 'Cooking me rabbit stew! That's all I'm asking at the moment. A little time to meself to eat me rabbit stew . . .!'

They bit their lips. Tony whispered in his ear. 'Do yourself a favour, mate. Don't go down that best meal ever route, eh?'

It stumped the skinny drummer for a moment. His overheated head boiled red, showing an angry bald spot on his scalp. He tried to regulate his feverish, vexated breathing and talk this out. 'We've just sat in a meeting there, where the geezer's told us we've made over six million quid . . .'

'*Turned over* six million,' Wheezer corrected. 'Probably more. But it's yet to be discerned how much of that is profit and how the profit'll be split.'

Keva had been quietly trying to discern that too.

'Whatever, Wheezer. There's no way that each one of us isn't gonna walk away from this with Brewster's . . . so why can't we just slow down a bit? We deserve a rest. We need to come back in a few weeks' time refreshed, ready . . . Why are we, like, killing ourselves? *Smash Hits*? Fucken *Granada Tonight*! Now's the time to be turning those things down! Real bands don't do *Smash Hits* . . .'

'That's a bit elitist, isn't it?'

'NO! It's common fucking sense! We've just been told we're getting a quarter of a million each . . . how much fucken more . . .'

'WOAH! Hang on!' Wheezer had his palms up. 'We haven't been told anything of the sort! No specific figures were mentioned and quarter of a million is a wild, wild guess . . .'

'So you're saying we won't see, like, a million between us out of six million turnover?'

'I'm not saying that, at all. I'm saying we'll know the precise figures after Christmas.'

Beano went mad. He went stark raving bonkers. 'THIS is supposed to be Christmas! THIS was supposed to be rest and recouping for the band!' His eyes were shining out like a slash-movie anti-hero.

'Recuper-*ayshun*,' Tony muttered under his breath.

'But THIS . . .' he picked up the screwed-up itinerary off the floor and rolled it out again, flattening the corners down emphatically. '. . . is a fucken heavy-metal itinerary!' He started doing a funny, mannered little giggle. 'For the Grams! This band was never about doing fucken world tours! I'm telling you . . . I'm not fucken doing it!'

He looked at them all in such a way as to have them believe he was serious. Deadly serious.

Keva stood up. He looked them over and said, very calmly, 'That's OK, Beano. It's not a problem any more. Because I'm not doing it either. Not with you cunts. I'm splitting up the group as of now . . .'

They all turned to him, flabbergasted.

'I've had enough of this shit. No cunt except me does any fucking work.' For all his invective he remained inanimate. 'No cunt except me has their own fucking four-page addendum to the itinerary because there's so much *extra* they have to do. You're happy enough to fucking carve up the money I've made for you . . . but whenever you're asked to do anything, *any* fucking thing to justify your existence on this blessed fucking groovy train there's a fucking riot. Someone's having your kecks off you. See you.'

He walked out without even a gesture to Wheezer.

'*Gravy* train,' muttered Tony.

He'd meant it, too. Making the short walk along Clerkenwell Road, strangely elated, to Tony Wolfe's offices just off Theobald's Road, he'd determined to himself to see this through – break up the band, stop all this madness, this mad life of his. The twinkling Christmas lights and decorations, the thrilling blue promise of a December twilight with its dirty cold air gave him a sense of anticipation that'd been missing. The Grams had ground him down, gradually, inevitably. He'd had enough, for now. And he'd had enough of everyone taking a ride on his back. He'd pay them off, pay them well – but he just couldn't be doing with them any more. The Grams. Where'd it all come from anyway? They were a band, together, because they'd met by chance. Not because they were, all of them, the Greatest. Tony and Beano were just average session men. Below average. No way should they be getting an equal share of the Grams' poundage. And as for James . . . Keva reckoned he'd done well to call it all off before James fucked it for them anyway. It was the only way. If he felt like writing again in the New Year, whenever, he could do it. Find a real band. Go solo. Whatever. Eyeing up the fire-haired Australian receptionist with a hunger he hadn't felt in a while, he sat back and waited to be summoned, feeling on top of the world.

'I promise – I had not the faintest inkling . . .'

The band gathered around him, confused, wanting some sense of it all. Wheezer, in shock, pulled out a proposal for Grams-brand condoms.

'I hadn't even told him about this . . .'

'If you decide it's what you still want, of course – I'll be happy to represent you. But this isn't so unusual, you know. In fact it'd be unusual if the singer *didn't* break up the band halfway through their first American tour, sack the manager, get rid of the drummer, whatever. All the great bands have been through that. And survived it.' He bent forward, conspiratorial. 'Now. We have a slight conflict of interest, here, in so far I've been retained by Wheezer and Guy on certain projects.'

Pprrrrochggxxdzechs.

'But you interest me more, frankly. I can point Wheezer in the direction of some very reputable firms. Very reputable. But it's good that you've done this now. *Very* advantageous.' He was almost gurning, his unkempt Denis Healey eyebrows giving him a debauched look. 'What this sets out, quite clearly, is who is really in charge here.'

Keva was fascinated by his 'r's.

Ghrrrreeee-lee in charge.

He gave the 'r's a pretentious guttural raking, like Tom Stoppard, rolling them hard to give an impression of intellectual ferocity but sounding like an Albanian halfwit.

'When you *ghrrrreturrrn* to the gloop . . .' He couldn't manage two phlegmatic 'r's so quickly in succession. '. . . IF you return . . . it will be on terms of your decree.'

Dexkkghrrrreee. Was he using words with prominent 'r's in, Keva wondered, just to make himself stentorian? And what about that receptionist? She'd let her eyeline flicker down to his dick, just for a second – and given him a cool little come on. Just . . . nothing, really – an incline of her head, a brief holding of eye contact, a way of reaching for the phone that made the fabric on

430

her top stretch tight against her tits. Nothing at all. But she was up for a night out. He knew it. He was going to set something up with her on the way out. Wolfe's bronchial consonants brought him to attention.

'With a minimum of fuss we shall establish a hierarchy – that being that the Ghrrrrams is *your* gloop, *you* are the leader and your share of all income is commensurate?' He looked up and smiled. 'Remember that the group is on the verge of *considerable* success overseas, Keva, mainly thanks to your doing. If you were to leave things as they stand now, the other members of the group might reap a disproportionate benefit, from the American situation in particular. But if you were to strike a deal with the band, now, ride your album for all it's worth in the States, Japan, everywhere – make a name for yourself . . . then you're in a much better position to call your next move. Your group – your move. Yes?'

His next next five words were delivered with the distracted ease of a doctor, short, meaningful pauses between each word. 'Does. That. Sound. Fair. Ee. Nuff?'

'Yes. That's fair. If I keep the group going, what will we do about the publishing?'

Wolfe smiled dazzlingly. 'You tell me, Keva.'

So Keva told him.

He was knocked out by her, stone in love, straight away. He felt special, with her. She'd made him remember that he was a Superstar. A Rock God. He forgot that sometimes. Maybe there was something to be said for keeping the band together – for now. So long as he was unambiguously the top man. It could be done. It was all in the fine-tuning.

The girl, Kiara, had kept him laughing all night, drinking her way through the MTV party, ripping into everyone – then taking him back to her flat and collapsing, stupefied with drink. He loved her with all his heart.

As she slumbered, he kissed her shoulders and her neck. Hardening, he pressed himself into her back, rubbing his cock and balls around the top of her buttocks, simulating a slow, limbo-fuck, squeezing her breasts hard from behind. He kissed right down her spine, still massaging her tits, running his tongue over her bum, down her salty crease, darting it up her arsehole, making her oscillate with him, tensing her bottom and pushing down into the bed. She rolled on to her back. He caressed her hard belly, tracing it down to the tiny, manicured delta of flaming mott. He kissed around her hair, licking stridently up and down the lips. She let out a long, urgent moan and clutched his head hard, banging it down fiercely into her fanny and fucking his face madly, squeezing and mauling his aching skull.

Exhausted, bruised head resting on her ginger mound, he looked up at the smiling Kiara.

'The future's bright,' he grinned. 'The future's orange.'

When they'd bumped into the band at the party, Keva had just waved off their anxious advances.

'Business as usual,' he laughed. 'We'll talk over breakfast. This is Kiara. Isn't she the most beautiful thing you ever saw in your life?'

She was, too. He was mad on her. And because he wanted to walk her to work and arrange to meet her for lunch and take her shopping and fuck her standing up somewhere, he missed breakfast with Wheezer and the boys.

So, when he caught up with them, sitting round in the hotel bar drinking coffee – *coffee!* – and tea – *tea!* – they found him in an excellent mood. He'd bounced in there, happy as anything, confident, determined to stand up for himself but feeling, now, that he'd see them all right. He thought he might as well offer them something they could accept happily, with dignity, rather than something he just foisted upon them and which they'd have to sign because they had no other choice. He should have done this from the start. It was easy. The Grams was his band. He sat down.

'Sorry about all that yesterday, boys. Well . . . not *sorry*, but – you know.'

They nodded, Beano notably more enthusiastic than the others.

'Erm – this is gonna hurt, so let's get it done. I should probably see Wheezer on his own, to speed things along. OK?'

They nodded again, but nobody moved. Keva, grinning expansively, motioned them upwards with his hands. James and Beano jumped up, keen to please, while Tony slouched along behind

432

them, not looking as though he cared much. Wheezer fixed his beady stare on Keva.

'So. This has all come somewhat out of the blue, hasn't it?'

'Out of the blue. How true,' smiled the singer. 'Look. I'm sorry to have just dropped all this on you, just like that. I don't know what happened. Beano really got to me, I don't see why I should have to take that shite . . . but I've got to say, that was just the catalyst, really. This has been building up . . .'

'Well . . . in a way, I'm glad. It brings certain things to a head, doesn't it. So . . .'

So Keva told him. He wanted it properly acknowledged that this was his band, and proper acknowledgement was going to come in the form of a major share of the cash. He wanted to take seven-twelfths of the recording income, with a quarter going to James and a twelfth each to Beano and Tony. Of the publishing, he would take nine-twelfths, with two twelfths to James and the other two splitting a twelfth. Wheezer swallowed hard at this last. Keva saw him gulp.

'It's actually over-generous. They should get none of the publishing. James, perhaps, a twelfth for certain arrangements of my songs, but the others . . . I was going to take eight-twelfths of records, too . . . I think I'm being quite soft with them . . .'

He studied his nails.

'None of this affects your own twenty per cent, like. However you want to tell them is fine by me, mate – though obviously I'd prefer it if you were to stress my generosity, like. But, you know, whatever, Wheezy – this is it. This is what I want to get. If they're not having it, no problem. There's no group. Not with me in it anyway.'

Steve Double had thought the poses were magnificently moody, but the band weren't pretending. There'd been an atmosphere since before the Peel session. The boys were looking at Keva with a sullen reverence. They felt, not out of spite but out of a new fear of him, that they couldn't, shouldn't, go and talk to him. He'd sat alone, brooding.

He had reason. Wheezer and the band had accepted his proposals with little resistance, and the surge of joyous release that came with Keva's realising his new Grams dawn, was followed by a deadly low when he phoned Kiara. Rippling with energy, tingling with joy and relief and happiness for this great new life which was his, he took to his captain's role with fervour. He was going to be Big, he was going to be a real frontman and he was going to lead from the front.

He couldn't start by sacking a Peel session so that he could go shopping with his girlfriend. Indeed, now was more than probably the right time to let her know how things would be with them. They'd be great together, she'd look fantastic in pap pictures, at parties, making people laugh, making them love her, making them wish they were Keva, with her. They'd be a great rock 'n' roll couple. Keva and Kiara. They were made. But she was going to have to cut him a bit of slack. Last-minute cancellations come with the job, baby. It's just the way it is.

'Hi,' he crooned.

'Hey, stud-u-like . . .' She was almost dismissive. He couldn't tell whether she was pleased to hear from him.

'Listen. You're gonna hate me . . .'

'Oh, good! I love hate . . .'

That threw him. He was going to string out her disappointment then steam back in with dinner at Quaglino's and a sleazy night of drug abuse at Brown's. Then, Saturday morning, when he had to run off to *Smash Hits* rehearsals he was going to ask her to go out and buy a flat for him. Maybe in Notting Hill. She said she liked Notting Hill.

'No, really. I can't make lunch with you.'

'Too bad.' She didn't sound bothered. She didn't want to know why. Why not?

'I've got to do a John Peel Session.'

'Cool! Well, no worries. A girl can hold her head up, huh, getting blown out for John Peel. Anyway. Call me one day. It was fun.'

She put the phone down. He looked at the mouthpiece, put it down, paced about, troubled. What the fuck . . .? He called her again. This time there was definitely a tone to her voice. Keva tried to be smooth with her.

'Hey! I wasn't trying to let you down lightly, you know . . . I mean . . . what about tonight? What are you doing later on?'

Silence.

'I, uh . . . Keva, sweetheart . . .' A pause that lasted three centuries. '. . . I don't really wanna get *in*-to anything, right now. Like, it's Christmas? There's loadsa parties going down?'

Statements-as-questions. He was doomed to be fucked up by funny, horny, sexy bints who could make him love them with statements-as-questions.

'You said yourself you're off touring the world first of the year? My work permit runs out in March? It doesn't exactly have Meant To Be stamped all over it, does it?'

God, he loved her. Just the way she spoke. He could picture her little nose, wrinkling as she made each barbed remark. He could have listened to her all day.

'I hope you're not fucking me off here, madam?'

'Aussie Secretary Fucks Off Lovelorn Rock Star. Yep. I guess that's about the size of it. It was fucking unforgettable, though. Thanks for having me.'

He wanted to keep cool about it, go down nicely, but he couldn't let her go. He stayed on the line, hurt, bitter, smarting. 'Lovelorn! Don't flatter yourself? You just wanted to fuck someone famous, didn't you?'

'Oh, for sure, mate! That was part of it, deffo – I'm a starfucker! Listen . . . don't take it all so seriously. There'll be some other little temptress wrapped around your neck tonight. You should fucking lap it up? Enjoy it. I did.'

She put the phone down. His soul plummeted down, down, down. He dragged himself out to meet the band in reception. Off to the Peel session. He'd lead from the front then. Lead by example.

Guy, enjoying the whole dizzy topspin of a London Christmas like never before, wished he had not answered the telephone.

'Season's Greetings, youngest sibling,' trickled William.

'Big Brother. What a delight.'

'That's not terribly Christian of you now, is it?'

'What do you want?'

'Nothing. To congratulate you, if anything. And to wonder out loud whether you might be joining us for Christmas?'

'*Re* first: nothing to congratulate, as yet. On course to repay loan, but costs huge. *Re* second: almost certainly not. Presence of father precludes. Acceptance of kind Turnbull offer much more likely. Enquiry: state of health – wife, family, etcetera.'

William laughed his deep, rich, plummy laugh. 'Oh, you're incorrigible. I love you!'

They hung up on each other.

The idea of a ReHab Christmas party, which Guy had been playing with, was ruled out once and for all.

'Where you gonna go for Chrimbo, like?'

James had been trying to jolly him out of it all night. Anyone'd think it was him who was getting a half of a twelfth of the publishing. He was going to be a millionaire, for fuck's sake. Keva McCluskey, from Waterloo. A millionaire.

'Haven't thought about it. Have you?'

'I'm just gonna go round to me mam's for a few days. She's buzzin' off all this, you know. Me dad's into it all too, on the sly. I'm sure he fucken grunted at us last time I went round . . .'

Keva showed no interest at all, but he soldiered on.

'She loves it, me mam . . . our James this, our James that . . . calls us Jimmy, now, you know? Think she's expecting us to turn up in a fucken stretch limo an' that, like that monster in LA . . .'

'L.'

'You what?'

'Thought it was called L, now.'

A slight grin with it, just for a second.

'What about you? You going to see your mam?'

'No.'

Wrong thing to ask. He knew it. It killed the flickering exchange bone dead.

'Get off my fucking stage!'

Wheezer pretended he hadn't heard the big, beardy twat and carried on walking. The bloke in the sweat-soaked black Page & Plant T-shirt – *real* tour, *real* gigs – came running towards him from the side he was trying to get to. He was halfway across the vast, footy-pitch-sized stage now. He would've looked stupid turning back. He decided to back the angry roadie down with sang-froid. Fishing his AAA pass out of his pocket he swiped it casually in the guy's face, looking past him, not even breaking his stride.

'I'm the Grams' manager,' he droned, expecting him to fall at his feet and beg for mercy – or least put on a phoney, embarrassed laugh and say 'Sorry, mate' and allow Wheezer to reply 'Don't even think about it, mate – you can't be too careful with all this gear lying around.'

But none of that happened. What happened was that he ran and slammed his gut into the oncoming Wheezer like Friar Tuck bouncing the Sheriff of Nottingham, knocking him down on his backside. Wheezer blinked up at him, winded.

'Are you fucking DEAF!'

Wheezer picked himself up, dusted himself down. A few humpers and roadies stopped what they were doing to watch. Believing that he couldn't have seen it properly last time, Wheezer, holding his side, waved his pass at him once again. The fat bloke snatched it out of his hand and hurled it on to the floor.

'I don't give a FUCK who you are! *I* am the fucking stage manager of this event! *I* control the stage! NOBODY sets foot on my stage without my say-so!'

Wheezer hadn't felt violent towards anybody since his last run-in with James. As a lad, he'd been a fair scrapper, allying his nimble, athletic balance to a vicious Irish temper. This big, bearded cunt, now, represented everything he hated about backstage, about touring, about road crews. He was the sort of cunt who called a club a 'gig'. He'd call any venue a gig, whether it was Buckley Tivoli or Wembley Arena. He was everything he used to hate about Marty. He had that superciliousness – the sort a backstreet car mechanic uses to bamboozle unwitting customers with cocksure jargon. He wanted to make ordinary people feel inadequate. He was a cunt. So Wheezer butted him, fast as a bullet, right in the nose. The big fella collapsed in a heap, covering his face with his big, hairy hands. He was going to fill him in good style, when a flash in the corner of his eye reminded Wheezer there were onlookers. He looked up and caught each one's eye, individually, staring them out until each jerked his head down and got on with whatever he'd been doing before the dispute. One gave him a big thumbs-up. The stage manager sat there, snivelling, blood trickling through his sausagelike fingers. Wheezer crouched down, looking the other way for effect then catching the bloke's face betweeen finger and thumb, squeezing it.

'If there's any comeback on me or my band tonight, you're fucking dead. Yeah?'

He nodded. Wheezer went for a little walk all round his stage to give his racing, shaking heart chance to slow down again, before going where he'd been going before – to the Production Office.

They were more like a group again. Sitting in the dining compartment drinking chilled wine before they'd even looked at the menus, everyone could sense how much they had to be thankful for. They had things to look forward to. In a year of change, this was still Keva's constant, the credo to which he clung. Keep looking forward. Don't look back, or you die.

'It was me last time, wasn't it?' grinned Beano. 'Sulking on the train because me bird'd fucked me off . . .'

'Ay, skinnyarse, who's fucken sulking? Not me, matey. I'm the King of Rock 'n' Roll!'

They were all still twatted from the night before. James had been snorting throughout the whole thing with a Very Big radio personality, while the rest of them had hung around with Robbie Williams, the Special Guest Presenter Host, who had the keys to the hospitality caravan and who'd had them in stitches all day. He was cool, Robbie. He had a rather too large head, but they loved him. He was funny.

The shrieking from the crowd had been mind-splitting. Ten thousand recently-pubescent girls with their mums, aunties, big and little sisters, all squealing and screaming and shrieking, turning it up louder and louder, the nearer they got to climax time.

Climax time had been Boyzone, who'd shuffled around backstage, suitably amused and embarrassed by it all, killing time by making improper suggestions to the girls on the production team. They were a hoot too. Everyone was all right, but Boyzone and

438

Robbie Williams were top geezers, shrieking along backstage for the benefit of James's Shriekometer. Afterwards they all headed off to a massive post-awards party at the Hanover Grand, where the Grams hugged each other tearfully, wondering how all this had all happened so quickly. Ronan Keating got tipsy enough to ask Keva for his autograph.

'You're the king, man.'

'No, mate. You are. You're ace, you are.'

'No, man. I do what I do. But you're the king. The King of Rock 'n' Roll.'

'Shut up and buy us a bevvy . . .'

They were sound, all that *Smash Hits* mob. All the staff were dead nice, but the bands too – probably because they weren't in any kind of direct competition with the Grams, but nonetheless. They'd all come over and said hello, and they'd all been lovely. Everyone was blissfully blootered, but it'd all given Keva quite an unexpected lift. It was Christmas. Everyone loved him. Everyone loved each other. He didn't feel quite so cynical as he had done on Thursday and on Black Friday. Ah, Kiara . . . another one to push him away, just when he needed you most. Still, it would all be over soon. The day of reckoning loomed.

'Where'd *you* get to last night, Jimbo?' asked Wheezer. 'You missed a riot in the bar . . .'

James wiggled his eyebrows. Tony and Beano cringed, heads on forearms on the table. The train rattled on, taking them forward, and back.

'No! Don't! Please don't make us go through this again . . .'

Tony and Anita and Beano had just got back to their bedroom. They'd all been in the Gore's Green Room, where the dregs of the party had held sway until five fifteen when Anita, the new *Smash Hits* receptionist, had asked the time. Beano led a discordant punk a cappella version of The Who's '5.15' which, finally, snapped the patience of Steve, the night porter.

Anita followed Tony, drunk, stumbling up against him in a gauche attempt to let him know it was OK to fuck her. He looked at her dyed red hair, cut short, her hazel eyes, intense and close together, her slightly protruding top lip and he saw her wanting to be part of it all, wanting to be a mad one, a party animal. He couldn't do it. Not while she was so drunk. He tucked her up in his bed, kissed her on the forehead and watched her fall fast asleep, smiling. He turned to Beano.

'Room for an ample chappie?'

'Koff! Ample . . . fit three of you in here! You're normal, lar – I'm *thin*!'

And then the phone had gone. James. 'Listen to this . . .'

They'd heard the clunk of the phone being dropped on the bedside table, then a muffled, fervent, rhythmic slapping, like the punching sound in westerns but faster, really fast. Then came the noise, like a banshee in the manner of Norman Bates as his mother. It was a mad voice, almost a man's, a cracked, old man's voice. James was driving his victim wild.

'Oooooogh! Cok-cok-cok-cok! Yeeeegh! Ogh, cok! Ogh, cok! Ogh, cok-cok-cok! COK!'

If that wasn't enough to scare them, just as they were about to hang up, a young girl's voice drifted in. 'Save some for me, Jamie. Mum. Save some for me.'

Mum!

James beamed at Wheezer, whacked out of his mind, proud as punch. 'Mother and Daughter Act. Number Two. Could've had untold Sister Acts, but it's old hat an' that, that, innit? Even Snowy can get that . . .'

Wheezer shook his head admiringly. Beano peeped up from his hide.

'Is it safe to come out, yet?'

'Hey, you're just in time! I haven't told youse about her thrupennies, yet . . . fucking pure silicone! Fucking lovely! Had a few in the States who'd had little implants, had, like *essence* of implant, but these were gorgeous. Big hard squashy fucking cannonballs . . . *Xena* tits!'

Keva grimaced and smiled to himself, studying the menu through Armani shades on the Euston to Liverpool on the fourteenth of December. Just over two weeks now. And who the fuck *were* these people he was sitting with? What was this life of his? He couldn't say for sure, but he felt fine. And he still had things to look forward to.

Wheezer would've been lost without all this. That twenty-four hours when Keva had quit the band made this all the more wonderful to him – the faxes, the planning, the significance of his life and who he was and how his role in all of this would, in a small way, come to make a difference to people's lives. He loved it.

He read over the e-mail messages again, heart pounding, wanting to pick up the phone immediately and say YES! YES! YES!, but knowing that he couldn't. These messages, the big ones, always came in threes. Usually Knopf was first, him or Mel when it was to do with adds. There'd also be another, later on, from Amy, just being thorough.

This news must've come in just before close of business in LA last night. He'd checked into the office on his way to bed and there was nothing new, so this must've blown up last thing. There were four separate messages about it. Mel Parmese was first, timed at 18.18–2.18 a.m. UK time.

'Wheezer – Sensira just cancelled appearance at KROQ's Acoustic Christmas, Paramount Arena, 12/16. KROQ want Grams. Spoke Willard – no prob. flights etc. Just do it. Call me AS SOON as you receive this. ANYTIME. Just call – Mel.'

For a pulsating moment Wheezer had that old flush of inadequacy, that feeling of having been caught out. He'd slept like a bear last night. They were all probably trying to call him. What a nit! A real manager would've had a phone by the bed and sensors attached to his wrists to make him wake on the hour, every hour, to check whether he'd missed any critical calls.

Then, as he slowed himself down, he realised that they *hadn't* been trying to call. There were no messages on the ansaphone – and, anyway, what could he have told them at half-two in the morning?

No, the more he thought about it and the more that that first throbbing flush of excitement abated, the more Wheezer began to realise that this whole KROQ thing was untenable. It was tomorrow. It just wasn't fair on the band. He was going to knock it back.

But then, what if they think we're upstarts and refuse to ever play our records again . . .? Impossible! They were bound to see reason. Surely they knew that it was logistically, emotionally and creatively impossible for the band to just fly over and give a seamless acoustic show. They'd had no warning. No time to prepare a set. They'd be heroes if they could pull it off, but it wouldn't be the end of the world if they had to sack it.

The lists of radio adds and moves up the various charts seemed secondary. It was still a buzz to see those asterixes next to the sales and chart moves, indicating a bullet, a substantial rise over last week's move. Total sales of the album had shot to nearly 150,000. KROQ was key to all of this, he'd love to be able to thank them, but . . . it just wasn't on. He felt impregnable as he dialled up Mel to give him the bad news.

Keva leaned over Miles's shoulder, giddy with surprise and pleasure.

'That's IT! That's fucking IT!'

He laughed noiselessly in amazement and stared at the image on the screen, open-mouthed. He turned to Miles. 'You're a fucking genius . . .'

He'd been trying everything to regain the feel and the shape of 'Wellness'. He immersed himself in all the songs that suggested that mordant, despondent, decadent spirit. He went along to the Adelphi's fitness suite, hoping to find forlorn old hags labouring over the stepping machines but meeting only orange-skinned Cream-babes toning their midriffs.

He'd called Miles to talk through his idea for the sleeve art – a *Baywatch*-style line-up of radiant models in swimwear – but the models were going to be based on James's followers in the queue for the Roxy in LA. They were all going to be squatting in a line, Team Wellness style, but they'd be monopedes, paraplegics, obese teenagers, made-up old bags and haggard, sad transvestites. Miles had been cackling so much down the phone, loved the concept so much, that he told Keva he'd set about mocking something up immediately. He told him he'd have something for him later in the evening.

And he did. It was perfect. Even in rough form it was the sickest, cleverest, boldest, most ironic and eye-catching graphic since that amazing Diesel campaign. All it needed was a tune to complement it. He kissed Miles, who staggered backwards holding his heart like he'd been stabbed, and ran to get a cab back to Ivanhoe Road.

'Guy? Bob. Too bad about KROQ, man, but *que sera* . . .'

It took Guy half a minute to shake the sleep out of his mind, process the voice, try and recall who the fuck this voice belonged to, but Campione was already well away. He didn't even pause to acknowledge the unthinkable lateness of his call. As he slowly came to, Guy remembered Campione had been the only one to insist on taking his home telephone number. Rudy Wexner had *given* his and waited for the favour to be returned, but Bob had actually sat there with his organiser at the ready, waiting for Guy to give up the magic digits. He remembered other guys like Bob from before, when he was with MGR, guys who *had* to call you at home, *had* to call you out of hours, had to get this point across that they were totally dedicated to their job, that work was their life as well as their livelihood. He'd tried calling one or two them back, at mad hours, at weekends, at dawn, but each time it'd been: 'Guy! Hey! What's happening, man?' And always in the perkiest, brightest voices. At least Campione wasn't being perky. He was grave and gruff and macho, as always.

'. . . and, I mean it's not a *praaa-blem*. We can *live* with it. But . . . hang! I'm being stoopid, right? You know how it is. You're with me on this, right?'

He glanced at his clock. It was 3.47 a.m. That was after hours, even in LA. Fucking Campione was calling him up, needlessly, from the comfort of his own armchair as though it was a totally normal thing to do. And for what . . .?

'I mean, it means nothing to American kids. Ay to zed. Ay to zed! What the fuck is that to a kid in Minnesota?'

'What're you telling me, Bob? Please don't tell me that you want Keva to change his lyrics . . .' He starting laughing at the idea, hard. '. . . you want him to sing Ay to Zee, right?'

Campione was momentarily silent, then continued like a total fucking pro. 'NO! What, are you nuts! This guy's gonna sell six, eight, ten million albums for me . . . you think I'm gonna piss his nuts off by asking him *that*? NO WAY! We can do it right here in the studio. I've already booked the guy, Marty Looker – he can match, to the minutest degree the pitch, *every* nuance of Keva's voice. He doesn't have to leave his front room . . .!'

Guy was no longer guffawing. He was, all of a sudden, overcome with a dense, thickening fury. It was a general, spreading fury cocked at many ills, but this, from Campione was the most acute. Tony's words, by an alchemy of justice, drifted into his consciousness.

You don't have to smile at any cunt if you don't want to . . .

'Bob, stop it will you, please . . .?'

'Tell me that ain't fantastic, hey? Tell me you don't love it . . .'

'Bob. Fuck off.'

'One more, before we brave it?' squeaked Tony. He felt weak as fuck. Not ill, nothing like that, but fearful, timid every time he had to interface with the public, like he had no insides – just querulous space.

'Yeah! Come 'ead – one more!'

'Dunno, you know. I think we'd better just get down there. There was a fuck of a crowd outside when I came past before . . .'

They were sat in the Post Office in School Lane, an unfashionable old pub just up from the Bluecoat. They'd arranged to meet there *because* it was so untrendy. Another fifty yards, into Hanover Street and the golden square marked out by Bold Street, Berry Street, Duke Street and back along Hanover, and the Grams would have been unable to move. They'd have been celebrated to suffocation point. The bars and joints along Wood Street and Fleet Street were heaving with young drinkers, all lapping up the city centre Christmas craic. But down there in that little side street, within spitting distance of Central Station and Church Street and Clayton Square, the Grams and Wheezer sat unmolested, laughably got up in Puffa jackets and woollen hats to allow an extra level of anonymity.

'It's mad, innit? You go to fucken America where no cunt knows you and you get fucken mad security minding your arse for you, and you get back to your own town and it's . . . it's *scary* an' that, innit?'

'We shoulda got Burger up . . .'

'Why? People just want to shake your hand. They don't want to kill you . . .'

'Oh, aye? You want to see the ones who hang round outside our house. Ay, Kee? Are they fucken psychos or what?'

'They just . . . *watch*.' He pulled off his hat and scratched his head. 'Don't they? They *look*. Whatever time it is, they're out there, like, just . . . looking.'

'Sure they're not bagheads casing your gaff?'

'Fucken notten to rob in ours . . .'

Wheezer stood up. 'Shall we do it, then?'

Three of the others got up with him, draining glasses, eager to get out and do what it was that they did. Be recognised. Be pointed at. Be praised, thanked, touched, asked things. Tony stayed seated, looking down, holding his thighs.

'I can't do it.' Statement. 'I can't go out there.'

They'd spotted her, all of them, straight away. Her red coat and rouged cheeks and fearsome red lipstick flagged her up, but it was the outrageous beehive hairdo that made her outstanding. She was about seventy, and quite nuts. She waited in line cheerfully, cheerfully leaning out to aim a gummy smile at the group. Eventually she was there before them. She gurned at them. The boys smiled back. The queue behind pushed up, impatient. James broke the ice. 'Have you gorra CD you'd like us to sign, love?'

She beamed back at him. 'No.'

'Oh. Well, tell you what, queen, don't you go queuing up all over again.' He was talking very loudly. 'I'll get one brought over for you. All right, love. Is it for a prezzie, is it, girl?'

She blinked back. She had not a clue who he was. 'No.'

He scratched his head. Keva busied himself signing a young student's CD, his head kept resolutely down.

'Well, like . . . I don't know what to do to help you an' that, love. Why've you spent all that time queuing up an' that?'

She looked at him adoringly. 'You're faymush!'

He couldn't say which of the documents in front of him excited him most. One was a financial statement from Guy, listing all expenditure and income, and showing that, even after repayment

445

of the initial loan from Farquhar deBurret, after their distributor's cut, MCPS, tour deficit, wages, advances to band, studio costs, videos, pressing, artwork, pluggers, press, strikeforce, office, telephones, equipment and all the other costs they'd run up in pursuit of this dream – the band was due a cheque for over a million and a half quid. His heart had nearly come out through his ribcage as he'd got to the final few pages of the statement, eyes racing ahead, looking for the bottom line. 'Whadda we get! Whadda we get!'

When he saw it he actually swooned. He fell back in his big, comfy swivel chair and looked at the ceiling, gasping, like a sparrow that's just been shagged by a crow. They'd sold over 400,000 albums in the UK alone. They'd probably do another 100,000 over the Christmas period. The dealer price was over eight quid per CD – a gross of more than three million pounds, and rising, just in the UK, just on the album. Factor in the staggering success of 'Beautiful' and all the PRS royalties it'd brought in from radio and elsewhere, plus the sales from Germany, Spain and Japan in particular, and you were talking pay dirt. And then there was America.

The second document on his desk, the one which had made him jump up in the air after he'd ripped it from the fax and read it, was from Mel Parmese. Fuck knows how he'd got the news before anybody else – he'd sent it at 3.23 a.m. UK time. And it was news about MTV.

Dear Wheezy,

Great news! Buzz Bin on MTV from first week in January. Buzz Bin guarantees a minimum of 14, 15 plays a week – maybe more – then who knows? If the album carries on like this we'll go into major rotation.

Congratulations to yourself and the boys. You deserve it, you bunch of English freaks!

Your admiring co-conspirator

Parmese

There was a follow-up message on the ansaphone: 'Oh, uh, Wheezy, listen – that shit about MTV, you might wanna keep it to yourself, huh? I got the info hot off've the computers from an MTV source, but . . . when you speak with Campione and Nancy . . . you have to be *real* surprised and *real* delighted, yes? You ain't heard a thing about it. Good work. Over.'

You might wanna keep it to yourself! Bollocks! One of the few perks of this thankless job apart from getting indecently well paid, was breaking good news to ever more dependent news-junkie band members. He called Keva immediately and told him about MTV.

He didn't mention Guy's statement, though. He needed to talk to Guy about that first – clarify it. No cheque had accompanied the statement. He'd brought the account right slap bang up to date, even though he was only obliged to account up until September – their first six months of trading. Clearly, the bulk of the income had been generated after the release of *Powder* in September. If Guy had only shown figures up until then, they'd probably still be unrecouped. So what was he doing? Maybe he was just showing what was *due* next year, just to mollify them, to let them see that all the hard work was paying off. They were getting richer by the day. If that was the case, Wheezer was going to have to squeeze a hefty interim payment from him, just to oil the wheels, get them through this turbulent gear change. Each one of them had approached him about money in the past few days. Each one except Keva. Wheezer was going to have to get on top of it later.

First, though, he was going to allow himself a little pleasure. He pulled out the Rand McNally USA Road Atlas he'd bought in Melrose Avenue, and spread it open on the floor. Then he gathered up the third document from his desk – Todd's confirmed route for the American tour, plus offers from a dozen bands for buy-ons on to the UK tour.

He didn't know what the boys'd have to say about the thorny issue of buy-ons. A chuckling Purvis had told him the other day that it's a sure sign a group is doing well when they start getting moralistic about their earnings. Tracks being used on telly adverts. Compilation albums. And buy-ons. Making little groups pay for the privilege of supporting big groups on their big sell-out tours. Often, the real big groups would fuck off the buy-on, pissing off their managers by inviting their mates' bands on to the tour, or bands they just liked. Purvis loved all that stuff, bands going mad and having ideas of their own and making cunts of themselves.

Himself, he had it all justified in his own mind. Bigger venues. More spectacular lighting. Chunkier PA systems with sub-bass and all the trimmings. It all cost money, the crusade to put on a show to remember for the general public. If they could claw back some of those costs by charging an up-and-coming band a small consideration for the kudos and the exposure of opening the show for them – charging their very willing record companies, that is – then why not? A £25,000 buy-on was a bargain. £25,000 to play in front of 100,000 potential new fans. The same money'd barely buy you three full-page adverts. One band, The Velcro Puppets, wanted to pay £30,000 – but they were rank. He'd talk it all through with the guys on the way to London and pop in and see Todd while they were rehearsing for Jools Holland – that's if Todd wasn't already waiting down at LWT for them. It'd be unlike him to miss an opportunity like that. Nice problem, anyway. He flicked open the atlas and studied Todd's itinerary. It was exactly what he'd asked for. They were going fucking everywhere.

January Dates

20	San Jose
21	San Francisco
22	Sacramento
23	Medford
25	Portland
26	Seattle
27	Vancouver
29	Spokane
30	Butte
31	Idaho Falls

February Dates

2	Salt Lake City
3	Las Vegas
5	Santa Barbara (Gia Demarco's First Friday*)

March Dates

26 Richmond
27 Norfolk
29 Raleigh
30 Wilmington
31 Columbia

April Dates

1 Augusta
2 Atlanta
4 Panama City
5 Orlando
* *Live Cable TV show from amazing natural arena Santa Barbara Municipal Bowl. Show goes into six million homes in California. Very prestigious and well worth doing. More TV will be factored in as and when confirmed. Expect LOTS!*

That was a *tour*! Fifty-eight cities, weaving in and out of the heartland, penetrating Mel's Secondaries and Tertiaries . . . It was twice the size of a Medsin tour. No other British band had attempted a tour like this since Bush – and look at them! By the time the band were taking their week off – maybe he could think about giving them ten days – they'd have played to over 150,000 new fans. 150,000 converts, all knocked out by the – what had Pat McIntosh called it? The *coruscating desolation* of the Grams. Once the MTV rotation was starting to bed in and have an effect on sales, Worldwide would be able to haul in all the right TV shows. Arsenio. Jay Leno. The band were going to go nuclear. They'd sell five million in the States alone. Easy.

He lavished over the itinerary again. It was mouth-watering. It was the mad places that excited him, the idea of the Grams going into Butte, Montana and Richmond, Virginia. He couldn't wait. It was a slightly more taxing itinerary than he'd led the group to expect, but . . . they were getting the hang of this. They were getting to understand that this, *now*, was the most crucial time in their short existence. If they could consolidate, make good all the foundations they'd laid – flog their arses for another six or nine months, basically, then they could go to ground. Do fuck all. Think about writing another album, but in their own time. The time scale of the second record wouldn't matter that much, so long as they got this one right. If they could crank themselves up a gear, find the strength and the will to fight through this draining, emaciating period and come to relish the situation they were in, they could transform *Powder* from being a huge success into a genuine modern classic. A phenomenon. Most groups'd fall by the wayside at this point. They'd see their figures and think, 'Fuck it! Who needs another million when you can have so much fun spending your first?' But he had no worries about the Grams on that score. Keva wanted to take the band as far as they could possibly go. He knew they'd be up for it.

They were strangely quiet on the train down. Wheezer had wanted to capitalise on his captive audience and run through all the outstanding things, ratify one or two untidy loose ends and make sure that everybody was fully in sync for the big push ahead in the New Year, but something told him not to push it. Tony was drinking already – it wasn't eleven yet – and James was staring into space. Beano had gone down last night, straight after the HMV signing, to be with Celeste. He felt for Beano, he truly did sympathise with the little fella, but he had grave misgivings about the course his true love was taking.

Wheezer was reading *Music Week*.

'*ReHab Goes Into Orbit.*' That was the second lead story on the front page. '*Grams hits stoke deBurret venture.*'

It was mostly about Guy and his past successes in A&R, his risk investment and the massive sales he'd achieved at home and abroad. He was in line for an Industry Award at the Brits. But the Grams wouldn't be at the Brits. They wouldn't be at MIDEM. They'd be in Japan and Australia, making Guy's reputation for him. It was annoying, no more. Praise was great, true recognition was better and the riches it could reap was best of all. But since the tricky stuff about money had been settled out, it was beginning to feel like a team effort once more. Guy seemed happy, he was interested again, but he wasn't interfering. Wheezer had a free hand. Things were OK. He'd enjoyed the *Music Week* acclaim as though it were his own.

Tony sat there, gripping the table, feeling the walls coming in on him. There was no Beano on board to calm him, just the others, himself and his can of Worthington. His breath came hard and quick. He felt hemmed in, threatened by some invisible, menacing presence. Someone was out to get him.

He got up, electing to walk it off, walk the length of the train until his head felt right again. No way was he claustrophobic – this was more . . . more of a dread sensation, a foreboding that something bad was about to happen.

He pushed his way through into the next carriage, relaxing a little, but then imagining that, as he made his way, people were looking up and recognising him and talking about him.

'There he is . . .'

'There's thingyo . . .'

'That's the fella from that Grams, innit . . .'

He accelerated, attracting tuts and looks from the passengers he knocked into or tripped over. 'They don't even know my name . . .' he gasped as he staggered ahead, panicked. 'They know me kite and that, they think they know me. Nobody knows my name . . .'

He stopped by a half-open window as the train rattled on through a tunnel, giving him the respite of a delicious swoosh of fast air. He saw the First-Class seats ahead and, feeling the luxurious chill of the air-conditioning, he knew he had to stay there until London. They couldn't get at him in here. If the ticket inspector wanted another hundred nicker off him, so fucking what? He was happy to cough up. He was more than able to cough up.

He slumped into a vacant seat. There were loads. He'd noticed that last week. The trains down to London were so-so busy, but the one they'd got back had been chock-a-block. They'd rounded on Wheezer for First-Class tickets, next time, or at least Silver Service. So much for that. Nineteen-pound Virgin Advance tickets, as per usual. He was off his head, The Wheeze. Two businessmen were talking in hushed voices. He knew why. They were talking about him. His heart vaulted again. How much further to Euston? He couldn't put up with this for much longer. Maybe he should confront the two blokes, ask them to say it to his face. No. It hadn't happened, yet. It might not happen. He only needed to deal with it when it happened. Until that moment, he should put them out of his mind.

He'd felt OK again since they got to Maida Vale, and now he felt as happy as a lark. Guy, Todd and Mack Hansen had turned up at the Lamacq recording with funny masks and a crate – a *crate* – of champagne. There was a lovely atmosphere down there. Everybody, the BBC team, band, everyone was having a great time. The more of them there were, the safer Tony felt, and the more he drank, the more he felt foolish for the way he'd been thinking before. Sitting in the calming ambience of I-Thai, sucking happily on his fourth Tiger Beer, a flushed Radio One researcher to his immediate left and the reassuring poshness of Guy to his right, he couldn't for the life of him remember what all the fuss had been about. He was looking forward to Christmas, to that precious bit of free time – but this was ace. He fancied he might throw the lips on the BBC girl, if it seemed like the right thing to do, later. Possibly.

They sat in the canteen at BBC Elstree studios, spotting the *EastEnders* stars.

'There's Pat Butcher!' gurgled Tony, too loudly, almost jumping out of his seat.

'Apparently she's dead posh, you know,' ventured Beano.

'Is she?'

'Yeah. *Really* posh . . .'

James's cherubic face lit up. 'Come 'ead! Let's go an' talk to her! See what she sounds like an' that?'

Tony looked down at his plate, bashful, his dark eyelashes fluttering as he tried to pluck up the courage. 'Nah! We can't do that! Can we?'

'Course we can. She'll be made up. I bet you – I *bet* you she's got a lad or a daughter or something who's a mad Grams fan. I fucken bet you . . . come 'ead! She'll love it! What's her real name?'

'Isla St Clair.'

The riot of laughter from their table could be heard all over the canteen. Everyone looked up to see what was so funny. When

Sensira saw who it was, they were even more nervous. Helmet scuttled off back to the dressing-room with his KitKat.

James stared in disbelief at the fantastic grey BBC carpet with yellow speckles for the third time in twenty minutes, shaking his head to help get his message across. Beano and Wheezer and Tony had heard it already, but these girls from *EastEnders* hadn't.

'Fuckinell! I hope they're putting the money they saved on this gaff into your pay packets, are they?'

'You're joking aintcha? We don't get paid fack all! Naffink like you rock stars . . .'

She was a little bit older-looking in real life, but cute as fuck. Perched on James's knee, pert as an apple, she kissed him right on the lips. 'This one's mine, anyway!' she cackled. 'NYAGH-HAGH-HAGH! He's got all the fackin charlie! NYAGH-HAGH-HAGH!'

James slipped his hand under her skirt and prised three fingers under her knicker elastic. He could not for the life of him remember her fucking name. He didn't even know which one she was off *EastEnders* – he just vaguely knew the face and knew that she was up for a walloping courtesy Love, J., Mr.

'OI!' she warned, jumping up in the most mocking of mock protests. 'Saucy! Keep yer 'ands to yourself!'

James kissed her neck. 'Just a bit of scumffin'. No harm in a bit of a scumff an' that, ay?'

His hand went under her flimsy top. It had a tiny Chanel logo on the join of the slight V-neck, but it was too cheap to be Chanel. You wouldn't get inside a Chanel that easy. She located and removed his hand patiently. 'Come on, love. Hands off, eh? Where we goin' later, anyway? What time do you boys knock off here?'

He admitted defeat. 'About nine, isn't it?'

'Supposed to be.'

'Nine, yeah.'

'Smashing. We'll wait for you, yeah?'

'Sound.'

'Got any more charlie, you tight Scouse sod? NYAGH-HAGH-HAGH!'

He echoed her love-call with his fullest-fruit chuckle and fished out the wrap. 'It *is* a disgrace, though. That fucken carpet is a fucken disgrace . . .'

Helmet, just about to come into the bar to try and make his peace, heard James's gruff Liverpool accent and heard the terrifying laughter and turned back down the corridor.

Wheezer was still breathless with excitement a full five minutes after Chris Cowie had left the room. Sensira had pulled out! They'd blown out *Top of the Pops*!

The way the producer had just explained it, Al Meredith and Helmet had been to see him about the running order. Wheezer hadn't even glanced at his copy – the Grams were on, that was all that mattered – but there it was in black and white. Sensira's was to be the final performance. They were closing the show. What was the problem?

Their problem was that closing *Top of the Pops* was seen by veterans of the show as the least prestigious slot. The performance was often shortened by the end credits. Sensira wanted at least as much screen time as the Grams. Indeed they were suggesting that the Grams close the show. Cowie had left them in no doubt as to where their suggestions would best fit. Helmet, apparently, had thrown a tantrum and stormed out.

'What I'd like you to consider,' said Chris Cowie. He paused and looked Wheezer in the eye, his Geordie baritone remaining even. 'I'd really appreciate it if you could perhaps do a longer version of the track. You know on the CD, there's that lovely extended mix? Lovely sort of acousticky intro? I mean, would you mind asking the band? It'd really help us out . . .'

Would he mind asking? Would he! Sucking on his inhaler, Wheezer skipped out of the dressing-room to find the boys and impart the sad tidings.

Wheezer sat in silence as the minicab picked its way through Borehamwood High Street. Mad that this utter nonentity of an anytown main road should provide the only way in to one of the UK's creative institutions. Too mad. Still, that was *Top of the Pops* for another six months or so. The Christmas Special was one more affirmation of how far the Grams had come. Only the biggest and the best were invited. Sensira were crazy to blow it out. They were losing it.

The plastic burn of flesh on hot vinyl signalled James and his friend squirming deeper into their embraces on the back seat. They'd been at each other since the moment the old Sierra had pulled away from the studios' security lodge. Wheezer, in a disoriented moment, had tried to give the two BBC security stewards a tip. They'd been totally baffled, staring from Wheezer to the proffered notes, back to Wheezer until he'd fled in embarrassment. As soon as the car had reversed and five-point-turned away, James had launched into his sexual improv show, as though the motion of the car was a necessary part of the act. Wheezer thought he'd leave it a moment, let them get into it a bit before copping an eyeful. There were some good noises coming from her now. Good nonsense from James too. Where does a – basically, a fat fool – get the confidence to come out with that shit? In the back of a car, in front of non-participants? In *Borehamwood*? Listen to him . . .

'Pull those wet . . . those wet fucking knickers right down for me . . . *yeah* . . . take them right off . . . mmmm . . .'

Didn't care a fuck about the cabbie. Or Wheezer. He chanced a look over his shoulder. Oh, nice! Nice . . . her little skirt was back over her belly, her arse was six inches off the seat, only heels and elbows keeping her up, and Jimbo's head was clamped between her thighs. Very nice . . . Wheezer adjusted the mirror on his useless sunscreen and settled back to watch. He was getting a stiffy and his band had everything to play for. He couldn't ask for more.

'Ah, come on, man! Play the white man! Don't hold out on me . . .'

'I swear to you, Ben – I haven't got none . . .'

Ben licked his lips nervously. He looked completely fucked, dark purple rings around his young eyes, like he hadn't slept for months. His nose was scabbed and seeping. The glamour drug was paying off.

'Well, here y'are. Lend's a score, yeah? Fuckinell, man – you and me used to be mates, yeah? Lend's a score. I'll get us sorted, yeah?'

'For a score?'

'He owes me. The guy owes me bigtime. Come on, man. I'll be two fucking minutes.'

Just as James was about to cough up the money, he spied the unmissable flaming head of Adam Rice with Ally Bland, coming right towards him. He almost leapt on them with gratitude. 'Listen!' he muttered. 'Sort this cunt out, will you! Just fluff him up! I'll see you right, like, I've got stacks, but I don't want him on me case all night . . .'

Adam stepped up to Ben, gripped his head in an armlock and snogged him passionately on the lips, for ages, until it looked like Ben was going to pass out. The second Adam relinquished his hold Ben gaped at him, then legged it.

'Easy,' shrugged Adam. 'Who wants some drugs . . .?'

They pimp-rolled like three warlords, thinking they were It, back past security, into the Red Room, nodding to Jarvis and Chris Evans. Gangsters were plying actresses with powder and champagne. Danny Baker was swallowing a pint of lager in one draught, to the huge amusement of Sid Owen and Ulrika Jonsson. Every single person in there was a Face. Everyone was drinking and drinking and drinking, laughing and laughing and laughing. The room hummed with the delirious energy of a hundred unhinged egos, all crackling and spitting, high on coke and bubbly and their own beauty and brilliance and fame and fucking good fortune.

'Grab a butcher's of your fackin singer!' Adam nearly pulled James's head off in his eagerness to point it at the spectacle in the corner. 'Fackin Chrimbo snogfest or what!'

Keva was in a different corner, snogging a different girl. He was eating her head off. He'd been eating another girl's head when James had popped out, only five minutes ago, to find Kanu, the bloke he'd been introduced to earlier. Ben must've seen him talking to him at the foot of the stairs, by the secret door. He must have walked over the tops of people's heads to get there as fast as he did.

'LOOK at the kant!'

Any other time he would've stayed with Adam and giggled at the spectacle of Keva McCluskey, lurching from girl to girl, from mouth to mouth, sightlessly fitting his lips over the next set of lips and giving them what for . . . But he wanted to find what's-her-name. She'd disappeared. Probably getting her hand inside Sid Owen's kecks.

'Here!' gasped Adam as James tried to sidle away. 'Watch this.'

He strode over, excused Keva's latest flame from duty and set about snogging him with all the passion of a B-movie swashbuckler. Keva was gloriously unaware who he was with, what he was doing, where he was. He was having a great time. That's all he knew.

The big security guy ambled over to Wheezer, smiling.

'Sorry to disturb you again, mate. This one's really persistent. You can usually tell the chancers, but this guy say's he's been with Keva all night . . . just popped out to get something for him . . .'

He rolled his eyebrows at The Wheeze. 'Sorry about this . . . can't exactly pull Keva, can I . . .?'

They both looked at Keva, lying on the floor now, writhing with a little black dress. Wheezer chortled. 'No problem. Come on. I'll sneak downstairs and have a peek who it is . . . it ain't *Burger*, is it?'

'Nah. Working the Arena tonight, innee?'

But Wheezer didn't even need to get halfway down the short flight of steps. He could hear Pat McIntosh, affronted, his sense of self inflated beyond any reason, demanding to be let in.

'I am Mr McCluskey's official biographer! He'll never set foot in this dump again when he hears about this . . .!'

Wheezer shrugged a patient disclaimer at the security bloke. 'Don't know him. I'd throw the cunt out . . .'

'Fine. Sorry about that . . .'

Out on the street, fucked, backs of eyeballs throbbing with fatigue but hearts fluttering and minds deluded, they found themselves the centrifugal force in a party of twenty or so who just wanted to carry on, anywhere. The Grams – James, Keva and Wheezer – were the aces in the pack. With their well-known faces, the rest of the gang knew they'd get in too, if they stuck close enough. It was a nice little crew, anyway – a handful of music people they semi-knew, friends of people they'd met somewhere or other, a few rampant trendies and a young couple, who'd like nothing more than to spend their last thirty pounds in the world on drinks for Keva and James. They'd walk home to Victoria Park, if necessary. This was a dream come true for them.

They stood out there, shivering on the corner of Long Acre, trying to make the right choice.

'Met Bar?' offered Gary Wilkinson, the producer. James had been promising the Grams' next album more sincerely as the night was punctuated with each new bump of coke.

'Too far,' said a voice. London via Norfolk. 'We'll never get cabs . . .'

'The End's open 'til eight, isn't it?'

'Is it? You sure . . .'

'Think so. Special licence . . .'

'It'll be fucking rammed, anyway . . .'

The voice again. Wheezer looked up, to appreciate him. He was marvellous. Six foot six, maybe six-seven, maybe even taller . . . He was about twenty, clear-skinned, with a detached aura about him, as though he were taking everything in, but slowly, processing everything that was said and reacting to it in his own good time. He seemed to know what he was on about. He was dressed, with minute accuracy, in *Clockwork Orange* gear. No make-up, though. He saw Wheezer clocking him. He offered his hand in a friendly shake.

'A'right, mate. Wheezer Finlay.'

'Alex,' he said. Uh-oh. 'We should go to the spiel, down Lisle Street.'

Other voices took this up.

'Yeah. Nice one.'

'The taxi place?'

'Yeah. New gaffers, though. Only been there coupla weeks. Shouldn't be too mobbed . . .'

'We can walk it in five minutes.'

So they did. Wheezer, more intoxicated by the knowledge that he'd be flying, by private jet, back to Liverpool in exactly eight hours than by the copious lagers and bubblies he'd accepted during the night – nobody'd let him buy them a drink – was determined to hang on until the end, whenever and wherever the end might be. He had that lovely, buzzing momentum now, that early-hours tingle of nicotine and booze and possibility, when all he wanted to do was to keep going.

Rounding them up was easy. Nobody had made it any further than the Green Room. They slept where they fell. Tony Snow still had his lips clamped around the breasts of Queen Victoria, whose austere bust he'd carried down from the landing at six this morning.

'Hey! Wheezer! I just called to wish you and the guys a good holiday . . .'

Did you fuck.

'Mr Knopf . . .! On Christmas Eve . . . I'm honoured!'

Too hesitant, too suspicious to even *sound* spontaneous, but no worries. They both knew where they stood.

'Yeah . . . I just kinda ambled by the office for an hour, and I just saw this itinerary for the Grams and I just wanted to tell you . . . I AM FLOORED . . .!'

'Isn't it cool?' Wheezer was flushed with pride, in spite of himself.

'Cool! It's *awesome*! That is a major fucking commitment to the USA, pardon my French. I gotta tell ya, that is the kind of commitment I am looking for from an English band that wants to break big in this country . . . I mean, with MTV and the kinda support Myra drummed up before her departure . . .'

There was an infectious liberation about Knopf's speech patterns. He wasn't shitting. He was full of enthusiasm for the Grams, all of a sudden. It was business, of course. He wanted to succeed and to associate himself with success . . . but the guy was at work, on Christmas Eve, *raving* about the band. He was unguarded, for once. He was letting it slip that English bands, with their poncy ten-day tours and their drug habits and their aversion to Meet 'n' Greets and their all-round slovenly, late-night, sleep-in, miss-the-interview routines were not his priority. But he was changing his tune, with this. He was joining them, instead of trying to beat them.

'. . . I gadda tell yah, Campione seems pissed at the band. Something to do with Guy? Leave me out of it . . .'

Wheezer could picture Knopf sitting back in his swivel chair, digesting statistics off his screen, talking into his headset, flapping both hands at thin air in denial.

'. . . I never told you that, right? But Willard is going to be so up his ass on this reckud, he *has* no choice . . . he's gotta *work* this fucking reckud. And if he don't . . .'

You'll be the new Head of Promotion, mused The Wheeze.

'Anyway. I guess that's what I kinda wanted to let you guys know . . . I just wanted you guys to know I am really with you on this . . . You have a Cool Yule, dude!'

Wheezer grinned to himself. Now people were killing each other for the band.

Keva felt wretched. The sniffles had started on Christmas morning, and by lunchtime he could add a poisonous sore throat, plummeting body temperature, shakes and shivers, stinging eyes and a thumping headache. That, at least, answered the question of which Christmas dinner invitation he was going to take up – none of them. He was going to bed with a hot-water bottle and a book. He was going to stay there, until he could feel the whites of his eyeballs again. Maybe he could get a message to Lorraine first – but her legendary annual dinner party at Keith's was a non-starter for him, this year.

He actually found a bit of a spring in his step as he bounced up to bed. The entire house was his for the next three days. He could just lie there, looking shocking, being ill. He could sleep and sleep and sleep. Claw back some goodness into a life gone wrong. His metabolism was crying out for water, sleep and vegetables. What he'd been feeding it was drugs, booze and debilitating late nights. Dirty sex and snogging, lots of snogging, in London, of all places. A city which feeds a year-round influenza epidemic, each new outbreak caught from the previous bug, the cycle never properly broken for more than a week as each new case infects another victim. He'd strode into a succession of small, overheated venues and snogged his way through the guest list, night after night.

It made his palate turn green just thinking about it. He'd

known, instinctively, for ages, that at the end of this mad December at the end of this mad year would come his thirtieth birthday, which he would spend alone, in bed, shattered. He threw himself onto the mattress and eagerly opened up *Filth*, which he'd been trying to read since August.

He couldn't concentrate. He knew that he was very unwell, and he felt wonderful about that. He couldn't fully take hold of the fantastic concept that he could do what he wanted for a few days. Hector wouldn't be back, probably, until New Year. He was off to be huge in Crosby. Fabulous! He lay back on his pillow, and revelled in his freedom. He revelled, too, quickly, in the idea of his dying there, alone. Of all his fans lining the route to the burial ground, inconsolable. Mountains of flowers, in spite of Wheezer's request that donations be made to Music Therapy. The convoy of cars, driving in slow procession, would stretch back miles and take hours to arrive. Paul McCartney and Tony Blair would read passages from the Bible and bewail this tragic loss to Britain's cultural richness. And the girls . . . wailing and gnashing their teeth, throwing themselves on his grave, distraught. Hannah. Kiara. Evie. Myra . . .

He sat bolt upright. Maybe a glamorous waste of his life was not called for, just yet. He'd been in bed ten minutes and his sense of freedom was starting to be replaced by the usual tristesse. What was he doing in bed on Christmas Day? Who would believe that rock music's brightest new light was forced to be alone on the most celebrated day in the calendar? How many other stars, here and abroad, were on their own on Christmas Day? Loads, probably. He slumped back under the sheets. His aching throat was killing him, but each glass of water sent his body temperature into the tundra. Shivering, hand trembling, he swallowed three Nurofen and glugged a bitter slug of Night Nurse, hoping it'd knock him out quickly.

Waiting for the soothing numb of unconsciousness, he flicked through Wheezer's end-of-year summation. He couldn't be arsed when he'd got in, last night. He'd got a cab into town with James and ended up trawling around the Mathew Street side of town. Looking at it, now, it was mainly a sign-off from Wheezer, to ease his conscience about going off for a week right before their next bout of touring. All the future plans, itineraries, contact names and numbers and financial computations were there. Bloody Wheezer was earning a fortune, that's for sure. No wonder he could afford to buy them all Armani jumpers for Chrimbo. Fuck! Just looking at those festivals alone – there was over three-quarters of a million quid's worth of fees there, for half a dozen appearances. That's . . . a hundred and fifty grand for The Wheeze, just for picking up the phone and saying 'yes'. Fuck!

Concentrating on it all only honed his consciousness. He wanted sleep. But the same little item kept invading his quiet. He sat up again and tried to take it in properly. If he was reading this right, the PRS and MCPS element of this statement – the publishing, basically – accounted for the best part of two million pounds. He couldn't remember. Had he signed the publishing over to Guy? He knew that 'Beautiful' was a big radio hit, but two million! Jesus . . . He'd felt angry enough about Guy and Wheezer conspiring, without him, after everything that'd been said, to dole out the fifty grand to everyone. He'd already made a date in his mind to confront Wheezer as soon as he got back about *that* little scenario. But *this* . . . it was unthinkable. His songs were keeping ReHab afloat. *He* was paying back Guy's loan to his brothers. Any other day and he would've got straight on the phone to the Wolfman. Jesus! He was so tired. So tired . . .

Only when his brain thumped with the relentless shiftings of decision did Keva fall into a troubled sleep.

As they'd said their farewells outside the airport on Christmas Eve, Wheezer had handed each of them an envelope.

'Don't open it until you get home,' he said.

'What is it? Our P45?' Tony had said.

But it wasn't. It was a bundle of information and statistics and phone numbers and, pinned to the topsheet, was a printout from ReHab showing that each of them had had £50,000 transferred into their accounts by Guy. Fifty grand!

James, now, was wasting no time in conspicuously consuming his own first chunk of the windfall. Two sleek navy blue Saab limousines had collected himself, his mother, his father, his sister, his brother, two aunties, two uncles and a grandmother from their

Crosby semi, where they'd been celebrating madly for the best part of two days, and transported them to Beecher's Brook restaurant. Everything was on James, and he wanted them all to order whatever and as much of it as they wanted.

'Bah! Humbug!' he chuckled. 'Fill yer boots an' that!' He looked down on them all ruddily, and beamed out his pleasure. Life was great. He tackled his lobster with gusto.

His dad, sitting next to him, thin and immaculately dressed as always, leaned into his ear. 'Chump? This is marvellous. I'm so pleased for you, lad . . .'

He put his arm around his father. He was almost in tears. 'This is just the start of it, Dad. I'm going to *well* look after you . . .'

His dad looked choked, humbled, not quite comfortable. He looked down at his napkin in his lap.

'But Dad . . . ?'

He looked up again.

'No more Chump, hey?'

He thumbed-up his son, who baffled him with a back-to-front clenched fist handshake.

Tony got off the train at Ormskirk and, after a cold, shuffling wait in the deserted terminus, took the first bus out, out through Burscough and on to Parbold. He felt more relaxed with each new stop, taking him further and further away from the teeming populus and the curious, threatening passers-by. His grip on the estate agent's details became less tense and, bit by bit, he began to breathe more easily. Wheezer's suggestion of the Ventolin and Beclazone inhalers was a help, but that wasn't the problem here. It wasn't his breathing. The problem was him – and other people. Other people were getting him down. Even on the ride up to Ormskirk on a mainly empty train, he'd set his head at the floor and hadn't moved it, through all the stiffness of a jolting half-hour journey, for fear of catching someone's eye.

Out, now, at Parbold Hill, he couldn't ever imagine being so traumatised. This was just . . . he breathed the cold fresh air deep down, pulled his woolly hat further over his ears and set off to get a feel for some of these little houses and cottages. This would do him – it really would. It would be, in every sense, his haven, his escape, his bolthole. From the first time they came up here as kids he had sensed the great, ancient *immunity* of the place and now he could feel it pouring through him again, unravelling him and making sense of his stupid life. He wanted to laugh out loud, then drink twenty pints of bitter with a poacher. If his life, now, meant roaming around the world making the thud-notes in these songs that everyone was going so mad over, then he'd do it, happily, with energy, if he had all this to come back to. He sat down on the hillside and looked out. Liverpool was miles away. The little cottage he liked the look of – he and Beano had talked about nothing but cottages, and Aga cookers and real-ale pubs the longer the year had dragged on – was £49,500. Only two bedrooms, but so what? It bore the magic words: *In need of a full programme of restoration and renovation.*

What that meant was no UPVC double glazing; no fitted kitchen; no red-brown stained Canadian cherrywood-type doors with matching window frames and brass-effect door furniture; and no bloody lavatory suite in soothing champagne. What it meant was that, with any luck, the place probably still had coal fires. Probably had a cast-iron bath and bog. Might not have a damp course or central heating, but he could use these things to get the price down. Joey would be made up helping him get the place nice. He had every intention of spending his advance on securing that little cottage for himself before he left for Japan. Looking at it, now, it was obviously unoccupied. It was in probate, as sure as anything. Whoever the beneficiaries were, they'd be pleased to get forty grand on that place – so long as they got it quickly. It was all going his way, he felt. It was meant. If he could pluck up the courage to call up the estate agent and have a look around the place today, there was no reason why he couldn't turn all this around very quickly.

The sticky warmth of her blood came right into his dream. He was going down on Kiara, relishing her, and she was wildly into him. He was talking all through it, telling her how her cunt smelt, and then her smell came into the dream too. But it wasn't the smell of her love. She smelt of putrid, stinking shit. And, as she started to come, as she bucked herself higher to grind herself on his chin, her juices enveloped him. Thick, sticky juices, then dark, trickling, warm blood. He could not back away from it. She held his head there, the blood washing all over him as she laughed and laughed.

'*You came back for more! Hah-hah-hah! You came back for more . . .*'

He tried to reach out and claw himself away from this awful thing, which he knew, somewhere in his stoned, numb animus, was not real. And now, in this half-consciousness, in this haunting, feverish limbo, the tune sung out through the stifling, clashing nightmares. It was the whole tune – the all of it. Coming suddenly awake, awash with freely-running sweat and salt and stink, he groped for the light switch. The smell hit him full force in the eyes, stinging him, making him roll over the bedside, dry-retching, in agony.

He was covered in yellow-green shit. The bed was soaked in slick, spawnlike yellow faeces. But the tune was still there, it's plangent knell flooding him. He dragged himself up and out of the bed, padding his slop across the floorboards, and sat down with the Martin to write 'Wellness'.

He'd never been so glad to see James. Within moments of his being there, Keva was feeling better.

'Happy New Year an' that!' Fuckinell! You're yellow! It stinks in here!' He threw open the big sash window. 'How long you been like this an' that . . .?'

It made Keva laugh, faintly.

'You've got fucken . . . yella fever . . .!' He threw some mail on the bed. 'I thought you'd done one when I seen all these piled up.'

Cards. Birthday cards. It must be the day then. He'd been there, in bed, for nearly a week.

'Jesus, fuck! You're a skinny cunt at the best of times, but you look . . .' He trailed off, shaking his head in dismay. 'I'll get a pan of chicken soup on the go. Loadsa noodles. That's the best thing for . . . whatever you've got.'

He sifted through the cards and letters, tons of them, postmarks dating back weeks. Wheezer must've redirected a bundle. There was the usual spread of goofy boys wanting to tell him how he'd rescued them from the slough of despondency, inspired them, connected with them and, some of them, made them realise it's OK to be gay. There were letters from boys and girls who'd started bands, enclosing cassettes of their baleful, often laughably bad songs, asking for support slots on the new tour. He tossed them all in the bin. He didn't even want to think about those people – the Helmets of the world.

And then there were the porno letters. Mainly from girls who sounded young, under twenty – though some of them were clearly older. One or two of them he read and reread, dick in hand, one eye on the bedroom door.

Dear Keva,

I've just opened NME *and saw that you're coming to Brum on 25 April. I'm counting the days because that is the night I will finally feel your dick inside my aching cunt. I'll be right down the front wearing my pink Wonderbra with my lovely tits pushed together so you can see everything. God I want you to stick your big hard dick in between my tits and fuck them till you come, then stick it my mouth so I can swallow your lovely seed. I swear to God I'll swallow every drop then get you hard again so you can fuck my tight cunt until I'm out of my mind. God just thinking about your hard dick going inside me is making me come . . .*

She left a half page, a big greasy patch smeared across it, then took up where she left off.

Sorry, I just had to go and strum myself off – here's a little sample of what'll be waiting for you, my darling . . .

It got a bit religiose after that, and he got bored. He stuck the letter in his 'keep' pile, consisting, so far, of two letters and a card.

The card was from his mother. His first instinct was to hurl it into the bin as soon as he recognised her flamboyant hand, but his curiosity haunted him. He thought she'd given up the chase. He had not heard from her, by post, telephone or intermediary, since just after he and Jimbo moved into Ivanhoe. He'd been bracing himself for another flurry of activity from her after 'Beautiful' took

467

the nation by storm. If she'd seen his *e.p*, it would have torn her apart. But there'd been nothing from her. Nothing.

He read the card again. Beautifully precise, as always. Dramatic, but with not a word wasted. Except one. The word 'we'. That was one word which, in the context of his mother and her new life as Mrs Wilson, held only horrors for Keva McCluskey.

My Keva, my baby, always my boy. Is it so long since then? I hope so dearly that your life is all that you want of it and send my love, a mother's love, on your birthday. I miss you terribly. In spite of all that has passed, we feel so proud of you, so much a part of all that you do.

God bless you, child.

Your loving mum

His fat tears splashed on to the card, a Medici print of a Virgin and Child. The hauntings would have begun, had he the strength to let them in. But he still felt weak. His eyeballs were grey and their backlight was dim. His legs still ached and his skin was clammy. But it would be soon. Soon he would open up that door and walk through it. It had been coming. It had been coming back. And now, as never, he was ready. After sinking himself into the bath at last to scour away a week of seeping mania, he barely had the strength to towel his back dry. But he was getting better. Tomorrow he'd be stronger again.

He'd forgotten about the Peel session. He'd been tinkering in his room, trying to polish the structure of 'Wellness'. He was determined to get it down, just the basic form, on that same mono recorder he'd demo'd with from his very first songs, before he lost the pattern again. He turned on the radio to blanket his chicanery from James. Straight away it was Peel's voice. Not the last bit of the Festive Fifty that Keva was somehow expecting, but them. The Grams. Their version of New Order's 'In A Lonely Place'. And it was stunning. When they'd done it at Maida Vale, laying it down live, as a group instead of individually, everyone connected with the studio, everyone there from motorcycle couriers to production assistants had stopped what they were doing. It was a leviathan, the sense of loss aching from every tremor of Keva's voice. The mood and the build of their cover was more sumptuous than the original, but Keva's bleak vocal was sublime.

'*How I wish you were here with me now.*'

Waking now finally from his illness, however long it had been, he knew he was falling into a mood and a time when his songs would come. 'Wellness' had come and, hearing this now, the germ of another was appearing. It was folly that he was to go to Japan next week, then Australia and then that depraved tour of America. He couldn't think how he'd given that his blessing. It was madness. He was still weak, only just regaining some of his stamina. He knew what he had to do. He had to scrub Japan and Oz. Too soon. Too far. Too taxing. And no matter, anyway, because he was going to be writing new songs. Songs as good as 'In A Lonely Place'.

He thought of loved ones he'd had, loved ones he'd lost as he listened and tuned his guitar to the tone of the song, and he found himself smiling at the thought of Kiara's world-weary dismissal. She was right. Tomorrow is a long time coming. He croaked a battered vocal into the Pye recorder. His mother had given him that exactly thirteen years ago yesterday. And in thinking it, having dismissed the same thing yesterday, he decided just then that now was the time.

He was there, all through the visit, wanting to please, hanging in the background like a beaten dog. Walking back through that door had taken his breath away for a moment, but he wasn't devastated by it. He wasn't haunted.

Roger had opened the door himself. That dreadful, shouting, hitting monster who had just . . . *come downstairs* one morning and changed the course of his whole life. It was he who had come to the door, head bowed, knowing it would be Keva. He didn't try to shake hands or say anything much: 'We don't get many visitors. Your mother'll be so pleased . . .'

That had been all.

He couldn't hate the man now. The man who had ripped his posters from the wall. The man who scoured his eyeliner off with a scrubbing brush and shampoo, still scrubbing and scrubbing, long after Keva had no cries left to cry. The man who burnt his black jeans on a bonfire in their scrap of a garden on a Saturday night and made him sit in the bedroom and watch. The man who beat Keva's skinny arse until he screamed himself unconscious, beat him with his own studded belt because it was a 'greaser's belt', then took them all for a picnic next day. The man who took the stylus off his record player. The man who told him to be a Man.

This man was his mother's choice, her choice to sit where once his father had sat. His father who, when Syd next door told him, laughingly, that Keva was a prodigy, bought him his first guitar. Who used to be there when he came home from school, with toasted teacakes ready. Always there, until that day he came home and no one was in and he sat on the step and cried and cried. Mum found him there, later, when she got back from the hospital. She told him Dad had got poorly and had had to go away. He never came back.

He sat and looked right into Roger's eyes. The man who'd smashed his beloved guitar. The guitar Dad gave him, smashed to nothing on his bedroom wall. He was so overcome with power and strength that he had it in him just to tell the man that it was all right, he didn't hate him, he'd done what he thought was best, back then. But he sat there instead and looked at the poor bastard in silence, looked at his fearful eyes flickering around the room.

'She'll be back any minute,' he stuttered.

Roger got up and went to the kitchen and only came back in when he heard Mum's key in the door. This man had once terrorised Keva. He had been awful to him. Now he was a stooped, balding, broken old man in a nylon shirt. How could he have done it to him?

He'd gone pretty easy on his mother. It was left clear that they'd see each other again, obviously not there, and piece by piece they could maybe pick things up. He only stayed a short while, not to hurt her but because, sitting there, more things came to him, more music, more lullabies. There were things he needed to get down and things he needed to do.

Walking back in the rain, the boot polish started to run down his face. At the last minute he'd run a dabful through his hair, just to cover up those few white ones. It mattered to him that he should not look older to his mother. He put his three middle fingers to the trickling black streaks and started to cry passionately. He couldn't stop. But it was over now. That much he knew.

James had left a note out:

Yo! King of Rock 'n' Roll

Got hold of Todd. Not happy. Can't bin Japan until tomorrow but wants to speak with everyone first. He's on Wheezer's case.

Back later.

Hector Lovett

Keva was angry but not surprised that Todd was kicking and screaming about Japan. The thing he hated more than anything in the world was to have to cancel gigs. Other agents, other bands seemed to do it all the time. People get ill, whatever. But Todd couldn't hack it. It was a bad reflection on him and his rep as an Up-and-Coming. He decided to call Mr Hotshot there and then and stymie any lingering hopes he might have of rescuing this 'situation'. He was bound to say 'situation'.

Fatigued after only an hour or two of writing, heart drained and nothing left to give, he wandered down to the huge, frozen slab of a kitchen, put the kettle on and flicked on the portable with the remote control. *Stars In Their Eyes* special. Nice one! Pity Jimbo wasn't there to see it. One of their cult favourites, in the days when they used to stay in with a Pot Noodle and watch TV.

He padded back over to the steaming kettle and held his face over the scalding mist for as long as he could bear it, easing out a couple of miniscule plugs from his pestle. Waiting for the tea to brew, he turned to face the telly, arse dug back into the old marble work surfaces. Fucking Todd. He'd kicked and screamed all right – in a voice that he'd tried to keep even. Keva had almost laughed, at one point, when he actually started squeaking. He sounded like Mickey Mouse issuing a kidnap threat: 'OK. No problem. Cancel

Japan. But let me tell you, Keva. We'll never go there again. We will not be invited back. Japan will not deal with this group from now on . . .'

The dickhead. Did he think that Keva wasn't ill? That he just wanted a holiday? As always, he backed down completely, grovelled for forgiveness when Keva, finally, snapped at him and put him straight on why the Grams *could not* fulfil their obligations. But then he made his apology into nothing by pausing meaningfully and saying, 'I'm a winner, Keva. I guess I just hate to lose.'

Prick. Keva poured his tea. Good colour. Could feel the heat of it on his cheeks. He took it across to the big, solid table in the centre of the kitchen, scraped out a chair, banged up the sound on *Stars In Their Eyes*, sat down and nearly choked on his drink. The guy on the TV. The skinny, ugly, knicker-thief with the bug-eyes and the lank hair, throwing his arms around like fucking Morrissey, sticking one hand on his hip-bone and shagging the mike – it was him. There was a Keva on *Stars In Their Eyes*.

When the telephone went for the eighth time in an hour, Keva let the ansaphone pick it up. Another delighted acquaintance wanting to make some predictable remark about his 'greatest performance yet'. He could understand it – it must've been hilarious to anybody who knew him. Hilarious to *anybody*. But it was fucking spooky for him, sitting there, watching some . . . *lunatic* taking him off. Fucking bad impersonation too. Nothing like him. He didn't throw his arms around. Not that much.

So he was surprised to hear Guy's voice, distracted, almost monotone on the machine. Keva leapt to snatch up the phone before he hung up. 'Hey! Guy! It's me . . . whoops! Hang on – just managed to chuck the whole fucking phone system on the floor. What's up? Don't tell me . . . Todd King?'

'What?'

'Ah, nothing. We had to bin Japan and Australia. I don't suppose you'll have heard . . . I've been in bed with . . .'

Guy cut in, staccato, sounding very frightened. 'My father shot himself this morning.'

*

'I'm really glad you came down. Thanks.'

He'd said it three or four times, now.

'I would've come sooner but, trains and all that. Bank holiday. Crazy.'

'No . . . no. This is . . .'

He was distracted, but not through grief. There was a lot he wanted to say to Keva. He wanted to get it all out, in the right way, in the right order.

'I mean, I was thinking, you know?' He looked up sharply. 'Your songs have . . . it's been my salvation. I didn't even think about it, but now . . . I often think we're . . . we're not dissimilar, are we?'

Keva told him, that night up on the Hyatt roof when they'd sat up and talked about everything, told him his dad had died, and how maybe that had shaped his view of life. Nothing else. And he'd *loved* his dad. It was nothing like Guy's thing. They weren't similar, not at all. He didn't know what to do. He wanted to take his hand – but he couldn't.

'I, er . . . when my dad died . . .'

Guy didn't seem to hear him. He sat there, glassy-eyed. Keva felt sick for him. He knew too well that dull thud of a pointless heartbeat. He thought back, again, to their rooftop conversation, Los Angeles and their lives glittering way below. He hung his head, clasped his hands together. He could save this boy's life.

'This is awful, what I'm going to tell you. The timing couldn't be more . . . bad, like. But you'll want to know this. I don't think you'll hate me. Remember you told me, that night, up on the roof in LA . . .?'

Guy nodded, dumb.

Keva sighed out loud, a long, despondent sigh. 'I'm such a fucking arsehole. I could've told you then. I don't know . . . I just wanted . . . it was soothing, sort of, knowing that somebody else was fucked too. D'you know what I mean, though . . .?'

Guy nodded, not knowing at all, but coming back to his senses, sensing something.

'And I didn't know if I was still in love with her – for myself, like. It was never conclusive. I always thought, like, you always do,

473

don't you . . . I hoped she might be someone I'd go back to, one day . . .'

'Who?'

'. . . cos she has that sort of effect on you, doesn't she? You just, fucking . . . *fall* for her . . . she's so . . . *needy*.'

'Evie?'

He couldn't say anything. He couldn't even look up. Guy leapt to his feet, eyes fierce with hope. 'Keva!' He grabbed him and forced him to look up. 'Is it Evie?' he whispered.

Keva nodded. 'I'm sorry.'

Guy's face, ash grey a moment ago, was a furnace of exhaustion and joy. 'Oh my fucking God! Evie . . . I mean, she's *alive*? I mean, how do you . . .'

Keva held his hands up for hush, relieved that he was, at last, doing something good. 'Here y'are, just . . . sit down again and I'll tell you everything.'

He told him everything. Everything Evie had told him. Guy just sat and nodded, a dumb realisation dawning as answers came tumbling from Keva's lips to questions which had haunted him for years. He had to see her. He had to see Evie now.

Wheezer was surprisingly fine about Japan and Australia. He was much more interested in hearing about the new songs, excited to get over and see Keva and hear his demos.

'You're in Tim Speed's place?'

'As per always.'

'Good. I'll er . . . I'll bring you updates on everything.'

Guy sounded elated.

'I'm meeting her on Thursday. God! It's been such a fucking ordeal these last few days . . . But thanks. Thanks so much.'

'No *praaablem*!'

They both laughed, out of awkwardness, or sheer relief that it was all out in the open.

'I mean . . . I feel as though this is all meant to be. Does that sound pathetic?' He sounded incredibly posh. Keva hadn't noticed it so much for ages. Maybe it only came out when he was excited about something. 'I mean . . . Pa completely cut me out of his will. Blames me for everything . . . Ticky . . . the decline of Western civilisation. Ma can't be consoled, but it's fantastic, you know. I'm a Gram. I've got no baggage, I'm travelling light, I'll just go wherever the wind blows me . . .'

'You fucking hippie!' laughed Keva. But he was pleased for his friend. It felt weird that Guy and Wheezer had stolen up out of nowhere to become his best friends. Weird.

'Hah! Not quite, though! There *is* the little matter of the business to consider . . .' He gulped audibly. 'I mean, I am totally sure about this. I've thought about nothing else. I'm sure of two things. That I will find Evie and we'll run away together. And that I want nothing further to do with this business. No offence, Keva, but I was right the first time, when I got out of Vermeer. I need, I've always needed . . . well, it's not commerce, anyway. I don't need that. Even if I'm the most shit poet in the world, I'll be happier . . .' He paused to reflect, trying to picture Keva on the end of the line, all those miles away. 'The Artists' Label, hey? The grand vision didn't quite happen.'

'You're fucking the label off?'

'Don't say it like that. You'll be *so* much better off. I mean, a new band, OK, you get fucked. But the Grams – you can write your own prescription. And you get your own publishing . . .'

Keva hardly heard the rest.

'. . . you'll get a two-million-pound advance. I just want my outlay back from Worldwide, to live on. I mean, I *have* to sell to Worldwide, it's part of the agreement . . .'

They talked for another hour and a half, but he could only remember the publishing bit.

The moment he dragged open his eyelids he knew today was a big one. Wheezer loved Wednesday mornings, but this was an extra special one. This was their first batch of pop radio adds from the States.

Mel's fax was there. Knopf was strictly an e-mail man, and all the others at Automatic, too – but Mel liked the physicality of paper for his important messages. Lots of the big stations were in already – they'd been working on them right up to the Christmas break and now the conversions were totting up.

Z100 – *New York City*
WPLJ – *New York City*
KIIS-FM – *Los Angeles*
Q106 – *San Diego*
WXKS – *Boston*
KMEL – *San Francisco* ·
WPLY – *Philadelphia*
WBBM – *Chicago*
KKFR – *Phoenix*
WPGC – *Washington DC*
KRBE – *Houston*
KDWB – *Minneapolis*
WHYT – *Detroit*
KQKS – *Denver*
WBZZ – *Pittsburgh*

Fifteen in the first week! Each and every one of them a choice, pick-of-the-pops P1 . . . this was an immense start. With MTV and these new stations, the Grams were probably, right now, being exposed to a populace of over one hundred million. It was staggering.

Mel's fax added that there were other, smaller stations still to come in as well as one or two unconfirmed reports, but he was cock-a-hoop. With the tour starting in ten days and all the cities they were visiting to come in with radio support, the album was going to be phenomenal. Even on paper he was radiant. He was a fuck of a guy, Mel, a real enthusiast, a worker and an ally. Wheezer wanted to call up Guy immediately to thank him for making him see sense.

He couldn't believe Pat McIntosh had done this to them. Was this all because they'd cold-shouldered him at Brown's? Wheezer looked at the thing again. It wasn't the end of the world, but it drastically undermined their credibility.

It was the *NME's* New Year issue. Lots of funny little

predictions, Ones-to-Watch in 99, and a couple of pages full of Sadly Missed, Gladly Missed and Cheerios. The Grams were a Cheerio. All it was was a big photo-caption. The words said:

Farewell to overrated doom-angst merchants the Grams? Almost certain to self-combust as egos run out of control on daunting Stateside jaunt.

The picture showed the group, a gurning, multichinned James looking like a melonhead in the foreground, dressed in formal evening-wear and cummerbunds. How the fuck had they got hold of *those* pictures? The boys looked like a cabaret band. It was bad. It was *very* bad.

'Hey, Wheezer! What about these stats . . .'
  Knopf.
  'Aren't they something?'
  'We'll pass gold before you guys even get out here.'
  'You think so . . .?'
  'Euw – for sure! It's not even a question. But, ah – there is something . . .'
  Here we go, thought Wheezer.
  'Lemme tell you this one thing that concerns me a little . . .'
  His one little thing was that some of his stations, the huge commercial modern rock stations like XRT in Chicago and the Edge in Dallas and, obviously, KROQ were well past their shelf-life with 'Beautiful'. The track was burnt-out. They do what they want to, these stations, everybody looks to see what they're playing and, just when you have a nice, consistent pattern they've broken away in another direction, with a brand-new track. You can't control them, you just try to work with them.
  'I was just talking with Norm Winer in Chicago a minute ago, and he's totally behind this band. OK? He's not saying to me, like, don't call me about this band ever, right? He's a fan. But he has his listeners to think of. They all want something new from the Grams. Now, that for me is the worst possible scenario, just as we finally have a story, here, we have loose cannons going off in all

477

directions all over the country and we're suddenly fighting a rearguard . . .'

Wheezer could sense something atrocious coming.

'*So* . . .'

This is it.

'I'm thinking, we can't have them getting a signal from us that it's OK to just rape and pillage from the reckud. What if I commission some *mixes* . . .?'

It didn't sound like mass murder.

'Erm, what kind of mixes, like? Not dance mixes?'

'No! God, Wheezer, please! Listen, I have Mordecai Bender sitting with me right now . . . say hi to Wheezer Finlay, Mordecai . . .'

'Hi there, Wheezer! I am *floored* by this band! I can't wait to work with you guys . . .'

That's where it got weird. Mordecai Bender sounded five years old. Knopf came back on.

'Mordecai has been listening to a lot of classic sort of seminal angry grunge, right? The real extreme stuff, Nine Inch Nails? The early Lollopolooza sound . . . Jane's Addiction. Fishbone. He envisages a real demented mix of "Beautiful" . . .'

'Real furious . . .' came the pre-pubescent voice.

'"Beautiful" is a ballad,' ventured Wheezer. 'It's an idealistic ballad.'

'Sure,' insisted Knopf. 'So we turn it on its head.'

'Right!' squeaked the kid. Wheezer started to envisage a toddler sat on Steve Knopf's lap, enjoying a Sherbet Dip.

'Erm . . . Mordecai . . . ? Who *are* you?' spluttered Wheezer.

Keva felt a strange but deeply satisfying detachment from the rest of the party. A lot had changed in the short time since they had last flown that way across the Atlantic, but it was the encroaching knowledge of himself, and that this was all about him, that was soaking deeper and deeper into his consciousness.

They were going back now, so soon and with such a lot to say, because he had played his part so well last time. He could hear their stupid shouts, voices raised so that everybody else on the plane knew they were important. How soon they'd forgotten their blinking disbelief when he quit the band a few weeks ago, and their grovelling acceptance of his terms to come back again. They'd learnt nothing, any of them. Nothing about themselves, for sure.

Still tiring easily, Keva drifted in and out of consciousness, eased by the brandies, trying to get a shape of all this, of what had happened in his life. Each time he closed his eyes he saw Roger. Until his birthday, he hadn't thought of him in years. Even in Ibiza, with the deluge of memories Syd had dislodged, he'd blocked him out.

His birthday. He'd been alive for thirty years and no one on this plane knew it. Not even Marty. He totally accepted Keva's explanation that, as frontman, he was susceptible to more curiosity, more cranks, more danger than all the others, so he preferred not to let his passport out of his hands. He was happy to arrange his own visas and take care of his own immigration details.

Thirty years. What had he learnt? He closed his eyes again, to try to think of one thing that he could say was true. What would be the thing he'd want to pass on to his own son? What?

'Don't take it all too seriously, son. It means fuck all.'

He smiled to himself. It was all right, being thirty, now . . . now that he *was*. If he thought anyone would have believed him, he would have jumped up and announced it. It was like a clean start for him. He'd laid his ghosts – for now. He could even, almost, conceive of being grateful to Roger. For terrifying him. For driving him deep down inside himself. For driving him away. Roger, with his sadistic pursuit of manliness, had made a man of him.

Mel was waiting for them at the airport, big grin, holding aloft a copy of *Radio and Records*.

'This, my friends – this is the Bible. Accept no substitutes.'

He showed them the back page. The American Top 40. The most famous chart in the world. And they were on it. There they were, at number 37. With a bullet.

'I don't know what to tell you, guys. It's happening!'

He burst out with the most infectious guffawing so that,

immediately, the whole party was standing around in the arrivals hall, bent double, cracking up with laughter. It was happening.

Wheezer had never tasted dim sum like it. He'd never *seen* dim sum like it. A whole gigantic crab, bigger than a frisbee, cracked open and served plain with ginger. An unbelievably good taste, so good that he didn't care, he just dug in and ate more and more and more of it, with seaweed, and pork dumplings, and *tiny* salted pork ribs.

'This is dim sum, Mel? It's a bloody banquet!'

Mel beamed at him, pleased that he was pleased. They'd left the band to wander around Chinatown while they sat down to go through statistics, changes to the itinerary and interview requests for the next few days. Keva was going into KITS later in the afternoon.

'Well, kid – we've made one helluva start. We have twenty-one new adds this week, fifty-seven in total, over half are PIs. It's exceptional. Sales just rocketed after the first of the year. MTV, all the big guns coming on board first week . . .'

Wheezer found himself tittering inside, impatient to know how many albums they'd sold. 'Knopf reckoned we'd do 500,000 by now,' he said, rolling his eyes to show incredulity.

'And some!' grinned Mel. 'Nearer 600,000, my friend. Five-eighty something last time I looked. You can see that baby going round like a milometer, though. For real. There's someone buying this album every minute somewhere in the States . . .'

Wheezer felt faint. 'Fuck! I guess we owe you chaps some trigger money, what?'

'Oh yes, sir!' Mel guffawed. 'Oh yes indeedy, sir!'

Keva was enjoying his time at KITS. Rich Sands himself was manning the telephones as he came in. He turned to wave hi to Keva, holding his hand up in the air like Sitting Bull, asking him to wait.

'. . . In fact, Rob, you will not believe this but the man we have just been talking about has just walked in to the room . . .' He turned full-face to Keva. '. . . hey! Keva McCluskey!'

'How's it going, Rich . . .?'

'Do you suppose you could come here and say hi to Rob from . . . San Jose?'

'No problem.' He crossed the room, mouthing the question to Rich. 'Are we on air?'

Rich shook his head.

'Hello? Rob?'

'Oh . . . man!'

'How's it going, Rob?' He could almost see the kid shaking his head in dumbfounded disbelief.

'Awesome, man.'

'Cool. You coming along to the show tomorrow?'

'I'm going to all of them, man. San Jose, San Francisco, Sacramento. I can't fucking wait . . .'

'Please don't curse. I'm a Catholic.'

'Shit, man, I'm sorry! I . . .'

'Only kidding. So, well . . . er . . . if you leave your name with reception here at Live 105 I'll try and get some goodies left out for you. Nice to talk with you, man.'

He handed the phone back. He could hear a distant: 'No way! *Cewlllll!*'

The opening couple of gigs were good, if unspectacular. Wheezer, watching from behind the mixing desk at a stoked-up Warfield Theatre, sensed that Keva was holding himself back. The band were tight, no doubt about it. The crowd fucking loved them. But he'd seen Keva, so often, take a crowd like this, a big, fanatical crowd and completely fuck their minds up. He could do whatever he wanted with them, when they were like this, and he wasn't doing it.

He elected to leave well alone. Things were going just perfectly, they had an enormous journey ahead – there was nothing to be gained by trying to get inside with Keva, so early into the tour. They had a bigger crew, this time round, an American production manager, Tam Haines, and two of his crew, lighting director Lee Fforde and drum technician Peter Waller. This freed up Marty to advance the tour and co-ordinate with venues and local crews, while Rory could concentrate on guitars with Crapston solely in charge of the mix. There was a tour accountant, Bryan Hedges, working with Marty and the Rope boys, swagging their first major American tour. They were travelling in Hotel California, a huge touring bus with twelve berths, front and rear lounges, fridges, TV, video, sound system, of course – and two toilets which no one was allowed to crap in. The bus was reputedly owned by the Eagles and its exterior was a huge mural of the *Hotel California* album sleeve.

'I'm not fucken going *nowhere* in *that!*' spat James when he saw it. But he loved it. They all did. When the bus was surrounded by curious onlookers as they waited to make the short drive to Sacramento, they all realised that the bus was going to be a shag magnet.

Wheezer looked out at the flat farming land on the periphery of Sacramento, looked at Tam and Marty, making earnest calls by mobile, and thought about the gigs again. It was all too finely-balanced to risk upsetting Keva. The whole thing was bigger now, and getting bigger every day. No. There'd be nothing to gain from tackling the singer.

'I wasn't being critical, you know . . .'

The two of them were waiting in the reception at KWOD, Sacramento's modern rock station. Keva didn't mind going up there himself with Elsa, Worldwide's local rep, but Wheezer had insisted.

'I don't really want to get into it, Wheeze,' he said. Finally he looked up, and faced the manager. 'It'll come. It's fine. Yeah?'

'If you say so, mate.'

Keva cracked a smile. 'Don't worry.'

'But I do. I do. Just, like . . . if it gets too much – let me *know*. All right?'

'Sure. Ta. But I'm fine.'

The DJ, a pale-skinned girl with ocean-green eyes, had Keva eating of her hand. He was relaxed, almost hypnotised, answering her questions with a candour which surprised him. He wasn't *trying* to be cool. That was the difference. He didn't care what people thought of him.

A young researcher came in, blushing like mad and slipped a

note to Gwen, the DJ. Not so long ago, Keva would've got off on the effect his mere presence, his celebrity had on people. Not now.

'Wow!'

Gwen read the sheet again. She faded the track. 'Sorry to all you fans of Hed-Pe to cut the track short – we'll be hearing a lot more of those boys, don't you worry about it. Big, big news though. Just off the net, like, *minutes* ago I have news from England that Sensira has sensationally split. There's not much more detail. Helmet has *not* made a comment, but we understand he's been booked into a clinic. Wow! Keva McCluskey. How d'ya react to that?'

Keva was stunned, elated, relieved, disappointed. Disappointed not to have the opportunity to really kick Sensira into touch. 'I dunno, really. I suppose I'm pleased if I'm perfectly honest. I don't like Helmet, that's no secret. But more important, I always thought the band were wrongly praised. They were not a good band. Even this ending is too rock 'n' roll for them . . . he'd probably like to die in there.'

'Keva McCluskey!' she teased. 'That's not very generous.'

'They've had more than enough generosity.'

'D'you care to choose a track for Helmet? A tribute?'

He gave it some thought. '"Desert Rain". By the Grams.'

She stabbed her tongue at him and played the track.

Beano, Tony and James all climbed back up on to the bus, chattering excitedly.

'I'm going on that Twister ride! have you seen that? I seen it on *Wish You Were Here*! Looks fucken awesome . . .'

'I fancy the Tower Of Terror . . .'

'I just like the look of the water attractions. River Country and that. Typhoon Lagoon.'

'Bit fucken parky for the beach, innit?'

'Nah! Florida? It's always nice there. Anyway, it'll be April when we get there . . .'

Keva looked up from his book, still prickly. 'Are you geezers talking about what I think you are?'

Wheezer got up and went to see how Catering was coming on inside the venue.

Beano grinned. 'Fuckin right! We're going to the Magic Kingdom.'

'Disney?'

'And Universal!'

'Erm . . . that's in, like, three months' time, guys . . .'

'Yeah, well – you need something to keep you going, don't you?'

'Something to aim at . . .'

Keva stood up and looked at them all. 'I can't believe you lot! We're not even three dates into the fucken tour and you're planning your holidays . . .!'

'Well . . . what's wrong with that . . .?'

'Er, nothing – except that there's a little matter of a ball-breaking tour to concentrate your minds in the meantime. I mean, don't you *want* to do this? It isn't like it's hard work for you . . . all's you have to do is plug in and go through the motions. Some of us have to worry about the bigger picture . . .'

'Oh aye, yeah, but it's worth *your* while, isn't it?'

Keva looked psychopathic as he rounded on James. 'Meaning . . . ?'

'Fucken ball-breaking is about right, lar. Breaking rocks while Massa McCluskey cracks the whip . . .'

Beano joined in. 'Too fucken right! This isn't a band no more – this is US working for YOU! We're your workers . . . you're as bad as fucken Helmet!'

Keva looked at each of them, individually. Tony looked away. Beano and James glowered back at him.

'We *have* had a cosy little chat, haven't we?'

He walked to the front and hopped off the bus.

'You have a choice, Wheeze. It's one or the other. You can fly me to the gigs, put me up in hotels and I'll meet you at the gigs. Or you ban everyone from the front of the bus. That is *my* space and the touring party does not violate it . . .'

Wheezer hung his head in despair. 'Keva, mate, please, I *appeal* to you – whatever was said, you know . . . it can all be sorted out. People say things. We all say things we don't mean . . .'

'Oh, they fucken mean it all right. They've had a fucken union meeting . . .'

'Look. I'll sort it, right? You can't let this get out of hand. Believe me, separate living quarters will only make the situation worse . . .'

'You don't get it, do you? I don't *give* a fuck! I don't *want* to sort it out . . .'

Wheezer looked like he was going to burst into tears.

'They've had their say. They've made their bed . . .'

The drive up to Medford was fine. The band, all three of them, stayed at the back playing *Zelda* while Keva sat at the front, strumming the Martin. Last night's gig had been special. Sacramento did not know what had hit the place. All that anger and tension and strife came blistering to the surface in a violent, spectacular, unforgettable performance. Even now, Wheezer was breathless thinking about it. It was the best show he'd ever witnessed. Tony Snow, mild, unassuming Tony went beserk on stage, pogoing madly, kicking over amps and throwing himself madly into every song. 'Beautiful' sounded closer to what Mordecai Bender had in mind, corrosive and contaminating. The crowd would not let them go.

Their adrenalin fuelled a wild night's clubbing, which culminated in James trying to smuggle a stocky, diminutive woman on to the bus.

'Are you a *dwarf*?' asked Tony, sloshed. 'C'mere, Miss Dwarfie . . .'

She sidestepped his lunge nimbly and brought a thunderous karate chop down on his shoulders. Thuck! He was on the floor, gaping at her.

'Mizz Dwarfie, if you don't mind . . .' She sounded like one of the Krankies.

Marty stood up front, imperious, and addressed the bus in general, but Mizz Krankie in particular. 'Bus Rule Number Seven. You get on the bus, you *do* the bus . . .'

She nodded eagerly, little fat head going a dozen to the ten. People were starting to look nervous. James beamed out, face ruddy even in the half-light of the front lounge.

'Oh aye, she's game. She's up for anything. She'll blow the lot of us, won't you, Lucy?'

'It'd be my solemn pleasure,' her crackly voice crackled.

Marty was having none of it. 'I'm sorry, my darling, any other time, but . . . I'm afraid we're carrying our full capacity. California State law . . .'

'Ah, fuck the law! This is rock 'n' roll!'

To great cheers, she was carried from the bus, kicking and spitting and trying to get Marty's flies down. All but Keva stayed awake, drinking, and their good spirits spilt over to the next day.

'Hey, Wheeze! Medford! Is it a good *market* an' that?'

Squeals of laughter. Maybe Wheezer would have a role to play, after all. A big role. Only he could keep the band together. He sighed at life's rich contradictions and took up with his tour hobby again. Staring out of the window.

Guy's call came only a few minutes after they arrived at the Holiday Inn, their day rooms for Medford.

'Hi! Wheezer! You sound like you're next door . . . I tried about an hour ago . . .'

'We just got here . . . set off quite a lot later than anticipated . . . what's happening?'

'Oh, you're all over Radio One news again. Keva's come up trumps!'

'How come?'

'The stuff about Helmet? One of the radio stations out there has given Radio One the story – wishing the bloke dead and all of that . . .'

'Jesus! Does it hurt?'

'Hurt? It's fantastic!'

'So, erm – what record label are we on today, Monseigneur deBurret?'

Guy told him. The transfer of the company to Worldwide was almost complete. Willard's affiliate company in the UK would take over the day-to-day running of the project as soon as contracts were signed. Overseas territories would come on line as and when their option periods expired.

'Hey, I know this is a bad time to lay all of this on you, old man,' he continued. 'But I have to get this out of my hair. It's best for everyone . . .'

'Sure.'

'So, erm . . . this really needs pushing through at your end, Wheezer. I can have Willard's office pouch the actual contracts through to you for close scrutiny, be with you tomorrow, but if you can bear it, or if you have time, maybe I could whang the Heads through to you now . . .? D'you mind?'

'I'll do my best, man. If I can get the boys to where they're supposed to be first, then maybe I can salt myself off somewhere. Bung it through anyway, and I promise I'll get to it.'

'Thanks, Wheeze. I really appreciate that.'

'No problem. You're welcome.'

So they were off ReHab. So soon. Guy had promised substantial financial emoluments for the Grams – a great big whack of dough – but somehow the whole deal felt irrelevant. The fight, the dream, the inch-by-inch progress, all the things they'd been aiming for – it all seemed to have gone a bit limp. Even the shit with Sensira was an anticlimax. He expected Todd to call any day to confirm that the Grams would be headlining Glastonbury in June. Headlining. Glastonbury. The Grams. The Biggest Band In The World. Great stuff, but just now it felt like a hollow victory. The telephone went again. A cheerful, familiar voice.

'Is this Wheezer Finlay? It is? Marvellous! This is Matthew Wright . . .'

'Let me assure you, my friend,' laughed the cabbie. 'Those guys had to totally rethink their *modus operandum* when I pulled out the monkeywrench from under my seat . . .'

As usual in the States, the taxi driver was immensely intelligent and highly articulate. They all were. Every cabbie from JFK Airport to Sacramento had read more books and used more syllables than Keva wanted to even think about.

'You want to know what those guys did? They paid. Ah-hah. Those guys paid me every cent they owed for the ride they commissioned. No tip, though . . .'

He laughed again. The cabbie was letting them know, in as charming a way as possible, that he was not to be trifled with. Keva wasn't taking a blind bit of notice. He was too busy seething about his manager, his dim-witted, overstretched, totally exposed, run-of-the-mill manager.

He knew what Wheezer was up to. Fuck him. He should know by now that he had no influence over all this. Did he think he could *advise* Keva? Did he? He probably fucking did, the tithead. The taxi pulled up outside KTMT, Medford's R&R station. Wheezer, Joni the rep and, last of all, languorously, letting his hips roll insolently as he mooched into the building, Keva, in a stinker again.

Wheezer had told him about Matthew Wright. The *Mirror* had got hold of the cummerbund shots and paraphrased Pat McIntosh about the Grams losing the plot out here.

'You might want to tread a little carefully for this one . . .'

That's all he'd said. Not exactly a final warning. No stroppy I'm-the-manager shit, just Wheezer trying to point him in the right direction. But it irritated the shit out of him. The way he said it, that half-American mid-Atlantic drawl he'd affected for the past few days, and . . . just the fact that, that he actually thought he could say things to Keva that he'd listen to and act upon. Wheezer thought he had his ear. He thought he could influence him. What a fucking joke. He reckoned he might go in there and tell the DJ he'd become a Seventh Day Adventist. That'd guarantee a few more column inches back home.

That was the thing Wheezer completely failed to grasp. Keva did not give a flying one what anybody back home said or thought about him. Back Home. *Home.* What high concept! He did not care a fuck if he never saw Britain's septic streets again. A small, jealous, restrictive, nasty place – why should he care? He could feel it, right now, from here. He could feel the slow puncture starting to take the diamond-honed velocity out of his rocket to the stars. The cracks were appearing. It would take months, years for the momentum, now, to arrest itself. From now until the last person ever to walk into a shop, Back Home, and ask for a CD by the Grams was *years* away. But the countdown had started. Instead of today being bigger than yesterday, it was only just as big. The day would come, soon, when today would be smaller than yesterday. And it was nothing to do with the real things. It was nothing to do with music.

He looked at Wheezer, the manager, so anxious that everybody should form a good impression of him, think him a great guy, a real pro – and a bit of a maverick. These things *do not matter*, he wanted to tell him. He wanted to not be even doing this, any of it. He wanted to write a whole new batch of wheedling, sick, ingratiating songs, starting now, later, tonight. But he was in Medford, with Wheezer and the Grams. They were all feeding off him. Parasites. All of them. Well not for much fucking longer, they wouldn't be.

James was doing that noiseless laugh; his contorted, agonised face made Wheezer want to punch him.

'What the fuck *is* this place?'

'It's where you're playing, you tit! Keep your voice down!'

James was still bent double, chipped tooth on display, killing himself laughing. He turned to the others. 'Who do they think we are? The fucken Judds?'

The venue was a down-home, rough-and-ready cabaret lounge. There was a stage with a small dance floor below it. Next to the dance floor was a gathering of wooden tables and chairs and behind that area a raised platform with more, bigger tables and a blackboard saying: 'Bob's Hot Vittles. Drink With Food Only Beyond This Point. Warning – You'll Need It!

Medford lies on the periphery of the great North Western Grunge Belt, but this place was more suited to line-dance marathons and duelling banjos than a tortured rock 'n' roll roadshow from Liverpool, England.

'It's a place to play, isn't it? The radio station here has been banging merry hell out of you bastards since 'Desert Rain'. Show them some fucking respect, will you . . .?'

'Ah, do one you, you tithead!'

Wheezer turned on him, maddened with grief. 'I swear to God, knobhead, I'll fucking *kill* you . . .'

James trembled his lower lip with his three middle fingers. 'Ooh, ay – I'm bricking it . . .'

Wheezer, furious, ran in to head-butt him, but James sidestepped smartly and helped The Wheeze on his way with a little trip.

'The manager,' muttered James, watching him scrabbling among the mops and buckets.

Wheezer sat there without moving. He could not have felt worse.

It got worse. He knew it was something awful from the way Keva summoned him. He'd never, ever heard a voice so lifeless, so killing and he'd never known Keva to ask for a 'little talk'.

'I need to speak with you, Wheezer. Somewhere private. Just a little talk.'

They went to sit on the bus. Keva got straight to it.

'I don't want you to think this is personal. It genuinely isn't. Everything's got to change. Everything's going to change . . .'

'What did you have in mind . . .'

Keva cut him off by holding up a hand for quiet. 'No. Please. I mean you've done well out of it. Really. You're made for life. But it's just . . . it's not appropriate any more. None of it. It doesn't make sense. It isn't . . . *right*.'

Wheezer's soul hit the floor on the word 'right'. Only he and Keva knew what he meant by that. Wheezer was out. His time was up. Keva was getting rid of him.

'But . . . *why*? I mean . . .'

Again, cold as death, the hand was raised. 'No. Don't. There's nothing to gain from it. We'll have a drink when I get back, yeah? Meet in the War Office. Talk it all through.'

And that's when it hit him. It was over. Wheezer was going right now.

'I can't . . . I don't . . . you don't know . . .'

Guy smiled down at her. 'I do. I do. I know it all, now.'

His fondness for her was almost paternal. He held her, his little waif, in his arms, his stomach flat against her back, stroking her fine, bony shoulders and kissing her stooped nape. Still, so long after the last of the tears, the shudders shook her frail body. She forced her face around to see him.

'But . . . you . . .' He shushed her. 'You won't go away from me, will you? Please don't ever leave me.'

He wanted to be solemn, to be earnest, to be the rock and the

490

truth she wanted, but he could not keep the soaring joy from his eyes and his voice. 'I won't ever leave you, Evie. I promise you.'

Marty explained courteously and simply that he was, for now, if they could conceive of such a thing, the band's acting manager. Wheezer was already heading for a connection to San Francisco and from there onwards back to Heathrow. Everything would be properly sorted when they got back home but for now, if they would, and for everybody's best, he'd recommend and appreciate heads-down, no-nonsense, mindless hard work – and play – from now until Florida. He didn't fully know why Wheezer had gone – but he had gone. James grinned.

'Nutter! Knew he wouldn't be able to take it . . .'

Beano glowered at him, then Marty, but said nothing.

'I suppose we've got no choice, have we?' said Tony, thinking: *Get me through. Get me through to the end. Give me my money. Then let me be.*

'Does Keva know?'

'I should imagine they've spoken, yes.'

'So soon, eh?' said Beano, shaking his head. He looked up at Marty and enunciated every syllable. 'So. Fucking. Soon.'

Again, Keva worked out his anguish on a wild-west crowd. Then, after a truculent encore, he shut himself in the club's tiny production office to enable the band to do whatever they wanted to do without feeling beholden to include him. He stopped to sign some posters and CDs – James was already moving in on the bonny, gum-chewing blonde who had stayed seated at her table throughout, with her mom and pop.

She was never twenty-one. The law was twenty-one, for licenced premises. She wasn't even fifteen. She had big, blonde, sprayed, backcombed hair and a prominent jaw, rigorously exercised by the gum-chewing. Her dad looked like Joe Dan Baker. Maybe he was the mayor – he was certainly somebody. The promoter, two guys from the radio station and another, older man surrounded him with handshakes and backslaps, polite greetings to wife and daughter, then tugged him away to the bar. James seized his opportunity, flattering up to the mother, a tense, sinewy, worried woman.

He sensed out with heat-seeking precision that there was no give in the situation. Not with the mother, anyway. She wasn't even listening to his compliments: 'Your eyes, you know, Eileen – they dance. They really do. Your eyes dance.'

'Eew?'

But the daughter. Maggie. She was hot. Her laser-blue eyes were all over him, appraising, surmising, anticipating. He didn't even need to butter her. No patter, no nothing. As soon as Anxious Eileen got up to go and hang by her husband's side, James raised an eyebrow.

'Would you like to see Hotel California?'

Beano was nervous, but determined to see it through.

'Keva?'

He knocked out of respect, but also in case he had a girl in there.

'That you, Al?'

'Yeah. You all right?'

'Just tired.'

'Just wanted to see if we could maybe . . . you know. Just wanted to talk, really. Haven't talked to you in ages.'

Keva pulled back his curtain. 'What's up, like?'

'Oh, nothing, you know. Loads. The band.'

'Wheezer?'

Beano nodded. 'Never really liked the fella. But, you know . . . It feels weird. He's gone, like. Wheezer's gone. I mean . . . what happened, like? Where's this band going? What *is* this band?'

Keva slumped back down, head on his pillow. 'Dunno, matey. Don't fucking know. But Guy's gone. Hannah's gone. I just want to . . . I want to strip it all down to nothing again. I don't even know what I'm looking for. It's . . . I need to stop it all. D'you know what I mean? I want to freeze it all and have a proper look . . .'

Beano put his hand on Keva's shoulder, truly glad that he wasn't him.

She hadn't *not* swallowed; it was not a gallant, principled stand against swallowing. It just didn't stay in her mouth. When the first volley just dribbled back down her chin, he pulled his knob out, held his bell tight for a second, closed his eyes and masturbated viciously. He could feel the full force of the second coming. He threw his head back, eyes closed, laughing and Maggie laughed too, shouting 'Cooooool!' as he sprecked over her.

So it was only as the engine started up on the bus and she gathered up her denim jacket and ran to join her mother and father, waiting for her, chatting with sycophants in the well lit foyer of the club, that he noticed the spunk in her hair. No. It was *on* her hair, most of it. Laying perfectly flat on her hard, lacquered, big hair were winking pearls of insouciant cum. As she ran to hug her father and turned to wave to a hysterical James, he could see the old man actually stoop to poke his nose at her hair, blinking, unwilling to believe that he could smell what he thought he could smell.

From commencement of landing right up until now, in the queue for EC passengers, Wheezer had been clutching his passport open at his visa page. It had been magical to him when it came back from the US Embassy, like a glorious, stamped, watermarked validation of who he now was. The big, bold, crested eagle, bearing the motto in its majestic beak: *E pluribus unum*.

More magical still, though, was the typed entry next to the petitioner section: *Worldwide Records Inc.*

It was there, on his visa, in his passport. Wheezer Finlay, man of means, man of mission. And now what? He had no tears left to cry. His bottom lip was bitten raw. His soul dragged with a desperate want, as he tried to envisage a future which started, now, in a few hours with his key back in the front door at Parkwest. But all he could think about was yesterday.

Keva wouldn't even listen to him. He doubted he could ever, ever forget the contempt in Keva's eyes when he started crying. He was so hard. So hard. He just shut him out, just like that.

Transferring for his domestic flight back to Manchester, and the end of the road, he ducked into W.H. Smith to stock up on newspapers. *Billboard* was in. With shaking hand he picked up the bulky mag and went to pay.

493

The Grams were mentioned in seven different sections. They were charting all over the place. They were happening, and Wheezer could not, yet, regulate his emotions. He was still as proud as punch. He could not have ever prepared himself for the inside back page, though.

Bob Campione, a – presumably – worried and insecure Bob Campione, had dipped into his promo budget to try to tack himself back on to the joyride, reassert his fraying relationship with the band. He'd taken out a full-page advert, sent as though by fax, on Worldwide letterhead:

20 January 1999

Dear Program Directors and Music Directors,

Why is a naive, simplistic ballad propelling sales of an album into the Millennium and inspiring requests from everyone from teens to retirees?

Why have KIIS-FM, KMEL, WBBM, WXKS and WHTZ added out of the box a record which might seem to be out of format for those stations?

Why do my wife and son demand that I put on the Grams each time we get in the car?

The reasons:

KIIS-FM – 'Immediate adult requests and major impact at retail.'
PWR 96 – 'The biggest reaction record so far this year. #1 requests.'
WHYT – 'Right into power rotation. Every other call is for 'Beautiful'.

'Beautiful' is the track that all America wants to hear. The early CHR play is being reinforced by constant television exposure with the video in heavy rotation on VH1 and MTV Buzz Bin. In addition 'Beautiful' is the highest converting record in the Top Five of R&R's AC chart as well as a breaker at Country.

The retail success of the Powder *album after only ten weeks is incredible. Following a five-day sales figure of over 300,000 units*

the album has already achieved gold status and is lighting a trail
towards platinum. This week it moves from 23* to 9* on
Billboard's Pop Album Chart and is set fair to become this year's
key breakthrough album.

These are just statistics. The point about this record is that it
touches the emotions of listeners of all ages, whether they hear it on
pop stations, alternative stations or country stations. The first time
Willard Weiss played me 'Beautiful' my spine tingled and I had to
dry my eyes with a handkerchief. I get that same feeling even now,
every time it's played. I'm sure that this is the effect this track is
going to have on all listeners for years to come, regardless of age or
radio format, as 'Beautiful' beds itself down as an American
classic.

'BEAUTIFUL' IS A RADIO PHENOMENON.

Regards

Robert J. Campione
Senior Vice-President, Promotion
Worldwide Records

He read it once more, with a creeping sickness in his guts.
Platinum . . . 300,000 . . . Radio Phenomenon . . . American
Classic. *American Classic!*

The call for boarding came and Wheezer shuffled up with the
formless rabble. American Classic. *He'd* done that. Him. The
Wheeze. Mr Michael Wheezer Finlay. He was overcome with a
debilitating sense of loss. He recalled his handkerchief prank, with
Guy, when they first went out to LA. An age ago. Like Bob
Campione, Wheezer was in tears again over the Grams.

The tedium of the overnight from Spokane to Butte was broken by
speedy, fragmented conversations about sex and titty-bars, and the
now nightly robbing sprees. Every night the bus pulled up at an
all-night store. Gus, the driver, sat down to coffee and muffins,
while the band and the British element of the crew sidled through
the aisles, pocketing plastic daggers, rubber vampire bats, biro
pens, sunglasses, chewing gum – anything crap. When they got to

the checkout they would order but one item. Mini Thins. Available without prescription from roadside stores like this, Mini Thins were an instant hit from the moment Lee the Light had pointed them out, amazed that the Grams knew nothing of this legal speed.

'It's, like, a slimmer's thing, originally, I think. Maybe asthmatics, whatever – but they sell them in places like this for the all-night drivers . . . you know.'

'And it's amphetamine, right?' spluttered Beano.

'I don't know about whether it's amphetamine, all I know is that these little bastards kick. Don't take too many. Your heart'll be jumping through your ribcage . . .'

Beano and Tony loved them, cramming handfuls down every night before the show and more again afterwards.

'I'm addicted,' squealed Beano. 'I'm a Thinhead!'

He started singing: 'I don't wanna be a Thinhead no more/I just met a girl that I could go for . . .

Gus raised his eyes to Our Lord in Heaven above, willing him to make the days tick faster. This band was the biggest pain in the ass he'd ever known. They were like kids.

Wheezer sat there, in the office, twitching to do the hundred things he automatically did, every day. Call Mel. Call Guy. E-mail Taurus. Speak to Simon Moran. But there was no need. He was surrounded by Grams memorabilia, redundant. He opened up a box of the extra white-label EPs he'd ordered up. Wonder how much they'd be worth now. He might need the money soon. Fighting back tears, he reached for the phone to tell Guy what had happened.

'I mean it, Marty,' said Keva. 'Don't even think of trying to fuck about with me, telling me there's no flights. Don't let that thought even enter your head. This is America. There are flights . . .'

'But . . .'

'No buts! Just do it!'

'Hey . . . !'

'Look, I'll make it *this* simple, yeah? I will never set foot on that bus again, ever, period. You and it are free to travel hereafter in

496

Jerky Boy heaven. Have Cheech and Chong to your heart's content. It's yours. I'm out of there. If you want this tour to continue into the merry merry month of Feb, I will be needing flights from city to city from now on, transfers to and from hotel and venue and airport, a separate, sole-use dressing-room and a per diem of one hundred dollars. Got that?'

Marty decided just to ride with it. Fuck him – they could afford it. Bryan Hedges told him in Spokane that the Grams were selling 75,000 albums per *day*. A few flights, hotels, a few hundred dollars – if it kept the show on the road . . .

'None of this is a problem, Keva. None of it . . . I just. I'm just worried for you, Keva. That's all . . . I . . . I've seen groups just self-combust in these circumstances. Just . . . BANG! They can't take it any more. I . . . if you want me to pull a few of the dates, give you some breathing space . . . would that make things more tolerable?'

'I don't think you get it, man. This is all *very* tolerable. But it'll be a whole lot more tolerable still, the less I have to see of the supporting cast . . .' He was walking Marty out of the door, just walking him backwards with his shoulders and chest.

Marty took a deep breath and let it out again, slowly. 'I'll go and book the flights then, shall I?'

'Yeah. Oh – Marty. No DC10s, please. Check it with the travel agent, whoever. No DC10s, period. If it means sending me to Salt Lake City via Miami, just do it, yeah?'

'No problem.' He walked away, shaking his head. The time bomb was ticking. Keva had lost it.

'But maybe that's *why* he's being an arsehole. We don't get it like he does, do we?'

'We don't get the wedge he gets, do we?'

'Ah, come on, boys. We're a band. We stick together, eh?'

'Wouldn't that be nice,' grunted Tony.

'Come 'ead. We'll all go and talk to him once we get there. Take him out, like. Make him cancel all his shite an' that. There's nothing we can't sort out, eh?'

'Worth a try, I suppose,' said Beano.

'I doubt it.'

497

'Come 'ead, Tone. The lad's head's probably gone to bits. Cut him a bit of slack, eh?'

Tony swallowed a handful of Thins and turned up his Walkman.

Wheezer found himself standing there, in the little park opposite the Simkins Partnership in Whitfield Street, bedazzled. He must have lost, what? A minute? Ten? He'd stepped out from his meeting with Jules Trouttman and, with a fierce *déjà vu*, stopped still in a dead trance. Except this was no *déjà vu*. This was where he'd walked, with Keva, that damp sweet pre-light morning last spring when they'd just finished 'Beautiful', when the world was theirs, undulating with possibilities. They'd come out of the studio, so full of what they had made and what it would come to mean, and they'd stumbled in silence as far as this little park before realising they'd taken the wrong turn. But, full of everlasting strength, they weaved on through the side streets, avoiding main roads, walking on and on, aglow, until they hit Seymour Street and Marble Arch and Hyde Park.

'Spare us a quid for a cuppa tea, mate.'

Wheezer came to. He smiled at the filthy old drunk. Was he old? It was impossible to tell through the stateless pallor of living rough on the street.

'Must be a big cuppa, eh?' He dug into his pocket.

'Whatever you can spare, sir.'

Wheezer could spare a quid. He could spare a hundred. Trouttman had just told him he was worth two million, just on commission from Keva – and he could carry on billing him for twenty per cent of band income, income derived from the first album, for another five years. Four years, three hundred and fifty-six days, at least. Wheezer was rich.

He was happy, but not because of that. Jules had told him that Wolfe would try to buy out the contract, that Wheezer was holding all the aces, that bands and labels would form a disorderly queue for his services. He told him, basically, that this was just the start. He had a future. But that wasn't it.

What made him happy was the *déjà vu*, his experiencing fully that whole mystical shudder of anticipation, that significance, that unspeakable *excitement* once again. He had not known that for a long time. It had slipped away, without telling him, to be replaced with a more frantic, hungrier sort of thrill. One that could not be savoured. That he had known that other, and known it fully and deservedly, made him at peace with everything else. This was something good that he had done. He gave the wino a two-pound coin.

'God bless you, sir! Be lucky!'

Wheezer was overcome with a strong and positive spirituality, a rising sense of the good that was him and his. He glanced at his watch and decided that, just like they'd done on that electric dawn, he'd walk it.

'Hannah Brown, please. Yes. No – no e.'

He didn't get the double bonus for keeping the funds in for a year, but the high risk tracking fund he'd used for Lord Turnbull's windfall came out quite well. His five thousand pounds was now almost seven – and it was Hannah's. His intention, now, was to see Guy for lunch then just drop in on Hannah, a real flying visit before the train back, try and build bridges at least. And he was determined to give her this money which belonged to nobody, after all, to help with her new company. He'd pretend it was an investment if she got uptight about it. He wanted to make things better. Keva had treated her like shit, and he'd let him.

The clerk handed over the cheque without even looking up so Wheezer swanned out of the bank without saying thanks or goodbye. He quickened his pace towards St John Street, stopping only to post Keva's letter, care of Steve Knopf in LA.

By any definition it was a tragedy. The Salt Lake City crowd, like all the crowds, greeted the Grams with religious fervour. They were here to worship and from James's first intro they'd piled forward, frenzied, fanatical. The young lad with the mohawk launched himself from the stage before security could get to him. It looked like a bad fall to Keva, and when the crowd parted and paramedics came streaming in he knew the boy was dead.

Nobody spoke as the bus made its way through the Utah–California borderland. Keva, back in his bunk, could find no order to his thoughts. A flickering slideshow of images played on his aching mind. Nothing made sense to him.

Santa Barbara was warm, even with the breeze. The bus had pulled in by a tree-lined beach road after the overnight from Las Vegas. Gus, hugely fond of his bacon, eggs Benedict, grits, hash browns and French toast in the morning, had a favourite café in every town. This one was right on the beach by the old baths, with only a jogging path separating its terrace from the sand. The gradual slowing of the bus as they entered the city limits had woken half of them, and the gush of warm morning air as he wooshed the pneumatic door open brought James and Keva to their feet. Tony and Beano had not long dropped off, after talking deep into the night, wanting to quit the band while knowing they would not.

'Gus! Hang on, mate! I'm starving!'

Praise the Lord, thought Gus. He turned back towards James, pointing. 'It's right here! I'll order you up some orange juice, yeah? And some coffee.'

He lumbered away, his huge legs quivering with every step, his stance turned inwards by the mass of his fat thighs. James, then Keva joined him at the outdoor table after placing their orders at the counter.

'Crazy life, eh, Gus?'

'Sure is.'

Keva leant his head back and drank in the smells of the ocean, mingled with the abundant bouquet of flora which stayed on the breeze only for moments at a time. Whenever he thought he could fill his lungs with it, get a sense of it, it was gone again, drifting in and out and away.

Wheezer let himself in, stepped over the letters, of which two, he could tell, were cheques. He was tired from the day in London, but he knew he wouldn't sleep. He couldn't stop thinking about Hannah. She'd hugged him so powerfully when he got up to leave, and held his hand for ages. 'You're lovely,' she said. Maybe there was hope for him yet. He opened up the boys' PRS statements, which, even under Keva's formula, gave them each another tidy sum to tuck away.

Steve Knopf arrived at soundcheck, wearing his hair in a slick, short bob and his pipe-cleaner legs in enormous khaki shorts. His emaciated chest was clad in a Calvin Klein camouflage shirt.

'Fuckinell!' whispered Tony. 'Baden-Powell!'

Knopf ambled over. He was accompanied by a boy, about ten or so, his kid brother or some precocious relative.

'Hey! My supremos! Is the godlike Keva McCluskey anywhere to be found . . . ?'

Beano looked at Tony. Tony looked at Beano. Steven Knopf, VP Contemporary, had rarely spoken to the two grafters before, let alone addressed them in this flattering, familiar way. The kid grinned, impressed by his uncle's contacts.

'Eeow, I'm sorry. Guys, this is Mordecai Bender. He's the hottest mixer in town right now . . .'

Mordecai held his hand upwards and outwards to the disbelieving two, still stopping a distance short of contact. He was a metre tall. They looked from him to Knopf and back and down to their amazing shorts, speechless.

'He's with Gia,' spluttered Tony, jerking his head up towards a sort of balcony to the side of the stage. It was a glorious, natural amphitheatre with banked terraces going way back up the slope, big enough for five or six thousand. Maybe more. Conscientious, bald-shaven, goatee-bearded young men in camouflage shirts and gigantic shorts bustled around with self-importance, asking folk if they could see their passes, if they needed anything, if they might wanna go and get something to eat. Tony and Beano just sat out front by the mosh-pit, taking it all in, waiting their turn.

'Doing the interview,' added Beano.

'Cool,' said Knopf, turning on his heel. 'Catch ya.'

'Hey! Don't say I never give you nutten . . .'

Knopf handed Keva a Jiffy bag and an envelope. The envelope was addressed to him, posted in England and bore Wheezer's hand. He opened it slowly, warily and with sinking heart. He half-expected to find Wheezer's ear in there. Or, at least, a lock of his hair. Keva spluttered as he opened up the letter.

'What is it?'

He handed Knopf the chain letter. The letter he'd slipped under Wheezer's door a year ago had made its way back around the globe to beguile him. When the letter had got to him, on the morning of the Ticky Turnbull gig, he knew that it was the start of something. Maybe now it was the end, too. Maybe it was time to go home.

It was Guy.

'Wheezy! Hey, listen man, bad one! Willard's pulled out. Yeah. No – blown the whole thing. Dunno. Dunno. They just lost it, apparently . . . who cares? Listen. Can you get down here, pronto? I have a minor proposition for you . . .'

Wheezer's spine tingled. He went outside to bring in the milk. It was going to be a glorious day.

Kevin Sampson

AWAYDAYS

'The dark side of Nick Hornby's *Fever Pitch*'
NME

'An acutely observed rite-of-passage story about a teenage hooligan who follows Tranmere Rovers in the heady days of 1979...the Pack rampage at away matches, beating up rival fans, slashing faces with Stanley knives and looting local shops...brilliant at evoking the period when the casual movement was just gaining momentum on the terraces... Sampson looks closely at what motivates their dysfunctional behaviour, it comes as a relief to read a rounded evocation of a time and a generation which has too often been reduced to cliches'
Independent on Sunday

'Kevin Sampson's excellent debut novel...set around Liverpool, is funny, hip...Sampson is a fine storyteller...He has a fantastic ear for the Liverpudlian accent...Nasty stuff, brilliantly told'
Guardian

BY KEVIN SAMPSON
ALSO AVAILABLE IN VINTAGE

☐ **Awaydays**	009 926797 7	£6.99
☐ **Leisure**	009 928515 0	£6.99
☐ **Outlaws**	009 942223 9	£6.99